TEMPLE MAZE: DARK SHIFTER ROMANCE
COMPLETE SERIES

ANNA FURY

© Anna Fury Author

Paperback ISBN: 9798867681203

All rights reserved. No part of this publication may be reproduced, stored or transmitted in any form or by any means, electronic, mechanical, photocopying, recording, scanning, or otherwise without written permission from the publisher. It is illegal to copy this book, post it to a website, or distribute it by any other means without permission.

This novel is entirely a work of fiction. The names, characters and incidents portrayed in it are the work of the author's imagination. Any resemblance to actual persons, living or dead, events or localities is entirely coincidental. However, if I get the chance to be in the middle of an Ayala Pack sammie, I'll say a quick prayer of thanks.

Editing - Kirsty McQuarrie of Let's Get Proofed
Proofreading - Marcelle of BooksChecked
Cover - GetCovers & Linda Noeran
Maps - Darren DeHaas (@theadventurousfuryk)

❦ Created with Vellum

A QUICK NOTE

Temple Maze is a dark omegaverse romance series, and omegaverse often deals with difficult topics like generalized violence, possessiveness, physical dominance, lack of consent, mention of parental death and more. This series has that in spades. It is intended for mature audiences due to prevalent dark themes.

It's never my intention for a reader to feel triggered by something in these pages. If you need more specifics from what's listed above, please send an email to author@annafury.com.

NOIRE: A DARK SHIFTER ROMANCE
TEMPLE MAZE LEVEL ONE

MONSTER GUIDE

While I made up some of the maze's monsters, some are loosely based on existing entities. For the sake of those not familiar with monster lore, I'll quickly lay out the monsters you'll see and hear about in this book.

Vampiri - humanoid with exceptional senses, incredible speed and occasional psychic ability. They are pale-skinned with black claws, lips and fangs. Vampiri are venomous and drink blood.

Rohrshach - humanoid with a featureless face, covered in an inkblot-style black blob that morphs and changes like the famous Rorschach mask. Not as strong as vampiri or shifters, so they hunt in packs.

Manangal - loosely based on the mythical filipino manananggal, a vampire-like winged creature that could separate it's lower half from it's upper to fly in search of prey.

Maulin Fox - I made these up, knowing I wanted something between a cat and a dog, but utterly wild and blood-loving. Tiny black foxes whose jaws split open to lock onto their pray and drink blood.

Minotaur - A 15-20-foot tall cross between a human and a bull with a humanoid body covered in fur but a bull head, complete with horns.

Gavataur - I made these up. Vaguely humanoid body with two arms and legs, but very tall and thin with saggy skin and a bull head, complete with horns. Ancient, wilder forms of the more modern minotaur. They are cannibalistic and non-communicative with hybrid monsters.

Naga - Half human and half cobra, naga have humanoid upper bodies with a flared hood behind a distinctly snake-like face. Their lower half is that of a snake.

Kurasao Dragon - I made up these snow dragons with long snake-like bodies and short limbs. Of all the monsters in the maze, they would be the largest and the least seen.

PRONUNCIATION GUIDE

Noire - Nwar (rhymes with car)
Diana - die-ANNA
Renze - renz (like friends)
Tenebris - TEN-uh-briss
Cashore - CASH-or
Ascelin - ASK-uh-lin
Liuvang - L'YOO-vang (like hang)
Vampiri - vahm-PEER-ee
Naga - NAH-guh
Gavataur - GAV-uh-tar
Manangal - mahn-ANG-ahl
Lombornei - LAHM-bor-NAI
Tempang - TEM-payng
Siargao - See-ar-GAH-O
Rezha - RAY-zhuh
Vinituvari - vin-IT-u-VAHRI
Deshali - deh-SHAH-lee
Dest - rhymes with west
Sipam - SAI-pam (like dam)

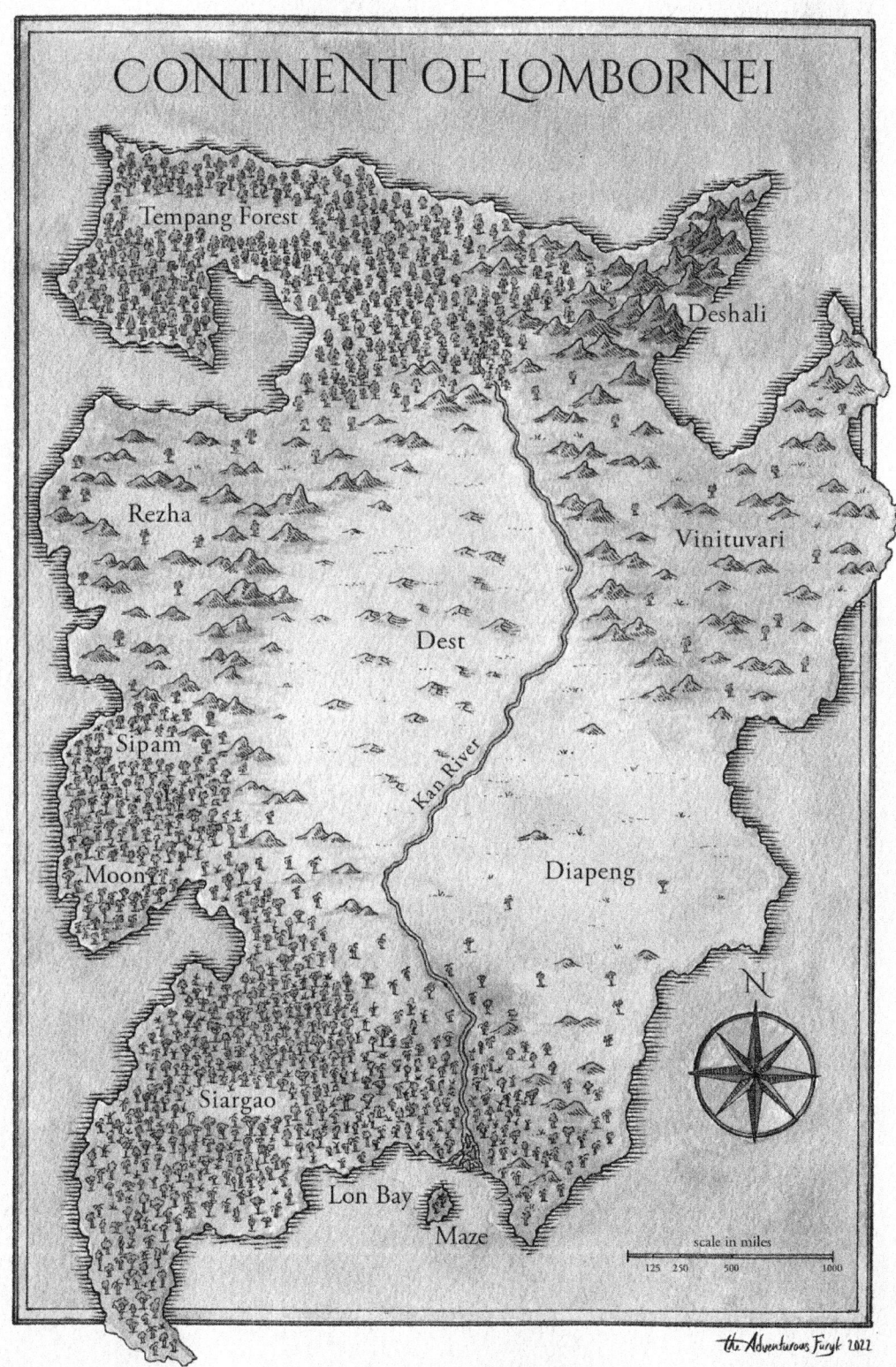

A SHORT HISTORY LESSON

In the early days, the continent of Lombornei was ruled by humans, and it was lawless. Monsters kept to the shadows of the Tempang forest, living far from the human element and never mixing.

Eventually, a direwolf and a human woman fell in love. The wolf shifter sired a son, and the first alpha was born. Those hybrid genes spread quickly, and other monster crosses emerged as humans and monsters bred for the first time in history.

This new generation was less content to remain in the Tempang, and they desired freedom to roam and settle across all of Lombornei. Hybrids were bigger and stronger than humans, and within five hundred years, every province on the continent was a mixed region of monsters, hybrids, and humans together.

Most provinces lived in relative harmony, but not all monsters were thrilled at this new world order. Hybrids and humans built the province of Deshali on the edge of the Tempang forest, right within claws-reach of every dark shadow that remained in the forest.

The villain of our story was born and grew up in Deshali, her soul twisted and torn by life among true monsters–eventually turning her into the very worst one of all.

PROLOGUE - NOIRE
SEVEN YEARS AGO

Standing in my personal car on the river train, I lean up against the window, watching the green jungle and glittering high-rises morph into the gritty Riverside District. The houses here are practically falling into the Kan River, some even propped up on stilts. The train jostles from side to side, but where most people would sit for this ride, I've always preferred to stand and look out the window at my kingdom.

A deep voice breaks through my peace. "Noire, Alpha Rand from Deshali is at the next station requesting an audience with you."

"Alpha Rand?" I glance up at my younger brother, Oskur, my enforcer. "What does he want?"

Oskur growls, "Says he has critical business with you, and in the name of Ayala pack, he is requesting an audience. Invoking the pack name to ensure a meeting is such a stupid fucking tradition."

Next to Oskur, my brother Jet rolls his eyes. "It's old-fashioned, but I think we should hear him out. He came across an entire continent to speak with you, and I thought he was killed when Deshali was decimated. I'd like to know how and why he's here, wouldn't you?"

I should listen to Jet when it comes to things like this. He's the strongest strategist in the family, always looking for approaches I wouldn't normally consider. Water flashes by the open windows as I inhale the beautiful waft of the Kan riverside–fried fish, dirt, common people. There's something strangely calming about the stench. I may live in a beautiful tower up in the verdant foothills, but riding the train down here along the river is where I get my best thinking done.

Sighing, I nod to Jet and Oskur. "Let's hear what he has to say."

Oskur nods and leaves the passenger car to make arrangements to stop as I look out the window, Jet coming to stand by my side. Like this, we're eye to eye.

"Last we heard from Rand, monsters were coming out of the Tempang to attack Deshali. I'm surprised he's still around," Jet says. "We haven't done a tour of other alpha packs in years, Noire. Maybe it's time to get a sense of what's happening in the other provinces again, as Father did."

"I don't give a fuck what's happening in the other provinces," I remind him. "Father cared far too much about the rest of the continent, forgetting Siargao has resources the rest of the continent needs. If you control Siargao, you control Lombornei by default. He focused too broadly, and it made him ineffective. We are better than he was, far better."

Jet nods, but I can see the wheels in his head spinning. The truth is I fucking hate traveling. I don't want to leave my part of the world because the rest of this continent and its people don't matter to me. My place and my rule are here. And it is firmly fucking cemented.

I growl when the train slows at the next station. Normally, when I'm on board, the train runs from up in the hills where I pick it up, all the way down to the mouth of Lon Bay. I'm intrigued why Rand has come all this way, though, even if it means my train has to make an atypical stop.

When it slows, Rand gets on. Standing by the window, I get the first whiff of an omega alongside his deeper alpha scent. Hers is heady, dark, enticing. It seems Rand has brought either a beauty to offer me, or something he thinks I lack. When Oskur enters the train car with Alpha Rand and a woman in tow, I narrow my eyes at them.

"Alpha Noire. It has been a long time," the older alpha murmurs, looking at me where I stand up against the open train car windows. I know what he sees: an alpha in his absolute prime. Rand, on the other hand, has not aged well. His skin is burnt by the sun, peeling off in many places, his hair nothing more than splotchy patches.

Rand is sick and dying. That much is clear.

If he were part of my pack, I'd have put him down by now. But he's not, so I take a step forward and glance at the omega behind him. Her eyes are downcast, as they should be, but she peeks up when I look at her. Long chocolate hair, stunning green eyes. She's gorgeous, although a little older, older than me by probably ten years, heading into her late forties. When I look closer, the hint of a faint scar slices from her hair down to her chin. It's barely there, but still noticeable.

Not that it would stop me fucking her.

I glance back at Rand. "You requested an audience, so let's hear it."

Rand's hands grip a cane he's using to hold himself upright, but he takes one hand off it to gesture to the omega standing behind him. "This is my daughter, Rama. I came to offer her hand in marriage to you, if you'll take it, Alpha Noire."

I bark out a laugh. "What leads you to believe I'd accept such a random, unbidden proposal?"

Rand nods. "It isn't traditional, to be sure. Deshali is devastated, overrun by monsters, and we have fought them for generations, Alpha Noire. You know this already."

He's referencing how he's called me for help twice in the past, and I did not grant it.

Rand continues, "I'm dying, as you can see. I need to cement a place for my daughter in this world, and Deshali has no marriage prospects for her."

I snarl as Jet comes to stand next to me. "So you thought you'd foist this omega on me simply to help you because you're dying?"

"No, alpha," Rand answers, lifting his head higher. "My daughter is brilliantly inventive, and the only reason we've hung on so long is because of her inventions to belay the monsters' advance out of the Tempang forest. But we can only do so much. However, we've recently discovered a gold mine in our kingdom, and we are reluctant to leave that, as you might imagine. If you marry Rama, you will get access to Deshali's natural resources. Plus, a beautiful omega who will birth you many pups to spread the Ayala name."

"Prove it," I snarl, not bothering to look at the hapless omega, even though she's staring at me now with open, curious eyes. "Prove a single fucking word of this bullshit, Rand. What this sounds like is yet another plea for help. I didn't grant it the first two times because you were foolish enough to build a city on the very fucking edge of the Tempang, the one place on our entire continent where the old uncivilized monsters still live. That's your problem."

Rand blanches but reaches into his thick coat and brings out a bag. Already, I hear coins rattling. He hands them to me, but I don't take them, waiting until he can't hold them upright any longer and the bag falls to the ground. The omega winces but looks up at me.

"Please, Alpha Noire," she whispers. "I would be a good mate, and there is plenty more where this came from." She gestures to the bag of coins at my feet.

There's something about this omega I don't like. The way she spoke without being spoken to. The way she said "please." My alpha intuition pings as I take a step closer and grip her arm, tugging her out from behind Rand. He holds back a growl as I circle the woman, leaning in to scent her neck and the back of her shoulders, which she's left exposed. She shudders when I touch her, and not in a good way.

No. This omega wants nothing to do with marriage, and anything she says to the contrary is simply meant to fit her father's narrative.

She darts back behind her father when I finish my inspection and take a step back.

"No, Rand. Once again, no."

Rand's watery eyes meet mine as he brings both hands up. "Please, Alpha Noire. I am begging you to take her off my hands, to give her a place to be of use. Help her regain our homeland because there are riches there beyond your wildest imaginings."

The omega brings her head up, her expression carefully guarded. I don't like what I see and sense–a dark, deviant mind hidden behind her elegant features. There's a reason this omega is single. My guess is she's run off every potential suitor with the general air of distaste that wafts from her like a poisonous cloud.

I glance back at the father, narrowing my eyes. "You have nothing I want."

"Please," Rand continues. "She is exactly the type of mate a powerful alpha needs–beautiful, connected, and powerful in her own right. She can help you cement your foothold in the west."

I whip out a hand to grip his throat. "I already own every inch of Siargao, which means I own this whole continent. Every man, woman, and child does exactly what I wish them to do. This place was lawless before I took over from my father, but the city thrives under my rule. If I *ever* take a mate, I'll take one with her own assets." I glance at the omega, whose eyes narrow at me. "You and your daughter have nothing to offer me aside from a pretty face, and my pack is already full of those."

Behind Rand, the omega snarls, clenching her fists together. She's likely to be an absolute hellcat in the bedroom. Normally, I'd take her and enjoy her once or twice before they leave, but there's no way in seven hells I'm mating this beast.

"Your father would–" Rand barks. One glare from me halts him in his tracks as I loom closer. At his age, he's already sunken to half the size he was when I met him as a younger male.

"It doesn't matter what my father would or wouldn't do because I killed him and took his place. The only thing that matters is here and now, and I am fucking bored of this conversation. I won't make the deal because I have no incentive to."

"But," he blusters.

I step closer to him, pushing my chest to his, looking down at him, a reminder of how fucking powerful I am. I'm an alpha in my prime. My claw-tipped hands could rip his head from his shoulders in a second. There's no patience left in me for this topic.

Rand reaches down for the bag of gold, but I put my foot on it with a tsk. "That's staying with me for this colossal waste of my time."

"It's all I have left; I have to take it to the next place," he spits, suddenly full of vehemence. "And the next and the next until I secure a place for my daughter. I cannot mine more without he–"

"Not with this money," I snort. "And not with that daughter. Not a single thing about her screams that she wants a mate, so you've got more problems than a lack of assets. Go, *now*."

He stands and glares at me but reaches for his daughter's hand, leaning on her for support. One dark brow travels upward, his eyes sad as he takes me in. "I'm sorry, Alpha Noire."

Confusion curls in my chest at that. Sorry? He's…sorry? It makes no sense.

I glance over at my brother, Oskur. Of the four of us brothers, he's the biggest. Tenebris is still a pup, but I don't think anyone will ever outweigh my second-youngest brother. Oskur grips the omega by the back of the neck hard and guides her to the door. The father follows as Jet drops to a knee and opens the bag at my feet.

As he pulls the strings open, I'm happy to see it actually is full of gold coins, thick gold coins. Jet hands me one, and a quick sniff tells me they're real. I'm surprised this wealth existed in Deshali, but it's not worth fighting the monsters who remain in the Tempang.

Nobody trades in gold any longer, but these will still have value in some circles. I'm thinking of the alpha group I hunt with at the club on Fridays. A few of those males are collectors of ancient treasures such as this. I pick a coin up to examine it and realize it's printed on both sides with a pattern.

Jet rubs at the grime that coats the coin's surface as I frown. The pattern isn't a pattern at all; it's a labyrinth of sorts with an eye in the center. How… odd. I'm familiar with many of the old coins used in our history, but I don't recognize this.

That makes it more valuable. Already, my mind spins with ways I can use this to push and pull Siargao's seedier citizens around my personal chessboard.

Smiling, I go to put the coin in my pocket when I realize the pattern on the front is fading.

No, not fading. *Bubbling, melting.* I drop the coin back into the bag and peek in just as Oskur returns to the carriage.

"We were examining this coin, but it started bubbling—watch, Oskur," I bark.

Our brother strides over and picks up the coin as Jet takes a step away. "Toss them all out the window. That can't be a good sign."

As soon as the words are out of his mouth, the coin in Oskur's hand evaporates in a puff of smoke, filling his eyes as he coughs. Half a second later, Oskur drops to the ground as Jet roars.

I reach for the bag, kicking the fabric back over the top of the coins. But the second I do, the rest explode, filling the train car with curling black smoke. Jet and I roar, and then there's nothing as the train car's floor rushes up to meet my face.

∼

My head is pounding, my heartbeat a steady thwomp in my chest. Even my fucking eyeballs are throbbing in my head. What in the fuck...

The black smoke. The omega. The godsdamned gold coins.

Glancing around, my eyes narrow. On the bed next to me sits a pile of gold coins, the same fucking coins with the labyrinth and eye pattern. These are all shiny, the eye winking at me maliciously.

Rand. Rand apologized on the train. Is this what he meant?

I jolt upright, only for stabbing pain to send me doubling over my lap, grunting in pain. I roll off the bed and sink down onto the floor, putting one hand out to steady myself. Glancing around, I don't recognize anything. Black stone floor. Black carpeting. Black stone walls.

Gripping the side of the bed frame, I manage to get myself upright as my alpha senses kick into overdrive. More grunting and cursing reach my ears. Oskur.

There's a door to my right, and I head there, expecting to find it locked. But it's not, so I stride through, peeking into a long hallway.

"Oskur," I call out quietly, knowing my brother will be able to hear me. Our alpha senses are incredibly strong.

"Here," he grunts. "Dying."

I stride up the hallway, the pain starting to fade from my head as I fling another door open. Another dark bedroom. Oskur lies on the floor, both hands on his head. "What the fuck was in those coins? Where are we?" His big chest heaves with exertion.

"Don't know," I bark. "Get up; you're not dying."

I turn and leave the room, listening for Jet. I find him the next room over, walking around the room with his hands balled into tight fists. "I don't recognize this place, Noire." Jet frowns, dark brows pulling into a tight vee over dark eyes. He looks so much like Father that I do a double-take for a second.

I leave his door and stride up the hallway, which ends in an open room. Living quarters with a kitchen on one side and a giant arched doorway on the other. Several more hallways lead off the main area. "Search," I bark to my brothers, tension building between my shoulder blades. I know every inch of Siargao, and I don't recognize anything here.

No doors, no windows save for the open doorway on one side of the room. It looks like another hallway. Jet and Oskur take a hallway each as I stalk toward the kitchen area, trying to get a sense of my surroundings. More dark stone, dark appliances, dark furnishings. Everything here is black. Behind the island, a small figure lies on the floor with a bag over his head.

Oh, fuuuuck. Dropping down, I whip the bag off and growl as I look into the face of my youngest brother, Tenebris. He's just a pup, barely eleven.

"Ten, what the fuck are you doing here?" I bark. "How did you get here, alpha? Answer me right the fuck now."

Ten's lower lip trembles as he looks up at me. "A woman led a bunch of guards to the house last night. She...she killed everyone, I think, Noire. I tried to escape, but she took me. The pack was running when she took me, and nobody could save me. Why did she take me, Noire? Where are we?"

I roar for Jet and Oskur, and make Ten repeat his story twice. Oskur questions the boy within an inch of his life as I jog for the arched stone entryway at the front of the quarters. Another hallway. I jog down it. Another hallway, and another, and another. I don't want to get lost here, so I jog back and find my brothers, still questioning Ten as he sobs and curls in on himself.

"Enough," I snap, anger churning my stomach. Something is very, very wrong. "Ten, stop–"

"Good evening, Noire," a silky voice echoes through the cold room, stopping me in my tracks.

I whip around to find one section of the wall lit up like a television screen, a woman's sneering face the only thing on it.

The fucking omega from the train. Not Rand but the omega.

Balling my fists, I turn toward her but say nothing. This is her doing. I know it.

"No smart retorts, Noire? No scathing commentary about the state of my father's health or my utter inadequacy as a mate?" She doesn't wait for a response before she continues, "It doesn't matter because it was all a ruse anyhow. A ruse to keep you from looking skyward as my city approached yours. It was easier than I expected, to take it over from you. And now I own you, and anyone else who defies me."

There's so much there, I don't even know how to begin to unpack it, but boiling anger roars through my veins as my vision clouds, my fangs descending. I'm barely holding back the need to shift and rip something to shreds.

"Tsk tsk, Noire," the omega warns. "I'll make this very clear for you. You didn't help us when we needed it, and you could have. I'll never forgive you for letting Deshali fall when you had the resources to swoop in and push the monsters back. So now, you're in a maze of my own design. It's impossible to escape. And you will live there for the rest of your life. Not only will you live there, but you and the other monsters in the maze will do my bidding."

"I will never do your bidding," I snap.

The omega laughs. "Oh, you will. Take a look at your wrist; see the disk embedded there?"

I flip my arm over. A metal disk is now implanted along the underside, and it's flashing a red light at me. Godsdamnit all to the seven hells, I didn't fucking notice when I awoke. I scratch at the edges of the disk, sending a shooting pain up my arm.

The omega gives me a sinister grin. "That disk will tell you exactly what you're allowed to do and not do, every day for the rest of your godsdamned life. You work for me now, Noire. All of you do, even little Tenebris over there. But you're not alone in the maze. So be careful, or what remains of your life could be pitifully short."

"Let me the fuck out of here," I snarl. "Or you will rue the fucking day you came onto my train with those motherfucking coins."

"Oh, I don't think so." The omega laughs. And it's the laugh of someone who knows she's won. "Welcome to the Temple Maze, Noire."

CHAPTER ONE
NOIRE
PRESENT DAY, SEVEN YEARS LATER

Striding across the open living area of our rooms, I scent the air for Jet and Tenebris. Sensing Ten, I head down the long hall toward my brother's quarters, growling at the way the security cameras pan to follow my every move. When I turn the corner, a screen inlaid at the end of Ten's hall shows a countdown timer. Only an hour and a half before tonight's hunt.

I'm certain the screen is not only a timer but a camera too. I spit at the tech and flip it the bird before knocking on Ten's door. His gruff bark is the only response he gives. Twisting the ornate metal handle, I push my way through and close the door behind me. Glancing up at the ceiling, I take note of the pinhole cameras in every corner of my youngest brother's room. Rama didn't install the swiveling globe-shaped monstrosities from the common areas in our quarters. The way she watches us is less noticeable here because the cameras don't follow.

Doesn't mean I'm any less aware of the truth. There is nowhere in this godsforsaken prison we can go that Rama's eyes don't see us.

Fuck Rama and this maze she's trapped us in. Seven years here haven't dulled my intense drive to get the fuck out.

I don't realize I'm snarling until my younger brother looks up from his chair. He's seated in front of the enormous black stone fireplace that lines one entire wall of his bedroom.

Sighing, Ten snaps his fingers in irritation, getting my attention. "I was hoping to finish this book before the hunt, but it's clear you need something, alpha. Spit it out."

"Watch your mouth. Why are you so tense?" I slide my hands into the pockets of my black jeans as Ten takes me in, pale eyes traveling down my body and back up. I take the opportunity to really examine my younger brother. He's grown up here in the maze, and these days, he's all alpha. Nearly as big as Oskur was. Bigger and brawnier than Jet. Mouthier than I'd like.

Ten sighs but bows his head, an apology of sorts. "Not tense. Alert. And invested in the ending of my book."

"Where are you tonight?" Anger prickles along the back of my neck when I think about Ten going into the maze for the hunt. It's not that an alpha is ever really in danger, but this fucking maze is full of all sorts of monsters. I might be the worst, but Ten is most definitely not. He's less of an asshole than Jet and me, even though he came of age in this hellish labyrinth.

"Maze too." Ten nods, chocolate hair falling across his light eyes. He's the only one of us brothers without the jet-black hair of our father and the dark eyes of our mother. "If we're down here, then Jet must be…" He breaks off as he gestures up at the ceiling.

"Yep. He'll be up in the Atrium tonight, balls deep in rich virtual-reality pussy so he can please the bored housewives of Siargao." I'm not bitter. I want nothing to do with that scene, but Rama rarely allows the three of us to be in the same place at the same time, with the exception of our quarters. Just another way to fuck with us.

Ten doesn't respond, but a lot goes unsaid between my brother and me in that moment. How he hates the way we're nothing more than assassins and prostitutes in here. How he'd give almost anything to escape this place.

"One day, brother," I whisper, low enough I'm sure the cameras won't pick it up. Alphas have extraordinary hearing. Ten doesn't bother to agree. He's not harboring hope we'll ever escape this prison. I don't harbor hope either. I harbor ill fucking will toward the woman who enslaved us here in the first place. If it's the last thing I ever do in this life, I'll get out of this place and destroy the woman who put me here.

∼

Leaving Ten to his novel, I use my senses to locate my middle brother, Jet. He's at the opposite end of our quarters in the hallway we use for knife throwing practice. He likes to use it for other recreational activities because covert alcoves line the entire hall.

The sloppy sounds of fucking ring off the stones as my pupils dilate, nostrils widening. I round a corner to see Jet screwing a panting woman bent over a black velvet sofa. She could be anyone. A bored wife. Someone's daughter in need of a lesson. A junkie looking for the thrill of bedding an alpha male in his sexual prime. This sort of private, one-on-one show with Jet is one of the many ways Rama exerts her dominance over us. Jet has no more choice in this than any of us do, although he likes to pretend this is his preference.

We all have our skills, and Jet is exceptionally creative while fucking.

The woman is chained, arms stretched along both sides of the sofa's back as Jet rails into her viciously. The chains are meant to amp up his alpha libido, the same way the drugs they provide him get him ready to fuck rich women upstairs in the Atrium all night.

Jet turns his head only slightly to the side as I lean up against the dark stone wall and wait for him to finish. He pounds into the woman's dripping pussy over and over, cum pooling on the floor in a steady stream as she screams in ecstasy and he grunts his release.

I don't say a word as he slips out of the woman, wiping his still-hard dick off with a towel. Throwing the sticky fabric on top of her back, he presses a button set into the stone wall of this particular alcove. The woman's faint, satisfied moans ring in my ears as Jet rolls his eyes, walking past me. He doesn't turn to look when steel bars close down over the alcove and the back wall opens. Black-clothed and masked helpers come in, unchain the woman, and drag her away. We'll never see her again. Nobody ever risks coming back twice.

I tried to get out this way once. Killed three of Rama's beta workers and nearly got my leg hacked off by the descending bars before Ten dragged me back into the hallway. I'm a fucking lion pacing in a zoo cage. One day, I'll get out and raze everything to the ground to kill the bitch who threw me in here.

I follow Jet back into the main living room area of our quarters, frowning as I glance around. Our quarters are beautiful, or they would be if they were mine by choice. Knowing we're stuck here just makes me hate every black velvet sofa, every black stone on the wall, even the black fucking rugs. I suspect Rama made it beautiful because everything in the maze is for show. It's all one huge production for her rich clients. They want to see monsters being monsters in beautiful, seductive surroundings. They want to touch us and taste us from relative safety. They want to watch us do their dirty work.

Jet stalks to our fridge, still nude, and grabs water out of it, downing it with one great gulp. His broad chest still heaves from the exertion, his cock swinging around like a damn baseball bat. "Rama wants me in the first show for her VIPs, so it's ten solid hours of sex for me tonight."

"I didn't say anything, brother," I murmur, training my eyes on him. He glares back until, finally, his dark eyes flicker away. He still blames himself for touching those fucking coins. Reaching into the fridge again, he grabs a vial of purple liquid and downs that too, grimacing at the taste as it goes down.

I despise that he takes uppers to deal with his nights in the Atrium, but it is what it is. Jet needs it to handle the shit they put him through upstairs. I can't fault him for that. My pack is in survival mode the longer we're restrained here. Lesser alphas would have gone certifiable at this point.

Jet pulls a cigarette from a pack on the counter, fishing a lighter off the island at the same time. His shoulders shrug upward as he continues, his pupils blowing wide as the uppers hit his bloodstream. "I never thought I'd get bored of sex, but I can honestly say I am reaching my limit." Jet frowns and sighs again, sucking at the cigarette before releasing pale rings into the air.

It's not that Jet is bored, not really. It's that nothing will ever ignite or sate an alpha's intense sexual need but an omega, ideally our bondmate. I assume Rama knows enough about alphas to be aware of that. Maybe not, though, or she'd be dangling omegas in front of me constantly. A reminder of how her father offered her to me seven hellish years ago.

Jet's dark eyes find mine again. "I heard Rama put a fucking naga in the lower levels."

"Godsdamnit," I bark out. "She must be going deep into the Tempang. I've never heard of a naga settling in any of the provinces, unless the outside has changed..."

Jet shrugs again. "One of the rich bitches from upstairs told me someone tried to get out through the lower levels, so Rama found a fucking naga from somewhere and threw him in the basement to keep us away. Looks like your theory about the lower levels is probably right."

A dull ache spreads between my eyes as I pinch the brow of my nose. I've theorized the entire seven years we've been stuck in here that the lower levels hold the key to a way out. So far, I haven't found it, though. Sounds like I'm not the only monster with a bone-deep desire to leave.

A naga complicates things. I had planned to stalk the very lowest levels of the maze tonight during the hunt, but I won't risk a naga until I learn more. It's too dangerous, and nagas are too fucking big for me to take on without an army.

Once you become Rama's puppet, the only thing you're good for is fucking or killing the marks she sends in, or both. And Rama controls every moment of it through orchestrated bullshit and the disks buried in our arms. I have no army here, and never will.

"Where are you tonight?" Jet questions, handing me his cigarette after a deep puff.

"Maze with Ten."

Jet laughs cruelly. "Guess you're not off Rama's shit list after that stunt you pulled last month?"

"Hardly a stunt to kill her favorite handler when she dangled him the way she did. I've never *not* been on the shit list. She won't kill me; she has too much fun fucking with me."

"Still, you've been on maze duty ever since." He laughs. "Out there stalking and killing. Fucking is far easier, and you get to come."

"Who says I don't come when I stalk and kill?"

Jet ignores that, rolling his eyes. "Where's Ten right now? Shouldn't he be getting ready?"

"He's reading."

Jet's eyes soften for a moment. I know he'd never admit it out loud, but he worries for our youngest brother. Jet and I can handle this place, but eventually, it'll break Tenebris. He doesn't have the vicious, cruel, violent streak we do.

"We've got to get him out, you know." Jet's voice is thoughtful, quiet enough that I wonder if he's simply thinking aloud and not expecting a response.

I growl at my middle brother. "Finish getting ready, Jet; it's almost time."

Jet nods and takes another slow sip of the purple uppers, sucking in a hiss when the bitter taste coats his tongue. Snarling, I turn and head for my room.

Thirty minutes later, I'm armed to the teeth with weapons, zipping up a black leather coat, when Ten strides into my room without knocking. He takes a look at my leather. "Not planning to shift tonight?"

Shaking my head, I strap a serrated knife to my forearm, growling at the metal disk that flashes the fucking countdown back at me. It's embedded in my skin, tying me permanently to all the computerized systems and gadgets that make this godsdamned maze work. I despise not knowing precisely how much Rama knows about me because I'm unaware of what the disk does, other than count down to the hunt and give me permission to kill–or not. It's her own version of psychological warfare.

Glancing at Ten, I frown. "Don't feel like shifting tonight. Stalking in human form is just as fun."

Ten rolls his eyes but laughs. "I was going to run as my wolf, but I guess I'll stick around like this. Someone's got to keep you out of trouble. Not that you listen to me…"

"I'm never in trouble," I counter as Ten lowers his gaze, waggling his brows at me as he gestures around at the maze itself.

Growling, I snap my fangs at him. "Point taken."

The five-minute warning alarm sounds as he and I head toward the front of our living quarters. We can go anywhere in the maze at any time, but we tend to make a competition out of it amongst ourselves by standing in the doorway to our private quarters and waiting for the hunt alarm to go off.

Next to me, Ten snarls deep in his chest as he bends both knees and crouches, watching the screen that's set into the wall opposite the entry to our quarters. With two minutes to go, the screen comes on, and Rama herself smiles broadly at us, just like every other fucking night. A sheet of black hair hangs over one eye, the other done with wildly suggestive makeup designed to make her appear younger than she is.

"Your mark tonight is this man," Rama purrs. A photograph flashes up on the screen of an overweight white man's face. A tiny goatee lines his pudgy chins, expressive brown eyes looking at a camera he probably didn't realize was taking the last ever photo of him alive.

Rama continues in a raspy voice that grates at my sensitive ears, "Our client prefers the mark to meet his end via dismemberment or decapitation. Torture and play suggested but not required. Happy hunting, my children."

My eye twitches at her condescension. Deep in my mind, I picture her face and then my claws slicing her head from her shoulders. And I smile because, one day, I will make it happen.

There's never much more from Rama than a brief description of the evening's mark, but it doesn't matter. On my personal shit list, she is at the very top.

"Wonder what he did…" Ten muses as the screen flashes a sixty-second countdown.

"Don't know, don't care. I'm in the mood for violence." It's an easy retort.

I crouch down next to Ten, snarling when the countdown numbers move to the corner of the screen and the view changes to a room full of the wealthy elite–Rama's customers. Someone in that room paid a lot of money to get our mark thrown into the temple maze tonight. Someone wants that man dead. The reason could be anything–he had a secret, he fucked someone's wife or daughter, he had political aspirations, or saw something he shouldn't have.

I'll never know, and frankly, I don't care. But like every night, I memorize each face on the screen. Those are the people who get off watching monsters kill in the maze. Those are the people who profit off my suffering. Some faces I recognize from my time ruling Siargao, but most are new, the wealthy from other provinces farther inland. I will see them dead if it's the last thing I do.

Rama's so confident the monsters will never get out that she lets us see the clients. It's a mistake. Because when I do get out, I will hunt down every fucking one of them.

The buzzer goes off, and Ten sprints up the hallway into the black depths of the maze with me right behind. When he and I hunt together, I always bring up the rear to have his back. It's how alpha packs work. The alpha brings up the rear, just like wolves.

We use our senses to sweep our way through the levels closest to our quarters, but there's no one here. Rama's minions must have dropped the mark somewhere in one of the lower levels or the other side of the maze where the vamps and rorshachs live.

We prowl up hall after hall, the mark's scent nowhere to be found until we get to the enormous maze's large stone chapel. The scent of fear is strong here, although the mark isn't here now. A quick breath tells me he *was* here, probably dropped here, but he's gone now.

The alpha urge to hunt overtakes the more logical side of my brain. My body focuses on finding the man we're meant to kill tonight.

Growling, Ten and I turn as one and jog through the chapel, along the pews, and out the back door into another dark hallway, following the man's scent. The floor is slick with piss, so he definitely came in here. A cackling laugh rings up the hallway as a human grunts and then screams.

The fucking rorschachs. Pushing in front of Ten, I sprint up the hall toward the smell and sounds of a fight. With my alpha eyesight, I make out the mark at the end of the hallway. He's surrounded by three of the monsters we call rorschachs. Their faces are eyeless, noseless masks of ever-changing textures and patterns, just like the famous inkblot masks from history. But they've got the ability to take on anyone's face for a minute or two. They were there the night Oskur was killed. They're the reason he's dead.

When I see them, murderous need overtakes all reason in my mind.

Bellowing up the hall, I sprint toward the group. The mark's eyes go wild when he sees us, and he scrambles to his feet and hauls ass as the rorschachs turn toward me. We're not supposed to kill other monsters in the maze; Rama makes sure we can't do that without retribution-starvation, pain, physical attacks. Not that monsters don't occasionally die here in one way or another.

I've never given a fuck about the repercussions. If I get a chance to kill something, I do it. Fuck her and fuck her maze. She wants to torture me far too much to kill me. I barrel through the group of smaller monsters, knocking two to the side but focusing on the largest of them. Ten backs me up immediately, blocking the smaller ones as they scramble upright and hiss.

I don't know their names; they don't speak unless they're speaking in the voice of the face they take, but this is the one who sacrificed one of his people to kill Oskur. He's still got a long scar down one mottled arm from my claws. I fuck with him every chance I get.

Slashing black-clawed hands across his chest, I roar with satisfaction as he screams in pain, a high-pitched sound that fuels my predatory instinct. The rorschach reels backward and takes off to get away from me, followed by the other two.

Ten stops beside me, chest heaving. "I suppose you're never planning to get off the shit list?"

"That was for Oskur."

Ten sighs.

I don't bother to say anything further as I jog up the dark hall after the fleeing monsters and our mark. Mere seconds later, we're in the opera house room. I'll admit, for a good show, this is a great place to end a life. Rama clearly thought of the cinematic aspect when she built the Temple Maze because there are all sorts of beautiful rooms to kill someone in. The opera house has great acoustics. The screams ring beautifully along the high, paneled ceiling.

The mark is in the middle of the stage, all lights pointed at him, his face a mask of terror as the rorschachs, and then Ten and I, push him toward the middle. Unfortunately for him, the vampiri stand in the shadows at the opposite side of the stage. This mark didn't put up much of a chase, but the sheer amount of aggression in the air now that we all surround him is enough to get my hackles rising, my competitive nature taking over as I stalk closer to the trembling human.

When I hear shouting, I look up the opera house's central aisle. The human contingent comes through the front door swinging baseball bats. The leader sees the collection of monsters on stage with the mark and frowns. He hates dealing with us, and we hate dealing with him. But the human element in the maze is the largest of the monster groups. Alphas are the smallest. Yet another way Rama continues to make fucking with me her personal mission.

I don't grace the humans with another look, but they turn to go as a group. If a monster finds the mark first, the humans have got no chance of being the ones to take him out. Rama's got it all planned out.

Onstage, one of the rorschachs morphs his face into a beautiful woman, although his body remains monstrous. The mark's eyes go wild as he shakes his head, stumbling backward as he screams, "No," over and over again. The rorschach stalks around the mark in a circle, berating him verbally before turning into its typical form again. The unfortunate man throws his arms over his face and screams into them, rocking on the floor like a child.

I should feel compassion, probably. If I were normal, I would. But I'm not. I'm an asshole and an alpha. I've seen thousands of men cry just like this. At the end of the day, all of us monsters have one job in this place: to do Rama's bidding or lose our heads. Honestly, the hunt is the only part of the maze where I get to still feel like myself. Stalking, hunting, chasing. The blood.

Gods, I love the blood.

Next to me, Ten stands quietly, watching the show play out as the rorschachs fuck with the man over and over until he's a bumbling mess of snot and tears. They swipe at him with long blue claws until he's bleeding all over the stage. Just surface cuts, nothing severe. Nobody has permission to kill him yet. But the man is falling apart. And the smell of blood only serves to amp up the waiting tension in the room.

My mouth waters as I hover around the edges, watching the lesser monsters fuck with the mark. The timer disk embedded in my arm pings, and all the monsters look down at their own forearms at the same time. Apparently, the client is ready for the grand finale. The disk counts down from thirty as we all crouch, looking at the mark. He must sense the impending attack, because dark, pleading eyes fly around at us, begging for his life.

We can't help you, little man, I muse. *We cannot even help ourselves.*

My eyes wander across the stage to Cashore, the vampiri king. He's a mean motherfucker, probably the closest thing to me in this place. But we have an agreement–I don't go near his quarters, and his people don't come near mine. He tips his head at me with an evil smile, waggling his forearm to show the fucking disk that's approaching zero.

Go time.

An alarm sounds, and my disk flashes red, per usual. Not my turn. Godsdamnit. Next to me, Ten visibly relaxes. I could swoop in anyhow, but then I'd have a bigger fight on my hands.

Across from me, all the vampiri disks flash green as Cashore roars in triumph. His people spring across the stage and descend upon the mark, ripping into him with black claws and sharp teeth. His large body jerks once, twice as he screams, the sound of claws drawn across flesh ringing across the opera stage. There's a deep grunt from the mark and then the squishy noise of intestines hitting the wooden floors as the man groans.

Still seeing red, I watch a vampiri rip the mark's arm from its socket with a loud pop as the man screams, gurgling around a mouthful of blood. The monster brings the severed arm to Cashore with a bow as the vampiri takes it and looks across the stage at the rest of us.

Breaking the arm in half, Cashore sucks the marrow out of the bone, grinning at me before walking across the stage and tossing the arm at my feet. "A little consolation prize, Noire. It wasn't your night, but then again, it rarely seems to be. I wonder when Rama will ever find another client willing to pay the price for you to finish a mark..."

I snarl as I kick the arm toward the rorschachs, who descend upon it in a crazed fury.

In the middle of the stage, the mark's screams have slowed to the occasional grunt. He's not dead, but he's barely hanging on, drowning in pain. He won't last more than another minute or two, and when the vampiri are done, he'll be an eviscerated, dried husk. Mission accomplished for Rama's client.

There's a delightful ripping sound, and a slab of fat gets thrown out of the frenzy, landing with a squelch next to my shoe. I snarl at the vampiri as they rip into the man, balling my fists as I urge myself to hold back from taking over. Tonight is not my fight.

Next to me, Ten steps forward, growling, "Let's get outta here, Noire."

He's right; we should, but the dominant look on Cashore's face calls to the alpha side of my brain. He's challenging me the same way he always challenges me, every fucking night we hunt. I don't know if he's bored or just can't help himself.

Let's run the middle levels, Ten sends me through our mental bond. *Everyone is up here; it's a good time to examine some of those hallways again.*

I don't bother to nod, but Cashore cocks his head to the side as I back away from him, his expression triumphant.

The sounds of flesh tearing follow us as Ten and I head out of the opera house and through dark hallways toward the entrance to the middle levels. Already, the maulin foxes who clean up after the monsters flit in the shadows, waiting their turn to pick at the bones. Smiling, I wish them the best. They, at least, seem happy to be here.

We run for hours, examining doors and fake windows and looking for something, anything that might mean a way out. But like every night we do this, I can't find a single godsdamned thing that leads me to believe there's even a way out of this hellhole.

When we finally return to our rooms, I shower and lie in my bed, looking up at the dark stone ceiling. Every night I return here, temporarily defeated in my attempt to find a way out, that ceiling seems a little lower. I dread the day I wake up to find it right above my head, ready to crush me to dust.

Liuvang, I pray to the deity I scorned my whole life, *send me something, some sign. I have got to get out of here.*

CHAPTER TWO

DIANA

I sort through the photos on my computer, searching for the perfect one. It's an in-the-moment shot of my subject, taken just days after he was thrown into Rama's maze.

Even the word "maze" sends a jolt of terror up my spine. It's shrouded in secrecy and rumors, but if you are put in, you never come out. It's Rama's dumping ground for anyone who defies or betrays her. Or anyone she simply dislikes. Now her wealthy clients have access to the maze too, paying her great sums of money to dispose of anyone they want.

I find the picture I'm looking for, sucking in a breath as I look at my subject. Dark hair is slicked back, revealing elegant, angular features and a square, masculine jaw. Everything about the way he's standing, looking across the hall toward the camera, indicates deadliness. He's intent, poised, the predatory look in his eyes seeping right from the file on my computer screen, sinking deep into the marrow of my bones.

This is a dangerous male. The most dangerous monster ever to rule Siargao. Before Rama took over, anyhow.

Alpha *Noire*.

Even his name means darkness, something I've always wondered about. When he was born, did his parents take one look and know their son would be the most ruthless alpha to ever rule this province?

I met him once after he killed his alpha father and took over the Ayala pack. He came to meet my father to present himself as the new ruling alpha—a long-standing tradition amongst rulers. Our pack's province is on the far

29

side of Lombornei, but Noire came anyhow. He nearly bowled me over with alpha dominance then. I was only seven at the time, but meeting him is a permanent imprint in my mind.

I drag the photo to the top left of the profiling document I'm working on for the client. She wants a full and complete picture of Noire. Who he is, every crime he's ever been implicated in, everything he's ever been convicted of, everything about his family and pack, and the details surrounding his abduction and entry into Rama's maze. I'll combine this with a full scene suggestion report, recommending to the clients how best to utilize Noire's talents to kill their chosen mark.

The work is gruesome, being the stage director of innocent peoples' final moments, but I have no choice in this—none at all. I'm certain Rama forces me to do it because it's a way to ensure death is always around me, and at her direction.

Staring down Noire's list of crimes, I shudder as icy prickles drag down my spine. Dismemberment, murder in all three degrees, assault with and without a deadly weapon, decapitation. He was once accused of sending a man's head to his wife in a box after the stupid male betrayed Noire. If a crime can be committed, Noire has been accused of it.

He's been in the maze for seven years, though, and Rama is in charge now. There's no more government, not that they had any power when Noire was in charge, or so I've heard. The client has asked for a complete profile of Noire, and I'm the very best at dredging up every nitty-gritty detail there is. In the few years I've had this shitty job, I've never been asked to profile him. He is almost never chosen to kill the marks, unless he was before I got the job. Nobody can afford what Rama charges for Noire. Until this client, apparently.

Satisfied my report is finished, I download the whole thing onto a thumb drive and ring a bell.

Precisely thirty seconds later, there's a rap at my door. When I open it, one of the street urchins who frequents this block shows up with his grimy palm held up. He knows the drill, the same as I do. We all work for Mistress Rama in one way or another, even Siargao's children. I hand him the thumb drive. "Straight to the docks with you."

He rolls his eyes as if it's obvious where he should go, and I suppose it is. Rama's goons litter the docks. They'll take this drive and deliver it to her so she can deliver it to the client. My job is done. It's on the tip of my tongue to remind the child to be careful, but I hold that comment back. I was a street urchin once, and I wasn't careful enough. That's why I'm stuck here now, working for the woman who rules this city under her bejeweled, elegant thumb.

Not that I've seen her in person in a very long time. But she appears nightly on every screen in the city for evening prayer. A prayer with her well-being and power front and center. A prayer that happens right after every screen in the city turns on to televise the maze and the mark's demise. Another reminder of how very much she owns all of us.

The child snatches the drive and goes, and I watch my project disappear with him. Once he's gone, I turn back into my dismal apartment and walk to the window. Looking out, I smile when I see clouds rolling in over the hills. It's going to rain soon, and that's my favorite time in Siargao. Everyone else huddles inside, but I can put on my running shoes and sprint through the streets, along the shoreline as I watch the train crawl its way along the Kan River.

I run for miles when it rains. I run until I forget the memory of my dead pack and my dead twin brother. Everyone dead. I run until my emotions quiet into a simmer deep in my chest. Reaching into the secret compartment under my desk, I bring out the only photo I have of my twin, Dore. We're only seven or so in the photo, our arms slung around one another as I peck him on the cheek.

Our birthday. A happy time. Eventually, he and I were on the run from Rama's invading army, fighting for our lives, fighting for our freedom. She caught us, of course. With her superior technology and devious innovations, she caught *everyone* and subtly took over the Vinituvari province. And then she came here to Siargao and took it from Noire's Ayala pack overnight, dragging Dore and me along with her.

Lost in horrid memories, I reach down to my left arm and stroke my way along the intricately angular tattoo that goes up my entire arm and elbow. Father gave Dore and me matching tattoos when we turned eleven. I've often wondered about the timing; did Father know what was coming? Rama murdered him right after my fourteenth birthday.

I've always loved the tattoo's design, even though knowing Dore had the same one sends a knife straight through my broken heart.

Glancing out my window, I look at the floating city that glitters in the gray sky above Siargao's river valley. Rama's up there now, entertaining the wealthy. They live among beautiful, bright towers there and in Siargao's foothills, while the rest of us scrabble to stay alive down here by the riverside, praying for someone to relieve us of the woman who terrorizes us at every turn.

Growling, I head into my room, searching under my bed for my running shoes. They're threadbare at this point. I've nearly worn holes in the bottoms of them from my late-night runs.

A crack of lightning streaks across the sky, the clouds opening up to pour rain down on the valley. Smiling, I open the window to my back porch and raise the awning, providing a small, dry space. Moments later, a maulin fox slinks out of the growing shadows and hops up onto my railing, picking its way along until it's close to me.

The fox's lower jaw separates as he drops a tiny bone in my hand. He's been bringing me bones for years just like this, usually when it's rainy and he wants to come out of the cold. I scratch behind his ear and tickle under his chin as he rubs his cheek along the palm of my hand. When I'm satisfied he's happy with his spot perched on a dry section of my porch, I head back inside.

Moving my TV stand aside, I pull a panel off my wall and extract a large box. Taking the top off, I look at the hundreds of bones the fox has brought me over the last seven years. I toss the newest gift in with the rest and close the box, shoving it back in the wall and placing the TV stand back where it was.

I join the fox, lacing up my running shoes as he licks one paw slowly. Vibrant golden eyes meet mine as he cocks his head to the side.

Be safe, my friend, I think.

I imagine he understands me when he dips his head and focuses on me again, his gaze intent. We sit that way as the rain pours until finally the itch to run wins out. Stroking the tip of his chin one more time, I tell him goodbye and head to the front of my apartment just as the TV clicks on. There's no warning, but a man's screams ring out through my apartment. They ring through my open window too as every neighbor's television blares the death of tonight's mark.

Turning, I watch the beginning of the televised massacre. The clients nearly always agree with my scene suggestions, and I suggested the opera house for this man's final moments. The empty seats, the old-timey wooden stage, the velvet curtains–it's a beautiful place to die.

Plus, the vampiri in the maze always do the opera house justice, and I selected them to be the harbingers of this man's death.

I don't stay to watch them kill him. I can't. "I'm sorry," I whisper under my breath to Rama's latest victim.

If I could help you, if I could change this, I would.

Holding back tears, I open my door and step out into the hallway. I jog down a set of stairs and out into the rain, pulling a hood up over my head as I look across the street. Two of Rama's goons stand there, watching me in the way they often do.

"Evening, gents," I snap, flipping them double birds as they growl. Everywhere I go, they're there. This whole town works for Rama in some way, and she loves keeping an eye on me because of who my father was. Just a reminder that she took everything away from me, and I have no choice but to live in her capital city and work for her. Controlling Siargao means she controls the whole continent, with the exception of the Tempang forest, of course. But the other provinces need the thick oil that's pumped out of the ground here.

The street is full of people scrambling to get inside, away from the deluge. I walk down the center as it empties, smiling as I lift my head for the rain to hit my face. It slides down my cheeks and neck, into my shirt. My smile deepens. This, at least, is something Rama can't take from me. The joy of a nighttime run in the rain.

Across from me, my neighbor, Trig, cooks bao in front of his restaurant. The rain is good for his business. When I turn his way, he looks up at me and blinks twice, slowly. Then he turns away, eyeing his patrons.

Still, I've received the message loud and clear. Two blinks for a need to meet.

I may be forced into servitude, crushed under Rama's boot, but I'll die before I give in and accept my current fate. Turns out I'm not the only one, and there's a growing movement of people who want to rebel against her somehow. Small, but growing.

I pick up a jog, heading toward the shoreline, and then I run along the Kan, people watching from dry porches as I pass. I push my muscles hard until I reach the mouth of the river where it empties into Lon Bay. Across the bay, an island stands, a solitary sentinel for the entire Siargao province.

The maze.

My father built the labyrinth, then Rama grew an island on top of it, and dragged the whole thing here, settling it at the mouth of the river once she took control. I can barely comprehend how she managed it.

"I miss you, Dore," I whisper to my brother's ghost as I look out at the maze island. It's as tropical as everything in this province, but seeing it makes me long for the rolling green hills and valleys of my homeland, Vinituvari. I miss the delicate, detailed architecture my father was famous for designing. I miss the hand pies. I miss riding my horse, Dove. I miss every fucking thing about where I came from. Shit, I even miss the cold.

"One day, Dore. One day, I will get retribution for what she did to you. I promise you that," I whisper again, more to myself than my brother. I don't know how I will, but something's got to give.

I watch the maze island silently for a while before turning and jogging up into the hills toward the graveyard near the end of the Riverside District. It marks the last bit of wildness before glittering towers take over as skyscrapers replace the trees, heading up the valley into the low, rolling mountains. The wealthy live safely in those buildings, using the big airport on top of one of the skyscrapers to travel to and from Rama's city in the sky.

Fuck all of them.

Slowing to a stop, I pick my way through the graveyard, to the spot where I collect rocks in memory of Dore. I didn't get to bury him; Rama made sure of that. But she can't tear his memory from my fucking memory banks, so this is how I make sure he's gone but never, ever forgotten.

I grab a small purple stone from my pocket and lay it gently on the pile, dropping to both knees. "I miss you, Dore. One day, Liuvang-willing, I will see you again, brother." I whisper that last prayer to the goddess under my breath. Praying to the fox goddess, Liuvang, is a sin, according to Rama, punishable by death. The only one anyone is allowed to pray to is Mistress Rama. She's a damn psychopath.

A sudden whirring noise whines behind me, the faint brush of wind brushing my blond waves aside, despite them being soaked. Whipping around, I'm shocked when an entire floating office, complete with a woman sitting at a desk, slides out of the dark clouds and descends until it's in the middle of the road. Inside the office, Rama sits at the desk, watching me, hands clasped together on the desktop. I haven't seen her in person in several years. Two at least, maybe three.

This is a bad sign, that she's here in person.

I stand, rain sluicing down my face as air pulses from underneath the floating office. Already, heady nerves bundle in my stomach, and I force myself not to clench my jaw as I pick around the gravestones and approach her. It's what she wants; I know that well enough from being forced to grow up under her thumb.

"Hello, Diana," she purrs, her voice throaty and seductive. I want to slice my claws across it and separate her fucking head from her shoulders.

"Hello, Mistress," I speak up, dipping my head. *Mistress bitch*, I add silently in my mind.

Rama stands in the office, and it maintains its floating position easily as she crosses the room. I see a faint distortion on the surface. It looks like I'm peering into an office with only three sides, but I'm sure there's some sort of force field across the front to protect her.

God, if only us regular people had access to tech like this. But she keeps most tech under lock and key, and nobody leaves Siargao.

"I'm sure you're wondering why I came down here personally, Diana,"

Rama begins, examining her nails before clasping both hands in front of her waist.

Not really, I want to bark, but I grit my jaw instead. "Was there an issue with my most recent profiling report? I sent it about an hour ago with one of the kids..." I trail off, unsure where to go from here.

"No," Rama laughs, "the client wants Noire's profile, and she's got Noire's profile, thanks to you. You've outlived your usefulness as a profiler, Diana. I have other plans for you now." Her face splits into an evil smile as I hear footsteps behind me.

When I whirl around, I see the goons, the same two who always follow me. "What's going on?" I bark as Rama hisses and points a dart gun at my face. She pulls the trigger, and before I can even register the anger, something pokes into my neck.

My knees give out, and I sink to the pavement, spinning as I fall to my back, the rain peppering my face like a hail of bullets. Distantly, I'm aware of Rama laughing as she directs the goons to do something. My hearing goes fuzzy, and the last thing I see before darkness takes me is a man's face.

One of the goons. He's got both middle fingers up and pointed straight at me. And he's smiling, his teeth black and crooked, his breath foul.

"Gotcha," he snarls. "It's finally your turn, little omega."

∽

Voices surround me as I struggle to blink my eyes open. My mouth is one enormous cotton ball as I open it to say something and nothing comes out. The back of my head feels like a split log, pain radiating to the front of my face. My fangs descend, a protective move that happens involuntarily sometimes.

Snarling, I feel saliva drip down my fangs, coating my lower lip. Everything is fuzzy until I blink three or four times, and a black room comes into view. Black walls, black ceiling. I move to sit, but...I can't. I grunt as something pokes into me. Blinking hard, I glance down to see a corset.

A fucking corset. I'm wearing a cornflower blue corset and below that, a matching skirt.

"What do y'spose she did?" a harsh voice grates at my ears as I continue blinking, struggling to wrap my mind around the corset and matching skirt and a black room I don't recognize.

"Doesn't matter," a softer voice murmurs. "Not our place to guess. Finish prepping and keep your mouth shut."

"Where...where am I?" I grunt, finally finding my voice, even though it sounds like someone dragging me across gravel.

"The maze, of course," quips the first voice cheerfully. Then, a little more solemnly, "You go in tonight."

The maze. The fucking maze.

Struggling against whatever binds me, I bite at a hand as it comes close to my face. I still can't fully see past a foot or two, but there's a yip before someone backhands me, my head snapping back against something hard. Pain blooms at the back of my throat as a snarl rumbles out of my mouth.

"Try it again, bitch," the quieter of the two voices snaps. "It's our job to prep you, and you'll never make it out, so start praying to Mistress Rama that it's quick for you. Bite my hand again, and you'll go in missing a finger or two."

A mist of something that smells like pure sex hits me straight in the face as I try to leap back and can't, still strapped to some kind of platform, tilted upright so the two people can do whatever the hell they're doing.

The mist coats my face and hair until it drips from my eyelashes, and I start to get a sense of the two women in the room with me. The quieter one sprays a steady stream along my neck and shoulders as the second one watches her with a wary, guarded expression. "That seems like enough, Heti. Don't you think?"

"Mistress Rama said to coat her, so coat her we will. You don't want to answer to the Mistress if you forget a single part of the mark prep process, Del. I can promise you that. Finish her hair."

The chattier woman steps closer to me. "Please don't bite me, okay? I can't help you. I'm just doing my job."

I snap again, but she sighs and presses a button on a table beside her. Immediately, a strap goes across my neck, crushing my windpipe so hard, I can't even turn my head to the side. Another one flies across my face, slipping between my teeth as the woman grumbles, "I didn't want to do that to you. Why'd you have to fight?"

The quieter of the two huffs out a disbelieving breath and sets the mister bottle down. "No point talking to the marks, Del. They're dead, remember? Just do your best to keep your chin up and your head attached to your shoulders."

I struggle against the thick bands crisscrossing my body and neck, but I can't move as the worker fusses with my hair, piling it all on top of my head with metal pins that definitely couldn't double as any sort of weapon.

The fucking maze. I'm going into the fucking maze.

That bitch.

The wheels of my mind spin so fast that I can practically hear my brain heating as I struggle to think through this process.

The helpers finish messing with me, despite my struggle. Watching them clean up their tools sends my anxiety into overdrive, like their cleaning is a countdown timer to throwing me into the fucking maze to be killed.

And they continue cleaning, glancing at a clock on the wall that indicates the time. The room is painfully silent until the platform I'm chained to creaks and moves, sliding forward on a track toward an archway cut into one side of the room. The track seems to disappear off into the darkness like a horrible roller coaster ride from hell.

Despite knowing they won't help me, I can't resist the urge to beg them to let me out. "Please," I attempt to choke out around the strap. "Please, don't do this." Fear has my spine locked tight as the one called Heti smirks and Del's face falls a little. She clasps one hand over her heart as they follow my platform along the track, waving a sad goodbye to me as the platform heads through the archway and disappears, leaving the black room behind.

"No!" I try to scream. "Let me the fuck out of here!" My words are muffled around the thick leather between my lips. Gooseflesh crawls across my skin as freezing air slaps me in the face. The platform I'm strapped to rumbles noisily along the track, through a long dark hallway until it comes to a stop in front of a black stone wall. In front of me, a screen whirs to life, Rama appearing with a smirky smile on the brightly lit screen.

"Your mark tonight is this woman. The client wants her tortured and pulled apart in every possible way, drawing the death out as long as possible. Happy hunting, my children."

My face flashes across the screen for a few long seconds. I look…normal in the picture, as if they took it while I was walking down the street. Blond hair, blue eyes, freckles. There's a tension in the crinkles at the edges of my eyes, but I look…average.

The screen goes blank as I struggle against the bindings, although there's no point. This maze isn't designed for marks to get out. I've never heard of someone coming back from the Temple Maze. The platform creaks and begins moving again, floating through pitch darkness like a macabre circus ride. The blackness even eats up the light from the screen behind me until there's nothing, and I can't even see my body when I look down. I suck in deep breaths, certain my heart is pounding loud enough for the entire maze to hear.

When the platform rounds a corner of the track and another stone door opens, there's a little bit of light. Then the stench hits, all unwashed bodies and filth. My mouth dries up as I struggle against the bindings, huddled in the middle of the platform. It continues creaking forward, until I'm able to see slats in the stone walls, claws and arms reaching through.

Oh God, the track here is only as wide as my platform, which isn't that wide. Every arm reaching through will be able to touch me. The monsters. Oh fuck.

Liuvang, please help me, I pray to the deity.

Most of the arms end in claws of all shades, and horrifyingly, there's a viewing window of sorts where I can see mouths, snouts, teeth, gnarled hands coated in sores. A few of the viewing holes have erect cocks poking through, deep grunts emitting from the monsters those swinging cocks are attached to.

I struggle not to scream–when a black-clawed hand grabs my hair and yanks it hard, snarls ringing through the small, cold hallway. Another hand reaches out and grips my breast through the bodice, squeezing hard enough to elicit a scream from me. That's what she wants, Rama. She wants the terror, the tease of how violent and ruthless the maze's monsters are. This is a prelude, something to terrify the maze's marks before the monsters play with them. Something to scare the shit out of me because, shortly, there will be no stone walls separating me from them.

I force myself to look forward, focusing on the end of the hallway as hands grip and tear at me, claws scratching at my skin until I'm bleeding from multiple stinging wounds. The monsters hurl insults and innuendoes like bricks, their filthy words sinking into my mind as I focus harder on the end of the hallway.

After what seems like hours, my platform reaches the end, and another stone door shuts behind me, enclosing me in darkness once more. It moves forward with a click and a hiss and then travels downward, the floor underneath me opening into a brightly lit room. My eyes struggle with the sudden explosion of light; everything here is golden and opulent. A gigantic circular bar enclosed inside a golden cage holds extravagantly dressed men and women, drinking.

Their heads swivel as the lights dim, and I see a stage. This has never been televised to the general public; I don't know what I'm looking at. But if I had to guess, this is a way Rama's wealthy patrons can enjoy the maze's monsters without being in real danger. The entire caged bar is full of wealthy-looking people, dressed to the nines and turning toward the stage. Small caged rooms line one side of the bar, and inside, it's easy to see men and women in various stages of getting fucked by monsters. But the monsters shimmer and shake like they're not real.

Virtual reality? Is that what I'm looking at? A safe way for the rich to experience the maze's beasts without worrying over their safety?

My stomach ties itself in knots as I resist the urge to be sick, my platform traveling down through the room and finally pulling to a stop. The people inside the bar's safety cage look up at me, pointing and laughing before the lights dim further, and a velvet curtain slides up on the stage. I can't pull my eyes from the scene as a huge alpha male stalks from the shadows, an erection clearly visible in his pants.

Noire's brother, Jet, the one he's closest to in age. I've profiled him a few times over the years, but seeing him in person is a shocking experience. He's fucking enormous, far bigger than I remember my own alpha father being, even in his prime. Jet slips his shirt off as the people in the cage take their seats and wait.

His pants slide off next, and then the crowd is presented with his naked form, his erect cock straining toward a woman chained to a table that pops up out of the floor. Jet shifts into his wolf and stalks across the stage, shoving his nose between the woman's thighs as she screams in terror.

My heart pounds in my chest as he paces around the table, scenting her before he shifts into human form again and unlocks one of her ankles from its chain. The woman brings her legs together quickly, but Jet yanks them back open wide and slaps her pussy with his thick cock.

Below me, the crowd goes wild, cheering him on. And then there's at least half an hour of him taking her in every possible way a woman can be taken. He's inventive and creative, and the crowd is crazed as the woman comes multiple times, despite her screams for him to stop.

Every now and again, the patrons glance up at me and point, snickering and laughing. I'm obviously just here to be presented to them. For them to know these are my last hours of life. I can't stop looking around the room, but my eyes return over and over to Jet and the way he fucks the woman in ways I could never have even imagined.

This room is debauchery in all its possible forms, and I'm so sick to my heart from watching it that I'm not even terrified for my life at the moment. I want to rage and scream and do something. But as the platform holding me shifts to move again, I can't resist another backward look at the performing alpha on the stage.

The woman is limp and catatonic at this point, but another platform comes up out of the stage, a muscular man tied to this one, his ass up in the air for everyone to see. Jet drops the woman and stalks across the stage to the man, but a door opens up in the wall above the stage, and my platform exits through it.

I hold on to that little bit of light from the ostentatious room, knowing it's the last light of any sort I'll ever see. With a click, the chains holding my arms and legs snap open, and the platform dumps sideways. I hit the ground hard enough to pull a grunt from my body, but then the floor opens up below me, and I *fall, fall, fall.*

When I hit the ground, the air whooshes from my lungs, my hair in a pile around me. And the very first thing I hear is a clicking hiss.

Oh gods, I'm in the fucking maze.

Not a single thing stands between the monsters and me.

CHAPTER THREE
NOIRE

nother night, another hunt. Slipping a simple black tee over my bulky frame, I turn when I hear Tenebris coming down the hall. Striding across the room, I open my door and gesture for him to come in. The look on his face is carefully neutral as he inclines his head toward me, a respectful gesture from an alpha to *the* alpha.

"I went up to see the mark tonight." Ten's voice sounds easy, but there's a tense quality to it that lifts the hair on the back of my neck.

"Why? We never preview the marks."

Ten shrugs and walks across my room, leaning up against the black stone mantel with his arms crossed. "I've actually been up a few times this month. Just looking for something…different."

I lift a brow. "You went up alone? That's fucking foolish, Ten."

He shrugs again. "Everyone's too focused on the mark to bother one another. Anyhow, the mark's an omega. They doused her in enough pheromone to take down an ox, so they want her played with."

I bristle again. "An omega, are you sure?" We've never seen an omega in the maze. Nearly all omegas in Siargao were part of my pack or one other. I know every single one of them, and if Tenebris' early story is true, Rama killed everyone. "Do we know her?"

Ten shakes his head. "I couldn't place a scent through whatever they coated her with, but I didn't recognize her either."

My wheels spin as Ten stands, keeping quiet. Is it circumstance that

Rama's putting an omega into the maze tonight? There's never been one the entire time we've been here, and I don't believe in circumstance.

Turning to my brother, I nod. "Where are you tonight?"

Ten smiles, but it doesn't reach his eyes. "Maze again with you. Which is a good thing. I'd like to see the omega a little more closely. Tall, delicate, blond, blue eyes. She's beautiful. Are they all like that? I can't remember anymore..."

"She's a dead woman walking," I remind him. I don't need to know anything else about her. And unless we get out of here, Ten will never take an omega. Maybe we can, at least, give him a good time tonight with this one.

Ten shrugs his shoulders. "I think this is the first time I've been excited for a hunt."

Whipping my head up, I cock it to the side and examine my youngest sibling. He leans casually against my fireplace, but there's a tension in the set of his shoulders and muscular frame. There's a predatory agitation about the sense I read from him right now. He wants to hunt this woman.

"What is it about her?" I snap, my alpha bark rolling over him as he bows his head to me.

"Nothing." It's a grumble, but it's a lie.

"Don't lie to me, Tenebris. What is this omega to you?"

He looks up, head bowed with respect. "She feels...different from the other women who get put here. Maybe it's just because she's an omega, and we haven't seen one this whole time."

The wheels in my head spin as I look at my brother and think about what he's saying. The more I think, the more certain I am that Rama sending an omega in here is no coincidence, just another way she can think up to try and fuck with us, me in particular.

For the first time, I regret not going to preview the mark. I'd like to get a sense of this woman before we hunt her tonight. In the end, it won't matter. She will die like so many others before her. It's just...curious.

The disk at my wrist flashes the five-minute warning. Ten shifts up off the fireplace and pads to the door.

Grabbing my favorite knife, I slide it in the holster across my chest and follow him. I spit at the screen outside my room that flashes the countdown timer like every other fucking night. Ahead of me, Ten chuckles low under his breath.

As we pass through the kitchen and living area, Jet holds a glass of purple liquid up to us in a mock cheer. "Just popped back down on a short break between performances. Happy hunting, my children!"

I frown, and Ten snorts while Jet downs the entire glass of uppers. It's so fucking much that his pupils blow wide almost immediately as he snarls at us both, tossing the glass into the sink.

I'll need to do something about this later. The increasing amount of drugs Jet's pumping into his system every night is getting out of control. He's going to become a problem if this keeps going.

"You and I need a chat later," I bark as Jet bows his head, mocking me as he bats his eyelashes. That's the drugs talking because no alpha would ever disrespect his pack alpha in this way.

I cross the room with swift intention, gripping Jet by the neck and throwing him up against the fridge. He dents the door and sinks to the floor, but hops back up with a raging howl, fists balled. The smell of uppers hits me hard when his mouth opens, but I don't back down. I never back down. I'm the fucking pack alpha, even of this sorry three-man pack in this fucking maze.

Siargao was my kingdom before getting put into this goddamn place, and it'll be mine again if it's the last thing I do. But for now, the maze is mine. And this high-as-fuck alpha is mine too.

"You forget your place, brother," I snap as I step into Jet's space, invading it as I whip a hand to his throat and squeeze hard enough to bruise his windpipe.

The alpha bark causes his eyes to lower, but he still struggles against the bond. That's the drugs talking again. Unless it's something more sinister, something deeper. Something like this place finally fucking with pack dynamics enough that my own brother thinks it's okay to challenge me.

I slice my dark claws across Jet's top two ribs and dig them under his skin, snarling in his face as he yowls at the pain. "This is a warning, brother. You know better."

Sweat slides down Jet's face as he squints his eyes against the pain. For him, it's hardly more than an irritation, but getting stabbed by our claws still hurts like a bitch. I slip my claws out, relishing the sound of bone on bone as Jet winces. Blood flows from the wound as he sucks in a deep breath.

The disk in my wrist flashes the sixty-second countdown as Jet's eyes go wide. "I've got to get upstairs. Can't be late. Can't be late. Can't be late."

When he repeats himself again, I narrow my eyes to observe him. There's an anxious tension scratching at our mental bond.

What happens if he's late? Something, clearly. I file it away for later investigation. For now, I drop his throat and indicate he can go.

He sprints for the door as Ten's eyes meet mine, full of sorrow. I don't return the look but head for the door to await Rama's nightly message.

Just before it comes on, Ten turns to me. "Did you have to do that? He's strung out."

"He disrespected me." That's all I need to say because, when I turn to look at Ten, he dips his head an appropriate, respectful amount and nods.

The screen inlaid across from our front entryway blinks several times, then we see Rama herself, looking smug as fuck as she begins her evening's directions.

"Your mark tonight is this woman." A picture flashes up on the screen, and I can see what Ten meant about her earlier. She's stunning. Clearly an omega, even from the little of her shown. Something in the focus of her eyes. If you know what to look for, pack omegas are just different enough from normal human women to be noticeable to an alpha.

"The client wants her tortured and pulled apart in every possible way, drawing the death out as long as possible. Happy hunting, my children."

Rama smirks on the screen, black hair swinging. I always imagine she's speaking directly to me when she comes on the screen. And that little smirk? Someday, I'm going to swipe it right off her face when I slice it from her body with my claws.

"As long as possible?" Ten turns to me as the timer flashes down from ten.

"Someone hates this woman," I grumble as he and I crouch in the front entryway.

Ten huffs. "Let's get to her first."

I turn to look at my brother as he crouches next to me, entirely focused on the dark hallway ahead of us. This maze is finally changing us, who we are, what we want. Ten's never been excited for a hunt before. I'm almost proud, although his interest amps up my competitive nature.

I want the omega first.

The buzzer sounds, and Ten takes off like a shot, me following up the rear, same as I always do. Tonight, Ten is focused. He doesn't bother sweeping the levels closest to us; they almost never drop marks at our doorstep. Instead, he heads right for vampiri territory. For whatever reason, marks often start there. Or in the middle levels where the humans can chase them for a while.

We round a corner, heading toward the chapel, and a scent hits me so hard I stagger and fall to my knees, sucking in deep, gasping breaths. Ten is frozen next to me, doing the same. Omega pheromones. I've never smelled them this strong before, although they usually prep female marks with some level of this. The scent sets off a livewire reaction in my body, every inch of me going rock hard in anticipation of whoever's giving off that smell.

This scent is blood in the water to a school of sharks, me being the biggest and baddest of them. This time, it isn't a general pheromone for monsters; it's specific to alphas. The mark smells like an omega in heat.

If I had any doubt Rama wanted to fuck with me, that doubt is gone. Someone wants this woman dead, and Rama's aware she's an omega, so she wants to torture me with this woman's presence for a while by rubbing it in my face—which means we aren't meant to kill this woman either. It'll be the vamps or rorschachs probably, maybe even the humans. Rama will want me to see this delicious-smelling mark ripped out of my hands for someone else to toy with.

I think not. Leaping back to my feet, I race through the hall, through the chapel where the scent gets stronger. But then other scents come to me. *Vampiri*. Competitive anger slices through the forefront of my brain as Ten growls next to me, panting with the intense need the pheromones produce in us both.

Far away, I hear footsteps and desperate breathing. The omega. She's running.

Sprinting in her direction, I calm my thoughts, ensuring my footsteps are silent. She'll run right into us, focused as she is on whatever she's running from. An omega should be able to sense two alphas ahead of her, but an omega running for her life could miss the danger she's about to run into.

I hope she does.

The vampiri hoot and call happily when they hunt, and those noises ring up the long hallway toward us as they chase her slowly, playing with their food.

Peeking around a stone pillar, I can just begin to see her coming up the hallway. She's dressed in an old-fashioned blue dress. A tight bodice pushes up ample breasts so they spill out of the top. She's covered in blood already, blond hair falling out of the bun they put it up in. Tears stain her cheeks as she pumps her arms hard, flying up the passageway toward us.

A body barrels out of the shadows and knocks into the omega, slamming her up against the wall.

Rorshach. It screams in her face as its own begins to morph and turn. But before it can finish shifting, the omega bellows in anger and slices her arm upward, driving a knife up under the rorshach's chin. It screeches and hisses and stumbles backward as she yanks the knife out and gets to her feet.

She killed it; I'll be damned.

It's haunting to watch prey run right toward me, knowing when she gets to me, I will take her. In all the ways, I'll take her. Because I want to and I can. Watching her get murderous does things to my cock, stirring my natural need.

Across from me, Ten tenses. "More monsters are coming."

We're far enough away from the omega, and she's crazed with fear enough not to focus on us sprinting up the hallway quietly. She moves gracefully, long arms pumping as she steadies her breath, sucking air in quietly as blue eyes, the color of her dress, dart from side to side, scanning for danger.

I'm right here, female, I whisper to myself. *Keep coming.*

Ten and I hover in the dark shadows, watching as the omega skids out of the hallway and into an open room with dark stone pillars holding up the ceiling. Behind her, the vampiri hoot and call out to one another, and a rorschach snarls.

The omega pauses behind a pillar, taking a peek behind her as she grips the knife tighter in her bloody hand. She opens pink lips and sucks in a deep breath, scenting the air as her muscles tighten under the dress. I watch gooseflesh crawl its way along her skin as she glances around, starting to ascertain that Ten and I are here.

Next to me, he pants and tenses, centered entirely on the beauty now crouching down as she scents the air and prepares to run. Again.

Calm yourself, brother, I snap through our mental bond. *The chase is the best part of all this. Enjoy it.*

Ten nods imperceptibly and shifts forward onto the balls of his feet.

The omega glances around the dark room, looking up the nearest hallway, the one that leads almost directly to our quarters.

My dick leaks in my pants as I watch her look for the danger—me, the biggest threat to her in this whole fucking place. It's obvious she realizes she's not alone in this room, that the threats to her life are multiplied here.

Stay, I mentally bark at Ten as I step out of the shadows and into the room.

The omega's eyes widen as she sucks in another deep breath and grips her knife tighter, eyes traveling up my frame before she snaps her mouth shut.

I ball my fists as the noise of the other monsters' approach rings up the hallway. The omega's blue eyes dart to one side as she crouches, eyes flickering back toward me. Smirking, I cross the stone floor quietly, stalking toward her as my muscles bunch and harden in anticipation of taking her.

She'll run. I can sense it. And she should. *Not that it will help; I'll just enjoy it more.*

When I'm fifteen feet from her, I stop, cocking my head to the side as her chest heaves, accentuating the fullness of her breasts. She's so pale I can see the blue veins throbbing under her skin.

"I'm going to enjoy this," I growl as she blinks once, twice, her body already lighting up for mine. For a long moment, blue eyes lock onto my darker ones, and her gaze turns assessing, then wary. She's probably wondering if she can reason with me since we're the same species.

She can't.

"Run." My alpha bark washes over her as her mouth drops open, her body drawn to my alpha nature, despite knowing she needs to run from me.

She takes off like a shot, and I watch her go as Ten jogs toward me, panting heavily as he watches blue skirts disappear into the darkness. "Why'd you let her go? Godsdamn, Noire. She smells so fucking good; I'm losing my mind."

"Calm yourself," I snap. "And wait."

Behind us, the vampiri hoots come closer as need and lust amp up in my system. My cock strains against the front of my pants as my vision narrows to the hallway the omega disappeared inside of. Next to me, Ten whines and pants, shifting from side to side.

"What are we doing?" he groans. "Why are we waiting?"

"The chase is the best part of hunting an omega, brother," I growl as Ten groans again.

When the vampiri flood into the room behind us, I look at Ten.

Go, I whisper into our mental link.

He takes off like a shot, sprinting up the hallway after the omega. Like all omegas of our kind, she's fucking fast, and we gave her a head start.

I hear Cashore roar behind me as he watches us track the omega, running up the hallway.

Knowing other monsters are running just behind us sends my libido and natural dominance into overdrive. I follow Ten as he snarls and pushes toward the omega. We follow her up hallway after hallway until she makes a mistake, turning into a dead-end room.

She slides to a stop with an angry scream, spinning around with the knife out as Ten and I round the corner and pause. "Fuck you," she barks out, the force of her words slamming into me. She's strong, this woman. It's rare to find a mark with fight.

She's fucking godsdamned beautiful too.

Out of the darkness above her, a rorschach drops from the ceiling and throws the omega up against the wall. Her head hits the stone with a loud crack, the smell of blood permeating the air. The rorschach turns, creepy textured face morphing from face to face to face. It draws inspiration from the mark's mind, but when it turns into Rama and rounds on us, I'm shocked.

Instinct takes over then, and I dart across the small space, whipping out with my claws, separating the monster's head from its neck, reveling in the blood that sprays me.

"What the fuck are you doing?" hisses Ten, even as he reaches down and grabs the groaning omega, slinging her over one shoulder.

When we turn, Cashore is there, surrounded by dozens of vampiri. He leans into the room and sucks in a deep breath before glittering black eyes fall to the floor and take in the dead monster at my feet. "That was a foolish move, alpha. Rama will have your head for this."

"I don't think so," I snap back, stepping in front of Ten and squaring my shoulders.

Cashore's fake smile falls. "The mark is not for you. We all know it. The disk gave us the green tonight."

"And yet my brother has her, and we're taking her back to our rooms to play. So she *is* mine until the moment I say she's not. You heard the instructions; the client wants her played with. I'll take care of that part."

Cashore snarls, piercing black teeth flashing from underneath his equally black lips. "Hand her over, alpha."

I step closer to the vampiri king and snap my teeth in his face, reveling in the way one eye twitches as he shifts ever so slightly back. "Don't make me fight my way out of here, vampiri. You will not win, and I will get the girl anyway. Tenebris and I wish to play with her, per the client's instructions. You can collect the mark later when I am good and sated."

Cashore snarls and takes a step back. "You're outnumbered, alpha."

Gesturing to the dead monster on the floor, I smile, letting every shred of malevolence I feel into my wicked smile. "I don't give a fuck. As you can see. If I come out of this room swinging, some of your people will die. Do you want that?"

I see the moment he gives in and takes a step back. He doesn't want to lose anyone to my anger. He realizes just how few fucks I have left to give. I've broken the cardinal rule of the maze–don't kill the other monsters. I've broken that rule time and time again, and still, Rama doesn't come down on me as hard as she could.

Flicking my eyes to the side, I gesture for him to get out of my way, staying between the vamps and Tenebris as my brother sidles out of the room and heads up the hallway, the limp omega over his shoulder.

Raising my middle finger to Cashore, I give him my back and stalk up the hallway after my brother, eyes locked onto the blond hair dangling down his back. There's a red smattering of blood at the back of the omega's head. The rorschach flung her into the wall pretty hard. Hopefully not too hard because I want to play before it's time to end her. I'd rather her be awake enough to keep fighting.

Rama might be hoping to fuck with me by dangling this pretty thing in front of me like a toy. What Rama doesn't realize is precisely how much I'm going to enjoy this breakable doll before the disk embedded in my arm reminds me to give her up.

CHAPTER FOUR
DIANA

As I come to for the second time tonight, I shoot upright, then fly back down as pain blooms in my head hard enough to send black stars shooting across my vision. It blurs as I struggle to process voices. I'm not dead, thankfully. But I am laid out on top of a wooden table.

Turning my head to the side, I grunt in pain as my eyes blink open. An alpha–Noire–sits in a chair in front of me, one ankle crossed over his knee, fingertips steepled as he looks at me. I haven't seen an alpha male in years until I saw Jet earlier. I forgot just how big they are, how dominant they feel. Noire is enormous in real life, far larger than I could have realized from the profile I put together.

A second alpha comes into my view, but when I look up at him, Noire growls, a deep rumble that demands I return my gaze to him. When I do, a wicked smile marks his face, thin lips turning upward in a dominant smirk. When he speaks, his voice is so deep, I feel it all the way to my core and lower. "You came from outside the maze. Tell me about the city, omega. What of the Ayala pack?"

The Ayala pack, the famous alpha pack Rama decimated when she took over Siargao. I've never met anyone claiming to be from the pack, although I've never left my area of the city either. "I don't know." My voice comes out small, barely a whisper as he leans forward.

"Don't lie to me. If you screwed someone over enough to get sent here, you know my people. Which means you know where they are if they're still around. Out with it."

His voice is a deep bark I can't resist and can't dance around. It's one of the bullshit things about being an omega, being physically subservient to the growly alpha males of my species.

"Ayala pack hasn't run Siargao since Rama took over. I don't know where they are these days, and that's the truth."

The alpha snarls and sits back as if he suspected this was the case but didn't want to believe it. He's been here for seven long years. Seven years is surely enough time to drive an already monstrous male to become something sub-alpha. If my research is accurate, there was no compassion in this male to begin with.

Dark eyes travel slowly back to mine. "Rama's never sent an omega into the maze. Why you and why now?"

It's another alpha bark that makes me want to roll over and show him my belly. He knows it because he leans forward in the chair and snarls again, and a whimper leaves my mouth at how that noise lights up my body. I'm tonight's mark. These males *will* kill me.

"She sent me here to fuck with you," I blurt out. It's probably the truth.

The alpha laughs, gesturing at my dress. "Why? Where have you been for seven years?"

"I worked for her," I admit. "Everyone does in one way or another. But apparently, I've outlived my usefulness." A bitter taste coats my mouth as I think about Rama's cruel words when she snatched me.

You've outlived your usefulness as a profiler, Diana...

"Wait," I moan, sensing the value of my life decrease as Noire stands from his seat and steps into my space. I'm assaulted by his masculine scent, all warmth and heat, and something so intensely sexual, I have to squeeze my thighs together as slick coats them.

Noire reaches out, gripping my neck with one huge fist, black claws digging into my skin as the pain throbbing in the back of my head increases.

"Things are different outside the maze," I gasp out as he squeezes my throat. "Everyone works for Rama now. She is the Queen of Siargao. Nothing happens without her hand in it."

The alpha snarls as Tenebris comes into view, younger, although I can barely tell with the pain in my head hurting so damn bad.

"Let her down, alpha," Tenebris urges, dipping his head submissively even though he's nearly a head taller.

Noire's eyes scan my face, looking for what, I'm not sure. I'm looking at the former King of Siargao. He ruled everything with an iron fist, controlling the politicians, controlling the elite, controlling the seedy underbelly. This alpha ran every facet of Siargao society until Rama swooped in and yanked it out from under him, throwing him and his brothers into this maze.

Seven long-ass years ago.

Tenebris turns to me. "What did you do for Rama?" Even though he's younger and not in charge here, he's still an alpha. That fucking urge to roll over for him hits me hard, a whimper leaving my mouth as he snarls and steps closer, dragging his nose along my collarbone.

"Good, she smells so fucking good," he pants. "Do all omegas smell like this?" His voice is a deep whine. He's not much younger than me, and he came of age here in the maze. Plus, I know from profiling all the marks who've gone in that he hasn't seen an omega since he was young. In all my time in Siargao, I've never met another omega either, or an alpha, for that matter.

Noire leans in, one arm coming to either side of me as he gets right in my space. His nose goes to the base of my throat first before fisted fingers drag my head back, pulling a squeal from me as my head throbs. He doesn't care but sucks in breath after breath as he works his way up the column of my throat, under my ear, and back down along my collarbone.

"It's been a long time since I scented an omega." His voice is a deep growl as my thighs open of their own damn accord. "They're making her smell like a heat."

The young alpha whines again, wanting to step in and scent me, but he won't do it with Noire here.

Noire snarls and lets me go, rounding on his brother. "Tenebris, go upstairs; tell Jet to come down early if at all possible. I want to enjoy this omega before we have to turn her over to the vampiri."

Tenebris doesn't hesitate but stalks across the black living space and disappears out a side door.

Noire glances up at the cameras in the ceiling. "Rama wanted to dangle you in front of me. I'll ask you one more time. Why you and why now? I want details." He pulls his shirt over his head, revealing a thickly muscular body with a knife holster strapped to his chest.

My breath comes in huffy pants as his dark eyes lock onto mine. "I suspect she wants you to want me, and to watch the other monsters rip me away. Just another thing you can't have because of her."

Noire smirks and shakes his head. "I figured that part out on my own, omega. It won't be a hardship to enjoy you, but I will hardly care when your death happens."

"Maybe you should care," I snap back before I can rein the words in. "Because I can get you out of here."

His smile falls, turning into a furious scowl as he grips my neck and yanks me to the edge of the table. "What the fuck do you mean?"

CHAPTER FIVE
NOIRE

This fucking omega wants me to believe she can get me out? I've never believed in luck, and even if I did, this is too far-fetched. I'm done listening. I'm ready to take and take and take until I'm sated. Rama did one thing right; the pheromones she sprayed on this hapless omega are riling me up like no other mark ever has.

"My tattoo is a map of the maze," she blurts as I lean in. *Fuck*, she smells so godsdamn good, my mouth is watering, fangs fully descended. She must sense the direction my thoughts are headed because she keeps talking. "I can get you out, Noire. Please…"

"Open up." It's a simple alpha command that sends her body rolling up into mine, her hips pressing against me at the edge of the table. She's tall, even for an omega, probably close to six feet. But she's delicate and tense. She's prey, and every inch of my body knows it.

What she'll say next is anybody's guess, but this bullshit story about getting me out of here? I don't believe it for a second. She got put into the maze; she'll be dead tonight. And I want to have some fun first.

I reach for my knife and slice my way up her bodice as she gasps. It spills open immediately, pale breasts tumbling free. She moves to cover herself, an age-old instinct that doesn't mean shit in here. "Hands on the table. Keep them there."

She whines as she obeys my command, chest heaving as I lean in close to her. With both hands, I drag the bodice open, getting my first look at a semi-nude omega in years. I had no trouble warming my bed as the pack alpha, but it's been a long time, which is obvious based on how much pre-cum is pooling in my jeans already.

I need inside this woman, now. I need to fill her with my seed, to take her and possess her like the delicate toy she is. And then I need detail about this whole getting-me-out-of-the-maze plan. I don't believe her, but I want my brothers to hear what she has to say. After I fuck her.

Striking fast, I leap on top of her, slamming her upper body down on the tabletop. Before she can scream, I sink my teeth into her throat and flip us both, wrapping a leg around both of hers as I hold her tight to my chest. She's caught, the perfect, predictable prey that she is. Caught in my bite. I could crush her throat like this, and having her blood flow from the wounds to fill my mouth is almost more than I can take.

Like any good omega would, she fights the bite, despite the fact that it's a turn-on for us both that I could hold her here as long as I want. Her hips rock against mine even as she struggles against my teeth.

The godsdamned pheromones are making it nearly impossible to think straight though. This close, with her blood coating my tongue and sliding down my neck, her natural scent peeks through the shit they sprayed on her. She's all moonlight and grass and ferns. She's the scent of a midnight run, and it hits me so hard: if I don't bury myself inside that smell, I'll lose my mind.

Rolling off the table, I release the bite and grab an arm, pulling her up off the ground and dragging her toward my room. She whimpers and yanks against me until I turn, snapping my teeth in her face. She flinches as I haul her roughly to my chest. "Your alpha father did a pitiful job teaching you to obey, omega."

"I wasn't raised by a fucking alpha, you assho–" Her words cut off as I yank her up by the hair and throw her over my shoulder, slapping her ass twice until she falls silent.

I stalk into my room, tossing her onto the bed as I take my pants off. She hits the sheets and flies to the headboard, chest heaving, which only accentuates pale pink nipples I ache to bite and mark.

Gods, what precisely did they spray her with? My libido is off the fucking rails looking at her in my bed. I've never been so anxious to fuck in my entire life. I watch her eyes spring wide at the crisscrossed bars that pierce the tip of my cock. The piercings were a coming-of-age gift for the future queen I'll never have, a way of paying homage to the pleasure I'd bring my omega when I eventually took a mate.

"Wait, please. Just look at my tattoo, and I can show you," she begs, and that plea is like a physical tug on my dick. I want her begging and pleading underneath me, screaming for my knot.

It's been far too long.

Hopping up onto the bed, I crawl my way across it, grabbing her ankles and yanking her down toward me. Rama's probably watching this right now, and even that turns me on. Let her watch me fuck this pretty little thing she dangled in front of me. Let her see I don't care when I dump this omega with the vampiri to take care of.

Snarling, I use my knife to cut away the front of her skirt, ripping it open. I'm unsurprised to find there's nothing underneath the dress. It was just for show anyway. Something to make her appear more feminine and delicate. It worked.

Between her thighs, a patch of blond curls is already damp with slick. Leaning in, I drag my nose through her folds, her unique scent exploding across my senses like a bomb. The omega freezes then whimpers as I grip her thighs hard enough to bruise. I need a taste before I go mad.

Leaning in, I slide my tongue through her folds, circling the nub at the top that drives all omegas wild. Slick gushes from her, coating the bed as I growl, sucking air in deeply as her scent lights a fire in my core.

Focus eludes me as I lean in and lick my way down from her clit, down her entrance, lifting her hips with my hands to circle her back hole. I want to possess every inch of her. Snarling, I flip her and spread her ass cheeks, growling at the pucker that greets me. I want her here first.

Reaching between her thighs, I coat my fingers with slippery slick and run them along her back hole. This woman is just a plaything; I won't tease her the way I would a willing omega in my bed. But I want more than just shoving my dick inside her. I want to experience and savor in a way I haven't been able to. Touching her feels right, especially with the way her body betrays her. I want to soak in every scent, every vision of her. My mind, my eyes, my mouth–they're all fucking greedy and want a piece of her.

Glancing up, I laugh at the look she throws me over her shoulder. Abject terror, complete arousal. The warring sensations are too numerous for her to process. She's on the verge of coming and pleading for her life, all in one breath. "I can prove I know this place, Noire. Look right here." She points at a curve on her tattoo. "This is your–"

Without waiting for her to respond, I slide two fingertips inside her mouth. I don't believe this tale for a second. She chokes around my thick fingers as I revel in the soft heat of her mouth. "Silence," I growl as she sputters with my fingers pressing her tongue.

I laugh again as my need ramps up another level. Snarling, I gather more slick from between her thighs with my other hand and coat myself. Spreading her ass, I grunt as I slide the tip of my cock in and watch it disappear. She screams around my fingertips at the intrusion, locking up around me as pleasure shoots from the base of my spine all the way to the top of my head.

So tight, so fucking hot.

Removing my fingers from her mouth, I slide further in, pushing past the omega's resistance as she begs and pleads for me to stop, to listen. But I won't, not until this insatiable desire has blown my need away, not until the fire burning in my core is reduced to embers. She's asking me to stop even as her body takes over and calls to me in the way only an omega can. It's deep and primal, and her need rages through me like a hurricane.

Leaning over her, I slam my way home, heavy balls slapping against her as she grunts in pain. And that sound turns me on because I'm an asshole.

The omega grips the sheets as I slide out and back in, picking up a fast rhythm. Her ass is perfection. Hot, tight, gripping my cock harder than I remember this being.

Omegas are built for dominance, so even though this clearly hurts, based on the stiffness in her stance, her body produces more and more slick, coating the bed and her thighs as I take her. Reaching one arm around the front of her, I grip her hips and use that leverage to pound into her as she grits out a huffy series of curse words.

I teeter on the edge of orgasm, every inch of my body attuned to the pliable woman beneath me when I realize my brothers hover in the doorway. They know better than to come into the room of a pack alpha in the middle of fucking. But they're concerned; I read it in our bond.

I push those thoughts from my mind, focusing solely on the warm body beneath mine. The omega clenches around me as I fuck harder.

An orgasm slams into me with the force of gunshots, my body rocking as ropes of cum line the omega's asshole. The sounds of our sloppy fucking amplify as I fill her, her cries growing louder, my hips punching her into the bed. I can't stop looking at my thick length leaving her and entering her again, the way her skin molds around me like her ass was made to take my dick.

To my surprise, an orgasm builds again as I look at her, the need to bite her coming out of nowhere. Leaning over, I start up a fast rhythm again as I tug the corset from her body and toss it onto the floor. Her back is all creamy, smooth pale skin with the exception of my earlier bite mark. Until I sink my fangs into her shoulder, her entire body squeezing tight around me.

I release the bite and move to where her neck meets her collarbone, and sink my teeth in there again. And again. And again. I bite until her shoulder is nothing but blood and bruises, tears streaming down her cheeks as another orgasm blasts down my spine.

In my doorway, Jet risks entering as I slip out of the omega and flop onto the bed.

"What's going on, Noire?"

Behind Jet, Tenebris scowls. I know he craved her. But as alpha, I get everything first, including pussy. Snarling at Ten, I hop off the bed and ball my fists. "Why are you in my room?"

Jet holds his hands up. "You asked Ten to come get me, remember?"

Did I? The omega sits up in the bed, her face a mask of pain, and it takes everything in my body not to leap on top of her and fuck her again. My brain feels fuzzy and cloudy, and the only thing I can focus on is the naked piece of ass in my bed. I need inside her again.

But a threat is in my doorway, leering at her with greedy eyes.

"We aren't a threat to you, alpha. You look ready to pound us into the ground. Whatever Rama sprayed her with is throwing you into a rut. You can tell, can't you?" Jet's voice is reasonable as his words sink in.

A rut? I haven't had a rut since before the maze.

When he takes another step into my room, inching toward the omega, I launch forward, barreling into him as I take my brother to the ground.

"Don't touch her," I snap as Jet's fist connects with my chin.

CHAPTER SIX
DIANA

In the room in front of me, Noire scuffles with his middle brother, Jet. I've profiled him as well, and I know that, of the three brothers, Noire is closest to Jet. Tenebris leaps through the doorway, tackling Noire as he and Jet fight.

My entire body is wound up tight, ready for release, slick and needy despite being taken in a way I was entirely unprepared for. I've never been taken back there, and now that first will forever belong to the alpha fighting tooth and nail just in front of the bed. Not that it matters. I'm likely to be dead in a few hours anyhow, based on how well my explanation of my ability to get the alphas out is going.

Jet bellows as Noire clamps fangs into his neck, ripping ferociously as blood sprays them both. The younger one leaps onto Noire's back as they fight. I press myself quietly into the headboard, not wanting to draw any attention to myself after what I just experienced. Slipping off the opposite side of the bed, I creep for the door.

Mid-punch, Noire's eyes flick to mine, and he snarls, throwing both alphas off him like they weigh nothing. He stalks across the room with big, purposeful strides, yanking me up into his arms and pressing us into the wall. All I can do is flail and plead as he drags my legs open and prepares to thrust inside me again. He's totally fucking unhinged as I scream and beat my fists against his chest.

"Omega," he snaps, bringing his lips to hover just above mine before a huge arm comes around his neck, dragging him away as I fall to the ground in a flurry of the remainder of my skirts.

"Stop, Noire, it's a rut. You've got to come out of it, alpha. We can't risk this now, not in the maze. She's the fucking mark, asshole."

The alpha drags Noire out the door with the help of the younger one, who gestures at me.

"Come."

It's one word, but damnit, my body complies because it's that fucking alpha command. I hover behind Tenebris as they drag Noire into the main living area. They manhandle him to the nearest wall, clamping huge thick cuffs on his arms before they let him go. He sprints to the end of the chains before being yanked viciously back by the immovable wall.

"Omega," he roars again, eyes intent on me where I hover behind the other two. Shit, fuck, I am in so much trouble. I never imagined he would be like this, that if we came face to face, he'd be so...alpha. I never imagined he wouldn't listen to me either, to what I had to say.

Turning to Jet, I put my hands up. "Please, I can get you out of the maze, all of you." My entire body is wired to run again, but I know they'll just enjoy the chase. And what they will do if they catch me won't be good. My heart gallops in my chest as I beg Jet with my eyes.

Please don't hurt me.

He laughs and grabs me by the throat, tossing me on top of the dining room table again. "You won't believe the amount of pure shit people start talking about when they get thrown in here. The amount of times marks tell me they can help me, or pay me, or get me money, booze, women. You name it. They think we can or would help them. But we can't, and we won't. You're already dead if you're here."

Shaking my head, I point to the tattoo that takes up my entire left arm. "This? This is a map of the maze. The entire maze. I know this place like the back of my hand."

Two pairs of eyes laser focus on me as Noire bellows behind them. "Start talking," snaps Jet, glancing over his shoulder at Noire.

Licking my lips, I show them both the underside of my arm. "Years ago, my father was forced by Rama to build this place, long before she took over Siargao. He built it, but Father knew I'd be in danger, so he tattooed a map of the maze on my arm and taught me how to read it. Rama killed him and the rest of my pack and brought me to Siargao. I've been here ever since."

Jet looks skeptical. "I don't believe a word coming out of your mouth right now."

"I can prove it," I counter as Noire's raging grows louder and louder.

Renewed concern for my physical safety slaps me as I shift backwards on the table. "What's happening to him?"

Jet grunts. "Whatever she dosed you with is throwing him into a rut for some reason. We need to get him out of the rut before we entertain any of what you're saying."

The younger alpha looks at him. "Jet, how the fuck do we pull Noire out of a rut? I've never seen this."

Jet frowns, looking over at where Noire bellows, pulling against his chains. I swear I hear a stone crack, but I must be wrong.

"Jet?" the younger alpha prompts him again.

Jet turns to me with a wicked grin. "Anger, Tenebris, that's the only thing that can pull him out long enough to gain control again. Right now, he's lost to lust, and if he goes all the way down that rabbit hole, it'll be a week before he comes back out."

Turning his attention to me, he smiles. "Good thing we've got Noire's plaything right here at the ready. Let's make him nice and mad by having our way with her for a while. If we take it far enough, he'll slip out of the desire long enough to want to beat our asses. There's a chance we can reason with him then."

I freeze as I take in his meaning, moving to slip off the other side of the table as both alphas turn their focus on me.

Tenebris, the younger one, licks his lips as he stalks slowly around one side of the table. Jet chuckles as he watches the younger alpha, winking at me. "Ten hasn't seen an omega since he came of age. He's going to thoroughly enjoy his first taste."

"Godsdamnit," I huff. "There are a few ways out, and Rama will try to stop us. Look at the fucking tatt–" The words cut off in my throat when Ten springs from his position and lands on top of me, crashing us both to the ground. I struggle under his incredible weight, but he's easily got two hundred pounds of muscle on me, despite my tall frame.

Ten pulls to a stand, one big arm around my waist and the other gripping my hair. My skull still feels like split kindling, but that's nothing compared to the terror of being at the mercy of two alphas.

Jet stalks closer to Noire, nodding in our direction. "Bring her over here, Ten. Let Noire get a good look at what we're gonna do to this soft little omega."

"No, no, please, we should hurry," I start as Ten snarls and drags me screaming across the carpet, throwing me down in front of Jet.

I back away instinctively as Jet tsks and shakes his head. "Don't get too close to Noire, little omega. If he gets his hands on you, I won't be able to get him off you a second time. Any logical thinking left in him is nearly overridden at this point."

Glancing behind me, I'm filled with terror at what I see. Noire strains against the chains, roaring as his eyes rake over me from top to bottom. His erection strains obviously, swinging and bobbing as precum drips steadily from him onto the floor. Despite my horror, my body recognizes a powerful sexual partner, and slick coats my thighs as I look at him.

Ten chuckles and sucks in a deep breath. "Ah, the body doesn't lie. Despite his violent taking of you, you want more, don't you? Fuck me, you're a pretty thing."

My gaze darts back up to his. "Please wait. Let's just leave, right now!"

"We can't, not without my alpha hearing this in the right frame of mind. Now, open those pretty thighs for me, or I'll open them for you."

At his compulsion, I spread my thighs open even as my stomach tumbles in knots.

Ten's eyes fall to my thighs, his pink tongue coming out to lick his lips as Jet continues talking, "Goddamn, there's nothing like omega pussy, nothing in this entire world." He falls to his knees in front of me, running both hands up my bare thighs as I shudder, falling back onto the floor. Already, my body wants him, his touch, his knot.

Jet turns to his pack alpha, gesturing between my thighs. "See this, Noire? See what I'm going to take? You think it's yours, but you're mistaken."

Noire bellows as Jet gestures for Ten to come closer. "Ten, stick your dick in her mouth."

I get ready to beg again, but the younger alpha straddles my head and takes his cock out of his pants. He's fucking huge too but unpierced.

Jet peers around Ten, dark eyes meeting mine. "Suck him off, omega."

There's no option as the younger alpha feeds his cock down my throat. He's surprisingly gentle, even when I hollow my cheeks and attempt to take as much of him as I can. A spurt of cum hits the back of my throat as he grunts and throws his head back. But when he starts moving, and I hear the rustle of Jet moving too, I make the mistake of looking up.

Noire screams in anger as Jet grabs my hips and shoves his thick cock inside me in one swift thrust. I groan around the dick in my mouth, unable to focus around the sensation of alpha cock in my pussy. I may have been terrified to come here tonight, but everything about their dominance and possessiveness was made to turn me on. I can only get past my biology so much.

Both alphas taking me at the same time is too much for my body; an orgasm racks my frame as I rock my hips to meet Jet, sucking Ten deep into my throat. Shockwaves ripple through my system as I scream out my pleasure, Noire raging as Jet laughs.

"I stole her first orgasm from you, asshole, and she feels so fucking good. I'll steal the next one and the next one until you come to take them from me."

Ten grunts as cum splashes against the back of my throat, his hips rocking slowly as I struggle around his thick cock.

"Get the fuck off her. She is *mine*," roars Noire as Jet slips out of me, hopping to a stand. Ten follows, grunting when his thick cock leaves my lips. He brushes the backs of his knuckles across my cheeks and holds out a hand to help me upright. It's surprisingly tender given what just happened. My mind is a mess of conflicting emotions.

One of the chains holding Noire back rips out of the wall then, and he uses his incredible strength to rip the other one free, stalking across the living space. He drags both chains behind him, chunks of stone still connected to them as he gets in Jet's face and lashes out, dragging his claws across the other alpha's chest, red ribbons of blood welling up immediately.

Jet flinches but bows his head. "Alpha, are you back with us? This is urgent."

Noire bellows, an angry roar that shakes the floor as I force my spine straight to watch the brothers' standoff. Ten steps in front of me protectively, shielding me from Noire's gaze, although I can't help peeking around his huge frame.

Jet keeps his head low, but his eyes glance up at Noire. "Alpha, this could be big. Are you here?"

Noire snarls again but presses his forehead to his brother's, his big chest heaving. "Barely. We need to talk."

Jet nods, not moving from the oddly gentle gesture. "Sit, alpha. I'll get you a drink. Ten, get those chains off him."

Noire nods and snarls at Ten, who steps to Noire with his head bowed, unlocking the chains. Noire comes to where I stand and leans in to drag his nose up my neck. "You need a bath. You smell like other alphas. But it'll have to wait."

I can't do anything but whimper. My entire body is bruised and worn from tonight's numerous assaults. Still, I let my forehead fall to Noire's chest as a rolling purr rumbles from between his thick pectoral muscles.

If the other alphas are surprised to hear their brother purr, they say nothing but watch in silence as Noire picks me up, sets me in a chair, and steps back, the sound stopping immediately. I'm ready to beg him to start it back up when he sinks into the chair opposite mine. Jet comes to his side with a glass of something amber, and Noire throws it back in one gulp.

"Talk." It's a one-word command I know better than to ignore.

"My tattoo is a map of the maze," I repeat, unsure how much he caught before.

"Your father built it; Rama killed him. What next?"

"I can get you out," I say simply. "And I want you to kill her for me."

Noire laughs, shaking his head. "In exchange for getting out of here, you mean."

I hold my breath, nodding.

He huffs out a breath as the other alphas sit next to him, one on either side. Seated like this, he looks like a king of the underworld, his loyal subjects flanking him, ready to do his bidding. Dark eyes land on mine, but there's no mirth, no joy in his gaze. "Why wouldn't I just force you to tell me how to read this map and then kill you and be done with this?"

He gestures at the elegant surroundings, his beautiful, dark prison.

"There's more than just this," I reply, keeping my voice low and even. "The maze is only part of Rama's temple. There's more to it."

"Why do you want her dead?" Noire's voice is ice-cold as he sits forward, placing one big hand on the table. His gaze never strays from mine.

"She killed my father." My voice comes out in a whisper as Noire frowns.

"So? Alphas aren't known for being kind and gentle fathers. Hard to believe you'd hold a grudge about him dying. Try again."

"That's it," I snap, harsher than I intended to as I run my fingertips along the tattoo, the same one my brother Dore has. *Had*.

"Try *again*, omega," Noire snaps. "I can taste the lie. You aren't here because of your father. Don't make me ask again."

Hurt and pain well to the surface of my heart as I ball my fists and think back to that horrible fucking night that set all of this into motion.

"I loved my father, you asshole." I don't mean to let the curse out, but it comes out anyway as Noire leaps to a stand, growling at me.

Noire grips my chin hard between his forefinger and thumb, eyes roving my face. Alphas have incredible intuition, but I let the truth of what I just admitted show through by not lowering my eyes from his.

"It's the truth," he whispers, more to himself than anyone, before turning on me with narrowed eyes. "Here's the thing. Rama has a habit of concocting situations in the maze to fuck with me. So I'm trying to understand what's behind your appearance here, the first omega we've seen in seven years."

I can't help the frustration that infuses itself into my voice. "I don't know why she put me in here now. Does it matter? Let's get the fuck out and ki–"

Noire's teeth clamp down on my neck so fast I don't have time to hold back the scream that burbles out of my throat. When he lets go, I round on him, but he brings his lips to hover just above mine. "I'll allow that one time because an alpha didn't raise you. But never speak to me that way. Do you understand?"

"Yes, alpha," flies out of my mouth so fast I can barely stand it. When Noire's dark eyes meet mine, there's nothing but command and possession there. No compassion, no caring, no excitement for the reason I'm here. Nothing at all but a stone-cold monster.

CHAPTER SEVEN
NOIRE

In front of me, the omega winces when I snap my long fangs in front of her face. She smells like slick and cum and my brothers, and it's so wrong, I want to burn the entire maze down. I'm far too close to my rut, and I'm barely hanging on to my sanity. Every inch of her body is calling to me. From the way her head is cocked slightly to the side, baring her neck, to the flare of her nostrils and the way her chest rises and falls. She sways slightly, blood coating her lips from where she spit it out.

Leaning in, I lick her lower lip first, the bright scent of her blood slamming into my senses. I groan as I press harder into her, one hand going to her throat as the other grips her hair possessively. Bending her backward, I nip and suck at her lips. I want every ruby-red drop of her blood on my tongue.

"Open," I command, her lips parting. I suck her tongue between my lips, tugging at it with my teeth as she moans. If I'm on the edge of a rut, and she's the only omega in sight, the sheer amount of pheromones I'm giving off right now are probably enough to send her into heat.

I can't have that. But it takes a herculean level of effort to step back from her when Jet's eyes meet mine, worried.

"I don't buy a word of your story," I snap as Ten and Jet come to stand next to me, leering at the panting omega as she slumps against our dining room table.

Blue eyes are nearly black as hormones rock the omega, sending her body into overdrive. But she sucks in a deep breath and closes her eyes, breathing slowly before opening them for me again. When she does, I'm surprised at the renewed focus in her gaze. It reminds me of how I underestimated Rama and fucked up my life. I will never underestimate a woman again, and there's a thread of strength in this one that doesn't match her delicate, frightened appearance.

"I can prove it to you," she begins, lifting her tattooed arm and pointing to the alcove Jet fucked a woman in last night, just viewable down one of the hallways extending from this room. "These alcoves all link to a common area meant for the beta workers to come and go from. There are many layers of security, and it's not our best path out. But I'll show you that I know this place, or how it was designed, at least."

When I cock my head to the side and look at the omega, really look at her, she sits up straighter, covering her breasts with her arms, not moving her gaze from mine. Even when Jet speaks up next, she doesn't turn to look at him.

"There are cameras and microphones everywhere. How do you expect to get past Rama? She'll see us coming from a mile away. She's probably watching us right now."

The omega snarls, a wicked smile tilting the corners of her lips up into a vicious line. "What's she gonna do, send me in here twice? The cameras aren't as good as you think; there are blind spots. And in the event of a catastrophic revolt in the maze, it takes upward of twenty-four full hours for Rama to mount a response due to the way the security system is configured outside the maze. It's built that way to keep you from escaping, but it limits her ability to respond if you don't behave."

"Keep talking," Jet snaps as I take another step away from the omega. I'm barely hanging on to my sanity, and between her scent and the sass, I'm ready to drag her by the hair back to my bed.

She pushes off the table, but I keep my eyes on her face, resisting the urge to watch her full breasts jiggle. The front of the skirt is still ripped too, but she acts like it doesn't bother her as she looks at her tattoo, running her fingertips along a jagged curve and then striding to the alcove.

"My father built a few ways out of the maze, some easier than others. But what he did a really detailed job of was ensuring that, even if you accidentally stumbled on a way out, there'd be so many levels to the maze that you'd never get free before Rama could get you back in. Escaping here has to be an inside job; there's no other way."

Jet, Ten, and I stand just outside the alcove. My brothers are tense as fuck, ready to spring if this is all some bullshit to mess with us. The omega examines the stone wall inside the alcove and then presses lightly on the stones in a specific order.

To my horrific surprise, there's a telltale click, and the passage opens, just like it does when the beta maze workers remove the women Rama sends here for Jet.

Without a backward look, Diana steps into the darkness and disappears.

"Fuck," barks Ten. "We go in after her, right?"

Diana peeks her head back out of the darkness, winking at Ten. "You coming in here to verify I'm not lying or what?"

Ten huffs in shock at the omega's snark, but one growl from me, and the smile broadens as she winks.

My Gods, this female needs a healthy dose of punishment.

I go into the darkness first. I'm the fucking alpha, and I won't send my people somewhere I wouldn't go myself. It takes no time for my eyes to adjust to the pitch black as I follow the long corridor. Diana comes to my side and points at green paint on certain stones throughout the tunnel.

"See this? Where there's green paint, these stones can be removed but still appear to be there to you, allowing the workers to physically look in on any room in the maze. Nearly the entire maze works this way, except for the lowest levels."

"So despite the cameras, they can spy on us like this at any time?"

"Yeah," Diana confirms then seems to rethink her response. "Yes, alpha." Her voice is tight as she gulps hard, her throat bobbing.

I'm still raw from falling into the beginnings of a rut and getting yanked out of it with that bullshit Ten and Jet pulled. My need to fuck is amplified in the small, hot space of this hallway, and her response to me isn't helping. "Show me more."

Diana's eyes flutter as she sucks in a breath. "This isn't a good way out."

"And what about this?" I lift up the arm with the disk embedded in it as Diana nods.

"Rama made sure no one person ever knew everything about the maze; that's why she killed my father. He designed the maze and its security, and I'm sure she added on top of that. I don't know if she can kill you with that. I know she can hurt you, and I know her first plan of attack is always to turn the monsters on one another if someone needs to be controlled. That's what happened with you–" Her voice cuts off as blue eyes fly up to mine.

Hot fury rockets through my system as I take in her meaning. Grabbing her wrist, I squeeze hard as she yelps, dragging her behind me back out of the alcove and into the living area. "Speak," I bellow. "The whole thing, the entire fucking thing. What happened with Oskur? How do you know? Be precise."

Diana shudders and reaches for both halves of her corset, but I yank the entire thing from her and shove her, reveling in the grunt that leaves her when she hits the nearest wall and slides partway down it.

"She gave the monsters you call rorschachs betas to play with for a full week for killing your brother. It was their reward for doing her bidding. She televised all of it, his death, the betas, everything to remind the common people how brutal the maze is, and how terrified we should all be of it."

Behind me, Jet roars in anguish, always having known there was so much more to Oskur's death.

Stone-cold fury lands in my stomach like a ball of dried cement. I can barely breathe around the anger, but when I look at the omega, I know one thing is for certain—I will get the fuck out of here, no matter what I have to do to her to make that happen.

Diana's quiet for a moment before looking up at me with wide blue eyes. "She'll do it again, knowing I'm trying to get you out. She'll offer the humans or vampiri something to come and finish off the mark and maybe kill you all too. Or kill one of your brothers but leave you. She will want retribution for you even attempting to escape. You're right about her watching us, she probably is."

"Maybe we should kill you and be done with it then," I snap, fisting my hands as I glare through narrowed eyes at the omega.

She surprises me when she stands taller, pale breasts pebbled in the cold of our private rooms. "I fully accept that this might not go well, that I might lose my life. I've already lost everything else important to me, so if that's the direction you want to take it, I'm ready. I can't promise I won't fight you, because even I've got a survival instinct...but I made my peace with this a long time ago."

"You're a crazy bitch," Jet snaps, coming to stand next to me with his back to the omega. "Can we talk about this? I snuck out of the Atrium...but if this is all a fucking ruse, I need to get back. Not that they don't know I'm here but still."

Not looking at Jet, I grab the omega once more and drag her back to my bedroom, throwing her inside. "Don't come out," I snap, pointing a finger at her.

She nods once, eyes narrowing at me as I close the door in her face.

When I stalk back into the kitchen, Jet and Ten are already seated at the dining room table. Jet's got a glass full of uppers in his hand, lifting it to his lips as he taps his foot rapid-fire under the table.

I grab the glass and hurl it across our rooms. "No more, not tonight. I need you here with me. Understand?"

Jet snarls but bows his head and nods before looking up at me again. "Do we believe her?"

"You saw the passageway." Ten sighs, gesturing toward the dark hallway with the alcoves. "But I don't believe the father story."

My brother's intuition is excellent; he'll make a good pack alpha one day in a pack of his own. *If I get him the fuck out of here.*

"One thing she's right about, Rama won't let us go easily. We're already in over our heads by not fulfilling the mark duty. Do we buy the tattoo piece?"

"I don't know," Jet says, hopping to a stand and pacing. "But she doesn't strike me as a liar. It's just a sense though. The story in and of itself isn't believable."

"I'd like to get more information," I admit. "If she's lying then maybe we're all fucked. If she's not, well, we'll never get another chance like this. I'm inclined to take it."

My brothers are quiet, torn, but they'll go along with whatever I say. Standing, I turn from them. "I'm going to question her, but prepare yourselves to go. If I'm happy with her answers, we're going."

I hear Jet mutter out a long string of curse words as he and Ten head for the small weapons room that Rama keeps just stocked enough for us to fuck with the marks. "Don't fuck her again, Noire. We need your mind right." His warning echoes up the hall as my body stiffens in anticipation of opening my door and scenting the beautiful omega again.

I am in deep. Far too deep. Because fucking her is almost all I can think about doing.

CHAPTER EIGHT
DIANA

Footsteps along the hallway send me scurrying from the door where I was listening back into the center of the room. I fold my hands in front of my lap, trying to appear nonconfrontational when the door opens quietly and Noire stalks back in. My ass stings, my entire body tense and sore. But when I look up at him, my body clenches with need, slick dripping down one leg.

God, omega hormones are such assholes, and Noire is so incredibly potent. Alpha dominance rolls off him and smacks into me with a tidal wave of pleasure. Dark eyes meet mine and don't move as he goes across the room and opens an armoire. Inside, I see both doors are lined with knives. I know Rama allows weapons in this place, and he's got quite a few of them.

"Tell me about where you came from, omega." It's not a request, and I sense he's struggling to believe my story about getting him out of here.

"My name is Diana," I whisper. "We don't have a lot of time, Noire," I begin as he slips a knife out of his armoire and into the chest holster he's still wearing. Another goes in right next to it as he looks at me, demanding an answer with his intense stare.

"I'm listening, omega, and I won't ask again." Noire turns and grabs two more knives, strapping them along his belt. One in the front, one in the back.

"I wasn't lying about her killing my father and my pack; she did that years ago."

"I already know that," Noire grunts. "Where did you come from? What pack?"

"Winthrop." The last name I haven't used in nearly a decade slips off my tongue as I choke back a sob.

Noire's eyes go wide. "You're Edson Winthrop's daughter?"

Tears fill my eyes as I think back to my childhood. It wasn't perfect, but despite Noire's earlier proclamation about alpha fathers, mine was good and kind—until Rama slaughtered him and my whole pack. Dore and I escaped to the streets until she found us and took us in. First by force, but eventually we fell into line because we were children, and we had no other options.

"You had a twin," Noire says, but it's not a question.

A sob does leave my throat then as the first tears spill down my cheeks. "I did. Yes."

"Other siblings?"

I shake my head as my lip trembles, heat flushing across my neck and chest as Noire crosses the room to me, his face an unreadable neutral mask.

I refuse to beg for comfort from this alpha, but I want it. His heat, his warmth, his strong arms. They call to me as we stare at one another, neither of us looking away. What do I want from him? Retribution for my family? Comfort? Understanding? Because Rama took everything from both of us.

Noire steps in close, lifting my chin so I'm forced to look into pitch-black eyes that betray no emotion. "Get changed, Diana. We're going. Now. We are going to follow you, but if I sense at any point this will hurt my brothers, I will end you. Are we clear?"

Without saying another word, Noire hands me a black shirt. Numb, I nod and take it, sliding it over my head, following in silence as we exit the room. As soon as we do, the screen just outside his door flicks on, and Rama's face comes on.

Noire turns and smiles at the maze's cruel mistress, his big body blocking me from viewing the full screen.

"You're not minding the rules, Noire," Rama purrs, her voice syrupy sweet. It claws at the memories buried in the back of my mind, slamming home how she tortured my brother, Dore, before slitting his throat.

Noire doesn't bother to respond as Rama sighs, her smile growing wider as she cocks her head to one side.

I peek around Noire, but when my eyes meet hers, a feral snarl leaves my throat. It's an animal growl that sends one of Noire's dark brows upward as he glances at me and then Rama.

"I want her dead, Noire," Rama says in a bored tone. "Blood play, dismemberment, those were the client's wishes. If you do not comply, I'll hurt your brothers. And then I'll kill you and this woman will die anyhow."

"Make me," purrs Noire, squaring his shoulders as Rama's eyes narrow.

"If you don't kill this woman, I'll send someone else, and there will be consequences." Rama speaks as if she's talking to a small, petulant child, and the effect it has on Noire is nearly instantaneous.

His entire body stiffens, but he doesn't bother to respond as he turns us both, placing his hand on the back of my neck as he steers me up the hallway.

When Rama huffs behind us, he turns on his hip, and I whip around in time to see him throw a knife up the hallway with incredible speed. It buries itself right in Rama's forehead before the screen sparks and clicks off.

At the same time, the disk implanted in his forearm lights up bright red, and his eyes find mine. "Let's go. I'm calling her bluff."

When we reach the open living area again, Jet and Tenebris are there, knives crisscrossing their bodies. Jet looks up at Noire, gritting his jaw. "It looks like we're going, then? We've got the weapons; what else do you want to bring?" He takes a beat, pointing at me with the tip of a knife in his hand, sending a shudder through my frame, although I stand taller to mask it. "Are we really doing this, Noire? You believe her? The disks are flashing red, we don't know what it means."

"We have to chance it," Noire snaps as he steps to the bag beside Jet on the table, opening it and looking in. Jars of a purple liquid shine from the interior of the bag. I don't miss the way Jet winces but straightens as Noire's eyes meet his. The big alpha says nothing but barks at Jet to get water from the fridge too.

When he turns to me, I meet his gaze and lift my chin. It's a bunch of bullshit the way alpha dominance makes omegas behave, and while these alphas are terrifying, I can't just roll over. I'm not built that way.

"Where to, omega?"

"We need to take the most direct route to the lower levels. Unfortunately, that means we'll probably cross some of the other monsters because the most direct route goes through other living areas."

Tenebris curses under his breath as Jet rolls his eyes. "Of fucking course." He turns to Noire again. "Noire, talk to me. Are we really following this fucking omega?"

Noire barks out a string of words in a language I don't understand, but Jet nods and turns for the door, taking the lead. Tenebris goes second, then me, and Noire follows behind me, silent as a ghost.

I take a quick look at my tattoo, tracing the intricate symbols that map out the maze. The map's legend exists only in my mind. Walking to the front of the alphas' living quarters, I find a stone inlaid in the ground with a small symbol on it. When I locate that symbol on my arm, Ten growls. "I knew these fucking symbols meant something."

"You're right," I agree quickly, nodding at him. "They do, but not without the map and the legend."

Tenebris grits his jaw but says nothing, hiking a bag up over his shoulder as he passes me. "Where to? Do you need anything before we go, omega?"

"Diana," I whisper. "My name is Diana. And, no, water is enough. We need to head to the left, through the chapel, and then there's a passageway there we need to take." Ten smiles gently at me as I whisper a thank you under my breath.

He nods and turns, Jet following him. I risk a glance at Noire, but his face is a mask of intense focus. His pupils are still wide from the rut, his body focused on me in a predatory way that calls mine to stand at attention. I freeze when he stalks the five feet or so between us, not stopping until he bumps into me, his warm skin heating mine through the thin cotton of the shirt he gave me.

My nipples harden into diamond nubs against his chest as he purrs and backs us into the nearest wall, lifting my tattooed arm to examine it. Black eyes flick back to mine. "You'd better be telling the truth about all of this." He looks up and gestures around the maze and toward his brothers' retreating backs. "If this is a ruse of some sort, and it hurts my brothers, your death will be nothing but slow pain. I'm saying it again because I want to make sure you are clear. Do you understand me?"

"I just want to get out, Noire," I whisper. "I want to get out and stop having to hide from Rama everywhere I go. I want to be truly free. I want *Siargao* to be free."

A shadow of understanding crosses Noire's face before he grunts, indicating I should follow the other alphas into the darkness. And follow I do, with the worst monster of all stalking at my back.

My body is a livewire as we walk purposefully through the dark halls of the Temple Maze. All three alphas are on high alert, but given that Rama knows I'm trying to get out, I know she'll send other monsters after us.

By the time we get to the chapel, I know for certain she's fucking with us. It's far too quiet. We step through the chapel's doorways, the haunting scent of the black Alborada roses that grow throughout the maze blasting my nostrils. They're genetically modified to need no light, another feature of the maze my father put into place. He was a brilliant engineer and planner, but it makes the maze a real bitch to get out of.

As we enter the chapel, Tenebris snarls, "Where to, omega? I scent humans."

I sprint toward the altar, referencing my tattoo and the rim of the huge stone block itself until I find what I'm looking for.

"Hello, Blondie," I hear as a man emerges from one of the alcoves, brandishing a steel bat, a relic of human history so far in the past, I don't even know what the tool would have been used for. Now it only signifies incoming pain. I've seen televised sessions of humans killing marks. It's a frenzy of group violence I am not ready for.

Tenebris steps in front of me as Noire comes around the side of the altar, not paying the man any mind. "More humans are coming. We need to move fast. We can fight them in shift form, but if they all come, it'll be harder. Move, Diana."

Urgently, I scan my tattoo until I find the matching symbol on the underside of the stone altar.

"Now, Diana," snaps Noire as more humans begin to pour through the front door of the chapel, their catcalls ringing off the black stones.

Depressing the stone with the symbol on it, I glance at Noire as the altar slides on tracks toward the front of the dais. He's not looking at me but at the throng of human men who now pour in through the open doors.

Tenebris and Jet stand in front of us, snarling, when the first wave of humans attack. They're no match for the much bigger, faster alphas, and they go down fast in a flurry of black claws. But then more and more come as Noire starts roaring for his brothers to leave it. They're lost to the madness of the fight, slicing and roaring and ripping into the human men like they're nothing but meat.

When the first human gets a knife between Tenebris' ribs, Jet and Noire go wild and strip their clothes, shifting into the enormous black wolves that alpha males have access to. Noire barrels into the closest group of humans, knocking them to the side as Jet grips Ten by the back of the neck with his teeth, dragging him to the altar.

"In here," I scream at Jet as his wolf helps Ten to his feet, the younger alpha holding the knife as he grunts in pain.

Tenebris goes into the dark space below the altar without looking back, Jet gesturing for me to follow. I risk a glance at Noire, but he's still wolfed out, scattering pieces of the humans around the church as they attempt to overtake him.

Jet barks something out again in that language I don't know, and Noire roars loud enough to shatter some of the stained-glass windows on one side of the chapel, glass exploding everywhere as the humans take cover. The moment they do, he turns and sprints for us, shifting mid-run as we all pile into the dark space under the altar.

As soon as Noire is in, I feel for the symbol on the wall, and the altar trundles closed above us with a heavy click.

Flying over to Tenebris, I examine the knife in his side and slide it out as he hisses. Without looking up, I rip my shirt over my head and bite it, tearing it into long strips as Ten watches, his jaw gritted and eyes intense on me. Jet stands protectively to one side, looking up the hallway as Noire hovers behind me, an ominously naked presence.

I wrap the fabric around Tenebris' broad torso, tying it tight. "This'll sting, but as long as the bleeding stops, you'll heal fast." He nods and grunts as Noire reaches out and hauls his brother to a stand.

Turning to me, his eyes travel down to my bare chest, the way my nipples harden in the cool air of the passageway.

I know Noire's libido is still running on high from the near-rut when he steps forward, leaning in to drag his fangs up my neck, nipping under my ear. My hips rock up against his as he snarls and runs both hands up my back, sucking in deep breaths along my throat, down into the hollow along my collarbone.

"Noire?" Tenebris' voice is tentative but urgent.

With a growl, Noire snaps his eyes toward his younger brother and stands taller, sighing. Reaching into his pack, he hands me another shirt before leaning in to nip at my ear and pulling out his own clothing.

I hold back a needy whine at his suggestive dominance and nod, pulling the shirt over my head. Noire puts his hand on my lower back and urges me forward to follow his brothers again.

The passageway is pitch black, but alphas and omegas have incredible senses, so we can see anyhow. I reference my tattoo from time to time, directing us from one dark hall to another.

"Wait, it's here," I say, quickly checking my tattoo. "When we go through this door, it'll drop us right into the middle of a living space, the one on the far opposite side of the maze from you."

Jet lets out a string of curse words as he rounds on me. "The fucking vampiri live there. Is there another way?"

"Yeah," I snap back, unable to keep the anger out of my voice as Noire comes up behind me, big body bumping into mine. "Yeah, we can take the long way around and do a tour of every single monster in this place, and hope we don't all get massacred after Rama offers them Gods-knows-what to kill us. Or we can go this way and directly to the lower levels, which is the best fucking way out."

Jet snarls and clamps a black-clawed hand around my throat. I don't know where my sudden vitriol has come from, but Noire growls in my ear as Jet squeezes, "What have I said about speaking to alphas like that, Diana?"

I might have a death wish, but I also want us to keep moving. The longer we stay in the maze, the greater our chances of dying. "You said not to speak to *you* like that again. You didn't mention your brothers."

To my surprise, Noire's booming laugh rings around us in the stone hallway, echoing off the black rock as Jet's grip on my throat tightens. Noire shoves his brother's arm away and turns me to face him. "Don't pretend you didn't know what I meant, omega. Another snarky remark and you'll deal with me."

It takes everything in me to resist snarking something at that precise moment, and Noire knows because he raises a brow and cocks his head to the side, challenging me to say something.

Stepping out of his grip, I look at Tenebris and Jet. "Let me go first. We need to go through the quarters here, so we'll have to speak with the vampiri if they live here."

Noire curses behind me. "Hate that. I'd rather go a longer way."

I shake my head and turn. "We don't have much time now that Rama is aware I know more than she thought. She has a stable full of monsters she can mobilize quickly. This is our best option, I promise."

Noire's brows furrow, but he steps aside and gestures for me to continue. When I depress the stone with the correct symbol, a floor panel creaks and opens. Gathering up my tattered, dirty skirts, I hop down into the darkness, followed by my three alphas.

Did I just call them my *alphas? Ugh.*

The moment I land and stand up, I sense monsters. It's the same way any prey knows they're being stalked. The hair on the back of my neck rises as Noire, Jet, and Tenebris snarl and surround me. My breath comes in short pants as I look around, even though I can't see anyone.

The panel above us closes as two vampiri step out of the shadows. There are more, I'm sure. Of all the monsters my father built the maze to hold, the vampiri scare me nearly as much as the alphas.

Stepping around Noire, I put my hands up as one of the monsters snarls, "Hello, little mark. Nice of you to bring yourself to our doorstep."

I've seen him televised before; he's the vampiri king's second, Firenze. Up close, he's even more terrifying than on-screen. Firenze is pale like all vampiri, blond hair pulled into a tightly woven braid that curls down the nape of his neck. This close, I see his teeth are black and translucent, dripping with…something. Venom, maybe? Oh Gods. There are so many ways this could go horribly wrong.

"I need to speak with your king," I respond, mustering up confidence from somewhere. Fake it 'til you make it, I suppose. "It's urgent. I have information for you."

"The only thing urgent in this place is our desire to feed," the vampiri barks back, taking a menacing step toward me as Noire snarls and comes to stand by my side.

The vampiri's eyes move to Noire as Noire takes another step fully in front of me. "Take us to Cashore. Now."

The vampiri's blank white eyes find mine again, and he shrugs. "We will tear her apart either way; you know the disk chose us this evening."

I shudder, knowing he's referencing the disk that picks which monsters get to kill the mark. It was them. Rama meant for this male, and the one next to him, and all the rest to rip me to shreds.

Noire barks back, "The mark is mine until I say she isn't. Cashore. *Now*. I won't ask again."

Both vampiri snarl but turn, and we follow them along two long halls to a large wooden door, intricately carved with interpretations of the Alborada roses that thrive in this part of the maze. Double-checking my tattoo, I nod at Noire when his eyes find mine, asking the silent question.

The vampiri turns the door handle and opens it, and I see into a room full of his kind, fake moonlight shining down on them. Ignoring Noire's warning growl, I follow the vampiri in with a nod, looking up at the ceiling in these particular living quarters. The stones here are inlaid in such a way that a faux night sky peeks through, a cruel reminder of just how close the monsters are to the outside world, yet somehow not close at all.

Tenebris and Jet pace around in front of me, Noire still behind in a protective triangle formation as my heart pounds in my chest. There's every chance this could go badly. My only hope is that I know a few things about this maze that could be useful to its monsters. My only item of value is my knowledge, and I have to pray the vampiri will listen to me long enough to hear what I know.

Monsters fill the room, coming in from deep alcoves I know stretch back into individual rooms, although vampiri typically sleep in mating pods together—a random fact I know from profiling them now and again. Snarls ring through the room, several of them crouching down as if readying themselves to chase prey. Every cell in my body screams at me to run, run, run.

Ten and Jet pause, both holding knives in each hand, crouched slightly. Behind me, Noire doesn't stop until his chest is touching my back, a deep growl rumbling from his warm body. "Where is Cashore?"

His alpha bark rolls over the vampiri, and even though they're a different species of monster entirely, it's easy to see the way his dominance affects them. Looking around, I'm surprised to see the majority of the vampiri step away from the deep roll of Noire's command.

The monsters part, and a taller vampiri with pitch-black waist-length hair and ice-white skin comes forward, hands folded behind his back. Calculating white eyes framed by pale lashes don't blink as he comes closer to us, cocking his head to the side as he assesses us. "The mark looks surprisingly unaffected by several hours in your quarters, alpha. I believe there were some client requests regarding entrails and blood play. Or have you forgotten our gods-forsaken duty in this place?"

It's easy to hear the anger in his voice about being in the maze. I don't know where Rama found the vampiri, but there are probably close to thirty of them in this room. Far more than there are alphas.

Noire growls. "We need passage through your quarters."

The vampiri he called Cashore smiles, but there's nothing friendly about the way his lips pull wide, exposing black gums and black teeth. A clicking hiss leaves his throat, and another vampiri steps up next to him–a woman. She glares daggers at us as she steps to Cashore's side, holding a wicked-looking sword in a belt at her hip. Dark hair is braided along the sides of her head, falling free in the back, all the way to her waist. I'd call her beautiful if she wasn't so fucking deadly. I've seen them destroy marks when Rama televises it. The vampiri are horribly cruel.

Cashore steps forward. "That's hardly an explanation, alpha. It was foolish of you to come here. I allowed you to leave with the mark earlier because, as you said, my people may have suffered. But I cannot allow you to come into our quarters and demand...well, anything at all."

Another click leaves his mouth as the female stalks across the space, stopping just in front of Noire as Tenebris comes to my side, snarling. "Step away if you want to keep your pretty head," he growls at the female, brandishing a knife in each hand.

While all this is happening, Noire stands as if he owns this entire fucking maze, a king even here in this destroyed, devastated place.

Lurching forward, I raise my hands as though I'm surrendering, praying I can get them to just listen for a moment. "Stop, please. I know I'm the mark, but I have information that can help you, information about getting out of the maze."

Quick as a flash, the female vampiri shifts and moves, snatching me up by the hair before I have time to shout. Noire and Ten turn as one, but the vampiri moves again, and my head whips back. As soon as I can yank it upright, I realize we're across the fucking room already.

Oh shit, oh fuck. She was so godsdamned fast, I barely tracked the movement.

"Wait," I shout out as Noire stalks across the black stones with his fists balled. His eyes meet mine, full of alpha anger, ready to rip something apart to get to me.

Wait, I beg him silently. *Please, trust me, alpha.*

I know Noire can't hear me, but an understanding passes between us as he gets closer but pauses, looking directly at the female vampiri. "You touched what's mine, and I will shred your flesh from your bones if you hurt her."

The fist in my hair tightens, but the woman clicks at Cashore before kicking the back of my knees and forcing me down in front of the vampiri king.

Finding Cashore's eyes again, I put my hands back up. "Do you find your psychic ability dulled in the maze?"

Shock and awe cross his face before furious anger replaces it. The female yanks my head back so I'm forced to look up into Cashore's face. I can't help the squeak that comes out of my mouth. The back of my head is still tender from earlier.

In a second, Noire is on the female, slicing his claws toward her as she ducks away from him, roaring in anger but letting go of my hair. In front of me, Cashore looks bored as Noire rounds on the woman. "I warned you about hurting her. Back the fuck up before you lose your head."

The vampiri woman snarls but steps next to Cashore as Noire holds his hand out, pulling me upright. "Talk," Noire growls in my ear.

Cashore watches us, lips pursed. "What do you know of vampiri magic?"

Standing up taller, I meet his eyes and square my shoulders, feeling more confident with Noire's big body behind mine. I shift backwards, so his chest brushes against my back, and I swear I feel his strength threading through me. "I worked for Rama. This entire maze is built to handle certain species of monsters, including vampiri. There are numerous measures in place to control you. The Alborada roses that grow in this section are genetically modified to give off a pheromone that inhibits your psychic ability."

Cashore steps back and shakes his head, snarling.

"I can prove it," I press, stepping forward with one hand up. "Burn the roses in your quarters and outside the door. I suspect you'll notice a marked improvement with them gone. There are other measures in place to control you, but this is one. Help us, and I'll tell you the others."

Cashore narrows his eyes at me but nods at the woman with the sword. She immediately barks out a series of commands, and four vampiri dressed like her in black leather grab torches from the wall and walk around the room, lighting the roses aflame.

A hissing sound echoes through the stone chamber as the roses catch on fire and go up, hissing and popping as they burn to ash. Cashore drops to one knee as the smell of the roses slams into us. The female vampiri hisses and clicks at him, obviously worried as he falls forward, covering the back of his head with his hands.

She rounds on me with a hiss as Noire pulls me close. The vampiri hiss and click in concern around the room as Cashore roars in pain. Fuck. The fire must enhance the scent of the roses, and it's hurting him.

Jet and Ten are a tense wall behind Noire and me where they joined us as Cashore fell to his knees.

The vampiri female barks out a series of questions to Cashore, not taking her eyes from us as he moans a response. Around the room, the roses are burning down to crisp, dead vines, smoke billowing into the room as Cashore rocks back onto his heels, closing his all-white eyes.

Deep in my mind, I feel a sudden intrusion. As if something is worming its way through the gray matter, eating me up as it goes. I squirm, gripping both sides of my head in my hands as I hiss around the pain.

Cashore blinks his eyes open. He looks too pained to smile, but his frown is equally terrifying. "Diana Winthrop, Edson Winthrop's daughter? My, my, my."

CHAPTER NINE
NOIRE

Edson Winthrop? So Cashore knows the famous alpha inventor? Winthrop was well-known in alpha circles, but to my knowledge, Vinituvari did not have much of a vampiri population. Jet and Ten bombard me with messages through our bond all at the same time, but Cashore looks over and chuckles. "You might as well be screaming your questions aloud, gentlemen."

Godsdamnit, why did the omega tell him something that gives him more power? I should have asked her what we'd have to give up to get the fuck through here.

Cashore closes his eyes and sucks in a breath. When he opens them again, he takes Diana's hand and pulls her closer. She goes willingly, allowing him to look deeply into her eyes.

"How do you feel?" she questions, her voice soft but curious.

Cashore's black brows furrow as he looks at her, his face inquisitive and concerned. "I have not had access to my ability in years, Diana. What other tricks do you have up your proverbial sleeve?"

Diana chuckles. "Can you not just read them in my mind?"

Cashore reaches out, drawing the back of his pale hand along her cheek as she stiffens.

Snarling, I step closer and pull Diana back to me. Her body relaxes when she hits my heat, and Cashore laughs.

"Oh, I see, alpha. This one is *yours*. All right. I'll allow it, for now." He turns back to Diana. "You did me a great favor, so I'll allow you through my quarters this once, but Ascelin, Renze, and I will be coming with you, wherever you're going."

Behind me, Jet and Tenebris growl immediately. The female, Ascelin, stalks around me, snapping her teeth. Tenebris turns to her when she passes him, taking an aggressive step in her direction as she pauses, eyeing him. There's a natural aggression between all the monsters in the maze, but I've seen Ascelin taunt Tenebris and Jet many times over the years.

Cashore clicks something at her, and she smirks, taking a step away from Ten, although she licks her lips as she does it. A tease of some sort.

"Let's go," I snap, urging Diana forward.

"Clear the room," Cashore roars as the vampiri scatter back along the hallways. Renze and Ascelin stay behind as Cashore turns to me. "I have questions, Noire."

"We don't have much time," Diana reminds him.

Cashore smirks. "No, *you* don't have much time, Diana Winthrop. Now, tell me more about your plans because I am highly interested in a way out of this maze as well."

Shit. She mentioned that, but he can read whatever she knows in her mind. Maybe even before she shares it all with me.

I snarl at the vampiri king, letting my fangs descend as he takes a step away from Diana.

She stiffens but nods, stroking her fingers along the intricately detailed tattoo. "If you knew my father, then you'll know he was a brilliant architect. When I was a child, he built this maze. Rama killed my entire pack once the maze was complete, and I've been living under her thumb in Siargao ever since." She lifts her arm. "This tattoo is a map of the maze. We're using it to get out. Right now."

Cashore blinks, bringing a palm to his forehead. "My gift is still murky, but I sense you tell the truth, Diana. As I said, I want a way out for my people. So if the way through is here, we'll be coming with you."

Diana looks at her arm and nods, pointing to the floor just beneath our feet. "Help me move this rug."

Gripping her arm, I give her a warning look. "We didn't discuss letting other monsters out, little omega."

Diana glances at Cashore and back at me. "We may not get out of here alone, alpha. It might be a good idea to work together."

We're between a fucking rock and a hard place. If I disagree with her, we'll have to fight our way out of the vampiri quarters, and they know what we're up to now. Shit, they might keep Diana and just read the way out from her fucking mind. I won't have it. Growling, I drop her arm and nod.

Cashore glances at Ascelin, and she and Renze go to the far corners of the rug, Ten and Jet at the other side. With a heave, they remove the rug, ripping it back to show the floor underneath. Black stones lie in a circle around three eyes carved into the dark stone. Cashore swears under his breath as Diana crouches down, running her fingers along the mark and then referencing her tattoo.

The vampiri king's eyes meet mine, assessing as he frowns. He clicks something at Ascelin, and she leaves the room as Diana depresses a sequence of stones around the symbol.

Ten and Jet come and stand next to me as the symbol stone sinks and clicks over to the side on a track. More stones fall away and disappear as a set of stairs opens up in front of us.

Ascelin comes back into the room, handing Cashore a vicious curved blade that he straps to his back. "I do not like this, my king." She's using English to make it clear that she doesn't trust us. She gestures at Diana and my brothers, and sighs.

Cashore turns to her as Renze comes to stand on his other side. "Lissette is due soon, Asc. If we can help her, we must. At any cost."

The vampiri warrioress pales at his words as I try to absorb their meaning.

Due? The vampiri are procreating in the maze? I've never seen a child, though, and I've traveled every inch of this maze thousands of times.

Jet and Ten send a flurry of messages through our blood bond, but if Cashore hears them, he doesn't bother to respond.

"Due?" Diana questions Cashore. "With a child?"

Cashore nods, his face sad as he looks at Diana. "It is a long, sad story, Diana Winthrop. But if Ascelin, Renze, and I determine you are not lying, I will call my people so we may all leave this place."

Diana nods, not probing any further, and encourages us to move by taking the stairs first. I snarl when Cashore attempts to follow her.

He steps back with a huffy laugh. "Apologies, Noire. I did not mean to crowd your omega."

My omega. The words ring in my mind as something scratches at the edges of it. He doesn't know that all alphas train to deal with other monsters' abilities when we visit other provinces, so diving into my mind will be harder than he thinks. I dealt with a small contingent of vampiri in Siargao when I ruled. I am aware of their abilities.

Jet and Ten stiffen behind me, but I pace down the stairs after Diana as Cashore chuckles and follows. The dark engulfs us once more as Diana walks ahead of me.

For half an hour, we walk in near-complete silence as Diana mumbles to herself, checking her tattoo every other hallway or so.

The quiet gives me a chance to observe her unencumbered by everyone else looking at me. I'm still at the very edge of a rut, ready to give in to that heat and take her for days. This is not the time or place, and my primary goal is to get out of this maze. But I can't deny that the way Diana's hips swing as she walks is a fucking distraction.

She looks over her shoulder, her elegant profile clearly visible to me. I let my mind wander to how she felt wrapped around my cock earlier, something I'd like to do again in the very near future.

If I get out of this maze tonight, there are three things I'll do, in order of importance:

Kill Rama.

Get my brothers to safety.

Fuck Diana until she's screaming my name and clenching around my knot in the throes of orgasm.

Behind me, Cashore chuckles in the quiet.

"Fuck off," I snap as he laughs again. He's not reading my mind, but I'm sure my focus on the beautiful omega in front of us speaks volumes.

Ahead of me, Diana pauses and finds a symbol on the wall. She turns to our group with a quick nod. "This should put us out into the lower levels. Do you know what's down there now? It's meant for larger monsters."

Ascelin comes forward, running pale hands over the symbol with a frown. "I have heard Rama put a naga in the maze, but I have avoided the lower levels for quite some time."

Cashore nods, giving me a knowing look. "The lower levels reek of wrongness to me. I cannot explain it, other than to say I hear voices there, which is a bad sign among our people."

"Fuck," snaps Jet. "I've been to the lower levels thousands of times. There's nothing there but more darkness. And maybe now a naga. So how do we deal with a naga?"

Turning to my youngest brother, I smile. "Tenebris, care to enlighten the vampiri? How shall we deal with a naga?" Ten has always been the studious one, and he was fascinated by other monsters long before we came into the maze, always reading books about them. Even the maze library in his room is full of monster lore.

Ten smiles and glances at Ascelin before looking at Cashore. "Naga mate from birth, so if there is only one here, it will be wild with grief at being separated from its mate. Our only hope if we stumble upon one is to hold its attention long enough to get it to listen to us. We'll have to tell it we have a way out."

We all turn to look at Diana, but she stands up straighter. "The lower levels were designed to hold larger monsters–naga, minotaurs, gavataurs. The only passages out of the lower levels are too small for those monsters to get through. They're dropped in from above. It's a way of locking them in, so to speak."

Ascelin frowns at Cashore. "That's why I hear the voices down there. Who knows what monsters exist there that we have yet to see? I tell you again, I do not like this, my king. If Diana is telling the truth, there are parts of the maze we have never seen."

Jet snaps his teeth with frustration. "There's never been anything down there until now. I was in the lower levels a week ago, and there sure as shit wasn't a naga there then."

Ascelin ignores him. "My king, please. Let us rethink this plan. Is this worth our lives?"

I look over, bored. "Come with us or not, vampiri, but rest assured, we are continuing on."

Diana gives Cashore a half-hearted smile, but beneath it, a thread of darkness lurks. This pretty little mark has already managed to surprise me this evening. What other secrets hide behind her elegant features?

I ache to find out.

"Let's go, omega," I command as cornflower eyes find mine and spark. Despite my taking of her earlier and my reassurance there will be repercussions for speaking to me with disrespect, she has to force herself to hold back. Deep inside Diana's mind, we are somehow on even footing, and I cannot have that.

Stepping up next to her, I watch her depress a stone, and the black stone wall slides open to reveal a passageway that drops straight down. Diana gathers the remainder of her skirts and hops in first. I follow her, hissing in a breath at the temperature drop of the lower level. The rest of our group drops down behind me, Ascelin and Renze snapping at the temperature change.

Ascelin opens her mouth to say something but stops when Cashore clicks at her in warning.

Turning, I frown. "What? What were you about to say?"

Cashore smiles, but it doesn't reach his eyes. "We dislike the cold, alpha. It's far cooler down here, one of many reasons vampiri avoid the lower levels."

Diana steps up next to me and smiles. "Vampiri slow down in the cooler weather. If it's too cold, they'll drop like stones. That's why they keep torches on in their chambers."

With that pronouncement, she turns and heads up the hallway as I glance back at Cashore. His face is white with rage, Ascelin snapping her teeth next to him as Renze draws his sword with an angry hiss.

Jet snickers at the vampiri group. "If it gets too cold and you pass out, I'm not carrying you."

I smile at Cashore, who still looks livid, before turning to follow the surprising omega through the maze.

CHAPTER TEN
DIANA

Cashore stops rummaging around in my head as I pace up a dark hallway with Noire a wall of warmth behind me. Until we hear a bellow that shakes the hallway. It's inhuman, a roar and scream rolled into a growl that shakes my bones.

Noire grips my waist, our group falling immediately silent. In the darkness, he turns to me. "We need the nearest open space; something's coming fast." He says this as if he's not terrified of whatever just screeched up the hallway, but when I glance behind him, the vampiri all look horrified, Ascelin gripping her sword tight in one white fist.

"The throne room," I bark. "There's a door there if we can hold it off long enough."

Noire's fingers trail along my waist as he steps past me and heads up the hallway, his steps swift and sure. He knows the passages of this maze well, and that's clear when he takes two quick lefts and a right, dumping us out into a large hall with a throne at the end. Angular columns line the hallway, the stones here a slightly lighter color than the rest of the maze. There's not a great way out of this room if there is a naga, and it comes in.

"What's the plan?" hisses Renze from behind me.

Tenebris speaks up first. "We can't hide from a naga; they sense body heat, and they have incredible hearing."

"Our bodies are cold, alpha," snaps Ascelin, "let us use this to our advantage."

"Aim for the back of its hood," Tenebris continues. "Right between the eyes. It's the only place a weapon can penetrate naga scales."

"Split up," Noire commands our group. "Half of us on that side of the throne, half of us on this side. Something's coming; I can hear it, and it knows we're here. We must get it to listen to us."

Next to me, Noire turns to Jet. "If something happens to me, protect Diana at all costs. Get out of here. You know what to do from there."

Jet nods as I frown up at Noire, but his face is a carefully neutral mask as he tugs me behind him, standing just behind the obsidian throne.

You know what to do from there? The idea that Noire has a plan outside the maze that doesn't involve him eats me up. I hate the idea that he imagines not making it out of this place, but my heart warms in my chest knowing he told his brothers to protect me.

Long minutes pass where nobody says anything, and when I glance to the opposite side of the enormous throne, Ten, Ascelin, and Renze are poised there in obvious disquiet. When Renze looks up with a soft growl, my eyes fly toward the far end of the hall.

Shadows play in the dark doorway we first came in. *Something is coming.* Behind me, Noire slides his hand around my waist, up between my breasts to circle my throat. "Keep yourself safe, no matter what, Diana. Stick close to my brothers."

Nodding, I shift back into his heat as he stiffens and huffs out a breath along the shell of my ear. Goosebumps prickle down my neck and shoulders as Noire nips my neck. Someone hisses at us to be quiet—Cashore, I think— but I can't help the panting breaths that come out of my mouth as Noire grazes his teeth along my exposed neckline. "Even now, I'm half-tempted to take you, omega."

Throwing my head back into his shoulder, I expose my neck to him in the darkness of the maze, reaching to hold on to his forearms. I should be terrified of him. He's been nothing but rough and cruel to me. But somehow, unbelievably, I feel safe in Noire's arms, with his fangs at my throat. The worst monster is the one at my back, but I'm not afraid of him, not completely.

Noire pulls me tighter to him, growling low into my ear as his grip tightens. A terrible grating sound rings through the hall as my gaze shifts forward, heart leaping into my throat. It pounds so hard that I know whatever's coming can probably hear me, but Noire chuckles into my skin and plants a tender kiss at the base of my shoulder before straightening up behind me. His grip doesn't leave my throat, though.

I know he wants to keep me safe so he can get out, but it's easy to sink into his dominant possession.

Turning to the alphas, I nod toward the noise. "I need time to search the back wall, but the door is somewhere behind the throne. We need to keep him away from it. Deal?"

Ten and Jet nod, and Noire squeezes my hip.

A slithery grating sound rings louder up the hallway as our group prepares for whatever's coming.

Renze is the first to click in surprise when the head and shoulders of the monster come through the doorway. It's a naga—broad, red-scaled chest, a wide hood flaring behind slanted snake-like features. It's clearly a male by the set of his shoulders, his muscular stomach flowing into a thickly coiled body. He slithers into the room, and he's fucking enormous.

"It's a naga king," murmurs Ten under his breath, his eyes narrowed. "See the pattern on his chest? It signifies he's royalty."

I've never seen a naga before because they mostly settle in the dusty and uncivilized western part of the continent, but he's nearly as tall as the columns themselves, his head almost touching the ceiling. He must be twenty feet tall without even rising up on his body.

The naga's tongue comes out to scent the air, and he snarls, gripping on to two columns with enormous hands as he leans into the room. His tongue tastes the air over and over as the remainder of his coils slips into the room and bunches up behind him. "Prey…" he whispers, the sound ringing off the dark stones of the room.

Noire moves from behind me before I can say a word, striding out from behind the throne like a king. He comes to stop next to it, the naga's eyes whipping toward him as it slithers forward another ten feet.

My first urge is to scream at Noire to run; we can't fight this thing. I've never seen a monster this big. But Noire wants out of this fucking place as much as I do.

He must have a plan.

"Prey," the naga whispers again, sliding up the aisle toward us as Jet and Tenebris slink off to either side of the columns, forming a box as the naga gets closer. His eyes dart from side to side as he looks at them but throws his head back and laughs.

It's a vicious, cruel sound, pitched low enough to rumble the stone floor.

Without warning, the naga leaps forward, crossing the space between him and Noire in the blink of an eye. He swipes out with one enormous arm, attempting to knock Noire into one of the columns. But Noire is faster than I could have believed possible, gripping the naga's arm and climbing up onto its back.

It's hard to even follow the movements as the naga writhes and coils, trying to dislodge Noire. They slam into a column, and the rocks crash around us as the rest of our group sprints into the clearing. Jet and Ten leap onto the Naga's front, attempting to drag it down as the vampiri all do the same.

With an explosion of fury, the naga shakes them all loose, and monsters fly around the room, hitting walls and sliding to the ground.

The moment the naga dislodges everyone, it rounds on me and shoots forward to where I stand next to the throne. There's no fucking way we can get past this monster.

"We can get you to your mate," I shout loudly to ensure the naga hears me.

The male slams to a halt, tongue flicking rapidly against his red lips, his eyes narrowed and angry.

Everyone is frozen, pulling to their feet as I face the naga king.

"Where is she?" he roars, flying forward and wrapping me in his scales, coiling up so I'm caught in his powerful body. The coils pull tight, crushing the air from my chest as his face comes close to mine.

My heart shrivels at what I see there: fury, distress, longing. His pain echoes in my soul. I feel...bad for him. Another monster who'd prefer to live out his life away from Rama, dragged here against his will to serve as her puppet.

"Your mate is in the maze too," I lie. I don't know if it's true or not, but I'll say anything I must to get us away from him. There's no way we can get past him. We'll just have to go another way, if we live long enough.

"I can...get you...to her." I gasp as the coils wind tighter, my ribs beginning to crack under the pressure of his tightly muscled body. Black spots dance in my vision as the breath steals from my lungs, my head falling back.

"Where is she?" he roars in my face, tongue flicking against my neck as he tastes me.

I'm vaguely aware of Noire leaping onto the creature's head, stabbing him over and over as the alphas and vampiri attempt to take the naga down. He unleashes his coils, flinging me across the room where I hit the black, glittering throne and fall to the ground.

The naga rolls and snatches Noire and Tenebris in his coils, twisting up tight as he roars for his mate and rounds on me again. "Where is she? Tell me now, and I'll make their death fast."

I gasp for air around the crushing pressure still squeezing my lungs. The naga slinks closer, crushing Noire and his brother in his coils when I see

Renze and Ascelin fly through the air. The king senses them coming and whips his tail out, knocking Ascelin to the side, but Renze keeps coming, landing on the king's hood.

Almost faster than I can follow, Renze buries his sword in the center of the hood until it comes out through his mouth, the king roaring in pain as he releases the alphas and thrashes on the ground. Renze pushes off the king's head and leaps to the ground, rolling out of the way as he sprints behind one of the columns.

Noire and Tenebris jump gracefully over the thrashing king, careful to avoid a hooked barb at the end of his tail. Tenebris joins Renze behind one column, and Noire ducks behind with me, turning me carefully to face him. "Are you hurt?" Dark eyes scan mine and glance down to where I'm holding my ribs.

"I'll be okay," I whisper as he leans in and sniffs at my neck, growling into my skin.

The king flails in front of the room's throne, roaring as he scratches at the back of his hood, yanking the sword out and tossing it aside. He rounds on us, blood already streaming out of his mouth as he pants and surges forward. Noire, Tenebris, and I sprint for the other side of the room, crossing to where the rest of our group hides behind the other columns, but the king follows us in a macabre game of tag.

We round the throne just as he leaps up over the top of it, throwing himself down in front of us as we scramble back, falling over one another to get away. But his movements slow, blood coating his entire neck and chest, dripping down. He lashes out, his tail whipping Jet across the chest as he flies against the wall, crushing his pack behind him.

I hear the crack of the uppers in his bag and watch the purple liquid seep out as Jet roars with anger.

"Get out of his way," I scream just as Jet falls forward and leaps upright, snarling at the swaying naga. "Draw him away from the throne, Jet! The door is somewhere in this part of the room!"

Jet sprints away from the king, but the naga's eyes barely follow him. He sways from side to side once, twice, then falls to the ground with a heavy thud, knocking us all to the stone floor, Jet flying sideways once more.

"Oh fuck!" I shout, throwing my hands up in my hair. "He's down in front of the wall. The door fucking swings open."

"You must be shitting me, Diana," Jet snaps as Renze comes to stand beside him, his chest heaving under the leather vest.

"Get away from the naga," I direct, scrambling backward just as Tenebris' eyes widen in understanding.

"Back up—as far as you can," he barks at our group. Without asking why, we all turn to do so, but the naga's body gives a horrifying squelch, and a cloud of mist rains down on us as Tenebris groans. "Godsdamnit, I hope he's the only one down here."

"Why?" barks Noire. "What the fuck is going on here?" He wipes at his face in disgust, frowning when it appears the mist has even gotten in his mouth.

I turn toward the group and sigh, closing my eyes and squinting them tightly shut. "Naga release a pheromone upon death, and if it coats you, it sends a signal to other naga when you meet them that you were in a naga's presence when they died. They're all reclusive, so they take this as a sign that you killed one of their kind. It's an immediate death sentence if there's another naga down here."

"Well, we'd have seen one already, wouldn't we?" Renze looks confused.

I point to the king's coils. "He's blocking the fucking door. There's no other way out in this section. We have to backtrack and go out the other side of the maze, which means going back down into the lower levels there. Those levels are all designed to hold the bigger monsters. It's entirely possible there's another naga, or something worse, something even bigger."

"I ran the lower levels last week," Jet reminds us. "There was nothing there…"

Grimacing, I turn to him. "The maze is designed to make it easy for Rama to insert monsters at various levels. She knows we're trying to get out. The likelihood of her putting something in the maze on the other side, knowing we're headed there, is very high."

"So, what next?" Noire's voice is cool and collected as Jet snarls and runs both hands through his hair.

"We follow the omega," Renze purrs coolly. "We protect her at all costs, and we get the fuck out of here. We knew it would not be easy, and Rama has not even begun to toy with us. We should expect that she will, as Diana just mentioned."

I look at the vampiri male with the disconcerting, too-white eyes. He smiles softly, but there's a sadness to it. He wants out, but he doesn't believe this will work.

Noire puts one hand on my back and ushers me forward. "Let's go, Diana."

～

Our entire group is pensive and quiet as we trek through the lower levels, backtracking toward the side of the maze that houses the vampiri living quarters. We can take another route from here, but it will be longer, and we'll spend more time on the other side of the lower levels. I'd love to avoid that, but unless we figure out a way to move the dead naga, we have very few other options.

Cashore pulls up next to me as we walk, despite a warning growl from Noire. I feel Cashore's gift rummaging around in my mind as I snap my teeth at him. "Get out."

The vampiri king's eyes narrow, but he does as I say, folding his hands behind his back. "I will be blunt, Diana. I need to get my people out, and I need to know that you have another way. A realistic way."

I turn to him, confused. "Why are you following me at all if you don't believe I'm telling the truth?"

Cashore nods slowly. "It is not that I do not believe you, but when we pass the vampiri quarters, I will ask the rest of my people to come. That group includes younglings, Diana, remember? Younglings we have protected from the maze for seven years. I will not further risk them, and I would not mention them again at all if I did not believe this was our one chance to leave this place."

Jet speaks up from in front of me, turning to walk backwards as he looks at Cashore. "Why would you have children in this place? Are you out of your mind?"

Renze speaks first. "Vampiri reproduce quickly, and our power is derived from sex. We have no way to prevent children from being born in this place. To my knowledge, we are the only group with females in the maze."

Jet nods. "I'd never considered that, but you're right. Of course, it's hard to tell the men from the women…"

Ascelin hisses next to Cashore, grabbing a knife from her chest-strap and brandishing it toward Jet. "Watch your mouth, alpha."

Jet winks at her before turning back around. I continue to follow but glance up at Cashore, who still looks at me with a blank expression. This close, I can see his eyes aren't truly white; there's an iris and pupil there but covered in a white film like a shark. "I truly know a few ways out, Cashore. And I will do my level best to help you get your younglings out of this place. I can't make you any promises, but I think you know that. I am not lying to you, though."

Cashore smiles, showing me dozens of razor-sharp teeth as his black lips part. "Good, Diana Winthrop. Because if you are lying, I will greatly relish fulfilling my duty for this evening." He holds his arm up, the disk still glowing a faint green, a reminder that the vampiri were supposed to take my life.

Ascelin laughs next to him, but it's evil and mean and devious. "If our remaining younglings suffer because of you, omega, I will suck the marrow from your bones while your heart still beats. You will feel every moment of pain until we end you."

Noire lashes out fast, swiping his claws at Ascelin's face as she chuckles and dances out of the way, batting her eyes playfully.

I hold back a shudder while Noire wraps a hand around my waist, tucking me into his other side, away from Cashore. "Don't touch the omega, vampiri. She's mine, and if you get in the way of my people getting out of here, you will deal with me." He snarls as Cashore laughs. And then we're at the vampiri quarters once more, the maze around us quiet and ominous.

"We stop here," Cashore barks, Noire stiffening beside me.

"No, we keep going."

Cashore rounds on Noire with a snarl, fangs descended as the white coating his eyes takes on a red hue. "Diana has already told us the lower levels will likely hold larger monsters. Do you really want to go down there without better weapons than you've got?" He gestures to Noire's knives, eliciting a growl as Noire pulls me tight against his chest.

"Are you saying you have better weapons?"

"I do," Cashore purrs. "I need a moment to gather my people, but if you can grant me a little time to do so, I will happily give your pack additional weapons so we may *all* leave this place."

I turn in Noire's arms, searching his face for any sign of understanding. It's clear from the angry clench of his jaw that he doesn't want to stop, not for a second. "Please, Noire," I murmur. "The more of us the better. There are worse monsters than naga in Rama's stable. We've only got one shot at this, and our chances diminish without good weaponry."

He looks over my head at Jet. "What do you think, brother?"

Before Jet can speak up, Tenebris does. "We need all the weapons we can get, Noire. Any one of them could mean the difference between us making it out or losing Diana and our only chance to leave."

Noire glances at Jet, who nods and, for once, has nothing saucy to say. Noire nods once to Cashore, and then we follow the vampiri trio back into their quarters.

The first thing we hear is a deep, wailing scream that sinks right into the depths of my bones.

CHAPTER ELEVEN
NOIRE

The vampiri scream sets my teeth on edge, grating at my sensitive hearing as Ascelin hands her long sword to Renze and darts off down a long hallway toward the noise. Renze turns to our group. "Vampiri birth is quite painful. We have had a youngling due for several days now. By the sounds of it, she is coming."

Diana looks at Renze in rapt fascination. "How do you protect them? How many younglings are in your group?"

Renze frowns over at Cashore, but the king nods at him. "Ten younglings left."

"Left?" Diana barks. "There were more?"

Cashore peers at Diana with a frown. "As I said, omega, we have protected the younglings from the maze when we could. But we have not saved them all. The maze has taken from us several times."

"Oh my gods," she whispers, tears lining her blue eyes. I shouldn't notice the way her cheeks flush or the way she takes a step closer to me as if my presence comforts her. "Do you have bones we need to take with us? How can we remember them? What do you need?"

Cashore frowns, looking meaningfully at the roses before glancing back at Diana. "The maze has already claimed the bodies of our dead younglings, Diana. There is nothing to take with us."

She chokes back a distressed noise and presses harder into my chest.

I shouldn't comfort her. If anything, she should step away because, out of the maze's dangerous hallways, my attention is focused once more on her intoxicating scent. Nothing can be done about the pheromones they doused her with, and my libido rises as she takes another step toward me, her skin hot against my arm through the tee she's wearing. Curiosity threads itself through the forefront of my mind, wondering why the scent isn't affecting Jet and Ten quite like it does me. The smell of Diana in heat was enough to send me into an immediate rut.

That is highly concerning because it indicates compatibility on a far deeper level than simple alpha-omega dynamics.

Cashore turns to me, changing the subject deftly. "Shall I take you to the weapons, alpha? You may have your pick of what you can carry."

Nodding, I grip Diana's hand and tug her along with me, maintaining vigilance as we follow Cashore down a dark hall and through a door. I'm leery of following him with Diana dangling like a prize between us. But Cashore sighs and turns to me in the darkness of the doorway. "We have a better chance of escaping if we work together, alpha. I will not attempt to harm you."

"Good," I purr back at him, not loosening my grip on the omega. "Because I think you know it would go poorly if you did…"

Cashore ignores the comment but flips the lights on in the room, not that any of the alphas need it. I sense his gift scratching at the edges of my mind as my brothers pace the room, eyeing wall after wall covered in knives, swords, and chains. The number of weapons in this room is staggering.

"Get out of my fucking brain," I snarl at the vampiri king. "I won't tell you again not to try that with me or my people."

Cashore has the bad sense to laugh. Renze grips his own sword tighter as he steps closer to his king.

Just then, a high trilling sound echoes through the hallway and open door, into the weapons room. Cashore whips his head around and stalks out, calling over his shoulder, "Help yourselves to the weapons. The youngling is here, and I must greet her."

Renze stays in the room with us, his gaze traveling from me to my brothers.

I run my fingertips up under Diana's shirt, stroking underneath one breast as I lean over her back, bringing my lips to her ear. "Find yourself some weapons, omega. I'll stand guard."

She turns and nods once at me, moving quietly across the room, silent on her feet like all omegas. I back up a step, leaning against the wall by the doorway as I watch my pack, keeping one eye on Renze. He relaxes when I do, sheathing his sword and crossing his arms over his chest, keeping watch the same way I am.

I don't miss how his eyes continue to fall on Jet, how he watches him far more than Tenebris. Alpha intuition tells me to keep an eye on him, that his focus on my brother is more than a general interest in a competing male.

Diana comes back to me then, tightening the straps of a chest holder filled with knives. I reach out, moving her fingers as I loosen it, moving one of the straps up over her head to the other side.

"You've got this on wrong, omega."

She looks up at me, and it's easy to see she's resisting the urge to snark something. When I tilt an eyebrow up in challenge, she bites her lip and keeps quiet. I tighten the strap, unable to stop focusing on how much the leather accentuates her full breasts.

Diana's nipples pebble underneath the shirt as my mouth starts to water. The sharp edges of my rut stab at the base of my spine as heat rushes to my cock. Gathering Diana into my arms, I pull her close and tug her head back, dragging my nose up her neck.

Gods, she smells so fucking good. Even beneath the fake pheromones, her natural scent shines through. It's warm and inviting, and the way she arches into me despite the tension between us only serves to stoke the flames building in my core. She remains wary of me, even with my body calling for hers, teasing hers. I want to push and pull her in every possible way until she's screaming release around my cock.

The trilling noise echoes louder, and Renze coughs. "The cord is cut, and the youngling is presented to the king. I must go meet her now as well. Feel free to come with us, or stay here with the weapons." He strides out of the room, careful not to touch the door. I eye him warily to make sure he doesn't attempt to close it.

Jet comes back and smirks at me. "Gonna fuck the omega right here, Noire?"

Diana's face schools into a careful neutral as she steps away from me, playing with the straps again. She turns to me, ignoring Jet's comment. "Let's just get out of here."

Nodding, I gesture for Jet to leave the room first, then Ten, then Diana. I follow up the rear as always, watching my people and keeping a wary eye for anything amiss. When we get to the common room, the vampiri step aside, and their circle opens to reveal a female vampiri in the center, holding a writhing infant in her arms. It's coated in blood, and the mother looks exhausted, but it sucks happily at her breast as Cashore looks up at me, face guarded and wary.

The vampiri around us trill again, a noise I've never heard them make. It's joyous and happy, and for a moment, I'm taken back to my own pack, to the way we'd celebrate when pups were born. Despair crushes my chest in that moment as I close my eyes, remembering my people before Rama slaughtered them. Liuvang willing, some of them escaped.

I vow again to find them, if it's the last thing I do.

Hot anger builds in my system, rising until I channel it into focus—focus on getting out of here, on keeping Diana safe so I can use her knowledge. She watches the mother and child with rapt fascination, her pink mouth slightly open as she leans against the wall, cradling her ribs still. She turns slightly as if she can feel my gaze on her, body pivoting toward me as blue eyes find mine.

I don't know what to read in those eyes. Sorrow. Darkness. A twisted soul as black and complicated as mine?

Cashore comes up next to me with a meaningful look, his eyes flicking to Diana's back. "A word, alpha?"

Not taking my eyes from the omega, I nod, then turn to follow him. Through my bond with my brothers, I send them a clear message. *Do not let Diana out of your sight. I don't trust anyone.*

Cashore leads me down a hallway that's eerily similar to my own in the alpha quarters, opening a door and slipping in. I scent the room, looking for any signs of attack as he sighs. "It is just us, Noire."

Stepping in, I look around, but true to his word, there are only the two of us in the room. Not that I couldn't take Cashore in a fight, but this night is wearing my patience thin, and I'd prefer not to kill the vampiri king if I don't have to.

Cashore cocks his head to the side and smiles. "You think you could take me in a fight?"

"Stop reading my mind," I bark out.

He smiles again. "I'll have to thank Diana again for that tip regarding the roses. My full abilities are not back but are returning to me fast, despite your ability to ward against me."

I don't bother to congratulate him. An enemy who can read my thoughts sounds fucking inconvenient; although, for purposes of getting out of this place, it may come in handy.

Cashore nods, although the slimy feeling I get when he's reading me dissipates. "On the subject of Diana, it's clear she is multi-faceted in ways we did not foresee."

I bark out a laugh at that. Multi-faceted is one way to put it.

Cashore tuts at me with a smile. "Diana is...willful, but she's hiding something. Her mind is its own maze. Reading her is surprisingly difficult, even for me. That typically indicates years of psychological trauma."

Trauma. Somehow, when I think about someone damaging Diana in that way, rage fills my system. The mental image of Diana hurt and injured and afraid does not bring me joy. Earlier, when she was nothing but a mark to me, it was different. But tonight, she saved all our lives by distracting the naga. Still, a mark will often say and do anything to try to escape the maze. I still don't trust her, despite how wildly attracted to her I am on every possible level.

Cashore continues, "I won't risk my people, and I sense Diana has not been forthcoming with all the details around our exit from the maze. I believe it would be unwise for us to continue without a fuller picture of what she knows and why she's here."

"What do you have in mind? You've said she's hard to read…"

Cashore nods and smiles, a deeply wicked smile that reminds me how very predatory vampiri are. It grates my alpha senses as I stand up taller and snarl. Cashore snarls too, taking a step closer to me. "I need her distracted, overwhelmed. And while she is in that state, I will be able to read her more easily. I need to pick my way through Diana Winthrop's mind. You will be the distraction. Diana's memory is its own form of maze, Noire."

"Are you asking me to hurt her?" I growl out the words. Hurting her sounds far less appealing than it did a few hours ago.

"Hurt her, tease her–whatever you need to do to push her to a desperate edge. People in that state of mind are unable to hide their thoughts from me, despite training against it."

"Done," I snap. I won't risk losing another brother in this place, although I'll try teasing first.

"That would be a shame indeed," purrs Cashore, even though I didn't say that last part aloud. I whip a hand out and grab the vampiri king's chin as I press a knife to his chest. "What have I said about digging through my mind?"

"I am simply illustrating a point, alpha," Cashore smiles, his darkly translucent teeth peeking at me between black lips. Taking a step back, I nod in the direction of the common room. Trills still echo along the hallways. I'm ready to get the hell out of here.

When Cashore and I return to the main living area, Diana's eyes find mine, an odd mix of relief and anxiety showing through before she settles her face into a careful neutral.

The vampiri clears his throat, and as one, his people turn and bow their heads. "We leave tonight. Gather only what you must take with you. Go now to grab those items. We will continue this celebration when we are free of the maze." With that proclamation, the vampiri scatter along the hallways as my brothers turn to me.

When I find Jet, I reach into his bag for the purple liquid uppers, relieved to find one bottle still whole. I stalk across the room to Diana, handing her the bottle. "Drink it." It's a simple command, but I let the alpha roll through me and wash over her, smothering her with dominance.

Diana shudders but takes the glass. "Why?"

My gods, the sheer amount of disobedience from this woman.

Gripping her hair, I tug her head back and force her to look up at me. "Because there's plenty you're not telling us about who you are and what you're doing here, and I want to know every fucking detail. Right now. You're hiding something, Diana. I can feel it."

Cashore hisses from behind Diana, stalking soundlessly across the carpet as our eyes meet over her shoulder. Jet and Ten reach out through our mental bond, and I caution them to remain watchful.

Smiling, I nod at the vampiri, even though Diana can't turn and see. "You're gonna drink this, and then Cashore is going to read everything inside your mind, and we're going to see where that leaves us."

"Please, Noire, I'm not lying," she starts as I snarl and yank her head back harder. Cashore hisses again and comes to stand just behind her, leaning into her ear as I grip her jaw and pinch hard. Her mouth pops open as her eyes go wild. The vampiri takes the uppers and pours them down her throat as she sputters and coughs. Once she has a mouthful, I clamp her jaw shut and watch her swallow the purple liquid.

"Time to push her, alpha," Cashore purrs in a sing-song voice as Diana groans. I grip her jaw and force another few mouthfuls down her.

The effect is nearly instantaneous, just like with Jet. Diana's pupils expand until they overtake the blue of her iris, her chest heaving slightly as she balls her fists.

Jet and Ten come to stand just beside me; both are there if I need anything at all. They know better than to interrupt me when I'm in alpha enforcer mode.

I let a rumbling purr wash over Diana as I haul her close to my chest. It reverberates between us, her nipples pebbling for me, body tightening. She wants me. Despite how we got started. Despite how roughly I took her in my bed earlier. A responding snarl leaves Diana's pretty lips as her fangs elongate, peeking out of the corners of her mouth. She's angry. Good.

Seeing those sharp teeth sends pleasure throbbing through my system. What would it feel like for her to bite me? I find myself pondering it as she pants in my arms.

"Tease her," purrs Cashore, nipping at Diana's ear as she shudders away from him.

Wrong, wrong, wrong. She doesn't want his touch.

Good. Because this isn't about her pleasure. This is about overwhelming her until she gives up all the secrets she's hiding in that steel-trap mind of hers.

"Tell me," I bark out. "Tell me everything about working for Rama. Tell me everything you know about leaving this place."

Diana fights the uppers and the compulsion I read from Cashore. His gift is like nails to a chalkboard in my mind; I can't imagine what it feels like to the omega on uppers. Diana snarls and shakes her head as I take one step closer to her, her breasts smashed up against my chest.

I purr again as she whimpers, the scent of slick slapping me across the face as her arousal amps up. "Tell me, pretty little omega. Tell me all your secrets." Reaching into her torn skirts, I slide my fingers between her thighs, chuckling when she parts them ever so slightly for me. I find her clit and pinch as she doubles over, Cashore yanking her back upright with his hand around her neck.

Anger flashes in Diana's eyes at the rough treatment, so I do it again, pinching her clit as more slick floods from her. This is the way an omega should respond to an alpha's need, rough as it is. Something about this woman brings out my darkest desires for pain and punishment.

Cashore leans into Diana's ear again. "Tell us about working with Rama. In what way did you work for her…"

Diana gasps, her eyes squinting tightly closed as I tickle my fingers along her clit, rubbing with even, soft strokes as she squirms between two monsters. "It doesn't matter," she grunts out, eyes flying open to meet mine.

I resist the urge to bellow and rage. I need details. "It matters to me, omega." My voice is husky even in my own ears as Cashore's eyes meet mine. *Push her.*

"I was…her profiler," she gasps out as Cashore's jaw clenches. He nods. She's telling the fucking truth.

"And that means what, exactly?" my bark whips around the space between Diana and me as she grunts against the onslaught of it and Cashore's gift.

Diana snarls and snaps her teeth at me as Cashore laughs. "More, Noire. Push her more."

Leaning in, I sink my teeth into her throat, just under her chin, blood filling my mouth and dripping down my fangs as Diana squirms against me, her feet losing purchase on the floor as I lift her off the ground. I release the bite and snarl into her lips, "Details, Diana."

"No," she pleads. "Don't make me!"

I bite her again, this time on her chest, just above heaving breasts I ache to suck and lick. She's clearly hedging, and the breath leaves her in a whoosh when I shove two fingers deep inside her and stroke. Diana's cunt clenches around me as she rocks her hips to meet me. "Tell me," I growl as I release the bite and look for another place.

"I profiled the mark and the monsters," she grunts. A deep moan leaves her as I stroke her inner walls, finding that spot that'll drive her wild.

"To what end?" I bark.

"To what end," Cashore repeats, his gift stabbing at Diana and me both as she grunts against the onslaught of my fingers. I shut him out as the vampiri groans at the slim expanse of creamy neck presented just below his mouth. The fiery poison he carries in his fangs begins to drip off his teeth, landing on Diana's skin as she yelps and squirms in my arms.

"What else, Diana?" I command as she sobs. I watch Cashore's poison eat away at her skin, burning it red and blistering it as I rub inside her with three fingers. Slick coats my hand, my dick lengthening in my pants as I growl and bring my teeth to drag up her neck, nipping under her ear.

Diana groans, sinking into me as her arms fly up to encircle my neck. She surprises me at every turn. All this hurt, all this pain, all this dominance, and still she doesn't run. What depths does this omega hide? I want to uncover every layer of her.

"I suggested scenes for the hunt based on the mark and monster profiles," she mumbles, her head lolling to the side as I bite my way down her neck, careful to steer clear of Cashore's venom. I don't want that shit in my mouth. "I've profiled every monster in here at some point. I've profiled every mark. I orchestrated...everything. Every detail of every death..."

I bite Diana's shoulder as she hisses and rolls her hips against mine. Cold fury sinks along a connection between us. *She created the scenes.*

"So, every time I killed, it was because you chose it?" Cashore's voice is a deep bark as Diana sobs and nods.

"I chose it; I chose all of it. Every moment of every death in this entire godsforsaken shithole." She's sobbing, shaking and angry as her words sink in.

"Every death?" I spit out. *"Every* death?"

Diana's blue eyes flash up to mine, and she shrugs, once. She knows what I'm asking. I need clear fucking confirmation. "Almost every one," she whispers.

"So, when Oskur died..."

A sob leaves Diana's lips as she nods again. "I profiled that too..." Her voice is a hint of a whisper as I roar with rage, shaking the ceiling as Ten and Jet pace around us. They don't know what to do with this information. This fucking omega worked for the woman who put us here. She planned Oskur's death. He is dead because of her. He died in the way *she chose*.

"There is more, Diana, I sense it," Cashore presses, looking at me. He takes the chance to speak into my mind. *Keep pushing, alpha; that is not all from her.*

"You're a greedy little thing," I purr. "You like this adventure, this trip into the maze to visit the monsters. I bet you came in here to get fucked by me. Did you profile this too? Did you profile our escape?"

There's a moment's pause where her eyes meet mine, and the truth shines so clearly through them as my breath halts in my chest.

"I did come here for you." It's a faint whisper, so soft I'm not sure she realizes she even said it aloud. Behind her, Cashore straightens and nods. *She's telling the truth.* He speaks this into my mind as I run circles around what she just said, trying to comprehend it.

"Rama killed everyone I ever cared about," Diana sobs as her body clenches around my fingers. She's overcome with emotion, tears streaming down her cheeks.

I'm so close to finding out all her truths. I can't let up now, even though watching her relive the horrors of her past doesn't excite me in the slightest.

"Why?" I demand, stroking her clit gently again as she sobs, her head falling back onto Cashore's chest as her eyes squeeze shut.

"Dore and I ran from her for so long, but we were just children. She caught us and brought us to Siargao. It was…awful, but we were together. We forced the bad memories away so we could stay alive, but as Dore got older and stronger, he questioned Rama constantly."

Diana shakes her head, her breath coming in great heaving sobs as her body ramps up the tension. She's miserable, high on uppers, and about to come all over my fingers, even though we're talking about her dead brother. This omega may be as twisted as I am.

"I knew she'd throw me into the maze one day when it suited her. And I knew I'd come for you when she did."

"Why?" I press further. Something about this story doesn't add up. Why me versus any other available monster, and why now?

Diana screams as her orgasm hits her, her body thrashing in my arms as my name falls off her lips like a prayer. I withdraw my fingers from her as her chest heaves.

Cashore groans as blood wells up along Diana's shoulders. Her body curls in on itself as I draw her orgasm out with another pinch to her clit, her teeth gnashing.

I'm halfway to coming in my pants watching her like this. But as her release fades, the shuddering of her frame turns into great heaving sobs as she points one angry finger at me. "She killed my brother, you fucking asshole. She slit his throat and threw him on a garbage heap the day we turned sixteen. You were kind to me once, when I was a child, when you came to see my father. And so, I thought, if anyone, if any-fucking-one could help me, it would be someone who was just as angry. I thought if anyone would take her down with me, it would be you!"

Diana throws her head backward, head-butting Cashore as he bellows in anger. Shoving her way out of his arms, she strides for the nearest door and sails through it without a backward glance.

Blood flows from Cashore's nose when I turn to look at him. "What do you make of that?"

The vampiri chuckles, his laugh wry around a mouthful of black blood. "I think she's your fucking mate, you hideous asshole."

The moment he says it, I know it's true.

CHAPTER TWELVE
DIANA

Dore Dore Dore. How could you leave me to deal with this shit? I think to my dead brother as I stomp down a hall and into the backmost living quarters.

I knew the truth would come out; I just didn't think it would come out so violently. I don't know what I thought. I just knew I couldn't tell anyone when I first found the alphas that I worked for Rama so intimately. That I planned things that hurt them. But I had no choice…none at all.

But now? Now I need a godsdamned minute.

I know one thing's for certain: Rama will not want us to get out of this hellhole prison–no matter what. I obviously brought nothing with me into the maze, but my father didn't tell Rama everything about the maze's design either. Only I know every single one of its secrets.

A sudden pang at my shoulder causes me to double over in pain. The fucking vampiri venom. The only thing that can dissipate it is the sulfur baths in Cashore's primary living quarters, the room I came to. I suppose the good thing about knowing my way around every inch of this maze is that I can help myself more than a normal mark could.

I slip out of Noire's shirt and the battered, trashed blue dress Rama's minions outfitted me in, letting the ruined fabric fall to the floor. My entire body is tender. I'll heal fast because I'm an omega surrounded by alpha males–my body is built to take a beating and be ready for my alpha as quickly as possible. Even so, my ribs and shoulder are tenderized from the naga's coils and Noire's various assaults.

Tears slide down my cheeks nonstop as I look out across the enormous blackwater sulfur pool favored by the vampiri. My father designed the maze in some ways to placate the monsters, bringing in little bits of their home provinces as both a mockery and a comfort. Rama wanted them to remember what they lost, but to get complacent in the relative comforts of their quarters.

I step into the sulfur pool and stride across the black sand until I reach the very edge. The pool's edge drops off into a huge abyss that's miles deep and nearly half a mile across. At the very far edge, I can barely make out a black stone wall with various outcroppings. More monsters live there, more broken and battered heathens here to put on a show for Rama.

Fuck her.

Snarling, I whip around as the doors to Cashore's quarters open and shut with a small click.

Jet.

He meets my eyes but says nothing, ripping his clothes off as he hops into the pool with a big splash. I watch him dunk under, washing the blood from his body before swimming toward me and propping his back up against the ledge.

In that moment, he reminds me so much of my brother that my heart feels like it'll shatter in my chest all over again. If Jet senses what I'm thinking with his alpha intuition, he says nothing.

In the darkness around us, I hear chirping, and it brings a smile to my face. *Maulin foxes. My only friends.*

The tiny monster foxes who inhabit the maze are the scavengers. They're at the very bottom of the power totem pole, but they keep the maze clean, and they're wicked smart if you befriend them.

"We share a common ancestor, you know," Jet begins, nodding in the direction of the chirping. "Tenebris taught me that." His half-smile falls when he says his brother's name. He looks back up, and his eyes are bright with hope, hope that dimmed many years ago. Which I know because I've been watching him deal with this shit-ass maze for seven long horrible years, every time Rama televised the hunt.

Jet clenches his jaw before speaking. "Rama will not let us go easily. Whatever you do, get Ten out of here and away from this place, okay? Noire and I could handle being thrown back in here, but Ten is meant for something far better than his. He's brilliant, and that could be put to good use in the right pack."

"I can't promise to get any of you out. There's a very good chance this is a one-way ticket for me. But I'll do my best to get all of you out, especially Ten."

Jet nods and sinks lower into the water, dark eyes still tight at the corners when he looks over at me. "You planned all the hunt scenes? Really?"

"Is that so hard to believe?" I whisper, meeting his gaze. Jet's eyes narrow as he assesses me, almost like he's really seeing me for the first time.

"You put on a good show when you first arrived, acting like a scared little plaything who just happened to know a way out. Did you spill all your secrets just now?"

I sigh, placing my own head back against the rock ledge as my body knits my injuries back together.

Jet's next question surprises me. "Do you know why Rama always sends me to the Atrium? Why not Ten? I can guess why she doesn't send Noire…"

"She hates Noire with a bone-deep passion I've never fully understood. You're right, she didn't send him to the Atrium unless one of the clients specifically knew to request him because she didn't want him to experience pleasure."

Jet huffs out an angry growl. "So why me, then?"

Turning in the water, I muster up all the truth I can find and answer Jet honestly. "Your sexual creativity, especially on uppers, is unmatched, Jet. The clients love watching you, and doing that and interacting with you got them high in a way the maze wasn't initially designed to do. Rich people drunk on your pleasure often make bad decisions. You served as an incredible distraction for Rama to swoop in and get whatever she wanted. I profiled all of that too."

He nods as if he suspected it, but now that I've spent hours around him, I can read distress in his face. His voice is a bare whisper as he continues, "That night I was late when she had the guards shoot me over and over and then fuck that man, who asked for it? A client?"

The blood drains from my own face at his question. I'll never forget that night. "I don't know that level of detail. She televised it, of course, but that wasn't suggested by me. I can't really say…I just created the…"

"Profiles, right." Jet sighs and nods. "I'm guessing it had nothing to do with being late, and everything to do with psychologically attacking us at every opportunity."

"That's true," I whisper. "Even Oskur's death and the way it happened was meant to feel especially tragic," I say softly as Jet turns toward me.

"Tell me everything."

Sighing, I bring my legs up and wrap my arms around them. "Rama wanted you to fear the disks, to fear her power, to wonder exactly how much she was capable of. But I guess Oskur did something, and she asked me to profile you all for his death to have maximum impact. I lied, of course, to try to minimize it, but she does whatever she wants, regardless of my profile report. It doesn't always play out the way I suggest."

I'm an asshole for sharing what I did, but Jet's dark eyes close as he leans against the pool's edge. His jaw is tense, and it brings me back to watching them after the rorschachs killed Oskur. Remembering how Noire raged around the maze for weeks, destroying anything in his path. He destroyed their quarters too, but Rama put them back together as a slap in the face. She televised all of it so the citizens of Siargao could watch their former ruler reduced to insanity.

The chirping sound in the shadows intensifies, and I respond with my own series of clicks and kisses as a small group of the maulin fox dart across Cashore's carpet and leap up onto the edge of the pool. Two babies and their parents. I recognize them immediately.

Jet watches in disbelief as the foxes trot along the ledge and come up to me, nuzzling into my hand as I scratch their ears. "When Oskur died, I asked the foxes to bring his bones out of the maze. They can come and go, you know. They're so tiny. They brought bones to me for years. I've got them all collected on the outside, waiting to be taken to your family crypt if we get out."

"Where is the maze?" Jet questions. "If they've brought you bones for years."

Sighing, I turn to him. "It's underneath a man-made island in Lon Bay. The foxes swim the short distance to shore and bring me the bones, then they come back."

Jet grimaces. "We're underneath the fucking bay, so close to home?"

"Yeah," I affirm.

Jet opens his mouth to say something but thinks better of it and stalks over to me. The foxes break our touch and hiss at him, snapping and chirping as I soothe with little responding clicks of my own.

"Just be silent for a moment and hold your hand out," I instruct him, pulling him closer as the foxes hide behind my head.

The powerful alpha male at my side crouches down in the water, bowing his head as he extends his hand. He smiles beautifully when the two baby foxes hop up into his palm and begin to roll around, nipping at his fingers. A laugh rings out across the pool as I tilt my head back, baring my neck to the grown fox.

Jet's eyes grow wild in disbelief as the mother fox's lower jaw splits open, many-forked tongue poking out to slide along the wounds on my neck and shoulder. She drinks up the blood before clamping her teeth onto my neck. Her partner comes and does the same, and I let them because this is how we connect. This blood-sharing produces a bond between me and all the maulin foxes in the maze, something I learned the first day one came to visit me. I can share sentiments and needs with them, and while we can't speak coherently in one another's minds, they can understand me. I have been befriending the foxes since the day Rama brought me to Siargao.

"What do you miss most about being outside?" I whisper.

Jet frowns and closes his eyes. "I miss music. I miss how close Noire and I were. Not that we're not close now, but it's different. This place has changed us all. He and I were so tight growing up, and this place has driven a wedge in that."

There is no suitable response to his sadness, so I rub the back of his hand and close my eyes, pushing my desire to help him out into the universe and hoping he can receive it.

"I've never said this to anyone," Jet growls. "But you surprise me."

I smile as I close my eyes, letting my connection to the foxes grow and blossom as they steal blood from me and heal my wounds, all at the same time.

Some days, I surprise myself.

CHAPTER THIRTEEN
NOIRE

Standing in the shadows outside Cashore's room, I listen to Diana and Jet talk. I hear him ask about why Rama always insisted on him being in the Atrium. I suck in a breath as she talks about Oskur's bones, and I relive the rage from when he died. Knowing Rama did it simply to fuck with me cements my bone-deep desire to rip her head from her shoulders when I get out of here.

But something else stirs in my mind, now that Cashore said it.

I think she's your fucking mate, you hideous asshole.

My body knew it before my mind did. The way she accepts my particular overblown brand of violence as if she craves it. The way her body pivots to mine the moment I walk into the room. I've known her for mere hours, but when I look into those blue eyes, I feel like I've known her for far longer. I knew she was hiding secrets, and I knew how far to push her to pull those secrets to the surface.

I never thought I'd find a bondmate. I figured I'd meet an omega as devious as me who would serve the purpose as my wife because the likelihood of me finding a bondmate in a pack where I already knew everyone seemed unlikely. I had no desire to travel Lombornei to find a mate elsewhere.

I did not see Diana coming. Had I continued to travel to the other provinces, perhaps I would have met her when she was old enough. I remember meeting her as a child, but there is nothing left of the bouncy, happy pup she was when I met her in Edson's home many years ago.

The vampiri are gathering their things to leave, and while I'm anxious to be on our way, I need to have a conversation with Diana first. Things between us have changed because of Cashore's words. Already, I read a protective thread in Jet's mannerisms toward her. He's seated in the pool, but he's wary and watchful, keeping an eye on the entire room. I can feel it through our family bond.

He's protecting her because we all sense she's mine.

I open the door, my gaze finding Diana's as she tips her head up and looks at me. She's surrounded by the tiny maulin foxes that flit through the maze, scavenging off the mess the monsters leave behind.

When I stalk across the room and take my clothes off, hopping into the pool, the foxes suckling at Diana's neck snarl at me. They don't stop, though, which brings the sliver of a smile to her delicate features. I've never seen anyone befriend a maulin. They're wild and free, although my people tell tales of queens of the past who shapeshifted into maulins and ruled the world for a time before the first alpha was born.

Watching the fox and Diana connect is a near godly experience, my dick hard as a rock as she breathes softly in the pool across from me. Jet moves away from her and out of the water, nodding at me as he grabs his clothing and leaves. He shuts the door as I cross the pool slowly, watching to see the effect my proximity has on her.

Now that Cashore opened my eyes, I can't stop looking at her and thinking of her as something deeper and more connected than the convenient, stunning mark I thought she was. Sure enough, when I'm within a few feet of her, her back arches, nipples pebbling in the water as the foxes unlatch from her neck and skitter away into the shadows. I don't watch them go, but I can hear them licking Diana's blood off their jaws somewhere in the recesses of the room.

I reach under the water, parting Diana's thighs so I can step between them. She hisses in a little breath when my hard cock rubs up against her pussy. Knowing that I elicit this reaction from her is a heady feeling.

"You don't look ready to apologize…" she snaps as I lean over her, forcing her to tilt her head up to look at me.

A dark laugh pulls from my throat, an instinctual purr beginning to work its way up out of my chest, transferring goosebumps to her skin, her hips working against me already.

Natural. It's so fucking natural to do this with her. I need to know more. What will it be like to touch an omega, knowing the gods created this one to fit me? Reaching out, I stroke my fingertips along her collarbone and down between her breasts as she shudders, body rocking in the water as her hips find mine and punch.

The uppers Cashore and I forced down her throat are still running wild in her system, her inhibitions gone as she snaps her teeth. "If you came in here to tease me, get the fuck out, alpha."

Laughing, I wrap both hands around her throat and use that leverage to hoist her out of the water and onto the edge of the pool. Her upper body dangles above the void behind her, her chest heaving as she realizes how precariously placed she is. If I let her go, she could fall to her death.

I crave it, pushing her to the edge like this, knowing her life is in my hands, that she's at my mercy. Bringing one hand down, I grip her thigh and then release her neck, ensuring I have a good hold on her. I huff out a growl, hovering just above her clit as she whines and attempts to move her hips. She can't, and the pressure of my arms is the only thing keeping her from falling.

I want her to fall in other ways.

Leaning in, I lick between her thighs, dragging the flat side of my tongue from her ass all the way up and around her clit. I suck it between my lips then tug on it lightly with my teeth as Diana wails and pants, her hands finding my hair and threading through it.

"More," she cries out, struggling to move her hips to meet me.

"Your pleasure is mine, omega," I growl, nipping at her clit again as she gasps. "Mine to take and use. You'll come when I allow it. Do you understand?"

"Yes, alpha," she gasps as I suck at the sensitive skin between her thighs. Already her muscles tremble, and I find myself wondering how many times I can get her off before the vampiri are ready to go. I want to find out.

Teasing her entrance with my fingers, I slide two inside her and curl them as she gasps. Fireworks erupt between us as she screams my name into the void, over and over as alpha pride heats my core. *I* do this to her. I make her a slick-coated mess with the barest hint of my attention.

I need more, so much more. Now that I'm looking for a deeper connection between us, I feel it. That faint thread that ties us together in the most meaningful way possible. If I tend to that connection, if I stoke its flames, it'll become a fire that eats us both alive until we're bonded so permanently that even death can't separate us.

I've never wanted that, never thought it would be within my reach. I thought I'd take a wife for political reasons and pack connections. But then Diana came for me. She came into hell. My little liar came here *for me.*

Groaning, I hop onto the ledge, pulling Diana up onto her knees as I rub my cock head against her pretty pink lips. Her pupils dilate wider as she opens her mouth and sucks me down greedily, choking around my thick length. Watching her lips stretch and pull tight around me sends sparks down the back of my thighs as her tongue plays with my piercing.

"Diana..." I grunt out as she takes me deeper, the tip of my dick poking into the back of her throat as she chokes and coughs around me.

Fuck, I need more. I need to know how far I can push this little omega before she taps out. There's enough of a size difference between us that I curl myself over her back, essentially on all fours on top of her with my dick still in her mouth. This angle forces her ass up higher and her face down lower so she can keep sucking me off. But from here, I can slide my tongue between her thighs and eat everything that's already so wet for me.

Diana sputters around my dick as she rocks back onto my tongue, sucking in a breath before diving forward again and taking me deep into her throat. I pant into her ass, sucking at her pussy lips as she mewls around me, the vibration tightening my balls. I'm going to come so hard and so fast like this.

Reaching around her, I grip her throat with one hand, feeling her feed my cock down it. When she swallows around me, the pressure on my length is almost more than I can take. I squeeze her throat and hiss at the pleasure that rocks through my system. I feel how full she is of me, and gripping her throat is like squeezing my cock with my own hand all while it's trapped inside her heat.

It occurs to me as fire builds between my thighs that this omega may not have a limit. Because she's handcrafted for me, there may be nothing I can try with her that she won't fucking love.

That knowledge brings my orgasm shooting up through my system as I spill ropes of cum down Diana's throat. She coughs and sputters as I suck her clit into my mouth rhythmically, her slick drenching my face as she comes with me.

My hips pump up against her mouth, my cock buried deep in her throat as she chokes and gags, rocking backward to pull away from me. Growling, I grip her throat tighter. "Breathe through your nose, Diana. Easy, omega."

She groans but does what I tell her, my cock still spurting cum down her throat.

A needy pant leaves my lips as I sit back on my heels, giving her the space to move.

My dick leaves Diana's mouth with a noisy pop, sticky white release dripping from both sides. There are scratches down the length of my cock from her sharp teeth, but it only heightens the pleasure I feel.

Sliding off the precarious ledge into the water once more, I haul Diana into my arms and take her mouth. Kissing is dangerous. Kissing is a deeper connection than pure fucking. I don't kiss omegas. But Diana's pouty lips are swollen from taking me, and the need to suck at them drives me hard.

Diana is an enigma, devious and crafty and wrapped up in an irresistibly strong package. She could be my downfall, but right now? Right now, I don't care. Her lips part the moment mine touch hers, my tongue sliding alongside hers. The taste of my cum mixed with her unique flavor smacks into me as she groans, deepening the kiss with her arms threaded around my neck.

I need to fuck her now with my mouth on hers and her tight body pressed into mine. She fits me so fucking well. Our kiss turns needy, Diana devouring me just as hard as I do her. When she reaches down for my cock, lining it up with her entrance and spearing herself on me, I throw my head back at the ecstasy.

Diana takes that opportunity to bite her way up my neck, fangs sinking into my skin over and over as I buck up into her heat. Her pussy is omega perfection–perfectly hot and tight and responsive to every thrust of my hips. I could claim her right now; gods know my body wants it. But my mind spins with all the ways I underestimated a woman in the past, that move leading me to be stuck in this fucking hellhole.

My eyes find Diana's, but there's no blue left to them. She's still high as a kite on the uppers. I could probably ask her anything right now and get an honest answer.

"Did you recognize me?" she whispers as my thrusts take on a new force. "When you came to see my father all those years ago, we met. I was a child. But you were kind to me. You gave me a rose. Do you remember?" She grunts as I rock my hips harder. "Did you recognize me tonight?" Black eyes are bright on mine as her eyelashes flutter and her pussy clenches.

We're both about to come again. "No," I grunt. "You are a far cry from the bouncy, happy child I met all those years ago, Diana."

Shadows cross her eyes as she pouts, even while I fill her up.

"That doesn't mean I didn't recognize what you *are* to me," I grit out between clenched teeth. I'm on the edge of a sizzling orgasm that's going to obliterate conscious thought from my mind.

"Mine," she snaps as a grating noise thrums through the air.

Womp, womp, womp.

Anguish and irritation skate down our growing bond as Diana's eyes whips from mine to focus behind me. She leaps onto the edge of the pool, dripping water as she looks up into the dark area above us.

"Something is coming," she barks.

The warm air has changed, wind brushing lightly across my face as the thumping noise intensifies. It almost sounds like helicopter blades.

A dark shadow begins to come into view as I hop out of the pool and stand next to Diana. My body screams that something dangerous is coming, and I call to my brothers through our mental bond. *Get in here.*

"This is Rama's doing," Diana snaps. "She must be delivering something to fuck with us."

"What would it be?" I bark out. "Another monster?'

Diana nods as an actual helicopter appears from the dark depths of the abyss, flying down, down, down until it's level with us and I can see what's chained underneath it. A minotaur, a male, trussed up like a plaything but clearly fucking angry. It bellows when it sees us, and as the helicopter womps closer, I can see what's going to happen in slow motion. They're going to throw that fucking thing in here with us. It's enormous. My alpha nature bristles at the intrusion of another alpha male on my territory, in my space, interrupting my playtime.

Diana backs down into the pool, screaming for Cashore as the room's door flies open and monsters rush in: my brothers, Ascelin, Renze, Cashore, and a handful of others.

"What the fuck?" Jet roars. "Is that a godsdamned minotaur?"

Diana nods and turns to me. "It'll be on uppers and probably tortured prior to her setting it loose."

"Aim for the stomach and base of the spine," shouts Ten, drawing his weapons. He takes a step in front of Ascelin as the vampiri rolls her eyes and walks around him to stand by his side.

Gritting my teeth, I nod as the helicopter blades bring it close enough that we can see the pilot inside. He flips a switch, and the chains holding the minotaur begin to swing. When they let go, the monster lands with a splash in the pool, chains flying off him.

He's up far faster than I'd think he could be, bellowing his rage as he looks around the room. Someone leans out of the helicopter and aims an automatic rifle at the minotaur, unleashing a hail of bullets on his back as we all dive for cover to avoid them.

The minotaur roars in pain and leaps out of the pool, crossing the room impossibly fast as Diana leaps out of his way. He's easily twice my height with a man's body but a bull's head, complete with razor-sharp horns.

He came for her. He fucking came for *her* first. But she is mine. He's trying to hurt what's mine.

Red fury clouds my vision as I leap onto the minotaur's back, trying to get my arms around his neck, but he's huge. Probably fifteen feet of pure corded muscle. He reaches around and grabs me like a China doll, throwing me across the room as he rounds on Diana once more. There's a screen inlaid in these quarters just like the one outside mine, and Rama's face pops up onto it, a wicked smile curving her beautiful features.

"Tsk, Noire. Diana will never get you out of there. Best of luck to you, though; we are highly enjoying the show…" The camera pans to a room full of the glittering wealthy, eyes rapt on the screen as they watch the minotaur careen around the room behind me, tossing bodies in his wake, including my brothers'.

At this point I recognize every one of these faces.

I don't bother to tell Rama to fuck off as I turn to find both my brothers attacking the minotaur with their knives. Diana has one of the vampiri swords in her hand, stabbing at the minotaur's core as it roars and shakes the alphas off. It rounds on her again just as Renze and Ascelin leap onto its back, stabbing into its neck with their long swords.

Nothing fucking harms the monster, high as he is. With an angry scream that shakes the chandeliers hanging from the ceiling, the minotaur whips around and grabs Diana in both of his beefy hands, bringing her to his face as he opens his mouth wide.

He's going to fucking bite her. Moving as fast as I can, I barrel into him, knocking him down at the same time as Diana grunts in pain. I hear the cracking of bones that signifies a shift before I sense it in our threadbare bond.

She's fucking shifting. Very few omegas can do it; I've only ever met one—my mother. But right before my godsdamned eyes, Diana's body implodes on itself and a gigantic white direwolf stands in her place. Before the minotaur can right himself, she darts forward and clamps her jaws around his neck and shoulder, ripping into him with astounding ferocity.

He screams in pain as my brothers and I shift and attack at the same time. And then the vampiri get in on the action, stabbing until the minotaur leaps upright, shaking most of us off him.

Except for Diana. She springs off the minotaur's hairy back and bounds off the edge of the pool, using that leverage to catapult her back into his lower legs. He falls to the ground as she swipes her claws across the backs of his knees, ripping tendons as he bellows in pain.

I leap on top of his stomach, clawing over and over again as Diana leaps out of his way. The minotaur rolls fast, unseating me as he grabs her by the scruff and yanks her around to his front.

I hear a crack in her leg joints as her wolf howls in pain. The minotaur tosses her toward the ledge as I roar and fly across the room. I manage to intercept her trajectory as her body hits mine and slides to the ground, both of us narrowly missing the steep cliff's edge.

The vampiri rush the minotaur again, crowding on top of him like lions as he struggles against the torn tendons behind his knees. He goes down with a grunt as Jet and Ten join the fray, biting and clawing at his throat and stomach until he's a roaring mess of blood and torn flesh.

The sloppy sounds of sharp teeth ripping flesh from bone ring through the air as I cradle Diana in my arms. Her wolf whines as I shift back to alpha form and stroke her cheek. "Foolish girl, taking on that monster. Shift for me, Diana."

She obeys, screaming as her human voice returns. Her left arm dangles, clearly dislocated from its socket as Ten and Jet leave the fray and pace across the room, sitting to watch us in wolf form.

Looking up at Jet, I scowl. "Shift and help me with her arm."

A crack rends the air, and Jet's alpha form stands there once more. He crouches down by Diana as I start up a purr, tipping her chin to look at me. "Eyes on me, omega. Tell me what happened when I came to visit your father."

I remember what happened, of course, but I need to distract her while Jet resets her arm.

Diana grunts in pain when Jet grips her arm in one hand and places the other on her shoulder. Licking her lips, she looks up at me. "I was seven, and you had recently taken over. You came to my father for–" Her words cut off in a scream as Jet shoves her arm up swiftly back into its socket. The scream dies off into a sob as I haul her up into my arms, capturing her mouth.

I don't know how to be gentle, and frankly, I don't care to be that way. But in this moment, I devour her lips with a tenderness I didn't think existed in me. She sinks into my heat, tears streaming down her face as she pours pain and need into the strengthening bond between us. I take that pain and banish it with my kiss, and our connection turns into a tether, stronger and more insistent.

Comforting her is stoking the flames of what already exists between us. It's a dangerous game, but I find myself wanting to jump headfirst into that tie to bask in its glory. What could she and I be, if we unleashed one another?

"When did you first learn you could shift?" I murmur, stroking tears away from her cheeks as she smiles softly.

"You shifted and ran with your brothers when you visited our pack. I watched you and wondered if I could do it, and I could. But my father cautioned me that it's a rare ability and that alphas would want to control me. I've never shifted again until now."

"Still surprising us," Jet murmurs, alluding to his earlier comment in the sulfur pools beside us.

Diana's tears stop, so I stand with her still in my arms. Ten comes over with Diana's skirt and hands it to me. Without taking my eyes from hers, I lean in and wrap the skirt around her waist, clipping it in the back. She shakes her head and unclips it, letting it fall to the ground.

Tear-stained blue eyes flutter at the proximity of my lips to hers again.

I've got to get out of this shithole. I want space and time and safety to explore every reaction I can drag out of this woman. I want to know every fucking secret she keeps and holds close to her heart.

Diana moves quietly across the room, running her hands along the wall until she gets to a stone with two interlocked circles on it.

Jet snorts. "Don't tell me you've got an extra skirt inside the wall?"

She smiles at him as she depresses the stones around it in a sequence, and it swings out like a door. Diana reaches in and pulls out a small black disk, crossing the room to us as the vampiri crowd surrounds us to see what she's retrieved. "Ten, peel off the sticky side and put it in the middle of my back, please."

Ten glances at me for permission as I growl, but I give it because I'm curious to see what new toy she found that's been here in the maze the whole godsdamned time. She's so full of secrets that I'm not even surprised at this point.

Ten peels a sticky layer off the thick disk and places it gently in the middle of Diana's back, but she keeps her eyes on mine the whole time.

I take a step closer and tilt her chin up so she's forced to throw her head back and look at me. Diana's lips part as I lean in and nip at the lower one, but then I feel a rush of air and step back.

The disk at her back unfurls into long black ribbons that slide up and over her shoulders, crisscrossing over her breasts and down below her hips. Ten, Jet, and I watch in utter shock as the ribbons lock together with a zipping sound until they form what appears to be one complete piece of fabric.

A long-sleeved, skintight black shirt covers Diana's upper body, and the same fabric forms pants that extend all the way to her bare feet. The texture reminds me of shark skin but has the faintest of sheens to it. Reaching out in wonder, I touch the fabric and feel a slight electric zing.

Jet's the first to speak. "What the hell, Diana?"

"Nanite clothing." She winks at me. "My father never trusted Rama, and there are useful items here and there if one knows where to look."

I grunt my acknowledgment as Ten reaches out to touch the fabric in wonder. "I cannot wait to see what has happened in the outside world in the last seven years. This is…amazing. Is there more like this?"

Diana turns to him with a soft smile. "So many books, Ten. So much art.

There's a whole world for you to explore, and I will get you out of here to explore it, if I can."

Ten's smile broadens as he nods at Diana. There's so much hope in his face, and the skeptical side of my personality wants to remind him there's a very good chance we won't make it out of here. I'm a realist, but I find myself unable to squash that dream for him. So what if this is the end for us, and he lives it hopeful and looking forward to the future?

Cashore comes up to us, blood trailing down his jaw as he licks blood off his lips. "Mmm, minotaur is the delicacy I didn't know I needed."

Jet fakes a gag as Cashore winks at him. "What have you been eating this entire time if not the meat that comes into the maze?"

"Sushi." Ten chuckles, glancing over at what remains of the minotaur. Most of the vampiri are on their hands and knees at this point, ripping the last shreds of meat from the minotaur's bones as the maulin hover around the edges. The moment the vampiri are sated, the maulin will crowd in and pick the bones and floor clean, dragging what remains of the minotaur somewhere. In the last seven years, I've learned they hoard bones, but to what purpose, I'm unsure.

Except for the bones of my brother. Those they saved for the stunning omega standing in front of me in a skintight superhero suit.

CHAPTER FOURTEEN
DIANA

I'm surprised when Rama doesn't come back on the screen in Cashore's quarters to rail about the death of the minotaur. She's been saving him up for the right use for a while, torturing him with spiked chains and uppers. I couldn't do anything for him, just like I've been helpless to do anything for any of the monsters imprisoned here. I profile them; I recommend when to use them. I watch their psych evals come through and change and recommend them again.

Until now. I plotted and planned for years to get to the point where I could get the alphas out. It's my full intention to let the other monsters free if I can.

Turning my gaze back to Noire, I sense his mind is back on our mission: getting the fuck out of here. Despite renewed urgency, I can't stop my mind from returning to our time in the water. Noire is alpha perfection in the bedroom–dominant, strong, violent, playful. When he dangled me over the fucking ledge, I nearly came from the sheer terror of my life being in his hands. Rubbing my hand over my chest, I notice the connection between us is stronger now, clearer.

I wonder if it feels different to him? If it feels good…or if he's conflicted.

The minotaur was a distraction meant to slow us down. Rama is probably bricking up the few exits she knows about as we speak. Father made sure she never knew about them all, but I know she's smart enough to know she wasn't aware of every one of the maze's secrets.

She's a ruthless bitch, and she'll use every resource at her disposal to take me down, given what I'm trying to do. I'm simply evening the playing field by bringing the monsters to this war.

I turn to Cashore and gesture at his people. "We don't know what might be in the lower levels. Are you certain you want to bring everyone? Even the younglings?"

Cashore frowns, and I feel the scrape of his gift at the edges of my mind. "The families wish to stay until we are certain of what lies in the lower levels. It makes me...uneasy. But Renze, Ascelin, and I will go with you. If we determine it's not something else like the naga, we will come back for the younglings."

Ten winks at Ascelin. "Whaddya think, Asc? Ready to head into the fiery depths of the maze?"

"At least it's not fucking cold down there," Ascelin grumbles, Ten snorting at her comment.

"I'd hate to see you drop like a log and have to carry you out." His voice is a deep purr as Ascelin scowls at him.

"If you touch me, I'll chop your dick off and feed it to the maulin."

Jet laughs at their banter. "God, we need to get Ten in front of some omegas, stat. This is fucking painful to watch."

Chuckling, I take a knife from Noire's holster and slide it into a strap at my thigh as his brows rise.

"You have them all; I need one," I respond with a raise of my own brows. If Noire dislikes my sass, he isn't saying anything just now. Through the bond linking us, I feel something like wary interest. He isn't sure what to make of me after everything that's happened.

Good. I hope he never stops wondering if there are more layers of me to uncover. I want him to spend years unraveling every one of my intimate secrets. I've wanted that since I was seven and he was twenty. He handed me a rose when I met him in my father's garden. I knew he was mine then, and I've waited years for him. I should have been too young to think of him that way, but a bondmate is a rare and powerful thing.

I suspect the only reason he didn't know it then is because I was so young. He wouldn't have looked at me that way yet.

Turning back to Cashore, I gesture at Ascelin and Renze. "Your people aren't safe now that Rama knows we're working together to get out. Someone should stay to guard them, especially the younglings. The rest of us can go to the lower levels and open the gate to the next section that has an exit."

Cashore frowns and looks at Renze and Ascelin before glancing back at me. "What is Rama capable of that you think the vampiri here cannot defend themselves?"

I appreciate that he doesn't assume they're invincible. Nobody is. Not in this place. "There's every chance she's already inserting new monsters we haven't seen into the maze. She has a stable full that she's conditioned for years for situations like this, or if it's something the clients want. She has traveled nearly every inch of our world looking for monsters to kidnap and put here."

Behind me, Noire bumps my back with his chest and growls, bringing his teeth to my shoulder and nipping. "What is she likely to put in the maze next? Would you have any idea, profiler?"

I blanch at my former title but lean into Noire's heat, leveling my gaze on Cashore. "She's got manangal, fifty or sixty maybe? They were a client request, but he ended up being a mark before she needed them. I've profiled four or five types of monsters that clients haven't ended up picking, but I've always assumed Rama keeps them around just in case."

Cashore hisses in a disbelieving breath as he runs both black-clawed hands through his hair. Next to him, Renze and Ascelin snarl and glance around as if the very mention of the vampiric monsters gives them the heebie-jeebies.

"The fuck is a mangal?" snaps Jet, looking from me to Ten, who sighs as if he can't believe his brother isn't aware of every monster in the world.

Renze turns to Jet with a slow, deliberate frown. "*Manangal* are distant cousins of the vampiri. They can separate their upper body from their lower and fly. Throughout history, manangal and vampiri have fought, and vampiri were manangal slaves for thousands of years before a bloody war to free ourselves. There's a lot of history there. Manangal have never left the depths of the Tempang."

"They eat vampiri," snaps Ascelin. "One of the few monsters who would try that because of our venom. But manangal are strong, and our group is relatively small. We would likely not succeed in fighting fifty of them. Gods-damnit," she huffs, throwing her head back with a snarl.

Ten watches the frustrated warrior with a thoughtful expression on his face.

Renze reaches out and places his big hand on her lower back, the way a brother might, standing in silence as Cashore looks back at me. "Diana, are there ways for me to hide my people here in our quarters while we check the plausibility of the next exit? Secret passages or secret rooms? What are my options?"

I frown at the vampiri king. "There is a room above your quarters, but Rama is aware of it. There's no exit, so she couldn't put a monster in with your people, but they would not be able to escape either."

I don't think Cashore could pale any further, but he strides out of the room, I presume to speak with his people.

Ascelin and Renze follow him without a backward glance as Noire turns to face me. "Did you tell him the whole truth?"

Nodding, I meet Noire's eyes, willing the truth to show through. Through our blossoming connection, I push the knowledge I have, hoping he can read it.

A sliver of acceptance crosses his gaze, but his frown deepens. "Hear this, Diana. We may need the vampiri to get out of here, but if it comes to us or them, it's us. Do you understand? We cannot take on fifty of those monsters at once."

I nod again, tears filling my eyes when I think about children growing up in this maze. I grew up in a maze of a different sort, tortured and destroyed by Rama. I never want that for another child. I can't leave people behind if I have any choice at all, no matter what I'm saying out loud.

Noire cocks his head to the side as if he still doesn't understand me, but nods. As a group, we turn to leave the room. I click to the maulin who still linger in the shadows, waiting their turn with the minotaur's remains. When they hear me, they flow out of every dark shadow in the room and descend upon the battered body, ripping into what's left of the monster.

When I turn to my alphas, I see something like awe and interest from Jet and Ten. But Noire's face is a mask of controlled desire when he looks at me. It sends my thoughts to his rut, wondering if he's still suffering from being on the verge of it and getting pulled out.

Now isn't the time to test his limits, but I aim to–as soon as it's safe.

We leave the room to the sound of the maulin scraping flesh from bones behind us.

In the main part of the dark living quarters, Cashore speaks urgently with Ascelin, Renze, and three other vampiri. I've watched him consult them over the years. It's interesting to me that while Cashore is the equivalent of the king or alpha here, the vampiri rule themselves almost democratically. At least, if what's televised by Rama is any indication.

I'd laugh if I didn't find it admirable how devoted he is to his people, even after so many years in this place.

"Cashore, it's time," Noire barks out as the vampiri turns with a snarl, crossing the black carpet soundlessly as he snaps dark teeth at Noire.

"Go, I will catch up with you. I need to settle things with my people. It will take me a few minutes. If you cannot possibly wait a moment longer, just go. I know where you'll be."

Noire shrugs and turns, striding from the room without a backward glance.

Jet winks at Renze and then follows Noire out the door, although Ten stays with me, hovering protectively by my side. Odd how much things have changed since several hours ago.

Looking at the vampiri, I give them a sad smile. "I can't imagine the lower levels will be free of monsters. There's every chance this could go poorly, but I wouldn't leave your people here either. You're almost better to keep on the move. The faster we get out of here, the better. It takes Rama some hours to organize the manangal; they're difficult to control, as you know. But she's had hours at this point. She could put them in here at any moment. Or something else, something worse. She has many, many options."

Cashore grits his teeth and nods. "I sense your honesty, Diana, thank you. We will catch up shortly."

It's a dismissal, so I dip my head and turn with Ten, jogging until we catch up to Noire, who barks at me immediately, with Jet at his side. "Is there a quicker way down to the lower levels than through the chapel?"

I shake my head. "Not without going back down to the naga's room and through a long hallway. But the opening for the door is on the opposite side. There's no good way around this, and the next closest exit is in the depths of the trench outside the vampiri quarters. I want to avoid that level at all costs."

"Of fucking course," Noire growls. "Why the fuck did your father build this place this way?"

Anger flares in my gut then. Anger that my father worked for the monstrous woman who controls this place. Anger that he didn't see she planned to kill him. Anger at her for killing Dore and making me an orphan in every sense of the word. I'm suddenly angry at everything.

Rounding on the alpha, I snap my good hand out and jab a finger deep into his muscular chest. "It kept you in, didn't it? That was its only purpose."

Noire doesn't miss a beat, grabbing my hand and twisting it until I have to bend my entire upper body to follow my wrist. I yip as he uses the momentum to swing me up against the wall, my head cracking against the black stones.

Jet and Tenebris continue up the hallway, silent as church mice.

"Traitors!" I yell up into the darkness after them, tears springing to my eyes as Noire twists my wrist harder.

A snarl rumbles out of his throat, his fangs elongating as he brings his lips to hover over mine. "They've never seen me with an omega like this, but even they can tell when discipline is coming. They don't need to be here to see it."

Discipline?

"We don't have time for this, Noire," I snap as he sinks his teeth into my throat right under my chin. Blood wells up in my mouth, choking me as he squeezes tight enough that I can't breathe. One big claw slices a hole in the back of my godsdamned outfit, Noire sliding a hand in and down. He stuffs two fingers into my ass, dry, as he bites harder at my neck.

Black dots flash across my vision as I struggle to move, but I can't. His fingers probe, stretching and hurting as I struggle to find my breath around his bite. Noire growls, and the vibration of it rumbles my chest, my nipples pebbling despite the fact that he could kill me now.

Noire releases the bite as my head starts to fall to the side, my vision sliding to black. A slap rings out against my cheek as I suck in a deep, gasping breath, my head flying up. The moment my eyes find his, Noire smiles a wicked, evil smile that makes me want to back away from him. But I can't, because when I do, he slides another finger into my ass and moves, and the pinch fucking hurts.

"You feel that, Diana? That's a hint of what I'll do to your ass if you continue to defy me. You think you have some power here because you know the way out, but it's simply not true. I will always be the alpha when it comes to us."

I squirm against the invasion of Noire's fingers as he leans in and nips at my lower lip, tugging it so hard that I pant out a huffy breath as he chuckles. "You came down here for me; you came into this maze to find me and get fucked by me. Never forget which of us has the real power in this situation." He steps back, sliding his fingers out of my ass, which he slaps hard enough for the noise to ring up the hallway.

Gesturing in the direction Jet and Ten left, he snaps his teeth at me suggestively. "Go. Now, Diana."

Rubbing my ass, I hold in the grumble I wish I was brave enough to emit right now and trot up the hallway until I catch up with the rest of our pack.

CHAPTER FIFTEEN
NOIRE

I'm certain Diana isn't done testing me, not by a long shot. Even now with a sore ass and blood still trailing down her chest, lustful need rolls off her in pheromone-laced waves that have my dick hard as a rock in my pants.

I've been in this maze a long time, and it turns out even I'm not immune to the power of a beautiful fucking omega. Knowing my bondmate walks in front of me and I haven't claimed her as my own is driving me wild. My people told bedtime stories of fated bondmates, how claiming one another can unleash incredible powers, how it can make them both stronger and faster. How it changes the shift in ways that are different for every couple. I've only ever known two bonded pairs.

Diana moves quietly in front of me, glancing over her shoulder every so often as I stalk behind her, keeping my eyes on the maze. It's quiet. Too fucking quiet.

Diana leads us through the chapel, only pausing when we hear a scraping, scratching noise. Jet and Ten stop at the same moment as Diana.

"What is that?" Her voice is barely a whisper.

Around us, the chapel is eerily quiet. Even the maulin who have a nest here are making no sound at all. Light shines in through what remains of the stained-glass windows, illuminating the church in a dramatic glow. The maze is built that way to really put on a show for clients who want to see a mark finished here on the altar. Alborada roses crowd the entire dais, growing up the walls and framing the windows. It's a hauntingly beautiful, eerie place.

The floor is still littered with glass from the panes I broke earlier. One of the remaining stained-glass windows breaks with a deafening crash as Ten flings himself on top of Diana, knocking her to the ground. Winged bodies flood through the broken glass, filling the front of the chapel. Dozens of monsters leap in through the windows and turn as one toward us.

Rama's face pops up on a screen behind the altar, and she laughs. That's it; that's all.

They must be the manangals. Long, leathery splotched limbs hang from thin, emaciated bodies. Their faces have two small eyes and a huge mouth full of translucent dark teeth.

The creatures go wild at the sound of Rama's voice and begin to shed their lower halves, just as Cashore explained. We all watch in horrified disgust as the animals separate the lower halves of their bodies from the upper, legs and intestines hitting the ground with a squelch. Then the legs shudder and shift and stand on their fucking own, charging toward us as the top halves' wings beat the air. The monsters shriek and hiss, and the legs seem to respond, veering into formation as they attempt to herd us into a group.

"Shit, we need to hide," screams Diana. But where? The whole point of this place is there is nowhere to hide, except for the tunnel underneath the altar where we went down before.

Diana reads my thoughts at the same time, but the monsters hover around the altar, still splitting in two.

Monstrous lower limbs stretch and snap loose as one of the manangal rockets through the air toward us with a shriek. Its arms are too long, too thin, with pale skin stretched over impossible-shaped bones. It's the least human thing I've ever seen. The legs scuttle quickly toward us on the floor.

The monster heads directly for me, most likely sensing I'm the biggest threat. But Diana surprises it when she leaps on its back and slams a blade through its skull. More manangal separate and shriek toward us, but the majority fly straight past us for the hallway.

"They just want us out of the way, why?" snaps Ten as he stabs a creature and watches it fall to the ground, others barreling past us as the sound of their wings hitting the walls rings through the chapel. Even the detached legs brush past us with spider-like hitched movements, following the upper halves out the front door.

The last wave floods through as Diana's face pales. "Cashore. They're going after them. We have to go back!"

"No!" I snap. "Better for them to be distracted. Let's go."

"No!" she barks. "We can't leave them. Younglings, Noire. I said I'd help them get out. I said I'd help, Noire! There are children in there!"

"And I told you that when push came to shove, it was us or them. What do you imagine we'll do, Diana? Beat fifty or sixty of those monsters? Some or all of us will die in that process. I told you not ten minutes ago that we would leave them if we had to. Get moving. Right the fuck now."

Diana glares daggers at me, but I learned long ago that it's every monster for himself in the Temple Maze. I'm an asshole, but I need to give my pack the best chance of getting free. A huge pack of vampiri is not what we need slowing us down, giving Rama more time to get creative.

"I won't repeat myself," I bark at Diana, letting an alpha command roll off my tongue to slap her.

She blanches under that particular power but the vehemence in her eyes doesn't dissipate. If anything, she stands taller, but Jet and Ten are already trotting out of the chapel's side door as Diana faces off with me.

I let loose an angry laugh. "If you think I'm going to forget about this, you're wrong."

"I could say the same," she snaps, the earlier wound at her throat starting to bleed again as if even her body wants to remind her what crossing me means.

When I take a step toward her, she blanches and turns, jogging after my brothers.

"Having fun, Noire?" Rama's voice rings through the empty chapel.

Turning to face my greatest enemy, I smile at her, watching her own smile turn sharp and bitter. "I'll be having all the fun in the world when I rip that smile off your fucking face. See you soon, omega."

Rama's smile falls as she spits into the camera, her voice threaded with violence. "I'm toying with you, Noire. It's been fun to watch you scramble, watch you think you have a hope of getting out. But even Diana doesn't know everything about this maze. Just keep that in mind if you decide she's trustworthy. She betrayed me by trying to get you out; how hard would it be for her to betray you?"

I beam at Rama, throwing up a middle finger as I turn and stride through the chapel's side doors after the devious omega who could very well be my downfall.

Catching up to my pack fast, I urge us on. "Rama is losing her patience," I grumble as Jet nods, his jaw clenched hard. In silence, we move through the maze, down level after level until we're on the edge of the huge doors that mark the end of this part of the maze. After this, the levels are larger, more open. Big enough for a naga to slip through. Or something else.

Diana pauses outside the door, looking at me. "We need to be wary of whatever's down here. We should just assume the lower levels are no longer empty."

I nod my agreement, gesturing for her to continue.

"There's a big room down here with the hot springs pool area. There's a hidden stone gate there we can open with a lever across the pool. When we do that, it'll open into a new section of the maze you've not been into. From there, we've got a few options."

Jet growls next to me as we hear faint voices. The humans. They don't normally come to this side of the maze, but no doubt Rama's offered them something to come after us. I wouldn't usually worry about the humans, but in a large enough group, they're dangerous, even for us.

Diana hears the low voices at the same time we do and swings the door open to the lowest levels. If the humans follow us in here, and there are new monsters, they'll be in for a fucking surprise. I almost hope they do.

We follow Diana through the door, pacing quietly through the lower levels on high alert. I can't scent any other monsters. When we get to the huge grotto that forms the bottommost room, I finally sense something. It's the hair-prickling feeling I get at the back of my spine when there's another predator in the room.

"Something's here," I hiss as Diana pauses behind a column, looking around the room.

"There," she whispers, pointing to a steaming pool of water down below us, even as she winces from the shoulder injury. The entire underground lake is filled with rocks that spout steam into the air. When I look where Diana suggested, I see the very end of a coiled tail tucked around one of the rocks.

"Another naga," hisses Jet. "You've got to be fucking kidding me. And we're coated in that pheromone, right? So we can just assume it's gonna go wild when it's close enough to smell us?"

Diana bites her lip and nods as Ten runs his hands through his wavy hair, growling under his breath.

Suddenly, the hooting calls of the humans ring through the hallways. They did fucking follow us. This is an opportunity.

When I look back, the coiled tail is gone, but across the lake, a naga rises out of the water. Jet gulps next to me. "Didn't realize they could be bigger. This one's the size of a fucking house, Noire. We barely stopped the other one long enough to talk to him."

"Hush," Diana chides, pointing toward the far side of the pool. "See that side pool there? The door handle to open the gate between the two sections is there. That's where we need to go."

"Yeah, let me just stroll down there and see if it'll let me take a fucking swim, Diana. How do you propose we do this?" Jet glares at Diana, but she glances at him with a wry smile.

"Bait, Jet. We need bait."

"Well, the humans are coming," I offer, pointing behind me. Even now, their catcalls are getting louder as they follow us. I'm surprised Rama didn't let them in on what they're heading into, but I suspect at this point, she's throwing everything she can at us.

Diana looks behind me. "This is not ideal. Once we open that gate, it's just one long hallway to another large area. We don't know what's there, so if we get stuck between two huge monsters, we're fucked."

"I'm open to suggestions, omega," I bark back. "How did you imagine this going?"

She doesn't answer but looks up at Ten and Jet. "One of you lead the humans here, and I need the other to distract the naga. Noire and I will go across the pool and open the gate."

"I'll distract her," Ten offers.

"Her? How can you even tell?" Jet snorts.

Ten rolls his eyes. "Obviously she has a completely different shaped hood than the male. She's twice his size. She's clearly a female, probably the queen. Get educated, asshole."

Jet sighs. "I'll take the humans, I guess. Fuck." He barks out the curse as he trots back toward the dark hallway we came from.

Diana turns to me. "Remember, naga see heat, so stick as close to the steam as possible. There's every chance she'll notice us, but if she does, just try to stay ahead of her."

Nodding, I reach out and brush my fingers against the back of Diana's hand. She shivers but straightens her spine, pale lashes fluttering against her cheeks.

The naga lets out a roar as Ten attempts to distract it. Her pained screams echo around the room—she sounds almost heartbroken. Shit. The fallen naga king must have been her mate. This is bad, really fucking bad.

Diana and I sprint to the far side of the grotto toward the locking mechanism. I hear Ten shouting and pleading with the queen, even as Jet's footsteps echo through the chamber. He and Ten nearly collide as Ten sprints ahead of the female naga. Tumbling to the ground, she whips the end of her tail out, cracking it across Jet's back as he screams.

True fear for my brothers urges me on. *Get the door open; we just need to get the door open.* At that moment, a horde of humans piles into the room, roaring in triumph before they slide to a halt. They can't stop the momentum of the crowd, so the unfortunate males at the front go down in a tumble right in front of the naga female.

She screams in anger, whipping her coils out as she dives right into the group of humans, cleaving bodies in two as she throws men left and right. The humans scream and scramble, but there's no escaping her. Some make it back out the door, but I urge Diana on, leaping across the last pool dividing us from the gate lock. When I get to it, Diana screams for Jet and Ten as they flee the queen and run to meet us in front of the gate.

Humans follow them as the naga queen roars and fights off dozens of humans who stab at her with knives, desperately attempting to overpower her.

"Help me with the lever, Noire," Diana gasps as she grips it in both hands and yanks. It doesn't move until I put all the force of my body behind a push from the front of the lever. With a heaving crack, it gives away, and we hear the maze begin to rumble and change.

"Go, go!" screams Diana as we take off for the hidden gate, humans crowding in front of it with Jet and Ten, surrounding my brothers even as they flee the naga.

With horrifying speed, she coils down the hill toward the gate, bellowing her rage at the attack as a newly revealed stone gate begins to lift slowly.

"Fuck, fuck, fuck," Diana hisses out as we pile in a mass of bodies in front of the gate. But it's opening slowly, too slowly.

The queen gets to us first, whipping her tail out as she slashes across the gate with the barbed end. Most of us duck in time, but she manages to eviscerate a group of humans as they fall to the ground screaming. I shove Diana through the widening gap, shouting for my brothers to join us as we roll underneath the bars.

When we get through, Diana stumbles across wet stones and looks frantically at her tattoo, then at the wall. "Got to shut the gate; we've got to shut the gate," she repeats over and over to herself as Jet and Ten stand tense next to me, waiting for the queen to realize what we're doing.

Diana yips when she finds the right stone and depresses it, the gate beginning to creak closed.

The moment the noise starts up, the naga queen whips around, tossing humans away from her as she slithers impossibly fast toward us, heading for the gap that's now wide enough to let her through. The gate begins to slide back down as she slithers onto her side, her head and upper body sliding easily through the opening.

"Run, Diana!" I bellow as I shift and leap on the queen, raking my claws across anything I can reach. She crushes me in strong arms as Diana screams my name. I sense Diana shift before I feel her barrel into the queen and me, knocking us all into the wall. The queen's head hits the wall hard, and she slumps to the ground momentarily.

She shakes her head and starts to move toward us again but not fast enough. The gate continues its downward trajectory, and she doesn't get her coils out of the way in time. The black stone moves slowly as she begins screaming and thrashing, the gate slicing its way inch by inch through her body.

I nudge Diana with my nose away from the queen's thrashing upper body. I have no idea if a naga can survive this, or if we'll still need to fight her.

"She can't regrow an entire body," Ten says behind me, his voice mournful as if he hates to see a creature killed.

On the other side of the chamber, the humans glare at us through holes in the inlaid gate. Most of them lie in pieces on the floor, slippery with blood. But a hissed scream causes them to spin around as Diana sprints to the gate, darting around the naga queen's body as it twitches in the final throes of death. It could only be Cashore and his people.

Seconds later, vampiri stream into the room. In the front, each vampiri carries at least one youngling, Ascelin and Renze flanking the sides as Cashore brings up the rear. Behind him, the manangal hiss and roar, attacking from all sides.

The remaining humans flee around the side of the pools, heading for the far side to get around the oncoming monsters.

Diana scrambles to the stone in the wall, depressing it again as the gate slides back open. I know instinctively that she won't stop until she helps the children, and I find myself drawn to follow her.

"Let's go rescue the vamps." Jet chuckles, always trying to lighten the mood. "We'll never hear the end of it from Diana if we let a youngling get eaten, and they made it this far."

My brothers strip and shift fast as Cashore's group sprints around the large pool, nearly halfway to us. Diana gets there first, leaping through the air and taking out two manangal with a slice of her claws across their chests. They fall to the ground and flop around as two more separate and dive for her, their leathery wings beating the air as the group keeps running.

Jet and Ten sprint for her with me, Ten breaking off to cover the vampiri carrying the younglings. As soon as he does, Renze splits from the group and spins around, dashing alongside Jet to attack the remaining manangal.

Diana yelps when one of the beasts sinks its fangs into her side, and my vision clouds to red. I barrel into them both, knocking the creature aside before I leap on top of it and rip its head from its shoulders.

Turning to Diana, I find her already up and attacking the remaining manangal, but there are just three left at this point. They seem to decide it's not worth continuing to attack us because they wheel around in the air and speed for the door they came in through.

As a group, Renze, Jet, and Diana turn and follow the fleeing vampiri until we're through the gate once more, depressing the button to shut it once again. Inside the dark stone hall, the vampiri huddle together, hovering protectively around the younglings. Ten sits down like a big dog and nuzzles his way next to Ascelin, sniffing at each youngling, licking a few.

He's trying to calm them.

I wouldn't have expected it, honestly. But then I remember how young he was when Rama threw us in here. I imagine he's seeing himself in these children's faces. It's another reminder that, of my pack members, Ten is the only one with any kindness in his heart. I've got to get him out of here. Ascelin watches him with open shock and surprise on her angular features.

Diana shifts back to human form. "Thank you," she murmurs as she runs a hand up under my shirt. Her blue eyes fill with tears when I reach out and stroke a stray strand of hair away from her sweaty cheek.

"I did not think you would help us," Cashore says, coming around his group to stop in front of Diana and me. "I knew you would not come back when the manangal came for us. I would not have come back either. But I did not think you would help us just now."

Diana turns and stands tall before me. "I could not watch your younglings die, Cashore. I will protect them and see you all to safety if I can. I promise you that."

Despite his earlier assistance in pushing Diana, she seems not to be afraid of the big vampiri king. Cashore takes another step closer to her, too-white eyes narrowing as he looks at her, leaning down so they're face to face.

I snarl, but Cashore smiles, revealing blood-coated black teeth. "You surprise me at every turn, Diana Winthrop. I cannot wait to see how you change Noire for the better."

Diana laughs as I growl and resist the urge to slap the smile off his face.

Cashore smiles at Diana again. "See what I mean? No chest-beating. No grabbing me by my clothes and threatening to kill me. You have made progress already, little omega. He is nearly civilized."

Diana smirks at me but turns and walks to the crowd of vampiri, finding the mother from earlier. "You're still here?" she murmurs to the vampiri woman who responds with a curt nod, a tear sliding down her blood-stained cheek.

Diana reaches out and wipes the tear away, and the vampiri leans into her touch. "I will do everything in my power to get you and your child free of this place. Everything, do you understand?"

The vampiri nods and tucks the child tighter into her chest, leaning forward to press her forehead to Diana's. They hold that pose for a few moments as Cashore watches next to me.

We're frozen, all of us alpha males watching the only omega in this whole place comfort a grieving mother.

Mine. Diana is mine. My queen. A natural ruler. She cares for others in the way an omega should, a way alphas aren't wired to. I know it, watching her caress the child's face in a way that would never occur to me to do.

"That's right," Cashore whispers next to me. "She knows it. Now you know it. So do something about it."

The threads were there earlier, that insistent tug of my body demanding I recognize her. But I didn't allow myself to believe it, to fully accept it, until this moment. The ghost of a smile turns my lips upward. "Diana, what's next?"

Diana turns from the vampiri woman, reaching out to brush the back of her hand across the child's cheek. My thoughts turn to her belly swollen with my own child, watching her birth, feed, and raise my sons and daughters. That's the future I want, the future I will take if I have anything to say about it. She will be mine before this is done.

She looks down at the tattoo running up her hand, following a line as she looks around the hall and points to an open alcove. "There, we follow that for a long time; it takes us around the edges of the maze. I don't know for sure what monsters are down there these days, but we'll just have to be quiet and careful. It's designed for water-based monsters, if a client has a need for that."

"Like what?" barks Jet.

"Water?" Ten grumbles as he turns to Diana. "How would they get water-based monsters in here? I don't understand. I've never seen any water except for the hot springs."

Diana smiles, but it's sad. "The entire maze is a floating island, Ten. That's why nobody ever knew Rama was building it. She built it out at sea across the Vinituvari coast and dragged it toward Siargao. It now sits right at the mouth of the Kan."

Renze gasps. "Are you saying this entire fucking place is what, underwater?"

Diana nods as Ten barks out a laugh. "Have you just discovered you're claustrophobic, Renze?"

Renze snaps his teeth at Ten, but anxiety threads its way through our family bond. Jet actually is claustrophobic, not that I'd ever mention that aloud to anyone.

Renze snarls, "Couldn't be claustrophobic living in this shithole, but I didn't realize water was an option in here. Diana, how much of the maze have we not seen in our time here?"

She looks upward as she thinks, zipping her bodysuit back up. I want to whine when her soft breasts disappear behind the fabric.

I slap myself mentally. We need to get the fuck out of here.

"You've seen about half the maze, give or take?"

Jet and the vampiri collectively gasp.

Cashore's gift scratches at the edges of my mind, and when Diana blanches, I know he's doing the same to her. "Do we even want to know what lies in the other half?"

"Stay out of my omega's head," I snap out in warning as he chuckles and Diana's face relaxes once more. She gives me a grateful smile before pacing toward me.

Diana smirks at the vampiri king. "Probably not. So let's get the fuck out of here."

Threading my fingers through hers, I tug her into my side as we head into the darkest recesses of the maze.

We walk, our group quiet as Diana and I bring up the rear, saying nothing. But the whole time I focus on her, on what I can read from her. Fear, anger, determination, and darkness thread themselves through her emotions. I think back to Cashore's comment about reading her being hard because of likely psychological trauma.

Whatever I need to burn down to fix the world for her, I'll do it.

CHAPTER SIXTEEN
NOIRE

Our group is quiet, naturally falling into a circle around the vampiri carrying the younglings. It's odd to behave like a pack with the monsters who were my greatest competitors in this place. Cashore and I have been spitting insults at one another for seven years. Yet, now my brothers and bondmate protect his younglings.

He was right about one thing: Diana is changing me in ways I am unprepared for.

Yet I am not trying to stop it. If anything, the need to claim and mark her, to fully bond with her, is driving me wild. My father was a terrible alpha–heartless, callous, and cruel. I don't have to be that. I don't *want* to be that. I want to be something better for the omega who walks quietly in front of me.

"Where to, fearless leader?" Jet jokes as he and Ten hover protectively around Diana.

She's changing all of us.

Diana looks at the part of her tattoo that travels down her forearm, then points along the hallway. "We follow this for a long time, and then we'll come to a big cliff. We need to climb it, and there's an exit at the top."

"What could we run across monster-wise in this part of the maze?" I ask, tilting her chin up so I can look at her.

I need to claim you, I think, pushing my need through our bond, wondering how much she can read since we aren't formally tethered.

Diana's lips part, back arching so she sinks into my chest, one hand coming to my arm. We can't speak in one another's minds, but she senses my need.

She looks up at me, concern slinking its way along our blossoming connection. "The cold-climate monsters live on this side of the maze. It's almost completely cut off from your side, with the exception of this hallway and an area at the bottom of the abyss outside the vampiri quarters. I don't know everything Rama could have put in this side, but I've profiled kurasao dragons, gavataur, and there are some species of cold-weather naga, ironically."

"You must be shitting me," Jet barks out, shaking his head as he crosses his arms. "Dragons? Gavataur? Where is she finding these monsters?"

Diana frowns but steps out of my arms. "I assume she ventures into the Tempang for the monsters I've heard of but never seen... Some of the monsters she's caught and put in the maze are myths I heard of as a child. But most myths have some truth to them."

Tenebris nods. "Kurasao do actually live in the far north. I've never heard of a gavataur outside of ancient history though. Maybe it's from a time when the continents were split differently than they are now, so we have stories about them, but we've never run across them."

Cashore hisses at our line of questioning. "Let us continue on. We can't possibly know what she will put in the maze with us."

"Right," barks Jet, frowning at Renze. "We can assume it'll suck, and that's about it."

"And not even in a fun way," Renze quips back, winking at my brother.

Jet rolls his eyes but looks away, his eyes falling on Diana's tattoo as she references it once more. Looking up the hallway, she points. "We head in this direction for a while. It may start to get cold, so we'll stick close together, okay?"

Renze looks over at Jet again, so I growl with my sneer directed at him. I won't call out his attention toward my brother, but it has not gone unnoticed by me. Renze's black brows travel upward, but then he looks back at Diana.

Our group begins moving, Diana and the younglings safe in the center. Cashore and I bring up the rear, Jet and Ascelin on one side, Ten and Renze at the front.

Cameras embedded into the ceiling swivel to follow us, reminding me that Rama watches our every move. There may be some places in the maze she cannot see, but I'd bet they're few and far between. For half an hour, we walk without saying a word until we round a corner and light fills the stone tunnel ahead.

One entire wall of the hallway is an enormous plate-glass window, and outside that window, the waters of the bay teem with life. Fish swim; a whale passes lazily by. Life goes on, despite everything that's happened here in the fucking maze. It's...normal. It's the first time I've seen the waters of my homeland in any form since Rama threw us in the maze.

"Water," Jet breathes. "It's the fucking bay, isn't it?" He turns from the front, eyes landing on Diana as she nods.

Jet and Ten are enamored, going immediately up to the glass to peer out. Diana paces quietly to me as Ten presses his face up against the glass, clearly in awe of what he sees. Anger stabs at my chest, knowing he spent his formative years stuck in the maze with Jet and me, never swimming in the bay, never experiencing all the things he should have.

I growl as I grip Diana's neck, pulling her close to my chest. She sinks into my heat, a deep purr rumbling between us as I relax and bury my face in her neck, sucking in great breaths of her scent. Home. She smells like home, and peace, and everything I want for myself. She has surprised me at every turn with her resilient strength, bravery, and kindness. Diana is everything I could never be because it's not in my nature.

But it's hers. And I want to possess it and own it and fucking worship it with every inch of myself.

My fingers grip her throat tight as she gasps and throws her head back. Some of our group watch, but most are enthralled with the sea and watching everything outside the window.

"We need to keep moving," Diana rasps as I let up on her throat, brushing my lips across hers.

"Yes," I growl. "You are a distraction, Diana Winthrop."

"I know," she sasses. "I don't like being by these windows. Do you know how easy it would be to–" Her voice cuts off as an explosion rocks the hallway, knocking Diana and me both to the ground, along with the majority of our party.

We leap upright, whipping around to face the windows. But the long window has a black blast mark stretched across it, and a crack that's spouting water right in the middle of the fucking glass. As we watch, the crack lengthens along the middle of the glass, water spouting out from multiple places.

Something is shooting at the fucking window.

"Run!" I bellow, grabbing Diana and sprinting. The vampiri have already taken off, keeping the younglings in the center as the first big crack sends chunks of glass into the center of the hallway. Another crack springs wide and then another, glass flying across the hall like bullets.

Diana sprints ahead of me as I cover her from one side, protecting her with my back to the glass. We make it to the end of the hallway before the entire pane gives way, the sea rushing in, sending water to nip at our ankles as the hall starts to fill.

"How do we get out of here, Diana?" I growl, still running with her at my side. She looks down at her tattoo, pointing to a corridor up ahead.

"Go right! Go right!"

Up ahead, Cashore whips around with a snarl. "It is a dead-end, Diana. Are you certain?"

"Fucking go right!" I bellow as we sprint along the hallway, water up to my ankles already. The vampiri listen, and sure as shit, when we turn the corner, the hallway ends in a black stone wall crawling with roses.

Cashore snarls, grabbing his head before snapping his teeth at Diana. "If you are lying, so help me…"

"I'm not," Diana barks, striding past him and depressing stones in the wall in a particular sequence. They slip aside, revealing a much smaller hallway that we all crowd into immediately, pushing the younglings first.

As soon as we're all in, Diana presses a stone and the door slides up, although this small room is filling with water as well.

"Diana," Jet huffs. "The water isn't stopping at the fucking door."

"I know, I know," she barks back, eyeing her tattoo. "Give me a fucking minute."

Behind us, the vampiri click and hiss, nervous energy filling the small room as water continues to seep under the door. Next to me, Jet's eyes dart up to mine, and I could scream at what I see there. Concern. Suspicion. Terror. He's worried if this is all some elaborate ruse, and he's going to die in this fucking room, choking on seawater.

"Steady," I growl at him. It was always our code word for "stay calm, stay vigilant, never let your guard down."

The terror eddies away, his face relaxing as he nods at me, gripping his weapons tighter.

Diana depresses another series of stones, and a new doorway opens in the middle of the black stone wall. The moment it does, a blast of cool air hits us, and one of the vampiri groans.

"You must be shitting me," murmurs Renze. "Of fucking course."

"Hush," barks Ascelin, turning to Ten. "You know about monsters; what can we expect if Diana is right?"

Ten peeks his head through the open doorway, but we can't see anything yet, just more stone. "I'll tell ya when I see something to worry about. But most cold-weather monsters are quieter, so keep the chatter to a minimum. It's likely anything we encounter would see body heat, so you're less of a target than our pack."

"Good," she hisses, smiling wickedly at him. Ten winks back as I struggle not to roll my eyes. We've not been around the vampiri for long at all, and I dislike the interest they're showing in my brothers.

"Get moving," I bark as a few of the vampiri peek around the corner.

"More hallways," someone murmurs.

Diana rubs shoulders with the vampiri mother who still holds the child. "Let's get through here and shut this door. Both together should stop the water. Through here is a forest, built for the quieter monsters. We need to pass through it, and then we'll come to the base of a cliff. If we get separated, look for either ruins or a cliff. Both are safe places to stop."

Cashore turns to his people. "You heard Diana; move quietly and with purpose. If we are attacked, find the ruins or the cliff, and do not stop, no matter what you may hear." He turns to Diana with a frown. "An entire underground forest? How did she accomplish this, Diana? Do you know?"

Diana sighs as she looks up at the vampiri. "It could only be magic, although I don't know what kind or how she did it. But Father wouldn't tell me anything about it. Even then, he was scared of what Rama was doing."

"Let's go…" I murmur, pressing my hand against her lower back. I'll ponder the intricacies of the maze later, once we're free. But right now we are still in danger every minute we stand around.

I fucking hate going into a new part of the maze we haven't seen with a large group. We're practically screaming for attention, but I can't change it. Diana glances up at me, gifting me a soft smile as she follows the mother vampiri into the dark hallway. Nobody says a word as we walk, the hallway opening up into a forest.

The underground forest is dark, complete with snow, white-tipped pine trees and near-freezing temperatures. Renze mutters a string of curses under his breath as the vampiri huddle closer together. For half an hour, we pick our way slowly through the ghostly pines, and nobody risks asking Diana a single question.

Jet hovers by my side, Diana in front of us and Ten on the opposite side, when a sound rings out through the quiet–something is crashing through the trees. Something big.

"Run!" I hiss as Cashore spins in the direction of the sound.

The vampiri take off, led by Ascelin and Renze as Ten brings up one side the way I taught him to. Jet takes off when I nod, but a huge beast gallops out of the trees and follows Jet as Diana screams his name.

It's fucking disgusting, whatever it is. Ten feet tall or more, all saggy, crusted long limbs but a distended stomach. Its face is reminiscent of a minotaur but gaunt, skin hanging from bone. Wicked-looking horns sprout from either side of its head, curling back behinds its skull. The monster drops to all fours and gallops toward Jet, who dashes to the side but not quickly enough to avoid one of the antlers.

The force of the beast's headbutt throws Jet high up into the air, blood spraying the snow when he crashes to the ground as Cashore, Diana, and I run for him. Then all hell breaks loose. Jet manages to stab the beast in the eye as it whirls on him again, just as I jump on its back and stab it through the skull.

Cashore sprints ahead of us, slowed by the cold but still quick on his feet as more beasts emerge from the forest, attacking the group as we run through the trees. I jump off the beast's back as Diana drags Jet out from under the beast's bleeding head.

Turning toward the group, Diana yells, "Head straight for the ruins!"

Jet leaps upright and starts running, holding his bleeding side as he turns toward me. "Just a scratch, alpha."

Snarling, I push him forward with one hand on his back protectively, he and Diana right in front of me as we chase the monsters chasing the rest of our pack. I couldn't give less of a fuck about the vampiri, but Ten is surrounded by the slower monsters and whatever this shit is that's chasing us.

Diana pants with worry in front of me, and I know she, at least, is thinking of the younglings as well. Ahead of us, dark stone ruins loom in the forest. "Get in!" Diana shouts. "Get in and shut the fucking door!"

I watch as the monsters barrel through the group once, twice, flinging at least two vampiri high in the air and leaving trampled, bloody bodies as they follow the rest of the group. I don't bother to look down as we pass the carnage, still sprinting to catch up with everyone.

Up ahead, Ten watches the group enter the broad front doors of the ruins and looks at the monsters following.

"Close it!" I bellow, praying Diana is right, and this is the best thing to do.

Ten grunts but does as I ask, slamming the door. I hear a lock click from the inside just as the bull-beasts slam into the door, raging and scratching.

Diana veers off before we reach the monsters, sprinting through the woods along the ruined castle until we're on the far side. She slows and examines her tattoo, finding an appropriate stone and pressing it. Immediately, stones slip to the side, and she dashes in, reaching for Jet and pulling him in beside her.

As soon as I pile in beside them, she presses the stone again and the stones slide back into place.

"Jet, how hurt are you?" she barks out, leaning over his side as he groans, lifting his shirt. Even in the darkness, I can see he's deeply bruised, and there's a long slice down his ribs but no puncture, thank fuck.

"I'll survive," he groans, "but it stings like a bitch. What the fuck were those things? I don't recall that from any of my mother's bedtime stories." His voice is wry and angry as he looks at Diana.

"Gavataur," she whispers. "They've been in the maze from the beginning, but never accessible from your side. They're stuck here and fully feral, unlike the hybrids."

Jet snorts and rolls his eyes. "Feral gavataur. Kurasao dragons. I'm suddenly thankful we didn't have access to this part of the maze. This shit is wild."

Diana rubs his chest gently and nods. "Rama is a psycho bitch. Let's go up and find everyone else; Ten will be worried about you both."

I nod as she turns and heads up a painfully narrow staircase that puts us out into a big room where the rest of our group huddles. Ten sprints across the room and pulls Jet into his arms. "Thought we lost you, brother."

"Never," Jet whispers. "I'll always be here to bug you, you big asshole."

Ten smiles and claps Jet on the back as Cashore, Renze, and Ascelin come over, looking furious. Cashore is the first to speak as I step protectively in front of Diana. "What did we just witness, Diana? What else lies in this underground forest? We lost two of our own back there."

She surprises me when she rounds on the vampiri king with a snarl. "And yet we protected you so that most of you made it. I never promised we would all escape this place, Cashore. This is dangerous, even for us. You knew that when you chose to follow me."

Cashore stands up taller and snarls, poison dripping off his fangs and melting the snow at his feet. Without saying anything, he turns and strides across the room, checking in with the mothers who still carry younglings.

"Still fucking surprising me," Jet groans as he looks at Diana.

And I smile. Because she truly is the biggest surprise of my life.

CHAPTER SEVENTEEN
DIANA

Safe inside the ruins, I pace the room as the gavataur rage and scratch at the stone door. The vampiri huddle together, keeping the younglings between them as they mourn the loss of their people. I'm irritated at Cashore's anger, but I feel the need to do something. I cross the space to Renze, seeing that Cashore is busy speaking with one of his people.

Renze's white eyes flash when he sees me, and he straightens up off the wall to take a step toward me. "Do you need something, Diana?"

Hurt blooms in my chest for him and his people. So much pain, so much loss in just a day. "I don't know how to comfort your people, Renze. Rama never televised anything but violence, and I don't know the vampiri ways. Can we do anything for you?" Noire's eyes on my back are practically tangible as he watches me.

The vampiri warrior's frown splits into a sad smile, black teeth poking out from behind equally black lips. "Vampiri are tough creatures, Diana. We will mourn when we leave this place. For now, we need to regain some of our power." He glances behind me with a wicked smile, then leans in close. "Do you know how vampiri derive our power?"

I lean in with my own smile. "From being badasses?"

Renze chuckles at that. "That we are. But our power loves sex, Diana. Vampiri are highly lustful creatures. Sex unleashes our gift, so do not be surprised if you see an orgy begin any moment."

I choke back a laugh. "I'm not trying to yuck your yum, Renze, but I'm surprised anyone feels up to it."

The handsome vampiri smiles again and leans in close, keeping an eye on Noire, who I sense crossing the room behind me, unhappy about the vampiri's proximity to my neck.

"Sex is all about connection, Diana. Sex is life. Already I sense my people's need. Why not partake in a little fun of your own while we wait for the monsters to forget us?"

Noire reaches us then, wrapping one big arm around my waist and shoving his way between Renze and me. He says nothing but growls deep in his throat as he pulls my back to his chest.

Renze smirks and takes a step back, leaning up against the wall again, his gaze traveling from us to land on something across the room. I suspect, when I turn, it'll be Jet.

Cashore's gift claws at my mind then. *I am sorry I snapped earlier. Play with your mate, Diana. Join us as we recharge our abilities.* Hearing the king speak directly into my mind is unsettling.

My second thought is the younglings, huddled together quietly in the corner. But when I look over, most of them are asleep, several of the female vampiri standing guard quietly as the rest mill around.

I snarl at Cashore, turning to face him as he walks my way. "Stay out of my mind. I won't tell you again. It's rude."

"Shall I say it out loud then?" the vampiri king barks with a huffy laugh. "You two should go play."

"We need to get out first," I retort, but there's no real belief in what I'm saying. We're stuck inside the ruins for now, until the gavataur give up and leave.

Cashore smiles, a dark and devious thing that twists his black lips into a smirk. "It is just a suggestion, Diana."

Smirking back, I let Noire lead me across the room toward a quiet corner. Through a window that overlooks the abyss, Alborada roses grow, tumbling along the wall onto the ground where they sneak across the floor. I suspect they're the reason Cashore remains on the other side of the room. I lost my fire starter stone to burn them, but his gift will fade if he comes near them and we have no other fire source.

Noire leans against the wall and watches me, dark eyes locked on me.

I point at the roses, nipping at my fingertip before holding the wound over one of the flowers as I smile up at Noire. "Did you know they're carnivorous? They clean the maze of anything the maulin miss…"

A rich red drop of my blood drips down onto the flower, which springs open immediately, greedily sucking the blood down into the center of the flower. I chuckle as the entire wall of flowers starts to shimmer and move. Noire frowns as he watches the roses rustle and shiver.

"These Alborada are the genetic memory of the maze, Noire. They take in all the blood, all the death, and they hold the memories of what happens in here in a sort of collective consciousness."

"They're thinking? Like a person?" Noire sounds highly skeptical as Jet comes over and watches the dark rose suck at my blood.

I think about the best way to explain it. "It's not that they're thinking so much as holding all that genetic material in a repository of sorts. If you could examine the genes of the roses, you'd find a mix of all the monsters and marks who have ever died here. Far more marks, of course, but still."

"That's creepy as shit," Jet deadpans, crossing his arms. "Is there anything Edson didn't think of?"

My heart breaks anew at the mention of my father.

I turn to Jet with a soft smile. "He didn't think Dore and I would ever be separated. He was always convinced that, because we were twins and so close, we'd leave this world together, the same way we entered it. He had the same tattoo I do."

Jet's face softens, and even Noire takes a step closer, stroking my cheek. My big alpha will never be a man of beautiful, romantic words. I know that. But he pushes sorrow for me through our bond, bringing the tip of his nose to mine, nuzzling it gently.

I smile up at him, bringing my hands to his chest.

And then I shove him–hard. Noire stumbles back, snarling, but as he moves forward, the rose vines wrap around his arms, dragging him back toward the wall.

I sense his irritation at finding they're strong. Really fucking strong. Tendrils whip around my alpha's upper body, spikes poking into his skin as I smile at him. Next to me, Jet holds his hands up and backs away. "I want nothing to do with this. But they won't like…eat chunks of him, right?"

I snicker as I wink at Jet, who bites his lip and turns as Noire bellows after him.

"Dare you to ask for help, alpha," I tease with a wink.

Noire struggles against the vines, but they tighten, dragging him right up against the wall as they snake around his thighs, neck, and chest. "What the fuck are you playing at, omega?"

I lean in, kissing the center of his chest. "You've fucked with me a whole lot tonight, alpha. I'm just reminding you that, regardless of what you say, no matter how many times you dominate me, I'm still a powerful fucking omega.

I will never let it go, never let it slide. It's like you told me earlier. Every little bit of sass from you is a rolling tally in my mind."

"And?" he barks out, sending alpha dominance rolling over me.

I shudder, my head lolling from side to side as a shiver racks my frame. "Gods, I fucking love it when you do that." Prickles along my skin send heat shooting through my core.

"The vines are attaching themselves, Diana," Noire grumbles.

"That's the idea, Noire," I chirp, dropping to my knees in front of him. "Let's mix a little pain with our pleasure, shall we? I feel our bond, and I want to feel it burn while I tease you."

Noire laughs then, a dark and devious sound that tells me I'm in trouble. "When I get free of this, you better run," he snarls as the roses begin to attach to his skin, their thorns slicing through his clothing.

Ignoring the threat, I pull his thick cock out of his pants, feeling it throb in my hand. The vines tighten across Noire's chest when he moves, eliciting a growl from his throat as he snaps his teeth at me, but can't reach.

"The fuck…" he complains, the noise cutting off into a grunt as I slip the tip of his cock between my lips and bite.

Noire bucks his hips as the roses tighten again. I tsk and lift my head, winking at him. "Be still, Noire. Be still, and I'll let you out faster."

With a swift move, I inhale his cock, sucking it deep into my throat as he gasps out in pleasure. I can sense the sting of my teeth alongside the prickle of the vines has his senses on overdrive.

"I'm going to punish you so hard that you won't be walking after this." It's a threat he fully intends to carry out at some point. Later. After I suck him off. Our bond is heavy with glittering lust as Noire huffs out a whine, trying to thrust to meet me but unable to move.

The rose vines yank tight as he strains against them. I sense he needs to move, to rut, to dominate–but I've taken that option from him. Anger heats our bond as I work him over, humming around his cock.

Awareness prickles at the edges of my mind as I snap my eyes open to find we have onlookers hovering to one side: a few of the vampiri, including Cashore and Renze. Noire groans as I cup his balls in both hands and tug them down, the roses biting into his skin at the same time.

Blood wells to the surface as the vines take from my alpha, all while I work at his feet to drive his pleasure higher and higher. His cock pulses in my mouth as I chuckle, and the vines yank tighter, dragging his arms out to the side as the flowers feed on his blood.

Out. He wants out. He wants to flip me over on all fours and take everything, to claim it all. Noire sends image after heady image through our bond until I'm ready to come from the strength of his desire. I don't know if he's even aware of the growing power of our bond, but I relish every fucking image.

His eyes roll back into his head as I moan around his thick length, deep throating it as I swallow. A hiss leaves Noire's lips when he looks down at me, imagining me planning this. That I chose to do this, knowing there will be repercussions, turns him on more than anything I've done so far. I read all that in our bond as it threads tighter, pulling our souls closer together as Noire's pleasure rises.

With a choked roar, my alpha explodes, filling my throat with release as shockwaves ripple through his system. Around us, other soft groans reach my ears. Our audience approves of the show.

My lips pop off Noire's cock as my eyes find his. I wink as a laugh rings out of my throat, Noire straining against the vines again.

I can feel him examining his feelings for me, looking at me like I'm a puzzle he can't quite figure out. When he speaks, the blood rushes between my thighs, my body lighting up. "I realize now why all the omegas I've met who bowed their heads to me and didn't talk back never interested me. I need a bondmate to push me, to challenge me. Someone as strong as I am. You," he snarls at me as I rise, "it'll only ever be you, omega."

I grin as I hunt around on the floor and finally find a piece of rock that could start a fire. I strike it against the stone wall, initiating a little spark. The vines react immediately, recoiling away from it. I repeat the action as they untwine themselves from around Noire's muscles until there are only a few left and he's able to yank himself free.

I step right into Noire's arms and run my fingertips up his exposed skin, tickling at the blood that wells from hundreds of tiny wounds. Innocent eyes flick to his, eyelashes fluttering as I pout. There's a thread of deviance behind my innocent look. "Are you ready to get going, alpha? I don't hear the gavataur anymore."

A dark laugh leaves Noire's throat. "You know we need to address this before we go anywhere. Are you ready for me, omega?"

CHAPTER EIGHTEEN
NOIRE

Diana flutters her pretty eyelashes at me, but I hear her heart racing in her chest. Her pink tongue peeks out from between pouty, swollen lips to lick at the cum still coating them. Reaching my hand out, I run it up her back, tugging her hair gently as I bite my way up her neck.

Diana sinks into me with a needy moan. She's so willing, so pliant in my arms. But part of me wonders if at any moment she'll pull more shit to try to test me. Not knowing for sure has me rock hard for her. This omega is a maze herself, her mind layered with inconsistencies and riddles.

"I want to pick apart every piece of you. I want to understand how you work," I growl into her ear.

Diana chuckles as I rip a length of rose vine partially from the wall behind her and wrap it around her neck. The laugh chokes off when I swing the vine up and over the nearest archway, hauling Diana's body up into the air, feet dangling inches off the cold, black stones.

She sputters and coughs, gripping at the vines as they begin to attach themselves to her, suckling at her porcelain skin.

Behind Diana, the vampiri and my brothers are rapt watching Diana struggle. Jet looks bored, and Ten looks…intrigued. The faint sounds of fucking ring out of one corner of the ruins, driving my need higher.

Turning my attention back to the omega, I find her face is flushed red and flushing deeper as I stalk around her in a circle. "Want to play a game, Diana?

Let's take this far enough that you pass out. Maybe I'll have my way with you like that. What do you think…?"

She doesn't respond, the swift thunder of her heart reaching my ears as she claws at the vines.

I stand there, monster that I am, and watch her until her movements slow, and then I unzip her catsuit and lean in to suck at her nipples, wrapping her legs around my waist.

Diana attempts to hiss in a deep breath as I haul her body up, both hands on her ass to bring her pussy right to my lips. I bury my tongue between her thighs as she rocks her hips against my mouth. Omega slick drips from her, coating my neck, chin, and teeth. Slurping noises ring around us as I suck Diana off.

Behind her, I hear grunts and groans. Cashore was right, the vampiri are fucking. I hear it. And knowing that Diana and my show inspired that encourages me to attack her clit, bringing her right to the edge of orgasm before slowly dropping her to struggle against the vines again.

She gasps for breath, straining to reach the ground with long, elegant legs as I glance behind her. I watch in surprise as Ten gets in Ascelin's face, tossing her sword aside and backing her up against a wall. The vampiri warrioress doesn't fight it but wraps her arms around Ten's neck as he takes her mouth.

I'm equally unsurprised when Renze turns to my brother and reaches out to cup Jet's cock, squeezing as he shoves Jet up against a wall. What does surprise me is Jet shoving Renze away, and then giving in when the vampiri yanks his head back to lick his way up my brother's neck. But then Jet pushes the vampiri from him and stalks to the opposite side of the ruins, pacing as he watches the vampiri warrior turn to observe him.

Interesting.

I turn back to Diana, her face nearly purple at this point, and spin us to face the party before picking her up again, granting her reprieve. "Watch our people fuck, Diana. Watch what your little show started. Watch while I bury myself inside you and take my pleasure from your body."

Blue eyes flick from me to the room, Diana gasping as she sucks in deep breaths, pupils blowing wide. Cries ring out behind us as the vampiri rage and Ten starts fucking Ascelin, grunting loudly as the vampiri warrioress hisses encouragement. The room is heavy with pheromones as the collective need increases.

Parting Diana's thighs, I slide into her with a quick thrust as she throws her head back and screams. I grip her chin, biting along her collarbone. "Watch them, omega." It's a reminder and a command, and her pussy clenches around me as she watches the show. I drop her lower so the vine cuts her breath again, but her heat locks onto me so damn tight, I barely stop myself from coming.

When she's at the edge of what she can take, I support her again. Her eyes never leave the orgy going on behind me, not even when Ten bellows his release. Diana clenches hard again as I punch into her, over and over. Reaching between us, I pinch her clit with light, teasing touches as she arches her back.

The move pushes her creamy breasts right into my face. So I bite. Over and over, Diana shattering around me as an orgasm barrels down my spine, sending shockwaves of need through me as I scream into her skin, into the blood and spit coating her as I fill her with ropes of my seed.

For the second time tonight, I imagine her body swollen with my pups, and I want it. I want that future where she is mine, and I am hers, and we build something together. My chest heaves with the aftershocks of pleasure as her head comes up, blue eyes locking onto mine. I feel her, feel that thread that binds us together. It shifts and moves in my chest, centering in a stronger way on the omega in my arms. I want to claim her, but not here. For bondmates, the claiming can lead to abilities, and while we could use the extra help, developing the abilities sometimes leads to temporary weakness. We can't risk it, so we wait.

With one hand, I keep her supported, and with the other, I detach the vines from her neck, reveling in the way she hisses as the rose petals release from her skin. She's covered in tiny wounds from the prickly flowers attention.

Hovering over her skin, I lick my way along her wounds, coating her in saliva. Because she's mine, this show of attention will heal her faster. Her forehead falls against my cheek as she rubs hers along mine, a sign of affection between mates.

"Want to watch the show, alpha?" Despite me halfway choking her to death, she's still in a position to tease me.

"Everything about you intrigues me..." It's an admission, something I wouldn't normally tell the woman I'm bedding. But this woman? She isn't like the many others who came before her.

Diana is...everything.

CHAPTER NINETEEN
DIANA

Noire and I watch in rapt fascination as the vampiri orgy rages on. Ten finishes fucking Ascelin and then carries her into a dark corner and starts anew. I watch Renze cross the ruins toward Jet, speaking low under his voice. I'm surprised when Jet yanks the vampiri to him with a hand around his throat and devours his mouth, slipping his tongue between Renze's black lips and sucking. They disappear back into the shadows, gripping one another tight.

It's impossibly hot, watching this connection happen. Through it all, Cashore stands in the middle of the room with his eyes closed, his head cocked to the side as if he's listening to the entire thing and is fucking thrilled about it.

Noire is all warm, sated heat behind me, holding me as we lean against the stone archway and listen to the madness.

Renze and Jet eventually join us, and I'm dying to ask what happened. If they took it further, or not. Based on the heated looks Renze is shooting Jet's way, I think not. But I know Jet's been the star of the Atrium for seven years, so his relationship with sex is probably complicated at this point. For the first time in years, he can choose who he wants to fuck.

And tonight is not Renze's night, it seems.

Jet looks over at me and frowns, shaking his head ever so slightly as if to say "don't ask me right now."

I smile softly and nod, wondering if the deepening bond between Noire and me will work with him like their family bond.

Can you hear me? I think, pushing it to Jet, making sure we're looking at one another.

A faint smile tips the corner of his lips up. *Gods, yes, but please don't start questioning me about this asshole trying to get all over me. We can gossip after we get out.*

I smile as Noire leans in and nips at my shoulder, Jet smirking as he watches us. Reaching out, I grab Jet's hand and pull it up to my chest, sending him comfort and affection the way I would Dore if he were still with me.

Tenebris stalks out of the shadows, Ascelin following behind him as she rebraids one entire section of her long hair. She looks...not put together for the first time this entire night. Her white eyes find mine as her lips break into the barest hint of a smile. *So the warrior woman has a softer side?* The moment I think it, her smile falls as if she's heard my very thoughts. Maybe she has too...

The orgy begins to slow around us, but I notice a small shadow slip over from the corner–one of the younglings. He's tiny, maybe four or five if he were a human child. He looks up at Ascelin with wide white eyes lined with tears.

Next to Ascelin, Ten drops to one knee. "What do you need, little friend?"

The child looks up at Ascelin, who nods once, and then back at Ten. "I woke up and I'm afraid. Are the big monsters still trying to get us?"

Ascelin drops to a knee alongside Ten and reaches out, stroking the backs of her claws along the child's face. Before she can say anything, Ten puts a fingertip underneath the child's chin and tips it up.

"We will protect you, young one. *I* will protect you. Ascelin and Renze and Cashore will protect you. Come here." With a soothing purr, he opens his arms, and the child steps in, lip wavering.

Behind me, Noire is a solid wall of heat and focus as he watches his brother behave so tenderly.

The youngling reaches up, throwing his arms around Ten's neck and burrowing his face just under Ten's ear. Ten hops gently upright and wraps both arms around the child, rocking from side to side as Ascelin watches him, a strained frown on her features.

For a long time, Ten rocks the child, purring deep in his chest as the orgy dies. Nobody says a word as the biggest of my alphas croons and rocks a youngling. When Cashore joins us, his brows tip up as he watches Ten. Next to Ten, I swear Ascelin's cheeks pink up a little.

Cashore turns from the scene and smiles at me. "I have not felt this powerful in many years. Thank you for getting us started, Diana."

Noire's grip on my hip tightens as he snarls. Choking back a laugh, I stroke Noire's forearm as Cashore chuckles.

"I no longer hear the gavataur," Noire purrs. "Let's get the fuck out of here."

Next to us, Cashore nods and hisses out a series of guttural clicks to his people. Several vampiri grab the sleeping younglings, and we head for the door. I open it using the code from my tattoo, and I'm relieved to see the gavataur no longer crowd the hallway leading into the depths of the ruins.

"I hope they're not right on the other fucking side of this wall," Jet whispers, coming to stand next to me.

"The old stories say gavataur are foolish and forgetful," Ten offers. "They didn't get in, so they'll probably move on. Still, we've got to be careful not to attract their attention. Keep quiet."

Our group falls silent as we make our way through the last bits of the tunnel, the air growing stale and cool. As we make our way silently through the pines, the cliff looming ahead of us, the vampiri slow. We're going half the speed we were, and while our group is surprisingly quiet, I sense Noire's mounting frustration as we get closer to the cliff.

They're too slow, he barks into my mind as I turn and stroke his forearm.

There are no cameras in this part of the maze. *Rama can only prepare for us to exit somewhere on the maze island,* I reassure him. This new ability to speak in each other's minds is insanely useful.

A hooting call rings somewhere off to our left, and Cashore whips toward the noise, baring black teeth in a snarl that drips venom. His movements are slower than they should be, slower than they'd normally be, and I know without a doubt that whatever is coming will reach our group faster than we're prepared for.

Dashing ahead through the vampiri, I run through a clearing and sprint through the forest, begging Noire to bring up the rear as fast as he can. Reaching into my pocket, I draw out the firestone I found in the ruins, pushing my tired muscles hard as I exit the forest edge and see a line of huge stone horses. The horses mark the very base of the cliff leading to the outside world, a decorative nod to my homeland.

I love you, Father, I send into the universe as I dash toward the statues. Alborada roses, oblivious to the cold, grow in thickets along the base of every statue, crawling their way up to the top. Striking my firestone against one of the statues, I smile when a spark catches one of the roses, the fire immediately traveling along the vines as the roses crackle and hiss.

My group exits the forest edge, Noire sprinting with three younglings in his arms. I'd throw myself at his feet in gratitude if a dozen gavataur weren't galloping through the trees, antlers lowered as they chase my pack.

Screaming in anger, I rush to light the remainder of the roses, a line of roaring fire separating me from my people. Too slow. The vampiri are moving too slow because of the cold. Pressing the button on my suit to undo it, I shift and jump the fire toward the group, just as Noire bellows for me to turn my ass around and run the other way.

I can't, alpha. I can't leave anyone. Please understand, I beg as I rush past him toward Cashore, bringing up the far rear. I watch the vampiri king turn to face the gavataur, who have now reached the very edge of the forest, coming into full view. They're just as horrifying as the first time I saw them, all saggy skin and long, cracked limbs ending in sharp claws, decaying teeth, and razor-sharp horns that are their greatest weapon. The last vampiri passes me, running for safety as I sprint for Cashore.

The vampiri king screams in anger, drawing the attention of all the gavataur as they pick up the pace, falling to all fours and running across the clearing toward him. I bark out a warning as I swoop in and grab Cashore up in my teeth, sliding to a stop and scrambling in the other direction. The vampiri king claws his way up my neck and onto my back as we run for the stone bridge.

Noire breezes past me, bellowing his rage as the gavataur crowd behind me. We run as fast as we can, leaping the fire again to cross the bridge. My only hope, my only prayer, is that the monsters are afraid of the flames. I don't wait to see if they stop, but when Noire brings up the rear, running just behind me in protective formation, my heart is full to bursting.

You are in so much trouble, little girl, he growls into my mind. *Stop risking yourself against impossible odds.*

Spank me later, I snarl back as we fly to the base of the cliff, grabbing my suit along the way.

"Where to, Diana?" Jet barks out as his eyes scan the cliff. If you didn't know what you were looking for, you'd never see the slight pathway built into the side of the black rock face. I fly past him and run up the first few steps as Jet curses creatively.

"This godsdamned place," he huffs, running up the steps as Ten, Renze, and Ascelin urge the rest of the vampiri on. Cashore leaps off my back with a quick pat on my shoulder as Noire shifts and grabs my snout, bringing his fangs right alongside mine.

"You are a wonder, omega."

A screech is the only answer as the first gavataur gets brave enough to leap over the fire and starts barreling up the stone pathway toward us. At this point, a dozen statues are aflame, the roses crackling and screaming as fire licks its way up them. The noise causes the gavataur to halt, and the next one that leaps over the fire backtracks, fire catching its coat and traveling up the beast's shoulder. It runs off into the forest, screaming, little licks of flame catching the trees.

"Go!" Noire barks the command as he grabs my suit and urges me up the path to follow our pack.

I follow the slow group until we're high enough off the ground not to worry about the gavataur leaping up to catch us. Several of them still pace near the fire, but the forest is starting to burn, and most of them have disappeared, trying to escape the flames. Pausing long enough to shift and put my suit on, I smile at Noire as we pace up the steep cliff.

"What next, Diana?" Ten falls behind to question me.

I smile at him. "A steep fucking climb and then freedom, Ten." I turn to Noire and find him smiling. A real smile, the hint of one, anyhow. A joyous smile too, not the wicked, devious thing I've seen many times tonight. "I can't wait for you to see the world again, Noire," I whisper as he reaches out, wrapping fingers around my throat and pulling me close.

A deep alpha purr rolls out of his throat as he brings his nose to my neck and sucks in a deep breath. "I can't wait to see it with you, mate," he whispers. "I want to rediscover every inch of Siargao with you at my side. I want to fuck you all over my city, Diana."

Chuckling, I wrap my hands in his hair and drag his face up so I can devour his lips. Noire presses me into the rock face and leans down, hoisting me up into his arms as he takes his pleasure from my mouth.

"You two gonna fuck right here, or shall we get the hell out this place?" Ten's salty proclamation draws a growl from Noire, but I rub his chest.

"Ten is right, alpha; let's get the fuck out of here."

Ten smiles. "We're almost free, Noire. I can almost taste fresh air. Can't you?"

CHAPTER TWENTY
NOIRE

My younger brother smiles, and it's the first time he's looked like himself since we got thrown into the maze. That smile reminds me of how he was a child when we were thrown in here, and how he spent all his formative years in this darkness. I don't know what lasting effect that will have on Ten, but we can unpack that later.

"Love you, brother," Ten whispers as he takes a step closer, bowing his head to me respectfully. I'm not even ashamed to find myself overwhelmed with emotion at the thought of getting the fuck out, of seeing my city, and freeing my brothers. Reaching out, I pull Ten into my arms and crush him close.

"I will see your wrongs righted, Ten. I swear that to you."

"I know you will," Ten whispers, clapping me on the back. "I can already smell fresh air, although maybe that's just the hope talking."

"Let's go," Diana urges. "At the top of the cliff, there's a hidden exit from the maze. Rama doesn't know about it, but it's safe to assume she knows we'll come out somewhere on the island."

I nod as Diana pulls herself up the black stone path fast, making good progress as Jet and I follow her closely. The vampiri are making their way slowly, but without monsters on our tails, I feel less ragey about hurrying them. Tonight's events have produced an unexpected partnership with the vampiri. I'm feeling far less inclined to kill them than I was earlier this evening.

The scent of fresh air is so heady that I don't even register it until Jet groans and picks up the pace.

"My gods," he sighs. "Crisp dawn air. Can you smell that, Noire?"

"We're almost there, brother. Keep going," I growl. I'll hug him at the top.

Jet nods and keeps pulling himself moving up, up, up until Diana disappears over a ledge, looking back over as we pull our way up next to her. Behind her, the stone is intricately carved with the black Alborada roses we've seen everywhere in the maze. Here, they grow again in plentiful bunches, surrounding the entire ledge and trailing out over the edge.

Cashore growls at the sheer abundance of roses as he turns to Diana. "Tell me please that the surface of this godsforsaken maze island isn't covered with these fucking things?"

Diana laughs, and I want to capture that sound and imprint it on my soul. What other happy noises might she make safe and away from this place?

"Just regular tropical forest." She winks at the vampiri as he sighs happily. She steps toward the stone and runs elegant fingers along the roses. When she looks back down at her tattoo, the part that wraps around her wrist, I find myself in awe of her.

Cashore's gift scratches at the edges of my mind, but this time I don't stop it.

Together, you two have a chance of taking Rama down, he whispers into my thoughts. *But you must claim her, Noire. Make Diana whole once more; her soul aches for yours.*

I smile at him as he turns from me to watch her. Around us, our group is anxious. Renze, Ascelin, Jet, and Ten still hover around the edges, ever watchful, ever guarding. I sense my brothers are strung out; they're in desperate need of several days of sleep.

Diana depresses four stones in a specific order, and they begin to fall away, revealing yet another black stone hallway. If I never see black stone again after tonight, it won't be long enough.

This is different, though. Moonlight seeps through the roof, cool dawn air coming through the holes in the ceiling. I haven't smelled real air from outside in seven years. Sucking in a breath, I find myself blinking in disbelief.

We're nearly out. In my line of work, hope is a luxury I never placed much faith in. There was always planning and being the biggest and baddest. It's what my father prepared me to do, and it's what I've always done. But now? Hope fills my chest. Hope for the future I might have with my omega if we escape Rama and take her down.

"I always thought I'd destroy this place once we got out," I murmur to Diana, stroking a stray pale hair back from her cheek. "But now, I want nothing more than to track down every person who ever paid to send someone in here, who ever watched with pleasure as we were forced into servitude. I want to throw every single one of them in here and watch them get destroyed by the monsters they forced here. What do you think, mate?"

Diana's smile turns wicked and cruel as she smiles back up at me, sinking into my arms. "I've had fantasies every day since I watched Rama kill Dore about how I'd destroy her. And it starts right here in the maze. There is nowhere that she and the wealthy can hide that we can't find them."

A laugh rolls up out of my chest then as I lean in to brush my lips across hers, sliding my tongue along her own as she leans into my attention. "You truly are the omega I didn't know I needed."

"Good," she murmurs back. "Because I came in here with every intention of claiming you, Noire. You're stuck with me for good."

"You can fuck later," Jet snarls from the hallway. "Let's get going. I haven't had a good martini in seven years, and I fucking want one."

Diana giggles. "Seven years without freedom and that's the first thing you want?"

Jet waggles his brows. "First among many things I want when we get out of here. Like a bath and a week of sleep."

Diana's smile falls at Jet's admission, but I thread my fingers through hers and pull her up the hallway toward him. "Let's go, then."

For ten minutes we walk, the scents of the outside world assaulting my nostrils for the first time. I smell salt, water, and grass. I can hear the faint wash of waves; we're close to the shore. Turning to Diana, I nod toward the sounds. "I smell the bay…"

She nods, weaving her fingers tighter through mine. "The island grew fast, so when we get out, you will see cliffs and the sea, and across the bay, you will see Siargao, Noire." Her gaze darkens. "And if you look up over the city, you will see Paraiso, her floating fortress. She entertains the wealthy there."

"I'm still amazed she was able to build all of this without anyone ever knowing…" grumbles Jet.

"We underestimated her," I bark back, my voice sour. "It will never happen again. We will take over this maze and island until we get the retribution we want, and then we'll burn it down."

Diana squeezes my fingers as we reach the end to find another black door, this one all sleek metal, although it's rusted with the passing of time and the salt air.

"You don't know where this comes out?" Jet questions, grabbing Diana's wrist to look at the underneath of it. She stays still for his perusal as I growl at my brother for touching my omega without asking.

Jet's dark eyes find mine as he reaches into his backpack, groaning when he's reminded the naga crushed all his uppers. "My mind is a top spinning around; I need some focus," he snarls as I growl at him again.

"Jet, you're done. You need to get free of that shit. I need you fully here with me, brother."

Jet snarls but glances at Diana, who reaches out and rubs at his chest gently, purring softly to him. His dark eyes flare, lip curling up as he looks at her, but her soft noise seems to soothe him even as I bristle.

"Let's get the fuck out of here," Diana offers, turning to me. She grabs the door handle and swings it open, stepping through into the light. Grinning at my younger brother, I step through after her, reaching out to put one hand on her hip as I follow her into the cool air.

The scents of a jungle assault me immediately, the early dawn light so bright that I nearly fall to the ground at how light it is. Around me, the vampiri bask in the sudden warmth, their faces turned up to the sky as if they can physically will the incoming sun to sink into their cold skin. Diana smiles at me, even as we blink against the light.

"We're deep in the jungle," she whispers. "We still need to get off the island and into town. I don't have a plan for that part, to be honest."

"That's alright, omega," I reassure her. "We'll figure something out." I've never reassured anyone in my fucking life, but I have a deeply pressing need to do so for my female.

Quietly, our group heads for the sound of waves, and my alpha intuition guides us toward the city easily. We're close enough to the mainland that I can faintly hear the sounds of the Riverside District coming to life. Still, my senses are running circles in my mind. Rama hasn't found us yet, but I'm assuming she could at any minute.

We trek through the dense jungle for a few more minutes, passing a series of horse statues identical to the ones deep inside the maze. "We had these back home," Diana whispers to me. "They remind me of my childhood. They're a nod to my favorite mare, Dove. Dore named her the closest possible word he could find to his own name."

I stroke her hair as we pass through a thick stand of trees and into an open courtyard of sorts. It looks like the ruins from inside the maze, but my senses scream at me the moment our group steps inside the open hall.

Something clicks, and a bright light shines on us, blinding our group as Diana yips and sinks back into my arms. Next to me, Jet barks out a curse as I freeze in place, trying to see ahead of us.

The light cuts off just as suddenly as it started, and when it does, a woman stands in front of me across the courtyard.

Rama.

She's paused right inside the ruins, not forty feet from me, hands clasped in front of her waist as if we're meeting for business.

"Hello, alpha," she purrs, smiling from ear to ear as if she couldn't be more pleased to see me. Not a thing separates us, although noise assaults my ears as soldiers drop out of the sky on impossibly long cords, weapons trained on our group.

My body freezes and tightens as I warn Jet and Ten to stay vigilant and get ready to run if we have to.

Rama cocks her head to the side, calling out behind her, "He's here, Arabella. You can come out now."

A human woman steps out of the recessed shadows of the ruins, watching me with barely concealed glee. That's when I notice there's a sheen to the air in front of us.

It's a fucking force field, Diana whispers into my mind, snarling as she steps closer to me. *Genetically coded to let through only who Rama wants.*

Jet, Ten, and the two vampiri warriors stand in front of the others, who still carry the younglings protectively.

Rama's gaze levels on Diana, her eyes narrowing. "You surprised me, Diana. Your adventure through the maze was costly, but we had an agreement, and I will honor it. Come here, child."

Angst stabs our bond as Diana steps away from me. I'm too busy processing the words that just came out of Rama's mouth to stop her. Diana passes through the odd sheen and stands next to Rama, her fists balled as she looks at the older omega.

Genetically coded to let through only who she wants.

"I'll take my information now," Diana barks, raising her head without looking back at me. Through my bond with her, I search for answers, but it's dark and cold.

She lured us here on purpose. Jet and I realize it at the same time as he roars, "How could you? You promised to get Ten out. You made a fucking promise!"

I refuse to fucking believe it.

Kill her, mate, I whisper into our dark bond. If Diana can hear me, she gives no evidence of it as she squares up to Rama. Anger rises in my chest as I leap forward to follow Diana, only to be blown back by the odd sheen coating the space between our group and Rama's.

Rama laughs as I stand and roar, "What did you do to Diana? What have you done to my mate?" I fling myself at the barrier again and again, blasted back every time, but raging as I try to get to my mate and can't.

Rama laughs and reaches out to tuck a strand of Diana's hair back behind her ear, but I don't miss the flinch when her fingers brush across Diana's face.

Psychological trauma. It's true then, what Cashore said about Diana. Diana balls her fists tight and lifts her head higher, ignoring my onslaught. "My brother. Where is he? You said you'd tell me the truth about him if I got Noire here. Tell me, right the fuck now."

"Your brother is safe, for now," Rama purrs. "I will give you his coordinates once our business here concludes."

Hot rage fills my system, my fists balling as I resist the need to roar at the sky for this fresh betrayal.

Rama laughs as she crosses the courtyard halfway, the human woman in tow behind her, both women smirking at me. Rama speaks first, "What a knife to the gut, Noire. You discover your bondmate, only to find she lured you out of the maze at my behest..." Rama smiles at me again as the other woman steps forward–the human.

"Why?" My demand for answers is an alpha bark that bowls the human over so hard she falls back into Rama, who rolls her eyes and waits for the other female to right herself.

The human, Arabella, rounds on me with a frustrated, angry gaze as the soldiers behind her lift their weapons higher. "You killed my husband, Andre. I hope you fucking suffered tonight. I hope you found your mate and actually thought she was saving you, you monster."

Snorting, I hook my fingers into the front of my pants. "If you say so. I don't know an Andre."

"How can you not remember? You ripped his head from his shoulders and sent it to me!" the woman screams, incensed as Rama watches, dispassionate.

I smile at the angry human. "What a devoted wife you must be, waiting seven whole years to avenge your husband's death..."

The woman screams again angrily, ripping at her own hair as she turns to Rama with a distraught expression. Rama taps the woman on the shoulder as tears begin to stream down her face. "You paid for his misery, Arabella; have you seen enough?"

"It will never be enough," the human spits, glaring daggers at me. "I scrimped and saved every day for seven years to afford this night. I want him to hurt as I did."

Rama smiles again. "Shall we remove his head? Better yet, we can put him in the Atrium and you can fuck him," she offers as the woman's lips curl up into a snarl.

Diana stiffens behind Rama but still doesn't look up at me, not even when the human female continues with a leer at my brothers behind me.

"What if we put the alphas together into the Atrium and make them fuck each other?"

Rama laughs at the suggestion, eyes bouncing upward in surprise. "Your mind is darker than I've given you credit for, Arabella. Perhaps you could come work here. We're always trying to think up more theatrics, although Diana has always been the best at that."

Arabella smiles at me as Jet crouches down. Through our bond, he tugs at me. *We need to be ready to run, alpha.* The vampiri are frozen, even though Ten, Cashore, Ascelin, and Renze stand protectively in front of our pack. I'm not ready to let this go, not ready to believe this was all a ruse simply to satisfy a wealthy human's whims.

"What now?" I bark, taking another step as Rama smiles at me.

"When Arabella approached me about targeting you, I knew we needed a creative way to make you suffer. Something more than just killing another brother. What better way than to dangle an omega in her prime and make you think you were actually escaping?"

Cashore speaks up, snarling as he looks from Rama to Diana. "Diana. You knew we'd end up here? You knew, and you let me bring the younglings. I will tear you to fucking shreds."

Diana straightens her spine and lifts her chin as Rama smiles at the vampiri. "Ah, you see, vampiri, I have something Diana wants: information about her twin brother. And my sweet little profiler was willing to do anything once I told her. I directed her to concoct whatever story she had to, to get Noire to follow her out. Her story was good, I'll give her that. You should not have come with her."

"You've got me here, now what?" I bark, unable to stand still any longer as I pace, rage clouding my vision as I watch Diana stand dispassionately next to the other females, refusing to meet my gaze or respond through our tether. Behind me, my brothers and the vampiri are moving, congregating to one side of the ruins as they prepare to flee.

"I think I'll watch you pace another minute before we toss you all back into the maze." Rama smirks back. "Tonight has been fun, seeing that you believed you would escape. But the reality is you're going back in. All of you."

Cashore bellows out an angry roar as Rama's dark eyes flick over toward him, lips splitting into a devious smirk.

"I underestimated you," I admit. "But I will never lie down and take this. If you put us back in, we will get out again, and again, and again."

Rama smiles. "Oh, I'm counting on it, Noire. Counting on us playing this little game until you lose for good. I've hated you since long before my father offered me to you as a prized broodmare. Deshali was overrun with monsters from the Tempang, and he begged for your help, alpha to alpha. He offered you money and connections, and you turned him down. We were nearly decimated until I put my mind to work creating inventions to kill and imprison monsters. And that gave me an idea, Noire. The idea for the maze. A place where the monsters do *my* bidding. A place where I never again have to rely on alphas to protect me.

"Here's the thing, Noire," Rama continues, pointing toward Diana. "I have a gift, an unusual gift, not that you ever bothered to learn anything about me."

Diana's blue eyes lift then, and she looks at me but says nothing as Jet tugs on our bond.

Something else is coming out of the fucking jungle, Noire. We need to go. This is a godsdamned trap.

I still can't bring myself to run, though, not with Rama so close and my lying mate right next to her.

Undeterred, Rama continues, "I can see mate bonds, Noire. I've known Diana belonged with you since the day I killed her father and took her and her brother under my wing. The thing is, I liberated her *from* alphas. She doesn't need you, and it was fucking glorious watching her make the decision to choose her brother over you. Because that's exactly what she did," she spits the words out, her voice full of venom.

"Is she telling the truth?" I turn my gaze from Rama to Diana, who lifts her head and walks across the courtyard, a guard following her with his gun trained on her.

Diana's blue eyes are filled with tears as she raises both arms up imploringly. "She has my brother, Noire. I'm sorry... I, I have no choice. Please understand? Dore is the only thing I have left in this world. She took everything from me." Diana's blue eyes plead for my understanding as I step back, feeling a knife bury itself in my soul and twist as our bond frays.

Behind me, I can hear faint footsteps. Fuck. I sense the approach of something big as the vampiri huddle together, Ascelin and Renze turning to face the forest. Jet is right. Something is coming. My muscles tense as I realize we have very little time left to flee. I'm not going to get any more fucking answers, and I'm not killing Rama today.

Snarling, I turn toward the forest as Rama barks. "What are you looking at?"

I whip back around as a laugh rings out behind Rama.

Diana.

My mate's head is thrown back as she laughs deviously, her eyes trained on Rama, narrowing to an angry slant.

"I have a gift too, bitch," Diana barks at the other omega. "A wildly inventive father who created mechanical horses that look a lot like statues. They're activated by fire, and they're coded for one fucking purpose–to protect me."

Rama narrows her eyes and sputters, but the swift beat of hooves rings through the jungle as our group mills around, facing the oncoming noise, unsure whether or not to run.

"They'll never get through the field, you useless witch," Rama spits as I pace in front of the force field, looking over my shoulder but unwilling to leave my mate, despite her betrayal. Arabella backs away from Rama and runs toward the soldiers as Diana faces off with the older omega, a gun still trained on her back.

I can't get to her. Fear for her life scratches at my mind as my brothers and the vampiri huddle around the younglings behind me.

"That's where you're wrong," Diana hisses, fists balled as her chest heaves. "You see, despite whatever you held over my father's head, he knew my life was in danger. And he wanted to protect Dore and me in the only way he could. The horses are attracted to electricity, the same electricity you use to power this force field, for example, and your city. And the horses fly, you know. So that weapons system I'm assuming you were smart enough to build—well, that will be a great target for them." Diana points upward to the floating, glittering monstrosity that hovers in the clouds up above the maze.

Rama roars in anger just as the first horse emerges from the forest with a horrible grinding screech. Jet, Ten, and I dive to one side, the vampiri sprinting for the edges of the ruins. The horse still looks like a statue, all gray mottled stone with burn marks crawling along its skin. Except now, it moves as if it's alive, heading straight for the sheen that separates me from Diana.

I snarl when the first horse runs straight into the force field, a loud explosion rocking the forest. The field shimmers once but holds. But when the next one hits, Diana laughs and depresses the button on her bodysuit, shifting into her wolf at the same time. Rama's eyes widen in terror as she sprints and screams for the guards who open fire on Diana as I rage and roar outside the force field.

Bullets pepper Diana's hide but don't bring her down as she bounds across the short space, following Rama and barreling through the soldiers, even as more descend through the sky on long cords, shooting at the horses. Immediately, two of the horses split from the herd and lift off the ground, galloping up toward the soldiers, attacking everything they can reach. Bits of the descending soldiers' bodies rain down on us as the horses scream and attack anyone within reach.

I pace in front of the force field, steering clear of the bellowing horses as I roar for Diana, Jet and Ten hovering just behind me. More horses emerge from the jungle, throwing themselves at the force field and starting to pile around the sides of it, looking for Diana to protect her and attracted by the electricity powering the field.

My brothers shift, sensing the field waver tenuously as Diana bulldozes through the soldiers, tossing body parts in the air as she tries to get to Rama. Rama is already hopping into a ship of some sort that's cloaked in the jungle behind the ruins. The human, Arabella, screams to be let in, but Rama pays her no mind.

The field wavers again as I turn to Ten and Jet. "The moment it's down, we go through," I bark urgently as Cashore and Ascelin join us.

"We are with you," Ascelin says simply. "We are with Diana."

The horses roar and scream as I watch Diana push through the last of the soldiers. They continue to shoot at her as her wolf lands on top of the ship Rama is flying, swiping at the top with black claws just as the horses break through the barrier.

With a whoosh, my pack swoops in, overwhelming the soldiers as more continue to drop down from the sky. Rama screams in anger within the small ship as Diana rips into it with angry swipes of her wolf's claws.

Diana, I'm coming, I bark into our bond as I read her furious intent. She's so focused on getting to Rama that she doesn't turn as I leap through the air and help her drag the ship down, the noise of cracking reaching my ears. Hundreds of soldiers drop out of the sky, peppering the ruins with bullets as my brothers and the vampiri fight.

Anger turns my vision red as Rama's ship falls to the ground and splits. I'm shocked to see that she's shifted into a wolf as well. She leaps out of the box, whirling around as Diana lands on top of her, sending the breath from Rama's lungs out in a whoosh. Soldiers round on us as the fight rages behind us, but I can't take my eyes off the fucking woman who terrorized my pack, my people, my mate.

This is my only chance to take her down. I pounce on Rama, knocking Diana out of the way as I send a message to my brothers. *Help me, brothers, if you can. Help me end this.*

The air rings with the sound of the horses as part of the herd merges to form a circle around Diana and me, attacking anything that comes close. Rama roars with rage when my claws slice their way across her wolf's face. I lunge out, gripping Rama's throat in my teeth and biting tight, crushing her airway. The vicious omega grunts as Diana leaps up from where she fell and swipes at the wolf's stomach, opening deep gashes as bits of intestine start to slide out of the wounds.

Suddenly, I'm flying through the air, breath stolen from my lungs as something blasts its way through the horses and hits us. Diana is knocked the opposite way, howling in pain as I struggle to comprehend. A deep whirring noise assaults my ears as I glance up, seeing small, manned ships flying through the air, shooting at everything. Even the horses were blown to the side, although they leap up quickly, several jumping into air to attack the ship as the rest congregate around Diana where she fell.

An enormous clawed scoop grabs up Rama's bleeding, broken wolf, closing and pulling up through the air, darting from side to side to avoid the flying horses.

Another claw darts out of one of the ships and grabs Ten and one of the horses, gripping them both as I roar.

The ships turn and flee, leaving behind dozens of soldiers. The vampiri descend on those left behind and rip them to shreds as we crowd together and watch the ships disappear up into the dawn, heading for the floating city.

Diana shifts and flies to one of the horses, ripping a panel open on its side and punching in a series of codes, clutching her chest as if she's in pain. "Reprogram. Got to reprogram. Got to get Ten," she mumbles frantically as I rush to her side.

"That bitch took Ten," Ascelin grits out. "She fucking grabbed him with one of those claws."

"Oh fuck," snarls Jet, running his hands desperately through his hair as Renze comes over, licking blood off his lips.

"What happened?" he barks out, gripping Jet's chin and turning my brother to face him.

"She took Ten," Jet sobs.

I'm out of my mind with grief as I rock Diana, surprised when Renze pulls Jet into his arms and squeezes him close. "We will get your brother back, *atiri*. I promise you this."

"On it!" Diana roars as she snaps the panel shut, the horse taking off like a shot, spreading metallic wings and galloping up through the air. At least half of the mechanical beasts take off after the first, soaring through the sky and attacking the retreating ships. They manage to take down a few, and then we see them climbing up the side of the floating city.

Explosions rock out above us as the horses begin attacking the fortress. I can scarcely believe it when the city begins to move, until it's picking up speed and moving off into the distance at a rapid clip.

"They'll take out…the…weapons systems and, hopefully, bring the city down," Diana groans before falling to the ground, covered in blood. In the fury of the fight, none of us realized how many times she was actually hit.

The soldiers shot Diana dozens of times, and we can see the damage now she's back in human form. At least a few bullets are too close to her heart.

Roaring, I fall to the ground with her in my arms, holding her close to me as a rattling purr vibrates through me. I can't do anything about this–she's dying in my fucking arms, covered in blood. I didn't get to her in time. I couldn't fucking help her.

"Why, Diana?" I question her as she turns her cheek into my chest, smiling at the purr.

When she looks up at me, blue eyes are filled with tears, but she reaches up and places a palm over my heart, blood beginning to seep out of the corner of her mouth. "When you c–came to visit my father all those years ago and gave me a rose, I knew you were mine then."

"You were a child, omega," I whisper, stroking light hair out of her face as she coughs. Jet and the vampiri mill around, and already, I feel the need to protect her from them.

"Horses…will…try…to get Ten." Diana's voice cuts off as her eyes roll back in her head.

Cashore looks from her back to me, kneeling down to place his palm over Diana's forehead.

She looks up at him, gripping his wrist in one bloodied hand. "You're free, vampiri. I promised you I'd do what I could. Help Noire take her down, get Ten back, and then burn this place to the ground."

Cashore smiles down as Diana looks at me again, eyes rolling into the back of her head once more.

Crushing her to my chest, I hold back a sob as I plead to the gods. I'll give anything, anything, to keep my bondmate here with me.

"I can save her, but it will come at a cost, alpha," Cashore purrs at me, sitting back on his heels as Ascelin hisses and comes over.

"My king, you cannot think of leaving us. Not now?"

Jet roars in Ascelin's face, "If there's a single fucking chance to save her and get Ten—"

Ascelin doesn't respond to Jet but drops to a knee next to Cashore, who puts two fingers under her chin.

"You are my successor until the Chosen is ready, Ascelin. You know what to do. There is nothing outside this place for me with my queen gone. I have always intended to get you all out and then follow Zel."

He turns to me, cradling a limp Diana in my arms. "I can gift her my life force, but it will change her in ways we can't foresee."

I growl. "She'd be a vampiri?"

Cashore smiles but shakes his head. "No, it's not a metamorphosis, it's simply a gifting of my soul, a transferring, if you will. She may take on some of my characteristics. It is rarely done among my people."

"It is a great honor," snaps Ascelin as Cashore hushes her, Renze dropping down next to his king.

In that moment, I find myself grateful to the vampiri for the first time. We worked together as much as we had to to get out, but he could easily be leaving this place right now.

"Please," I whisper as blood from Diana's wounds coats my hands.

"She may retain pieces of my personality or gifts," Cashore warns.

"Then when I fuck her, I'll think about you," I bark as Cashore throws his head back, laughing.

He pushes forward, taking Diana out of my arms to lay her on the stone floor. When he climbs on top of her, straddling her body, I resist the urge to yank him off my mate.

Cashore carefully removes his leather vest and long-sleeved shirt, placing Diana's hand over his heart before he turns to his people. "You heard Diana. Work with Noire to take Rama down so she cannot do this to anyone ever again. Return Tenebris to his family. And then thrive, my people. Thrive..."

Ascelin chokes back a sob as the vampiri gather around them, Cashore chanting a string of words in an ancient vampiri language. I studied it as a child, but I find I remember next to nothing.

Jet comes to stand next to me, shoulder bumping mine in solidarity. I wrap one arm around his shoulder, comforting him in the only way I know how. I don't have the words for losing Ten and Diana both at once. Around us, the remaining horses stand quietly, stony sentinels guarding my mate's last moments.

As we watch, light travels down Cashore's arms and lands on Diana's chest, seeping into her skin, where it disappears from view.

Come the fuck back to me, I urge her. *Come, mate.*

CHAPTER TWENTY-ONE
DIANA

I wanted more in my last moments, more connection to Noire, more love. But Rama took that from me too. I accepted I might not make it out of the maze alive, but I hoped I was wrong. I knew there was every chance Noire would kill me for my betrayal, even though I always had a deeper plan.

My senses slip away as my core and chest heat until my mind squirms to get away from the flames.

But I can't move, and maybe this is already the afterlife coming, but if it is–I've gone straight to the seven hells. Flames lick up my body, eating me alive as I scream and writhe at the burning. I don't think my body's moving, so it's all in my mind.

I push my thoughts to Noire, to the faint read I have on him as I slip away into death. Except that read is getting stronger and stronger until something punches through my core like a knife, my body doubling over on itself.

I'm vaguely aware of a vibration rumbling from Noire's big, hot chest into mine, but my entire body is screaming, stabbing over and over as whispers start in the back of my mind.

Please, gods, let her be fine. I'll do anything. Please.

Is Noire speaking? Or am I just hearing what I want to in my final moments?

My bondmate, don't touch her. She is mine, mine, mine.

Fire eats up my insides as a scream erupts out of my throat, the whispers turning into a rushing roar of blood, the sound thumping in my ears so loud I wish I could move my arms to cover them. The scream turns inward, and then pictures play across my mind: *Cashore being crowned king. An attack, so much pain and loss. And then I wake up in the maze, looking through Cashore's mind, seeing the sulfur pools in my room for the first time. I roar with rage, but the sound travels off into the abyss and disappears.*

My pulse gallops under my skin as feeling returns to the tips of my fingers until I can move them.

Diana. Come to me. It's Noire's thought, struggling to break through the heavy drumbeat inside my head.

I'm trying, alpha, I cry back, struggling to reach my hand up to touch him, to feel him. I never imagined dying would be like this, grappling and scrambling to hold on to the living world.

Try harder. I'm here, omega. I'm waiting for you. Deep in my mind, Noire's insistent purr grows louder and louder until the vibration of it tickles along my chest and neck. I feel him; I truly feel him.

Fluttering my eyes open, I find myself looking into Noire's darker gaze. His forehead is pressed to mine, the tip of his nose rubbing at mine in gentle, languid strokes. His lips crack into a smile as he brushes them over my own. The hint of a kiss is reverent, worshipful. Tender.

"You're back," he growls. "Never leave again. You are mine, Diana."

"Yes." My affirmation comes with a smile as I struggle to reach my hand up and drag my fingers along Noire's stubble. Except, at the end of my fingers, where there were red painted nails, there are now sharp, black claws.

Vampiri, my mind echoes.

"He is speaking in your mind, is he not?" Ascelin drops down next to Noire, looking at me. When I turn to face her, she hisses in a deep breath, searching my face for…something. A string of words in her language flows out of her lips, but I understand them.

"*Hefesh aft inayit,* Ascelin," I murmur, reassuring her wounded heart. *I am still here.*

Did I speak those words?

A tear slides down her face as realization rockets around in my brain. Cashore is present in my mind, but when I glance behind Ascelin, his body lies on the ground, unnaturally still. He's gone.

My gaze flies up to Noire as he strokes my bloodied hair away from my face. "What happened? Cashore?"

Next to Noire, Ascelin breaks down into heaving sobs as Renze drops to his knees and reaches out for my hand, taking it in his own. "Cashore gave his life force to keep you from dying, but that means you're infused with a vampiri king's spirit, Diana. Some things may be different for you, going forward. Like this..." He holds my hands up, flicking his fingers along the new black claws. "There will be more. We can't know yet what changes his infusion will spark."

Sorrow hits me as I look at Cashore's still form, Ascelin turning to lay her forehead on his chest as sobs ring throughout the room.

"We need to get going," barks Jet from somewhere in the recesses of the dark ruins. "Rama could be back any moment with a fucking army."

Shaking my head, I sit upright, watching extruded bullets fall off my skin as Noire wraps an arm around my back, helping me rise.

He leans in, kissing the top of my shoulder, his warmth infusing me as he pours his need and desire for me into a bond that now burns brightly in my chest. "She will most definitely be back, and we need to be ready for that. Diana, do you have any idea what she might do? The fucking city flew away."

"I don't know," I whisper honestly. "She took Ten and one of the horses. So if she's still alive, she will need to regroup. The remaining horses can stand guard, and I can reprogram them to protect Siargao. I don't think she'll further risk Paraiso by coming close, but we need a better long-term plan."

Ascelin turns to me. "Chosen One, we need to retire Cashore's body. You and I must do it together."

"Chosen One?" I'm confused. I don't understand why she's calling me that.

"We have much to discuss, Diana," Ascelin whispers, her lips parting into a soft smile. "Come." The warrioress holds out a hand for me, and Noire lets me leave his grip long enough to take her hand and follow her to Cashore's prone figure.

Nodding, I turn as the few vampiri who remain crowd around their fallen king, kneeling beside him. Somehow, I know what to do. We lay our hands on him, and Ascelin and I speak the words vampiri have used for millennia to send their spirits to their ancestors. Cashore's face is still and beautiful in death, white eyes closed with the hint of a smile on his inky lips.

As we speak, his physical body begins to shimmer and flicker, and then it crumples in on itself until there's nothing left but glittering dark dust. I speak the words over and over as each vampiri cuts a slit in their palm, dripping the blood onto the ashes. We each gather up that mix and draw a line from our foreheads down to our chins.

I can almost hear Cashore mourning alongside us, deep in my mind. I've got no idea how this infusion of his spirit is going to work, but it's something to figure out later. For now, it's oddly comforting, like a cool cloak wrapped around my mind.

When the vampiri are done, I whisper a new refrain, and the ashes lift off the floor into the room, floating away through the stone ruins, disappearing into the dawn light. Ascelin turns to Renze and the remaining vampiri, and they're quiet together in mourning. Even the younglings.

I stand and turn away from them, looking for my mate. Noire's mouth crashes onto mine the moment we touch. Moaning softly, I sink into his heat and return the kiss, grunting when he fists my hair and pulls my head back to scent his way up my neck.

"You smell…different," he purrs. "Deeper. Stronger. Your blood is singing for me, Diana."

Patting his chest, I smile. "It will always sing for you, alpha."

Noire chuckles. "Did you just pat me like a Labrador?"

I turn my eyes up to his, laughing when his widen at what he sees there. "I'm still me, Noire."

"Your eyes are rimmed in black now," he whispers back, his voice soft. "I need you, mate."

"Good idea," I snark with a wink as we turn into the room. I am exhausted and grieving but needy all at the same time.

Noire pulls me close, gripping the back of my neck as his lips tickle the shell of my ear. "Don't think I'm not keeping count of every time you talk back to me, omega. There will be punishment for it."

I roll my eyes, pointing to my head. "Never know what kind of shit I might be capable of with Cashore's help, alpha. You sure you want to start this fight?"

Someone snorts quietly in the back of the room as Noire's smile broadens, sharp fangs poking out from his lips. "Absolutely certain, omega. If you dish it out, I will take and take and take it. And then I will punish you for days."

I lean in with a conspiratorial wink. "I can't wait."

CHAPTER TWENTY-TWO
NOIRE

We hike quickly across the island until we come to a small building. "This is the only office on the island," Diana explains. "It's there if something happens to the city above. The entire maze can be run from here."

"So, we could let other monsters out?" Ascelin questions. "I have half a mind to let loose anything with wings. Minus any remaining manangal."

Diana sighs, rubbing the warrioress' forearm. "It's tempting, Asc, but we cannot control the maze's monsters. Our only hope is to eventually return them to their homelands or destroy the maze. First, we need to do something about the disks. We can deactivate them from here."

The disks, I'd fucking forgotten about the disks.

"How much can she really do with them, Diana?" Renze questions, holding out his forearm. The disk is dark like it usually is overnight.

Diana frowns, rubbing at the disk. "I have no way of knowing what she added to the disk technology, but when my father designed it, it was really just a timer. It's likely Rama made it seem like she could control you, but she was just using the maze for that."

"I want it the fuck out," I snarl. "What's the best way?"

"They need to be surgically removed," Diana admits. "If you rip it out, you'll damage your nervous system."

I growl at the dark disk buried deep inside my skin. "I know someone who can take it out, but can we deactivate them here?"

Diana nods, leading us through the small outbuilding until we come to a dusty office with an entire wall covered in knobs and buttons. Our group watches in quiet silence as Diana powers on the wall of buttons and presses her palm against a reader. We watch as a panel of lights flashes then dims, and Diana turns to me with a smile, holding up her hand. "Deactivated! My fingerprints are an override for the maze. If Rama hadn't had her goons follow me twenty-four-seven, I could have swum over here years ago and turned this fucking place off."

I think about the years of emotional trauma Rama caused my omega, and I know with renewed certainty that I will rip this place to the ground.

Snarling, I look at my exhausted pack of two. "Can Rama follow us with these deactivated? I have a place we can go. But I do not want to lead her there for whatever comes next."

Diana shakes her head. "I can never be positive with Rama, but I'm as certain as I can be…"

"I'll take it," I murmur, kissing her forehead. "Let's go. When we take Rama down, we will come back and deal with this place."

Diana nods and smiles at me.

∽

The vampiri refuse to leave us now that Cashore's spirit is infused into Diana's. The dozen or so who remain are piled onto a rubber speedboat, crossing the warm waves of the bay toward the mainland. Siargao glitters ahead of us, and I can practically feel it welcoming me home. I have a few immediate priorities–claim Diana, get some rest, retrieve Ten, take back my town. Not in that order.

The fact that we're free still hasn't sunk in. Not for any of us. The vampiri sit quietly behind Jet in the boat, but Jet's jaw is slack as he lets the air fill his lungs, the wind whipping his dark hair around. He's never looked so peaceful, not since Rama put us in the maze. And despite the fact that we're missing another brother.

When we land on the opposite shore of the bay and I touch Siargao dirt for the first time, something in my dark heart blooms and bursts with joy. This was my home, my town, my kingdom. When I look up, the gray and black spires of the city loom tall above us. The city's skyscrapers gleam and flicker with light, just as they always did. There's a huge jet pad attached to one of the buildings now–it wasn't there before. The first of many new things I'm sure I'll notice.

"That must be how the rich fucks get up to Paraiso, right?" Jet questions.

Diana nods and squeezes my arm as I growl. That is a problem for another day.

The Riverside District is as run-down and decrepit as ever, but to be honest, it was always my favorite part of my home province. Riverside is gritty and resilient and glorious.

There's only one person I trust now that I'm back, and we need to get to his home if there's a chance he's still alive. Our group follows me in silence as we head up the riverbank and into the depths of the city. I step into the street and flag down one of the small buses that used to haul workers back and forth from Riverside to the Towers, the area the wealthy live in.

When the driver stops, his eyes go wide with recognition when he sees me. He bows when I give him the address, eyes widening once more when the vampiri follow me up into the cab and take their seats.

The cab takes off toward our destination, but our group says nothing as I turn to the driver. "Tell me what has changed in the seven years I've been gone." I'm curious to hear this from a fresh perspective.

He blanches but straightens his back and glances over his shoulder at me. "Mistress Rama controls everything, alpha. Ayala pack is scattered, as far as I know. Nearly everyone in the city works for her in one way or another."

"Including you?" I purr, letting my dominance roll over him as he jumps in his seat.

"When I have to," he admits, unable to lie to me.

"What's it like with Rama in charge of the province?" It's something I've wondered about. I ruled Siargao with an iron fist, but I was fair to the common people, good even. I took a share of every transaction in the city, so it made sense to ensure the city's businesses thrived. I highly doubt Rama rules that way, but I'd like additional perspective. Diana has eluded to some of what's gone on, but I am eager for more news.

The driver sighs. "She plays with people simply for the sake of her own entertainment. She's needlessly cruel and terribly unpredictable. She fucks with people for fun. She's a psychopath."

His words make me think of everything Diana has endured since she was a child. Rage at her treatment blisters my soul as I vow, pressing my lips to her forehead, that Rama will never fuck with her again.

The driver stops in front of a long row of low-slung houses. I owned every one of these houses before I left. I wonder who owns them now? I'm praying the alpha I knew before somehow escaped the slaughter. He was out of town visiting family when I was thrown into the maze, although I don't know if he would have even tried to come back here.

The vampiri follow Jet and Diana out of the aircab as I pause by the driver.

"I have nothing to give you in thanks, but I will not forget your help this evening. Spread the word that I'm back, please. And find me if you ever need anything. I owe you a favor."

The cab driver's eyes widen, but he nods, a splash of relief darting across his face. "Thank you, alpha," he murmurs as I stand and hop down out of the bus.

Gripping Diana's hand, I walk up the middle of the street, watching as people peek out and close their windows when they see us coming. Ah, I still strike fear in peoples' hearts then. I imagine seeing me walking up the street with a vampiri pack in tow, all of us covered in blood, will do that. It's a good fucking feeling. An older alpha comes out of the last house on the left, staggering when he looks up the street and sees me. He yells over his shoulder into the house for someone, then jogs up the street.

When he's close enough, he falls to a knee in front of me, head bowed. "Alpha, you escaped."

Laughing, I reach out to give him my hand and lift him back upright. "It is good to see you, Thomas. I thought you might have stayed abroad. I had help getting out. This is my mate, Diana."

The alpha who raised me when my father couldn't smiles broadly at my mate and reaches out to shake her hand. "It is so incredibly wonderful to see you." Thomas' eyes dart over Diana's shoulder, a growl rumbling out of his chest at the vampiri contingent behind us.

Jet comes forward, wrapping Thomas up in a hug. "They're with us, Thomas. They helped us out of the maze."

Thomas turns to me as a woman flies out of the house and barrels up the street toward us. I smile, opening my arms as she flings herself up into them, squeezing my neck so tightly I can barely breathe.

"Maya, Maya! I can't breathe, woman."

Rheumy sobs ring in my ears as she refuses to let up, crying into my neck with her arms crushing me. I glance at Diana to find her biting back a smile.

So you're a big softie? she asks in our bond.

There's not a single soft thing about me, omega, I bark back into her mind. *But Maya and Thomas are family.*

Maya finally stops crying long enough for me to put her down and introduce her to everyone. She cries again when she sees Jet, throwing herself into his arms too. "Where's Tenebris?" Her voice wavers as she asks the question.

"Tenebris was taken by Rama during our escape," Jet says the words, and they're a dagger to my chest. I went into the maze with three brothers and came out with one. I'll never let this stand. Rama is playing a game with me, a game that's going to eat her up.

Maya sobs quietly as she looks at me. She was a mother to the four of us when our own died and our father lost his way to insanity without his bondmate. He came out of it eventually, but Maya and Thomas raised us in the meantime. They're practically my grandparents.

"Let's get inside and get you settled," Thomas encourages, waving at the vampiri. He waits for me to nod my agreement, and then we follow him up the steps I played on as a young pup, into the house so many of my happy memories were made in.

You grew up here? Diana asks the question in my head as we walk down the hall, past the stairs, and into the kitchen at the back of the house.

For a time, mate. I'll tell her the whole story later, but for now, I have questions that need answering, and I sense everyone is ready for food and rest.

The vampiri need sleep, Diana whispers into my mind again. The feel of her connection is a lick of smoke curling along the edges of my consciousness, warm and comfortable. I want to press her into the wall and tease her until that smoke becomes a raging bonfire big enough to burn me to ash. It wasn't that long ago I was on the edge of a rut because of her, and now that we're out, my predatory need to take her is starting to eat at me again.

Maya flits around the kitchen, gathering food to heat. Jet howls with excitement when she pulls his favorite roast out of the fridge. He helps her, but I read how broken he feels underneath the busy exterior. He's coming down from the uppers and destroyed about Tenebris.

We'll get him back, I promise, I whisper into our family bond as Jet freezes, then relaxes.

Linking my fingertips with Diana's, I tug her across the kitchen, where I fall into a chair with her in my lap. "What do your vampiri need, mate?"

When Diana doesn't react to the fact that I called them hers, I smile. Cashore's spirit is already changing the dynamic of our group, tying us together in ways we couldn't possibly foresee. The vampiri are Diana's, and she is mine, so they are all mine now.

She hops up off my lap like a naughty girl and walks across the kitchen, going straight to the vampiri with the child. "Do you prefer to bathe or rest?" Diana's fingers stroke across the baby's forehead as the mother's eyes flutter from exhaustion.

"Rest, my queen," the woman whispers.

At the word "queen," Renze sucks in a breath before hiding it behind a cough.

There's going to be an interesting dynamic here. Cashore's spirit lives inside Diana, and clearly, at least some of the vampiri are taking that to mean Diana's in charge. I'll sort that out later, figure out how we can use it to our advantage to destroy Rama. I glance over at Ascelin, but her eyes remain trained on Diana, her expression unreadable. Whatever Diana being their Chosen One means, I can see Ascelin will be a big part of that.

Thomas sets bread and butter on the table as he watches Diana warily. "What do they need, alpha?"

"Is the house next door ready?" The house next to Thomas and Maya's was always a safe-house of sorts when I was a child, always ready should one of our brethren need a place to stay at a moment's notice.

"It is." Maya grabs the key, handing it to Jet. "Jet, honey. I'll finish this and have it ready for you. Why don't you take them next door? Everything is in the same place."

Diana's eyes find mine, unsure.

You don't want to part from them? How curious. I cock my head to the side and watch her nibble at her lip. *I promise they will be safe there.*

I'll go with them, just to make sure they feel settled, she whispers finally into our bond.

Stay here, I bark back. When she raises her brow in challenging irritation, I add a *please* to my command. I've never said please to anyone, except for maybe Maya and Thomas when I was a child.

Diana nods, rubbing the vampiri mother's shoulder before pressing their foreheads together. She kisses the child, who yawns and blinks up at her with huge all-white eyes.

Maya crosses the room and smiles at the mother. "The house is not stocked for young ones; can I get you anything for your child?"

The vampiri smiles, but she's clearly exhausted and grieving from everything that happened tonight. "No, thank you. She feeds from me, and I just ate. Rest is the best thing for us."

Maya nods as Jet passes her, gesturing to the vampiri. I don't miss the way Renze's eyes follow my brother again–hungry and wanting. I thought it was the heat of the maze orgy, or maybe how few options we had for connection. But there's obviously something deeper there. I'll unpack that later with Jet. I'm still not sure how I feel about the vampiri thrusting themselves on my pack because of Diana, but if Jet could find a real connection, I would be happy for it.

Now that I have that bond and know what it is, I would never begrudge him the feeling, even if it's with a vampiri warrior.

Thomas watches the vampiri go before clucking the way he always does when he's thinking and unhappy.

"Speak, Thomas. What are you thinking?" My alpha command rolls over him as dark eyes flick back to me.

"The world has changed in seven years, alpha," Thomas begins as Diana comes back to my side, wrapping her arms around my neck. Reaching up, I stroke my fingers down her forearm as her warmth seeps into my back.

"Talk to me about what has happened while we were in the maze. Who is left from Ayala pack?"

Thomas blanches. "When Rama took you, she destroyed most of the pack. I've heard some escaped, and I've looked over the years, but I've never been able to find anyone. You know we were abroad, and we came back before the news spread of your capture. But we couldn't bear to leave, so we remained here–quietly."

"No one is left?"

Thomas nods. "An alpha from Dest passed through here once and stayed next door. He had heard whispers of some Ayala pack settling there. But it is difficult to leave the city, so I haven't traveled there to see if that's true…"

"Dest? That's on the far side of Lombornei," I murmur as Diana starts up a soothing purr behind me. She senses my distress. I can't believe my pack is gone. Actually, I refuse to believe it. Why would Rama decimate an entire pack when she could use them somehow? I add it to the long list of things to explore quickly. Every move Rama makes has a purpose, it seems.

When Diana speaks next, the news sends my blood hot through my veins. "I was never allowed to roam far from the riverside district, but I've heard rumors that *this* maze is one of several. That Paraiso is another maze of sorts, even though Rama entertains the wealthy there."

Thomas' eyes narrow as he looks at Diana. "You know this how?"

I dislike the bark in his tone. "Diana is my bondmate, Thomas. Treat her with the same respect you treat me. She worked for Rama but spent years planning how to get us out. It is only because of her that we are here today."

Maya blanches but sets steaming food on the table, nudging it toward Diana and me. "Eat, please. You must be exhausted."

Am I? Behind me, my mate feels vibrant with energy, with need. We should be exhausted; we've had a hellish fucking twelve hours.

Diana unwraps herself from my neck and sits next to me, piling a plate high with food before placing it in front of me. "Eat, alpha." It's an omega command that washes over me the same way mine does her, a rolling tidal wave of omega dominance, the way only a bondmate can do. Our connection compels me, and I take the food, spearing a piece of roast before offering it to her first.

She bites it daintily off the fork before making a second plate for herself. Thomas and Maya watch us the whole time, guarded but interested.

They've never seen me like this with an omega, and even among our people, bondmates are rare. Most packs marry for money and stature, and that works. But bondmates are nearly unstoppable together; the joint power that connection unleashes is a force of nature. Diana and I will become stronger and stronger together. And when I claim her with my bite, either or both of us could develop powers.

Shifting in my chair to ease the building pressure between my thighs, I begin eating.

Thomas leans back and sighs. "Rama doesn't come into Siargao as much as you'd think. She spends the majority of her time up on the sky island Diana referenced." Maya rolls her eyes, placing more food on the table and pushing it across to Diana as Thomas continues.

"In her absence, Rama created something called the Council, and the Council took over the prior Siargao government, taking directives from her. They're a bunch of fucking assholes. You know them all, but they stay up in the Towers."

"Who?" I bark out.

Thomas lists off the names of every smaller pack that wanted what I had when I ruled Siargao. Packs that take and take and take and give nothing back.

"And how is the city doing under this rule?" I question.

Thomas looks around with a frown. "It isn't thriving the way it did when you were here, alpha. The common man is crushed under the Council's heel. Nobody can ever excel because, the moment you make something of yourself, the Council and Rama swoop in to take it. The best of the best everything goes up to the sky island, Paraiso."

I can practically feel Diana rolling her eyes next to me, irritation skating along our bond before she tamps it down.

My need for her builds as her anger grows. I want her to unleash it on me. I'm done talking for tonight.

Turning back to Thomas, I smile, showing him the disk in my arm. "This needs to be surgically removed. Jet has one as well. Can you do it?"

Thomas pulls his glasses to the tip of his nose and examines the unlit disk, poking at the edges as he frowns. "It looks very intricately placed, alpha. I can do it, but it'll take me a few hours for each of you. Do you want to do that now?"

Shaking my head, I glance at my mate. "Diana deactivated them, but even so, I want it out soon. Let's get it done tomorrow, unless Jet returns and wants you to do his. For now, I need space and a room. Where do you prefer we go?" I ask because I'm going to be fucking Diana for hours, and my pseudo parents may not want to hear it.

"Stay here," Maya offers immediately. "Thomas and I will go across the street."

Turning to Diana, I smirk. "We've had a long night, omega. I think it's time for bed."

CHAPTER TWENTY-THREE
DIANA

Time for bed. Noire's words are full of the dark promise of the pleasure in front of me this evening. I should be exhausted; we both should. But instead, I can't wait to be alone with him, outside the maze for the first time. I've fantasized about this since I was much younger, too young to fantasize about the alpha in front of me. He was mine the moment he handed me a rose all those years ago. And I've spent every moment of every day plotting and scheming to get him out of the Temple Maze.

Maya stands and smiles at us both. "Please feel free to finish your meal, and leave the dishes. I'll clean up in the morning. Do you need anything before Thomas and I go?"

"Did you keep any of my things?" Noire's deep baritone travels straight to my clit. I thought I was doing a good job of being polite, but knowing everyone is leaving to give us space sends a feral need through my system. I want to throw Noire across this table and take him.

Rein it in for sixty seconds, mate, Noire chides through our mental link. *I'm going to lose my mind.*

I struggle not to let out a whine as Thomas nods at Noire. "Your chest is at the foot of the bed in the first guest room. We've never opened it."

Noire chuckles aloud. "Good, I would hate to scandalize you both."

Thomas snorts. "Had a mating chest myself once, you know…" His voice trails off as he looks at me, but I sense he's happy and relieved. "Do you need anything else, alpha?"

Noire doesn't turn to look at me but shifts in his seat, leaning forward. "I need a piercing kit, Thomas."

Maya muffles a giggle behind the back of her hand as my head whips to Noire. "A piercing kit?" *What the fuck are you talking about*, I scream into our bond. I know better than to question him aloud; he's my alpha. But a piercing kit? That's a big hell no from me.

Noire doesn't bother to respond as Thomas turns from the kitchen and disappears into the depths of the dark house. Across from us, Maya sucks at her teeth and holds in a smirk, refusing to meet my eyes as I glare daggers at the side of Noire's fucking face.

I start tapping my nails against the kitchen table, but I don't miss how Maya's eyes fall to the unusual black tips before Thomas comes back into the room, carrying a small wooden box. "Everything's here, alpha. I don't know if there are any fittings though."

"Thank you, Thomas." Noire's voice is a thanks and dismissal all at once as he turns in his seat toward me. I barely notice Thomas and Maya leave quietly out the front door. Instead, everything in me focuses on Noire, on the way his pupils overtake his iris as he leans forward in his chair, setting the box on the table.

I'm going to bed, I hear in my mind. It's Jet. *I'll catch up with you both tomorrow?*

Bed is the perfect idea, Noire purrs back into our family bond.

Ugh, don't start with a play by play. I don't want to hear it.

I snort, but a moment later his voice rings softly through my mind again. *I can't reach Ten through the bond. I can't feel him at all.*

Noire growls but speaks down the bond to both of us at once. *Tonight we will rest and regroup. Tomorrow we get the fucking disks out and make a plan to retrieve our brother. I will not stop until we get him back. You have my promise, Jet.*

Thank you, brother, Jet whispers back to us. *Night.*

Distress and longing snake their way along my bond with my alpha. I reach up to run my fingertips along his forehead, smoothing out the wrinkles from his scowl. "We have a few more tricks up our sleeves, alpha. I'll do everything I can until we get him back."

"I need to claim you," Noire whispers. "Bond you to me for good. Tomorrow we will plan for everything else." He reaches out, stroking my cheek as I lean into the touch, purring like a godsdamned cat in heat. My mate chuckles as I slide off my chair and into his arms, straddling him as my hips rock up against his hard length.

"I'm mad about the piercing kit, but I want you," I grumble into his lips as he throws back his head and laughs, a deep laugh I haven't heard from him yet. I love it, and I want more of it, this bright and unbridled joy.

The moment Noire's neck is presented to me, I lean in and bite my way up it, his laugh morphing into a groan as he brings his claws to the front of my suit and shreds it with two swipes. The top half of the black fabric falls away as Noire hoists me higher in his arms, bringing one nipple to his warm mouth and biting hard enough to bring blood welling to the surface of my skin.

Hissing and moaning, I punch my hips against him, a moan rising out of my throat when he tugs my nipple between his teeth, standing with me wrapped around him. Noire holds me with one hand, and grabs the kit with the other, heading for the front of the house. He takes the stairs easily, still nipping and sucking at my chest. At the top landing, he heads right, down a long hallway, up another few stairs into a room with a steep angled ceiling and tons of windows.

I can't take the time to enjoy the simple beauty of the room because all I want is my mate, undressed completely in front of me. A thread of sorrow is still buried in our tether, a reminder of how much we lost tonight. But I want us to claim one another, to grow in power and tear Rama to shreds, once and for all.

Noire tosses me into the bed roughly, smiling as I bounce and yell through our bond.

"Every little bit of sass will earn you a punishment, mate," he purrs, letting the vibration travel through the room. His promise lights me up as I arch my back on the bed, shimmying out of the remainder of my destroyed suit.

"Promise?" I whisper as he chuckles. When I'm fully naked, Noire drags me to the edge of the bed, pressing my legs open as his eyes devour me. Already, slick wets the sheets, dripping out of me as he licks his lips and breathes, heavy and deep.

My mate leans over me, holding my thighs wide as he licks a path straight up my core, my scream echoing off the rafters.

"Godsdamn, Diana. You're so ready to be claimed."

"I am, mate. Please." I'm begging at this point, but I've wanted him for years, and the scent he's giving off makes me want to eat him alive. We're as safe as we can be, for now, while Rama licks her wounds. The horses will stand guard. And I *need* to take my alpha.

Noire nibbles at my clit, sucking it into his mouth as one hand strokes my entrance. And then he stands and stalks out of the room through a different door as I whine and protest. The sound of water cutting on hits my ears as I hop to a stand and growl, following him into what must be the bathroom.

My mate pulls his shirt over his bulky frame and crooks two fingers at me. "Come, Diana."

"I'm trying to!" I shout back as he laughs again, that same deep belly laugh I'll never get enough of.

"And come you will, dozens of times before I'm done with you. But we both smell like the fucking maze and the roses and the vampiri, and I want to smell nothing but you and me. I don't want the distraction or the reminder."

"You did promise me a bath at the beginning of this adventure," I huff out, crossing the room into his arms as he purrs.

"You have a need, omega, and I'm going to fill that need. You won't leave this room wholly unsatisfied. I promise."

"Do you always keep your promises, alpha?" I snark back as Noire's smile falls, fingertips gripping my chin hard as he turns my face up to look right into his eyes.

"I don't make promises lightly, Diana. Which is why I can promise you now that we will take Rama down together. We will find Tenebris and bring him home. And you will not leave this bathroom without screaming my name."

So many promises. So much to do lies ahead of us.

The warmth of Noire's mouth over mine surprises me. His kiss is far from gentle, a demanding push that forces my mouth open as he sucks on my tongue and nips at my sensitive, still-bruised lips. Blood wells along the cuts and bruises at the corners of my mouth as Noire groans and licks the blood away.

He lifts me bodily, setting me in an ancient claw-foot tub, hissing when he steps in after me. The water is scorching hot, but Noire is gentle as he soaps a sponge and commands me to turn. I sink my back into his chest as he rubs the sponge along my shoulders, cleaning the dried blood from his and the maulin bites. He rubs soft circles along my arms, my chest, using his fingers to part my legs, and washes there too. He's careful around the still-healing bullet holes, the hot water burning my sensitive skin.

And then he pushes me forward to scrub my back and the base of my neck. His breath tickles along my skin as I pant and whine. He's so close, so warm, so hard behind my body. Reaching between my thighs, I grip his cock and nestle it between my folds so I can tease myself as he washes me.

Noire's first grunt of pleasure encourages me as I rock my hips along his length, reveling in the way his piercings tickle my swollen folds.

My mate pours water over my hair and turns his attention to that next, fingers rubbing at my scalp until I'm gasping at every touch. Truthfully, I'm half a second from coming right here in the tub, all over his thick cock. And he's barely teasing me. When he punches his hips against me, rocking himself between my thighs as he reaches with one hand and pinches my clit, I do come.

The wave of pleasure hits me as my back bows off Noire's chest, his fingers still tugging at my clit as his dick rubs between my legs. I can't tell if I'm screaming or just gasping for air as my body lights up from the inside, hot tingles traveling down my spine as I struggle to make sense of it.

When my orgasm fades, I fall back onto Noire's chest with a huffy pant. "That was...so good, mate," I gasp out as he reaches down, taking my hand and placing it on his cock, rocking his length through our joined hands as he groans.

"We're just getting started, my queen." Noire's whisper against my neck lights me up as he fucks himself through my fingertips, grunting as he gets close, and then stopping to shift us both up out of the tub.

I whine with need as Noire wraps me around himself, dripping water as we fall into the bed. Without further preamble, he parts my thighs and slides in, burying himself to the hilt with a deep growl.

"Mine," he snarls, snapping elongated fangs into the air as his jaw clenches. Noire falls forward, pulling my left knee with him for a deeper stretch as I moan underneath his big body. I'm caught under him, taking his thick cock, his knot already swelling between us.

"I'm going to pierce you tonight," Noire growls, nipping at my chin before turning his attention to my nipples. "First here and here, and then down below."

"Fuck no," I bark out as Noire pulls out of me. "No, Noire..." I cry, desperate to feel his incredible knot lock us together.

"You get to pierce me too, mate," he growls, reaching for the box on the bedside table. He rummages around in it before turning to me with a glittering needle, a curved half-moon-shaped gold trinket attached to the end of it.

"Why?" I bark. "Is this a thing alphas do? My father never gave me that particular talk."

"Mhm." Noire chuckles, pulling out and flopping onto his back on the bed. "Get on my face, Diana. Ride me, and I promise I'll make it good for you."

"I think the good is gonna stop the second you stick me with a needle, but we'll see," I grumble as I straddle Noire's neck.

He slaps my ass with a deep growl, eyes sparking as I yip and move my hips forward, settling them on his stubble. Noire brings one hand to my ass, playing with it with his fingers there as his tongue slides along one side of my clit, fire traveling to my core as his other hand plays with my nipple.

My mate brings me to the edge over and over and over again until he's covered in slick and I'm ready to scream and demand things. And then I feel the needle, the sharp prick at my nipple, and searing, burning pain as he slides it through the sensitive skin, tugging until the bearing is firmly lodged. At the same time, he sucks my tender clit into his mouth rhythmically, sending me into an intense wash of orgasm just as the bite of the piercing dulls to roaring pain.

I rock my pussy against Noire's face as I ride out the orgasm, heat and pain and pleasure confusing my system as I scream. Does it feel good? Does it hurt? Noire is all of those things. But as the orgasm fades, he groans, and even that threatens to make me come again.

"Good girl, Diana," he purrs, tapping at my tender nipple with two fingers. "Take a look at the first of many ways I'll claim you tonight."

Panting for air, I look down at the golden, glittering half-moon piercing that enters one side of my nipple and leaves the other. I'm wholly unprepared for Noire's teeth to close on my nipple, sucking it into his mouth before tugging gently with his teeth.

"Owwww..." I scream as pleasure and pain rocket through my system, warring with one another at the forefront of my brain.

Noire nips at my other nipple then, and before I can protest, he slides a needle through that one too. I pant at the heat and sting as he reaches into the box, twisting a second half-moon piercing onto the end of the needle. He sucks my clit into his mouth again before pulling the piercing through and tossing the needle onto a bedside table.

The moment that's done, he flips us so he's on top again, rubbing his cock through my folds as he groans. "I need you at least once before I pierce this." His fingertips come to the nub between my thighs as I spread my legs wider. My nipples hurt like a bitch, but he feels so good. I'm confused, horny, and needy.

"You're going to run out of things to pierce, Noire," I growl as my mate smirks at me.

"Oh, I think you'll find me highly creative about the various types of pain I can inflict on you, mate."

I grumble again as Noire leans forward and bites his way up my tummy and chest until his beautiful lips find mine. His tongue demands expert entry into my mouth, taking and possessing until I don't know where he stops and I begin. The first pressure of Noire burying himself between my thighs has my body producing enough slick to drown someone.

I grunt into the kiss when he bottoms out inside me, his knot partially swollen.

"I need to claim you, mate," he murmurs. "We'll get to the piercing later, I think."

"Good," I bark as I push up onto my elbows and throw my head back. It's a plea and an invitation, and I'm ready to beg when Noire simply chuckles and presses greedy, teasing nips to my neck.

"Gods, Diana. You smell so fucking good." Noire's voice loses some of its command and takes on a raw edge as he thrusts rhythmically between my thighs. His lips, his touch, his incredible thick cock–they're all sending warring sensations through my brain.

Noire collars my neck and flips us in one smooth move, parting his thighs for leverage as he grips a hip and starts punching up into me. This angle hits differently, stroking along a different part of my walls, and an orgasm builds fast as I clench around my mate.

He groans as if the connection isn't enough, not nearly enough. Wrapping both arms around me, he hops to a stand with me still impaled on him, trying my best to get friction and get off.

Stalking across the room, Noire thrusts me up against the plate glass windows that overlook the city, tugging my arms above my head in one of his big hands. Black eyes travel down my chest, his lips curving into a wicked smile as he looks at my new piercings.

"You're bleeding, Diana. And the sight of that pretty red blood does things to me."

"Wanna lick it off and make me feel better?" I pout for my best effect as he laughs, capturing my mouth again.

The first hard punch of his hips shakes the window, rattling the glass with its intensity. Noire grunts as he does it again. All I can do is be captured in his arms, taking what he's got, Noire's particular brand of violent dominance. Through our bond, I send him my desire, my need, the connection I've felt for years waiting for him. I think about all the nights I went to my bed with my toys and hands between my thighs, thinking only of him.

Need builds between us as sensation and emotion overtake Noire. He's all gnashing teeth and clenched jaw as he works my body like an expert, bringing me to the very edge. He'll fall with me, locking us together.

"Noir–" I gasp out, his name cutting off as an orgasm hits me with the force of a hurricane, my head hitting the glass as he leans in. My mate's mouth descends on that sensitive flesh where my neck and shoulder meet, fangs sinking deep into the muscle as he roars into the claiming bite. Hot seed bathes my womb as Noire's knot balloons and locks us into place.

His voice is ragged against my shoulder as he clenches harder into the bite, pain rocking through my system along with his incredible pleasure. The orgasms are a continual tidal wave of fire as he rocks into me, coming and biting, cementing us to one another for the rest of our lives.

When Noire releases the bite with a gasp, my hands fly up to the wound. It hurts like a bitch, but touching it also sends pleasure straight to my clit, causing me to rock hard against him.

"Easy, mate," Noire growls. "You're knotted, and you could tear if you're not careful."

"I can feel you," I whisper, searching his face, flushed from pleasure.

Noire pulls my hands down from over my head, placing them over his heart. "I feel you too, mate. Deep in here. Where you belong."

I'm half-tempted to make a joke about him going soft on me with those sweet words, but I'm a little scared he'll decide to get into more piercings if I do that.

Noire laughs as if he read every thought. "I haven't forgotten about the piercing, Diana. It's happening because I want it."

"And if I don't?"

"You will," he counters. "You get off on my dominance, mate. The day I stop pushing you is the day a crack rocks our foundation. I will always strive to be at my best for you."

"I think I'm gonna cry," I tease, wiping a pretend tear away as Noire throws his head back to laugh. But something about seeing that muscular neck sends heat through my core, and I lean in to bite him hard.

Noire grunts as my teeth sink in, his hands going to my hair. "Claim me too," he whispers, letting his head fall to the side, eyes fluttering closed.

I release the bite and look at his neck, running my fingertips along it, looking for the perfect spot. "Maybe I'll just leave you hanging. It's kind of cute to watch you waiting for me like this." Another tease. I'm probably going to get punished for poking the bear.

But Noire simply smiles. "Don't think I'm not counting every time you sass me, Diana. I've got plenty of piercings in that box…"

Leaning over, I find the perfect spot along his collarbone and sink my fangs into his hard muscle, pouring my want and need into our bond. Noire bellows, pushed into release by my bite, rocking me hard against the windows as connection burns bright between us.

Feeling his pleasure sends me over the edge with him as I bite harder, reveling in the blood that wells to the surface of his skin, dribbling into my mouth. He's all dark temptation, pure sin wrapped up in a big, dominant package. Deep in my mind, I recognize a more fervent need for his blood, and I assume it's because of the vampiri spirit. I want to suck Noire's deep richness into my mouth and revel in his taste.

We come together until that sharp need fades, his knot deflating as I retract my fangs from his muscle. He's bruising already, but I bring his fingertips up to skate along the edges of the mark. He groans at the way it feels to touch it. Our claiming bites will be an erogenous zone for us going forward.

When I lean in and nip at the bite, Noire shudders and grunts, dropping me to the floor long enough to spin me so I'm facing the windows. "Hands up high, mate," he snaps as both of his come to my waist, lifting me back up until I'm crushed against the cold glass. "I'm gonna finish this night the way I started it, Diana," he groans. "Buried in your ass, fucking you within an inch of your life."

The first press of his cock against my back hole has me clenching, but Noire nips at my shoulder. "Open. Relax."

His cock sliding into my ass prompts a pained grunt from me. He goes far slower than the first time he took me here, but I've taken a lot of abuse this evening. When he shifts out and back in, that pain dulls to throbbing pleasure. A mewl leaves my mouth as I press my hips back into him.

Noire chuckles as he slides back in. "There's nothing like your ass, Diana. Hot, perfect, so fucking tight around my cock. Look out at the city while I fuck you, mate."

I struggle not to let my eyes roll back into my head, looking out the window at the glittering, dark high rises of Siargao.

Out and in, Noire slides, his growl turning into a deep groan of pleasure. "This city was mine, Diana," he grunts, rocking hard into me as I pant in response. "Now, this city will be ours. We'll destroy Rama, and we'll make Siargao something new, something better."

"Yes, alpha," I beg. "More, I need your knot again. I need your bite."

"You're gonna finally get that rut you were angling for," Noire growls, crowding me hard against the glass, teeth grazing along my shoulder as his thrusts take on a faster cadence, my hips crushed against the cold surface. "I will burn this world for you, omega," he whispers into my ear. "I will destroy everyone who ever hurt you, whoever forced you into something you didn't want. And then I will rebuild my kingdom with a throne for you to rule from."

Another orgasm hits me at his words, the city disappearing behind my eyelids as I throw my head up against Noire's. He bites my neck and shoulder over and over, all claiming bites, all bruising and bleeding as he comes with me.

When that finally fades, Noire bathes me again as my head lolls. I'm done. Absolutely done. He tucks me under his chin in the bed and strokes my back until I fall asleep.

I wake in the morning to find Noire between my thighs, sucking and licking with a devious hint to his gaze. He brings his head up just long enough to wink at me. "Hand me the piercing kit, Diana."

Not bothering to disobey, I lean over and hand it carefully to my mate as he sits up, slick coating his face. Noire wipes it off his mouth and rubs it along his chest and neck, over the black bruises of my claiming bite.

Fierce pride rockets through my system when I look at him. This incredibly powerful alpha male, locked to me for all time.

"All mine," I growl as Noire's dark eyes find mine and light up.

"Always," he agrees. "Now spread those legs for me, mate."

CHAPTER TWENTY-FOUR
JET

I thought I'd sleep for days after we escaped from the maze, but between coming off the uppers and my terror for Tenebris, sleep eludes me. Noire is in the house next door, fucking Diana six ways from Sunday, having a great time, I'm sure. I can't begrudge him this happiness. Liuvang knows he deserves it, and I'm sure he's thankful he'll never need to have a marriage of convenience.

Lying in a bed in one of the guest rooms, I growl. It's early morning, and I'm done attempting to sleep. I need to move. My body is sweaty, my palms clenching and unclenching themselves as pain hits my core.

I've been on uppers for seven years, and we lost my bag with the uncrushed bottles somewhere in the pine forest. The next week or so is going to be a fucking hellscape of pain and night sweats.

Snarling, I hop into the shower to wash the sweat off, then dress and go outside for some fresh air. Faintly, I hear Diana screaming Noire's name from next door. Gods, he must really be working her over.

The main street is already busy and bustling with people commuting or doing whatever they do now that Rama rules everyone. That needs to change. This city didn't run scared when we were in charge of it. It didn't look frayed and desecrated around the edges the way it does now. Ayala pack ruled with a heavy hand, and we took plenty. But we kept people safe, and we kept order. We committed every crime imaginable, but the city thrived because of us.

I sense Renze come onto the porch, despite how quietly he moves. He stops next to me, looking both ways up the street before leaning against the brownstone's half-wall. "Couldn't sleep?"

I grunt my assent, not turning to look at him. We did things in the maze, deeply sensual things that awakened something in my soul. I had a lot of sex in the Atrium, Rama's clients using me for their shows, for their own pleasure. But I took the uppers so I wouldn't have to feel.

And then Renze and I kissed, and something clicked and changed in my chest. Even now, it's twisting its way through me, making me want more.

"I feel it too, *atiri*," he growls, taking my hand and spinning me to face him.

I yank my hand back immediately, growling at him. "There's nothing, Renze. What happened in the maze should stay in the maze, all right? I don't know what an *atiri* is but don't call me that. I don't want anybody getting ideas about us."

Hurt and anger flash across his face before he frowns. For half a second, I feel guilty, but I squash it down. "We have a lot of work to do to take Rama down. We need to find Tenebris and the truth about Diana's brother. Let's focus on that."

"If you say so," he growls before leaning into my ear, a shudder racking my body when his breath tickles my skin. "I'll give you the space for now, but we aren't done with this conversation, alpha."

I growl again when movement catches my eye. Across the way from us, a woman exits a brownstone, dressed in a simple wrap dress that highlights her thick curves. Renze pivots to watch her at the same time I do, his lips still too fucking close to my neck.

She pauses at the bottom of the steps, green eyes flicking from me to Renze and back again. She cocks her head to the side, assessing, before catching herself staring and turning to move up the street. I watch her go, even when I feel Renze's eyes on me, asking a question with his gaze.

When she rounds the street corner, she passes a man who stands just in the shadows. They nod at one another as she walks by, but he doesn't watch the beauty go as we did. Instead, he looks at me, eyes locked onto mine.

He's an alpha, a pack alpha. That much is clear from the aggressive stance and the eye contact. He steps out of the shadows, and I get my first look at him. Tall, taller than Noire by a bit. Thickly muscled. The next thing I notice is a jagged scar running from one side of his neck to the other. Someone slashed his throat, but he survived.

Renze follows my gaze and growls. Before I can say a word, I'm down the steps and heading toward the alpha with Renze at my side.

The alpha smirks, sliding both hands into his pockets, then turns and heads into the busy street. Renze and I pick up a jog, but when we get to the corner, there's no way to see him among the crowd.

"Who the fuck was that?" Renze barks, running both hands through his dark hair.

"I don't know, but a pack alpha for sure. I have no idea what's changed in the last seven years, but it looks like we have a lot to figure out. Like who the hell even lives in Siargao anymore." I dislike being out of the maze and not recognizing my city. There could be new packs in charge; anything could have happened. Already, people are watching us now that we've returned. This is just the beginning, really.

Renze cocks his head to the side. "We will figure it out, *atiri*. I feel we should tell Diana and Noire, but they are still busy."

Grimacing, I turn. "We'll talk to Thomas about the city later. You can hear Noire from here?"

Renze smiles. "Vampiri kings are able to spread pleasure among us all when they experience it themselves. Diana probably doesn't realize she's doing it, but we've all been buzzing since last night."

"That explains you trying to get all over my ass then," I grumble as Renze's smile falls. He purses his lips but follows me back toward the brownstone as irritation and anger swirl away in my gut. We're not out of the maze a full day and it begins.

Siargao is its own unique brand of maze, just in a different way from the one we came out of.

Renze stares around at the quiet side street before opening the door for me. "Welcome to the maze, level two," he grunts in a sarcastic tone as I sail through the door, bellowing for Noire.

Level two indeed.

~

Half an hour later, Noire and Diana emerge, my brother looking happier than I've seen him...well, ever. Even before the maze. There's a lightness to his step, and the way he pivots to keep an eye on the omega is shocking. It's like they're magnets, perfectly attuned to find one another in a room.

It terrifies me. There's never been something for Noire to focus on other than Oskur, Ten, and me. And now, Ten is gone. Oskur is gone. There's just me. And Diana.

Noire was less than thrilled to hear about the alpha we saw and grilled me within an inch of my life while Diana bathed somewhere in the depths of their room.

Now I'm standing on the stoop outside Thomas' house, watching my alpha lead his mate out of the kitchen and toward the front stairs. Renze stands across from me, silent in the porch's shadows. He hasn't said much since this morning, but I can tell he's anxious to do something, anything, now that we're out.

Noire opens the door and pulls Diana out, smiling as he tilts his face up for the beautiful Siargao sun to warm it. "Godsdamn, it feels good, brother." When he turns to me, I see a smile I haven't seen since we were children.

Noire is happy. Truly happy. Despite what lies ahead of us.

"I think it feels a hell of a lot better for you two than the rest of us," I grunt. Noire chuckles and pulls Diana into his arms, sliding his tongue into her mouth suggestively. She sinks into his touch, ignoring Renze and me. Over Noire's shoulder, Renze's dark lips part, eyes on my brother and his mate.

"Liuvang-be-damned, keep it together, would you?" I snap at Noire. "We got out. What's next? Rama won't take this lying down, if she survived."

"Oh, she survived," Diana murmurs. "She's too much of an asshole to simply die on us. She was deeply injured, though, and she'll need time to recover. I suspect she won't want to risk Paraiso since the horses already attacked the city. So she'll pick apart the one she got to figure out how to disarm them."

"Why wouldn't she just blow this whole place up?" Renze asks. It's something I've been curious about as well. "With one word, Rama could probably destroy us. Why hasn't she?"

The frown lines around Diana's pale eyes deepen. "She thrives on playing with peoples' lives. Plus, we've got the horses. She didn't see that coming, so I suspect she's trying to learn more about what else my father might have created before she takes another step."

I glance up the street to where one of the horses stands at attention. It gazes up and down the street as if it's alive, and a shudder travels down my spine. "It's creepy as fuck," I murmur as I scowl back at Diana.

She huffs out a laugh. "I never knew what Rama held over my father for her to force him into architecting the maze. But I knew he would never leave Dore and me completely without protection. The horses were his way of looking after us in any way he could, knowing he wouldn't always be around."

"You had a much different childhood than we did, omega," Noire whispers into her lips.

"All alphas don't have to be asshole fathers," she murmurs back, nipping at

Noire's lower lip. He closes his eyes, sinking into her caress until finally opening them and turning to look at me, his stance all alpha command again.

I fall into it the way I always do, straightening my shoulders and spine, standing tall next to him just like we used to before the maze. "What do you need, alpha?"

"I want to bury Oskur before we do anything else." Noire's voice is all alpha, but there's a thread of sadness that sinks like a dagger into my chest.

"Do you want us to come help?" Renze asks from the shadows. "Or would you prefer to do this with your pack alone?"

Noire turns to the other warrior. "It would honor me if you came, but if everyone is still resting, I understand." I don't think I've ever heard Noire say anything so...thoughtful.

Renze dips his head. "We will be there, alpha."

"Even the kids?" gasps Diana, whipping around toward Renze. There's an odd moment where she pauses, cocks her head to the side and then relaxes.

Understanding passes over Renze's face. "Are you remembering vampiri customs, Chosen One?"

Diana shrugs. "I'm not accustomed to Cashore's presence in the back of my mind, but hopefully Ascelin can help me."

"I would be happy to," Ascelin says, emerging from the house next door and leaping over that porch and onto ours, settling herself in the shadows next to Renze. He turns to her with a soft smile.

"Get some sleep, Asc?"

"Not hardly," she barks back. "I cannot stop thinking about what Rama might be doing to Ten, how she might try to use him against us. And I am sorry. Sorry that we could not save him."

Noire snarls, but it's not directed at the warrioress.

"I echo that sentiment," I bark in response to my brother. "Let's go bury one brother and make a plan to retrieve the other. Others," I clarify, looking at Diana. "She will try to use the information about your brother to hurt us."

Diana frowns. "She has used Dore to hurt me for years, Jet. It can't stand in the way of us getting clear of her once and for all."

We head for the main street as Diana smiles. "How about a walk, alpha? You can see your city once more, and the people can see you and know you're back."

Noire nods and looks at me.

As always, I know what he needs without asking. I walk beside Ascelin, Renze taking up a position across from us as the vampiri begin to file out of the house. In a group, we walk through the riverside streets of Siargao's river district. The scents of the wild jungle surround us–wet leaves, brightly colored birds, raindrops everywhere. So much has changed, and nothing has changed. It's disconcerting.

For half an hour, we walk until we reach Diana's apartment. She stops in front of the door, looking at the bao vendor across the street. I watch her blink slowly, twice, a big smile crossing her face as he leans his head back and laughs. It's clearly a signal of some sort. "Chat later?" she asks the man.

He glances at Noire, and the smile falls a little. "Later, Diana. It seems you didn't share everything about your plan with us."

Diana nods. "I'll find you."

I have questions. Many, many questions. But we'll get to those as soon as we bury Oskur.

There's a resistance of sorts, Diana whispers into the family bond that more easily connects us all now that Noire bonded her. *We should meet with them as quickly as possible.*

I follow Diana and Noire up the stairs to the second floor of a shitty, shabby three-story apartment building. It's seen better days. When we ruled the city, we were controlling assholes, but nobody lacked basic necessities. Nobody lived in run-down homes. Noire put our pack first, but Siargao thrived under his strict rule.

Angst curls in my stomach when Diana opens her door and strides across the room, yanking her television stand out of the way. Noire follows her, keeping an eye on her open patio window and glancing around the apartment. He's keeping an eye out for her.

Diana yanks a panel off the wall behind the stand and pulls out a box.

It's small. It's horribly fucking small. "Oskur's in...that? All of him?"

Diana shakes her head. "I don't know if it's all of him. Gods, that's fucking horrible to say. But there are hundreds of bones here, so it's got to be close...."

Noire and I stare at the box like it's a viper, but he reaches out first, opening the box slowly. The first fucking thing I see is a skull, and I know it's Oskur immediately. He was in a terrible accident as a child, and there was always a knot in his skull afterward. There's clearly a lump in this skull in exactly the same place.

Anger and the need to rage fill my chest until Noire comes across the room and presses his forehead against mine, getting right up in my space. "We will avenge this, brother," he whispers, wrapping his hand around my wrist and pulling my hand up to his shoulder. "I will never let her do this to Ten. We will get him back. And we will honor Oskur's memory. I need your help to do that. Are you with me?"

"Of course," I bark. "You know that."

"I know that," he repeats, using his fucking alpha purr on me. "We need to let you detox off the fucking uppers, and we need to make a plan. But right now, we're going to bury our brother. Come on."

Noire stalks out of the apartment as Diana crosses the room and threads her fingers through mine. Blue eyes are filled with tears, and as the first one falls, I'm compelled to reach out and brush it away. She's Noire's, which means she's ours—our pack's. Diana is Ayala now. I will care for her as if she were mine because she belongs to my alpha.

"I'm so sorry, Jet," she whispers.

"Let's go, omega," I bark, smiling when she lifts her head high and lets me tug her out the door to follow Noire.

When we get outside, the vampiri line the street, and the citizens of Siargao have filled the street too. The neighbor across from Diana's building, the guy with the bao shop, raises his fist high in the air above his head. "We stand with Diana!"

The rest of the people take up the chant, and my heart clenches as the city chants for her, Noire smiling as he watches her hug the neighbor and a few others who come out of the crowd to greet her. Whatever this resistance is, it's clear the city is in support of it, and Diana is somehow a huge part of it all.

Renze falls in behind me as Diana plays the politician, greeting the people and chatting. Noire cuts it short after about five minutes, turning to stride up the street with Oskur's box under one arm and Diana's hand wrapped in the other.

The vampiri follow us, and most of the fucking town does too, until we get to the graveyard at the end of the Riverside District. Up here, the hills start to roll, and skyscrapers pepper them. The wealthy live there. The people who took from us.

I snarl as we turn into the graveyard. Two shovels stand up against a tree. I grab one, and Renze grabs the other. When Noire moves to take it, Renze shakes his head. "Let me, alpha. Let the vampiri show their support of this new, joined pack." There's a moment where Noire says nothing, and I expect him to bite the vampiri's head off, but he nods and takes a step back, reaching for my shovel instead.

"Let me, brother," he whispers. "This is not your burden. I am responsible for Oskur."

I don't hand it to him though. "Step back, Noire. I've got it," I bark. Because I do. I couldn't save Oskur in the maze, and I can't save him now. But I will bury him.

Renze and I dig in silence for a quarter of an hour until there's a hole big enough for the box that holds Oskur's bones.

I'm surprised when I hear the clicking of the maulin foxes from the maze, but Diana murmurs and hisses to them, and they surround our group as we lower the box into the hole. One of the foxes trots forward, dropping a small bone into Diana's open hand before hopping up onto her shoulder and sitting like a damn bird.

We cover the box back up with dirt, and Noire speaks the words all alphas use to encourage our spirits to pass to the next life. "Oskuredad Ayala, may the goddess receive you. May she keep you. May you run free in the Dark Forest, Liuvang-blessed."

I choke back an angry bellow at my brother's death. A sniffle reaches my ears, and when I look over at Diana, tears roll down her cheeks. She stands stiff and tall next to Noire, her fists balled as she looks at the small grave. The fox on her shoulder leans in to rub its cheek along hers, the same way alphas and omegas do.

I told Diana once that nobody had ever surprised me in my life. And it was true–until her.

All I know is that, whatever comes next, I want Noire and Diana by my side for it. I want this new pack in all its glory.

And I will kill Rama and return Tenebris if it's the last thing I ever fucking do.

THE END

JET: A DARK SHIFTER ROMANCE
TEMPLE MAZE LEVEL TWO

MONSTER GUIDE

While I made up some of this world's monsters, a few are loosely based on existing entities. For the sake of those not familiar with monster lore, I'll quickly lay out the monsters you'll see and hear about in this book.

Vampiri - humanoid with exceptional senses, incredible speed and occasional psychic ability. They are pale-skinned with black claws, lips and fangs. Vampiri are venomous and drink blood.

Manangal - loosely based on the mythical filipino manananggal, a vampire-like winged creature that could separate it's lower half from it's upper to fly in search of prey.

Maulin Fox - I made these up, knowing I wanted something between a cat and a dog, but utterly wild and blood-loving. Tiny black foxes whose jaws split open to lock onto their pray and drink blood.

Naga - Half human and half cobra, naga have humanoid upper bodies with a flared hood behind a distinctly snake-like face. Their lower half is that of a snake.

Gavataur - I made these up. Vaguely humanoid body with two arms and legs, but very tall and thin with saggy skin and a bull head, complete with horns.

Ancient, wilder forms of the more modern minotaur. They are cannibalistic and non-communicative with hybrid monsters.

Velzen - Velzen are the vampiri court's version of a guard dog. Imagine a thinner version of a greyhound and fox mixed together, but all black with occasional white spots

Mermaid - We're not talking about Ariel, y'all. These mermaids have long, spindly limbs, rows of razor sharp teeth and hair/scales in all the beautiful colors of the sea. The mermaids in this book are carnivorous and hunt anything they can.

Meju Dragons - Tiny, carnivorous dragons that hunt in packs. They look sweet but they are mighty dangerous!

Volya - Volya are ancient creatures from deep within the Tempang Forest. Ten feet tall, their bodies are thin enough for their bones to be visible. A wide mouth features rows of conical teeth. Where eyes should be, a flat expanse of bone crosses their foreheads and then curls up and behind their heads. Horrifyingly, they've got leathery, claw-tipped wings as well.

PRONUNCIATION GUIDE

Renze - renz (like friends)
Tenebris - TEN-uh-briss
Achaia - uh-KYE-uh
Noire - Nwar (rhymes with car)
Diana - die-ANNA
Cashore - CASH-or
Ascelin - ASK-uh-lin
Liuvang - L'YOO-vang (like hang)
Vampiri - vahm-PEER-ee
Naga - NAH-guh
Gavataur - GAV-uh-tar
Manangal - mahn-ANG-ahl
Lombornei - LAHM-bor-NAI
Tempang - TEM-payng
Siargao - See-ar-GAH-O
Rezha - RAY-zhuh
Vinituvari - vin-IT-u-VAHRI
Deshali - deh-SHAH-lee
Dest - rhymes with west
Sipam - SAI-pam (like dam)
Nacht - KNOCKED
Arliss - ARR-liss

PRONUNCIATION GUIDE

Sante - SAHN-tee
Etu - EH-tu
Dore - Door
Velzen - VELL-zehn
Volya - VOLE-yuh

THE VAMPIRI COURT

REZHA PROVINCE

OASIS

NORTHERN DEST PROVINCE

NACHT

NORTHERN DESHÄLI PROVINCE

the Adventurous Furyk 2022

CHAPTER ONE

ACHAIA

I hover just inside the glass-paned front door to one of Thomas and Maya's brownstones. I suppose it's my brownstone too, but since I've only lived with my adoptive family for three years, I think of it as theirs. In the street outside, two half-clothed males fight. It's the same wicked, wild dance they do every day, practicing for the war to come. And like every day, I can't pull my hungry eyes from them.

Jet, the darker, brawnier of the two, shoves the more elegant male hard to the ground before leaping atop him to scuffle. Jet's weight alone is a weapon. He's all bulky, corded muscle, belying his direwolf shifter heritage.

Renze, the vampiri, is taller and leaner. There's a sophistication about him that's impossible not to notice. Something about the way he moves is different from Jet's efficient, deadly jabs. It's so smooth and practiced it could be slow motion.

Case in point. He punches Jet in the ribs and slides out from under the huge alpha gracefully, slipping upright with a shift so fast that my eyes barely follow. His long blond hair is braided along his scalp, like always, in an intricate series of twists and knots that must take hours to fabricate. It's beautifully perfect. Just like every other day, I wonder if the design means something. Each of the vampiri living across the street does it a little differently.

I'd swear Renze is a mind reader when he turns from the fight, all-white eyes locking onto mine. They're striking with no iris or pupil but still somehow horrifyingly expressive when one blond brow curls upward. Thin black lips split into a smile as he sidesteps Jet, grabbing the alpha's arm and yanking him into a brutal headlock.

Without moving his eyes from mine, Renze leans into the alpha's ear and whispers something, chuckling.

Jet roars in anger and throws Renze bodily over himself onto the ground, flat on his back. In a flash, Renze is up and on the alpha's back, punching him in the neck with ferocious intensity.

I clench my thighs together at the heat their sparring produces. It swirls in my belly, the juncture of my thighs throbbing as I watch them.

At that precise moment, a shadow appears at my door, startling me—the female vampiri, Renze's friend. I smirk as Ascelin peers in through the glass with a devious smile. "Open up, little one. I need to speak with Thomas."

The first time she popped up like that, it surprised the shit out of me. Now, I'm accustomed to the vampiri warrioress. She loves to tease me for watching the males fight. I haven't stopped though. Even now, I urge her wordlessly to get out of my way so I can keep peeking out the front door.

Ascelin clears her throat, drawing my gaze back to hers. Pure white eyes narrow at me as I swing the door wide, stepping partially behind it as I avert my eyes from hers. The vampiri are all intuitive, but Ascelin seems to see more than most, especially if I let her stare at me.

Stepping gracefully inside, she looks down at me with a small smile. She's far taller than me, over six feet, I'd guess. I press my back harder to the wall as she tips my chin up, forcing me to look at her.

"Do I scare you, little one? Even now?"

I lift my chin. "I'm not scared; I'm wary. I watched you in the maze for years." I don't look away from her. She's a predator, and turning my back will only make me look weak.

Her smile morphs into a wicked, haughty grin. "True enough. I have killed and eaten women just like you. We all have." She looks over her shoulder at the males still fighting in the street. "But I have had plenty of chances to eat you since we escaped, and I have not done so yet."

"Thanks," I laugh, jerking my chin out of her black-clawed hands, unsure why she doesn't just go find Thomas. She didn't come here for me, and I've got things to do.

Ascelin crosses her arms and cocks her head to the side. "Curious," she murmurs, scanning my face as if I'm a puzzle she's missing a piece from.

Just then, Thomas comes around the corner with a suspicious glance in Ascelin's direction. "Achaia, you alright?"

"She is fine, Thomas," Ascelin croons, slipping up the hallway in that horrifyingly fast way vampiri do. She's in front of me one moment, and the next, she's disappeared in a stream of smoke and mist all the way to the end of the hall.

Thomas gives me an apologetic look before turning to follow her into the kitchen.

A grunt rings out from the street, and I turn to watch Jet and Renze fighting. Despite my typical fascination with them, my mind wanders as it sometimes does. I wonder what Ascelin found curious about me today. She seems to make it a personal mission to figure out the puzzle of my life, but she can get in line for that. Sighing, I grab my basket from a low bench by the door. I've got chores to do.

Leaving for the market means I'll have to pass Jet and Renze. Lifting my chin, I gird my loins and open the door. I don't like to be the object of their focus. Oof, that's a lie—I like their focus a little too much if the wetness between my thighs is any indication.

Outside, the sounds of their fight are far louder, echoing between the row of brownstones I live in and theirs across the street. Deep pained grunts, angry growls, and furious expletives reach me. There's an achy place inside me that wonders what males like that might sound like in the bedroom. I'll admit to imagining it when I'm alone in my bed.

Heat spreads outward from my core as I force myself up the street toward the main road. The sounds of fighting stop, and Renze appears in front of me, dripping sweat and blocking my path. His pale chest heaves with exertion, although he relaxes enough to slip both thumbs into the wide black belt at his muscular waist.

"I'm calling that a win!" shouts Jet from behind us.

"Noted," Renze murmurs, glancing over my shoulder before returning his gaze to mine. "Your beauty astounds me daily, Achaia, but this day, you are especially radiant."

I never know what to say when the seductive vampiri compliments me. But he finds time to say something delicious at least once a day, sometimes two or even three times. I don't know what to do about it. I've never had a man, not that I remember anyway, and he doesn't seem like a smart choice for my first. Renze is a predator in every sense of the word. I think I'd need someone kind and gentle.

Goddess, I haven't responded. When I open my mouth to do so, Renze takes a step closer, his eyes falling to my neck. I can hear my heartbeat pounding in my ears, and his kind drinks blood. I probably look like a perfect, delicious snack to him. Rage rises in me as I think about how mad I'll be if he tries to–

He takes another step toward me, reaching out to collar my throat with long, black-clawed fingers. They squeeze gently as his thumb swipes over my thick lower lip.

"Where are you going, little one?" Such an innocuous question while he touches me in such an intimate way.

Reaching up, I grip his wrist to pull his arm away, but Renze laughs and brings a second hand to my throat, squeezing tight. He leans in, black lips tickling the shell of my ear as I shudder. Like this, his forearms are pressed to my chest. He's not warm like me, or like another male might be. His skin is neither hot nor cold, but his possessive touch does things to me. My large breasts brush his arms as he chuckles.

"Your blood smells of the sweetest berries, Achaia. Will you grant me a small taste? I promise it will only bring you pleasure." His resonant voice draws goosebumps to the surface of my skin as I shudder in his grasp. I don't mean to rock my hips against him, but he chuckles and nips at my ear. "Do that again," he commands, his mouth tickling the shell of my ear.

I release a breathy pant, unable to break the hold he has over me. But every inch of my body is on fire with a sudden, desperate need to break a dam somewhere inside me.

"Let her go, Renze," snaps Jet, appearing to my right. I didn't see him join us, but when Renze drops his grip and steps back with a frown, I risk a look up at him. Jet's fists are balled, his broad, tanned chest coated in sweat from their practice.

"I would not hurt her," Renze croons to the alpha. "You know this."

Jet cocks his head to the side, glaring daggers at the vampiri. "She did not ask for your touch. You're frightening her."

"Am I?" Renze turns back to me. "Because it seems to me that she aches for my teeth. Is that not so?"

Looking between them, I summon a backbone borne out of rising irritation. "I *ache* for nothing. If you're done inspecting me like a scientific specimen, I've got errands to run."

Jet shoots Renze an "I told you so" look as I sidestep the vampiri, walking quickly up the street. I push the desire in my core out of my mind, willing the slickness between my thighs to dissipate. Every time Renze approaches me, my body reacts in ways I'm unprepared for. I can't ask Thomas, and I won't ask Maya. This feels too personal, too intimate. As a human, I should be more wary of a growing attraction to two monsters. Maybe I would if I had any memory of my life before the last three years. As it is, I don't always react to things the way I probably should.

Growling out of sheer frustration, I cross my arms and hurry up the street toward the main road. Even this early in the morning, it teems with people bustling about their lives.

"There is a marked difference in the feel of this street, is there not?" Renze appears at my side, now wearing a tight-fitting black vest. He's so fucking fast.

I gaze around at the main road before nodding. "People are adjusting to Rama not holding sway over Siargao any longer. It was quiet when she ruled the maze, but now..." I trail off, wondering if I should not have brought up Rama's Temple Maze. The vampiri and shifters have only just escaped, nearly killing Rama in the process. She may be physically gone from Siargao, having fled in her sky city, but an edgy undercurrent remains nonetheless.

The city itself seems to be waiting with bated breath for the other shoe to drop.

Renze is quiet for a moment before speaking. "We failed in our mission to kill her, and she is a psychopath. It is only a matter of time before she seeks retribution." He says it so matter of factly that I have to wonder if living in Rama's Temple Maze for seven years stole his ability to feel emotion. It would almost have to, in order for the monsters she imprisoned to survive its halls.

Per usual, he seems to read my thoughts. "It is not that I do not feel, *atirien*," he muses, his voice low and lilting. "It is that I choose to focus on what I can control. Like now. I can accompany you on your errands."

"You don't need to," I hedge, shooing him away with one hand. I curse myself inwardly when he grips it and pulls my wrist up to his nose, breathing in deeply. His nostrils flare, the tip of his black, forked tongue slipping from between his lips to snake along the inside of my wrist. He lets out a contented sigh as he tastes my skin.

It's a move so intimate I scarcely know what to do with myself. Heat blooms outward from my core, my body tightening in anticipation of him. Gods above, I want to feel his tongue everywhere.

Long moments pass as he kisses his way up my wrist to the crook of my arm. Moments in which I long to flee from him, hoping that if I do, he'll give chase. What the hells is wrong with me?

Warm awareness spreads along my cheeks as Renze drops my hand gently. "You would like to play chase, *atirien*?" His voice is deep and gruff, less formal than usual. I wonder what he'd sound like unhinged in the bedroom?

"Are you reading my mind?" I don't realize I've asked the question aloud until Renze smiles, a cunning smile that tells me I'm walking into a trap.

"Let me taste your blood, and I will tell you."

"Ugh," I roll my eyes. "Never mind. I'll just work on the assumption that you are."

"Someday, you will beg me for it," Renze murmurs, folding his hands at his lower back as he turns toward the market. He looks back over his shoulder. "Are you coming, *atirien*? Or shall I whisper in your ear a while longer…"

CHAPTER TWO

JET

I watch Renze follow Thomas and Maya's daughter toward the main street. Her thick hips sway under the wrap dress she favors, and despite the fact I am not at all interested in sex with another person, something about her stirs me. Maybe it's the innocence in those big green eyes or the way Renze plays with her. She screams prey, but there's also a backbone there. I'm an alpha–I'm wired to hunt, and I sense she'd fight.

I haven't chased anyone since the maze, and I'm alpha enough to admit there's a part of me that longs for that.

A bead of sweat rolls down my face, and I swipe it away angrily. It's always fucking hot in Siargao, but this is hellish. In the Temple Maze, Rama supplied me with uppers so I could perform sexual acrobatics to please her wealthy clients. I've got seven years of that bullshit in my system.

My pack omega Diana risked her life to get thrown into the maze as our mark. She got us out, though, the clever little minx that she is. Now Rama's gone, licking her wounds, presumably. And there *are* no more uppers. Withdrawal is a fucking nightmare.

I head into my brownstone to shower. My body is sore from training with Renze every day, or maybe it's the withdrawal. I can't be sure, but I need to be at my best for the coming war. Rama won't take our escape lying down.

"Jet!" my older brother, Noire, barks up the stairs. "Get down here."

"I'm in the godsdamned shower, Noire," I snap back, unusually irritated. I imagine I'll hear him stomp up the stairs next, ready to remind me that he's our pack alpha, and as his strategist, he needs me for something. There's probably some fucking *strategizing* to do.

But right now, all I want is to feel clean. I haven't felt that way in years. The dirtiness under my skin goes much deeper than surface level.

There's a yip followed by a growl, and I hear Diana's voice. Noire's displeasure spreads through our family bond like wildfire.

"Good luck, asshole," I holler toward the open bathroom doorway, knowing Noire can hear me. He's lucky to have found a bond mate in Diana, and the additional power development accompanying their claiming has been wild to watch. She is hyper-aggressive with my brother, and she's getting stronger every day.

I love watching her hand Noire his ass. I never would have thought there'd be an omega who matched Noire's alpha dominance, but Diana is perfection.

I finish showering and step out, wrapping my bulky frame in a towel when she appears in the doorway with a soft smile. "How are you feeling?"

Pacing across the small room, I stop right in front of her and lean into the doorway. Alpha packs are usually affectionate, not that we grew up that way so much. Our father was a fucking asshole, and then Thomas and Maya had to take us in when he was no longer fit to lead. Still, I'm drawn to be close to my brother's mate, just as I'd be drawn to any omegas in my pack if Rama hadn't decimated it.

Diana reaches out and rubs my forearm gently. "You're kicking ass, Jet. I'm really proud of you."

Pressing my forehead to hers, I whisper so low it's barely audible. "I'm so tired, Diana."

"I know," she murmurs back. "But you're going to be fine. You'll be through this bullshit soon."

I pull away from her with a wink, forcing normalcy back into my deep voice. "Cashore telling you that?"

She laughs, a joyful giggle that I'm elated to hear. "When he died to save me, I thought sharing his spirit would be so weird, but I'm learning fast."

There's so much to unpack there. "Any new power developing now that you're half vampiri king?"

She shrugs, blue eyes crinkling as she plays with her long blonde waves. "I get glimpses of peoples' thoughts, and I'm reading emotion like Renze and Ascelin do. But that means I feel your exhaustion, brother. Noire wants to talk to you about the resistance. He'd like to go today. But take it easy, okay?"

I run both hands through my hair with a sigh. "There's a lot of work ahead of us."

"Mhm," Diana confirms. "Gonna be a lot of fun. We're gonna murder the shit out of Rama once and for all. That bitch will pay for imprisoning you and forcing you to kill for fun. I will never rest until she's gone. She hurt you."

"I adore this protective side of you," I admit as she slaps me on the chest.

"Good, because it's getting worse by the minute. If I had wings, I'd fly up to that fucking city and kill her myself."

That makes me laugh because it's all bluster. Rama may be psychotic, but she's also brilliant. So is Diana. She orchestrated a scheme of epic proportions to unleash us from the maze. Rama nearly died in the process, but she'll never let Diana's betrayal stand.

"Want to run with me later? I think I might finally beat you." Diana gives me a saucy wink, followed by an exaggerated waggle of her blond brows.

"No fair when you're channeling vampiri power," I complain, returning the wink. "But I'm certain I'm up to the task."

"Renze didn't give it to you hard enough this morning?" She's asking the question in that fucking way on purpose, knowing that Renze and I shared a degree of intimacy when we were escaping the maze. Diana is convinced there's more to it.

There's not.

"Out!" I bark, pushing Diana out of my way as I shove past her, her laugh following me up the hall to my room. I change quickly, holding back a frustrated whine when sweat immediately begins to roll down my face. Glancing into the mirror, I take a quick assessment of what I see. It's something I started doing in the maze to remind myself that no matter what, I'm still me. Nothing Rama forced me to do will ever change that.

I see my father in my dark eyes and my mother in the smattering of freckles along my shoulders. Father's near-black hair and tanned skin are something all of us Ayala brothers share. My eyes drift down, fingers probing at a scar on my stomach, courtesy of Rama's fucking goons. Shrugging off that particular memory, I dress and head downstairs. The kitchen sits at the back of the house, and I can hear Noire tapping his foot.

Vampiri younglings play quietly as an elderly omega, Maya, bakes cookies. Noire sits in a chair, his dark eyes on me as I emerge from the hallway. He's kind-ish to the younglings but not gentle with them like I am. Not like our youngest brother, Tenebris, would be if he was still here. I choke back a worried growl when I think about how Rama took him so easily from us.

Diana passes me and seats herself next to Noire, which is where I always used to sit. Now, I find a place opposite him as Thomas and Ascelin come in the front door.

"Where's Renze?" barks Thomas. "I thought he'd be here."

Ascelin purrs, needling Thomas with a grin. "He will meet us at the bao shop. Right now he is accompanying your daughter to the market." Thomas's eyes narrow as he sits in a chair, crossing his big arms as he gives Ascelin a look. I know that look. It's the "you better not be saying what I think you're saying" look he often gave me when he took us Ayala brothers in.

"If he hurts her…" his gruff tone trails off the higher his brows go up his forehead. I hold back a snort watching them.

"What will you do, Thomas?" Ascelin questions with a sadistic grin. "Rip my head from my shoulders? I would slice yours off before you even managed to remove your ass from your chair."

If he is threatened by Ascelin's harsh words, he doesn't show it. Instead, he smiles at her. "You would do well to remember whose home Alpha Noire came to when he needed shelter after your escape, vampiri. Whose steady hands removed Rama's tracking disk from your arm so you could move about Siargao freely. I may not win a physical fight with you, but that doesn't make me any less powerful or important."

Ascelin's face falls as she lifts her arm, looking at the gouged flesh where Rama's round tracking disk was embedded. I've got my own healing scar from the same thing.

Fuck Rama and her tech. Fuck the Temple Maze and my time there.

I clear my throat, turning the attention on myself. "We need to do a few things in short order. First, we need to head into the Towers sector and see who's left. Rama left too fast to have taken her wealthy patrons with her, and they might know something about where she went. Plus, to fully retake Siargao, there can be no one left to challenge us."

Noire and Thomas nod in agreement before my pack alpha continues, "That's step one. As soon as we've got enough information to formulate a plan, we'll hunt her down and return Tenebris to our pack."

When he says it that way, it sounds simple. But the reality is far worse. We have no idea where Rama fled in her sky city, Paraiso, or what she's doing with Tenebris and the mechanical guardian horse she stole.

The possibilities are endless. And none of them are good.

CHAPTER THREE
RENZE

Next to me, Achaia walks stiffly with both arms crossed. A coping mechanism, it seems. One she often employs in an effort to discourage me from accompanying her—not that it would ever stop me.

"Achaia," I murmur, turning my head to watch as my voice rolls over her. Pleasure floods my system when goosebumps make their way along her arms, her nipples pebbling under the soft fabric of her dress. A pink tinge spreads along her cheeks and chest. I ache to unwrap every fold of that dress and reveal her naked figure to my hungry eyes.

After a heavy pause, she turns to look up at me, and I find myself lost in the depths of her green eyes. Every color of the sea is visible in the flecks surrounding her pupils. I have never been obsessed with eyes, but I am obsessed with hers. They narrow as she frowns at me.

"You're staring at me, Renze. Must you?"

"Oh, I think you know why I do," I chuckle, stopping in the road and tugging her against me. I wrap a tendril of auburn hair around my finger and pull on it. "I stare because you are breathtaking. I stare because I ache to taste you. I *stare*," I emphasize the last word as I lean in close enough to brush my lips along hers. "I stare because I'm imagining you tasting me."

She shudders and steps away, but my grip on her hair tightens as I wrap my fist in it, angling her head back. Achaia bends into my arms as I drag my teeth along the base of her neck. A breathless sigh escapes her plump lips as I nip my way up her throat. Her scent assaults me, rushing over me like a tidal wave. Heady arousal reaches me next, my emotive gift singing in response to her body's seductive invitation.

"Did you know vampiri gain strength from sex?" I whisper between us as those bright eyes land on mine, full of wonder.

"Is that why you're such a flirt?" she quips, suspicion evident on her delicate, round features.

"No," I confirm. "I court you because I want you, and I will have you."

"I'm not a conquest," she snaps back. "Something to be conquered now that you're free of the maze."

I live for the saucy side of her personality. It is hidden below many layers of skepticism, no doubt brought on by her lack of memory. She does not know who she is, so she struggles with her persona.

"*Atirien*, you are the *ultimate* conquest," I remind her.

Pale lashes flutter at the vampiri word. "You've called me that several times. What does it mean?"

I chuckle, dropping her hair as I clasp my hands behind my back once more, turning from her. "I will tell you another day, Achaia. Let us make a game of it. The first time you allow me to taste you, I will tell you."

She rolls her eyes. "Ascelin will tell me."

I quirk a brow upward and smile, but she trots up the street toward the market.

For a few minutes, we walk in silence. I take the time to admire Siargao. It is hot and humid here, unlike my home province of Rezha where it is mild year-round. Still, it reminds me of home in the way foliage spills from the forested hills all the way down to the banks of the Kan River below. In fact, foliage spills out of every crack and crevice in every ramshackle building in this part of Siargao. It's as if the forest is retaking the city, despite monsters, half-breeds and humans taking up residence here.

Brightly colored birds call out above our heads as I soak in the sun, smiling when it warms my pale skin.

"I would have thought vampiri hated the sun," Achaia muses aloud. "But you seem to enjoy it—like a lizard."

"The lizard comparison is not far from the truth," I murmur. "Vampiri are cold-blooded, so we adore the sun. Although I'll admit my favorite time of the day is when the moon is at its peak. We are creatures of the night, although we do enjoy a good sunbathe. Naked, preferably."

Achaia sighs as if my constant attention is absolutely exhausting, but the scent of her arousal still lingers in my nose. Anticipating her is the most fun

I've had in years. I cannot wait for that blessed moment when she breaks and gives in to me.

"Why did Jet stop you this morning? I didn't think alphas were really bothered with consent." She doesn't look over as she asks the question.

The question itself shocks me, so that I stop in place, turning to face her once more. Her green eyes are wide and curious. I can tell her only some of the reasoning behind Jet's actions.

"There are parts of Jet's story that remain his to tell, Achaia. But I am sure you saw much of his experience in the maze televised, did you not?"

She nods once, clipped. "I've only ever seen the hunting and killing of the marks. There was more?"

"Much more," I whisper, thinking back to the horrors in Jet's recent past. "Within the maze, there was a room called the Atrium. A high-end bar for Rama's wealthy clients. It was a way for them to enjoy the maze's monsters without being in danger of losing their heads. The primary entertainment was sexual, so many monsters spent time in the Atrium, including me, but Jet was Rama's favorite. He performed almost every night, nearly all night."

"Oh gods," Achaia moans, her delicate hand coming to cover her mouth. "So, he was forced to have sex just so they could watch?"

I nod. "Imagine seven years of that, and perhaps you can begin to understand why the concept of consent is important to him now."

She nods and begins walking again, lost in thought. There is more I could tell her, how Rama threatened Jet hundreds of times if he didn't perform certain acts or service her rich clients. How she once speared him through the gut and forced him to fuck a dying man. Then there was the time she slid hooks through the muscles in his back, flying him over the audience high on uppers while his blood rained on the deep-pocketed fucks below, safe in a gilded cage. The number of times she hurt him is a permanent sickening tattoo on my heart. I cataloged every single one.

I will never forgive her violence against him. Of all the things I feel the need to get retribution for, Jet's pain is top of my list.

A somber cloud lies over Achaia, brought on by the response to her question. I follow her through the market, admiring her beauty as she completes her shopping for Thomas and Maya. It is not until she has acquired everything she needs that she turns to me with a renewed and curious expression.

"You and Jet seem close." She picks through bright yellow *vaya* fruit as I think about how to respond. Ah. Even now, she senses there is more to my relationship with Jet than simply friendship. My smart little female. I would love to tease her about how she spies on us when we spar, but I sense she is not ready for me to call out such a thing.

"We formed a friendship in order to escape." It's as much as I will admit to her in this moment because the truth would frighten her greatly.

I intend to have them both, and I will not rest until I do so.

CHAPTER FOUR
ACHAIA

I don't miss how Renze fell silent after I asked about Jet. I've spied from the shadows of the front door many times to watch them fight. I'm certain they know and also certain I don't care. The intensity between them is palpable compared to when Renze spars with others, even Ascelin. He's focused and intent in a different way when he spars with Jet, and when Jet goes alpha savage on Renze, biting and snarling, Renze seems to relish it.

I haven't missed the way Renze gets hard when they fight or the way Jet notices but ignores it. It makes me wonder about their history from the maze, but that seems so outrageously personal to ask. I want to, because I'm nosy, but I can scarcely imagine the horror of what they went through.

The events Rama televised nightly were enough to give anyone nightmares, enough to terrify our entire *province* into subservience. She ran Siargao with an iron fist until Noire and Renze's group escaped and freed us, albeit temporarily, from her rule.

Renze tickles my side playfully, causing me to yip and jump, whipping around to scowl at him. "I sense you have questions, Achaia. I would love to answer them, but alas, we are at my destination."

I look up as Renze smirks, pointing to a bao shop. Outside stands one of the giant metal horse statues that aided the monsters in escaping the maze. Diana's father built it to protect her, and now it protects the city.

Shuddering, I look up at the statue. It stands silently, and like this, it truly appears to be made of stone. It's not until Renze gets close that the horse turns, recognizing him. Renze gives it a curt nod and grips my fingers in his. He pulls me into the bao shop. Inside, I can hear Noire, Diana, and a few other voices.

Ascelin appears at Renze's side, a quick flash of dark smoke emerging as she leers up at the considerably large warrior. "You are late, Firenze. Noire is in a dark mood this day."

"Moody and dark are his state of being, Ascelin," Renze replies. "He is lucky the Chosen One is his mate, or he and I would not get along at all."

His comment brings me back to three years of watching the vampiri and alphas fight in the maze. They were enemies there, until they weren't. Somehow, they banded together to escape, and in doing so they became a united pack. I don't understand it, but I can hardly ask about it either.

Ascelin smirks before her white eyes flick over to me, her smile falling. "Why have you brought *her* to this meeting?"

I bristle at the condescension in her tone, but Renze simply laughs. "*Shef inrepit min-atirien*, Ascelin."

"What does that mean?" I bark.

Ascelin frowns, ignoring me. "Are you certain, Firenze? She is not strong."

Renze reaches out and wraps one hand around my throat, meeting my gaze with an intense stare of his own, a soft smile on his black lips. "I am absolutely certain," he says to me more than his fellow warrior. White eyes bore into mine when his lips part, and a forked tongue snakes out to lick at them.

I shift backward, although I can't escape his grip on my neck. Instead, I meet Renze's gaze with my own, lifting my chin as I ignore Ascelin's rude commentary.

It's true I can't remember my life, but I don't lack strength. I'm simply not a warrior like she is. I urge myself to remember that she has just spent seven years fighting for her life in Rama's maze. I'm sure I look like a mark to her.

Ascelin's glowers at us for a long, heated moment before she throws her head back and laughs, dark braids swaying from side to side as she turns and heads into the depths of the bao shop.

"I see your strength," Renze whispers, bringing his black lips so close they nearly touch mine. "I want you, Achaia. And I will have you."

I hiss in a breath at his seductive words. My body aches for what he willingly offers. I have more pressing concerns than mind-blowing sex, though. I know nothing of who or what I am, and I am desperate to find out.

Renze sighs, sensing my straying thoughts. Still, he wraps his fingers through mine and pulls me with him into the bao shop's dark storeroom.

Noire, Diana, Ascelin, Thomas, and Jet are there already. The shop's owner, Trig, stands at the head of a table, an aged map spread on the wood in front of him. I don't miss the hatred in his dark eyes when he notices Renze. I pull my hand from Renze's, but he simply steps closer until his hip touches mine.

"Do we need him?" Trig barks at Noire, who stands tall and growls at the human. It's easy to see Trig struggles against how impossibly dominant Noire is, but I sense he's trying not to look weak despite a physical disadvantage. It's always been this way, though. Lombornei is a mix of monsters, humans and half-breeds—the humans are always the lowest rung on the power totem pole.

"Every being in this room is here because I need them." Noire's command leaves no room to argue.

Renze smirks at Trig. "Did I kill someone you cared about?" His deep voice is haughty and dismissive, but Trig turns with a frown. My heart hurts for him when he balls his fists tight. I've known Trig for three years. He's polite and thoughtful; he's a kind person.

Trig growls, "You killed my brother in the maze. He was innocent. He should never have been thrown in."

"Did I eat him as well?" Renze's question shocks me as Ascelin chuckles. Noire glares from the vampiri back to Trig.

"We all killed in the maze. It was our only option. Trig, tell us about the Resistance." My heart pangs again for the shop owner. I don't know if I had or lost a family, but I've seen Rama throw plenty of innocents into the maze to be torn apart by her monsters.

The very monsters who are here in this room now.

Noire's omega mate, Diana, croons and rubs his chest with her palm. Apparently, she used to live across the street from the bao shop, so she was aware of the Resistance against Rama already. I've overheard as much listening to Ascelin and Thomas talk.

Thomas has done an admirable job teaching me about Siargao's inhabitants in the hopes it'll spark my memory. It hasn't, but in the process I've learned plenty about the Ayala brothers. Noire's the alpha, which makes sense —he's an over-the-top jerk. Jet is his strategist and is meant to look at all angles and help Noire lead. Their enforcer, Oskur, was killed in the maze. And the youngest, Tenebris, was taken by Rama during the fight to escape. The rest of their pack was killed by Rama when she threw the Ayala brothers into the maze seven years ago.

Jet speaks, interrupting my thoughts, and every head turns to him.

"We need to take care of a few things in order. We need to know what happened while we were escaping, from an outside perspective. We need to retake Siargao so Rama lacks access to our resources. Finally, we need to make a plan for finding and killing her. Every day we remain here gives her time to reverse engineer Diana's horses and show up with better weaponry."

I've wondered about this myself. The giant metal horses that now guard the city are under Diana's control. They were instrumental in the final fight that allowed her to free the alphas and vampiri from the maze, but Rama was able to capture one. I know Thomas is incredibly concerned about what she'll do with that remarkable feat of engineering. She cut power to the entire continent seven years ago, throwing Lombornei back into the dark ages. Now she controls everything.

Trig nods, pulling his angry gaze from Renze. "The Resistance had no hope of overcoming Rama when she was physically here, so our focus was on building information networks. We have connections in every province at this point, including the very edges of Deshali, Rama's home province."

Diana huffs out a laugh. "But how do you communicate? Rama controls all the tech; she cut Siargao off long ago."

"That's true," Trig agrees. "But it's possible to travel if you wait for the right time. I have ventured to Dest and back twice. As of now, information comes slowly because it requires someone to physically go from province to province."

"Who knows if the information is even accurate by the time you do that," Noire snarls, shifting forward to look at Jet. "What do you make of this, brother?"

Jet's hands tremble slightly as he clenches them into tight fists and crosses his arms. I know coming off the drugs Rama pumped him with has been challenging. I'm dying to know more about the quiet, broody alpha. I'm in awe of his resilience, especially in light of what Renze shared earlier.

"We don't have a choice, Noire," Jet responds. "After we clear the Towers and find out what we can, I think you and Diana should go to Dest and seek allies. On the off chance anyone else from our pack survived, there's a possibility you'll find them there."

"You don't plan to come with me?" Noire looks surprised.

Jet's eyes flick over to Renze, who steps forward and points at the Rezha province on Trig's ancient map. "We will go to the vampiri court in Rezha. While I do not relish parting from the Chosen One, the vampiri nation is large. They would make formidable allies in the fight to come."

Ascelin cocks hers sideways as she considers the plan. "I will accompany the Chosen One, of course."

Jet looks toward Trig as he crosses his enormous arms. I zip my lips tightly shut to avoid gaping at the way his forearms pop with muscle. "We need to learn more about Paraiso. How did Rama build it? How does she power it? How do we take it down and get access to her? I see only two possible paths forward—we take the fight to her or wait for her to bring it here."

Trig gasps. "Let's not do the second of those things. If she brings the fight to Siargao, there will be nothing left once she's done. I can help with information about Paraiso. A vampiri came through here once, claiming she knew of the being who created the sky city. He calls himself the Builder."

"And what happened to this vampiri? Why did she come here?" Renze's voice is deeply skeptical as Trig turns to him with an apologetic look.

"She came to see about releasing the vampiri from the maze, she claimed. But after several days of inspecting the maze island from the mainland, she left. At the time, she said she was going to the Builder next to learn what she could about Rama. We never heard from her again, though. That was a year ago, maybe a little more…"

Ascelin growls as Renze sends her a heated look. It's clear they have thoughts about what Trig is sharing, although they don't enlighten the rest of us. Next to me, Renze is frozen but tense as Trig continues on.

"She had a theory that the Builder lives in a compound in the northern part of Rezha in the sand country. I can point out a general area on this map, but that's all I've got. Over the last year, I've had operatives agree to go look for this compound. Unfortunately, no one has ever returned."

Thomas sighs and crosses his arms, looking at the map. "That does not bode well for us. Plus, northern Rezha will take days to get to. I've got an old aircar I can lend you if you insist on this path forward, but I dislike this plan."

Jet rolls his shoulders, cracking his neck from side to side. "Our plan is incomplete, but we lack critical information. We'll do the best we can with what we've got."

I wince at his words but don't necessarily disagree. Rama's heinous clients paid to send people into the maze. They did it for political extortion and fun. They did it so they could drink and watch the maze's monsters rip their marks to shreds. And then Rama televised the whole fucking thing every night to scare an entire continent of people into submitting to her will.

If anyone can take her down, I have to believe it's this group. I've never seen Noire kill anyone, but I can imagine the bloodbath it would be. I wish I could say I ignored the television every night when it powered on to broadcast the nightly hunt. But the truth is I was glued to the scene every time, fascinated by the maze's prisoners and how they stalked and massacred so easily.

I've watched Renze eviscerate a man and eat his innards as he screamed for mercy. This room is filled with dangerous, heartless monsters. I don't know what it says about me that I'm enthralled by them and not half as terrified as any sane person would be. For all I know, I could be worse than all of them put together.

CHAPTER FIVE
JET

We settle on a plan to go up to the Towers, the glittery skyrise sector of Siargao. Huge buildings rise out of the thick, wet forest to kiss the sky. I used to love living there, looking out over the entire hilly valley and down to the Kan River, running all the way down to the Lon Bay.

We say our goodbyes to Trig, and the rest of my pack heads out of the bao shop.

A scent breaks through my thoughts then, a delicious scent. A scent I've tried hard to ignore since I first became aware of it a week ago. It reminds me of a gentle sea breeze, lemons, and deep water.

Our group dissipates, and I move quickly around the table to walk behind Achaia. It's her; I know it is. That fucking scent. It's beautiful and comforting and calls to me on a primal level. I want to ignore it; I want to ignore *everything* sexual after seven years of performing in the maze. But Achaia's scent flips a switch in my brain.

I wonder how much more potent that scent is in the hollow at the base of her neck or between her large breasts. I'd wager it's strongest between her thick, juicy thighs. My mouth waters as my fangs descend. Renze turns to me with a knowing smirk. When his white eyes flick back to her, the smirk grows into a full grin, although he says nothing.

The tall vampiri steps out into the sunlight and throws his head back, breathing in the smells of the Riverside district. We're closer to the Kan here, so it's all fried fish, salty bao, and river water. I fucking love it, even after living in the Towers. Riverside always felt more normal to me, people simply living their lives without politics. The Towers was a maze of its own, filled with the rich fucks who catered to our pack before Rama screwed us and threw us into her Temple Maze.

Next to Renze, Achaia lets out a little chuckle and slaps his arm playfully. "Okay, lizard. Can I get back to my errands now?"

Renze laughs as he tilts her chin up, stepping closer to her.

My blood heats; he pushes too hard. But then the smell of lemons explodes all around her, suffocating me as her hips angle toward his. Nipples pebble prominently under her wrap dress as Renze lets out a breathy sigh.

I clamp my hands on my thighs as I resist the urge to cage her in from behind, to press her to Renze and feel that round ass up against my cock. She smells godsdamned delicious—clean and inviting and cool.

"You may continue, *atirien*. But I will find you later." Renze's voice is deeply sensual every time he speaks to her. She's so obviously attracted to him, although she fights it. Any smart human would. We're monsters.

She nods once and turns from him, his eyes hungry on her as she sashays through the shop and out into the bustling street, shapely hips swaying.

"I see you've moved on from getting all over my ass." I hope the words don't sound like I care.

Renze turns and pushes into my space, our chests practically touching. He leans forward until his black lips are almost pressed to mine. I don't step away. Renze didn't scare me in the maze, and he sure as shit doesn't scare me now. How many times did we fight when we were imprisoned? Dozens. Maybe more.

The large vampiri smiles. "I would love nothing more than to throw you up against this building and take you, Jet. But I will never force something you are not eager to give me."

My godsdamn dick jumps in my pants at his words, despite my anger at him saying them. As if he could force me to do anything.

"I don't want that," I counter instead, bumping his chest with my own, an angry growl leaving my lips as they hover closer to his.

"You do," he counters, gritting his teeth as his white gaze meets mine. "Do you remember when I found you in the Maze Chapel, and I fucked your anguish away until you came in my hands? That was no chance meeting, *atiri*. Even then, I watched you."

It's one of my worst memories. That was the night Rama speared me and forced me to fuck a dying man, something one of her clients wanted. I nearly died from the injury, but she pushed enough uppers into my system that somehow, I managed to do her bidding. When she finally let me go, I stumbled to the Maze Chapel, hiding in a dark corner where the maze's cameras couldn't see.

I curled into a ball and sobbed my heart out before Renze showed up. I remember bristling as I leaped upright, trying not to show how obviously injured I was. My first thought when Renze found me was that Noire and Ten couldn't afford to lose another brother.

But then he tossed all his weapons aside and lifted his hands. White eyes met mine and I could see the understanding in them—not sympathy, never that—but recognition.

He wrapped both arms around me in the first and only hug I ever had in the maze. And then he threw me up against the wall and fucked all that pain away. He took my mind off how fucking dirty I felt. For a short time, I forgot I was stuck in the maze. It was the most connected, passionate sex I've ever had. We never did it again, but I'd be a godsdamned liar if I didn't admit to thinking about it all the time, even now.

Renze's deep voice breaks through my thoughts. "I will leave you with an enticing morsel to ponder for the rest of the day. *Atiri* and *atirien* are the male and female forms of the ancient vampiri word for mate. You and Achaia belong to me. And I will have you both. Not only that, but you will have each other. So, the next time you wish to bury your face in her hair and breathe her in, consider that it's because she belongs to us, alpha. Consider that I could take you while you take her, and we three could connect in all the ways that matter. We have a chance for happiness, Jet. Do we not deserve it?"

Heat floods my system at the vision he's dangling in front of me. Then my knees buckle—the fucking uppers still run rampant in my system, bringing about random moments where all the strength seems to disappear from my body.

I'm reeling from what he just shared. Mates? Hells fucking no. Not now. Not ever. There's a wholesale difference between wanting to fuck someone and keeping them forever. Taking a mate feels like something for future-Jet to worry about. Today-Jet is focused only on healing and rescuing Ten.

Renze says nothing more, but a low, throaty chuckle is his reminder that he's not done with this conversation. Sweeping gracefully past me, he heads out into the street and slips away.

For a moment, I pause and collect myself, willing the strength to fill my legs again. They're trembling, beads of sweat rolling down my face as I struggle to get my shit together. Growling, I shove off the wall, wiping the sweat off my brow. I jog to catch up with Noire and Diana. As always, Noire glances from side to side, always on the lookout for a threat. Diana walks with her hand on his back, inside his shirt, and I admire how beautiful they are together.

Bondmates. Most alphas don't get the chance for that, so they choose someone they can find happiness with despite not having a fated bond. I've only ever known one other pair of bondmates—my parents—and it killed my father when my mother died. Not right away, of course. But he went from distraught to angry to depressed, taking the four of us brothers along with him. Eventually, Thomas and Maya took us in when Father couldn't be trusted to raise us.

When Noire turned eighteen, he killed our father and took over leadership of the Ayala Pack and, eventually, all of Siargao.

I watch Renze walk up ahead. If, and it's a huge if, what he says about Achaia and me is true, I won't ever have a bondmate, either. Because the only thing I know for certain is that Achaia is not a direwolf omega. I scent no wolf under her skin, and she lacks the lanky muscularity of our kind.

Still, I refuse to be trapped or pushed into any sort of mating. I'm irritated by his words, though, because I did want to bury my face in those auburn waves and count the colors in them. They range from sunshiny-yellow to a deep, dark blood-red.

"Jet, want to run when it cools off?" Diana turns and walks backward, smiling at me.

"It never fucking cools off," I grumble, growling as I dab my forehead.

"Might as well get sweaty then, right? Well, sweatier…" Her happy tone pushes the ache in my chest away.

"Fine," I agree as Noire turns to glance back at me, snapping his teeth. It's his pack alpha way of reminding me that whatever his omega wants, she gets.

Without Tenebris here, our usual pack dynamic is fucked up. I should be next to Ten, with Noire bringing up the rear. That throws me into a spiral of worry for my youngest brother. We lost Oskur in the maze, and now Rama has Ten in her clutches.

Worry for my youngest brother hovers like a shadow over everything, pressure crushing my lungs when I think about how Oskur died. I can't let Ten meet that same fate. Tenebris is the best of us—the smartest, the kindest, and the most family-oriented. Noire and I are committed to getting him back, to giving him a chance for a full life.

I reach deep inside to turn that worry into anger. Anger will become action, and action is how we'll get him back.

When we arrive home, we split up to change. Minutes later, Diana and I stand on separate stoops, grinning at one another. She rolls her shoulders as she winks at me. "I'm feeling really fucking fast today, alpha. Think you can keep up?"

I snort. I've never failed to beat her when we run, but she's developing that wild vampiri ability to slip from spot to spot in a rush of wind. If she's as fast as Renze or Ascelin, she'll kick my ass.

Proving my point, she slips from her spot on Thomas' front porch down to the middle of the street, shimmying her hips in a little omega victory dance. I roll my eyes at my packmate. "This hardly seems fair, Diana."

"Fair has never been my MO, brother. I know you know that," she laughs back, slipping up the street as I sprint after her.

I follow my brother's bondmate through Siargao's humid, musty streets, keeping my eyes open for anything amiss. But there's nothing. No sign of a trap, no sign of anything to worry myself over. Even so, one of the horse statues canters behind us, always protective of Diana. I'll never forget that moment in the maze where she activated them with fire, and they came alive and saved our asses from a herd of gavataur.

Gods, was that just a week ago?

I lean harder into the run, thankful that my muscles are cooperating. I keep up with her for a long time, but eventually she pushes slightly ahead. We barrel through Thomas' sector all the way down to Riverside, along the Kan, until it empties into Lon Bay.

Diana slows as the maze island looms in front of us, just far enough offshore that I wouldn't risk a swim to it. Not that I'd ever fucking go back.

The horse trots up behind us before stopping next to Diana. There's a slight creak, and it freezes, looking just like a godsdamned statue again. Diana watches it with a soft smile. I'm sure she's remembering how her father created it when he was forced into building the maze for Rama. He did it to ensure Diana had protection if she ever got thrown in.

Which she did. On fucking purpose.

Diana flops down on a huge boulder and brings her knees up to her chest, wrapping both arms around them. Her face is pink with exertion, but she smiles up at me. "When you were still in the maze, I used to run when it rained. I always came down here to remind myself that I needed to get you out. And I'd talk to Dore."

Ah, her twin. The twin Rama used as leverage to force Diana into the maze. Little did she know Diana wanted to get in specifically to get Noire out. These days, we're unsure if Diana's brother lives or not, but I think she's holding out hope that Rama wasn't lying about that.

I look out at the tropical island, imagining the maze's dark halls far below the serene surface. "Think the monsters have killed all the humans in there yet?" I fold myself down next to Diana as she shrugs.

"Fuck all of them; I don't give a shit about the monsters in the maze still. There's not a single one of them who wouldn't have killed us, given the chance. But the monsters in Rama's stable? Some of those are sentient like us. I'd like to free the ones we can."

I give her a knowing look. "Have you spoken to Noire about it?" I'd bet my ass she hasn't, and that's why she asked me on this run. Divide and conquer is the oldest trick in the book.

Diana nibbles her lower lip and glances over with a beseeching look. "I haven't because I know what he'll say. That's why I'm bringing it up with you. Some of the monsters Rama held could be allies under the right circumstances. It can't hurt."

I consider the consequences of unleashing caged monsters into Siargao, but the reality is that Siargao is already full of hybrids and humans. All that aside, most monsters would probably return to their homes, given half a chance.

"Let me think about it. My first inclination is to agree with you."

Diana pauses for a moment, then agrees.

A sudden chittering noise reaches my ears, and Diana clicks her tongue in response. A tiny black fox trots out of the greenery to Diana's left and hops into her lap.

"The way they follow you is wild," I murmur as she sits the fox on her shoulder. Its tiny jaws unhinge and the lower one splits open, its teeth sinking into Diana's shoulder muscle as she sighs.

"If I hadn't befriended them like this, they wouldn't have helped us in the maze. We wouldn't have Oskur's bones to bury. They are teeny superheroes."

"They are." I laugh. "It's just crazy to me that you thought to befriend them."

"They're often underestimated," she murmurs, stroking the fox between the eyes as it devours her blood. "We can find allies in so many places, Jet, if we look for them."

Diana falls silent as the fox unlatches, hopping down onto her thigh to lick his lips clean. When he's done with that, he licks each tiny foot before nuzzling her stomach like a cat.

I click my teeth like she did, wondering if I can befriend the small animals the same way she has. Diana tickles her fingers along my knee, teasing the fox, who pounces on her hand and rolls over for a belly scratch. She grabs my hand, placing it on the fox's tummy as I rub gently. He's full and sated, still licking his lips as I stroke him.

A hissing sound comes from the bushes behind us, and the fox leaps up and darts away as Diana laughs. "Guess we only get one visitor today. Goddess, they're fucking adorable." Diana turns to me with a sad smile. "I'm so glad we're out, Jet. But sometimes, when I think about what lies ahead of us, I feel exhausted."

"Same," I admit. "But then I remember Ten and all the things he represents to me. I won't rest until we get him back because he's the only good one out of the four of us brothers."

Diana gives me a look, but I shrug. "Noire is your bondmate and my alpha, but he's a fucking asshole. Ten came of age in the fucking maze. He never had a normal childhood. He deserves so much more than he's gotten. He's a scholar, for Liuvang's sake."

Cocking my head to the side, I let the sun beat and batter my skin. It's so strong here on the southern end of our continent. I sigh before continuing. "We cannot rest, Diana. Not until we kill Rama and bring Ten home."

"I know," she gripes. "But I'm still fucking tired."

Laughing, I wrap my arm around her, letting my head fall against hers. We sit for a long time before jogging back home. The horse trails us, and I can't help but wonder what Rama's doing with the one she took.

CHAPTER SIX
ACHAIA

The following morning, I stay home as Thomas and Maya go across the street to help the alphas and vampiri prepare. Today, they go up into the hills to see if Rama left any of her wealthy patrons behind. Thomas agrees with Jet that while it's unlikely, there's a chance some of Rama's people have insider information that can help them form a better plan.

Noire is intent on fully taking back Siargao. Controlling this province means he'll control the rest of the continent since ninety-five percent of Lombornei's natural resources originate here—one of the reasons Rama took over seven years ago, from what Thomas has shared.

Anxious for something to do while everyone's gone, I head to my room and eye my wild hair. It hates the heat in this province, which leads me to believe that I'm probably not originally from here. Not that I can remember any detail of my life, despite spending the last three years desperately trying to jog my memory.

Frustrated, I sit in the chair in front of my mirror and part my hair. I've watched the vampiri braid their locks many times, and it's a little fascinating. I wonder if I can recreate any of their intricate designs? Biting my lower lip, I try a simple braid from my forehead down my hairline and up over my ear. It's easy to tuck back behind in case–

"It is stunning, *atirien*."

I shoot upright, whipping around toward my window, where Renze now sits, holding an apple in one hand and a knife in the other.

"A little warning that you're there would be nice," I shout, crossing my arms as the huge vampiri shrugs, peeling a chunky slice off the mottled red fruit. He stands gracefully and crosses the room, holding the apple toward me, still pierced on the end of his blade. White eyes meet mine as he takes another step closer, overwhelming me with his presence.

Renze touches the apple to my lower lip, grinning as his black lips part in a seductive smile.

Gods, I want to tease him, to play back like he plays with me. It's probably stupid, but when my eyes meet his, I know I'm about to give in to the heat. Just for a second.

I lean forward and lick my way along the thick slice of apple, not moving my gaze from his. His smile falters, black lips parting as his fangs elongate. I bring my lips to close over the piece of fruit and tug it gently off his blade. Renze lets out a deep, hungry growl and throws the knife without looking. It embeds in my wall with a loud thud as he wraps a hand around my waist and pushes me back.

One moment, we're standing in front of my mirror, and the next, we've slipped across the room, and my hands are above my head, my body pressed into the corner. Renze's hips are pressed firmly to mine, his obvious arousal rubbing against the front of my thin dress. My head falls back as he thrusts hard, snarling as he snatches the apple from between my lips and tosses it away.

His eyes lock onto mine as he scans my face for something. He pants as if it's taking all his strength not to unleash himself on me right here. When he takes my lower lip between his teeth and tugs, I lose any perceived ability of holding back. With an echoed growl of my own, I slant my lips over his and suck his tongue, swirling my own around the tip.

My gods, a kiss; my first one, maybe ever. Renze's cool tongue tangles with my own as he presses me harder into the wall, devouring me as if his life depends on it. He's masterful, pulling me into the kiss as his tongue plunders my mouth. It's all I can do to remain standing as my body tightens for him, desperate for more.

Renze is everywhere, his intoxicating scent overwhelming me as he takes and takes. I'm caught with my hands above my head, desperately thrusting my hips against his as he matches the movement, my ass bouncing against the wall from the force of our play.

It's not until someone calls his name from the street that he stops with a soft huff into my swollen, tender lips. "I must go, *atirien*. But we are not done with this." I imagine he's going to look at my body like he can't wait to tear into me, but he never pulls his eyes from mine. Instead, he leans in and presses a gentle kiss to my lips.

I resist the urge to close my eyes and sink into that kiss. When he nibbles softly at my lower lip, I give in and moan, pressing my body closer to his chest. I stifle a needy groan when Renze steps back, dropping my hands.

"Look what you did to me, *atirien*," he teases, pointing at the front of his pants.

Goddess help me, I look down to see his hard cock clearly outlined against his leg. Renze lets out a throaty chuckle and strokes it, a series of clicks issuing from his throat. He sounds so fucking pleased with himself that I have to laugh.

Someone calls for him again, and his brows furrow into an irritated scowl. He plants a kiss on the tip of my nose, then slips quickly out the window as I cross the room to watch. My core is on fire from the feel of Renze's giant body caging me in, taking pleasure in touching me. Gods, he was just as fucking good at it as I imagined he would be, even if my lips feel bruised by his. When he leaves, I'll have that memory to warm me at night.

The thought of him leaving and not being here to tease me every day sours my mood.

Down in the street, the alphas, Ascelin, and Diana all stand waiting. I can't hear any particular conversation, but Jet watches Renze join them. When they're standing side by side, Jet leans closer to Renze and inhales deeply, a surprised look crossing his face. When he looks up at my window, dark eyes flashing, I find myself unable to tear my eyes from his.

I wonder what he thinks about all this?

∼

Hours later, I sit in Maya's kitchen, helping her peel potatoes for dinner. A resounding bang jolts us as someone knocks on the front door, Maya leaping upright as she drops her knife. I stand and put an arm around her shoulder to steady her.

We turn toward the sound and see Renze through the glass panes of the front door with a man slung over his shoulder. Flying to the door, I swing it open and realize he's carrying Jet. My heart stops in my chest as I look him over. There doesn't appear to be any blood, thank fuck.

"What happened?" I demand.

"He will be fine," Renze murmurs to me, although tense lines dip between his pale brows. "Please come and bring smelling salts if you have them."

Without another word, he stalks across the street where the vampiri younglings play and into the brownstone next to Noire's. Well, technically Thomas owns this whole street, but I suppose it was Noire's before the maze happened.

I realize my thoughts are straying like they sometimes do when I'm faced with something unexpected. Frowning at that unfortunate trait, I turn, but Maya's already there with her medical kit and a large bottle of smelling salts under her arm. "Let's go, child."

We quickly follow Renze across the street and up the creaky stairs of the brownstone. I hear him in the last bedroom, the attic bedroom that's similar to mine across the street. Maya jogs through the doorway first; her hands pressed to her hips as Renze lays Jet out on his bed.

"What happened?" Maya questions the big vampiri.

"He passed out while we were at the Towers. I assume this is a side effect of his withdrawal period. He has been pushing himself hard, too hard." Renze's tone is bitter as he goes to the foot of the bed, pulling Jet's shoes off and tossing them aside. "Come, *atirien*. Help me."

"What do you need from me?" Maya asks, her tone softening as she leans over and strokes a stray dark hair from Jet's forehead.

Renze smiles gently at the elderly omega. "I require Achaia's assistance. We need only watch him and care for him when he wakes. I am aware you have other duties, Maya."

Maya glances at me and then back to the vampiri, so I put a hand on her weathered arm. "I'm fine, Maya. I promise."

She looks over at Renze, pursing her lips. "I'd lay a cool cloth on his forehead and change it continuously. He needs to slow down for a day or two. He's going to resist that, you know. Jet has been an extremely noncompliant patient ever since he was a boy."

Renze nods sagely as Maya lingers next to me. But with one final, concerned look in Jet's direction, she turns to leave. When she goes, Renze drops down onto the bed. "Help me to undress him, Achaia."

"Will he appreciate waking up naked?" I ask the question even as Renze reaches for Jet's shirt

"We do not have to remove every stitch of clothing, *atirien*, but enough to make him comfortable." Renze bends over Jet's chest, undoing each button as I chide myself for being thrilled at getting a close-up peek of Jet's muscular chest, covered in fine dark hair.

I help Renze roll Jet onto his side, sliding the shirt down his arms. When we lay him on his back again, I gasp when I see the puckered scar just below his ribs. It spiders out from an angry red center. I look up at Renze, who's staring bitterly at the wound.

"I thought alphas healed incredibly fast? Did he sustain this injury when you were escaping the maze?"

"No," Renze murmurs, "he has had that for quite some time."

Fury on his behalf fills me. I watched him murder people in the maze, but I have trouble reconciling this male with the one I regularly saw on my television screen.

Renze reaches for Jet's belt, unbuckling it. We slide his pants down to his ankles, and I fold them at the foot of his bed. He's left in nothing but tight briefs that hug his thick, tree-trunk thighs. I try hard not to stare at his beautiful, powerful form. He's hurting and needs help, and I can do that.

Jogging into the bathroom, I fill a bucket with cold water and grab extra washcloths. Renze waves smelling salts under Jet's nose, but nothing happens.

"Perhaps he simply needs deep rest," I reassure him as he frowns, taking a cloth from me and submerging it in water. He wrings it out and wipes sweat from Jet's neck and collarbone. Renze makes his way down Jet's chest and stomach as I lay a second cloth on Jet's forehead.

We sit quietly, changing his washcloths every so often. We sit long enough that the sun eventually travels across the sky, Jet's breathing deep and even. Eventually I realize we've missed lunch, and my stomach growls as I take notice.

Renze looks over at me. "I will bring food, *atirien*. Will you stay with him?"

I nod as Renze leaves the room. A crazy racket next door lets me know that Noire, Diana, and Ascelin have returned from their work in the Towers. I'd be concerned about some of the screaming, but everything about Noire and Diana is wild and untamed.

Renze returns with two bowls of chilled soup as I lean over Jet again, replacing warm rags with fresh, cool ones.

"How long will he be like this?" I question the imposing vampiri. "Not just passed out right now, but withdrawing from the drugs?"

Renze frowns. "I believe this to be the worst of it. Jet has pushed hard these last days, so his body is forcing a shut down and reset. When he wakes, I am hopeful he will be vastly improved."

There's a sudden rustle, and Jet curls onto his side, although his eyes don't open. I lean down to look at him, willing him to wake and be alright, but instead his arm snakes out to the edge of the bed, his fingers touching my knee. When his fingertips brush against the fabric of my dress, he grips it and wraps his fist in it, resting his forehead against his fist.

Renze and I watch with bated breath, but even like this, Jet doesn't wake up. We eat in silence, watching Jet's broad shoulders rise and fall with deep, even breaths. His mouth is slightly parted, his chocolate hair sticking up in every direction. Like this, the look on his face is almost childlike. It's a struggle to remind myself that Jet is a shifter—he's dangerous for a human like me.

The tricky thing is, I've never felt in danger around him or Renze. I just feel...*enthralled* might be the most accurate word.

Eventually, Thomas joins us to check on Jet and remind me of my evening lessons.

"I'll skip them tonight," I offer, looking at the sleeping male, still peacefully holding onto the fabric of my wrap.

Renze shakes his head. "Do not skip on Jet's account, Achaia. I will watch over him."

Thomas smiles kindly at me. "How about we do our lesson downstairs? That way, you can come back quickly if Renze needs any help." I know he can sense my indecision, and he's throwing me a bone. It's been hard to feel truly useful in my new life, but Thomas is always quick to help me in that regard.

Thomas turns from the doorway, and Renze stands and rounds the bed. When he grips my throat, my head falls easily backward, baring me to his hungry gaze. Renze's lips come to the hollow at the base of my throat and he kisses me once, gently. "I'll find you if he wakes, *atirien*. He will be just fine."

I let out a soft chuckle. "What does *atirien* mean, vampiri?"

Renze steps back with a haughty smirk, blond brows arched high as he thunks the tip of my nose. "Remember our deal, Achaia. When you invite me to taste you, I'll tell you."

"I never agreed to that," I chirp, reaching out to thunk him back. Before I can even comprehend that he's moved, he's in my space, my arms both wrapped around his neck as he takes my lips forcefully, just like he did in my room.

Time loses all sense of meaning until a helpful throat clearing from the direction of the stairs reminds me that Thomas is waiting.

Renze and I part, and he slips back to the opposite side of the bed, grinning at me as he changes Jet's rags once again.

Sighing, I turn from the males who have captured my fascination so easily, and head downstairs.

Time for the godsdamned lessons. Usually, I insist on them, desperate to learn anything that might help me figure out who I am. But right now, all I want is to be upstairs with the monsters who should terrify me but don't.

Shit, maybe that's a clue about me, and I'm a monster, too.

CHAPTER SEVEN
JET

I'm floating in the sea, surrounded by cool water and the comforting sounds of waves lapping softly on the shore. There's no pain, no angst, and no worry. Everything smells of saltwater, right down to the sand underneath my palms.

Except, there's no sand. As I become aware, I feel a wet sheet under my hand. And then reality crashes in on me, pain flooding my system as I grunt and surge upright.

"Easy, Jet," Renze croons as I fling a hot, wet rag off my face. It hits the wall and slides down to the floor with a squishy thud.

"What the fuck happened?" I bark, struggling to stand as Renze places two cool hands on my shoulders and urges me to lie back. The look on his face is a mixture of concern and relief.

"You passed out when we raided the Towers. I carried you home, and you have been resting for hours. Please relax; your body is processing its trauma. You–"

"Don't tell me what I need," I snarl, shuffling upright, pain lancing through my stomach so hard that I double over and fall to my knees. I'm going to puke. And puke I do, explosively and violently, as Renze rounds the bed and hands me a bucket without a word.

Frustration builds as I snatch the bucket from him. I'm a godsdamned alpha. I'm Noire's fucking strategist. I cannot afford moments of weakness, not with what's coming in our future. Not with Ten's life on the line.

I fucking passed out? I don't even remember…

"I must find Ascelin," Renze murmurs. "Please relax. Achaia will be back soon." He slips silently out the open door, leaving me to the tornado of thoughts spinning around in my brain.

Achaia.

My muscles quiver and give out when I attempt to sit up again. Gods-damnit. Groaning, I flop back onto the bed, setting the puke bucket down. I lay there in utter misery until I can't stand it any longer. I don't need Achaia to come help me stand on my own two fucking legs. Hauling myself into the bathroom, I shower and throw clothes on before heading slowly for the stairs. My body is a limp noodle. Weakness isn't something I've ever had to deal with. I'm a strong-as-fuck alpha in my prime.

Ten is counting on me, so I shove the weakness away and push myself to make it to the top of the stairs. I stop there, gripping the railing so hard it splinters. I need a moment to collect myself before I figure out what I missed.

Cocking my head to the side, I listen, cataloging the house's sounds like I always do. Outside, the vampiri younglings play in the street with some of the adults who escaped with us. Downstairs, I hear Thomas talking about...geography?

With my interest piqued, I struggle slowly down to the first floor and pause outside the kitchen, peeking in.

Achaia sits stiffly in one of the kitchen chairs, her hands folded in her lap as Thomas points to a map in an ancient-looking book. Her back is to me, long auburn hair curling down over the seat. It swishes side to side as she taps one foot rapidly against the floor. Ah, she's irked by something. I find myself curious about what.

Thomas has a gentle look on his face, one I remember seeing many times when he tried to knock sense into us Ayala brothers. "While the Tempang Forest is not technically a province, we treat it as such when we think of geography. Since it occupies the entire northern section of the continent, it forms an effective border between the forest, its dangerous monsters, and anywhere else."

Achaia nods, but it's clipped. Thomas looks at her, seemingly checking in before he continues, "Northern Rezha borders the Tempang and is home primarily to the vampiri courts and the sun-loving monsters, naga, and the like."

"What other monsters love the sun?" Achaia questions, leaning over the map to study it.

"Why?" Thomas asks, his voice taking on an urgent tone. "Do you remember something? Does the idea of the sun seem familiar to you, child?"

"No," she whispers, slumping back in her chair. "I find it interesting, but I can't think of a memory correlated to the sun. I've got nothing, Thomas."

"You have no memory?" I don't mean to ask it aloud, but Achaia whips around in her chair, red hair falling in a sheet over her shoulder as seafoam-green eyes find mine. I knew she hadn't lived with Thomas for long, but not that she had no memories. I'm intrigued. I wonder if Renze knows this about her? I'm sure he does. Discomfort settles in my gut for some fucking reason.

"That's right," she responds, a tight, fake smile on her face as I join them, falling into the chair at the head of the table. I'm fucking exhausted from simply coming downstairs.

Thomas stands and pours a cup of coffee, sliding it across the table to me as Achaia continues leveling me with a cautious smile. Finally, Thomas speaks. "Achaia, may I?"

"By all means," she mutters. "You've got more details than I do."

My surrogate father pours her a cup of coffee, adding a touch of heavy cream before placing it near her hand. She takes it with a slight nod of thanks as he settles back into his chair. "Three years ago, our daughter had an emergency with one of her pups. We heard there were smugglers helping people out of Siargao for a price. We managed to get to our daughter and stay for a time, but on the way back, we came across a small caravan of mercenaries. They had Achaia strapped to a table inside a cage, hoping to smuggle her somewhere. I'm old, but not too old to kick a little ass, and they were simple humans. We brought her back with us, and she has been here since."

Seven fucking hells.

The story is shocking and weird, and I have a million questions.

"Why smuggle you?" That's the first and most obvious one.

"I don't know," Achaia says despondently. "I don't remember that. My first memory of my life is waking up in Thomas and Maya's house, asking where I was."

Thomas nods. "That's right. And each day since then, we talk about the provinces and Lombornei's history. We pore over every book in my library, hunting for something, anything, that might jog Achaia's memory."

"So, is Achaia your real name?" I sip the fresh coffee, willing it to work its way into my system and kick my ass somehow.

She shrugs, green eyes flickering down to the tabletop, where she picks absentmindedly at a gouge in the wood. "I don't know. Apparently, I repeated it over and over and over when Thomas found me. So that's what I go by now."

"Why bring her back here?" I question Thomas. "Alphas aren't known for our savior complex." It's a rude question, and she blanches when I ask it, but this story is a little too unusual for my liking. If Noire came across a group of smugglers, he would simply carry on.

Thomas smiles. "I could not leave her. She needed our help then, and we were happy to give it. I won't stop until she's able to regain her history and memory." He shoots me a wry look. "You may remember me taking in four scrawny alpha boys when their own father became too drunk to care for them. It's entirely possible that *I myself* do have a savior complex."

I chuckle at that. He's not wrong. He raised us when Father couldn't, then wouldn't. Good riddance to that fucking asshole.

"How are you feeling?" Achaia asks, turning the attention from herself to me.

"I've been better," I grumble.

"Let's get you back upstairs, then," she offers. "I'll grab more washcloths."

"I'm fine," I bark, even as sweat starts rolling down my face again. Achaia rolls her eyes but stays seated, not giving in under my dominance. She's right, though; I need to get back upstairs. I'm woozy from the journey down. Stupid. This is so stupid.

I stand and grip the table's edge to keep my knees from buckling. I've got to fucking get it together. We have things to do, pressing things like murdering Rama and rescuing my brother.

"You're not fine," Achaia says kindly, rounding the table and wrapping her arm around my waist. "Come on." Her hand is up under my shirt, finger splayed across my skin. It's an intimate touch, but I don't hate it.

I sense Thomas' dark eyes on me as I let her lead me out of the kitchen and back upstairs to my attic bedroom. By the time we get there, her sea-breeze scent fills my nostrils, and my dick is getting hard. It sways heavily against my thigh as we reach my room. I practically fall onto the bed, and to my embarrassment, my cock juts straight out, clearly visible, even through my jeans.

Achaia glances down before heading to the bathroom. A flash of pride hits me at the way she looks at my dick, but then I gasp when pain stabs between my eyes. Wrapping an arm over my forehead, I grit my teeth as sweat pours down my face.

She returns with a bowl of cold water and washcloths as I urge the pain to go away. When she reaches over to place a washcloth on my brow, her large breasts brush along my chest, pulling goosebumps up along my forearms and shoulders. I let out a groan. Lemons. She smells like lemons. A sudden need to know if she *tastes* like lemons overwhelms me.

"Leave me," I bark, unable to look into her eyes. I don't want to see sorrow there—or understanding. I don't want to see pity. So I snarl and snap at her fingers as she yips and takes a step back.

Achaia gets right in my face after the outburst, gripping my chin as she glares daggers at me. "Listen up. I've been here all day caring for you because you're fucking healing after going through hell. It would be nice if you did us all a favor and chilled the fuck out, so you can get better faster. You can't rush it. If you could, you wouldn't have passed out today during a godsdamned operation. So simmer down. Am I clear?"

I'm fucking shocked at her show of dominance, but my own rises to match hers. Reaching out, I grip that long auburn hair in my fist and drag her on top of me, snapping my fangs in her face. I nick her chin, blood welling up along the cut to trickle down her neck. She lets out a gasp and brings her hand to her face, swiping at the sticky red blood as her expression morphs from surprise to fury.

"Don't presume to dominate me, Achaia," I purr. "I'm a fucking alpha. I do the dominating." Her mouth is nearly pressed to mine, caught like she is with her hair around my fist. Goddess, she's so fucking soft pressed to my body like this, those plump lips hovering so damn close.

"Oh, yeah," she purrs, ignoring my fangs. "You did a shitload of dominating while passed out and thrown over Renze's shoulder like a limp rag. Great job, *alpha*."

Embarrassment and rage war in the forefront of my mind as I consider whether to bite the shit out of her, spank her, or just toss her out of my room. While I'm mulling it over, she yanks her hair from my fist, shoves off my chest and heads for the door, throwing the pile of washcloths in my direction. "Do it yourself," she snaps, the command in her tone rolling over me as my hackles rise, my wolf threatening to burst forth and chase her down for the insolence.

I snarl as she leaves, with my dick still leaping in my pants at the way it felt to manhandle her. My libido didn't die in the maze. I've always been the horniest of the Ayala brothers. But after everything Rama forced me to do, I can't stand the thought of someone touching me if I haven't asked for it. Still, my dick is weeping from the lack of attention.

For a long moment, I stand in the doorway and listen to her stomp down the stairs, huffing about rude-ass alphas. The front door slams, and I seriously consider chasing into the street to drag her back to my room and have her like a caveman.

The desire comes and goes like the stab of a knife. I'm not ready for a woman to touch me in pleasure.

I lock my door. I need to get off, to feel good, and that interaction with her has my dick pulsing. Ripping my clothes off, I cross the sparse room and flop onto the bed. Thanks to my nightly acrobatics in the maze, I'm plenty creative.

Rolling onto my back, I slide both hands down my abs, feeling along the dips and valleys as I appreciate my own touch. I'm in prime shape, at the peak of alpha physical strength in my thirties. As soon as I get past these fucking uppers I'll be back to my old self—powerful and dangerous.

When my mind dredges up how delicious Achaia felt against me, I snarl and force it to the memory of being fucked by Renze in the maze. Gods, he was masterful the way he hit every achy place inside me that needed touch.

No. I don't want to think of him either. Right now, I just want to be alone.

Curling my lip back, my fangs descend as I grip my cock, rubbing roughly at the hard length. I flick the two bars buried just behind my cock head, groaning when zings of pleasure shoot up the base of my spine. The piercings were a coming-of-age gift to my future mate, a way to ensure sky-high pleasure for her. Although they feel really fucking good to play with.

Pleasure and pain mix together as I tug at the ring exiting the tip of my cock, pulling the bars simultaneously. The dueling sensations have me sweating already. My mind wanders to Achaia's huge breasts. What would they look like spilling out of my hands, or Renze's? Are her nipples pink or darker?

The thought comes to me completely unbidden, but nobody is here to know I'm fantasizing about the very thing Renze has told me he wants. My imagination takes over, helpfully supplying a vision of her sucking me off as he takes her from behind. He leans over her back to kiss me as I pant with need.

Reaching down, I grip my heavy balls, rolling them in one hand as I work my cock with the other, using precum to coat myself. My strokes are always fast and rough; most alphas get off on some degree of pain, and I'm no exception. A whine builds in my throat as I imagine how wet she'd be for us, how pliable and willing. *Or maybe she'd fight.*

I know I'd like that.

My chest rises and falls steadily as I yank, claw, and play, my dick swinging fat and heavy in my hands.

Every night I performed in the Atrium, I came over and over. And every time I came was at Rama's discretion because she orchestrated the entire show. She selected my partners. She picked the playbook. I had no choice.

But I have a choice now. So I play and stroke for a long time before the need to come overtakes me. I imagine shooting a load and covering my body in my own seed, and the groan I've been holding back issues from my throat.

Curling my legs up over my torso, I prop one foot against the headboard and grip my sack, pulling my cock toward my mouth. I lick the tip once, groaning at the flare of pleasure that streaks along my thighs. It's hard to maintain this position for very long, but I pull harder, sucking the tip between my lips and giving it a light tug with my teeth. Stretching hard, I swirl my warm tongue, moaning as precum coats it.

Tasting my own cum has always turned me on. Maybe it's the knowledge that I'm a freak, and proud of it. Being able to fuck myself gets me hard. I've sucked my own dick more times than I can count and plenty of times on stage for Rama's clients' viewing pleasure. But this is better because this pleasure is mine alone.

I suck and lick as I stroke my sack, rotating between deep pulls and playful bites. Sliding my hand behind my balls, I use precum to slip two fingers easily into my back hole, heat building in my system. But I don't want that crest yet. I need more.

Unfurling myself, I stroke with two hands until I'm panting with the aching desire to come, and then I curl my hips back up over my head and use both hands to push on the backs of my thighs. Capturing my cock between my lips, I suck hard as three or four inches fill my throat. I'm leaking so much at this point, lapping up my own precum as my ramrod straight shaft begins to throb in my mouth.

I'm going to come so fucking hard like this. Gasping around the pleasure, I go wild on myself, sucking and biting my rock-hard length.

What would Achaia look like with those pretty lips wrapped around my cock instead? I imagine my teeth and my lips are hers, and I explode with a bellow as stars shatter behind my eyelids. Opening my mouth wide, I shoot myself in the face, swallowing as much of my salty cum as I can. My cock spurts for a long minute until my balls empty, and I slowly lay flat again, panting with intense pleasure.

Holy fuck. I haven't come that hard in years. My entire body is coated in a fine sheen of sweat. I let out a pleased laugh when I think about what Achaia might say if she knew how hard I busted a nut imagining her on top of me.

My second thought is to call her to come and help me clean up. I imagine the look on her face, the way her nose would scrunch up in fury, and I want it. I want to fuck with her.

Reaching for a towel, I clean up, debating if I should go for round two and think about her again. Nobody's here, nobody has to know.

A knock at the door draws a growl from my throat, but I stand and pull pants on, swinging the door wide. Renze strides in with a fresh stack of washcloths in his hand. His neutral expression morphs into something more devious as he leans in close to my neck and breathes in deeply. Elegant nostrils flare when he backs up and shoots me a predatory look.

He knows precisely what I was up to but chooses to say nothing. Instead, he drops the washcloths onto a chair and grins. "Good to see you're feeling improved, Jet."

CHAPTER EIGHT
RENZE

"I am. I'm fine," Jet purrs, heat splintering through my chest as he watches me. He is waiting for me to comment on the obvious scent of his pleasure. But his pleasure is his alone until he wishes to share it. Still, pheromones assault me as I force my own desire down deep.

Jet takes a step closer to me, a purr deepening in his chest as his eyes flash to mine. They sparkle for the first time in years, so I return the look before speaking.

"I started something earlier with Achaia. Do you wish to watch me finish it?"

Jet's eyes widen, his black pupil overtaking the walnut brown of his striking irises. He glances out the window. "I pissed her off while you were gone; doubt she's going to be in the mood."

I can only laugh at that. "I have been teasing her for days, *atiri*. It is a delicious torture, and she is ready to be taken. I would like you there."

"Why?" Jet's tone is light as he taunts me. "You don't need me to help you bed a woman."

"Of course not," I agree. "But I think you might enjoy *watching* the show for once. What do you think?"

Jet shrugs, but I sense my words intrigue him. Vampiri intuition and emotion reading is a gift, certainly, and I employ it daily in my quest to win him. War lies ahead of us, and I do not want to go into it without Jet and Achaia by my side. I will not.

And so, my conquest continues.

Flashing Jet a cheeky grin, I slip out the window as he grumbles behind me, heading for the stairs. A minute later, he joins me on the front stoop. "And how do you propose to begin your adventure for this evening, Renze?"

I call out to one of the vampiri younglings, who smiles at me as she bounds towards the stairs with youthful exuberance. Anger fills my chest when I think about what she and the other younglings endured in the maze, trapped and hidden from the other monsters. It was no way to live. I am once again thankful that Cashore, my king, took the opportunity to align our court with Noire's pack to escape.

Now, this youngling will know the feel of the glorious sun on her pale skin. She is to be protected at all costs. She is our future.

"*Fazhet hapish*, Firenze?" she chirps. *May I help you, Firenze?*

Because she is younger than me, she uses my full given first name as a sign of respect. I tilt my head to the side in thanks, leaning down to press my forehead to hers, our standard greeting among court family. Zephyr hops from side to side, smiling at me.

"I need you to take this note to Achaia for me, please. Now, my sweet, if you will."

Zephyr lets out a happy squeal and grabs the paper from my hand, inclining her head once before bounding across the street and up the stairs of the opposite brownstone.

Jet sighs. "Sending notes via kid delivery is sure to get you into Achaia's pants. Well done, Renze."

Smirking, I turn to my sarcastic mate, pressing my chest to his, our lips nearly touching. He doesn't back down, but hooded eyes drop to my black lips as I lick them suggestively.

"Lucky for me that Achaia does not wear pants," I murmur. "I intend to have her this evening, Jet. Do you want to watch me chase her or not?"

His focused gaze flickers to mine again. "Yes," he whispers. "Yes, I do."

Snorting in amusement, I cross the open street where our court's younglings play and stand in the shadows of the small alleyway between Achaia's townhome and the one next to it. I feel rather than see Jet cross the street and stand at the corner, watching me. My mate is aroused, watching me wait for the beautiful female. And I am aroused knowing what I'm about to do will turn him on.

I focus when the brownstone's side entry opens, and Achaia pops out, looking from side to side. She does not see me in the shadows, hidden as I am, but descends the stairs gracefully and looks around. I watch her turn toward

JET: A DARK SHIFTER ROMANCE

the street and notice Jet there. She opens her mouth to question him, but I slip behind her, so close that my chest touches her back.

She whips around, one hand flying to her hip as the other points a finger in my face. Before she can say a word, I lean in and nip her finger hard enough to make it bleed. She squeaks and moves to pull her hand back and examine the wound, but I grab her wrist and pull it to my nose, inhaling deeply.

Ruby-red blood drips from the fresh wound as I breathe in every scent I can place. "Sweet berries, clotted cream," I murmur, bringing her finger to my mouth and sucking hard.

Achaia gasps as I swirl my long tongue around the bleeding digit, reveling in how she tastes. "You are a brisk wintry breeze over the open ocean, *atirien*. I have teased you long enough. Tonight, I will have you."

"Is that so?" Her voice is a sultry purr in response to my attention. Behind her, Jet steps into the alleyway, pupils blown wide as he watches. We chased the same marks in the maze. In fact, he and I have stood across from a trembling mark hundreds of times, waiting for that moment when Rama let us know who should kill. I have seen the look on Jet's face for the last seven years.

Want. Lust. Need.

Good. I want him dying to touch us. I will push and shove my mates across my personal chessboard until I've got them right where I want them—all over each other and all over me. Permanently bonded and fucking as much as possible.

Smiling, I yank Achaia forward, up over my shoulder as I turn and stalk toward our townhome. Noire and Diana are in the middle of an unfortunately timed heat and rut next door, so they will be unavailable for a day or two. Diana's horses stand guard at the end of our road. Thomas and Maya are busy making plans with Ascelin. I have ensured that no one will need me for the next few hours.

Achaia grumbles over my shoulder as I rest my hand on her ass, stroking between her cheeks while I cross the street. Jet follows us, a silent shadow despite his unmistakable fascination.

I stalk up the stairs, opening the door to Jet's simple room. Crossing the plush carpet to a bed stacked with thick, white pillows, I toss Achaia in. Above, a skylight lets in the fading sun's rays, highlighting her burnished skin as she sits up on her knees and glares at me.

Behind us, Jet closes the door and locks it. I shoot him a haughty grin before dipping down onto the bed on my knees. In one swift move, I rip

Achaia's soft dress open, unveiling her gorgeous breasts to our greedy eyes. Jet hisses in a ragged breath. Good. I will not force him because of what he endured in the maze. But I want him to need this like I do.

Achaia's back arches as I drag my black claws down her chest. Parting my lips, I spit venom on her breasts, coating her heaving chest as she yips in surprise. Then I yank those incredible thighs wide and spit venom between them, too. She jerks upright, attempting to cover herself as I shift off the bed and take a step back.

"What the fuck was that?" she demands as Jet comes to stand next to me. Her lip trembles as she looks down, swiping at the venom which now drips from prominent, dark pink nipples, visible through a thin bra.

"How does that not hurt her?" Jet's voice is a low murmur, his eyes locked onto a now-snarling Achaia. "I've seen grown men fall to the ground after you spit venom at them."

I open my mouth to answer, but Achaia roars in anger. Her muscles begin to tremble, and she clamps her thighs together as her lips part.

"No."

No sooner has the word left my mouth than a desperate cry issues from her throat. Her body convulses as she falls back to the bed, both hands coming to her breasts.

"What...what did you do to me?" she gasps. "Fuuuuuck." Her chest heaves as Jet looks over with a concerned expression.

I give him a devious look. "Vampiri venom is an aphrodisiac for our mates; only for our mates."

If Jet is surprised by what I've said, he doesn't show it. Instead, his intrigued gaze flickers to our female, who now writhes on the bed, ripping at her panties, oblivious to what I just shared.

"If you decide to join me," I murmur to Jet, "I would welcome it."

Jet declines again, backing into the corner of the room as I turn toward the bed. When my weight dips the edge of the mattress, Achaia's thighs spring open. She regards me with an angry glare. "You fucking did this, whatever this is. Fix it. My skin is on fire, Renze."

"You need me, *atirien*," I purr. "Ask me to taste you."

"Please," she begs, her pretty lips forming a bow as she drags her fingers down her breasts, plucking rosy nipples.

"Please, Renze," I correct as she grunts in annoyance.

When my dark lips close over her nipple and tug, she bows off the bed, her hips thrusting hard to meet mine. My tongue is different from an alpha's; longer, slimmer, and capable of doing things Jet would not be able to do to her. I wrap it around her nipple and tighten it as she screeches and grabs the end of my braid, gripping it in her fist.

"I'm so godsdamned mad at you," Achaia shouts. "Fix whatever you did. It hurts, Renze."

"It does not," I snark back, moving my attention to her other nipple. Using my dark claws, I shred the lace of her bra and expose her fully to me. Goddess, help me. "You are absolutely stunning, *atirien*," I whisper in appreciation. "Every inch of these curves." I run both hands up her thick breasts. They spill out around my fingers as I knead them gently.

My mate's hips brush against me as I make my way down her body, licking and teasing her as she whines and commands me for more. But I want to draw this out, to enjoy my first true taste of her. When I slide to the edge of the bed, I drop to both knees and spread her legs wide, my fingers stroking along the sides of her pink, wet center. Auburn curls hide nothing from me as I lean in and breathe her scent, letting it wash over my senses.

Lemons. Sweet berries. The freshest of cream.

"Look how beautiful she is," I call over my shoulder. "Aching to take us."

There's a soft groan behind me and a sound that can only be Jet's pants unzipping.

Feeling triumphant, I lean in and slick my tongue around her clit, tugging on it as my lips close around that sensitive bud. Achaia screams and clamps her thighs around my head as her muscles quake. She's close, so close so fast. I do not want that. I've always been highly fond of teasing and edging, and I am not ready for her to come. I've only just begun to take her.

I lean back, massaging her thighs as she shifts up onto her elbows with a glare. In one swift move, I fall to my back and yank her hips up, setting her on top of my face. Goddess, being surrounded by her scent has me so hard and ready. My tongue finds its way between her legs again, sliding deep inside that wet heat that is so needy, so desperate for me.

Achaia rocks her hips against my mouth as I slide my tongue deeper, probing until I find a rough patch inside her.

"Yes!" she shouts, grabbing my braids and using them to ground herself as she fucks my tongue. I wanted to edge her for longer, but I find myself desperate to know what she tastes like when she comes.

Growling into her pussy, I slip two fingers into her as I wrap my tongue around her clit and squeeze hard. Achaia freezes for one long moment, muscles tensing before her back arches, her sweet honey flooding my mouth as I snarl. I never stop stroking her, not until her cries crest and she comes a second time. She's sunshine and tart summer berries, cream and salt. I will never get enough of this taste.

I pull at her clit until she becomes oversensitized, and then I flip us in one swift move, shoving her hands up on the headboard. "I will have my pleasure now, *atirien*," I command as another groan rings out from across the room. I do not turn to Jet because his release is his alone until he chooses to share with us. It is the one thing I will not negotiate on. Where usually I'd dominate a mate in the way I dominate Achaia, I cannot do that to him. I will not.

Humming with anticipation, I yank her tattered dress down her back, ready to sink into her sweet pussy. But what I see stops my heart. An intricate tattoo covers the entirety of her back. The dark design begins at the base of her neck and continues in jagged stripes along her spine, spinning out into flowers that reach either side of her back. A bitter, metallic taste coats my tongue.

Magic. This tattoo is magical somehow, but it's a dark magic that my gift senses is utterly wrong.

Jet joins me as Achaia looks over her shoulder, suddenly wary of how we have paused behind her. She moves to cover herself but I stop her. I cannot pull my eyes from the incredible, intricate detail of the design.

"What is that?" Jet breathes. "It's almost…iridescent. The color changes slightly in the faded light. Across the room, it appeared red, but up close, it's almost pure black."

I reach out and touch the tattoo, but Achaia jumps when I do. Immediately, a painful zing transfers from her skin to mine, sending a shockwave of pain all the way into my skull.

"This is no ordinary tattoo," I murmur as I lean closer to look it over. Under me, Achaia trembles, silent as I examine her. "This has magic infused in it. Achaia, do you know how you came by this?"

"No," she whispers, slumping forward as Jet reaches out and runs his fingers along it. He hisses when the same pain stabs him, yanking his hand back with a low growl.

"I've never seen anything like this," he admits. "Not in all my time as our pack's strategist."

"I have lived hundreds of years," I reply. "And only once have I heard of a magical tattoo, but it was not like this. There is one being who may be able to provide insight, but I have not seen her since before the maze."

"Who?" Achaia barks, whirling around to face us. "Who would know about my tattoo? It could be a clue about my identity, right?"

"Perhaps," I muse, pulling her dress back up over her shoulders. Frowning, I stand and pace from side to side, mulling over what this means.

After a moment, I turn to Jet and Achaia as they watch me. "Cashore was the vampiri king, but when he transferred his consciousness to Diana to save her, that effectively ended his reign by one definition. While my court would consider him alive and well through Diana, other vampiri courts may see this as an opportune time to take his throne for themselves. In fact, there is every chance one of the vampiri lords did so the moment Cashore was thrown into the maze.

I cannot be certain, but we should take Achaia with us on our way to the Builder. It will not add time to our journey. There is an old friend at court who may know about this."

Achaia sits up in the bed, seafoam eyes flicking to Jet, who looks torn. "I don't want to take away from you rescuing Tenebris. As much as I'm dying to learn what I can, I won't get in your way."

Jet says nothing, but it's clear she's echoing what he's worried about.

"Tenebris comes first," Achaia reiterates softly, sliding off the bed as she pulls the fabric of her dress to rewrap it.

Jet sighs and grabs her arm, spinning her around as he slides the dress down her back to her waist. He runs his hand down the tattoo again, a muscle in his eye twitching when the tattoo zaps him. He examines it top to bottom, and along her sides. Her eyes flick up to me, worry and stress evident on her elegant features.

"Tenebris would know what this is," Jet murmurs to himself. "He knows everything there is to know about Lombornei and monsters and magic. He's fucking brilliant."

"We will retrieve him," I reassure Jet. "We are all committed."

Achaia sinks into Jet's touch as he pulls her dress back up. He spins her around and drapes the fabric over her curves, tying the belt as she and I watch him. I wonder if he's even aware that he's fallen into such a tender moment, tending to her like this.

He seems to come to the realization at the same time, clearing his throat as he takes a step away from her.

Achaia crosses her arms. "And how is the new vampiri ruler, whoever that may be, going to feel about you showing up and mentioning Cashore lives within Diana still?"

"Not well," I admit. "Cashore was beloved, but vampiri adore power and sex, in that order. Any hint of a weakened ruler results in fighting until someone strong replaces them. Cashore existing only within Diana's spirit will be seen as a weakness. For that reason, I would not take the Chosen One there."

Jet looks at me with an angry frown. "There are too many holes in this plan, Renze."

"I agree," I begin. "But we have to do something, do we not? The only thing that could unite infighting among the vampiri is a common enemy. And we have that. We need allies, Jet."

We fall silent until Achaia finally crosses the room to gather a pile of dirty washcloths. She picks them up and scoffs immediately, turning to Jet with a scowl. "This is covered in jizz, isn't it?"

I hold back a laugh as Jet shoots her a deviant look.

CHAPTER NINE
JET

The information we just uncovered about the link to Achaia's potential past has my head spinning in circles. Already my strategist gift kicks in, thinking about how Thomas rescued her. Add in a strange magical tattoo, and there's a lot more to her than meets the eye.

"Noire and Diana need to know about this." Renze gives me a meaningful look as Achaia twirls her hair anxiously around a finger. She nibbles at her lower lip as I start reworking our current plan, formulating our stop in Rezha to include her. It's not ideal to bring her, though. She's soft and delicate, and I don't have time to protect someone while I'm focused on rescuing Ten.

I jog downstairs and head next door, rolling my eyes when I hear my brother roaring Diana's name. He's mid-rut, which is hardly the best time to discuss strategy. But this can't wait. The longer we remain here without movement, the more likely Rama will have time to retaliate. We can't afford to stay here.

When I bang on his bedroom door, Noire snarls but stomps over and yanks it open. I give him a wry look when he bellows angrily at me, pupils blown wide as his chest heaves. He's not in his right mind, consumed by the rut, but I can see he's trying. *Sort of.*

"What the fuck can you possibly need?" he yells, gripping the door handle so hard the frame splinters. Claws tip his fingers as he snarls, snapping at me. It's dangerous as fuck to get near any alpha in a rut, but my brother is the absolute worst. I wouldn't bother him if I had any other choice, but now that I'm recovered, we need to get moving.

"Renze and I are leaving," I inform him. "We'll make the stop in Rezha. You go to Dest, find our people if you can. Meet us at the Builder's compound, and we'll decide where to go from there."

I watch as Noire processes everything, but he learned long ago to pay attention when I outline a plan. He nods once, fangs fully descended as Diana whines from somewhere behind him.

"Go," he commands. "Diana and I will meet you as quickly as we can."

"There's something else," I barrel on, knowing I'm about to lose his attention. "Achaia's got a tattoo on her back that's infused with magic. We're taking her with us to see if the vampiri have any insight."

"I don't give a fuck about a tattoo!" Noire shouts. Without another word, he slams the door. I grin when he opens it back up and gives me a brusque hug. "Be careful, strategist." I bow my head respectfully, and he brushes his cheek against mine.

Diana lets out a keening wail, and Noire turns from me, shutting the door once again. I hear him bound across the room, and then Diana squeals as the mattress creaks. Hearing their pleasure drags me back to what happened with Achaia before we discovered the tattoo. Goddess, Renze was so close to fucking her.

And my question about her nipple color was answered.

Smirking, I head downstairs and across the street to the townhome where she lives, shouting for Thomas.

"We're in the solarium, Jet!" Maya shouts up at me.

I stalk through the kitchen, passing into the small sunroom that overlooks their back garden. Maya stands, wrapping me in a hug as she reaches up to brush hair out of my face. "You look good, Jet. Clear-eyed. How are you feeling?"

How am I feeling? It's a complicated question for me. Physically, I feel improved after the rest. Emotionally and mentally? It's a rollercoaster. I'm focused one minute and highly distracted the next.

I mull over the best way to answer her, but opt to pull her in for a hug instead. I bury my face in the top of her head. She still smells like the soap she always used when I was a kid. Maya is home for me, and I'm sad to be leaving that behind.

"Trig is on his way over with information," Thomas shares when I glance over at him.

Maya pats me on the chest and drops back down into her chair with a sigh. I follow her and lean against the solarium's back door. "Good. Renze and I are leaving for the Builder as soon as possible."

Maya gives me a worried look. I'm sure it's hard for her to have us brothers back for the first time in seven years, only for us all to leave again. I'm about to say something when there's a cool breeze, and Renze slips up the hallway. He bends at the waist and plants a tender kiss on Maya's cheek.

I've seen Renze eviscerate a man. I've seen him break limbs and crack bones to suck the marrow out. Somehow it still surprises me to see how kind he is to my adoptive parents.

I'm curious to find out what else I don't know about him.

Thomas flashes Renze a wary look and moves from his place to stand next to me, leaning against the wall.

"Have you spoken of Achaia?" he addresses the question to me.

"I hadn't gotten there yet," I growl.

"What about Achaia?" Thomas snaps, glaring at the both of us.

"Do you know anything about her tattoo?" Renze questions. His tone is low and commanding, sending Thomas bristling as he balls his fists.

"How did you even know about it? She keeps it covered."

"It was not covered when I saw it." Renze smirks. "I have examined every inch of it, and I believe it to be imbued with dark magic."

"Oh, gods," whispers Maya, her hand flying up to her mouth. Her eyes flick up to Thomas as his face turns red with rage. But I watch him school the look into something slightly more neutral when Maya pats his arm to get his attention.

Eventually, he sighs. "I've scoured every book I have for a mention of a tattoo like hers, but I've never found anything. It hurts her, though. Sometimes she'll wince when she moves, like it never healed—"

"Achaia is coming with us when we leave," Renze interrupts. "A contact in the vampiri court might know about her tattoo."

Thomas' face goes from red to purple, but finally, he hisses in a breath and nods, all the fight leaching out of him. "I knew it would come to this eventually. We've cared for her to get her on her feet, but she's a grown woman, and she has questions. Hear me on this, though," he growls, pointing a crooked finger at Renze. "She's special, and if you hurt her, I'll—"

"You will do nothing," Renze says casually, dominance clear in his voice. "I am hundreds of years old, Thomas. I could snap you like a twig if I chose to do so. You are right about one thing, however. Achaia *is* special. I will guard her with my life, but do not presume to threaten mine."

Maya looks nervously from Renze to Thomas, but eventually, Thomas flops into a chair with a tired huff.

Next to me, Renze smirks as I ponder his words. *Achaia is special.* The room is tense when the front door opens, and Trig jogs up the hallway, his scowl deepening when he sees Renze next to me. Achaia comes through the doorway after him, crossing the room to stand between Thomas and Maya's chairs. Her blue-green eyes flick to mine when I speak.

"We're leaving tomorrow. We'll pass through the vampiri court and then on to the Builder. Trig, you have new information?"

Trig frowns and leans in the doorway. "We don't know much about the Builder, frankly. Just whispers here and there, so you'll have to uncover information along the way. But a contact arrived last night from Dest. Already there are whispers of your escape from the maze."

Hope flashes hot in my chest. If anyone remains from our former pack, Noire will find them when he goes there.

"There's more," Trig murmurs, voice steely and low. "Rama's flying city, Paraiso, has been sighted off the northern coast of Vinituvari. That's Diana's home province, the same place it was built. My contact has a theory that it's a recharging spot of sorts for the city. Rama would have had to use magic to build the maze and its island as fast as she did. We assume she returned to that specific place for a reason."

My mind processes this new information. A charging spot of sorts. I need to ponder it, but it's as good a lead as any. And the fact that the city is still there means we've got a little bit of time. When we tried to kill Rama but failed, she escaped to the flying city and left, but it's not fast moving. That would mean she's spent days trying to get to this specific location.

Curious.

"What else is there?" Renze barks at Trig. "It appears that you wish to say more."

Trig shoots Renze a pointed look. "The Builder is dangerous. Be careful. It's through sheer, random luck that we even heard about him. He's secretive, quiet, and presumably magical if he helped Rama build Paraiso. That's the rumor, anyhow."

"Why isn't he dead?" I question aloud, thinking through this. "Rama forced Diana's father to build the maze but then massacred the whole province afterward. Why would the Builder be allowed to craft Paraiso and still live?"

Trig shrugs. "Diana never shared much about her family with me before she was thrown into the maze. I can't even begin to surmise why Rama killed them, but the Builder lives. Maybe he's just a myth to draw unsuspecting people in so Rama can murder them. I wouldn't put it past her to allow small resistances to grow and gather hope just so she can crush them. It certainly fits her MO."

That's a devastating thought. But I can't cling to it. Rama's a shifter, flesh and bone, just like I am. Just like Diana. She's one being. And while she's incredibly powerful and horribly brilliant, she's also a fucking asshole. There must be plenty of beings in this world anxious to bring her down like we are.

"We need more allies," I murmur. "As well as the resistance here. Maybe even some of the monsters who remain in the maze." I look up at Thomas. "Diana wants to go back to the maze island. Rama kept a stable of monsters there. According to Diana, most of them are sentient and she wants to release them."

"You must be joking," Maya huffs.

"If there's any chance we can find allies or information about the Builder or Paraiso, we have to try," I remind her. "I'm not asking you, I'm telling you we need to do it."

"Great," Trig complains. "Let's just unleash a shitload of monsters on the town and pray that goes well."

Renze slips across the room in a second, tossing Trig up against the wall as if swatting a bug.

"We have bigger issues than a few stray monsters, human," Renze snarls. "Our plan has far too many holes. If we can fill a few, we should. Stop complaining and start helping. What sort of Resistance do you lead if you are unwilling to risk anything for it?"

Trig gulps, the room tense as Trig's eyes move to each of us. When we don't immediately help him, he nods at Renze.

"The vampiri court is a good starting place," Renze answers, looking over at me. "The vampiri nation is powerful, and our gifts are many. If we can retain the vampiri loyalty, it would go a long way to helping with what comes after we formulate a plan."

I look around the room. "I won't bother with long goodbyes. Thomas, Maya. I pray to the goddesses that I will see you soon. Liuvang-willing, we will toast to our success when I return." The fox goddess is a shifter's patron goddess, and I've prayed to her thousands of times for the safety of my pack.

Maya grits her jaw, her eyes filling with tears as she stands and wraps Achaia in a hug.

"When will you leave, child?"

Achaia tucks a stray strand of auburn hair behind her ear. "As soon as Jet and Renze want to."

"In the morning," I confirm, looking over at Renze. "We'll go in the morning."

CHAPTER TEN
ACHAIA

After dropping the bomb that I'm going with Jet and Renze, I leave the neighborhood. I can't stay there a minute longer; I need to walk and think. I pace through the streets toward the market, knowing the hustle and bustle there ironically quiets my mind. Maybe because the market feels so normal, and the sights and sounds keep me from focusing inwardly quite so much.

When I pass the first fruit stand, an older human male smiles at me, tipping his head in my direction.

"Hello, Effen," I greet him, waving as he offers me a bright yellow, ripe vaya fruit. I take it with a grin, inclining my head in thanks as I continue. The people of Siargao have been kind to me in the last three years. I've always hoped someone might recognize me, but it never happened.

I pass stall after stall filled with tropical fruits native to this province. The market is busy all day and all night, the offerings changing according to the time of day. As the sun sets, many vendors will sell alcohol and late-night snacks as people stroll along the Kan River. The night market down here in the Riverside district is the very best one, and this is the last time I'll see it for a while, maybe ever.

I walk for several hours before prickling awareness causes the hair on the back of my nape to stand. Stopping at a stall, I examine the woven reed baskets as I peek surreptitiously to one side. A giant male appears next to me, command rolling off of him in waves so strong I grip the edge of the cart to avoid my knees buckling. The urge to run hits me so hard that I can barely breathe.

Gritting my teeth, I turn and straighten my spine. Everyone knows you don't run from a predator. When my eyes connect with his, I fight to maintain my composure. He's an alpha, like Jet, and horrifyingly handsome. Slicked-back blond hair, dark gray-blue eyes, and high, elegant cheekbones frame a hooked nose. My gaze travels to a puckered scar extending from one side of his neck to the other.

"Ugly, isn't it?" he purrs, taking a step closer to me.

"I've seen worse," I hedge as he laughs, a deep, sinful rumble that shouldn't be quite so sensual.

"Hurt like fuck when she tried to kill me," he murmurs, blond brows pulling into a vee as if he's lost in a memory. The expression morphs fast into a cruel smile. "I'm still here, though. And I've been wanting to speak with you."

A chill races down my spine. *He's been wanting to speak with me?*

His shirt is partially unbuttoned, dark metal spikes sticking out as if he's got some kind of metal implant in his chest muscle.

"Is that so?" I question, not taking a step back. Somehow, I know if I back away from this monstrous alpha, he'll give chase. Everything about the tenseness of his stance, the way he's focused like a predator, all screams danger. There's something not quite right with him.

"You're a beauty," he says softly, white fangs descending from behind thin lips as I urge my muscles to remain loose and ready.

"You're following me. Why?" I summon my inner bluster and pray he doesn't read any fear in me. If I can just get back up to the main road, there's a chance I'll see someone I know. Of all the godsdamned times for Renze not to accompany me.

"I find you fascinating," he replies with a shrug. "I'd like you to come with me somewhere. To bed, perhaps." He smiles again, reaching out to grab a lock of my hair and twirl it around his finger.

Alarms trill in my brain. To bed, my ass. This is how women get murdered.

"I don't think so," I reply coolly. My eyes flick behind him as my cheeks heat. I wish like hell there was someone here to protect me.

Almost as if on cue, one of Diana's horse statues stalks up the street, looking from side to side. She programmed them to protect Siargao's citizens from violence. Thank fuck it's here. Relief fills my chest as I back slowly toward it.

The male follows my gaze and grins, slipping his hands casually into his jean pockets. "He's not here to help you." He sing-songs it like a fucking crazy person as I take another step. The mechanical horse is almost level with us now. The alpha steps to my side and grabs my chin, directing my gaze to the horse's withers. "See, little one?"

I can't help but look where he's pointing me, and that's when I notice the horse's entire back and stomach is inlaid with metal spiders about the size of a hand. The alpha reaches out with the hand not holding me and depresses a small button on the horse's neck. There's a mechanical creak, and I watch in horror as the closest spider's legs begin to unfurl and straighten, feeling around its metal dock.

One by one, the rest of the spiders seem to come alive as I rip my chin from the alpha's pinched fingers. Goddess, what the fucking hells is going on?

The alpha laughs as the spiders begin crawling up out of the divots they're secured into in the horse's metal side. In droves, they begin to pop off the horse, falling to the ground and scattering in every direction along the street.

Shocked cries ring out as the alpha grabs one of the spiders and slaps it against my chest. "We will have your truth, little one," he whispers, leaning in.

At that exact moment, a huge shadow barrels into us, knocking the alpha to the ground. The spider skitters away as I look up.

Jet.

Thank fuck.

But then the screaming starts in earnest.

Out of the corner of my eye I see people begin to run in every direction, swatting at the mechanical insects as they start crawling up peoples' legs and arms.

The blond alpha cackles as Jet leaps a second time, knocking the other male down onto the cobblestone street. Jet pounds the alpha's face as the blond roars. Next to me, the horse snorts and lowers its head, stomping at the ground as its red eyes focus on Jet. "Jet, watch out!" I scream. "The horse!"

It takes off like a flash, barreling toward where Jet and the blond alpha roll in the dirt, biting and punching. Jet leaps off the male at the last moment as the horse gallops toward them, metal teeth bared. The blond grabs a handle that protrudes from the horse's stomach and swings himself onto its back.

People are still running everywhere, trying desperately to flee the spiders. But when the horse disappears up the street, the spiders rise as one into the air like tiny drones. They take off after the horse, leaving a whirl of confusion in their wake.

Jet rushes to me, running his hands along my jaw, down my arms, and over my hips. "Are you okay?" His voice is angry, so angry, his dark eyes locked onto mine as his big chest heaves.

Renze appears next to us at that moment, slipping in a swirl of black shadow as I try to process the events of the last few minutes. "What happened?" he barks, pulling me into his arms.

Jet removes his hands from me and runs them through his hair. "I don't know," he admits. "I came down here for one last walk through the market, and an alpha showed up. He was stalking Achaia."

Renze wraps an arm around my waist and pulls me close. "Did he hurt you?"

The whole story comes out of me then, what the alpha said, the horse, the spiders. Not a single one of the mechanical bugs remains, and the horse was too fast for us to give chase. The street clears as people flee from the scene.

"Did you recognize the alpha?" Renze doesn't look at me as his white eyes scan the dissipating crowd.

"No," I confirm.

"I did," Jet growls, stroking a dagger in a holster strapped to his thigh. "I have seen that male once before," he shares. "So have you, Renze. When we first escaped the maze. He was standing at the corner one day, watching you and me. Achaia passed him, walking to the main street, but he stood there, watching us. It's Rama; it's got to be her doing."

I bristle at that. "You think she's using me to get to you somehow, then? Why? Why send spiders into the crowd?"

"A diversion tactic, maybe?" Jet replies with a growl. "It doesn't fucking bode well that we're seeing him a second time. When we get home, Achaia, pack your shit and come to the brownstone Jet and I are in. Stay with us tonight, and we'll leave first thing."

I shudder, thinking about the dangerous male I just met. "There's something off about him," I tell Renze. "As if his mind was there but not. He had a scar across his neck, mumbling something about a woman who tried to kill him."

Jet and Renze share a look.

"What?" I question. "Do you know who that is?"

Jet sighs. "I can't say this for sure, but it seems too coincidental not to be true. Rama sliced Diana's brother's throat in front of her and left him on a garbage heap when they were teenagers. Many years later, she told Diana she hadn't actually killed Dore. It's part of how Diana was able to get herself thrown into the maze. I think she's always assumed that Rama lied about Dore's death and that he was really gone. But...that might have been him."

I don't know how to respond to that or how to tell Diana that her twin might still be alive, but he's crazy as hell and trying to hurt me.

JET: A DARK SHIFTER ROMANCE

When we finally reach our street, Renze turns to Jet. "Do you wish to share this news with the Chosen One, or shall I?"

Jet frowns. "She's mid-heat with Noire. Let's tell Ascelin. That or wait until the heat is over."

"Ascelin can deliver the news," Renze confirms. "She will do it tactfully."

~

Hours later, I'm sitting in Renze's room with him and Zephyr, watching in rapt fascination as he braids the youngling's hair. The everyday action is such a stark contrast to what happened earlier this evening. I'm shaken, but more resolved than ever not to get in Jet and Renze's way. Rama is the most dangerous threat to all of us. Something must to be done.

Finding out about my past has to come second to rescuing Jet's brother.

"Ouch, Firenze," the youngling complains, pulling me back to the present as she grits her teeth. Renze yanks her dark hair tight, his fingers flying along her scalp in swift, practiced motions.

"*Sitep*, Zephyr," he growls in his beautiful language. "Calm yourself, young one. Push through the pain, for when you are grown, you will do this every few days. Pain in your scalp is hardly something to concern yourself over."

I note how he grins slightly as Zephyr harrumphs and crosses her arms with a tiny grumble. Eventually, he finishes the intricate braids up over her ears, leaving the length of her hair untouched. When she scampers away, he pats her now-vacant chair.

"Come, *atirien*. Allow me to braid your hair next."

"I don't know," I laugh. "Zephyr makes it seem pretty painful." Plus, I'm still on edge from what happened in the market. Reliving it with Thomas, Maya, and Ascelin when we returned home was exhausting. Although it did make one thing clear—when Noire and Diana are done with their heat, they'll go to the maze island and free the other monsters. The more enemies Rama has, the better.

Renze rolls his white eyes with a huffy chuckle. "Come now, Achaia. I will not ask nicely again."

"Oh, is this you asking nicely? I missed that," I tease as I step into his space, my breasts brushing across the soft leather of his vest. Gods, it feels good to do something normal, and I'm craving closeness with Renze after my near-miss with the blond alpha.

Renze's gaze falls to my chest.

"It is times like now I wish for Jet's ability to purr," he says quietly, reaching out to stroke underneath one of my breasts. "I would love to watch your nipples harden as I purr for you." He leans closer, brushing his lips across mine. "One day, I will command *him* to purr for you. Then perhaps, I will fuck him as he fucks you, and I will revel in every godsdamned second of it."

I choke in a breath, willing my lungs to fill as Renze pinches both of my nipples with a self-satisfied smirk. "And there we are. I must resort to filthy words to arouse you, but it *does* work."

"How can you be thinking about sex after what just happened?" I question, turning to settle myself in the empty seat. I watch Renze in the mirror. Black lips part as translucent black fangs descend from behind them. His smile entrances me as his white gaze meets mine.

"Vampiri power is bolstered through sex, Achaia. When things get dangerous, we become nearly insatiable. I wish to be all over you, *atirien*," he murmurs.

I cross my arms and try to look serious, but the reality is this news doesn't surprise me. Everything about Renze is so incredibly sensual. Like now. He brings his black claws to my scalp and scratches, pulling a breathy moan from my throat. Goddess, he feels so fucking good. He makes me feel *safe*.

"Hair play is a favorite tease of most vampiri," he offers as he scratches gently along my scalp from front to back. When he gets to the back of my neck, he pushes my head forward and massages my muscles. "Most vampiri mates braid one another's hair, and it is considered an intimate moment to do so. When we arrive in the vampiri courts, never allow another to touch your braids. It is offensive and disrespectful to me. You will have to show you are mine while we are there."

"I haven't agreed to be yours," I counter. "Spitting venom on me so I'm out of my mind with lust is hardly consent."

Renze chuckles as he scratches at my scalp, bringing his fangs to nip at my earlobe. "I do not require your consent, *atirien*. But if you want to be safe in a vampiri court, you will have to act as if you are mine in every way."

When I harrumph, he laughs again, standing tall. "You will see sex all over the court. We do not feel the need to wait for a bedroom, *atirien*. Bondmates and pleasure mates may take one another anywhere and anytime."

My blood heats as Renze parts my hair down the middle. I'm unprepared for the pinch of pain as he begins an intricate fishtail-style braid along my scalp. Somehow, he turns it into multiple braids that weave through each other before cascading freely at my back. I say nothing as I watch him work, not even when Ascelin joins us, eating an apple as she smirks at me.

She questions Renze in their language, but he answers her with a hiss and a baring of his fangs. Her white eyes find mine, black lips parting as she grins. "Take care in our court, little one. Vampiri are lustful, and Renze is likely to lose his mind when other males try to take you."

I scowl up at Renze when she unleashes that tidbit of info. "Try to take me? Forcefully she means? Unless I act like I belong to you?"

Renze glowers at Ascelin, who shrugs. "It would be better if you were formally mated. You should mark her, Renze."

"I am aware," he snaps as I widen my eyes, hoping it's clear that I need more information.

"Who said anything about formally mating?" I barrel on. "I *might* consider the idea of fake dating while there so I can stay safe."

Ascelin's lips pull into a broad smile, dark fangs peeking from behind them. "Wait until you see the vampiri court, pretty human. You will be begging for Renze to fake date you right into actual matehood. If you are not a vampiri, and you are not claimed, then you are food."

Ascelin shrugs as she cuts a slice of apple and hands it to me on the tip of her knife. I take it with a grumble, which causes her to laugh aloud.

Just then, Jet joins us, sniggering at my hair before he beams at Renze. "Wanna do mine next, vampiri?"

Renze laughs but doesn't look up as he moves to the other side of my head, beginning the painful braiding process there. "I would do yours anytime you wish, *atiri*."

Jet's smile falls as Ascelin roars again, taking a bite of her apple before handing me a second piece.

"Watching the three of you together is a most excellent comedy," she chuckles. "If I was not committed to guarding the Chosen One, I would be anxious to see how your trip to the vampiri courts goes. Best to get your fake mating story straight before you enter the court."

"Fake mating? What do you mean, Asc?" Jet laughs, not having been there for the conversation we just had.

She rolls her white eyes and hands me the whole apple as Renze growls at my back.

"I mean that vampiri do not value weakness, and this whole fake mating charade will make Firenze appear weak. You are both liabilities to him if you show up without accepting him as yours."

Jet rolls his eyes, too. "I am no one's mate, Ascelin. So it will not be an issue."

"As you say," she chirps, shrugging her shoulders. "But remember that when you think no one is looking, and your eyes drift to Renze's lovely cock.

Because if I have noticed that you gaze at it fondly, then Sinan and others will also notice."

I'd laugh if Jet didn't look so simultaneously horrified and pissed.

Ascelin breezes out of the room, knocking into his shoulder with hers as she goes. I think I fall in love with her a little bit at that moment, but Jet scowls at Renze without saying a word. Renze is as cool as ever, unruffled by Ascelin's abrupt commentary, his black lips curled into the tiniest of smiles.

"Time for a road trip!" I chirp, hoping to break the obvious tension in the room. Renze's smile deepens as he tugs at my hair, but Jet simply growls from the doorway, muttering under his breath.

This is going to be so awkward. Part of me can't wait to see how it turns out.

CHAPTER ELEVEN
JET

Achaia insisted on remaining with Thomas and Maya for the night, reminding Renze and me that she was just across the street if the alpha showed up again. As a result, I sleep like shit, my mind poring over all the possibilities of what could go wrong on our trip. In fact, we lack so much critical information that I'm practically expecting everything to head south the moment we leave Siargao.

When the sun rises, I growl and grab my packed bag, stalking across the hall. I lift my hand to bang on Renze's door, but he opens it swiftly, shooting me a lazy smile. My heart whomps in my chest as he licks his lips, sending my mind back to the way he took me in the maze that horrendous night. Renze is capable of dispensing indescribable pleasure with that tongue, and I'd be a fucking liar if I didn't admit that seeing it now makes me hard.

He knows it, clearly, because he leans in the doorway with a satisfied look on his face. "We have time for pleasure before we leave, Jet. Allow me to remind you how good I can make you feel, *atiri*."

I inhale deeply, my body moving closer to his, drawn by a magnetic, primal pull. "*Atiri* means mate?" I'm focused on his mouth as I ask the question.

"Indeed," he confirms as I shake my head.

"I'm not," I growl.

"You are."

"No." It comes out in a whisper as Renze leans forward and presses his forehead to mine. It's a standard vampiri greeting, but when his lips brush along my own, shards of white-hot heat streak through my system, my lips parting.

"You are fated to be mine, Jet, in the same way that Achaia is fated to belong to me. It is the same incredible way she is fated to belong to you. But I have said it before, and I will remind you now. You will choose me. And I will not have you until you do. Because above anything else in this fucking world, your happiness and your choices matter."

"Why?" I press. "You're as dominant as Noire or any of us alphas. We take what we want when we want it. Consent is hardly something we concern ourselves over."

Renze's lips brush along mine again as he murmurs, "I am observant, *atiri*. I read your emotions, and forcing my brave, strong alpha would not endear you to me. I will revel in the slow burn between us because when you give in to it, the pleasure will be so godsdamned incredible."

I let out a soft moan as Renze holds still, waiting for me to make any sort of move or show any type of encouragement. But something pulls me back into the darkness of my mind. I remember all the times Rama threatened to hurt my brothers if I didn't do exactly what she wanted, and a sour taste fills my mouth. I think of Ten lying chained and broken somewhere, and I can't focus on the heat between Renze and me.

Stepping back, I force myself to look at the big vampiri, expecting to see disappointment in his expression. He should be disappointed because if I *am* his mate, I'm a piss poor one. My mind is like a locked box, shut away from everything, and I don't know how to even begin fixing that.

To my surprise, Renze gives me only a sexy, sultry smile. "Come, Jet. Let us find Achaia."

He brushes past me, not touching me as he goes. But I ache. I fucking ache for his hands on my body, even though I pulled back when we got close just now.

Gritting my teeth, I run both hands through my hair to keep myself from yanking him back into my arms. I don't know how to fix the constant push and pull in my mind, I just know I've got an intense, all-consuming need to both fuck him and flee at the same time.

I grab my bag and follow him downstairs and into the street. Next door, Diana screams Noire's name. I can't begin to fathom what sex would be like with an omega in heat while in a rut yourself. One day, I hope we're all safe and happy, and I can tease Noire about it. It's horrible timing, but he was on the edge of a rut when we met her in the maze. There's no stopping it now.

Outside, Thomas has already parked his black aircar in front of our brownstone. He looks up at me, his wrinkled face breaking into a worried smile as I follow Renze down the steps.

The aircar trunk is already open, so I toss my bag in and round the side with a cheeky grin.

"How old is this thing, Thomas? You buy it when you came of age?"

He shoots me the middle finger. "Barely *had* aircars when I turned eighteen. I bought this when I knew I was getting grandpups, but then Rama took over, and we could hardly even sneak out of Siargao to visit. Only managed it the one time and haven't tried again."

Renze carefully sets his bag in the trunk before coming around the aircar, his head inclined respectfully at Thomas. Despite our tense conversation yesterday, they seem to have a cordial relationship, if not the beginnings of a friendship of sorts.

"I will get Achaia and be back in a moment."

Thomas looks up at the brownstone. "She's not a great sleeper and usually rises later. If you can give her another hour or two, I'm sure she'd be grateful."

Renze frowns at that but turns from us and heads for my brownstone.

Thomas growls and turns to me. "Guess another hour of sleep isn't in his plans."

I shrug. "You said she doesn't sleep well, so I suspect that's all he can focus on."

Thomas rolls his dark eyes. "What do you make of all this vampiri mate stuff? Renze seems pretty focused and I've been eavesdropping a bit."

A heated blush spreads across my cheeks as I crack my neck from side to side, hedging. "I think if she's his mate and they both know it, I'm happy for them. But I'm focused on getting to the Builder, so we can figure out how to take Rama down and bring Ten home. That's what I care about above everything else."

"I meant more the obvious connection between you two," Thomas says pointedly.

Thomas may have raised me, but my relationships are none of his business. He wasn't with us in the maze. He was relatively safe out here. He doesn't understand a godsdamned thing.

He must sense my rising ire because he puts both palms up in the air. "I didn't mean anything, Jet. You know all Maya and I want for you is happiness. If he brings you that, I'll be glad. But vampiri aren't like us. Interspecies mingling is...difficult."

The door to the brownstone opens, and Renze slips through with a yawning Achaia behind him. He's got two bags slung over one shoulder, and he reaches for her hand, guiding her down the stairs behind his much larger frame.

My own body heats watching them. He's tender with her, so opposite to the way he was in the maze where we fought for our lives. I sense Thomas turning to watch them too, but I don't pull my eyes from the sight of them descending the stairs. Achaia's auburn hair is still braided intricately along her brow, disappearing up over her ear.

Renze's white eyes meet mine, the hint of a smirk still evident on his handsome face. I want to touch him when he reaches us. But I also don't. I'm not ready. Rama fucked me up when she forced me into sexual servitude. I survived for seven long years, but I don't want things the way I used to. I'm drawn to them both and don't want them at the same time.

The helpful devil on my shoulder supplies a quick reminder of what she looked like naked, spread on the bed under Renze, and I grit my teeth to hold down a groan.

I open Achaia's door, but she throws herself into a tight embrace with Thomas first. He begins purring for her, a deeply comforting noise that reminds me of my childhood as she sighs happily and promises to return safe and sound. But the sound of him purring makes me want to rip his head off. He raised me. He raised all of us brothers when our fucking father couldn't. But right now? I'd like to forcefully remove Achaia from his arms, rip them off his godsdamned body, and present them to her as gifts.

Renze stands next to me, cocking his head to the side. "Down, boy."

I snap my teeth in his face, but the warrior doesn't flinch. He never did, not even in the maze. Of all the creatures we were imprisoned with, the vampiri were the only ones that ever seemed as strong as our pack.

Renze chuckles, and we wait silently as Achaia pats Thomas' forearm. His eyes are filled with unshed tears. I wonder if he's thinking of how he raised his own pups, me and my brothers, and now this woman as well. How has Thomas turned into the father of everyone in this fucking province?

His dark eyes flick over to mine, and he nods once. "Take care of her," he snaps brusquely, squeezing Achaia's hand as she looks over at us.

"Until I draw my final breath, I will," Renze confirms.

Eventually, we manage to extricate Achaia from Thomas' affection. I take the driver's seat of his aging black aircar, and Renze hops in the back with Achaia. I haven't driven in years, and even before the maze, I had a driver.

"This should be interesting," I mutter under my breath.

Sighing, I punch the button to start the engine. A throaty hum fills the aircar as it lifts up off the ground. I step on the pedal to accelerate, and the car leaps forward, Achaia yipping in the backseat.

"Godsdamnit," I mutter, frazzled. "Quiet back there."

"Well, don't kill us," Achaia bites back as Renze holds back a grin. We make it up the row of brownstones and pull out into the early morning traffic. After a minute or so, driving comes back to me, and we make it easily past the morning market as Achaia gazes out the window.

I'm focused as we move through the streets, only the faint hum of the aircar's engine a constant in my ear. I drink in the sights of my home province, saying a quick prayer to the fox goddess, Liuvang, for Noire and Diana's safety on their journey. I don't like splitting our pack further, but there's no time. We can't wait for Rama to make another move, especially after the attack on Achaia yesterday.

We pass the market and its brightly colored stalls. Giant narra trees cover the market in shade, dropping fragrant yellow petals on top of the vendors' carts. I'm struck with a sudden nostalgia so hard that it stops my breath for a moment. I grew up here. I ran these streets as a child. And then Ayala Pack ran Siargao with an iron fist until Rama forced us into the maze. We underestimated her when we met her. *I* underestimated her.

And my pack has paid a high fucking price for that.

We pass through the Eastern Gate at the far end of the market. After that, there's nothing but dense tropical forest for hours before we leave Siargao's borders. I've felt a certain sense of relative safety here at home, despite knowing Rama ripped me out of a similar complacency seven years ago. Still, Siargao is mine in a way that the rest of Lombornei isn't.

A slight sigh reaches my ears, followed by the sound of weight shifting on the leather seats. When I look in the rearview mirror, Renze is focused on Achaia next to him.

"What?" She questions as he leans against the seat, staring at her as if she's the most beautiful creature he's ever seen.

I force my eyes to the road, but they drift back to Renze again. His hand snakes over to her in the back seat. I can't see everything, but her red lips part as pink tinges her cheeks.

"Godsdamnit," I bark at him. "We're not in the aircar an hour, and you're fucking."

"Not fucking," Renze murmurs. "Not yet. Simply enjoying. No need to pull over, Jet, unless you intend to join us. We have a long drive ahead, and I need her pleasure."

"Again, I haven't agreed to give it to you," she reminds him, but it's easy to see she's overwhelmed by how thoroughly seductive Renze is.

The fucking aircar fills with the scent of Achaia's arousal. It's a tidal wave that surges and wanes; it's like crisp salt air and the fragrant *exan* vines that grow along the coast, but different still. It's unique to her, a scent that tugs at my own desire, wrapping tendrils around my need even as I fight not to be so wildly attracted to her.

"Open those pretty thighs, *atirien*," Renze growls as I grip the steering wheel tighter.

"You will have to do whatever I ask at the vampiri court," he reminds her. "Appearing weak is dangerous."

Achaia appears to war with that pronouncement as I look out at the road, and quickly back to the rearview.

"Let me remind you why being fake mated to me will be so much fun." His voice is a deep rasp as he grips her throat, holding her steady. Renze's black tongue slips down into the front of Achaia's thin shirt. I can clearly see it wrap around one prominent nipple, squeezing as she jerks in the seat, grasping onto the pale, strong forearm wrapped around her waist.

"Lay back, *atirien*. Let me please you, and I will tell you what that word means, finally," Renze commands as Achaia looks up, her eyes meeting mine in the rearview mirror.

Goddess, I'm barely looking at the fucking road. I wipe a hand down my mouth and chin, trying desperately to center myself as her viridescent eyes flash with a challenge. She's taunting us, her red lips pursing as she looks from me to Renze.

"No."

He laughs aloud, throwing his head back before spinning her bodily on the leather bench seat. He pushes her down hard on the center console, her upper body right alongside my thigh as she squeals.

"Help me, Jet," he demands. Without thinking, I replace his grip on her throat with my own, my chest heaving as her eyes flash in anger. But then they squint tightly closed as a cry leaves her lips, her throat bobbing underneath my fingers.

I yank my hand from her as I hiss at Renze, "She said no."

His face is buried between her thighs, and goddess help me, I watch the look on her face as he eats her. Her body jerks to one side as she screams. I want to know precisely what he's doing. No. Scratch that—I *need* to know. She told him no, and he's pleasuring her anyway, and I want to watch.

Slamming the aircar to a stop, I throw it in park and turn in the seat to watch him. Renze's upper lip rubs side to side over her clit, but when I look closer, I see his tongue down between her ass cheeks. Gods, he can take her both places at once, just with his mouth.

Achaia's nails dig into my hand as she rolls her rounded hips up to meet Renze. He lets out a deep, commanding growl, and I watch in fascination as her entire body tenses, the faint hint of abs showing underneath her bronzed skin as she screams aloud. The depth of her scream sends a shudder wracking my frame; it's as if I can feel it in my bones when she does it.

My dick leaps in my pants, spurting cum I wasn't even fucking ready for. She screams my name next, surprise sending heat barreling through my system. I want more. I want to know what it sounds like when she breaks apart on my knot. I'm quickly losing control as I watch Renze force ecstasy from her pliable, soft body.

Renze's eyes move to mine. "Would you like to know how she tastes, *atiri*? There is nothing better on this continent than her release."

I nod. I'm desperate to know and not ready at the same time. I wanted to watch, but...

Renze leans between the seats, his massive body on top of hers as he puts one hand on the steering wheel and the other around my headrest. I'm effectively caged in as he hovers his lips over mine.

"I will not kiss you unless you ask me, *atiri*. But I am absolutely covered in her scent."

My nostrils flare as I look at him. Moisture from her release covers his black lips, his tongue peeking out from between them. Their combined scents are driving me wild, a possessive whine making its way out of my throat.

Renze says nothing but licks his lips once, watching as my eyes follow the seductive moment.

A dam breaks in my head, demanding I seek more. I lean in and bury my nose in Renze's neck, sucking in breath after gasping breath. Achaia's scent is everywhere, combined with his. If I give in to Renze right now, he'll take everything from me he can, from her and me both if I want him to. I know without a doubt that he would claim us if we asked.

I'm not ready to give in to that—I'm no one's mate.

I feel Achaia's eyes on me, pulling my attention to her. What I'm doing, scenting her on Renze's skin, it's turning her on. When I look down, her lips are swollen, and her chest heaves as she nips at her lower lip. I read her emotions well. She's frustrated, turned on by Renze and me together, and aching to be filled by either of our cocks.

Or both, whispers that helpful devil in my mind. *You could take her together.*

It's nothing I haven't done before in the Atrium. But that was for others' pleasure. This would belong solely to us. Renze shifts into the back seat as Achaia looks up at me.

I sense her agonizing need for more, for something to fill her deeper and thicker than what she got just now. She came, but she's not sated. She shifts up onto her elbows and eyes the hard bar in my lap and the wetness at the front of my pants.

"May I taste you?" she whispers. Renze focuses on me, awaiting my answer.

I pause. I want it, but I don't. I don't even know what the fuck I want. My mind is a confusing whirlwind of emotions after watching Renze drag an orgasm from her and then shove her beautiful scent right at me.

"*Atirien* means mate," I blurt out, wanting the attention on anything other than my cock. I shift back into my seat, away from her. Hurt and then shock flashes in her eyes. She sits up and slides into the back seat, well away from Renze, as he gives me a cool look.

I put the car back in drive, relieved they're focused on one another again. Although one part of me—one rock-hard part—wanted to say yes to her, to feel those pillowy lips caressing my cock.

Instead, I hurt her.

"I'm sorry, Jet," she whispers from the back seat. "I shouldn't have asked to touch you. It won't happen again."

CHAPTER TWELVE
ACHAIA

Mate? *Mate*! Emotions too numerous to process hit me as Jet drives in absolute silence in the front seat. Renze sits at the other end of the back seat bench. He brings one leg up and turns to face me, his forearm resting on his knee. "Shall we discuss what Jet shared, Achaia?"

I notice he doesn't call me *atirien* just then.

"Why didn't you tell me before now?" That's my first question. It's not as if he hasn't hinted at it, looking back. But shit, he just escaped from a monster-filled maze, and he was locked in there for seven years. I figured a conquest when he got out was just par for the course, maybe.

Renze smiles at me, his dark lips parting. "I was planning to work it into a night filled with pleasure, to take you and tell you at the same time. I wanted you shattering around my cock when I shared that particular truth."

Jet remains silent as the grave in the front seat.

My mind makes a leap, then. "You call him *atiri*. That's the same thing, isn't it?"

Renze's smile broadens, and he nods his assent. Jet shifts in the front seat, the leather crinkling under his weight.

I sit up taller, knowing this conversation is making Jet highly uncomfortable. If I'm good at anything, it's reading people. Jet doesn't want this. Or he does, but he isn't ready. Why did I even let Renze do what he just did? There's so much more at stake here than the strength of our erotic connection. I can't risk my heart or the chance to get answers and rescue Jet's brother, not for Renze. Not for anything.

I look back at Renze. "And if I don't accept?"

"I will wear you down until you do," Renze laughs, shifting forward on the seat to bring his lips to mine. They brush me with the faintest hint of seductive touch. "The stars fated us to belong together, *atirien*. We will have you, and you will ache for us and no one else."

When I don't respond, Renze slides back to his side of the aircar. The aircar is completely soundless as we leave the tropical, verdant forests of Siargao. For hours, we pass through the provinces of Moon and eventually Sipam. I gaze out the window as the sun begins to set. My stomach finally grumbles once the sun has disappeared behind the lush tree line, and Jet looks over his shoulder.

"We should stop in Sipam for the night. There's a hotel I've been to with my brothers. If it's still there, it's as good a place as any to stay."

Renze nods his agreement as I watch the dense forest morph into tiny towns here and there, finally giving way to a city that seems to spring right up out of the jungle. It's a mixture of tall towers and what appear to be treehouses built between trees that are wider around than our car. I've never seen anything like it. Every building is natural shades of wood and foliage. It's stunning.

"Does any of this seem familiar to you, Achaia?" Renze questions gently. "You seem enthralled with the scenery."

I shake my head. "Just admiring how similar it is to Siargao, yet different still. It's almost like they moved the whole city up into the trees to avoid being on the ground."

Jet laughs from the front seat. "That's exactly what they did. You're safe in Sipam in the daytime, but at night and on foot, the Meju dragons will eat you alive."

"The what?" I bark.

Renze lets out a throaty chuckle. "Meju are tiny dragons that hunt in swarms. They look for easy prey. We are safe in the car but will not linger outside the hotel long."

Suddenly, the beautiful city outside my window looks menacing, all dark alleys and even darker tree limbs that seem to jut out of nowhere.

We drive through a hole bored straight through the center of one of the giant trees, and then Jet makes a left down a well-lit street. Cozy-looking restaurants and hotels line both sides, but I notice now that glass tubes connect the treehouses above with the entrances to each store.

"We will not let the meju eat you," Renze laughs. "But if you see an adorable tiny dragon the size of your palm, do not touch it. They are devious little miscreants, and where there is one, there are most assuredly hundreds."

Jet pulls the aircar into a brightly lit hotel roundabout. The moment he enters, a net slides down from the roof above us, caging the car in. Protecting us, I suppose.

A man jogs out from the entrance with a friendly smile. "Welcome to the Naveen Hotel. May I park your aircar?"

Jet hops gracefully out of the front seat and hands the human his keys, eyes moving from one side of the hotel to the other. I recognize this as what it is—he's performing his usual pack function, even though it's just the three of us. There's an anxious but focused set to Jet's shoulders, but when his eyes land on mine, he schools his face into something devoid of emotion.

"Come, Achaia," Renze croons, wrapping my hand in his as he extracts our luggage from the trunk. I attempt to remove my hand to carry my own bag, but Renze simply chuckles. "You are shocked by what Jet shared in the car, *atirien*, but make no mistake—you are mine, and while I am here, you will never carry your own bags."

His white eyes crinkle at the corners as he tugs me toward a door. It's lit on either side by beautiful lamps, built in a style I've never seen before. When we enter the lobby, I'm shocked anew. Everything here is curved, with not a single angle to be seen. It's beautiful. I search deep inside to see if this feels familiar somehow. I'm disappointed when it doesn't.

Jet takes care of getting us a suite, and then I'm led up an exquisite, curved staircase of burled, dark wood. Renze keeps hold of my hand and the luggage, and Jet stalks behind us, a comforting presence to me even though tension radiates from him.

He rounds us to shove an ancient-looking, golden key into our room's door, and when he swings it open, he enters first. Renze and I wait in the hallway for a moment before he reappears and grabs the bags.

The room is heavenly, all neutrals and whites. I gasp as I cross the room to a wall of windows that make up one entire side. Outside, the jungle smashes right up against the window. Limbs crisscross my view, giant leaves and flowers of every shade just out of arm's reach. I cock my head to the side when I realize there's no way to open the window. Perhaps because of what Renze shared earlier.

On cue, he joins me, sitting in the window seat and pulling me onto his lap. I don't want to sink into his chest. We haven't discussed what they revealed to me in the car, but his arms around me are so familiar and comfortable that I can't help myself. In a world that feels horribly certain, Renze gives me clarity and peace. I don't want to sink into it and encourage him, but I can't help myself.

Renze threads his fingers through mine, lifting our arms together as he points outside. "See there, *atirien*? See the glow of eyes in the shadow? If you wait long enough, a meju will appear and give you a sweet look. Just know its brothers and sisters are waiting to suck the marrow from your bones."

As if to highlight his point, he bites at the skin where my neck and shoulder meet, a soft groan leaving his throat. "I need to hunt," he murmurs. "I can smell the blood coursing through your veins, and I want it, *atirien*."

"You're not about to drink her damn blood, are you?" Jet quips from across the room. "I don't wanna watch that."

Renze shifts us upright, letting go of my fingers. "The sharing of a blood meal is customary among mates, Jet, but I will hunt instead."

"Where?" I question. "You've just said we can't go outside."

"I am not worried about the meju, Achaia," Renze laughs. "I am far older and far faster. I will not be gone long. Apart from hunting, I want to see if there is any trace of that alpha following us. I would not think so as far and fast as we came, but we cannot be certain."

Remembering how the alpha tried to attach the mechanical spider to my chest, I shudder. Lifting my chin, I meet Renze's eyes. "Be careful."

"Do not worry," he croons. "I will return safely to you, and then perhaps I will eat *you* before bedtime. What do you think?"

"I think we need to have a conversation," I counter. "Because you haven't been entirely forthcoming, and I want to know everything before we get to your court."

Renze dips his head, bringing his forehead to mine. "You shall have my truths, Achaia. As soon as I return."

Without a backward glance, he sails out the room's only door, leaving me alone with Jet.

CHAPTER THIRTEEN
JET

I watch Renze go, loving that Achaia turned him down. She sits back at the window and peers out, looking for the meju dragons.

That's when I realize this is the first time I've really been alone with her and not ill. And she's studiously ignoring me because of what happened in the aircar. She offered me something and I turned it down, and now things are awkward. Leaning up against the four-poster bed, I watch her in the low light of the room.

Her hair is still braided along one side, but she undoes the knot at the end and begins to undo it.

"Why?" I question.

She doesn't turn to me, which sends a need for domination curling through my gut. "I knew Renze wanted me, and I was fine with that. But mates? I don't even know who I am, Jet."

"If he's right, then you have no choice but to accept the mating," I hedge, wondering if she now feels trapped like I do.

She turns, her hair in a tangle from the braid. Crossing the room, I sigh as I reach for it, using my claws to rake through the mess. I feel her pale eyes on me, but I don't look away from my work.

"Doesn't seem to me like you've accepted it," she goes on, her breath warm against my chest. My stomach clenches at the throaty timber of her voice. It's low and soothing. I don't immediately answer, focusing instead on the braid. As I unravel it, her hair goes wild, sticking out to the side. I tuck it behind her ear and notice a vein in her neck throbbing.

Her heartbeat races, her chest rising rapidly, green eyes still focused on mine. When I move my gaze to meet hers, I notice the way she nips her lower lip, and how delectably plump it is. "What are you thinking about?" I growl, a purr working its way out of my chest as the tips of her breasts touch me. She's so soft and so warm; her nipples harden to points as they brush along my front. I suddenly wish I wasn't wearing a shirt, so I could feel her more closely.

Godsdamnit, I need more of her.

Not waiting for an answer, I run my hand up into her hair, gripping it as I draw her head back, forcing her breasts to smash up against my chest. "Gods, you smell fucking good," I drag my nose up her neck. The scent of her arousal washes over me as one of my hands slides down her hip and over the swell of her round ass. I squeeze tight as she gasps but squirms out of my touch.

Sea-green eyes flash at me as she backs up a step. "No, Jet."

The desire to hunt her hits me so hard that I let out an angry roar.

Achaia stands taller. "Not only no right now, but no in general. No to being mates. No to all of it."

"All of what?" I press, my ire rising at her dismissal.

Her face falls a little, a sad expression greeting me when she looks up. "Renze may believe we're fated to be together, and maybe he's even right. I don't know enough about it to form an opinion. I do know I'm attracted to you both, that's why I tried to touch you in the car." Her face is sad as she lifts her chin. "I also know you haven't had a lot of choices, and your focus is your brother, which it should be."

She's inviting me to share more about my time in the maze, I can tell as much from the way she's phrasing this conversation. I'm just not ready. I'm hot for her, and I want to focus on that heat and the incredible way she smells, not all the very real, very awful shit in our near future.

"So, you'd like to take my choice away right now by making this one for me?" I snarl as I collar her throat and yank her back to me, my fangs snapping in her face.

She doesn't bat a godsdamned eyelid. "I'm saying no until it's not in the heat of the moment, Jet. I'm saying no until it's a choice you're making with a clear mind and not something you're pressured into. I'm saying no because I don't believe you're ready to be anyone's mate. Shit, I don't know if I am either. I'll do this pretend-to-be-mates thing at the court because we have to, but that's as far as I can take this."

Her words hit me, resonating deeply as I let go of her throat. She doesn't want it, not now, maybe not ever.

That should be so freeing for me. Achaia has zero expectations of anything to happen between us. So why do I feel like tearing something to shreds?

She turns from me and sits back down in the window, watching as one meju, and then two, pop up and play in front of her, teasing and taunting.

Resisting the urge to toss her against the wall and fuck that denial away, I turn into the room to unpack my bag.

An hour later, Renze returns with a smile on his face, arms wide as he greets Achaia. "Back safely as promised." There's slightly more color to his pale skin than before he left.

She gives him a little smile in return but turns to look back out the window.

Renze looks over at me, but I grab my bag. "You two should order room service. I'm going into the adjoining room to rest. Take first watch." He nods once, watching as I leave the room and head next door.

I hear him call for food, then sit in the window with Achaia. Eventually, I fall into a fitful sleep, but my dreams are full of enticing visions of Achaia spreadeagle before me, riding Renze's long cock and sucking my balls. I cannot stop fantasizing about fucking her.

This is going to be a problem.

CHAPTER FOURTEEN
RENZE

Jet retires to the second bedroom as I order food and join Achaia in the window. She smiles over at me, although I read her as troubled.

"Something happened while I was gone. What?" I question her gently as she pulls her knees to her chest, finally meeting my gaze with her own.

"I told Jet I didn't accept being mates, not now, maybe not ever."

"With him or with me?" I growl, sliding across the bench seat to pull her feet into my lap.

"Maybe both," she admits, leaning back against the edge of the window. "You withheld critical information from me, Firenze." The hint of a smile plays across her plush lips. "I thought perhaps you simply wanted a post-maze conquest, and as much as I'm attracted to you, that didn't seem like a good idea. But now? You want much more than that, don't you?"

"I want everything," I confirm. "And I shall have it, too."

"Not if I don't agree," she snarks.

I love the confidence radiating from her, but I am more than willing to push her in ways I won't push Jet, given his history in the maze.

"I will have you, whether you verbally agree to it or not," I assure her. "We" —I gesture between us—"are a foregone conclusion, my pretty thing. There is no if; there is only when."

Achaia pulls her feet from my hands and stands. "You'd force yourself on me, even if I didn't want that?"

I stand along with her. "I was saving the *atirien* conversation for a sexier time, but let me make this clear. You belong to me, Achaia. I belong to you. Jet belongs to both of us. If you tell me no, I will pursue you *relentlessly*. There is no escaping me."

She opens her mouth to say something, but in a flash, I grab her and slip to the bedside, tossing her in. Large breasts heave and sway as I climb on top of her and untie the knot of her wrap dress. I unveil her slowly, watching the dip of her stomach, the way her thighs clench together, her underwear hiding her sweet pussy from me.

"You need teasing for this insolence," I rumble. Sucking at my teeth, I spit venom at the juncture of her thighs and rub roughly at her clit with my fingers. She cries out, back arching as she shoves her breasts in my face.

"You're such an asshole," she grits out, rubbing at her nipples even as I nip her fingers.

"I will be if I must." I roll my hips against her thighs, knowing she can feel my hard length, even through the fabric. She cries out as I spit venom on each breast, rubbing it in with my hands, and plucking her nipples until they stand tall for me.

"Consider this, Achaia," I chuckle. "If you were not mine, my venom would hurt you terribly."

"Consider that just because we're fated to be together, it doesn't mean now's a good time," she counters.

"There is only now. Because we never know when our last breath will be. That is why I push you. And will continue to push you until you throw yourself headlong into our mating. Are you nearly there?" I tease as she thrusts up against me.

I slip two fingers inside her and stroke until she's mad with desire, my own rising as my cock twitches behind the uncomfortable fabric of my pants. As her panting cries grow faster and more desperate, I remove my fingers, licking them clean of her honey. "That is enough for tonight, *atirien*. Perhaps if you ask me sweetly, I will wake you in the morning with my tongue."

Achaia sits upright with a furious glare as I slide off the bed, removing my shirt. Her eyes fall to my muscular chest and lower still. I know she is on fire from the venom. Unsated. She will remain that way through multiple orgasms.

Still, she lifts her chin and wraps her dress carefully around herself, only wincing when the fabric brushes over her tender nipples.

I smirk as I fall onto my back, propping my arms behind my head as she lays down with her back to me. Rolling over, I give her plump ass a squeeze, bringing my lips to her ear. "If you cannot wait for relief, tell me, *atirien*. I will grant it the moment you accept me as yours."

"Not happening tonight," she counters. "We've got bigger fish to fry."

Laughing, I roll over onto my back, knowing Jet is likely listening to us. "There is nothing more important than one's mates. Not a thing in the world."

Achaia is silent for a moment, but then room service arrives, and I take intense pleasure in feeding her every bite. She fights me to do it herself, but I will continue to remind her what it is to be mine—as long as I am here, I will care for her in every way I wish to.

In the morning, I wake to find Jet standing at the foot of the bed.

"Did you find any trace of the alpha from the market when you hunted last night?"

"Good morning, Jet," I murmur as I turn to look at Achaia. Her nipples are two hard peaks under her dress, and her heartbeat is fast.

Good. I want her needy and aching with heat from my venom. It will make our 'fake mating' at the court that much easier. Not that it's fake to me. But if that makes it easier for her to accept, then I'll call it that for now.

I slip out of bed and cross the room for my clothes, kicking my pants off as I turn to Jet.

Jet's eyes are locked on my erect, swinging cock as I reach for a fresh pair of trousers. I said I would not push him, but I didn't say I wouldn't tease him at every opportunity to find me attractive.

He licks his lips slowly and follows me across the room, his chest bumping against mine. My cock pokes into his hip as he begins purring, his eyes dropping to my lips. "I asked you a question, vampiri." This is Jet in strategist mode—looking for all the information, all the angles, so he may formulate a plan.

"I saw no hint," I confirm. Every emotion I read from Jet right now is focused. I would give nearly anything to take his hand and place it on my throbbing cock, but I resist the urge, which gives me an idea. Looking down, I spit on my long shaft, hissing as my lips curl at the edges.

"Godsdamnit, you are really something," Jet growls, the purr stopping as I stroke myself with both hands.

"If my mates do not wish to take advantage of my skill, I will enjoy my own self," I laugh, snarling as precum leaks from my tip. Jet does not step away as I stroke harder, throwing my head back, knowing the alpha in him will relish being presented with my neck.

"You are hard to resist, vampiri," he growls, reaching out to drag his claws down my throat and my chest. He slides them all the way down my stomach, stopping just short of where I want his attention. My entire body thrums with need for him, this alpha who plays the long game in denying that he's mine.

A groan leaves my throat. Yet another excellent idea comes to me, and I drop to my knees in front of him. Jet looks down at me, nostrils flared as my lips hover just over the front of his pants. I tug hard at my cock, my fists moving faster as sloppy noises ring through the room. In the bed, Achaia stirs.

I pant as pleasure builds in my core, my balls tightening as Jet takes a step closer. My mouth is practically on his obvious erection, his piercings visible through the front of his pants. I reach out and nip his cock through his jeans, a shocked groan leaving Jet's mouth.

Orgasm hits me as I gasp, closing my mouth around his hard length, letting the force of my moan reverberate into his skin. He doesn't touch me, but a wet spot spreads along the front of his jeans.

"Fuck," Jet hisses. "Your godsdamn mouth, Renze."

Achaia is up in the bed, seated in the middle like a queen, watching us in silence.

With a final bellow, I spurt all over Jet's legs, fucking into my own hands as he presses his cock to my lips.

When ecstasy fades, I sit back on my ankles, my head falling back. What I read from Jet now is pure, focused intensity. He wants me, and yet he hesitates.

But all of that will change in the vampiri court because there is no room for weak mates there. He and Achaia will have to pretend to be thoroughly mine.

I cannot wait.

CHAPTER FIFTEEN

ACHAIA

I see Renze's actions for precisely what they are—the vampiri is playing dirty, as dirty as he can, to get Jet and me to give in. Somehow, that sparks my own need to do things my way, to not be pushed and pulled by external forces. And I find myself wondering if that in itself is a hint about my past.

Despite how fucking erotic it is to see them, I do my best to hide my obvious arousal and slide off the bed, walking into the bathroom. I take a quick shower, spending the whole time wondering if they're fucking while I'm in here. But I decide, ultimately, that that particular vision probably only exists in my fantasies.

Jet isn't ready for any of that, despite the fact that he clearly wants it.

We leave the beautiful Naveen Hotel by mid-morning, getting back on the road. Truth be told, I'm sad to leave the Sipam province. I'd love to explore more of it. To venture out at night, knowing I'm taking my life into my hands. To visit the shops and restaurants from the main road the hotel was on. I ache for more adventure, and I have to wonder what that says about my past, if anything.

The air outside our car begins to chill as we drive through the afternoon in silence. Eventually, the foliage changes from lush, multicolored flora to the darker, harsher blackwood Thomas taught me about.

It's not until the sun begins to set that Renze reaches up and taps Jet on the shoulder. "I should drive."

Jet nods, not questioning Renze but putting the car in park and rounding it to hop in the passenger seat.

Renze slips quietly into the driver's seat, turning to look at Jet and me. "The vampiri do not look fondly on weakness. Our arrival will be shocking enough. There is every likelihood they are not aware we escaped the maze or that Cashore died to protect Diana. I do not think that news would have made its way here yet."

A chill sneaks down my spine as Renze continues, "As I told Achaia, vampiri derive power from sex, so do not be surprised when it is all around you. Meetings and meals often turn into orgies. You will be surrounded by hundreds of very powerful, very old vampiri. Follow my direction without fail, and we will be fine."

Jet's lips purse into a thin line, but he nods. As an alpha, following directions doesn't come naturally to him.

Well, tough shit. Falling in line doesn't feel natural to me, either. But at the very least, I've got an extreme sense of self-preservation.

Renze puts the aircar in drive. I stare out the window in silence, watching the landscape morph even darker into shades of brown and black, the trees becoming sparse except for random clumps, and dark spines shooting jaggedly out of the ground like black daggers. Goddess, if the landscape itself looks this dangerous, what will its inhabitants be like?

Suddenly, I long for the steamy lushness of Siargao. I wonder if that means I'm not from this province because I feel no connection to it as we make our way through the stark, sparse environment. My thoughts spin in my mind while both males are silent as we enter a canyon of pitch-black stone.

"They know we have arrived," Renze murmurs, white eyes traveling to the cliffs that rise like walls on either side of the narrow road.

Jet is tense in the front seat, focused as he keeps an eye out for anything amiss. "Tell me this wasn't a grave mistake, Renze," he barks. "If shit goes south, we can hardly fight off hundreds of vampiri."

"Hardly," Renze agrees. "You will not need to fight, *atiri*. If it comes down to it, they would only expect me to."

"What do you mean?" Jet snaps, turning in his seat as Renze puts a palm up.

"We will be there soon. Say nothing until I tell you to."

Jet bristles and growls but looks forward again. The road takes on a sharp incline, around turn after turn until I think I'll be sick from the height of our precarious path. On the left side of the car, the black rocks now drop straight down into a gorge. Wherever the vampiri court is, it exists very high up.

I hate heights.

"Shit!" I bark out, realizing I just remembered something about myself, something I didn't know. "I hate heights!" I blurt it out as Renze smiles at me in the mirror.

"Aside from Lombornei's winged monsters, vampiri are one of few creatures who enjoy heights. It does not surprise me that you would not prefer them, *atirien*. Wherever you hail from, it is not here."

Falling silent again, I revel in that small victory. Little by little, I'm narrowing in on how things make me feel. It's by no means a giant revelation, but it's something, at least. I love lush tropical forests. I love color, and I'm fascinated by dangerous animals. I'm unafraid of monsters, even though I should be. And I *hate heights*.

It's not much, but it's more than I learned about myself in the three years I lived with Thomas and Maya.

For another half hour, we drive in total silence, the sun finally setting as the moon begins its climb above us. We round a bend in the gorge, and I gasp. At the far end of what I can see, a blood-red city is built right into the cliff. Black rock hangs out over it, making it clear the city wouldn't be visible from above.

Our aircar crawls along the gorge's only road, heading straight for the city. I realize this means the vampiri can never be caught unaware by visitors. Unless one could fly, there's simply no way to access the court unseen.

The closer we get, I see black windows, black stone roofs, and black spires jutting above the blood-red walls. Every so often, a platform opens wide with a huge doorway to the exterior.

Renze looks at me in the rearview but says nothing. Finally, we make our way up to a massive black metal gate. Carvings of winged monstrosities adorn the entire front of the entrance. Above the horribly disfigured creatures stand seven carved vampiri, each holding weapons to the throats of the creatures at their feet.

"Manangal," Renze mutters. "A vampiri's most bitter and ancient rival."

Jet releases a growl at that. "Fucking disgusting."

"Indeed," Renze deadpans, his lips pulled into a snarl. "If I never see another, it will not be soon enough."

I'm just about to ask when he saw one because the carving looks old as if it tells a story from many lifetimes before our own. But the black gates open, and a figure stands there, hands tucked behind his back. He's broad but elegant, just like Renze. Statuesque. That's perhaps the right word to describe the handsome male. He's regal.

"Stay in the car," Renze commands as he opens the door and slips out with predatory grace.

Jet snarls but remains in his seat when I plant my hand on his chest without thinking. "Give him a minute," I demand as our eyes follow Renze.

He moves with purpose, stalking up to the figure. The other vampiri smiles, but there's nothing friendly about the way he looks at Renze. His dark blue hair is braided intricately from front to back, long braids piled into a knot on top of his head.

From where we are, Jet and I can't hear a word they say.

Renze inclines his head and then speaks as the other vampiri barks out a string of questions. Renze stiffens but answers them and returns to the car after a few tense moments.

"What happened?" Jet questions.

"I will tell you in a few moments," Renze cautions, directing the car through the gates. The other vampiri has disappeared, but I don't miss the dozens of guards who line long, open hallways stacked on top of each other in a square around the courtyard we're now in. They all look down on us as we enter. Renze puts the car in park and turns. "Remember what I told you both. Quiet until we reach our rooms, then I will answer your questions."

He opens his door and slips out gracefully as Jet turns to me. "Stay close, Achaia."

I nod and leave the car, Jet hovering behind me like a protective, possessive shadow. I'd sink into his warmth if I wasn't so focused on the dozens of vampiri who watch us from above.

Renze pays them no mind but walks through a dark archway, indicating we should follow. Jet and I remain silent, soaking in the sights and sounds of a vampiri court. Renze glides up black hall after black hall, lit only with flaming torches. Everything here is so fucking ominous. I think about how much Renze loves the sun and its warmth, and I find it hard to reconcile that version of him with this muted midnight court.

After ten solid minutes of twisting and turning up obsidian stone halls, we come to a door and Renze sails through, closing it behind us. He lets out a deep sigh and presses his forehead to mine. At the same time, I feel him reach out to where Jet continues hovering behind me. We stand quietly for a long, heated moment before Renze's white eyes flick around the room, his lips pursed into a thin line.

Jet leaves us and paces around the room, examining the ornate red and black wallpaper, the black bed and bedding, and the intricately carved blackwood ceiling. It's…over the top. Stunning but cold.

"I have a hard time imagining you living here," Jet murmurs, turning to

Renze. "All of this black reminds me so much of the fucking maze." He stands, tense, as Renze slips across the room and presses up against him, bringing his lips to Jet's as he whispers back.

"I should have warned you, *atiri*. I did not think of it until now. Whatever you need, you shall have it."

"Don't treat me like a victim," Jet snarls.

Renze slides his hand between Jet's thighs. "Noted, alpha."

Jet's dark eyes move to mine, and he shakes his head as relief and disappointment war in my mind. The idea of seeing these big males locked together in passion makes me unspeakably hot. But this place feels wrong and dangerous to me. I want to leave as soon as we can.

Jet pushes Renze's hand away. "We came here for allies. Let's ascertain if that's even possible, and then get the fuck out of here."

Renze bites at Jet's lower lip, tugging it as the large alpha rumbles from deep in his chest. The noise lights me up as I take a step closer, Renze's hand going back to rubbing the length of Jet's obviously hard cock.

"Are you certain, *atiri*?" Renze presses. "I can sense your need. Perhaps a vampiri court will be easier to process if you come a few times first. I want to taste you." Renze has fallen so easily into treating Jet like they're in a relationship. This entire visit is going to be hard, I can already tell.

"Some other time," I agree with Jet, knowing he's not ready for this. "Tell us what happened at the gate."

Renze sighs in frustration and turns from Jet, pacing to the window as he beckons us to follow. I realize it's not actually a window but a giant open platform like a porch. It sticks out in a semicircle above the gorge, although other spires of the city are clearly visible through the arched opening.

Renze steps out and gestures around. "We are in the vampiri formal court, where vampiri sub-courts come to celebrate the solstice and engage in politics. This is the place the entire vampiri nation is ruled from. Most sub-courts live in their own small cities along this gorge. We only come here when the formal season is in session, which it is now."

He looks up, pointing to a spire above ours, hundreds of stories higher than our own. "Each sub-court has its own spire, and the higher up, the more your political power. Sinan is who I suspect rules now. He has chosen to put us in this castle wing because it is lower down. He is making a point to me that although I have returned, he does not regard my sub-court the way he used to. When I was free, Cashore was king, and so we always resided in the highest wing, way up there."

He points across the vast city to a beautiful crimson outcropping with multiple enormous archways. Even from here, I can see vampiri standing on the open platform.

"That is Sinan's court, according to the vampiri at the gate, so he has obviously taken on the mantle of king with Cashore locked inside the maze. It is as Ascelin and I suspected, so we must tread carefully. As Cashore's First Warrior, I am obligated to defend his honor."

"By yourself?" Jet deadpans, looking around at the wash of red and black that is our current view.

"By myself," Renze confirms.

Jet looks over at me with a wry smile. "Anybody else want a drink? This all sounds like a terrible idea."

CHAPTER SIXTEEN
JET

After everything Renze just shared, I can't imagine a scenario where Sinan will want to become our ally. Why would he? He probably has everything he ever wanted. Cashore is effectively dead, and Sinan is now king. I'm having trouble understanding why he would lift a finger to help us rid Lombornei of Rama's devastating rule. I can only hope that she's somehow a thorn in his side and that will bring him into our camp.

The reality is that this place doesn't appear to be devastated in the slightest. So it must be true then that she focused entirely on Siargao. Cut the head off the snake, and the snake dies. Isn't that the saying?

Renze looks at me. "I need to visit an old friend. I'd like to know more about Sinan's rule. The vampiri you saw at the opening of the gate is Elleph, Sinan's First Warrior. It does not bode particularly well that Sinan himself did not greet us. I need more information. I will return shortly." He steps to the platform's edge, his muscles bunching tight as Achaia sputters.

"Wait, Renze. You're just going to leap off? It's hundreds of feet to the other side."

Renze turns with a smile, pushing his way into Achaia's space as he grips her throat, stroking her plump lower lip with his thumb. "Vampiri do not fly, but we glide very well, *atirien*. In the same way that I shift to run, I am able to do it in the open air. I will return safely."

It's disconcerting to look out over the expansive gorge and the black wings built right into the cliffs, but I trust that he knows what he's doing. Not for the first time, I wish Ten were here. He'd know everything there is to know about vampiri customs and habits. I have so many questions that he could answer.

I shove my worry for him deep down because if I allow it to bubble up to the surface of my mind, I'll go crazy with fear for him. Wondering what Rama's doing to him right this minute makes me want to scratch my godsdamned skin off.

"Do you need us to do anything while you're gone?" I question the vampiri as he presses his lips to Achaia's tenderly. When he parts from her, he turns to me with a grin.

"I need all the power I can get, *atiri*. It would be most helpful if you'd fuck our mate so I may return to the heady scent of your pleasure. And then I would like to fuck you both before dinner. That is what you can do for me since you asked." He meets my gaze with a sensual, self-satisfied look.

Heat barrels down my spine as Achaia risks a glance over at me, her blue-green eyes narrowed and wary. She pushes at Renze's chest. "Go. We'll see you when you get back."

He crosses the short space to me and grips my throat the way he gripped hers. In the maze, we fought so many fucking times. I'd just as soon tear his arm from its socket than have him touch me. But outside? I want it.

"I have given you space, *atiri*. But your pleasure would indeed bring me power. Consider it please, for all our sakes." He says nothing else, but steps back and then leaps into the open space as Achaia hisses out a worried breath, flying to the edge of the platform.

I grab her at the last minute, wrapping an arm around her waist as she watches him. It's incredible really. "I can't believe he can do that," she whispers. "It's otherworldly, the way he slips from point to point."

We stand silently as Renze disappears into the depths of the dark city, obscured from our view.

And then I'm painfully aware of my now-hard cock pressed between the twin globes of Achaia's ass. Renze's suggestion spins in my head as I rock my hips once, watching the way my outlined length slides along the soft fabric of her dress.

She lets out a breathless sigh but pushes away from me. It's polite but firm.

I open my mouth to say something when a sudden knock at the door causes me to bristle. "Stay here," I command, jogging across the room to the door. Already. I have a knife in my hand. When I open the door, a vampiri woman is there with a rack full of clothes.

Her white eyes dart to the knife in my hand, and she sighs. "I was sent by King Sinan to bring you appropriate clothing for a welcome dinner this evening. Please do not attempt to stab me; it would be a waste of energy to disarm you."

"You could try," I snap, sliding the knife back into its holster as I grab the rack and drag it inside. When I look back up, she's slipping down the hallway in that same swift, smoky motion the vampiri are so good at.

Achaia peeks around the corner of the platform, crossing the room only when I nod that it's alright. She eyes the dresses like they're snakes. "Is it bad that all I can think of is what if there's some way to spy on us or poison us with clothing?"

I frown and toss the clothing onto the bed. "Truthfully, the same thought crossed my mind. I can only assume that this room is bugged, because it's what I'd do if a rival pack came to our tower back home."

"Do you miss it?" she asks softly, leaning against the bed.

"Miss what?" I press.

"Whatever your life was before Rama and the maze?" Her voice is cautious and low, her tone even and quiet. I'm conscientious enough to realize she wants to know me, to understand me, because Renze has her believing we're connected in some magical, fated way. She denied our matehood, but we're still drawn together like magnets.

She sighs when I don't immediately answer.

"Come here," I command, purring from deep in my chest. Renze's suggestion that I have her while he's gone takes up all the space at the forefront of my mind. I could do anything I want to her, and I suspect she'd welcome it as long as I chose it and initiated.

"Why?" she snaps, lifting her chin as she pulls back to a full stand.

"Because I said so," I growl, reaching for the fabric at the front of her dress and twisting it into a ball. I use it like a handle, yanking her to my chest so I can look down at her. "When I tell you to come, come."

"Well, if you made it sound like fun, perhaps I would," she croons, eyes locked onto mine in a challenge.

"I don't miss what I had before," I retort, dropping the fabric of her dress. I reach up and pinch both of her nipples hard as she gasps. "I only miss being free to choose what I did with my time."

Achaia moves back, but I follow, bumping her with my chest, reveling in the way her huge tits sway as she falls onto the bed. I haven't fucked anyone but myself since we left the maze, and my libido is in overdrive after the tattoo incident and our car tease. If Renze can have her, why shouldn't I? It doesn't have to mean anything. It can just be a way to get off. There doesn't have to be any emotional attachment at all. Except, there is.

Those thoughts war with one another as Achaia snarls. "I'm not a fucktoy, Jet."

"Are you not?" I question. "You seem happy to be fucked by Renze as long as it doesn't mean anything."

"You're right," she barks back. "He makes me feel good. Physically, emotionally, mentally. Even so, I haven't agreed to be his. At least he's charming. You're looking at me the same way you might look at a glory hole in a public restroom—just a means to an end."

"What in the hell are you talking about?" I bark. "A glory hole?"

"You've never seen that? You stick your dick through to get sucked. You just don't know who's on the other side…" she muses aloud.

"I've never seen that. If I found a hole in the wall in the maze, I sure as shit wouldn't stick my dick through to see what happened."

"Maybe it's something from my past," she murmurs. "I'll ask Renze if he's heard of that when he gets back."

She's lost to wondering about who she is again, and I don't have those answers for her. I hope like hell that glory holes aren't a huge part of her past persona, but there's just no way of knowing.

I'm hard and I want her, and I hate that she ducked her way out of an interaction with me. I was so torn days ago, but when she told me no at the hotel, it flipped a switch somewhere in my brain.

Eventually, I break our heated stare-off and look at the rack of dresses. "How do we feel about dressing up?"

Achaia shrugs. "Feels like bullshit, but I'm a sucker for sequins and beads."

I laugh at that, rounding the bed and pulling the rolling rack closer to her. A dozen floor-length dresses hang from the bar, all in dark shades of red and black and gray. Next to that hang formal suits, along with dark leather vests.

"Let's have a little fun." I wink at Achaia. "Might as well enjoy ourselves before we let Sinan know his rule isn't real, but we'd like his help."

She snorts out a laugh but slides off the bed and fingers the dresses, examining each one before landing on a charcoal gray number.

I'm entranced watching her decide.

"Take your dress off," I direct before I even realize I'm doing it.

She lifts her chin but undoes the tiny knot at the front, slipping the dress off her shoulders. Underneath, black lace holds back her beautiful, round breasts. My eyes fall on the way her waist pinches in, then flares out into big, juicy hips. Her scent hits me then, not just the usual sea salt, but her earlier arousal and Renze's venom.

Licking my lips, I step closer and unclip her bra, letting it fall to the ground.

"Won't be able to wear that with any of these dresses," I murmur as her eyes remain locked on mine. "Let me help you into it."

She cocks her head to the side, perhaps trying to decide if I'm hitting on her again, or if she needs to rebuff me. Instead, she hands me the dress, and I drop to a knee in front of her. I hold the dress open so she can step in.

"You look good down there," she purrs, placing both hands on my shoulders as I resist the urge to bury my face between her shapely thighs. I want to scent every inch of her. I give in, just for a moment, running my cheek along her inner thigh and biting at the juncture of her leg and hip.

Achaia yips but stills, her grip on my shoulders tightening. We're walking a fine line. She's told me no multiple times, and I'm beginning to hate it.

"Again," she whispers, blue-green eyes focused on me as her pupil begins to overtake the color.

I rub my lips along the front of her thigh next, letting my fangs drag down her bronzed skin as she hisses in a breath.

Slowly, I stand, pulling the dress up over her hips, dragging my claws along her skin as I go. Her eyes don't move from mine, her gaze confident as I pull the thick straps up over her shoulders.

"Turn," I tell her, reveling in the way goosebumps pepper her skin. But she does as I ask, pulling that sheet of red hair up over her shoulder to reveal the back of the dress to me.

Except there is no back. The shoulder straps travel long and low, meeting just above the dimples in her ass. Her entire back is exposed, her tattoo on full display.

I slide the zipper up over her hips, grimacing at how the dress covers next to nothing.

"How do I look?" she questions, taking a step away from me and spinning.

"If vampiri get drunk on sex," I grumble, "they're going to lose their minds seeing you in this."

She preens under my attention, a pink blush traveling across her round cheeks. I wonder how pink they'd get after a few hours in bed together? I know dozens of ways to get a woman off, and a growing part of me wants to do that with her.

"I'm going to touch you," I murmur, surprising myself and her as she looks over her shoulder, one dark red brow sliding upward.

"Is that so?" she teases. "We agreed not to pursue this, Jet."

"Friends can tease each other and fuck," I counter. A muscle twitches in her jaw as she grits it tight.

I consider what it might feel like to eat her out and have Renze show up to see what we're doing. That idea sends heat flooding through my system as I glance at the bed behind her. Am I choosing to touch her right now?

I fucking am.

Just then, I hear a noise on the exterior platform, my eyes focused over Achaia's naked shoulder.

Renze slips gracefully into the room with a knowing smile. "By all means, continue," he encourages. He stops in his tracks when Achaia crosses the room toward him. I'm entranced watching her luscious curves move under the beaded fabric of the charcoal dress she picked. Her whole back is bare and inviting as Renze takes her hand and spins her once, eyeing the exposed skin.

"Absolutely stunning," he whispers, placing her hand on his obvious erection. "See what you do to me, *atirien*? I need a taste of you before dinner. I want my brethren to smell your release all over me."

Achaia laughs as she turns to look at me, Renze pulling her into his arms as he wraps them carefully around her.

White eyes meet mine, sending my natural aggression into overdrive. I cross the room to the beautiful couple and grip Achaia's throat, squeezing it tight. She's caught between Renze and me, but she looks fucking thrilled about it.

"I wasn't done," I growl.

Her brows curl upward mirthfully as she challenges me with a self-satisfied look. "You looked pretty good on your knees, Jet," she teases as Renze lets out a deep snarl.

"Jet got on his knees for you? That is something I would dearly love to see," Renze purrs, pulling Achaia's hair to one side and kissing her shoulder. "Sadly, we need to prepare for a welcome dinner Sinan is throwing in our honor—word traveled quite fast of our arrival."

I sigh and take a step back, shoving my hands into my pockets. "So, fake mates?"

CHAPTER SEVENTEEN
RENZE

Vampiri courts have long been rife with political intrigue and drama, but it seems this has worsened under Sinan's rule. When I visited an old friend just now, it became clear Sinan is reaping the benefits of Cashore's absence without actually behaving like a king. The likelihood of him wishing to become our ally grows smaller by the second. Still, we must try. We owe it to Tenebris.

We will enjoy the formal dinner and dancing afterward. If I can sway Sinan to our side, I will. If not, we will leave first thing in the morning to meet Noire, Diana, and Ascelin and attempt to locate the Builder.

Being here without Asc feels wrong. She is Cashore's other First Warrior. She and I are meant to work as a team. I have not been without her in hundreds of years. It hits me hard now that I am in our home for the first time since we were imprisoned by Rama.

Jet walks behind me with Achaia, hovering protectively at her side. I sense he's focused on our surroundings, as always, as I lead them through hall after dark hall, heading for the large dining area of the formal castle. We pass no one on our way, and I am certain that is by Sinan's design. He wants me to know that he controls the vampiri now, that there are no friends for me in this court.

Fucking short-sighted asshole.

"What are we in for?" Jet questions a second time.

Angling my head over my shoulder, I risk a glance at my handsome mate. He selected a fitted three-piece suit, although he has left the top buttons open with his tan skin exposed. I want to rip the entire thing down the front and have him against the wall, but this is neither the time nor the place. Still, I will have him soon. I have given him space, but my need to dominate my mates is beginning to wear at the edges of my formidable control. We need to be strong in this court.

"Dinner is exactly as you would expect, but it is typical to dance afterward. I'd like to catch up with a few former allies if they are still at court. There may be contacts here who can help us sway Sinan to our cause."

I hear Achaia open and close her mouth, and I turn, walking slowly backward. "What is it, *atirien?*"

She blushes, a rose-tinted hue traveling across high, round cheeks. "I was going to ask about my tattoo, but I know that isn't why we came. I'm just anxious to find out something about myself if it's possible."

"I have a plan for that tomorrow, Achaia," I share. "We will visit another old friend. If anyone can tell us of your tattoo, it will be her." I smile at them both, changing the subject. "Vampiri are all gifted at reading emotion. Try to maintain a hold on yours while you are here, lest they pick you apart for fun."

Jet shoots me a satisfied, lazy smile. "Noire and I trained against that when we ran Siargao. I'll be fine, and I'll protect Achaia if you have to leave us."

I stop my backward momentum and take a step toward him, and Jet is unable to stop in time. Bringing my hands up to his chest, I shove him hard into the wall, smiling when I hear a stone crack under the weight of his bulky muscle.

Surprise and white-hot heat show on Jet's face as his fangs descend, plump lips curling into a snarl. Achaia watches us in silence, but the heady scent of her arousal permeates the air.

Without warning, I crash my lips to Jet's. I need connection, I need more. I have given him space, but I am losing the war for control. I have very little mercy left to gift him. Achaia has chosen to deny him, but I can no longer do so. Being in my home court has my need overwhelming everything else.

I wrap my longer tongue around his and tug on it as he lets out a possessive growl into my lips. We are nothing more than a clash of lips and teeth. Achaia stands with one hand on the wall to steady herself, her staccato heartbeat fueling my lust while she watches. Her muscles tremble with need as I bite Jet's thick lower lip and pull on it, a whine issuing from his bobbing throat.

Reaching out, I pull Achaia close; close enough that she is right in our space with her huge breasts pressed to Jet's arm.

"Kiss her," I demand as our lips part. He turns to the beautiful woman at our side, dark eyes falling to her plump red lips.

And then he wraps a fist in her hair and takes her mouth forcefully, bending her back as I snarl, my cock leaping in my pants. There has never been anything this sexually intoxicating for me. Seeing my alpha mate dominate our female is pure bliss. I slide a hand into the front of his pants and roll his heavy balls between my fingers as Jet throws his head back and growls.

"Don't stop," he commands me, taking Achaia's mouth again, both hands fisted in her hair. They were playing earlier, on the verge of touching. I interrupted them, but I want to see it happen. The needy, aching noises coming from them are gasoline on the bonfire of my lust. I feel like I could pull the entire castle down brick by black brick.

Jet's pierced cock throbs in my hand, precum leaking from him as I stroke, reveling in his velvety thickness. His passionate kiss with Achaia turns desperate and ragged before he throws his head back and lets out a low moan.

This is not the time and place to have them for the first time, but I am unable and unwilling to halt my actions. Jet must sense the direction of my thoughts because he smiles lazily at me and shifts away from my ministrations, pulling Achaia firmly into his arms. The kiss he dazzles her with is tender and deep, his tongue dancing along hers as his focus moves to her needs above his own.

Yes. This is as it should be. She is our treasure, a gift from the gods to us, and it is our sacred duty to protect and worship her. And fuck her constantly.

Jet bends down and hauls Achaia up into his arms, high enough to sling her legs over his shoulders as she wraps her hands in his hair. I step to his side, running a hand up her thigh, pushing the beaded fabric of her dress up, up, and up until her bare pussy is exposed to us.

"So fucking wet and ready," Jet growls. "You want to come on my tongue before this stupid dinner?"

I snarl as she nods assent, biting her lip as we both watch Jet. His focus is entirely on her as he leans forward and sucks in a ragged breath. "So good," he mutters. "So godsdamned good." He's lost to arousal, and I cannot tear my gaze from them.

Jet's warm, pink tongue slips between Achaia's thighs, running in a line from her sensitive clit before dipping into her sweet honey. She cries out as Jet groans, a deep rolling purr resounding from his chest.

Vampiri don't purr, but the resonant sound he makes has me leaking precum into my pants. I ache to shatter with them.

Achaia's cries grow louder and more broken as he continues a slow and delicious tour of her heat. He teases and taunts her, never losing control, never taking her roughly.

"More, Jet," she demands. "I need you wild. Please."

"You'll have me how I wish," he snarls into her pussy. "And I wish for slow and controlled."

"*No*," she gasps out, attempting to rock her hips against his mouth.

"May I join you, *atiri?*" I whisper into Jet's ear.

Our eyes meet, and he gives me a look that tells me everything I need to know. He wants me.

Leaning over his shoulder, I snake my tongue along his as he shudders, caged in between my arms. Jet releases a deep, needy cry as my tongue wraps around his and pulls. And then, I slide it up and around our mate's clit, lapping gently as he eats her from below. The dual pressure of our soft lapping turns her into a hellcat, demanding more—harder, now.

"Stop fucking teasing me, you bastar–*oh fuck*," she gasps out when I pull at her clit with the forks in my tongue. Jet unleashes on her then, thrusting several fingers inside her pussy as he attacks her clit with me. And then we are nothing more than a wild clash of wet heat on her sensitive bud as she screams our names, her body clenching and tightening.

Jet growls repeatedly before reaching over one thigh and pinching Achaia's clit. The effect is instantaneous, her back bowing as her screams ring along the dark, empty hallway. Anyone could come upon us here in the open, and that gets me insanely hot. It is the vampiri way, but watching my beautiful mate come down from that orgasm, I wonder if I could convince my mates to let me fuck them in front of a crowd.

I would like that very much, I decide. Very much indeed.

My focus is honed in on my stunning mates, on the way Achaia slumps against the wall, and Jet sets her down carefully, pressing his big body to hers until she looks up into his dark eyes. "You came so prettily for me, little one. Would you sound that lovely breaking apart on my thick knot?"

I am spellbound watching him actively taunt her, seeing a hint of who he could be when he escapes the hellish maze Rama has turned his mind into. Perhaps Achaia denying him was exactly what he needed to make him willing to take her. He reads as centered and confident like this.

Achaia lifts her chin and slips out of his embrace with a teasing look. "Tsk, alpha. I think the question is, how loud would you squeal if I climbed on top of you and took what I wanted. I don't care for gentle romance, Jet. I need violence."

Without another word, she turns from us and disappears into the dark depths of the hallway as Jet watches her go, licking his lips as her skirts vanish before us. "That was…"

"Breathtaking," I suggest. "Radiant. Enchanting. Perfect. If I could say fuck dinner, let us retire to our rooms, I would do so. But we cannot deny Sinan."

Jet swipes a hand over his mouth and jogs up the hallway, trailing our mate with intense focus.

I slip past them both to take the lead, eventually passing through a giant stone archway into the vaulted, elegant ballroom where formal dinners take place. Jet's earlier comment about the court reminding him of the maze is accurate—everything here has a similar dark gothic feel.

Long tables line the rectangular room with Sinan's glossy black table at the very end, facing his subjects. I bristle at that. He is not my king, and I will not address him as such. Not while Diana lives.

Nearly the entire room full of hundreds of my brethren turns as one, falling silent as I stride into the room. Elleph appears in front of me, glancing narrowly over my shoulder.

"Firenze," he addresses me by my formal name. "You are looking well, although what have you brought with you? Appetizers, I hope?" His condescending tone is designed to put me on edge. But I am easily a hundred years older than him, so I ignore the barb.

The vampiri court is a place of insults and intrigue. I will have to play this game, although I do not relish this part of being home. "You look much the same, Elleph. Not that I had much cause to notice you before."

He bristles and snarls, but I turn to my mates. "Come." It's a simple command they follow well as we pace the long, full hall toward the head. I wish Ascelin were here with me. As a First Warrior pair, it will appear meaningful that we are not together. Typically, we would never separate as long as our king lives. But our quest is greater than simply protecting Cashore's spirit. Still, I miss the Chosen One. I find myself anxious to return to her soon.

Jet pulls closer, Achaia nearly sandwiched between our bodies by the time we reach the end of the hall.

She comes to my side, Jet hovering protectively behind her as I see the self-proclaimed king of the vampiri court for the first time since I was taken.

"Firenze, welcome home," Sinan purrs in an easy, pleased tone. Crimson hair is braided intricately into a crown atop his head. I would wager he did this just for my benefit. I would like nothing more than to rip that crown from his head and present it to Diana with the severed remains.

"Sinan." I smile, cocking my head respectfully to the side in the way vampiri do for equals. I will not bow to him.

"You have missed much, Firenze. I am king now. A formal bow would do nicely."

I smile at that. "My apologies, Sinan, but I cannot. My allegiance remains to Cashore."

The vampiri stiffens and stands up from his ornate carved chair. "We heard he was killed attempting to escape the maze. Are you saying that is false?" His muscles quiver in what I assume is anger as I hold back a grin, despite knowing I will elicit his help shortly.

"Funny how news of his death traveled here so quickly. Tell me how that came to be, Sinan?"

He ignores my question as a crowd gathers around us. I watch his white eyes dart from side to side. He was a stupid asshole when Cashore was king, and it appears he remains so.

"The prophecy of the Chosen One has come to pass. Cashore is gone in physical form," I confirm, "but he gifted his spirit to a shifter, the mate of Alpha Noire of Pack Ayala. You may remember his father who visited us here when he first took control of Siargao."

Sinan turns apoplectic with rage, fury radiating from him. "I will tell you this, Firenze. If you came to relieve me of my crown, you will not succeed. The vampiri courts are loyal to me, and as Cashore is not able to grace us with his presence–"

I cut him off with a flick of my hand. "I have no intention of relieving you of that crown, Sinan. I am simply telling you that Cashore's spirit lives on in Diana Ayala, and thus, my loyalty remains to her as our queen and Chosen One."

There are gasps, followed by hushed whispers in the crowd. I sense my mates' wishes to pepper me with questions, but there will be time to answer them later. Jet is aware of the vampiri prophecy, but I don't know that Achaia is.

The crowd parts, and a stunning navy-haired vampiri female slips through. Her deeply cut black dress sways around her sensual hips. She approaches me, pressing her forehead to mine. "Welcome home, Firenze." Her voice is throaty and low when we part.

Turning, I gesture to Jet and Achaia. "*Min-atirien*, may I present Zara of Court Stellen, a long-time friend of mine."

I sense Achaia's immediate dislike of her, but she gives Zara a polite nod as Jet presents her with a rakish grin. "Hello, Zara. I'm Jet of Pack Ayala. This is Achaia."

"Pack Ayala?" Sinan's deep voice breaks through our reunion. "This is the pack you claim Cashore infused himself into?"

Jet turns with a nod. "That's the one. The Chosen One is my brother Noire's mate." Ah, Jet is catching on quickly by using Diana's formal title, as opposed to her first name.

Sinan leaps over the table, landing gracefully as he folds his pale hands behind his back, stalking to stand next to Zara who eyes my mates with something between bitter distaste and outright hatred. "Did I hear *'minatirien'*, Firenze? You are mated?" White eyes drift to Jet and Achaia's ears, and then back to me.

"I am," I confirm with a smile. "Blessed be the gods to grant me two mates." I expect Jet to stiffen, but he plays the part well, smirking at Zara and Sinan as they attempt to figure out what to do next.

Just then, a black shadow appears at my side, a soft whine reaching my ears. When I look down, one of the court's resident velzen has seated itself upon my foot, looking up at me with big black eyes. Seeing one for the first time in years, he reminds me of Jet's shift form, but far smaller and lankier. This one is pitch black, although most have white spots or white patches somewhere on their furry bodies.

The velzen's long black snout rests against my knee as my mates look at me curiously.

"What's that?" breathes Achaia, taking a step closer to me. I reach for her hand and pull her into my arms, dropping down to a knee as I bring her with me. I pointedly ignore Zara and Sinan. They are not my focus, and an initial show of power will go a long way to bringing Sinan to my side, if such a thing is even possible.

I try to see the velzen from Achaia's perspective. He's something between a cat, a dog and a fox, if I had to explain it most accurately. At this point, he is still small, thirty pounds or so.

"It's beautiful," she murmurs, stroking the velzen's elegant snout and pointed ears.

I gesture to the gold cuff around his front left foot, a chain wrapping around his leg and connecting to a collar at his neck. "Velzen are the equivalent of vampiri guard dogs. Fiercely loyal and highly destructive. See this?" I stroke the velzen's long leg, gesturing to the extra skin behind his elbow. He wriggles, his long black tail swirling against the floor as he turns to watch me.

"Velzen glide by, spreading their front legs, almost as if they had wings. You will see them all around the court. Once claimed by a family, they grow until they are quite large. If you notice any enormous velzen prowling the halls, do not be alarmed."

"Thank you for the lesson, Firenze," Sinan spits. "But we are ready for dinner."

"By all means, continue," I purr without looking up at the braggart who has attempted to steal Cashore's throne.

He and Zara both turn from us as Achaia rubs her cheek along mine. "I want you to tell me everything about them later. There's history there, is there not?"

I laugh and grip her chin as Jet hovers protectively behind her. "I like you jealous, *atirien*. It stokes the flames of my desire. If you like this velzen, you may keep him. A singular cuff means he is unattached to any court and available for taking. Velzen are attracted to our spirits, so if he expressed an interest in us, it may mean he is ours."

Achaia's face lights up as Jet groans.

"We didn't come here to get a fucking cat-dog, Renze. Or a fox? I can't tell what it is but we don't need it." I sense there is more he wishes to say, but he holds back when my eyes snap to his.

"Eyes and ears open, Jet," I remind him. "We will need to remind Sinan of the bigger picture if we wish to make allies in this court. Remember, we must be dominant and powerful. Being polite here will garner us no friends. We will request his help tonight and tomorrow we leave to meet our pack."

My imposing mate purses his plump lips into a frown but nods once at me.

"Good boy," I murmur in a teasing tone as Jet gives me a wolfish look.

Achaia runs one hand up Jet's chest seductively, gripping his throat as his dark eyes flick down to her. She's commanding like this, forcing his attention on her.

Like a queen. The thought runs rampant in my mind. There is more to her story, and although her background is not Jet's focus, I want every detail I can have about her. "Stay close to me, Jet," she commands.

"Of course," he purrs back.

At her feet, the velzen copies Jet's purr, his long black tail swishing side to side behind him.

And I laugh because even though I did not expect it, our misfit family is growing yet again.

CHAPTER EIGHTEEN
ACHAIA

Everything about this place sets my teeth on edge. It's clear there's history between the beautiful blue-haired vampiri and Renze. I shouldn't be surprised. He's exhilarating and authoritative and distinguished as fuck. Seeing him in his element is turning me on like crazy.

I'm not sure I really grasped the full meaning of him calling me *atirien* until we came here, but it's clear that being a vampiri's mate is a deep commitment. It's literally the first thing Sinan commented on. I don't know anything about mates; I have no memory of my people or what a mate means wherever I come from. I lack basic fucking context.

I mull all this over as the velzen curls itself around my ankles like a cat would. He's fucking adorable, all soft black fur and the most beautiful, sweet eyes. He follows us as Renze moves to the table closest to Sinan's, sitting next to him and Zara.

"Tell me how you came to be free," Sinan asks with a wry expression on his handsome face. He says free as if he wished Renze was anything but.

It's probably accurate, but Renze shoots him a brilliant smile. "A cunning omega got herself thrown into the maze to find and release Noire, Jet's eldest brother. Cashore, Ascelin, and I aligned with them in order to escape. Now, we are a court, or pack as the shifters call themselves. It is just as the prophecy foretold."

"How does that work?" questions Zara, ignoring Renze's comment about the prophecy. She spears a piece of asparagus, popping it delicately between her black teeth.

Renze's smile falls. "We experienced much tragedy in the maze, as you may be aware. Did Rama televise it here as she did in Siargao?"

Zara nods once, her white eyes filling with tears. What a joke. She reaches out, placing one elegant hand on Renze's forearm. "I watched every night, Firenze, hoping for a glimpse of you. We were devastated when you were taken."

Angry fire fills my veins, but I remember at the last second that she can sense my emotion. She's probably reveling in poking at me verbally. Two can play that game, however, and I find my desire for verbal retort suddenly *very* strong.

"It's a shame you didn't think to enter the maze yourself if you were so devastated at his loss." I keep my voice light, although my message is anything but. She narrows her eyes and snarls at me as Renze pulls his hand away, laying it on the back of my chair. There's a pleased expression on his face as I smile politely.

I'm not done, though. Reaching out, I slide my hand up Renze's thigh, gripping his thigh tightly as her white eyes follow the movement of my hand. "A single, unmated omega got herself thrown into the maze and rescued not only the Ayala Pack but all of the vampiri as well. It certainly sounds like fate, does it not?"

Zara snarls and leaps toward me, but Renze cuffs her throat with a snap of his dark teeth in her face. "Do not presume to touch what's mine." He shoves her back into her seat. Sinan watches the entire exchange with a displeased expression on his face.

"You have changed, Firenze," he murmurs.

"Seven years in hell will do that to a being," Renze counters. "What do you know of Rama's actions now? It seems news travels here quickly, Sinan. We are on a mission to rid Lombornei of her."

Sinan gives Renze a quizzical expression as Jet and I lean in, curious to hear what the vampiri has to say.

He shrugs his shoulders once, feigning indifference. "It is true we heard of the escape. We assume she occasionally retreats to her home province of Deshali, but we cannot confirm it. Our scouts have never returned."

Renze stiffens next to me. "You have sent warriors?"

Sinan agrees, "I have. She must be using magic to seal her province off from external forces. I do not know how she could do such a thing, but then again, how did she build a maze unbeknownst to everyone and grow an island atop it?"

This doesn't ring true to me, since Trig has mentioned having operatives at the edges of Deshali, but I hold my tongue. I already know the answer to

Sinan's question from my conversations with Diana, but it's clear that particular bit of news isn't known here.

To my right, Jet reaches for his full wine glass, throwing it back before pouring a second. I'm aware of the uppers he was on in the maze and his work to come down from those. Seeing him down a second glass of wine and then pour a third sends alarms trilling in my brain.

Dinner is quiet and formal. The vampiri talk only amongst themselves. Where I expected them to be curious about Renze's unusual mating arrangement, they aren't. The only exception is Zara, who eyes my hand on Renze's thigh as if she'd like to lop it off.

Renze and Sinan continue to talk, catching up as I tune out. Renze can handle this. He knows the innermost workings of this place far better than I do. So, I focus on Jet, turning in my seat to look at him.

He picks at the bloody meat on his plate, not eating, although his wine glass is empty again. I don't know how much booze it would take to make a direwolf shifter tipsy, but he's got to be headed in that direction.

I reach out and place my hand on his forearm. Mahogany eyes flick up to meet mine, consumed with something I can't quite put my finger on. Anger? Frustration?

"Talk to me," I murmur, sliding off my chair and into his lap as my arms go around his neck. It's forward, so forward. But after what we did earlier, I swear I feel him buried in my chest. Either way, Renze told us to put on a good show so he doesn't appear weak. I can do that.

Jet leans back in the seat and grips my chin, turning my head to the side, his eyes on my neck. He sighs and lets go as I lean in closer, looking at his plump lips. I want to taste him the way he tasted me.

"What are you looking for?" I question as my breasts brush up against him. The top four buttons of his shirt are open, and I ache for my naked figure to rub against his beautiful tan skin.

"Wondering how Renze feels when he looks at the vein that throbs in your neck here." He reaches out to drag his fingertip along the left side of my neck, down along my collarbone.

I let out a chuckle. "Alphas are no less predatory, isn't that right? Do you not have the desire to bite me, Jet?" I'm teasing him, but the hard bar beneath my ass tells me I'm on the right track.

Next to us, I sense Renze's focus has shifted from his conversation to what we're doing. In fact, all around us, vampiri are watching. I think back to what Renze has shared with us several times–vampiri power is fueled by sex. Playing with Jet will make Renze more powerful, and we need every bit of power we can get.

Jet's lustful gaze is pure deviance as he wraps both arms around me and crushes me to his chest, his lips hovering just above mine. "Bite, lick, suck, tease. I want all of it, little one." I'm unsure if he's putting on the show Renze suggested we should or if this is a continuation of what happened in the hallway. Either way, I want it, despite the red flags waving at me. Jet's mind is still a maze in its own way, and I don't want to damage that tonight.

Still, we came here to gather allies, and we both agreed to do this.

I clamp my thighs together as wetness seeps from me, my body heavy with the need for him. Flashbacks of what he did to me against the wall play through my mind as I lean in and tug his lower lip between my teeth.

Jet returns the bite, tugging my head back and licking his way up my neck with a satisfied hum. I look to our right to see Renze stroking his cock lazily through his pants, his hands wrapped around that gorgeous thickness.

Zara watches him with barely restrained need as I focus only on radiating confidence. Sinan grins murderously at me but doesn't look away.

Jet nips my throat hard before pulling me upright, our gazes traveling to where Renze shifts in his seat, big hips rolling into his hand as he strokes lazily with his eyes locked on us. I know Jet sees the way Zara practically salivates over him. He pats me on the ass. "Go play with Renze, little one. He looks like he could use some attention."

When my eyes meet Jet's, there's an assholish smirk there. He doesn't like her any more than I do, and he's telling me to send a clear message–get the fuck away from what's ours.

I don't bother to look at Sinan or Zara as I open the slit in my dress and straddle Renze. His white eyes crinkle at the corner, but they never leave mine as his black lips part, that talented tongue running along my mouth. For just a moment, we hover like that, and then I crash my mouth over his, taking and demanding, wrapping my arms around his neck as he growls into the kiss.

Renze's tongue tangles with mine, teasing as both hands come to my thighs and squeeze tightly. He slips one inside and runs his fingertips between my ass cheeks with a sure, confident touch. His kiss is practiced, slow, and thorough, a deep exploration of my lips and tongue as I close my eyes and feel him everywhere. A blush of heat spreads through my body when Renze lets out a snarl and pulls back ever so slightly.

"You have an audience, Firenze," Sinan chirps as we both look over. "Grant us a first look at how you take *tua-atirien*. I'll admit to being curious. It is so rare for a vampiri to mate outside our race."

It's a veiled barb, but I chuckle. "Renze has thoroughly, deeply enjoyed mating outside your race, Sinan." The would-be king snarls as Renze lets out a possessive growl.

Sinan continues with a bored expression. "Firenze, the platform is free. You should take your mates there and show us how this works. A good fucking would be most welcome."

Next to us, Jet throws back another glass of wine. Renze shoots Sinan a haughty look. "I am enjoying my mates here, Sinan. I do not need to parade them around on the platform. Someone else may go."

I know exactly why he's hedging. Jet's past, and the way Rama used him for others' pleasure, are at the forefront of Renze's mind. Jet's frozen in the seat next to ours, his breath coming in short pants. It won't do. I'd like to stab Sinan in the eye for suggesting it, but I suspect he's reading Jet's reluctance and trying to use it as a weakness against us.

I can be strong here and now to gain us allies. Jet doesn't need to do this. I slide out of Renze's lap and grab Jet's chin, kissing him once, deeply before I whisper in his ear. "I want to show everyone how a human fucks. Enjoy watching, alpha."

I hold my hand out for Renze. "Come, mate," I purr at him.

Sinan growls appreciatively as Zara's face pales, but I pay them no mind as Renze's white eyes find mine. He's barely holding back a laugh, but I sense how proud he is. He stands and undoes the buttons of his dinner jacket, sliding it off his big arms and tossing it onto the seat behind him.

"As you wish, *atirien*," he murmurs, threading his cool fingers through mine.

Jet says nothing, but his fingers trail along my side as we pass him.

I don't know why or how, but I am in my element like this—the political intrigue, the beautifully veiled verbal barbs? It's surprisingly comfortable for me.

Time to teach this court of assholes a lesson.

CHAPTER NINETEEN

JET

I'm employing every technique in the fucking book right now to not lose my godsdamned mind. I won't give these monsters the satisfaction of seeing me run scared. Unfortunately, everything about this place brings me back to the maze's Atrium. I'm reliving my worst nightmares. It's the most unmoored I've felt since we escaped. Air refuses to fill my lungs as pressure tightens my chest.

In front of me, Renze leads Achaia around the long rows of tables, and it's then I notice a stage of sorts built into an alcove that looks down into the dining hall. A fucking stage. What a bunch of pompous pricks.

Firenze ascends the stairs, Achaia's hand firmly wrapped in his as I stand and follow. Our mission is critically important. No matter what happened to me before, I have to set it aside to get Ten back. The wine I hunted for moments ago is forgotten as I think about my brother—everything we're doing here is to gain allies and get him out.

I don't want to go up on stage and perform. Achaia knows this—she went for my benefit—but I'm a godsdamned alpha, and I'm strong as fuck. Still, I stop at the bottom of the stairs as the edges of my vision blacken and narrow.

Most of the vampiri vacate their seats and mill around at the base of the alcove. The alcove itself is flat, with a high bed in the middle and a sofa off to one side. Flashbacks of the maze and our dark quarters assault me.

I push those visions aside, too, as Zara comes to stand next to me with an evil grin. "You do not wish to claim your mates?" She's digging for information, and I won't be a party to it. We can't show any weakness; Renze told us that at the very beginning.

"Fuck off," I command her, watching how my alpha tones slap her before she stands straighter and growls. She backs away, though, crossing in front of the alcove to stand with Sinan, who stares up at the platform with eager anticipation.

Zara whispers something in his ear, and he looks over at me with a devilish grin. I remind myself that we came here hoping for an ally, and we probably aren't leaving with one. But the more time we spend here, the more I realize it was a long shot. Sinan doesn't feel threatened by Rama; he has nothing at stake.

I resist the urge to rage and pull this entire fucking castle down, but then I hear a groan, and my eyes are drawn to the stage. Renze is on his knees, Achaia bent over in front of him. She sucks on his thick, erect cock as he runs his hands up her side. There's enough of a size differential between them that he can slip his fingers into her ass while she sucks him off.

Heat crashes through me, watching them, the way her lips pop off his rounded head, that pink tongue swirling around the tip before she nips at him. The moment she bites, he jerks, cum leaking from him and onto her tongue. Godsdamn, it's hot watching them. Renze ignores the crowd as clothes are removed, faint moans reaching my ears.

I can hear others joining in around us, but I don't turn to watch anyone else fuck because I can't take my eyes off the way Achaia works Renze over with unbridled enthusiasm. He rips the straps of her dress down, sliding it fully off her plentiful hips. She cries out when he spits venom on her ass, using his fingers to push it deep inside her.

Fuck, her ass must be perfection. She moans aloud, forgetting about his cock even though it spears the air right in front of her.

"Suck, *atirien*," he commands, slapping her lips with his swinging dick.

"Renze," she groans. "I'm so close. I need to–" her words die off as he grips her chin, forcing her mouth open and shoving his dick inside. She coughs and sputters but groans again, sucking while she rocks back to meet his hands.

They pick up a rhythmic pace together, Achaia's cries growing louder and louder as the crowd around me meets their vibe. When I turn toward Sinan, I see Zara in tears by his side. He rolls his eyes and grips her throat, forcing her to her knees as he unzips his pants. I smirk when he shoves his cock in her mouth. I hope she fucking chokes on it.

Onstage, Achaia explodes, legs quivering as she screams around Renze's big dick. He lets out a snarling bellow and a string of curse words, the sloppy sounds of his fingers in her ass ringing off the alcove's walls.

I'm so godsdamned hot watching them that I could come right here. My earlier worries still linger, but I can't stop my body's natural reaction to them.

Join them, my consciousness whispers helpfully. *You can join them.*

I take a step toward the stage, drawn like a moth to a flame, as Renze lifts Achaia into his arms and crosses the platform, tossing her roughly on the bed. My feet stop as I watch him spit venom on her neck and chest. The effect is instantaneous as she falls into the sheets, arching her back.

There are murmurs in the crowd when the realization that his venom didn't hurt her reaches our audience. I hear whispered, hushed voices as they continue their erotic show.

I'm entranced by how her big breasts sway, rosy nipples aching for sharp teeth and violent attention. I want her. I want him. I need it. I ascend the stairs but can't take that last step onto the stage, angst building in my system. Behind me, the vampiri are fucking; screams, groans, and the sloppy sounds of oral ring off the black stone walls.

In front of me, Renze now fingers Achaia with steady, hard strokes as he leans over her, murmuring something into her ear.

I want to know what he's saying. I have to know. Is he reassuring her that she's doing a beautiful job? Is he reminding her that he needs to prepare her because she's smaller, and his dick is huge? Maybe he's professing his undying love. I don't know. Out of the two of us, he is undoubtedly the gentleman.

I want to know exactly what he's saying.

When I take the first step onto the alcove platform, my body locks up. My chest heaves. I feel eyes on me, waiting for me to make a move. Lights that focus on the stage feel like they're pointed directly at me.

I can't do this without uppers. Taking a step back, I press myself against the alcove's wall and look around.

Sinan grins at me, shoving his dick in Zara's mouth forcefully as he watches me, unable to join my mates.

But then Renze lets out a deep roar that calls my eyes to him. His big hips piston between Achaia's thighs as he draws himself out, then shoves his way back in with a huge rolling thrust. He spits on his own cock before sliding back in. On the mattress, she's lost to pleasure, crying his name over and over as he fucks her.

But then her head falls to the side, her body jerking on the bed as he takes her. Her eyes find mine. "Jet," she whispers, so low I don't know that anyone else even heard it. "Mine," she mouths before her entire face scrunches up, and she comes again, screaming my name as Renze roars out a bellowed, "*yes, atirien.*"

I yank my dick out of my pants and stroke, leaning against the wall as an orgasm surprises me, overtaking me with such force that all I can do is roar my pleasure as pulses of heat batter me like waves crashing on a shore. When the surprise dissipates, I gasp for breath as I look toward the bed. Renze is now taking Achaia on her knees in front of him, both of them eye-fucking me as Achaia gets absolutely railed.

The vampiri rage around us, but all I can focus on is the way Renze grips the back of Achaia's neck and how she swings her hair to the side, presenting all that beautiful tan skin for his perusal.

I just came so godsdamned hard, but I'm ramrod straight again, watching Renze grab her throat and pull her nearly flush with his chest, careful not to touch her tattoo. He still fucks her from behind, his balls swinging heavily between her thighs. He looks up at me, sinking his teeth where her neck and shoulder meet. She comes immediately, locking up around the bite as he moans into it. Renze's movements turn jerky and erratic as he snarls.

He brutally rips his teeth from Achaia's muscle, blood spraying the bed and her chest as she grunts in surprise. And then his tongue is everywhere on her neck and shoulder, lapping at the ruby-red drops that spurt from the wound. He breathes hard and heavily, whining with pleasure as I watch her body quiver under the onslaught of his violence.

Achaia lets out a delicious cry as her head falls to the side, her body going loose in Renze's arms. He sucks and licks at the wound on her neck, his eyes focused narrowly on the throbbing vein he tore when he bit her.

Reaching down, I drag my hand up and down my length as he feasts on the beautiful woman who's quickly taking up residence in my chest. So strong. She's so godsdamned strong.

Renze fucks her through what sounds like another mind-numbing orgasm as I jack myself off watching them. I come a second time when they do, splattering the stage with ropes of my cum as they pant breathlessly in the bed. Pleasure fades, and I shove my cock back in my pants, my head falling to the stone wall behind me.

A sudden pressure on my leg surprises me. I haven't been paying fucking attention, focused as I was on Renze and Achaia. The black velzen from earlier curls his long, thin body around my leg. It sits itself at my feet and holds its paw up as if it wants me to shake it. I can't tell if it's closer to a cat or dog, but when I drop to one knee and examine its foot, it leans in to brush its cheek along mine.

My direwolf recognizes a friendly spirit, the velzen purring softly as it rubs its angular black snout along my cheek and neck. When I look up, Renze is putting his pants back on, smiling as he watches me.

He crosses the platform, still shirtless, and squats down next to the velzen and me. "He wishes you to gift him a bracelet, *atiri*. That is why he shows you his foot."

"He's an animal, Renze," I retort. "Why would he want a bracelet?"

Renze reaches out and strokes the velzen's thin side, counting the ribs there before he wraps its tail around his hand and tugs on it playfully. The velzen purrs and curls itself in little circles, playfully nipping at Renze's fingers. "A bracelet would indicate he belongs to our family. It would be a source of pride for him. You would wound him greatly if you do not gift him one."

I roll my eyes. "And I'm getting a velzen bracelet where? You got a gift shop here?"

Renze laughs at that and scratches the velzen under the chin as its purring intensifies. "It is bad luck to deny a velzen who chooses you. That he has approached us twice speaks volumes. I will procure us a bracelet, and you and Achaia may formally invite him later. He will appreciate it."

My eyes dart to Achaia on the bed, still boneless from release, her breasts swaying slightly as she comes down from what just happened.

Renze's smile falls. "I took her hard, *atiri*. She needs you. Come."

I hold my breath as I look at the stage, willing myself to step foot up onto it. But then Achaia moans from the bed, and that unhappy noise calls to me, tugging deep at my chest. She's not an omega, so I don't think we would ever bond like Noire and Diana have. But still, I feel her there. She's in pain. That pain pushes my worry down deeper.

Crossing the platform, I focus on her, grabbing her dress as I go. I slide it up her trembling thighs before leaning over her limp figure. She's covered in blood, the wound at her neck slightly swollen. She shifts up onto her elbows but falls back.

"She's exhausted," I murmur as Renze hops onto the bed, crawling behind her. He gently places both hands under her arms and shifts her up. I cradle her to my chest, swinging her legs up into my arms as I turn from the alcove. A rolling purr rumbles between us as she sighs and nuzzles her way inside my open shirt, her cheek warm against my chest.

I head down the steps, Renze a cool shadow behind me when I hear Sinan.

Renze and I turn as one, the fake king still thrusting rapidly into Zara's mouth. He yanks his cock out, splattering cum all over her face as she grunts in surprise. Renze puts a hand on my lower back as if to tell me not to say anything.

Sinan grabs his dick and rubs it all over Zara's mouth and cheeks, smearing his essence over her as she pauses. But you'd have to be an idiot not to see that she hates every second of it. He obviously doesn't care, though, as he slaps her once on the cheek and turns to us, stepping out of his pants and crossing in front of the alcove with his cock swinging.

He grins at Firenze. "You don't claim your alpha mate, Firenze? What does that say about your honor, old friend?"

Next to me, Renze laughs, low and evil. "Do not concern yourself with my honor, Sinan, and I will not concern myself with yours."

The vampiri snarls but laughs, glancing down at Achaia in my arms. "Your mate does not seem well-suited for vampiri libido, Firenze. Perhaps you should cast these two aside and take a woman who can handle you. You may have Zara if you wish. I am nearly done with her, and she will not be the woman to have my jewel."

Behind him, I see Zara pull to a stand, snarling at his back as she wipes cum off her face, shaking her hands to fling it to the stone floor.

Renze laughs again. *"Zephet ya min-atirien, Sinan. Vezhafet hissop."*

Sinan smirks but glances at Achaia and me. "If you say so, Firenze. It is hard to believe that a king's First Warrior could find fated mates such as this, but perhaps the fates do not look as kindly on you as I thought."

I school my face into a careful neutral, turning to Renze. "I'm taking her to our rooms. You coming?"

"No," Zara purrs, joining us as the rank smell of Sinan's seed permeates the air. It's fucking gross. "Firenze must stay. There is always music and dancing, and Firenze has not graced us with his talent in many years. It would be a gift for him to play for us."

An instrument? I glance at Renze to see what he's thinking, but he looks wistful as if he longs for what she mentioned.

"Let's stay," Achaia whispers from my chest, green eyes peering up at Renze. He looks down at her, stroking her hair off her face. I see this for what it is; she's trying to rally her energy to support us. It reminds me again how this isn't her fight, but she's chosen to aid us in it, anyhow. She continues to put our mission first, over and over again. I find myself in awe of her.

"*Atirien*, there is no need. We have issues of greater importance to tend to."

"Tonight?" she snorts. "There is nothing more we can do tonight. I'll rest for a minute, but I'd love to see you play. I bet it's sexy as fuck, and I'm going to need you again afterward."

I don't bother to hold back the smirk I shoot in Zara's direction as she bristles. Achaia seems undaunted by court life. As for me, the political intrigue and veiled insults are something I don't miss from my younger years.

Gods, I long to be free of the weight of Rama and her insanity hanging over our shoulders. I want my brother back, and I want to lean into the burning connection I feel building with both Achaia and Renze. I don't want my nightmares to rule my mind, despite how hard they're trying to.

Around us, many vampiri are still mid-fuckery, the entire hall filled with the sounds of a raging orgy. But there's a steady drumbeat beginning to sound from somewhere deep inside the stone castle.

Renze smiles at me, rubbing Achaia's leg. "Take a seat, *min-atirien*. We repurpose this area into a stage. Just rest."

Achaia gives him a big thumbs up, but he leans in and nips at her finger before sucking it into his mouth with a pleased sigh. "You taste good, *atirien*. My power is so strong right now. Your blood is a gift."

She giggles as I roll my eyes at them both. "What she needs is a massage and maybe a little tender ass-eating until she creams all over my face. And then a cuddle."

Renze laughs but reaches out to run a thumb along my lower lip. "That would be my ideal night as well, *atiri*." He looks down at Achaia. "You wish to stay?"

"I do," she confirms, patting me on the chest. "For a little while, at least."

We leave Renze with Sinan and cross to the nearest long wooden table. I pick the chair at the very end. It's all plush round velvet with gold buttons in a herringbone pattern. It's ostentatious, but it looks comfortable. Easing down into it, I arrange Achaia gently, continuing to purr as she intertwines her legs with mine.

She looks up at me from my arms, her eyes darker and more intense in the low light of the dining hall. "I love that you purr like a cat."

I open my mouth to correct her when the velzen hops onto the table next to my shoulder, leaning in to rub his cheek against my jawline.

"He recognizes a fellow cat," she sniggers, "or are you both more like a dog?" When the velzen lays down, folding his long black legs over one another to give her sad eyes, she laughs aloud. He begins purring, his tail swishing lazily on the table as Achaia's laughter turns raucous. "Oh my gods, you're both purring for me. This is fucking great."

It's so beautiful to watch her laugh that I can't even chide her for comparing me to our new lapdog. Lapcat. Is a lapvelzen even a thing? "Renze says it chose us, and we have to give him a bracelet and keep him or else he'll be offended."

"Oh gods, really?" Achaia laughs more, reaching out to stroke the thin animal's impossibly soft fur. "This hardly seems the best time, but I don't think he'd suggest it if it wasn't right."

"We came for allies and left with a cat," I mutter in her ear. "Think how pleased Noire will be."

"I sense your dismay, Jet," she murmurs low, sitting up just enough to wrap her arms around my neck, hissing as if she's sore. "This feels like a detour to you instead of going right to our next destination. I promise I'll do everything possible to help you get your brother back."

Her tender words rip my heart to shreds as I lean in and take her mouth. It's a gentle exploration as I focus on the building heat between us. She tastes like Renze, all darkness, blood, and brisk coolness. But she tastes like her too, that floral scent combined with the depth of the sea. I press harder into her lips, my tongue tangling with hers as that far-off drumbeat grows louder. I want to know her secrets. I want to know everything I don't already know about her.

We part, breathless, as she scans my face. "You stopped purring."

I hover my lips over hers, letting her see how focused I am on her, only her. "The velzen is purring."

"Two is better than one, though," she whispers, giving me a saucy look before turning toward the alcove. There are still vampiri fucking in groups all over the damn place, but the crowd parts, and a dozen new vampiri enter the room, banging on huge drums. The hollow noise booms around the large hall, echoing from the vaulted ceiling. It washes over us as they pick up a slow, thunderous beat.

More vampiri flood into the hall, carrying instruments I've never seen before. Zara appears on stage, handing Renze something I can only closely approximate to a guitar. The body is rounder, like a gourd, and the top features elegant wooden scrolling where dozens of white strings begin. They follow the instrument's body straight down and hang onto the floor in a pool at Renze's feet. It's beautiful, and Renze stares lovingly at it as he inclines his head at Zara in thanks.

She pauses for a moment but steps away as he holds the instrument and strums it like a guitar. So it's similar in that sense. Next to me, the velzen scoots closer and puts his head on my shoulder. Achaia snuggles under my chin, and I feel something close to peace for the first time in a very long time. We might be faking this, but it feels good.

It feels real.

Tension leaves my body as more vampiri leave the wild orgy and take up instruments until there are a dozen or more onstage and two dozen or so beating drums rhythmically along the wall.

Renze smiles at another tall male, and then they begin strumming identical instruments at the same time. Achaia and I are entranced, watching his fingers dance along the strings, pulling and strumming as the notes dance together. Renze plays the lower tones while the other musician plays the higher ones, and the beat of the drums changes, picking up in time with their song.

The velzen scoots closer still, his cheek pressed tightly to mine, both black paws hanging over the edge of the table as Achaia and I face the alcove. This is turning into a regular family gathering. I don't even know what to make of it.

Achaia hums along as the rest of the musicians join in, one by one, laying their melodies on top of Renze's, the song building to a rhythmic, pulsing crescendo. At the peak of the music, Renze pulls the instrument up under his chin like a violin and strums underneath it, sending a deep reverberation through the room. It's so loud I can barely comprehend how it's possible, but I feel it. Deep in my gut, that tone builds and builds until I'm hard again, Achaia starting to squirm in my lap.

"How do I feel that in my clit?" she moans, burying her face in my neck and nipping. "Gods, Jet. This music is intoxicating." My dick is solid against her soft curves. Her body is so pliable in my arms, so hauntingly beautiful. I haul her up higher in my arms so I can bury my face in the hollow of her throat, tasting her softly with my tongue. She smells so fucking good. The taste of lemons coats my tongue as I lick my way along her skin.

I shift uncomfortably in the seat as the velzen slinks off to give us space. Achaia's bites turn harder and needier as the drums and the instruments play an undulating, throbbing refrain. All around us, the orgy continues. The entire room reeks of sex and pheromones as I start to lose control. I'm ready to throw her on top of this table and have my way while Renze watches us.

"Do it," Achaia commands, looking up into my eyes.

"Do what?" I counter, gripping the back of her neck as I rock my hips along her ass. She's wearing far too many godsdamned clothes.

"What you're thinking of. Whatever it is, I want it," she growls, practically feral as the music builds to yet another peak, the room around us wild with revelers. This sex music has us both on the verge of fucking right here.

"Dance with me," I purr into her lips, my eyes falling on them. They're swollen and bruised from Renze's attention. I want that for myself. I want her to bleed for me. To run from me and scream when I take her in the dirt on all fours like an animal.

She slips off my lap, reaching her hand out as we join a throng of vampiri in front of the stage. Some are fucking, some are fighting, and plenty more are dancing wildly to the beats. I've never heard music that sounded so much like sex, but this is practically orgasmic.

I could get used to it. Nobody's looking at me; nobody's focused on me. There is only that steady drumbeat and the gorgeous woman in my arms.

And the fucking velzen. Sitting on the tabletop, watching everything.

CHAPTER TWENTY
ACHAIA

I'm so sore from Renze taking me. It was rough, violent, and perfect, everything I thought he'd be. I should be blissfully sated.

But the male who leads me onto the dancefloor and looks at me like he could eat me alive? I want that, too, especially after having his mouth on me earlier.

We said we'd fake our way through this evening, but this feels far too real, far too *good*. It's terrifying and intoxicating all at the same time.

Jet stops in the middle of the throng of wild dancers, pulling me in close as he wraps one arm around my back, low enough to avoid touching my tattoo. The other hand slides up my side as he grips the back of my neck hard.

And then he starts to move. And gods help me; I understand why Rama put him on a stage every night. Jet focused and seductive like this has me nearly coming out of my skin. His hips roll rhythmically with the music, his eyes on mine. They never move, never waver. And I realize if he kept this attention and focus up, I could come with minimal effort.

Jet growls into my lips, both hands sliding to my ass. He uses his command of me to drag my body along the hard bar of his cock, which juts up obscenely between us. His dress pants do nothing to hide that beautiful length. He smirks when I lick my lips and gaze down at it with open longing.

He leans forward to tickle my ear with his rough lips. "You want that, little one? Want my knot to fill you up?" We turn on the dance floor, swaying to the music, as Jet brings one of my arms up to his shoulder, my breasts crushed to him.

Jet swings us in a circle, hips still thrusting against me as he backs me into the table, caging me in with his arms. It's like he's dancing just for me, emulating what sex with him would be like. And it's so intensely sensual to have him focused like this that I'm about to beg him right here.

"I want you to come apart on my knot, little one," he murmurs, his mouth brushing mine. "Do you know what a knot is?"

I gasp in a breath but nod. "I've read about it, alpha. But I only want what you're willing to give." I don't know how to tell him that I can't fathom what happened to him in the maze, but I never want something he's not willing and excited to give me. I want Jet to be whole, healthy, and happy. I need that like I need air.

His gaze darkens. "Let's go to our room. I need you, Achaia."

I risk a glance at Renze. "What about Renze? He's so absorbed."

"He can join us when he's done," Jet purrs.

I nod once, looking up toward the stage. Renze's white eyes are locked onto us, and he gives me a cocky smile as he strokes the underneath of his instrument, sending a reverberating, intensely low note through the room. My back arches in pleasure as his smile turns into a grin.

Have fun, he mouths, winking at me as he goes back to the music.

Jet grips my hand firmly, somehow navigating our way back to our room. We're quiet the whole route, but tension simmers between us. I have no doubt he's going to unleash on me when we get there. I want it. I want it so badly.

The velzen trots behind us, his paws soundless on the black stone floor. The only noise is the slight tinkle of the singular gold cuff around his ankle. When we get to our rooms, Jet opens the door wide, sighing when the velzen trots through and makes a lazy perusal of the room.

"This has been a weird experience," he mutters, watching the animal hop into a chair and curl around himself, looking at us with big black eyes.

"Indeed," I murmur, slipping my dress off my shoulders and letting the heavy fabric fall to the ground.

Jet's eyes darken, the pupil overtaking his dark-brown iris as his eyes meet mine. "Go to the bed, Achaia. Lay on your back."

I shudder as goosebumps cover my skin but do as I'm told.

Jet follows me, and when I lay down, he parts my thighs, stepping between them. His hands move to his buttons, which he undoes deftly, slipping the shirt off his broad, stacked muscles.

A whine leaves my throat as he unbuttons his pants, sliding those down as well. Because now he's naked before me, and there's nothing about him that's not perfect. Down to the—

"Fuck me, what's that?" I bark out, pointing at his junk.

"It's a cock, Achaia." He smirks. "What's so surprising about this one?"

"There are bars everywhere, Jet. And a godsdamned ring through the tip. How did I not feel any of this when we were dancing?"

He shrugs. "You were lost to the music, little one. These piercings were a coming-of-age tradition, a gift to my future mate. Something to ensure exquisite pleasure when I take her. All alphas do this."

His smile falls a little, but I lean forward.

"May I touch them?"

"You may."

"They're beautiful. Did it hurt?"

"Hurt like shit. But it feels good to mess with them."

I can't tear my eyes from the dazzling cock that now leaks precum for me. Reaching out, I wrap my hand around his warm, hard length, sliding my tongue over the tip. I suck the fat head into my mouth.

"Tug on the ring with your teeth," he rumbles, his hand coming to the back of my head. When I follow his command, he hisses out a pained breath and shudders.

"Does that hurt?" I bark. "I don't want to hurt you, Jet."

"Hurts and feels good at the same time," he growls back. "I like pain with my pleasure, Achaia. Can you understand that?"

"I got that treatment earlier, if you remember," I snort as Jet presses me back onto the mattress. I'm dismayed when he grabs an extra blanket from beside the bed. It's thin but huge, and he tosses the length up over the bed's canopy so it hangs down like a tent.

"Stand up," he commands as I give him a curious look.

"Are we making a pillow fort?"

"Not hardly," Jet chuckles. "Are you going to question everything I do or pipe down and enjoy it?"

I bite my lip to keep from laughing as Jet puts a stern look on his face. It surprises me when he slides the ends of the blanket through my legs, wrapping them intricately around my arms and core and then back up over the bed's canopy.

He winks at me once and then yanks hard, and I fly upward, suspended like a trussed chicken by the godsdamned fabric.

"What in the seven hells?" I sputter as Jet ties the end of the blanket off on one of the bed's thick posts.

"I'm creative, Achaia. It's why Rama—" he pauses for a moment. "It's why she picked me to do what I did." His dark eyes cloud over as goosebumps crawl across his skin. I hate that he's remembering her now. I squirm to reach for him, but I'm caught. Even so, I capture his gaze with mine to give him an earnest look.

"You're with me, alpha. I only want what you're willing to give, whatever that may be. Even if it's nothing at all." My soft words seem to snap him out of his reverie, and he smiles again. And that smile is fucking breathtaking—confident and sure.

"I want a lot of things, little one. And I'm going to start with my mouth on this sweet pussy again. I want to taste him on you." He growls once as I shift in the thin fabric, but I can't fucking move with both arms pinned behind me and my legs spread wide.

Jet grips my ass and swings me toward him at an angle, burying his face between my thighs with a happy groan. That magical fucking tongue traces a path over my clit, then down my pussy before dipping inside. He purrs simultaneously, the vibrations sending waves of pleasure through me. I arch my back, but I can't move. I hate it.

I love it.

Whining, I attempt to roll my hips, but I have zero control like this, with my hands behind my back.

Jet's exploration deepens as he laps at me.

"You smell like him," he growls after a momentary pause. "You smell taken. I want that."

"Why?" I question. Renze told us we're all mates, but there's never been a single word from Jet to indicate that might be true. Plenty of sexual tension but nothing emotional, nothing to connect us in the way I'd expect from a mate. Maybe that's normal, although watching Noire and Diana together makes it seem like they're magnets, inexplicably bonded in all ways.

"I've never had a choice," he whispers finally, and his voice is suddenly so low, so sad, that all I can do is struggle to reconnect with him. He meets my eyes and looks away, his hands leaving my ass and flying to the puckered scar just under his ribcage. "No choice," he murmurs again softly, and then his eyes cloud over, and he frowns.

I watch his brows furrow, fangs descending as a suspicious look steals over his angular features. His eyes dart from side to side, his breaths coming rapid fire. He looks cornered, like a wounded animal. Oh gods, he must be reliving something from the maze. Rising concern burrows its way through me. I've got to get out of this sheet cage.

"You're with me, alpha. You're safe," I croon. I'm fucking losing him; I can see that. He's remembering something terrible, it's obvious from the look on his face.

"I had no choice," he mutters, stepping back and shaking his head from side to side. His hands go to either side of his head, and he squeezes his eyes tightly shut. "Don't." It's a one-word snarled command as his body tenses. "Don't you fucking dare." He shakes his head angrily as I struggle, suspended in the makeshift swing. Jet is lost in his nightmares, and I've got to do something.

Fuck, fuck, fuck. I need Renze, and I need him now. I think hard about him, knowing he can't hear me, but hoping beyond hope that his ability to read emotion extends this far. I don't want to shout for him in case it frightens Jet.

Abruptly, Jet falls to one knee, panting. He's having a fucking panic attack or a breakdown or something.

"Jet, it's me. Achaia. I'm here, alpha. You're safe. Please, Jet, come back to me!" My voice rises in pitch as pins and needles begin to stab up my wrists.

Jet leaps upright, fists balled as chocolate-brown eyes snap open. "Never again," he commands, his voice deep, dominant, and cruel as he points one finger at me. "Never fucking again."

Oh fuck, does he think I'm Rama right now? Jet's overwhelming like this, absorbed and furious. It's a side of him I haven't seen, the side he must have had to show in the maze for seven years to keep himself safe. He's throwing up brick walls around his mind, trying desperately to reclaim something I don't know how to give him. But if he sees her when he looks at me, I'm fucked.

My heart aches for him as Jet takes a step toward me, growling, but it's so menacing that I barely recognize him.

I do what I'd do with any predator, and when his body is flush with mine, I meet his eyes and don't look away. I'm caught, and if he's going to hurt me now, there's nothing I can do about it. He's hurting, and I want to dash all that hurt, to pull him out of it. "Jet," I murmur, rubbing the tip of my nose along his, my lips touching his. "It's me, Jet. Achaia. Come back to me?"

I don't look away when his mouth opens, fangs dripping saliva as a slow snarl leaves his mouth. The velzen flies across the room and leaps onto the bed, standing protectively in front of me with his hackles raised. He doesn't growl though, he simply watches Jet, who doesn't even bother to look at the diminutive animal.

"Please, Jet," I press in an even tone. "I need you to come back." His pupils are blown wide, nostrils flared. This is Jet in hunter mode. "*Atiri*," I murmur, wondering if a word from outside the maze will help. "*Atiri*, please, it's me."

Something seems to snap in his brain. Jet's eyelids flutter as he looks around the room like he's just realized where we are. He runs both hands anxiously through his slicked-back hair, whining as he sucks in ragged, gasped breaths. He looks at me like I'm his only lifeline, reaching out to shred the fabric and pull me into his arms as the Belsen whines.

"I'm so sorry," he whispers into my hair, big arms tightening around me as he holds me close. "I could have hurt you, Achaia. I was...reliving something. Gods, I'm so fucking sorry."

"You didn't, Jet," I reassure him, stroking his dark waves as he falls to the bed, pulling me on top of him.

For a long time, Jet says nothing. But his mouth is on my neck, his fangs dragging along my skin like he's tethering himself to me. His breaths come rapid-fire as he shifts me higher and buries his face in my breasts, groaning from between them. Rolling us carefully onto our sides, he nuzzles me with his nose. "Thank you," he whispers.

Gods above, my poor broken Jet. "You did it yourself," I remind him. "You're so fucking strong, alpha."

He groans again before focusing on my face. "You pulled me out of what I was remembering."

I run my fingers down the side of his square jaw. "You want to talk about the memory?"

"No," he whispers, capturing my finger with his teeth. Chocolate eyes flick to mine again as he lets out a plaintive groan. "Yes. I want you to know what happened to me. I've never talked about it with anyone, not even Renze. He found me afterward, but..."

Anxious energy churns in my stomach. I'm terrified of what I'm about to hear, but he needs this. I reach down and rub his big chest as the velzen stalks to the pillows, flopping down on top of Jet's head.

Jet sputters around the black fur tickling his nose and shoves the velzen off him. It scoots closer, determined to comfort Jet as well.

I hold back a laugh as it begins purring, Jet's dark eyes finding mine again as he studiously ignores our new pet. He's silent for long moments, but I sense he's simply thoughtful. Somehow, I feel him in my chest—his emotion, his strength, his power.

Sliding off him, I thread my legs through his and stroke his stomach as his muscles relax.

Jet talks for an hour nonstop, telling me about every fucking horrible thing Rama did to him and his brothers. How she used her own father to entrap Noire. How she threw the Ayala brothers into the maze when Tenebris was just ten years old. How she forced them to kill and torture and maim. How she shoved uppers down Jet's throat until he was addicted.

For seven years, she showed off his body in the Atrium room. Jet was her prized pony, good for nothing but the show ring. She forced him to fuck rich men and women. The memory that stole him from me tonight was the worst, though. Rama's goons stabbed Jet with a lance while forcing him to fuck a dying man. And once the man was dead, she forced Jet to continue.

By the time Jet's words slow, I'm a sobbing mess. My heart is shattered to pieces in my chest for what he endured. The velzen is purring louder and louder when Jet finally rolls over, bringing his forehead to mine. "I know it's horrible. But I wanted you to know. I want you to know *everything*," he whispers.

I can't say a godsdamned word as tears stream down my face. All I can do is stroke Jet's tan cheeks, down his angular nose, and along his forehead. "Tell me if you don't want me to touch you," I cry. "I will never take from you like she did. Never!"

Jet smiles and brings his lips to mine. It's the first kiss we've shared that's tender like this, a gentle but commanding exploration. His soft tongue teases mine as our kiss deepens. We part, and I'm breathless with how much I ache for him. "I will always want you to touch me," he murmurs. "Only you. Only Renze. I choose it, Achaia. I will always choose it."

Dark eyes flick over my shoulder, and the door swings open, Renze stalking through with a devilish grin.

CHAPTER TWENTY-ONE
RENZE

I stayed to play the mandelien, knowing my mates were fucking here in the room. I purposely did not intrude on their time, knowing how significant it was for Jet to choose this. To come back and find them so intertwined together was…unexpected.

Achaia's eyes are puffy from crying, but I sense they're relaxed, and that makes my emotive gift sing with pleasure. It would appear they shared something intimate, and that is even better than returning to find them mid-fuck. Because intimacy is the key to everything perfect with one's mates. Without intimacy, the heat holds no value. Without intimacy, it is only baseless lust.

Jet untangles himself from Achaia and slips off the bed, crossing the room as I slide my hands into my pockets. He looks from Achaia to me. "I'm going to shift and rest for a while. I'm all talked out. It was good, though," he shares, smiling over his shoulder at Achaia, who remains silent in the bed.

"Alright, Jet," I murmur, using his name rather than *atiri*. Something momentous happened in our room tonight, and I do not wish to press them. I lost control in the hallway earlier, but now is not the time to force the issue.

There's a flash of swirling, black smoke, and an immense direwolf stands in Jet's place. He's pitch-black like the velzen, longer and thinner than a normal wolf. With a low whine, he paces back to the bed and climbs up onto it, curling himself along one side as Achaia sidles up along his belly, burying her face in his fur as she marvels over seeing him for the first time.

The velzen wriggles in circles before hopping between them, nuzzling his way between Jet's furry front paws.

There is a rightness in my chest I can scarcely fathom. The perfect pieces of my soul lie in bed together in my home court. But I know, looking at them, that wherever I go will be home if they are by my side.

Pulling my clothing off, I toss it aside and round the bed. I press a button above the headboard, and the ceiling above us slides open, revealing the night sky. Stars twinkle as Achaia lets out a breathy, pleased sigh. Chilly air cools the room as she snuggles closer to Jet but pulls me to her side.

"I liked seeing you jealous this evening, *atirien*," I murmur into her hair. "Zara may never recover from your verbal sparring."

"Good," she chuckles from her place tucked next to Jet. "I hope she chokes on a dick."

Jet's wolf lets out a huffy snort as I match it. "She did, my sweet. Again after you left."

We fall into a comfortable silence as I bask in the peace of having Jet and Achaia together in bed. Eventually, I point to the stars, then bring my hand to her ass and slide my fingers along the seam until I find her sweet, wet center. Jet's dark fur tickles my arm as the velzen begins to purr quietly.

"Vampiri believe the stars write our destiny, that they pick our mate or mates. And when we leave this world, we will pass on to the next, joined together to become one of the stars in the sky. They are brightest at night because it is a vampiri's favorite time of day. So when they shine upon us, we feel the love of those who came before us. And I feel that with you both in my arms. I know the stars chose you for me."

Achaia sits up in bed, seafoam eyes focused intently on mine. "You believe that to be true?"

"I do," I assure her, my eyes flicking to Jet in his shifted form. "About you both, I do."

She follows my gaze, nipping at her lip before she turns back to me with a soft smile.

"There is something I would like to do one day, *atirien*," I murmur, reaching up to tuck her hair back. I stroke the shell of her ear, letting my fingers trace the delicate skin. "Vampiri celebrate their mating with a pierced bar through the ear from here—" I touch the tip of her ear, then the very bottom. "Exiting through here. It is a vampiri's greatest pleasure to gift his mates a jewel for every year they celebrate together."

"I never noticed that on any of the vampiri from your court," she whispers, reaching out to cover my hand with her own.

Sadness curls in my chest at that particular memory. "Rama stole them from us when she captured us seven years ago. There were many bonded vampiri in my court, but those jewels were taken from them. I would return them if I could."

"I'm so sorry she did that. It's a beautiful tradition," she sighs.

"It is called the binding," I continue. "When we are past this, after we uncover the truth of your past and rescue Tenebris, I would like to bind you both. It would be my greatest achievement to give you my jewel and to accept yours."

She breathes in a surprised breath but smiles, leaning in to kiss my lower lip.

I want her. Gods, I want her so fucking much in this tender moment, speaking of our future. Now is not the time to take her, not after what she and Jet shared. Still, my power is at an all-time high after having her earlier.

Leaning over, I stroke the velzen's pointy black ear. "Have you named him yet?"

Achaia shifts off my chest and turns to rub his chin. The velzen lets out a happy whine and closes his eyes, leaning into her touch.

"I'm thinking Rosu," she says. "I don't think it means anything, but I don't know. Maybe it's a word from my past."

A sense of knowing and belonging hits me so hard I have to grip the sheets to maintain my composure. "Rosu is the vampiri word for fate," I whisper, looking at the velzen as his black eyes open, his gaze connecting with mine.

"It's perfect," she whispers.

~

A sense of danger wakes me hours later, so pervasive and all-consuming that I shoot up out of bed to look around. The moment I do, both the velzen and Jet are up, growling. Achaia sleeps beside me, face down, with her hair flung across the pillow in disarray.

Something is not right.

I flip her over as she moans, and my heart freezes. Next to us, Jet shifts immediately into human form.

"Is that what I think it is?" he barks out. "Fuck, he's here, or he *was* here."

On Achaia's chest, there is a metal spider nearly the size of my hand. It is an exact mirror of the ones that attacked the market in Siargao—its legs muted shades of gray and the main body a blood-red. It is then I realize the coloring is because its taking blood from her.

"Get it off!" shouts Jet, reaching for the mechanical insect.

"Do not, Jet," I warn. "It rests over her heart. Let us examine it for a moment, but if it is sentient and tries to escape, grab it quickly."

I peer down under the spider's body, seeing where a needle dips into Achaia's skin, but it does not appear to be more than surface level. The scent of her blood thrills me, but the idea that this is stealing hers nearly throws me into a rage.

"I am going to remove it," I murmur. "Be ready, Jet."

He nods as I grip the spider's body. It is oddly warm to the touch, but when I pull, all eight legs curl in on themselves as if the machine is locking up or folding into a defensive position.

Just then, Jet snarls, cocking his head to the side. "I can hear someone coming. Sinan, I think."

I hand Jet the spider as Achaia's eyelids flutter open. "What are you two—oh my gods, is he here? Oh, fuck!"

She shoots backward, hitting the headboard just as the door to our room flies open, Sinan slipping through with his First Warriors and half a dozen others.

The would-be king is furious, his eyes are narrowed slits of white as he looks from me to my nude mate to Jet, who holds the mechanical spider.

"You!" he spits. "I woke to find spiders crawling my godsdamn room, sucking at Zara's blood. What is this tech? How did you come by it when Rama controls all such things? Tell me now, and your death will be swift, warrior."

"It was not I," I counter. "Look for an intruder immediately and possibly a giant metal horse. We were attacked by these in Siargao before we left. You cannot think I would purposely bring such a thing into our court," I hiss back, clicking out a warning as I stand from the bed, pulling Achaia off it and behind Jet and me. "I just removed the same mechanism from Achaia."

Sinan snarls, his First Warrior, Elleph, stalking toward us.

Behind me, Achaia sighs loudly and peeks around my body. "This isn't us. We must have been followed."

Sinan clicks angrily, white eyes flicking again to mine. "We detected an intruder several hours ago. My warriors gave chase but were unable to catch him."

"Your First Warriors could not catch one person?" I quip, unable to help myself. "Surround yourself with a better court, Sinan. Or you will not rule this one for very long."

"That is rich," Sinan hisses back at me. "You who come to my court with your so-called mates. They do not even claim you, Firenze, they have no bars, and you have no honor."

My blood boils, but I shove it aside. My mates are none of Sinan's business. "I am hardly concerned with what you think of that, Sinan. We came here for your help. This is Rama. Obviously! To what end? I do not know. But it is clear that she is preparing for war. I will ask you again: help us put an end to her reign. These creatures did not come only for Achaia or Jet or me. They came for you, too. You have lived in relative safety here, but if Rama has set her sights on you, then you must act *now*."

Sinan's eyes narrow again, but I sense he's conversing with his First Warriors. He should be able to do so without talking, as I was able to speak with Cashore when he lived. Although, Cashore's power of mindspeak was the greatest I have ever known.

Sinan steps between his warriors and crosses the room, pulling a small orb from his pocket. He hands it to me with a frown.

"All our technology died when Rama took over Siargao, and we have never regained any of it. We did not rest on our laurels, as you seem to believe, Firenze. We researched vampiri history and came across an ancient seeing orb that our ancestors used hundreds of generations ago. As it turns out, there were a few of these orbs buried deep in the coffers here. We sent warriors to Siargao, Deshali, and the coast of Vinituvari to plant orbs. From here, we can watch those locations, almost like a television."

I take the orb as he places a hand on it. "Vinituvari province."

The white ball turns clear, and then I am looking at Paraiso, floating in the sky over a vast blue sea. A column of water stretches from the surface of the ocean up to the bottom of the city.

"Why are you telling me this now?"

Sinan rubs his chin. When his eyes meet mine, I know he will not help us. "We will hunker down here in safety, Firenze. I am not willing to take Rama on directly. I am not ready. But I will point you in the right direction. I was not entirely truthful when I said we were unaware of what she was doing. You can see in the orb that Paraiso is drawing seawater up from the ocean below it. The city returns there on occasion. We believe it to be a resting place of sorts to recharge somehow. She returned here the day you left the maze. We saw that in the orb, as well."

Jet lets out a menacing growl. "What else has she been doing?"

Sinan shrugs. "Guards watch the orb day and night. Nobody has come or gone from the sky city since she parked it there."

"We need to move on," Jet barks. "We need to get the fuck out of here."

"What do you know of a man called the Builder?" I question Sinan.

Jet sucks in a breath at my sharing of that information, but Sinan nods.

"We have heard whispers of him, but I do not know anything concrete to share."

"And you will not help us," I press.

Sinan crosses his arms. "I will not help you, Firenze. And you are no longer welcome here. Get out. After this invasion from the spiders, we are putting the court into lockdown."

Achaia's arm whips out from behind me. "If you sit back and do nothing, you're siding with her. You understand that, right? No one is safe."

Sinan balls his fists but gestures to the door with a dip of his head. "Out. Right now."

"I must see the whisperer first," I retort as his eyebrows travel upward.

"To what end, Firenze?"

"It is a personal matter," I reply harshly.

Sinan laughs, gesturing toward Jet. "Ah. I suppose you want to see if this one truly belongs to you, given that he wants very little to do with you or the woman." I don't bother to answer him, but he nods. "You may visit her. She remains in the same quarters you are familiar with. Do not come back here, Firenze," he warns.

I nod as Sinan and the guards turn to leave.

Achaia looks at Jet, whose dark eyes are on the pinprick at her chest. A drop of blood wells at the surface of the wound. Leaning close to her, I slick my tongue out, capturing that drop as she sighs. "I wasn't ready to wake up, but I suppose it's a sign from the universe that it's time to go."

Jet turns from us, grabbing our clothing and bags and shoving everything together. We dress in silence, then leave the room as I call Rosu.

Jet whirls around in surprise. "After everything that's happened, you want to bring the velzen?"

"The others will kill him if we reject him," I tell Jet. "He would die slowly and painfully. Being accepted by us will help him grow into a formidable guardian for our pack. It is best we bring him. He is still young, but he will become quite large."

Jet's eyes soften as Rosu pads past him with his ears drooping. Achaia reaches down and pulls the skinny pile of fur up into her arms, padding gracefully out of the door. Jet sighs. "We came here for allies, and we're leaving with a dog. Noire's gonna love this."

CHAPTER TWENTY-TWO
JET

I throw our bags over my shoulder and trail behind Achaia as Renze leads the way down dark stone hallways. Every corner we turn reminds me of hunting in the maze—waiting for disks embedded in our arms to tell us if Rama preferred that we kill the marks that night or not. I can't wait to get the seven hells out of here. The vampiri home court is not good for my mental state, even though part of me is soothed after my connection with Achaia last night.

We make it to the car, but Renze passes it and heads into another wing of the castle, descending down, down, down skinny stairs. After the uproar this morning, I'm anxious to get on the road. Even so, it's clear the alpha followed us from Siargao, which means we need a plan. Otherwise, we risk leading him right to Noire, Diana, and Ascelin. That can only end in one outcome for us.

Achaia walks stiffly in front of me, the velzen still clutched in her arms. Its head hangs over her right shoulder, black eyes sad on mine as he cuddles her neck. I reach out and rub between them when we reach the bottom of the stairs and pause in front of a door.

Renze turns to us both with a look of warning. "The whisperer is ancient, and she has lived in this castle for hundreds of generations. She is a wealth of vampiri knowledge. Achaia, I would like her to examine your tattoo. Perhaps the answer we seek lies here. I must discuss a few other things with her as well."

Achaia turns to me with a meaningful look. "I promise we'll be quick, Jet. I know you're dying to leave."

I clear my throat and stroke her cheek, aiming to comfort her. "I am, but you need answers and so do we." She leans into my touch before turning and following Renze as he opens the thick, wooden door.

Entering the whisperer's room is akin to passing through a portal. The interior is lit up like the morning, even though it's still dark outside. Moss coats the entire floor, a small rabbit running across the stones as I glance around. A giant stone hearth roars with a banked fire.

Achaia sets Rosu down, and he trots across the room, Renze following just behind him. In a small alcove, there's a table, and behind it, a woman sits.

Maybe a woman. She is so old and grizzled that I can't tell. Stringy white hair hangs limply at her shoulders, which hunch over the table as she eats a bowl of something sloppy. When she looks up to see Renze, a smile splits her grizzled cheeks. "Firenze. You have returned home."

Renze drops to one knee at the head of the table before rising back up. "Not for long, I am afraid. Much has changed here, *min-hiren*."

"So it has," the crone agrees, white eyes flicking to Achaia and me. "Who have you brought me, Firenze?"

Renze smirks at that. "This is Achaia, *min-hiren*, and Jet."

"Fine mates," she murmurs, stroking her chin thoughtfully as she examines us. I hold back a growl at her lazy perusal, disliking the way she eyes me like a piece of meat. "Calm, alpha. I mean you no harm," she says kindly. "It has been many years since an alpha visited the court. Not since the time of your father, may he rest in peace."

Despite my surprise at her mention of my father, I snort. My father was a fucking asshole, and I don't miss him. Thomas is the alpha I think of as my father now.

"Your father was not always as you knew him," she murmurs. "But that is a story for another time." She turns to Renze. "You seek something, First Warrior."

Firenze nods. "We seek answers for Achaia and our journey. We were followed here by one of Rama's warriors. We cannot risk leading him to our pack. I need your help."

The woman stands and rounds the table, reaching out to pat Achaia's forearm. "Let us take a look at you first, my child." All-white eyes flick to Achaia and narrow, who turns and pulls her shirt over her head.

I'm presented with a mouthwatering view of her full breasts, which sway slightly as the whisperer lets out a clicking hiss. The old woman reaches out, yelping when she experiences the same painful zing Renze and I do if we touch the tattoo.

"A curse," she mutters under her breath. "A dark and powerful magic. This is a prisoner tattoo. It keeps you from your true form and it seals your memories away. Whoever tattooed this upon you does not wish you to know who you are or to have any memory of who you were."

Achaia looks over her shoulder. "What are my options?"

If she's surprised by this news, she doesn't show it. She's focused and resolved, ready to take action. I feel her in my chest, which is significant and meaningful. And that shocks the hells out of me because she's not an omega, or I never thought she was. But maybe she is one, trapped beneath the magic of the tattoo.

I can't help myself, pressing into her side as I stroke her stomach and purr.

The crone watches my movements before sighing. "You will have to cut or burn it off, my child. Or find the person who gave it to you so that they may remove it. That is rarely possible though, unless there is anyone around you who can identify that being."

"Fuck. Then only the first two are options," whispers Achaia, the first hint of tears filling her eyes. She glances over her shoulder again. "Have you seen what you need to see?"

"I have, child," the woman replies, patting Achaia's shoulder as they face one another. "I do not know your future path, but there is no better male to walk it with than Firenze. Stay close to him; allow him to guide you. He is a keeper, as the young ones say these days."

Renze looks distraught at the news. "There is more," he continues. "The prophecy of the Chosen One has come to pass. Cashore now lives within the mate of Jet's elder brother, Noire."

The crone whirls around. "Then he is one step closer to reuniting with his beloved Zel."

My blood freezes at that because being reunited sounds like something that should happen after death. Diana is very much alive. "Please tell us more about that," I press. "I'm my pack's strategist, and I need to know everything I can. Is Diana in danger? Well, any more than usual?" I tack that last bit on because none of us are safe while Rama lives.

The whisperer smiles. "The Chosen One prophecy is complicated, alpha. There are two halves. The first I received in vampiri tongue. It seems you're aware of that already through your connection with Renze. The second half came to me in a language I do not speak, a language of the monsters of the Tempang. In all my research, I have never been able to translate it."

She turns from us and crosses the room to a small desk, pulling a weathered sheet of paper from a disorderly stack. Folding it, she crosses the room and hands it to me. "This is the other half of the prophecy, written phonetically since I did not know the original language. It is the most help I can give you, sadly."

I take the paper as frustration builds under my skin. I can't help Achaia. I can't learn more about this potential threat to Diana. I can't do anything for Tenebris. Reaching out, I pull Achaia into my arms and bury my face in her neck, her scent grounding me and bringing me focus.

"We need guidance, whisperer," Renze murmurs. "We are being followed by an alpha we know works for Rama. A contact recommended we find a man called the Builder, but I do not wish to lead Rama right to our pack. It is bad enough we have been followed."

The crone grins. "That I can help you with." She crosses the room and opens a trunk, rooting around inside it until she finds what she's looking for. Turning to us, she gives us a wicked grin, holding up a small orb.

Renze laughs aloud. "Does Sinan know you have a traveling orb?"

The whisperer scoffs. "He does not, fool that he is." Her broad smile falls. "Cashore gave this to me the last time I saw him. He said, one day I may wish to finally leave this place, and the orb would deliver me wherever I wanted to go. A retirement spot of sorts."

Achaia throws both hands over her heart. "We can't possibly take that from you."

My mind churns through ideas, though. We could take it straight to Rama's bedside and kill her. But there are obvious flaws in that. We could go straight to Noire and use it thereafter. But I don't want to lead the alpha right to the Builder, and we still don't know precisely where he's located.

The whisperer places the orb in my palm, a soft smile on her wrinkled face. "Go to your pack, alpha. Use this to escape the man who trails you. It is my contribution to your cause, and to the freedom of our peoples."

"This is a sacrifice, and we are honored by it," Achaia murmurs, reaching out to grab the crone's fingers, pulling the woman's hand to rest over her heart. For long moments, they look at one another, and the only thought in my mind is how perfect Achaia is like this. She is the kinder, gentler serenity to my possessiveness and Renze's power.

Firenze stands and plants a kiss on the woman's cheek. "I have one last request, old friend." His eyes fall on Rosu, who sits patiently on Achaia's feet. When we all glance down, he begins shimmying from side to side, hopping from one front foot to the other as he yips softly.

The older woman nods and smiles, crossing the room to a second chest. When she opens it, golden cuffs spill out across the floor, and Rosu starts yowling happily, zooming around the room in circles like an overly eager puppy.

The whisperer crosses the room once more and hands Achaia the cuff. "This is yours to gift, my child. Through it, your bond with him will grow, and he will grow physically once you claim him. A velzen is loyal until death. He will never part from any of you, and he will always protect you and your younglings, if you choose to have them."

Achaia nods, the first tear streaking down her face as she kneels down on the floor. Rosu bounds up to her joyously as she looks up at the whisperer. "Do I need to say anything specific to him? Is there a proper way to do this?"

The crone smiles. "There is a saying in ancient vampiri. *Setep-vi-hyren*. It means 'my heart upon yours'. Your velzen will hold his paw out for you. Once you clasp the band on him, it will never unlock, and you will be formally bound."

Achaia looks at Rosu, who leans in and presses his nose to her arm with a soft whine.

"*Setep-vi-hyren*, Rosu," she murmurs.

Immediately, his paw flies up, quivering slightly as Achaia laughs and nuzzles his cheek. "Eager little thing, aren't you?"

Rosu whines again as my eyes find Renze. The look on his face is something I can only describe as joy. He glances over at me, and the smile broadens.

Achaia clasps the gold band around Rosu's thin leg, and then he zooms around the room in circles again, yipping at the top of his lungs as Achaia laughs.

"Go with the gods, my children," the whisperer intones. "I will pray for your safety in the war to come."

"Perhaps you can put a good word in with Sinan," Renze growls, shaking his head. "He is a fool."

The older woman sighs. "I will do what I can, Firenze. But I am not hopeful. Go, now."

Achaia hands Renze the traveling orb, and he smiles at us both. "Are you ready, *min-atirien?*"

Achaia looks over at me, reaching for my hand. "Ready as I'll ever be," she murmurs.

I take a step closer and slide her hand up under my shirt. "I've got you. I'll be right there."

CHAPTER TWENTY-THREE
ACHAIA

My heart beats so loud in my chest that it's all I can hear as the whisperer places her hand on the traveling orb. I've never heard of anything like this. It was never mentioned in a single book Thomas had me read. It must be incredibly uncommon. The fact that she's just *giving* it to us speaks volumes to me about the type of person she is.

Between claiming Rosu, the traveling orb, and the revelation about my tattoo, my emotions are a shredded mess. My fingers quiver as I place them on the orb. Renze and Jet's follow mine as the whisperer looks over at me. "Pick up your velzen, child. Else he will be left behind with me, and much as I love them, he would be highly distressed without you."

I reach down, Rosu leaping up into my arms and throwing his paws over my shoulder as he buries his face in my neck and snuffles. I put my hand back on the orb, and the elderly woman smiles. "I can send you to a place, or to a person. What details do you have?"

"All we know is that he goes by the Builder," Jet offers. "We don't know his real name. An informant suggested he lives in the northern part of Dest province, but that's all we have."

She smiles. "That is enough, child." She closes her eyes, and the orb fills with sand, swirling around inside it. The sand moves lazily at first, but as it picks up speed, she away from us. "May your journey be safe and your lives long and bound." She clasps her hands in front of her as the orb begins to expand, its outer shell enveloping our hands as I struggle not to feel trapped.

"Easy, *atirien*," murmurs Renze. "This is ancient magic. We will be fine."

My chest begins to heave as the orb grows and grows, expanding all the way up my arm as it draws us inside of it. It's warm and prickly, like being pulled into quicksand. Rosu whines into my neck as the shell touches him, and then it's like we've walked from the bright, musty room into a sandstorm. It batters us from side to side as I hold onto the orb's core.

Jet presses tightly to my side as the sand's torment yanks and pulls us. When it finally knocks me into Jet, he wraps one arm around my waist, pulling Rosu and me into his chest. I bury my face in his warm skin as he purrs. Behind him, Renze snakes a hand around to rest at my hip, holding us both.

I don't know how long the storm rolls over us. It batters us so constantly, sand fills my mouth and eyes, and I long to be done. But then, in the span of a moment, there's silence, and the sand drops to the ground. When I open my eyes, we stand at the bottom of an equally sandy dune.

"Liuvang, it's hot as fuck," Jet growls, looking down at me. He reaches up to brush sand out of my hair and off my shoulders as I spit it out of my mouth. I put Rosu down, and he shakes right away, sand flying everywhere. Jet turns from me and laughs. When I look around him, Renze has his face upturned to the sun, smiling as he soaks it in.

"Still a lizard, I see..." I tease as his smile grows wider.

"I missed the sun for seven years, *atirien*," he murmurs. "I will take every moment of its brilliance that I can."

My heart clenches at the idea of him and Jet trapped in the maze. I watched Rama televise the nightly hunts. I've seen these men torture and maim and kill. But it's clear to me now that they had no choice at all. There's so much more to their story than what we saw on the television.

Jet heads up the sand dune. "Let's go. We need to find this place and figure out how to get in." He turns from the top of the small dune. "Renze, can you sense Ascelin? I hope they were able to find this place too."

Renze's face is still upturned to the sun. "I cannot sense her yet, but that could mean they have not yet arrived. Or that we are not close enough."

Jet looks around in a full circle as Rosu and I trudge to the top of the sand dune. "There." He points off into the distance. "Built at the base of that cliff. I see color."

"You can see that far?" I grouse. "Why didn't the orb bring us straight to the front door?"

"We did not have sufficient detail for a front-door arrival, my sweet," Renze chuckles.

There is nothing around us but sand. Not a single plant or sign of life at all. In the distance where Jet swears he sees color, a sand-colored cliff juts straight out of the ground, rising up to block the sky and crossing the horizon like a plateau. I suppose if one were to build a city out here, that's as good a place as any.

"Come on," Jet says, tickling my side before he heads down the sand dune toward the cliff.

Half an hour later, sand is once again in every crevice of my clothing and person. Rosu trudges next to me with his tongue hanging out of his mouth.

"He's supposed to be a guardian one day, right?" I question Renze as we pick our way slowly up and over dune after dune.

"Yes, *atirien*," Renze laughs. "He is small now. All velzen stay that way until they are claimed by a family. Once that happens, he will begin to grow quickly. Eventually, he will be nearly as big as Jet's direwolf, and twice as mean."

Jet growls from in front of us, but there's no bite to it. I sense that the same way I sense his focus now that we're here. Rubbing my chest, I feel a tiny bump from the attack this morning.

I look over at Renze. "Hand me the spider, please. I'd like to get a better look at it."

Renze reaches into his bag and withdraws the spider that attached itself to me this morning. He hands it to me, our fingertips brushing each other's as I smile at him.

"We assume this is Rama because of the market, and because she controls this sort of tech, right?"

Renze nods. "But why she would target you and then others in the vampiri court is a mystery to me. Why Zara and not Sinan?"

I examine the body of the spider. It's full of red blood—my red blood—dozens of vials' worth. I look up at Renze. "Can you use your claws to help me take this apart?"

He nods with a smirk, black claws sliding from his fingertips. I try not to focus on how beautiful his long fingers are, or how good they felt inside me last night with his mouth on my clit. I hold back a needy whine as he examines the spider, its spindly metal legs still folded protectively beneath its body.

"Could it have implanted a tracker in me?" I question as he undoes the last screw, handing me the vial of blood.

It's a chilling question, and Jet freezes in front of us. "It's possible," he muses. "But if we find the Builder and make it in, maybe he'll help us."

"Oh, there are so many holes in this plan," I groan aloud. "I hope Diana, Noire, and Ascelin are here."

I pick the spider apart, piece by piece, careful not to lose any of them. There's nothing to indicate any sort of sensor or tech to it. I have to believe that whoever dropped the spiders in the castle didn't expect to have to go find them after they attacked, so there must be some way for the spider to find its way home. The ones in the market flew after the horse, but I doubt they could have made it very far.

"If we let it go, do you think it would go back where it came from?" I'm wondering aloud, but Jet and Renze both turn to watch as I screw the whole thing back together.

We fall silent as we mull over the questions that comment brings up. I hate that we have so many questions and so few answers.

~

Hours later, Rosu and I are being dragged along by Renze as we struggle through the heat. Rosu is a limp pile of fur thrown over my shoulder, panting loudly in my ear. Fur is stuck to my face, chest, and neck, and the only thing moving me forward is Renze's hand on my wrist, pulling.

"Gods," I complain, hating that I'm doing it but also completely miserable. "Wherever I'm originally from can't be a sandy place. This is fucking awful."

Up ahead of us, Jet's shirt is drenched in sweat, but he turns and smiles. "You need a carry?" He flashes me a cheeky grin as I point my finger at him.

"It wasn't that long ago you were complaining about the heat back home."

Jet's smile grows bigger as he stops. We catch up to him in moments, and then he's towering over me, smirking down from his superior height. I could almost cry at the shadow his body casts over mine. He leans down, brushing my sweaty hair away from my neck on the opposite side as Rosu. "I want even more heat than this, Achaia. Do you think you can handle that?"

A whine leaves my throat as Rosu sits upright in my arms and licks all over Jet's face with a happy whine.

Jet sighs. "Why do I get the feeling he's gonna ruin a lot of sexy moments for me in the future?"

I point down at my body, at the clothes plastered to every inch of me. "This is sexy?"

Jet growls appreciatively as his dark eyes scan my figure. He licks his lips as Renze watches us with a smirk. "Everything about you is sexy," he murmurs, reaching out to pinch my nipple lightly.

I find myself wishing there was a bed somewhere close by.

CHAPTER TWENTY-FOUR
RENZE

An hour later, a sand-hued compound looms large in front of us, built at the base of a steep cliff that juts straight up. A two-story stone wall guards it. In front of that, there's an ominously dark moat and a singular bridge that leads from the dunes right to massive front gates.

There is no getting into this place without an invitation. Using my gift, I search for Ascelin, but I cannot feel her. Frowning, I turn to my mates. "I do not think our people are here yet. Or they are here, and I cannot sense them." When I look around, there is nothing to indicate anyone has arrived. No aircar resting by the dunes, no sign of footprints. Perhaps we are the first to arrive.

Jet glances over at me. "We can't stay out in the sun much longer; we need water." His eyes flick to Achaia, who licks her dry lips as she assesses what's in front of us. He continues on. "I'm going to shift. My senses are better that way. We'll have to ring the doorbell, I suppose. I'm sure they're already aware we're here."

Achaia bites at her nail. "That bridge between here and the gate seems…" She pauses before looking up at me. "Like is the bridge just going to dump us into the water or what? It's a fucking moat, Renze."

"The situation is not ideal," I mutter. Still, I am faster than both Achaia and Jet, and we are limited on options at this point. "I will go alone."

"Hells no," Achaia shouts as Jet nods in agreement. She whirls around. "You're going to let him go alone?"

Jet gives her an understanding look, even though his posture is tense.

"Renze and I escaped the maze, Achaia. We've killed monsters and humans alike. He can do this—I promise."

"It is the least risky option," I agree. I pat Rosu once and kiss Achaia softly on the lips. Jet gives me a curt nod. Turning from them, I slip down the dunes to the dark metal bridge. Their emotions are a tempest that follows me all the way to the overpass.

This close to the compound, I cannot see any defenses. It could be misleading, but with nothing else out here in this part of Lombornei, it is unlikely the Builder receives many visitors. He is more myth than man at this point, so I am hopeful these protective measures are simply there for looks.

Jet and Achaia follow me down the dunes, standing at the very edge of the bridge as we gaze upon the front gate. I give them one last look.

Slipping quickly, I cross the bridge without issue. I lift my hand to knock at the gate, but just as I move to do so, a net comes out of nowhere, knocking me to the ground. It zips tightly around me until I am huddled into a tiny ball, barely able to move. I rage, slicing at the net with my claws, but nothing happens. It does not even shred as I begin to shout for help, calling for the Builder, for Ascelin, for anyone at all.

I sense Jet and Achaia's terror and immediate desire to help. Achaia sprints toward me, even as Jet's direwolf follows to stop her, knocking her down as he grabs her boot in his maw and begins dragging her back to the safety of the dunes.

Struggling against the net, I watch in horror as the river beneath the bridge begins to roil, waves bursting across the surface as dozens of arms in every color appear out of the murky depths. "Come no further!" I scream as bodies begin to pull themselves up out of the dirty moat and onto the bridge. Spindly arms reach for my mates as I bellow. The net I'm trapped in is yanked up by a long chain, and I swing slowly from side to side, giving me a view of the matted hair and thin arms of the beings rapidly crowding the bridge. The first emerges fully, landing on the bridge with a squelch as I see scaled legs ending in pointed fins.

Mermaids.

Oh gods, please, I pray to the gods I defied my whole life. *Please don't take my mates from me so soon.*

On the bridge, Rosu yelps as a mermaid grabs Achaia's leg and yanks her to the very edge. Jet's wolf snaps at the mermaid's arm, and she screams and lets go. But where she falls back, two more take her place. Claws in every glittering color snatch and grab at my mates as Rosu snarls and bites in their defense. The mermaids let out a chorus of yipping hisses, similar to the vampiri language but different—this is haunting. This is a battle cry.

Jet's wolf roars as he pulls Achaia between his legs, standing over her as he claws and slashes at dozens of long arms that reach for him, Achaia and Rosu. I watch in horror as a mermaid snatches at Rosu's tail, but Jet clamps his big jaws around the arm, ripping it from the socket as the mermaid hisses and clicks, revealing rows of spiky teeth as she screams in pain and falls back into the water.

Hands begin to reach in a frenzy for Jet, who winces and snarls, snapping at what he can reach. But he never wavers from his place above Achaia, even as blood begins to stream down the sides of his slick coat from dozens of deep gashes. Rosu stands in front of Achaia, just below Jet's chest, biting any hand that comes near them.

Too many.

There are far too many.

I roar as I slash at the net binding me, but there is no give at all.

More thin, bedraggled bodies pull up onto the bridge, and Jet seems to realize it's a losing battle. They can't stay where they are, despite how much larger his wolf is.

"Run!" I scream at him. "Run, Jet!"

If he can hear me, he gives no sign, but Achaia pulls Rosu to her chest as she kicks a mermaid right in the face, knocking it back into the murky water. My mate scrambles out from under Jet, and he noses her up onto his back as she clutches Rosu and clings to Jet's wolf.

Jet leaps to one side, knocking a slew of mermaids off the bridge as he barrels up it, despite clawed hands snatching at anything they can reach. The mermaids begin to scream, haunting, echoing noises that settle in my bones as I shout for the Builder, for Diana, for Ascelin, for anyone who can hear me. I claw at my net but make no purchase as I watch Jet leap over three mermaids and sprint for the dunes.

There are simply too many, and horror chokes me as a pile of the miserable creatures block Jet's way, hissing, their too-big eyes focused on their next meal. Jet lowers his head and charges through the row of mermaids, but they claw at him, Rosu and Achaia as blood flows in steady streams to the bridge's surface.

Jet's wolf bellows as he goes into a rage, biting and lashing out as mermaids fly in every direction. Rosu leaps from Achaia's arms to help him, biting every finger that gets near Jet. They work as a team, but they can't win. They can't...

Suddenly, I feel the slip of vampiri breeze upon my face. Ascelin darts past me, depressing a stone in the wall which opens the net holding me. She springs immediately down onto the walkway and roars.

"Hands off my court or I will remove them from your godsdamned bodies." The mermaids freeze and turn, and from somewhere behind the walls, a high-pitched whistle sounds. When the mermaids hear it, they grow agitated and throw themselves back into the water, although one makes a final mad dash for Rosu. Jet bellows and leaps on top of her, snapping her neck before he tosses her into the still-roiling water.

I cannot even be relieved to see my First Warrior partner. Slipping past her, I snatch Rosu and Achaia and press them both into Jet's heaving body. He's covered in deep gashes, and Achaia drags one leg. Even Rosu is bleeding from multiple wounds.

"Bet you've never been so thrilled to see me," Ascelin deadpans as she stalks up the bridge to meet us, glancing from me over the edge of the bridge. "Go the fuck away, they are not your food today."

From the water, a dozen heads look up at us. Maws open to reveal sharp teeth as the mermaids let out an earsplitting screech that echoes across the water. Achaia slaps her hands over her head as Jet wraps his big head around us, crushing us close to his body. Rosu snarls from under Jet's chin, struggling to get out of my arms.

Ascelin rolls her eyes. "Psychotic carnivorous mermaids. They nearly ate us the first day, as well. If we hadn't found out the Builder's name and shared it, we might not be speaking today. Follow me. You will be pleased to find Diana and Noire are here with me. We only just arrived last night." Ascelin cocks her head to the side, pointing at Rosu. "A velzen?"

I have questions. So very many questions. But my mates are in pain, so I gather Rosu and Achaia closer to me and follow Ascelin, who glances at the velzen with a quirked brow. "I take it Sinan is behaving precisely as we imagined."

"Unfortunately," Achaia offers, wincing as I sling her up into my arms. "He was unwilling to provide any assistance whatsoever. To be frank, I did not care for him."

Ascelin laughs, looking back at me with a joyous expression. "I take back my initial assessment of *tua-atirien*, Firenze. Perhaps there is a fire in her that I did not initially see."

"I'm right here, Ascelin," Achaia teases, reaching out and yanking Ascelin's long braid, stopping the First Warrior in her tracks.

Ascelin whips around with a furious expression. "Do it again, female. I dare you."

Achaia leans into Ascelin's space as Ascelin's fangs leak venom onto the sand. When Achaia plants a teasing quick kiss on my First Warrior partner's nose, I burst into laughter. Ascelin steps back in surprise and wipes the kiss away.

When she opens her mouth to snap back, Achaia gives her a pointed look. "We have had a long day, First Warrior. We are cut to shreds, we need water, and we're in desperate need of an update. Please lead the way."

Ascelin's mouth drops open as she turns to me with a frown. I shrug and beam down at my beautiful mate.

The way she commands Ascelin sends my cock leaping in my pants. I need Achaia, I need that hit of power her blood pushes into my system. I want them both, and after our rude interruption at the vampiri court, I believe I will have them soon.

It is said that patience is a virtue. I suppose I will find out.

For now, I am simply thrilled we didn't die.

The doors to the compound open wide, and I am shocked beyond belief at what I see within. There is a veritable oasis inside the gates. Water fountains, soaring palms, and people everywhere in brightly colored clothing.

A man clad in nothing but wide-legged pants runs up, handing us a basket of water bottles as Jet shifts back into human form. My mate runs his hands over Achaia's face before opening a bottle and lifting it to her lips. His dark eyes land on her injured leg, and even though he's bleeding from dozens of deep cuts, he leans over to examine her.

Diana and Noire are just inside the doors, and I sag with relief when I see the Chosen One. It is my duty to protect her, and though Ascelin and I agreed to split duties, it has weighed on my mind to part from Diana.

"Thank the goddess you're here," she murmurs, throwing herself in my arms as I set Achaia down. "You're hurt. And you've got a dog. I have so many questions, but come on. We need you to meet Arliss, the Builder, and then we'll get you a room."

Jet paces around Diana to his brother, rubbing his big cheek on Noire's arm. Noire pinches the tip of his ear with a growl. "Thankful to see you in one piece, brother. I want to hear about your trip. There's a lot for me to share with you."

We follow Ascelin, Noire and Diana along a stone path through a thicket of brightly colored flowers, replete with singing birds and even a troop of howling monkeys. It is almost as if someone crafted a desert oasis with magic. How else could something like this grow from nothing in the barren landscape of this part of Lombornei?

I have so many questions, and I intend to ask them all as soon as I can.

Diana hooks her hand in one of my belt loops, as if she's so relieved to be close to me again, we have to touch.

"Chosen One, how did you find this place?" I question as we make our way through the sprawling compound.

"After you left, we went back to the maze island and released the sentient monsters from the stable. It was dicey for a minute, but we met a harpy called Moriah, and she knew of the Builder. I guess she lived here for a time before moving on and being captured by Rama. She refused to come with us, but was able to draw us a map. According to Moriah, the only way to get in was to be accompanied by one of Arliss' group, or to find out his name. She gave it to us in exchange for her freedom."

I blink away my surprise. "I imagine there's a little more to that story, Chosen One."

"Oh yeah," Diana huffs, glancing behind us to Noire, who's already taken up his usual position at the back of the pack. "But that's the overview, and that'll do for now until we get you three taken care of. Liuvang, I'm so fucking relieved to see you in one piece."

Achaia shuffles in my arms to be put down, and I drop her gently to her feet. She gives Diana a pointed look. "We've got a lot to catch up on. The vampiri court was enlightening, to say the least."

Diana's half-smile falls, but she nods and continues. "Our host is… unusual, a man of many…." Her voice trails off as she waves her hands around, seemingly hunting for an appropriate word.

"He is a manwhore," Ascelin chirps, clapping me on the back. "Needless to say, we get along quite well. He might as well be a vampiri as much as he loves to fuck."

I smirk as Ascelin jogs forward and opens a door, ushering us into a bright hallway. The tiled floor is a vibrant, shocking blue, with tall columns opening into a forested courtyard. We head straight up the hallway as a group of scantily clad women pass us, tittering as they go.

"You'll get used to that," Diana laughs. "Arliss is…"

"*Yes*, my beauty. Fuck. Just like that," groans an impossibly low voice. I stiffen as Achaia grips my arm. Jet hovers just behind Achaia, growling softly as he wipes blood away from one eye. We round a corner into a huge open hall with arched ceilings. In the middle of the room, a massive black man with midnight hair braided in long locks down to his waist sits on a throne.

Perched at his side on a raised, tufted platform is a nude woman, her mouth bobbing up and down on his erect cock as he glances up at us with a grin. He lets out an appreciative sigh and rubs the girl's cheek. "Enough, my beauty. That was lovely, but I must concentrate. Let us continue later, shall we?"

The woman laughs and wipes her mouth, but plants a kiss on his cheek and hops off the platform, jogging out of the room without a backward glance.

Power rolls off this male in rippling waves. I don't recognize him as any particular sort of monster, but that is not to say something monstrous does not lie under his skin. He tucks his still-erect, enormous cock back into tight black pants and stands up from the throne. A loose sweater of sorts flows behind him as he descends the stairs, bare-chested, as Jet steps in front of Achaia.

Diana smiles as the male approaches, all predatory grace and enormous stacked muscles. This is a male in his prime; physically spectacular and clearly in possession of that same alpha strength that Noire exudes. I find myself surprised that Noire is not beating his chest and challenging the male to a fight, but perhaps even Noire is capable of change.

The male stops in front of our group, brilliant blue eyes giving Ascelin a lazy perusal as he licks his thick lips. "You are absolutely enchanting today, Ascelin."

I glance over at my partner. She puts one hand up, black lips opening to reveal her sharp fangs. "I had you once, Arliss, and once was enough. Move along, please."

The handsome male feigns a dagger to the heart, grinning wickedly at her. "You wound me, warrioress. I may yet win you over. I shall not stop trying, at the very least."

"Don't waste that lovely cock on me, Builder," she laughs back. "As I said, one frighteningly quick ride atop it was plenty."

So many questions rattle around in my brain, but my emotive gift is working on overdrive. My mates are hurt and exhausted, the rest of my pack is relaxed but focused, and this male who jokes with Ascelin feels like pure deviance personified. If Noire is an asshole, the Builder is even worse.

Arliss turns to me with an appraising look, his eyes moving from me to Achaia and finally Jet. He lets out a little noise as he folds both hands in front of his waist. He has judged us and found us lacking.

"We need a room," I purr, commanding rather than asking. "My mates are injured and I need a moment to care for them."

If any of my pack is surprised to hear me call Achaia and Jet 'mates', they don't say anything.

The Builder smiles, but there's nothing truly friendly in the way he opens his arms wide and looks around. "My home is your home. If you find a door locked, do not attempt to open it. Do not cross the bridge again unless you wish the merfolk to eat you. Noire has apprised me of your quest, and I have many, many thoughts. But please, *freshen up*, and we will reconvene for dinner."

We have been summarily dismissed. Without another word, he pushes his way through our crowd, stopping just next to Ascelin, his voice a low growl we can all hear. "Hear me on this, vampiri. I will have you again if I wish to. This is my home, my sanctuary. And here? Here, I am king."

"Is that so?" she croons back, bringing her claws to his throat. "You will have no more or less than I wish you to have. Now go, find a partner elsewhere. You do not lack options, Arliss."

"If I wish to tie you in my dungeon and fuck you senseless, then it will be so," he murmurs into her ear. "There will not be a thing you can do about it. Watch yourself." He crosses the room in silence as Ascelin rolls her eyes.

"Hot damn," Achaia chuckles when he has gone. "That man is sex on a stick. Ascelin, I don't know that I'd be so quick to turn that down."

Ascelin rolls her eyes at that comment. "Come. Let us get you a room so you may enjoy one another before dinner. You smell…off-putting."

CHAPTER TWENTY-FIVE
JET

To say I'm relieved to see my brother is an understatement. He's been quiet as Arliss greeted us, but our family bond is tense.

We have a lot to discuss, he growls into it as Diana sends her agreement.

Plus, we want to hear all about what happened at the court, she tacks on.

It's not great news, I grumble. *Sinan rules and is unwilling to join us. There's more. I'll share after we get settled. What happened in Dest? Did you find anyone from our pack?*

No. That's all Noire says, but it's a dagger to my gut as I grit my jaw, reliving their loss all over again.

A striking, golden-tan woman with long blue hair rounds the corner and gestures for us to follow as I shove my grief way down. I mourned my lost pack seven years ago, I've got to focus on Ten now.

Diana loops her arm through Renze's as we follow our guide through hall after sun-drenched hall. Achaia carries Rosu as I limp along next to her, my fangs still descended and ready. As always, Noire is at the rear of our group, and I bring up the side. I remain focused on our surroundings, looking for any hint of danger.

Diana strokes the back of Renze's hand. "Tell me, old friend. Sinan is now the king, so how was it?" There's an odd timbre to her voice, and when I look over, her eyes are pure white like a vampiri's.

I turn to give Noire a look before spinning back to the front. What in the world?

"My king," Renze whispers in shock. Ascelin laughs from the other side of our small group.

Diana continues on in that odd, otherworldly voice. "Not exactly, Firenze. Since we arrived here, I have been able to channel Cashore's spirit more fully. He speaks to me, guiding me. It's…incredible. I have his gift. I'm imagining so many ways it could help us for what's to come."

My throat bobs as I remember the moment Cashore gave his life to join his spirit with Diana's. Knowing there's a second un-translated half of the Chosen One prophecy makes my skin itch. Noire's gonna lose his shit when I tell him.

Renze sighs. "It is exactly as we suspected. Sinan remains a yellow-bellied coward, and he will not help us. There is more, but we need a moment to compose ourselves."

"Make it fast," Noire barks from his place next to Diana. "Fast-ish," he corrects when she gives him a dirty look. "Every moment we remain here is a moment Tenebris is still in Rama's clutches."

From Achaia's arms, Rosu lets out a deep growl, snapping his teeth at Noire as Diana chuckles. She reaches out, scratching under Rosu's chin as he licks her fingers. Our group is tense and silent after the fucking reminder of why we're doing this. My heart aches when I think about Tenebris and his love for books and learning. Liuvang-willing, I will return him to our pack, so he has the opportunity to learn to his heart's desire.

Eventually, we come to an extensive hall with doors running along one side. Our guide turns to us with a smile, pointing to the nearest door. "These two rooms connect, and you're close to your packmates. If you come straight down this hall, you'll enter the dining area." She hands Renze a small bag. "Arliss thought you might want this. The mermaids can be overzealous in their protection of Oasis." Without another word, she turns to leave.

Noire pulls Diana into his arms. "We'll wait in the dining hall for you." He grips Diana's hand and pulls her with him in the direction the woman indicated. *Make it fast, brother,* he growls into our family bond.

Renze opens the first door for Achaia, who limps through with Rosu still in her arms. My protective nature is on high as I pace the room, looking for anything that might endanger Achaia or Renze. When he closes the door, I'm alone with them for the first time since the mermaid attack.

I cross the room, pulling Achaia into my arms. My lips trace a path from her forehead down her nose, along her jawline, and down her neck. Then I take those plump lips between my teeth and suck gently.

Achaia moans softly into my touch, but she's trembling, her skin chilled. She needs to be cared for. I sense Renze watching us, but my focus is on her.

"You were so fucking brave on the bridge," I share as I examine the deep scratches on her arms.

"It was stupid to cross it," she sighs. "I put you and Rosu at risk."

"We fight for those we love," I say without meaning to. We all pause as the word *love* leaves my lips. My gaze finds hers as I drop to my knees and run my fingers over her injured leg. Blue-green eyes flash with intensity as I touch her. I look down when I feel sticky, red blood. It covers the lower half of her left leg. Angry gashes mar her tanned skin.

I look up at her and Renze. "Bathroom," I command. Renze reaches out and picks Achaia up. She curls into his neck, breathing deeply as his white eyes find mine, flashing with need. I want time with them, and I don't have it.

Rosu limps after us into the bathroom. I fill the tub as Renze sits on the edge, Rosu perched on his big thighs. Achaia fusses over the velzen first, cleaning the worst of his cuts before he flops down at the foot of the tub and falls asleep.

"You next," I murmur as I unwrap her dress and slide it off her shoulders. Her eyes come to mine, hooded with lust as the fabric drops to her feet. Renze joins me and slides his arms around her upper body. He pulls it away from her body and tosses it on the ground, growling low under his breath.

"Take the panties off," I demand, watching how my voice affects her. Her breasts sway gently as she leans down, grabbing the edge of the panties and sliding them down her big hips. When she kicks them down past her knees, Renze drops to his to examine the injuries on her leg.

His black tongue slicks over her blood-coated leg. She hisses in pain as I reach out and grab her. I pull her into the tub with me, lowering us both as Renze strips out of his clothes and slides in next to us. The tub is a giant, deep circle shape with a raised area around the edge. I press Achaia up onto the raised surface, and Renze lifts her leg.

His lips and tongue are on her, lapping and sucking at the blood that covers her wounds. I'd chide him not to hurt her, but the scent emanating from her in response to his touch is overpowering. The need to protect them, to protect everyone, chokes me as I press our bodies together and brush my lips against hers.

"Something snapped in my head when you told me no," I admit. "You gave me a choice, Achaia." Her green eyes blink as tears fill them, pink lips parted as I continue. "I may always be broken. You might lose me to my memories sometimes. But I will always find my way back to you. And I will always, *always* protect you."

She leans forward and presses her forehead to mine, tears streaming slowly down her cheeks. They make a track down her skin as I smile at her. "You need a thorough scrubbing. I'm going to do the honors."

"I thought I was losing you both," she whispers as I grab a bar of soap and begin to wash her. Running my hands over her body is a fucking pleasure. I'd love nothing more than to tease her and take her alongside Renze. Now is not the time, but I need just a few godsdamned minutes with them.

"Never," Renze reassures her, taking the soap from me as I pluck and pull her nipples. The need to cement her to me permanently presses at the forefront of my mind as Renze's hand comes to the back of my neck. When I look up at him, his white eyes are focused on me.

He leans forward, black lips pressing hard to mine as his claws come to my hair. He fists it as I sling both arms around his waist and pull him to me. Achaia lets out a breathy sigh as our kiss turns heated. Renze's tongue swirls around mine, tugging and teasing as I growl into the kiss. We fight for domination as I drag my claws down his back. He lets out a clicking hiss as his head falls back, baring his neck to me.

I bite my way roughly along it as he sighs with happiness. His head falls to the side, and I know he's eye-fucking her. I sense it in the way I can sense them both if I look deep inside. They're not direwolves like I am, but I feel them despite that fact.

"Gods, I don't want to stop the show," she gasps. "But please, can we pick this back up later? Watching you together is so hot."

I look up from where I'm biting Renze's neck, letting my tongue trail a path up his chin. I lick a stripe along his lips, his black tongue snaking out to wrap around mine. He tugs it back into his mouth as he devours me anew, pulling us down onto the ledge beside her. My erection throbs against his as Achaia slides her hand between us to touch us both.

It's my turn to let my head fall back, but it's her soft lips that brush against my skin. My dick leaps in her hand as Renze slides his hand around my back, playing with my ass. "Perfection," I whisper to myself, smiling when Achaia hums happily.

Rosu leaps up and growls when a sudden banging at the door announces Noire's presence. "Time's up," he snarls from outside our bathroom door. "You can fuck later. Get out here."

Renze sighs and slides his hands up my stomach. "Later, *min-atirien*. Let us pick this back up later."

∼

A few minutes later, we join a snarling Noire and smirking Diana in the dining hall. My brother paces as Diana speaks with a beautiful pale-skinned girl. Every inch of her is covered in brown freckles.

Diana's face lights up when she turns and gestures us over. "Come meet Sante. She's an engineer on Arliss' team, and she's just been telling us about the weapons system that protects Paraiso."

I feel my brows raise. "Arliss' team? Seems like very confidential information to share so freely."

Sante turns to me with a grin, her angular face breaking into a huge smile. "Oasis is a haven for philosophers, engineers, and technicians. Sharing amongst each other is kind of our thing. Plus, what's Rama going to do, come down here and blow us up? Not hardly. We designed all the tech for Paraiso. I'm sure she's layered in security on top of it, but she wouldn't fuck with us."

"What a privileged position to be in," I snap, thinking of the seven fucking years I spent in a maze, surrounded by Rama's tech. This girl might have had a hand in designing that.

"Jet," Noire barks. "Remember our end goal, brother." When I look over, there's a fire in his dark eyes that mirrors my own. But it centers me for my alpha to remind me why we're here.

"We're getting him back, Jet," Diana reassures me, folding herself into my arms. She rubs her cheek along mine in the way we do and sighs. "I wish I could purr to comfort you. It must be so fun."

I start up a deep, rumbly purr just for her as she giggles and slides back out of my arms. "Showoff," she growls, slapping my chest. "Sit. We'll get you food." *And tell me everything about you, Renze, and Achaia and the mates comment. The tension is palpable,* she adds into our family bond. Noire frowns and continues his predatory pacing.

Renze speaks up as Ascelin slips quietly into the room, nodding at him.

"Sinan is unwilling to help. He did, however, keep tabs on Rama through a vampiri viewing orb, an ancient technology I thought long gone. He shared that Paraiso is now parked off the coast of Vinituvari, and that it returns there, pulling seawater up into the city at regular intervals."

I look over at Sante. "What's the seawater for?"

Sante shrugs. "That I don't know. We've always assumed she made modifications after we delivered the city, but I can't think of a single reason she'd need seawater."

Achaia looks thoughtful. "If she always returns to that spot, perhaps it's not the water she's after, but the location. Otherwise, there's plenty of seawater in other places."

"There's more," I bark, tossing the spider we brought with us onto the table. "The male from the market attack trailed us to the vampiri court, somehow. He sent spiders into the court—we found this one attached to Achaia."

"How do you know he didn't trail you here?" Noire barks.

I bristle and sneer at my older brother. "There's a much longer story behind this, but we traveled here by orb. We stepped out of the court and onto a dune."

"Seven hells," Sante chirps. "What tech is that? I've never heard of such a thing."

"Vampiri magic." Renze smiles, trailing his fingertips up Achaia's arm.

Noire eyes the spider like it's about to leap up and stab someone. I get it, though. We could never trust anything about the maze. It was designed only to imprison and torture us. Anything Rama sends to us is an immediate threat.

Sante reaches out and drags the spider close, looking down at it. "I can probably pick it apart and tell you a little about its purpose if you're okay with me taking it to my lab."

"You have a lab?" I'm shocked to hear her reference such a thing, although Oasis sounds like it's been very isolated from Rama's destruction.

"Yeah," Sante murmurs, lost in thought as she turns the spider over in her freckled hands. "Part of our agreement with Rama long ago. We'll build the city, but leave us the fuck alone."

There's obviously more to that story, and I'd love to know it. Noire and I both growl, but Sante shrugs. "We're helping you *now*, aren't we?" She turns to me, holding up the spider. "I'm gonna go take a peek at this, okay?"

I consider it but nod. There's nothing I can ascertain about the spider that I haven't already attempted.

She jogs off with the machine in hand, and Noire and Diana turn to me as one.

"What else?" Noire spits.

Renze looks at Diana, his expression sad. "There is a woman in the vampiri court whom we call our whisperer. She is the most ancient of ancients, hundreds of generations old. She received the Chosen One prophecy long ago. We visited her to ask about Achaia's tattoo, but she mentioned that the prophecy we have always known was only half of what she received."

"Truly?" Ascelin rounds the table, looking highly concerned.

Renze nods. "Unfortunately, the second half was received in a language that is no longer spoken. It is a language of the monsters of the Tempang. We have no way to translate it, although she wrote it down for us."

Ascelin swears, and Noire's face turns red with rage as Diana presses her back to his chest. His hand goes around her stomach protectively. I'd give anything to remedy the sense of impending doom this news brings, but I can't fix it. Just as I can't fix anything else about our situation.

"This doesn't change anything, brother," I say. "We have to set that news aside and plan for what we know."

Diana nods, although she's clearly lost in thought. Her blue eyes flutter as she straightens her spine. She's so fucking strong, and I'm grateful again for the risks she took to save our lives. "Achaia, what happened with your tattoo? Did you learn anything?"

"It doesn't fucking matter," Noire snarls.

Achaia doesn't blanche under his vehemence. Instead, she gives Diana an even look. "It's a prisoner tattoo, a form of dark magic used to keep me in human form and bind my memories. I have no idea what I am, or why the spider took my blood. Perhaps, I'm someone important to Rama."

I see the wheels of Noire's mind spin as she shares that theory. He's suddenly interested in her.

"Can you remove it?" Diana murmurs, her voice full of pain as if she already knows the answer will be something terrible.

Achaia grimaces. "According to the whisperer, I can burn or cut it off, or find whoever placed it."

Noire lets his claws slide free of his fingertips. "Happy to do that right now if you want. Maybe you're a weapon, and someone sought to cage you because you're dangerous. Maybe Rama knows this, and that's why the alpha followed you."

I resist the urge to bark at my pack alpha and remind him the spiders followed others as well. Instead, I pull Achaia into my arms and away from his investigative gaze. Already, he's pondering ways to figure out why Rama would care about a kidnapped woman enough to track her across a continent. Achaia has suddenly become a far larger piece on Noire's imaginary chessboard.

He might be right, but I won't let Noire rip her to shreds to find out.

CHAPTER TWENTY-SIX
ACHAIA

Noire's harsh words ring in my head. Me, a weapon? I suppose it could be true. It doesn't feel like me, though. Who knows what I am underneath the tattoo that binds me? The only thing I do know for certain is that I want out of this inked prison. What if who I am can help Jet in his mission to free his brother? If I can do that, I will.

Just then, Arliss enters the room with his arms held wide and a big grin on his handsome face. "I've just seen Sante. She's thrilled to be examining the spider you brought. I imagine she'll have answers for you by the end of the evening."

Our host is dressed in form-fitting cerulean pants, a black long-sleeved shirt fit to his body but open all the way down to his navel. He stalks into the room, and I'm hit again with the alpha-like power that rolls off of him. It's so like Noire's, and so different at the same time. I square my shoulders against it.

Arliss seats himself at the head of the table, leaning back in his chair to steeple his fingers, elbows propped on the chair's arms. "What is this I hear of a tattoo that needs investigating?"

He wasn't here when we said that, so either every fucking room in this place is bugged, or he's some creature with incredible hearing. He's not human, but what he is, I couldn't say. The only thing I know with any certainty is that whatever he is, is something horribly powerful.

I turn and lift my shirt up to my shoulder. Arliss laughs darkly. "A prisoner tattoo. Very rare, very cruel. I know of only one being with the magical strength to craft a prisoner tattoo, and she died three years ago."

Despair crushes my chest. So much for that path to finding out my identity. "Can I assume she did my tattoo, then?"

Arliss beams again, wicked and devious. "Oh no, my child. She is the only being I have *met* who could craft such a thing. But the Tempang is full of monsters who could do it. The possibilities are endless there. I wouldn't advise taking a stroll in to ask, however, if you value that pretty face."

I sink back into my chair as Jet reaches out and slides his big hand up my thigh. His fingers move to the upper inside of my leg, and he squeezes tight. It's a reassuring touch, despite how focused he is on Arliss.

Renze lays his arm on the back of my chair, stroking my hair with his elegant fingers.

Diana speaks up from across the table. "Arliss, you mentioned there might be an opportunity to get up to Paraiso. Tell us more about that, please. We're anxious to rescue Tenebris as quickly as possible."

It's obvious they've had some conversation already about our quest. To be honest, I'm grateful not to have to hash all that out myself. Diana is clearly a woman on a mission.

Arliss sits back in his chair with a devilish grin. "I cannot guarantee your safety, obviously, but I can get you there and get you information."

"Get to the point," Noire growls.

Arliss smiles again as if Noire is nothing more than the slightest of nuisances to him. The intense need to warn Noire away from Arliss slams into me so hard that I grip the edges of my chair to resist saying anything.

Jet's grip on my leg tightens, his jaw clenching as he watches the exchange. As Noire's strategist, it must be uncomfortable to watch a power play between his alpha and another male.

Arliss watches all of this and laughs. "The six of you are so opaque I could practically tell what you'll say next." He turns to Noire, nostrils flaring as fangs show from behind dark lips. "Hear this, Noire. I help you only because, in doing so, I help myself. Let me make that abundantly clear. If there comes a time when coming to your aid does not further my personal interests, I will not do it. I do not give a single fuck about your missing brother."

"We understand, Arliss," I croon, anxious to soothe the rising tension in our group. If Arliss can help us, we need it. We risked everything to get here on the off-chance he had information we desperately need. "We're grateful for any opportunity to partner, and we're hopeful that our goals remain aligned. For a time, at least."

Electric blue eyes flick to mine, narrowed and assessing. My words appear to mollify the considerable male, and he sits back, looking at me as if I'm a puzzle to figure out. His brows lift in amusement, but he doesn't move his gaze away from me. "Rama is having a celebration on Paraiso in several days' time. As the creator of the city, I will attend with a retinue."

"What sort of celebration?" Noire presses, sitting back in his chair as he matches Arliss' stance.

"That I do not know," Arliss purrs, "but she is often celebrating one thing or another. This is not out of the ordinary. She may be a sociopath, but she is a masterful hostess."

Jet's claws sink into my skin as they emerge from his fingertips. I startle in my chair. I suspect Arliss' careless words are bringing him back to every time he was the entertainment at Rama's parties.

I'll kill her for what she did to him. But we need to get to her first.

Diana frowns at Arliss. "How do you propose to get us up there?"

"Getting you there will not be the difficult part," Arliss hedges. "Getting around the city will be harder, although this particular party has a masquerade theme. So, that helps."

"How lovely and convenient," Ascelin deadpans from her place next to Renze. "A timely celebration and a masked ball; it's almost as if she knows what we plan to do before we do it."

Arliss laughs, a big belly laugh as he reaches one hand into his lap and strokes his cock. "You could very well be walking into a trap, my beauty, that is true. And if you are, I will not help you out of it."

"Unless it benefits you," I press. "Isn't that right?"

"I stand corrected, lovely one," Arliss purrs, still stroking his cock as Jet starts growling.

"How can we ensure that happens?" I urge. Arliss' focus on me strengthens. I don't know anything about magical beings, but a sense of wrongness hits me as my skin crawls. It's like cockroaches skittering along my skin and inside my mind. He's doing...something. I just don't know what. I lift my chin higher and don't break his intense gaze.

Arliss pauses for a moment, seeming to debate what he's about to say. "I have a friend, a scientist, who works closely with Rama. She is not there by choice. My goal at this party is to retrieve her while you kill Rama."

"Why haven't you done so before now?" Jet questions.

Arliss looks over at him with a bored expression. "I could have, many times. And then what? Brought her back here and declared open war? That would have been foolish. But since you mean to kill Rama, the timing is ideal for my needs."

"Why not help us kill her, then?" I question. That seems the most logical path forward.

Arliss' snarky expression falls into a displeased scowl. "For reasons I won't share, I cannot do that. I cannot lift a finger against her. You'll have to do that part on your own."

"We understand," Jet answers in an even tone. "If we can help you achieve your goal, we will. Please tell us about this party and your plan to get there. I need to know all the options so I can formulate a plan for my pack."

The feeling of insects scratching at my bones intensifies, but I lift my head higher as I stare at Arliss. Whatever he's doing, he will not find weakness here. I will not be the broken link in the chain of my motley pack. I may not know who I am, but I can be strong for them.

With a painful pinch, the feeling evaporates, and I'm left with an oddly powerful sensation in my gut, like I could grow wings and take off into the sky. Whatever Arliss was doing gave me a heady rush of endorphins. The room spins as conversation picks back up, but I can't focus on it.

I need a moment. Standing, I murmur that I'll be back in a second, and I sail out of a giant arched doorway into the setting sun.

CHAPTER TWENTY-SEVEN
RENZE

Rosu trails Achaia onto the balcony as I watch Arliss' narrowed gaze on her voluptuous form. Next to Achaia's empty chair, Jet watches her go, despite having just asked Arliss a question. It seems the whole room is focused on my beautiful mate.

Without waiting for an answer from Arliss, Jet stands and follows Achaia, Arliss grinning as he watches the tall alpha go. While I'm drawn to cement our plan, I'm also drawn to my mates, especially after what happened on the bridge. I follow Jet onto the balcony as Noire scoffs behind me.

Asshole.

Outside, Achaia watches where the Oasis' moat trails through an opening in the wall, winding its way lazily through the lush courtyard just outside the dining hall. Even from here, the occasional ripple in the water belies the danger of the beings who inhabit that dangerous kingdom.

She shudders and turns when she senses us appear in the doorway. She gives me a lazy grin, her bright eyes traveling the length of my body and back up.

My cock twitches in my pants as I cross the balcony and wrap my arms around her, placing her gently up on the railing. I take her mouth possessively, using my tongue to taste and tease her, to remind her how completely hers I am.

Jet swoops in, gripping her chin to steal her kiss from me. "You need food, little one. You need energy."

She glances over his shoulder to the open door. "Alright. I want to remove the tattoo tomorrow. Whatever comes next, I want answers. It might be the difference between us saving Ten or not. I just…I have to know that I can help."

Jet brings his nose to her neck and breathes her in, his lips traveling a path along her clavicle. He bites her shoulder gently as Rosu winds himself around our feet.

Achaia looks up at me. "Will you remove it? There's nobody else I would trust to do this."

I hiss in a breath, clicking in frustration. But I nod. "Of course, *atirien*. For you, there is nothing I would not do. Understand me well when I say this. There is nothing, my love."

She takes one deep, steadying breath before reaching for Jet. "And you'll be there? Will you distract me?"

"Without a fucking doubt," Jet confirms. "All the more reason to eat up today since you may not feel like it tomorrow."

At that moment, a small shadow appears in the doorway. Sante.

"I didn't mean to intrude, but sound really carries around here, ya know?"

"Does it now?" Jet purrs, clearly disbelieving the diminutive human.

"Yep!" she chirps. "I heard you mention the tattoo removal. I've not been part of that before, but I'm a better-than-average healer, although it's not my first love. I'd be happy to stay on hand for…after."

"I'd like that," Achaia whispers. "I can't imagine it will be anything less than excruciating, although I generally heal quickly."

"That alone confirms you're not human," Sante remarks with a sly grin. "Takes me fucking forever to heal, and I always get scars. It's not pretty. You're lucky if you heal fast, though, because you won't be able to use any sort of anesthetic—that's the way these tattoos work, I'm afraid." She shrugs and looks back into the room. "I'm heading back to the lab to finish picking apart the spider. I'll catch up with you tomorrow, okay?"

"Thank you, Sante," I respond as she skips back into the dining hall. Achaia is miserably silent as she absorbs what Sante just told us.

"I could spend years picking apart the secrets of this place," Jet growls. "But for now, I need to get back inside and consider our options. We need a plan for Ten."

Achaia sighs. "It'll all be worth it when we get him back. And then when we kill Rama, everything will change."

When she lays out our focus so simply, I have to force myself to continue breathing. There is so much we must do right for this to work out. And there are so very many factors we can't possibly foresee. I was less terrified for my future when I was still imprisoned. I have far more to lose now.

Jet takes Achaia's hand and directs her back into the dining hall. I remain on the balcony, watching the sun dip behind the last craggy sand-colored dune, praying to the goddesses for the second time in an hour.

Please don't take them from me. But if they must go, let me go alongside them. Because I never want to be parted from either of them. Not for the rest of my life.

～

An hour later, we have eaten our fill. Despite Arliss' attitude, he is a decent host. I see to it that both my mates and Rosu eat while Arliss lays out a general plan for our approach to Paraiso. We will arrive for Rama's party, utilizing tech to mask our appearance. After that, he can get us access to the level where Rama keeps her prisoners. If Tenebris is there, we will release him. Getting out is likely to be the hard part. We cover option after option after option until late.

Arliss and Jet strategize about some escape possibilities when the noise in the room heightens. Music echoes from the hallway as servants clear the table. A figure catches my attention, a beautiful dark-skinned male. He's shirtless but wearing the billowy pants they seem to favor here. He crosses the room with his eyes locked onto Arliss.

Our host does not stop his conversation with Jet as the male approaches him but instead pushes his seat back and spreads his legs wide.

Without saying a word, the man drops between Arliss' legs and begins to rub his cock. Our host is still mid-conversation, although I don't miss the way Jet's eyes fall on the second man as he rubs and strokes, bringing Arliss' cock to life. It juts up out of his lap, the male pulling Arliss' pants down to release it.

His lips are upon Arliss' dick the moment it is free, and Arliss lets out a small sigh of happiness, winking at Jet.

"Etu is a masterful cock-sucker. Perhaps you would enjoy a turn after I finish with him?" He looks over at Diana. "Or perhaps you would, pretty little omega?"

Diana laughs. "Noire is more than enough for me, Arliss."

Next to Diana, Noire is silent, which shocks me. Jet's brother has never been one to let someone goad him in this manner. His dark eyes are locked onto Achaia, though, the wheels of his mind spinning with what's happened tonight. I sense he's calculating as he always does, hoping to figure out what piece she represents on this maze-like game board we travel.

I spit venom across the table in his direction, Ascelin laughing when he jumps in his seat and returns my angry indignation.

Arliss lets out a satisfied groan before laughing at us. "If you six cannot get along here, in the midst of sex, beauty and good food, how will you do it in the heart of Rama's city?"

"We have done it before," I retort, turning my gaze to him as Etu's head bobs up and down in his lap. "When the need calls for it, we work together. We did it to escape, and we will do it again to rescue our brother and free this continent from a madwoman."

"A noble quest, to be sure," Arliss laughs, the laugh turning into a deep moan as his hips begin to thrust up to meet Etu's mouth. He smiles at me, leveling me with a dominant gaze. "You and your mate should join me, Renze. I know the vampiri thrive off sex. We function in much the same way here. Anyone can enjoy anyone at any point in time. I fear we've been holding back just a touch with newcomers at the Oasis, but it is time to reveal our true selves to you. And our true selves really love to fuck."

Jet reaches for Achaia, pulling her into his lap. "Not a chance in the seven hells," he assures Arliss, his arms possessively wrapped around Achaia's waist.

"You already share her," Arliss purrs, both hands moving to the male's head as his hips begin to thrust rhythmically.

"Not happening," Jet returns smoothly. "She is mine."

Achaia looks between Arliss and Jet and then over at me. "Perhaps I am no one's. Perhaps I belong only to myself." She is teasing Jet, and I love to see it.

He turns her head to the side with a tight grip on her chin. "Mine," he growls, biting at her neck. "Mine to use. Mine to fuck. Mine to protect."

Achaia lets out a breathy moan. My mates are wired and exhausted at the same time.

Jet comes to the same conclusion I do, standing as he tosses Achaia over his shoulder. "We're going to bed. We can finish planning tomorrow."

I fully expect Noire to argue with us, but when I look over, his tongue plunders Diana's mouth. There is a desperate need for connection, born out of a terror for what's to come. He wants her because he does not know if their time is drawing to a close.

Next to them, Ascelin shoots me a barely-concealed grin. "What are you waiting for, First Warrior? Time for some fun with *tua-atirien*." Her white eyes flick to where Arliss' groans grow deeper. She licks her lips as she watches the male bob in his lip. Ah, my First Warrior partner is having a good time here.

Smirking, I take my leave, the sound of Arliss' impending release echoing in the room as others begin to join him in the festivities.

Predatory focus hones my body into a weapon, my eyes narrowing as I

JET: A DARK SHIFTER ROMANCE

stalk my mates. Achaia resists Jet at every turn, beating his back. "Put me down, you animal."

"No."

"Right now!"

"Never," he snaps. He knows the same thing I do. This pretend fight is turning her on. The scent of her arousal is a drug so heavy and potent I could drown myself in it.

We reach our door quickly, and Jet yanks it open, setting her down and pushing her through as I slip in behind them. He still has one of her wrists in his hand.

"I'm not a sack of potatoes to be thrown over your shoulder. Let me go, you assh—"

Jet's mouth is on Achaia's before she can even finish her statement, lips and teeth wild as he overpowers her. She presses hard against his chest, but Jet is an immovable wall of focus. His tongue dips into her mouth before he sucks on hers, drawing a whine from her as I slide one hand into my pants to stroke myself.

When Jet breaks the kiss, Achaia reaches up to slap him. "I hope you enjoyed that, Jet."

His focus never wavers as he snaps his long fangs in her face. "Enjoyed it. Taking more of it right now."

"You can't have me." She grins wickedly. "I don't accept what you're offering." She is teasing him because it riles him. Telling him no makes him wild with lust for her.

"A charade," he replies coolly. "Your body betrays you. Everything about you wants what I'm going to give."

I love this interplay between them. The fight. The resistance. It stokes my predatory tendencies. I want to throw fuel on their fire and watch us all burn to embers.

"If she says no, you should respect that, Jet," I warn. Another lie. I simply want to push this dynamic a little further.

He ignores me, reaching out with black claws to shred Achaia's dress down the front as she sputters. When she moves to slap him again, he catches her wrist, bringing it to his mouth. Jet plants a tender kiss on the inside before biting hard enough to draw blood. Dark eyes flick to mine. "Smell that, vampiri? Smell how right she is?"

The scent of my mate's blood fills my nose, my fangs leaking venom for her as I cross to them, lapping at the ruby-red richness on her skin.

Achaia moans when Jet and I both suck on the wound, even as she tries to pull her arm from his grip. When her green eyes find mine, she gives me a mischievous wink.

Oh, our female is highly enjoying torturing both of us. And it's working because telling Jet no pushes him past the barriers inside his mind. He is crushing the hold the maze and the Atrium have on him.

I laugh at her wink, Jet looking up at me with a knowing grin. Dropping Achaia's arm, I unbutton my leather vest and remove my shirt. The leather strap that holds my knives goes next, and I am halfway nude before my mates. Jet's eyes rake over me, hungry and on edge.

"If you want her, you'll have to fight me for her," I purr to the big alpha. "She told you no, and if I am anything, it is a protector of her wishes."

"She doesn't mean no," Jet laughs. "I know that. *She* knows that. If I dropped to my knees in front of her now, she'd spread those pretty thick thighs to let me feast."

Achaia is quickly losing her ability to taunt Jet when he utters filthy words about taking her. I slip across the small space between us, collaring Jet's throat as I bring my mouth to hover just over his. "She said no, *atiri*."

Jet snarls in my face, fangs fully descended as he breaks the hold and shoves me hard. I fly across the room, Jet leaping at the same time, but I manage to slip away at the last minute, crossing the room to stand in front of Achaia protectively.

This game is fun.

Jet roars, bounding across the room as I move to meet him. I throw a punch, catching him in the side of the head as he attempts to toss me aside to get to her. Jet is the more brutally muscular of us, but I am older and faster. We are well-matched in a fight.

I lock my teeth around Jet's throat as he pushes me into Achaia's space. But the moment I let my venom flow, his knees buckle and a heavy moan leaves his lips. Biting harder, I relish the way the venom affects him. I know it is working when his hips begin to rock against mine, Achaia pressed to the wall behind me.

Her scent explodes, watching us fight over her. I release the bite and flip us, shoving him up against Achaia as I yank at his pants. Spitting venom in my palm, I slide it between the muscular globes of his ass and press two fingers inside him, stroking slowly as Jet cages Achaia with his powerful arms. His forehead rests on hers, his lips brushing along her own as a desperate moan leaves his mouth.

Jet grips Achaia's chin. "You're driving me mad, woman. But you know that, don't you?"

He reaches for her breast, but I capture his arm and yank it up behind him

JET: A DARK SHIFTER ROMANCE

as he snarls, struggling against me. But he has no desire to leave this space—not really—so I add a third finger in his ass and stroke harder on the rough patch deep within. I am not gentle, but I do not need to be so.

Jet lets out a hungry cry as I remove my fingers and reach around to stroke his hard cock instead. When I pull at the ring through the end of it, his forehead falls to Achaia's shoulder. I hear her hiss out a breath as his lips trail along her skin, pulling and sucking at her neck as I work him over.

Shoving my pants open, I spit venom on my cock and slide it between his thighs. The venom is a perfect lubricant, and I slip inside my mate for the first time in too long. A self-satisfied string of clicks and hisses leaves me as I struggle around how tight he is, how good he feels.

"Mine," I hiss out as Jet throws his head back, baring his neck to me. I press him harder to Achaia, noting how her chest heaves watching us. Good. I want my little seductress to want everything about us. She is right where she should be.

With a quick buck of my hips, I thrust all the way into Jet's ass.

"*Fuck*, godsdamn, Renze," he bellows, pushing his ass back to meet me. When I thrust again, I fuck him hard enough to press his hips into Achaia's. I want to tease her with that incredible, pierced alpha dick. She's fucking with him by denying him, but I want them both wild.

I would love to savor this moment and take him slowly, building and building and edging him to insanity. But this moment calls for something more furious, more unhinged. So, I unleash on my alpha mate, taking him with hard, punishing strokes as he bites his way along Achaia's neck. She doesn't touch him, but he jacks himself as I grip his big hips and ride hard.

My own orgasm swirls deep in my belly, an impending rush ready to crest as Jet's panting grows faster, reaching higher and higher notes, until there—

"*Fuck*," Jet bellows out, his cock spurting ropes of cum onto Achaia's exposed belly as an orgasm barrels down my spine, a roar leaving my mouth as I clench my teeth and see stars. I line Jet's ass with cum until all I hear is the sloppy, wet noise of my cock entering him over and over.

Jet brushes his lips over Achaia's, purring into her mouth as I take his ass slowly, reaching around to stroke his cock as he cages her in once more. He gasps at the feel of my hand on him.

"Achaia," he murmurs. "Give yourself to me, *atirien*." He uses the vampiri word for mate, and it sends a thrill rushing to my cock.

"You think you've earned me, alpha?" she laughs.

Jet growls, gripping her chin. "I don't need to earn you, woman. But I think I'll punish this sass." He grabs her hand, bringing it to his cock as he uses it to stroke himself. "You know what? You're not getting this tonight; I'm going to make you wait for it."

The scent of her arousal assaults me as Jet reaches between her thighs, stroking with measured, steady movements. Achaia's head falls back as her large breasts heave. Reaching around Jet, I pinch her nipples as she arches her back.

"She is ready to explode, Jet," I hiss into his ear as he lets out an appreciative growl.

"Perhaps we shouldn't let her," he laughs as Achaia whines, bringing her hands to his forearm as her hips punch ever faster to meet his fingers.

"Don't you fucking stop," she commands as her cries grow louder, ringing out into the room.

Jet holds her with one arm, his ass still pressed to my front. "I'm going to bring you right to the edge, pretty one. And then, when you're ready to fall over, I'm going to walk away. If you ask sweetly, perhaps Renze will get you off."

"Asshole!" Achaia shouts, her breath coming in gasps as she prepares to ride the crest of ecstasy Jet brings her.

He lets out an evil laugh and slides his fingers out of her wet pussy, licking at them as he turns and walks toward the bathroom.

Achaia scoffs as he goes but turns to me with a pleading look. "Renze, please don't leave me like this."

Grinning, I follow Jet into the bathroom as she curses us both. I wash up quickly as she appears in the doorway, one shoe in her hand as she prepares to throw it at my head—or maybe his. He laughs when I slip across the room and throw her against the wall, thrusting into her with a quick punch of my hips.

"You can count on me, *atirien*," I murmur. "Gods, I am addicted to your heat." She clenches around me, so close to ecstasy. I fuck her slowly, dragging out the movement of my hips as her keening cries ring throughout the room. Jet watches us from across the room. When she falls over the edge, I let out a howl of pleasure as she milks my cock, soaking me with her sweet honey.

Jet laughs appreciatively as he fills the tub for us. "Come bathe with me," he commands. "You're both filthy."

Achaia falls against my shoulder with a huffy laugh. I pull away from the wall with her still impaled on my length, passing Jet to deposit her in the tub. Her eyelids begin to flutter immediately.

Jet pulls her into his lap and reaches for the soap. Behind us, Rosu hops onto the tub's ledge and curls up, watching us as he purrs happily. Jet works the soap through Achaia's hair as I clean myself, marveling at the change in him since we escaped.

"You look good like this, *atiri*," I offer quietly.

A smile ghosts his handsome face. "I *feel* good. Still focused on what's to come, of course, but this"—he points between the three of us—"feels like a blessing rather than something I couldn't choose."

Achaia has fallen asleep, so he passes her into my arms as he checks her injured leg again. It is healing fast, a definite clue that whatever she is, is not human. When he's done, I carry her into our room and lay her gently on the bed. She snores softly as I gather Rosu and place him up by her head. Instinctively, she reaches for him and pulls him to her chest so they're tucked together like spoons.

I roll onto my side to enjoy her, but Jet's hand finds my hip. He turns me on my back and straddles me, his hard cock bobbing against my stomach.

"I wasn't done," he growls, falling forward onto his hands as I rise onto my elbows. He lets out a snarl as I slick my mouth over his. The forked tips of my tongue tease him as he thrusts against me, leaking precum onto my quickly hardening cock. "I need you just like I need her," he whispers when we part.

"I know."

"I know you know. It just seemed important to say it. Don't be an ass," he chides.

Laughing, I pull his lips back to mine. "I've known since I first touched you, Jet. And I've known it every moment since. But hearing you choose me is the ultimate pleasure."

Jet rolls onto his side and holds me close, hips rolling in time with mine as our cocks spear the air. "I want to taste you, Renze."

I bring both arms behind my head. "Be my guest, *atiri*," I laugh, my cock throbbing when I think about how he will look perched atop it.

Jet slides down my body, growling as he runs his hands up my thighs, pushing one leg out wide so he can nip at my heavy balls. Heat streaks through my core at the feel of his soft lips and sharp claws. Even in the maze, he never came to me first. I approached him. I have never felt his mouth on me quite like this. Pleasure streaks through my system as he holds his palm up toward me. "Spit on it, mate."

Leaning up onto my elbows once more, I spit venom into his hand, Jet's dark eyes dancing as he slips his fingers behind my balls and strokes there. When he dips his head, sucking the tip of my cock into his wet heat, I nearly fall apart at the seams. Power roars through my veins as I read his emotions like a book—heat, desire, need, and confidence. Our connection pushes Jet to be more of everything he already is.

As he sucks teasingly on the tip of my cock, I concentrate on the power that radiates from him to me. If I focus, I can read every person in the dining hall from here. So much godsdamned power.

I laugh victoriously at the sheer strength of it as Jet surges forward, taking my entire cock down his throat. My laugh turns into a deep, needy groan as his teeth scrape along my sensitive skin, my length jumping in his mouth.

Jet hums as I fuck his face, exploding fast as power builds and builds in my system. When Jet's mouth pops off my cock, the pleased look he gives me tells me he feels the same.

"You are mine," he purrs. "All mine, Renze."

CHAPTER TWENTY-EIGHT
JET

I wake in the morning to find Rosu's nose touching mine at the edge of the bed. He lets out a soft whine, his black tail waving like a flag in the early morning light.

"Gods," I whine. "What do you need?"

"He wishes to go outside, *atiri*," Renze's deep voice rumbles from behind me. When I flip over in bed, he's on his back, Achaia tucked into his side, their legs threaded together. "I will take him if you hold her. She is sleeping so soundly."

"Don't move," I direct him. "You might wake her. I'll take him out and see if Noire or Diana are up. I'd like to know if Sante has uncovered anything about the spider, too."

Renze nods. "If she wakes, we will find you. I am anxious about the spider as well. So much of what is happening now feels too convenient. My skin is crawling." He looks down at Achaia, fast asleep in the bed. "Let us remove her tattoo as soon as possible. I am anxious to free her from this cage."

I nod because I feel exactly the same way. I have no sense of what she might be underneath that prison, but I'm anxious to find out. Rolling out of bed, I scratch Rozu's tapered dark snout. "Come on," I purr to him as he hops up and down in a circle, his tail swooping down to touch the floor. He's bigger today, several inches taller than when we met him. Renze wasn't kidding when he said the velzen would grow fast to become a guardian. I believe it, based on how he protected Achaia with me from the mermaids.

"I'm eternally grateful, Rosu," I whisper as I dress quickly and open the door for him. Rosu flies to the nearest courtyard and finds a plant to piss on, then trails after me toward the smell of food. I hear Noire there already.

At the breakfast table, Noire sits with Sante and others, although I don't specifically recall meeting any of them.

Sante's freckled face lights up when she sees me. "Hey! I was just telling your brother what I learned about the spider."

Noire growls at me, eyeing me in the way a good pack alpha does—he can tell something is different with me today.

Sante looks between us, then shoves the spider toward me. It's clear she's picked it apart from top to bottom. "This tech is purely for information gathering; it was never designed to return to its owner. The needle gathers the blood, which is stored in this chamber here." She points to the spider's round body as I shudder.

"We knew that part," I murmur as she flips the spider over.

"Right, that part is pretty obvious," she laughs, her tone excited. "But down here, on the underbelly. This panel hides a testing kit and transmitter. The spider was testing the blood for something and transmitting the results...somewhere."

"Can you figure out where?" Noire demands, his voice insistent and irritated.

"Hard to say." Sante shrugs, her excited tone changing as she looks at Noire. "It's most likely not transmitting to a specific location; it's just a specific *type* of transmission. So, anything capable of reading such a transmission could intercept it. If I had to wager a guess, I'd assume receivers for this tech are placed all around an area before the spiders are sent in."

"It flew, though," I muse as Sante nods.

"Couldn't go far though, it's not big enough for a large battery. So my guess is it flew to the nearest transmitter, and then its job was done."

"And you didn't build this—nobody here did?" I clarify.

Sante shrugs again. "This isn't really our sort of thing, to be honest. Oasis is a haven for inventors, builders, and scientists. But the torture-y side of Rama's business is something we steer clear of. We would never have built the Temple Maze, for instance."

"You wouldn't build the maze, but you built the city?" Noire deadpans. "The fucking flying city she lives in?"

Sante shoots Noire a look of irritation, rolling her eyes. "The city has defensive weapons underneath it, but the actual city itself is where she *lives*, Noire. It's meant to be a home base for her and her closest allies. It's a party town, basically. We do that well." She gestures at Oasis around us.

Noire runs both hands through his hair and growls, looking at me. "Somehow, every time I think of that bitch partying safely on Paraiso while we fought for our lives, I have to resist the urge to set something on fire."

Sante laughs nervously but looks at me. "So, there's your answer. She's looking for something in the blood. Impossible to say what that is, though, or if she found what she was looking for."

I mull that over but decide to share what Sinan told us. "The spiders attacked many people in Sinan's court, not just Achaia." I haven't mentioned this is the second time we've come into contact with the spiders.

Sante looks positively fascinated. "Perhaps Rama is looking for someone of a specific bloodline? And was Achaia just a hapless casualty or personally targeted? How would the spider even know to attack Achaia then, if even *she* doesn't know who she is."

"She's important," Noire rumbles, picking the spider up with one of his black claws. He eyes it suspiciously before tossing it back down on the table. When he looks up at me, his smile is as devious as I've ever seen it. "We need to find out who she is, brother. You didn't mate her yet, did you?"

For the second time in less than a day, the urge to rip Noire's head from his shoulders hits me.

"I dislike your tone, alpha," I snarl. "My mating is none of your gods-damned business. And if you do something to hurt her, you will have me to contend with."

Noire purrs but rises to a stand, not breaking our gaze. "You've changed, brother, and not for the better since you left Siargao. You were unequivocally on my side before…"

I grit my teeth, but Sante's cheerful voice breaks through. "You boys need to get out some aggression. Arliss is sparring this morning in the main courtyard. Why don't you join him? He's an amazing fighter. He'll give you a run for your money. Noire knows all about that already, right?"

Noire snorts in disagreement but brushes his shoulder against mine combatively. "Come on, Jet. We need it."

You've already fought him? I question through our family bond.

Had to challenge Arliss to get him to let us in, Noire barks back. *It was a draw.*

I rub my chest and think about Achaia and Renze, wondering what they're doing in our room. But Noire is right—being apart for days has distanced me from him, despite our typically close connection.

Sante winks at me and gestures toward the dining hall's side balcony. "We can head through here and cut through the main building out front. I think you'll be really impressed if you spar with Arliss. He's really fucking good."

Noire gives me a cocky grin and cracks his knuckles. He hasn't had many chances to fight since the maze, and I'm sure he's ready to blow off steam.

Plus, we're an excellent team. I'd like to burn off excess energy and then go over our plan another time or two. There are still far more holes than I'd like, but we're much better off than we were a few days ago.

We're coming for you, Ten, I think to myself. *Hold on, baby brother.*

Noire and I trail Sante outside and down a set of wide stone steps to yet another palm-filled courtyard. This fucking place itself is a veritable maze of big square buildings and open-air spaces filled with tropical flora. If it grew out of every crack and crevice, it would remind me a little more of home.

My heart pangs when I think of Siargao. I'd love nothing more than to go back to the easy days of running the province with a heavy hand alongside my brothers. Tenebris is big enough now to work with us. I hope there's a time in the future when we'll get to do that with him.

The deep sound of aggressive grunting echoes along a sand-colored hallway as Sante leads us through it and out into the bright sunshine again. A vast open courtyard dotted with trees and a winding, thin river is all that stands between us and the enormous front gate. I growl when I see it, remembering how they strung Renze up there while Achaia, Rosu, and I fought against the fucking mermaids.

Our host is shirtless, holding a dagger in one hand as he faces off against two enormous, muscular males. They charge him as one, splitting off at the last second. Arliss moves impossibly fast, slamming his dagger into one of the fighters, the knife slicing him open from shoulder to haunch as the man screams in pain. He falls to the ground as Arliss rounds on the other, leaping so fast that it's hard to follow his movement.

If I wasn't certain that Arliss isn't human, I'd know it now. No human is capable of moving that quickly or of tracking another predator quite so efficiently. He's almost faster than Renze, although I'll never admit that aloud.

Next to me, Noire lets out an enraged yowl. He's aching to fight, despite the fact that we just watched Arliss gut a man.

Brightly-clothed attendants jog to the fallen male, lifting him onto a stretcher as Arliss continues to fight the other. He dispatches that male nearly as quickly, shaking his head at what he must perceive to be poor performance.

"Hard to come by good sparring partners these days," he mutters, crossing the sandy ground to stop in front of us. He wipes his dagger across the front of his pants, sticky red blood wetting the fabric, before he slides the blade into a holster on his thigh.

Looking at Noire, he crosses his arms and sniggers. "You wish to fight, alpha? I sense a seething rage inside you. You would do well to unleash that before you accompany me to Paraiso."

I've known Noire my whole life, so I'm unsurprised when he doesn't bother to respond but dashes forward, wrapping one arm around Arliss' neck. Arliss lets out a snarl, long braids flying as Noire tosses him over his shoulder, the breath whooshing out of our host when he thuds to the ground.

Wild, raucous laughter leaves Arliss' throat as he shifts his body, leaping upright and spinning to face Noire. "I planned to ease you into it, alpha, but perhaps you will be a formidable partner for a time."

Predatory need burrows through my consciousness, pushing and pulling at the gray matter as my cells align with focus. Arliss. Prey. Think of him as prey. I stalk to Arliss' right as Noire goes in for the frontal attack again. Noire shifts mid-leap, his direwolf landing hard on Arliss as I dart in, snatching the knife from its holster before our host can reach for it.

Arliss bellows in rage and tosses Noire off himself, but I'm right there, throwing my weight behind punch after punch as my fists connect. Arliss dodges about half of them, giving as good as he gets.

I sense rather than see the rest of our pack join us, all eyes on Noire and me as we fight. I hit Arliss with an uppercut, his dark head flying back, right into Noire's grip. Noire twists Arliss around bodily and knees him under the chin. The hefty male falls to the ground but pushes up fast, letting out an unearthly roar. It's something between a scream and a battle cry, so deep and resonant I can hardly understand how such a loud noise comes out of a man.

But then his eyes roll back into his head, and his body goes rigid. Sante rushes past me as Arliss falls to his back, screaming bloody murder. It's a human-sounding voice again, but his teeth gnash wildly as his body starts to convulse and contort. He writhes in the sand as his eyes roll all the way back into his head.

"He's having a fucking seizure," I snap, dropping to my knees next to Sante. I lean across Arliss' chest as she shouts to the attendants who were here earlier. They rush over, jabbing a huge needle into Arliss' leg and depressing a bright pink liquid directly into his thigh muscle. Almost immediately, Arliss' eyes close, his muscles relaxing as a shudder wracks his frame.

Without a single fucking explanation, the workers roll him onto an oversized stretcher and jog off, carrying our fallen host as if it's every day that this happens.

Sante turns to us with an uncomfortable look. "We all have our demons to fight. This is his. Remember that he's helping you if you decide to try to use this against him."

I pat her shoulder. "We understand, Sante. Thanks."

Noire preens next to me as he scratches at our family bond. *We can use this.*

My alpha turns to me with a happy gleam in his eye as Sante leaves us. "Keep an eye open for any way we can use this information to our benefit, Jet."

Already the wheels of my mind turn regarding what just transpired. Strategizing and planning for my alpha the way I should be, I feel like myself for the first time in a long while. The only overwhelming thing is my need to recover Tenebris. I've got to ensconce him safely at home in Siargao, where I can watch him thrive and learn and do all the shit he *wants* to do with his life.

Suddenly, Achaia is there, her hands touching my face as she taps on my cheek. "Are you okay, alpha? I sense you need something."

A purr rumbles out of my chest as I wrap one arm around her waist and pull her in close, dropping my forehead to hers the way the vampiri do.

"You," I whisper. "I need you, *atirien*."

She smiles at my use of the vampiri word, but I use that moment to cover her lips with mine, my tongue making a lazy tour of hers. It's the kiss of an alpha who owns his mate, a reminder that I chose her, that despite the shit I put her through, I want us.

Achaia's tongue slides along mine softly as I pull her arms up around my neck. Noire stands next to us with Diana saying something to him. Renze is somewhere close by. I feel him. But all of that fades as my focus centers on the woman in my arms, her kiss growing deeper, more tender, as I devour her slowly, savoring the smooth silkiness of her mouth on mine.

"You gonna fuck right here? Or should we go over the godsdamn plan..." Noire growls, breaking through my beautiful moment. I part from Achaia's lips, planting one final nip on that plump lower one before turning to my brother.

"Today, we're removing Achaia's tattoo. My focus is there, Noire. When she's resting, we'll go over the plan again."

Noire opens his mouth to say something snarky, but Diana claps a hand over his lips. "We've got you, Jet." She smiles. "Let us know if we can help with the removal or do anything at all. Noire and I will revisit Paraiso's structural plans and look for anything we didn't see the first time. We're family, okay? There's nothing we wouldn't do to help you and your mates."

I nod and grip Achaia's hand, smiling at my brother's incredible omega. "Send Sante to help us once she's done with Arliss. I want to get this over with as quickly as possible."

Renze's eyes meet mine as I pass him, Achaia reaching for his hand. I sense distress from her. She's terrified about this process, and I'm terrified for her.

"Do you wish to eat, *atirien*?" Renze questions from his spot next to her.

Achaia shakes her head, auburn hair tickling my shoulder as I press my much larger body close to her.

"I'm afraid I won't be able to keep it down. Let's just get this done. I want to get this over with. I want to be helpful."

I stop in my tracks at that, pulling her to me as I tip her face up to meet mine. Pale green eyes spark with worry and distress, but she grits her teeth and holds her chin up.

"You are perfect," I murmur into her lips. "You don't need to 'help', Achaia. Just being here, just being you—that is enough. Do you understand?"

A single tear tracks down her cheek as she nods, Renze coming up behind her, sliding his big arms around her waist.

"I will make it as quick as I can, *atirien*. You are in good hands; I promise you this."

"I know," she whispers, blinking her eyes fast to urge the tears away. "And you'll distract me, Jet. Right?"

"I make an excellent distraction," I purr. "I promise to keep you busy, little one."

Achaia's forehead falls to my chest, her voice muffled when she speaks. "Let's get this bullshit over with."

Renze's eyes meet mine over the top of her head. For the first time in the entire seven years I've known him, he looks worried. But he purses his black lips together and gives me a look of determination as he turns and heads back through the sun-drenched compound toward our room.

I swoop Achaia up into my arms, her face still buried in my chest. And I pray to the goddess Liuvang, the fox goddess of all shifting beings.

Please, let this be quick. Let this be healing. Let this free her and answer her questions.

I'd be a liar if I didn't admit that part of me hopes she's a weapon, that whatever her tattoo is holding hostage is something monumental and dangerous.

We reach our room, and Renze closes all the doors and windows.

"I work better in the dark," he murmurs when I curl a brow up in confusion. "Do not ask me if I am certain," he barks when he sees the look on my face. "Strip the sheets from the bed, Jet," he directs. "We will do this there."

Achaia starts shivering in my arms, her teeth chattering as I set her in one of the room's curvy, comfy chairs. Rosu hops onto her lap and rubs her cheek, purring his heart out. He senses something terrible is about to happen.

"I'll be right back," I whisper into her hair before crossing the room. I pull the blankets off the bed, piling them on another chair but leaving the fitted sheet. Renze pulls candles from a box in the closet and lights them on both bedside tables.

I shoot him another look, but he doesn't explain. He simply crosses the room and lifts Achaia out of the chair, depositing her in the center of the bed and climbing up behind her.

Rosu lingers on the floor, pacing anxiously from side to side until I pat the bed next to Achaia. He leaps up quickly, curling into a ball in her lap with his head up on her shoulder. He snuffles her ear, licking it as she shudders and wraps both arms around him.

Already, I sense her retreating from us, trying to find a mental state capable of getting her through the horrific pain she's about to endure.

I slide onto the bed in front of her, crossing my legs as I move Rosu's long tail gently out of the way. Her beautiful eyes, shining bright in the low light of our room, are filled with tears that begin to spill down her round cheeks. Her obvious terror makes me want to pull the world down around us, to find whoever did this to her and tear them to shreds.

Behind her, Renze wraps both hands around her shoulders, leaning in to kiss her shoulder, right next to Rosu's nose. He piles her hair on top of her head, braiding it quickly to hold it out of his way. "I am going to begin, *atirien*. I may deposit venom on the wounds. My hope is that as an aphrodisiac, it will distract from the pain."

Achaia leans back into his embrace and nods, eyes focused on me as Rosu whines. "Just get it done."

CHAPTER TWENTY-NINE
ACHAIA

It's times like now I wish I knew how to meditate and enter another plane of consciousness. Because right now, I'm ready to come out of my skin with apprehension, and Rosu's tense body in my lap just reminds me how excruciating this will be. My tattoo is incredibly intricate and detailed. Renze will have to remove basically all the skin on my back.

Tears stream down my cheeks as I try, and fail, to find extra strength inside me.

Jet presses closer, his knees resting over the top of mine, Rosu's body sliding until he lies across our laps. His dark head rests between my breasts, his sweet black eyes staring up at me with so much love. I stroke the dip between his eyes, following it to the top of his skull, where I scratch him gently. He's a little bigger today, which is surprising, even though Renze told us he'd grow fast. I didn't realize it would be so noticeable day to day.

Jet grabs my free hand and brings it up to his face as Renze places both cool hands on my back, startling slightly when the tattoo zaps him. "Eyes on me," Jet commands, bringing his lips to the inside of my wrist. Behind us, Renze slips my dress down my shoulders, bunching it around my waist.

The first slow slice of Renze's claws on my back draws a scream from deep inside my body. His second movement follows his first as he carves a line from my shoulder to my spine. Pain shoots across my skin as I struggle to remain still, squeezing Rosu until he yips and leaps off my lap, hovering next to Jet as he licks his lips anxiously.

"Well done, *atirien*," Renze murmurs, kissing my shoulder as I suck in deep, gasping breaths. The tears fall freely as I slump forward.

"I can't do this," I cry out. "There has to be another way."

Renze doesn't answer, dragging his claws along the cut he just made as I scream again.

Jet tilts my face to look at him. "You can do this," he reassures me.

I leap forward as Renze cuts again, spitting venom on my back. The combination of raging lust and burning pain that it induces shocks my system, and I start to quiver even as my pussy throbs.

"Be still, my love," Renze murmurs behind me as I sob into Jet's neck.

"I can't," I scream. Jet wraps my legs up in his and falls to his back, only partially upright on the pillows.

"You can," he commands me. "You will, but let me distract you." Jet smiles at Renze behind me. "Remove her dress all the way for me, Renze."

I sob at the painful stretching of my carved skin as Renze shifts the fabric down over my hips as I cry out. I knew it would hurt, but I didn't realize it would be like this.

Jet's legs lock around mine, holding me in place as one hand strokes lazily down my side. His lips come to mine.

"Kiss me," he commands. "Let me distract you from this. Let me carry this burden with you, little one."

I open my mouth to say I can't, just as Renze spits venom on an open wound. I scream at the intense stabbing sensation until it fades to a deep, throbbing burn. But it's…manageable, so I press my lips to Jet's and pray for this to be over fast. Or to pass out. Passing out would be best.

When Renze slices another strip of skin from my back, I scream into the kiss, Jet freezing beneath me. He can't fix this; no one can.

Slice. Strip. A piece of skin is tossed to the floor, where it lands with a squishy, horrible noise. Rosu snarls at Renze, snapping his teeth, even as Jet begins to purr for us. "Venom," he demands, his arm shifting slightly underneath me as if he's holding it up.

I hear Renze spit, and then a soft moan leaves my mouth when Jet's hand slides between my ass cheeks, teasing and touching as the venom shocks my system.

So much pain. So much pleasure. They war for victory in my brain as Renze drags his claws down my back yet again, another piece of skin joining the first on the floor.

I screech as Jet's purr deepens, shaking my chest as he strokes my clit and ass, his fingers dipping inside to tease as Renze continues carving the tattoo from my skin.

JET: A DARK SHIFTER ROMANCE

"*Fuck*," I grit out when he slices across a wound he already made.

Jet grips my hair and drags my mouth to his, devouring me with so much possession, so much dominance, I can barely remember a time when I chose to reject him to give him back his choices. This male is different.

Jet nips at the tip of my tongue as Renze continues his horrific work, his claws moving faster as I heave and cry, the heat between my thighs building despite the shocking pain. How the fuck is it possible I could come while Renze shreds my back? I don't know, but vampiri venom and Jet might save me today.

Underneath me, Jet's kiss turns more frantic, his lust demanding my attention. Renze pulls another strip of skin from my back as Jet starts to roll his hips rhythmically against mine. His hard cock slides along my wet pussy as Renze deposits another stream of venom on us. I'm dripping with it as Jet moans, breaking the kiss. "More. Let me give you more," he growls as he slides his pants down, his pierced length bobbing up to meet my core as I sigh.

Claws drag down my spine as Renze murmurs. "Nearly halfway there, *atirien*. You are doing wonderfully."

"Focus on me," Jet demands, nipping at my chin, my neck, and my shoulder as he pulls me higher over his chest. Sharp fangs sink lightly into my skin as he bites me, sucking at the blood that wells from tiny wounds. Heat blooms in my belly as his cock rubs against my sensitive clit.

"Jet," I gasp out.

"We've never taken it all the way, Achaia," he murmurs into my lips. "But I'm wondering if this big alpha cock might take your mind off of things. Shall we try?"

I hiss when Renze pulls another bit of skin from my back, spitting venom on the wound as tears stream down my face.

Jet takes it as an agreement and reaches down, gripping his dick and pressing it to my opening. "Venom, *atiri*." His voice is a deep command, and Renze shudders behind me as he follows it. Flames spread along my back and shoulders as the big vampiri continues his gruesome work.

"Shall we count down, *atirien*?" Jet taunts me, slipping the very tip of his dick in and out of me so slowly I feel like I'm dying of need. I can't understand the pain at my back and the pleasure between my thighs. I'm losing my hold on reality as I focus on the huge alpha. Sound is beginning to fade away. I'm going to pass out. Gods, I hope I do.

"Three," he growls, sliding a little further in, the piercing through the tip of his cock dragging along my inner walls. When he pulls out, I whine until Renze continues on, and the whine turns into a scream of pain.

"Two, Achaia," Jet snarls, pulling my gaze back to him. Already, I'm wet and sloppy from the venom and the tease, my body fighting to focus on anything normal. I'm like a wild animal being eaten alive by predators—unsure whether to run or give in and pray to die quickly.

Jet grits out the last number as he bucks his hips, that thick cock sliding inside me so deep and so hard I'm practically choking on it.

Every ridged, pierced inch of him sends shivers through my pussy as I clench around the impossible thickness, desperate to get accustomed to his sheer size.

"This pussy is mine." Jet grips both of my ass cheeks and pulls me up off his cock before slamming it into me once more.

A noise between a shriek and a cry for help leaves my lips when he clamps his teeth around my throat and begins to fuck me with deep, steady strokes. He holds me still enough for Renze to keep shredding my tattoo, and I'm officially lost.

I've never felt pain like this. And I've never had pleasure like what Jet is capable of dispensing. He keeps up that delicious torture as my body trembles, my gaze growing darker. I pray to pass out even as I moan. I don't want to miss a minute of Jet taking me for the first time.

But then, blissfully, everything goes dark as Jet slows his thrusts and purrs loudly for me.

"Good girl, Achaia. Let go, that's it."

∽

I don't know how much time has passed when I blink my eyes. The doors to our small balcony are open wide, the night sky peeking through. Is it still today?

There was a knock, maybe. Something woke me. I hear both Jet and Renze and then a woman.

Sante.

Fur fills my mouth as I sputter and look up. Rosu is curled around my head like a hat, his feathered tail resting across my lips and cheek. I reach up to push it out of the way and scream at the pain that shoots across my skin.

"Easy, honey," Sante's voice encourages. "You're already healing, but I came to apply more salve. It's the best for shit like this. You're a fucking trooper. Lay still, okay?"

I bury my face in Rosu's soft fur as he begins purring for me. He snuggles closer around my head as Sante applies a freezing cold gel to my back. It hurts, but not as horribly as I would have expected.

"How's it look?" I ask, a little terrified of the answer.

"You're carved up pretty bad," Sante chirps. "But that's how this sort of thing works. Only one who is willing to go through this can break the curse of a prisoner tattoo. Speaking of which...how do you feel? Can you remember anything?"

I'd shoot upright in the bed if I could, but as it is, every movement sends searing pain through my skin.

I search my mind for anything, any sign of who and what I am...but... nothing. Tears fill my eyes when Jet drops to the bed next to me.

"Anything?"

"No," I reply. "I don't feel any different."

Sante pats my side. "That's okay. Healing takes time, and a prisoner tattoo threads its dark magic through your mind like a web. Your memories may take a while to return."

I hadn't considered that. Somehow, I assumed that once the tattoo was gone, who I am would come flooding back to me in a rush. That's what I wanted. What if we did this, and I just slowed down our plan to rescue Tenebris?

I grit my teeth against the frustration of that bit of news and hold back the cry that's desperate to come out of my mouth.

"I know you expected this to work differently," Renze murmurs from behind me. "But it will come back soon, Achaia. I have no doubt. The tattoo is completely gone."

"Rest, Achaia," Jet murmurs, stroking my hair from my face. "I'll grab us some dinner. All you need to do is rest and heal. Let your body do its job."

My eyelids flutter at his urging, his voice peaceful as it lulls me back under.

Hours later, I assume, I wake to the smell of food in the room. With Jet's help, I'm able to sit upright and stand while he changes the blood-stained bedding. I grimace when he and Renze pull it from the bed and replace it. It looks like someone got slaughtered.

Jet helps me back onto the bed, tucking my legs under me as he hands me a plate of steak and creamy potatoes.

"Eat something," he encourages. When I grab the fork and lift a bite of potato to my lips, I cry out and drop the entire thing.

Jet slides onto the bed next to me and takes the fork, spearing a bite and holding it out for me. I eat in silence under his watchful eyes. When I can't possibly fit another morsel in my belly, he helps me flip onto my side so I can rest.

At some point, a hard knock on the door tells us Noire is outside.

Jet growls but slides off the bed, exchanging harsh words at the door with his brother.

Renze winks at me. "I believe Noire was hoping you would immediately transform into an air dragon and burn Paraiso to the ground."

I chuckle a little at that. "I would if I could. Who knows…maybe it'll happen. Or maybe nothing will ever happen. And I'm just destined to never know who I am. That's a possibility, too."

"Unlikely," Renze murmurs, stroking the side of my arm. "Whatever you are will be perfect, *atirien*. Because it will be you. The memories will return. I have no doubt. In the meantime, shall we discuss how you finally got to ride our mate? Tell me how you feel."

He shoots me a cocky look as Jet closes the door, and Noire stomps off down the hallway.

Jet smiles when he slips onto the mattress next to Renze.

"Do tell, Achaia. How does alpha dick compare to vampiri?"

"Must we compare?" Renze mutters, slapping Jet on the side of the head. "We are mates. All dick is good dick. Am I not right, *atirien*?"

I chuckle, watching them, although even that small laugh hurts my skin.

"I don't know about all dick," I retort. "But I'm pretty happy with the two I've got."

Jet purrs under my half-assed praise and flops down on the bed, scooting his way over Renze's legs as he shoves his way between us. He pushes Rosu up onto the pillows as he lays his head in my lap, turning to the side so he can carefully burrow his way between my breasts.

"Fucking love your huge tits," he growls, his voice muffled from the positioning.

Renze smiles as he watches us, but he gives me an evil look as he leans over and nips Jet's shoulder.

"What if we give our mate something to watch while she heals, *atiri*? Perhaps she would enjoy dinner and a show."

Jet laughs but emerges from my cleavage, leaning in to bite one of my nipples. He sucks it hard into his mouth before releasing it and grinning up at me. "Would you like that, Achaia? Dinner and a show?"

"Yes," I breathe out as he sits back on his heels and beams at Renze.

"Good," he purrs, his dark eyes intent on our vampiri mate. "Because I want to give you that show."

Give it he does. Over and over, they give and take until they fall sated to the mattress, curling themselves around me protectively until I fall asleep once more.

CHAPTER THIRTY

RENZE

I stand on the balcony, more physically satisfied than I have been in my hundreds of years. Achaia's back is healing rapidly, and Jet and Rosu are curled around her protectively.

Still, I look at the white stars that blink in the sky and pray for a future that will bring us peace. I am resolute in my desire to rescue Tenebris and reunite my full court as quickly as possible. I never could have imagined that I would include direwolf shifters in my family, but now I cannot imagine it any other way. The Chosen One, Jet, Ten, they all feel like family. Even Noire does most days, although he is so irritable it is hard to think too fondly of him.

I don't turn when Jet slips quietly out of bed, padding across the lush room to join me on the balcony. He presses me to the sand-colored railing, his cock hard at my back as he nips my neck.

"You have come a long way, *atiri*," I laugh when he reaches around my hip to slide his warm hand inside my pants.

"You both gave me space, and I fucking hated it," he growls, cupping my dick. "This is mine. And she is mine."

I pull Jet's hand out of my pants and use the leverage to spin him up against the railing instead, thrusting my hips against his warm body as he throws his head back. I lick my way along his neck before biting his ear and tugging.

"I want my bar here, *atiri*. I want to gift you jewels and watch their number grow every year until we have to pierce the other side."

"If we make it out of this bullshit alive," Jet barks. "I want that too. And I want to breed her. I need to pump her full of our babies, Renze."

I grip his throat as he growls. Emotion floods my mind at the idea of her swollen with child. I must have it. "We *will* make it out, Jet. We have to. Because I have barely begun to love you both, and I need so much more time."

"Did you know what I was to you in the maze?" His voice is darkly seductive as I think back to those horrific years.

"I knew I watched you more than the others," I admit finally. "And I knew that on the rare occasion I was forced to the Atrium, I looked for you. But I did not allow myself to think on what it meant until that day I found you in the Chapel. I knew then."

Jet sighs and turns in my arms, his mouth slicking over mine. Our tongues tangle gently in exploration as Jet's hands slide down my backside. "I need you back here. I want it soon."

I let out a dark laugh at that. "You shall have it whenever you want, *atiri*."

He growls into my neck. "I want to make you scream while she watches. I want to fuck you while you're pinned between us, your cock buried inside our mate's sweet pussy."

A shrill scream breaks through our heated moment as Achaia shoots upright in the bed and falls off it to the floor. The sound of sobbing starts up immediately as Jet and I part, running into the room to help her.

Our beautiful mate is still nude but curled into a ball on the floor with tears streaming down her cheeks.

"Stolen," she whispers, eyes the color of a tropical forest finding mine. "I remember being stolen by...someone. But I don't remember where I was or who I was with. Just...violence. Being ripped from my home, my people. My people, oh gods, my people..."

Tears stream down her face as Jet lifts her carefully back into the bed.

"We expected as much," he murmurs into her hair, stroking it away from her face as she burrows her way into his thickly muscled chest.

"I know," she sobs. "But to have the memory of it is far worse than I imagined. Don't let me go, Jet. Renze?"

I sink onto the bed when she lifts a hand to reach for me, pulling it back with a hiss when it tugs the skin at her back. The salve is doing its job, though. Her entire back is a series of angry red scabs, but there are no more open wounds.

I thread my legs through theirs and kiss her neck, shoulder, and ear until she falls back asleep. Eventually, Jet's light snores join hers. Even Rosu snores, buried in the pillows above them.

Knowing with certainty that someone hurt her pushes ice-cold resolve into my veins, my fangs dripping with angry venom. When she remembers who it was, I will hunt them. And then I will kill them very, very slowly as she watches.

∽

The following morning, we finalize our plan with Arliss. Breakfast and lunch are taken in his office, where we pore over printouts of Paraiso's infrastructure. The city itself is built on three main levels and four pods that center around Rama's living quarters. Naturally, she made herself the very center of it all.

The only way in or out of Paraiso is by specialized hovercars that Arliss developed for the city. Oasis and Paraiso are the only places left on our whole continent with access to technology.

How odd it will be to see a live screen that's not telling me whom to kill. I cannot fathom it.

"We will enter the city here, in the Grand Hall," Arliss points out. "All incoming arrivals pass through security there. Next we will take a train to my personal quarters in the pod closest to Rama's. I travel with a group of ten or so usually. We will switch out some of my regulars for the six of you."

"What about the party?" Jet questions. Next to me, Achaia shifts on her feet and winces. Her open-backed shirt leaves her scabs open to the air to heal, but nearly her entire back is a crisscross of bright red wounds.

Leaning over, I kiss her shoulder as Rosu wraps himself around her feet.

"The party is a masquerade ball. There will be food and dancing, plus a show."

Jet bristles next to Achaia. I know he is thinking of the Atrium and the shows she forced him to perform there.

"It will be just like the Atrium," Arliss confirms, looking at Jet with narrowed eyes. "You'll need to keep your shit together, no matter what you see."

Jet growls but doesn't bother to respond. Arliss showed back up this morning as if he didn't have a seizure and fall to the ground yesterday, but I note the lines of exhaustion on his face, now that I am aware enough to look for them. Our host is not well, but Noire was unable to uncover any specifics yet as to why.

"What hold does Rama have over you?" I purr, curious to see if he will answer when off guard.

Without a beat, he grins as if delivering happy news. "Money, vampiri. A lot of godsdamned money." He laughs as he looks around my family gathered at his table. "Perhaps, instead of worrying yourselves over my weakness, you should focus on the fucking party. I can get you access to the lower level, which is where she keeps any prisoners taken on Paraiso. Admittedly, it is a party town, so most of her research and interrogation happens in Nacht."

"Nacht?" Jet asks the question just as I open my mouth to do so.

Arliss nods. "When Rama was younger, and the monsters were leaving the Tempang to attack her province, she and her father built a city called Nacht right into the mountainside. It was their only defensible location as monsters razed Deshali. Now, it is her home base when she is not on Paraiso."

Jet growls. "Back to the party. There's just one level for prisoners?"

Arliss confirms that to be true. "Prisoners are only held there. If your brother is on Paraiso, it is the one place she could keep him."

That comment chills my blood. We do not know for certain if Rama returned to Nacht after we escaped from the maze. From what we have pieced together, it seems she went straight to the Vinituvari coast to park the sky city. Still, it is possible Tenebris was delivered to Nacht first.

An uncomfortable silence falls over our group. After long, tense moments, Noire turns to Arliss with an evil gleam in his eye. "Hear me on this, Arliss. There are so many holes in this plan it is practically a sieve. But if you do a single godsdamned thing to put my pack in danger, I'll rip your head from your body. Do you understand me?"

Arliss' lips curl up, fangs sliding down from his jaws as he snaps them in Noire's direction. But Noire has faced down the worst of the worst monsters in the maze and survived them. I doubt there is anything that could scare my pack alpha at this point.

Noire grins like a maniac as Diana threads her small hand into his, kissing his shoulder. "We will get him back, alpha." She turns to Arliss. "And if we can help you rescue your friend, we'll do that too."

That comment appears to mollify Arliss, who slaps a fake grin on his face and returns to the schematics of the city.

We go over the details of our plan for hours, but there is a threatening undercurrent of anxiety now that it is nearly time to depart.

~

Dinner is the rowdiest it has been since we arrived at Oasis. Arliss' people are excited. For them, this event is a party, and that is thrilling. But among my pack, there is an overwhelming sense of doom. Tomorrow, we might go to our deaths in a final maze of sorts.

Ascelin hovers near Diana, and I find myself anxious to get past this mission so we can move on to the prophecy. I don't have the slightest clue how we'll figure out an ancient language, but there must be some way...

"Let us retire," I urge Jet and Achaia as they finish. Rosu hops off his chair and winds around my feet in a figure of eight, his bracelets tinkling softly. Jet nods and helps Achaia up, our beautiful mate lifting her chin with a devious expression.

"I'm so fucking ready to retire," she laughs. "Let's go, boys."

Behind us, Arliss fucks two women simultaneously on top of the table, thrusting into one as he feasts on the other. Diana sits in Noire's lap, stroking his cock while they watch. Ah, my little voyeurs. We are anxious for any happiness we can find before we leave tomorrow.

"Have fun, brother," Jet calls over his shoulder as we leave the dining hall's noise and head up the dark hall to our rooms.

My body is achy and needy for my mates. What if tonight is the last time I ever get to have them? What if our woefully incomplete plan goes to absolute shit tomorrow? What if I never get to touch them again?

Achaia sighs when I collar her neck from behind and turn her gently to face me. Her bright eyes dazzle me in the fading light.

"I know, mate," she whispers. "I'm terrified to lose you, too."

"Never," Jet reassures her. "We will never let it happen." He wraps an arm around her waist and looks at me with a big grin. "We need to show our woman how a vampiri and an alpha fuck their mate so good, she can't remember what she ever worried about."

"Agreed," I murmur, my eyes not leaving hers as she swipes away the tears that threaten to spill.

"Don't cry; you'll freak Rosu out," Jet laughs.

Achaia chuckles. "Renze, I thought you said velzen were protectors, but so far, I think we've just got a mix between a cat and a dog." Rosu begins purring on cue, and Jet purrs back until they're both sending loud reverberations into the hall.

We both laugh, and it's joyful until I lean close to her ear and bite it. "I cannot wait to put my bar here," I murmur. "To gift you that first jewel. The first of many, I hope."

"We're ready for that, aren't we, Rosu?" Jet purrs from next to us, crooning at the happy velzen. "Do velzen get bars too? I think he'd like one."

"It is uncommon but not unheard of," I admit as I open the door to our room, swinging my arm out to allow my mates to cross first. "Usually reserved for the most loyal and protective of velzen lines. If you were to gift Rosu an ear bar, it would be a shocking honor to him."

"Then I want to," Achaia confirms. "Sounds like you need to find three jewels every year, mate, because Rosu is part of this—no matter what."

"It would be my greatest honor to do that. I pray to the gods I get that chance," I answer.

I close the door behind us and turn to see Achaia's smile fall, but she hops up into my arms.

"Take me to bed, vampiri. Take me like you did that first night. I want to be that sore again, to remind me how fucking much I love you."

Jet crosses the room and plants Rosu in a chair. "You stay there," he commands, pointing at the chair as Rosu sits up, cocking his skinny head to the side. "You can snuggle after," Jet emphasizes as Rosu wags his tail and whines.

I set Achaia down on the bed, carefully removing her shirt before she leans forward, presenting me with an incredible view of her pussy. Growling, I lean in and bite both ass cheeks, squeezing as she sighs with pleasure.

Jet joins me, ripping his shirt over his head as he gives me a seductive smile.

"Join me inside her, mate," he murmurs. "Here." He reaches out and strokes his big fingers down her slit as the back of her thighs quiver.

"Not here?" I question playfully, stroking her back hole as she lets out a needy whine.

Jet guides my fingers lower to her swollen folds.

"Here," he confirms. "I want to feel your cock rubbing all over mine. I want your seed to mix with mine. I need to see it dripping from her after we use her."

I growl, leaning forward to capture his lips, even as I slide two fingers inside my mate. Jet groans into the kiss, shoving my pants down as our kiss turns deep and desperate. Heat flares along my spine, predatory focus on my mates as I kiss one and finger fuck the other. Achaia rocks back to meet my hand as Jet slides his fingers inside her along with me.

I whine at how wet she is, how easily she takes us as we stroke together, Jet parting from the kiss long enough to chuckle into my mouth.

"See, vampiri? See how beautifully ready she is." He bites my lower lip and tugs before deepening the kiss again, his tongue teasing mine until I lose focus on Achaia because playing with Jet is overwhelming me.

Vampiri are not highly emotional, which is ironic given our emotive gifts, but knowing I could lose my mates tomorrow sets my teeth on edge. I want to grab them and have them in every way I can to cement and bond us so that nothing separates us. Not even death if she comes on swift wings.

"I'm going to claim you both tonight," I purr into Jet's lips, stroking the back of Achaia's thigh as she whimpers. "I'm going to drink your blood, and then nothing will ever come between us—not even Rama."

"I want to wait until we're free of Rama before I mark you both," Jet admits, parting from me to hop onto the bed. He pulls Achaia gently on top of his nude form and captures her mouth, tenderly at first. And then more forcefully as he massages her ass, teasing her with his cock, showing me what waits for me.

"I can't do the slow teasing tonight," Jet admits as he pauses. "I need a hard fuck, Achaia. Can you take it?"

She sits up on Jet's lap, gripping his cock and sheathing him inside her wetness in one swift move.

Jet barks out a string of curses as he rolls his hips up to meet her, teeth gritted in ecstasy.

"I require it," she purrs, lifting herself off Jet again and rocking back down fast.

I watch his pierced thickness enter and leave her pussy, slick wetness coating his gorgeous cock as she gets hotter and hotter. When I dip onto the mattress and press her gently forward, she stiffens.

"You tease our mate, *atirien*," I whisper into her shoulder, careful not to touch her still-healing back. "What Jet meant was can you take all of this." I grip my cock, directing it to her pussy, moaning when Jet's piercings rub along my head and length. I push the first inch or two of myself inside her, growling as I watch her body stretch around us both.

"Godsdamn," Jet moans as I arrange myself between his legs and push another inch or two inside our mate. "You feel fucking incredible," Jet barks. "She's going to come too fast, Renze. Wait, *atiri*."

Hearing him call me *atiri* nearly sends me into release, but I pause and breathe deeply, relishing the feel of my mates. Using my knees to shove Jet's thighs wider apart, I spit venom on Achaia's pussy, watching it drip down Jet's thickness, down over his heavy balls. They tighten up as his body tenses with pleasure. I spit again, watching that aphrodisiac coat his back hole as they both writhe, Achaia's heat sucking me deeper still.

I reach down under my cock, sliding two fingers into Jet's ass as he bellows in pleasure. And then I stroke slowly, rhythmically, as my own orgasm builds from watching them.

Achaia cries out as I shift forward, my full length buried inside her as Jet's hips roll underneath. His piercings stroke my cock with every thrust of his big hips. Normally in this position, I'd be the one moving, but it's too hard when we both do it. Jet can't stop, his cries growing louder and louder to match Achaia's.

I hold myself impossibly still except for the hand taking Jet's ass, and I watch their bodies. The way Achaia stiffens and quivers, her thighs gripped tight around Jet's broad midsection. Every inch of her skin is flushed, her back hole an empty tease as I spit on it and slide two fingers in.

She screams at the intrusion, at being so impossibly full of us both. And when I slide out and back in, she comes, shattering as she drenches our cocks with release. Her citrusy scent blossoms as Jet pulls her forward and clamps his teeth around her throat. Not a claiming bite but a marking, most definitely.

Achaia screams Jet's name as I continue taking her, even as his body locks up in an orgasm to match hers. My cock slips out as he roars into the bite and rolls to the side, fucking her slowly as their chests rise and fall.

And I watch. I watch how they come down, her eyes fluttering open, pink lips parted as she licks the bottom, plump one.

Jet's focuses entirely on her as he strokes a stray auburn hair away from her forehead. "You are a gift," he whispers.

As one, they turn to look at me, my blood heating as Jet's focus changes.

"Show us how a vampiri claims his mates," my alpha commands.

Jet sits up as Achaia rolls onto her side and sits up tenderly.

I grip Jet's throat and push his head back with my thumb under his chin.

"Bare yourself for my teeth, alpha," I direct, watching my command roll over him as he bristles. Jet growls and sinks to his knees, his head falling back, his tan throat ready for my mark.

"Gods, that's hot," Achaia whispers as I lean in, my long tongue trailing a path from the dip of Jet's throat up to his ear. I bite my way back down his burnished skin, looking for the perfect vein.

"Will it hurt?" Achaia questions softly as I chuckle into Jet's skin.

"Yes," I confirm. "And it will also bring intense pleasure. Watch, *atirien*."

In a swift move, I slash my teeth across Jet's neck, ripping a vein wide open as his blood spills into my mouth. He grunts at the sting, but when I sink my teeth into that vein and pull his blood, sucking it deep, his cry turns to a deep groan of pleasure. His hips pump wildly against mine, his hard cock spurting cum onto my own as joint orgasms overtake us.

Achaia gasps aloud, watching as I push my devotion and love into the growing bond with him. Light flickers and explodes behind my eyes, and when I focus, he's there with me in my mind.

Jet, I murmur, relishing the new sensation of him startling.

You didn't warn me about this, he growls into the brand-new tether. *Speaking directly into my mind? Like alphas do?*

More fun to learn in the moment, I croon back, stroking him through that mental connection. *Vampiri can fuck their mates like this, too, Jet. A way for me to get you off even when we're not in the same room together.*

A lucky benefit of being yours, I suppose, he snarks before another orgasm overtakes him. He comes and comes as I stroke his hard cock, matching the rhythm while I stroke our bond. And when he finally comes down, I feel him in my chest. So strong and commanding.

Jet growls as he looks over at Achaia, pulling her gently into his lap. He starts nipping at her shoulders.

"Where do you think he'll take you, little one? Here?" Jet kisses a spot at the base of her shoulder before trailing his tongue to the other side, where a vein throbs. "Perhaps here?"

I laugh as I push them both back into the sheets, careful to keep Achaia on her side and avoid pressure on her wounds.

"How about here?" I murmur, spreading her legs wide as I point to a blue vein that runs along the inside of her thigh.

"You can't be serious," she laughs, green eyes scanning mine as Jet laughs. "Oh gods, you are?"

"I am," I confirm, leaning in to lick cum off her swollen pussy lips, groaning at the combined flavors. Within my chest, Jet's presence heats me from the inside. He finds this incredibly hot.

"Steady yourself, mate," I whisper.

CHAPTER THIRTY-ONE
ACHAIA

I'm fucking sore everywhere, but I can't get enough of my handsome mates. Jet holds me carefully, nipping at my neck and shoulder and whispering dirty shit in my ear as Renze lifts my left leg up, exposing my bare pussy once more.

"Hold her leg for me, *atiri*," he commands Jet, who reaches down and grips my knee, spreading me impossibly wide.

"Perfection," Renze growls, white eyes finding mine as a devilish grin splits his handsome face. Without another word, he leans in and licks a path from my clit along the juncture of my thigh and my pussy. He tortures me until I'm ready to come again, that talented tongue covering my whole slit and dipping inside. And then there's a sudden movement, and fangs rip at the vein, blood splashing Renze's face.

I buck at the sudden slice of pain, but his teeth clamp down on my skin, and I *feel* him. So fucking deeply. As if he's pulling the soul right out of me with every suck of my blood. A groan leaves my mouth as my body contracts, clenching around emptiness as Renze growls and pulls harder with his teeth. An orgasm overtakes me so hard, so strong, Jet's dominance overwhelming me from behind and Renze's from the front.

"I feel you," I gasp out. Where I've always sensed Renze, this is new. Depthless, aching, and perfect.

A sudden intense sensation travels down my core as a laugh echoes in my mind.

And now we are bound, purrs Renze into my mind as I gasp, struggling against his bite and Jet's hand holding me open. I come again as Jet laughs low in my ear.

"So beautiful when you unleash," he purrs into my skin before continuing in my mind. *Perfect in every way.*

I'm reduced to nothing but sensation as my mates nip and bite and pleasure me from the inside out. I lose track of how many times I come until I fall back onto Jet's chest and hiss at the pain from my wounds.

Rosu growls from across the room as Jet gently shifts me up, laying me down on my side in the bed, a spent fucking mess.

Then a dark face appears at the bedside, and I laugh, patting the bed. "Come on, Rosu, sweet boy."

Rosu hops up onto the bed, licking my cheek before turning his attention to Jet's neck. He licks away the blood as Renze laughs.

"Do we need to bite Rosu?" I ask curiously, watching the velzen clean Jet's wound.

Renze laughs and strokes his elegant fingers down Rosu's fuzzy back. "We do not, *atirien*. He is as connected as he can possibly be."

My heart is so fucking full, and even though I still don't remember most of who or what I am, I'm okay with it for the first time. If that information is meant to come back to me, it will. I pull Renze down on the bed, climbing on top of him as Rosu continues cleaning Jet.

"Make out with me," I demand as Renze sits up against the pillows, pulling me closer to his cool chest. He's covered in our blood. It drips from his fangs and dark lips, and he's never looked more handsome to me.

"Any time, *atirien*," he hums, opening his mouth for my tongue to dance along his.

Next to us, Jet feigns indignation. "You two are making out while the dog licks me? Fucking rude." I turn to him with a grin, watching him cross his arms as Rosu perches himself on Jet's chest. "Well, don't *stop*," he says emphatically, gesturing for Renze and me to continue.

Rosu starts purring and licks his way along Jet's collarbone, cleaning the spilled blood as Jet's head falls back on the pillows. He watches us make out for a long time, enjoying, touching, and loving.

It's the best connection I've ever had, and I am terrified to lose it.

"We cannot take Rosu," Renze says softly as I stomp my foot the following morning.

"We can't leave him here; what if they're not nice to him?" I demand, looking to Jet for backup.

The look on Jet's face tells me I'm not going to get it.

"We can't protect him up there, little one," Jet reminds me. "Plus, bringing a velzen would make it obvious that someone in Arliss' group is a vampiri. We can't risk it. He'll give us away if someone threatens you."

Rosu whines as if he can already sense what's going on. I drop to a knee next to him and crush him to my chest, even though my back hurts when I move that way.

I don't bother to agree with my mates because I sense their distress in our vampiri mate bond. They fucking hate the idea of leaving Rosu behind. But they're right. We can't protect him on Paraiso. And when I think about Rama possibly capturing him, I know I'd burn the godsdamned city to the ground to get Rosu back.

He stalks quietly beside us as we leave our room and head for the dining hall.

Arliss grins at us when we enter, spreading his big arms wide. "Today is the day. Are you ready?" He cocks his head to the side and looks at me. "I see you cemented your bond. Good. That may come in handy. How is your back, Achaia?"

How can he even tell? It is yet another mystery surrounding our enigmatic host.

I shrug. "Improved but still painful."

"Yes, well, slicing most of your skin off will do that," Arliss deadpans. "Still, I suspect your memories will return soon."

I roll my shoulders again. "I've gotten a few flashes here and there, but nothing terribly concrete. I need to thank Sante for the amazing healing gel."

"You're welcome!" Sante chirps, sailing into the room with a basket in her hand, vivid green skirts flowing gracefully behind her. She hands me a small metal disk. "Put this just behind your ear and depress the button in the middle. It'll insert itself into your skin."

"Why?" Renze questions, taking the disk from me and handing it to Jet to inspect.

"It is a piece of tech we have been working on for quite some time, my skeptical friend," Arliss croons. "With this tech, we can simulate a false appearance. It's not perfect, but this is as good a test as any. You wanted a disguise, and this is it."

Jet growls. "What's not perfect about it?"

Arliss shrugs. "The battery life is less than optimal, but making you look like a completely different person is hard work…"

"Maybe you shouldn't go for completely different," I mutter. "How about just different enough?"

Sante shrugs. "Not a bad idea. Leave your skin color, but change your hair, eyes, and maybe the shape of your nose. Make you slightly shorter or taller or thinner or fatter. It's the skin that's so hard."

Arliss grins seductively at Sante as she crosses the room and plants a tender kiss on his lips. "I love watching you in action," he murmurs, biting her lower lip.

"There will be plenty of time for action later," Ascelin barks as she enters the dining hall. I love seeing her needle Arliss, and I'd swear there's something between them, even if she seems to have moved on.

Sante parts from Arliss with a small grin then tosses a disk to Ascelin. "Goes on your neck." The diminutive inventor turns to me, dropping to one knee and stroking Rosu's head. "You're coming with me, little guy."

Rosu whines as I lean down and pick him up, hugging him tightly. Jet and Renze join me as I pepper the velzen with kisses.

Sante sighs wistfully. "You're so cute with him; you're like a little family. I promise I'll take good care of him. It'll be like a kid going to their cool aunt's house."

"Alright," I whisper into Rosu's dark fur, squishing him so tight he wriggles out of my arms. He gives us a sad knowing look, his long tail arched down to the floor as he leaves us to stand next to Sante. She reaches down and strokes his ears before pulling a piece of meat out of her pocket and handing it to him. For half a second, he ignores her, then he gobbles up the treat and looks back at us.

"Time to go." Her voice is cheerful as she beams at him, patting her slender thigh. Rosu looks longingly at us again and then follows Sante out of the dining hall as I choke back a sob.

Jet pulls me into his arms, burying his face in my neck as he bites me. *How did you get so attached in a few days?* He teases me in our new bond.

Tell me you're not attached, I counter.

I'm not attached, he returns immediately. A beat passes. *I'm not attached* very much.

I manage to avoid crying as Renze places one of Sante's disks behind his ear, just under an intricate blond braid. He depresses the button and shivers once as the disk clamps onto his skin. Half a second later, a different person stands before me. He's now shorter and broader with wild navy hair. A ring adorns his left nostril, a chain trailing along his cheek before it connects to a larger bar through his ear.

He's incredibly handsome. But it's not Renze. I let out a shocked huff as Jet releases his bite and turns around, growling at Renze before he realizes it's him.

"Liuvang-be-damned, that's weird," he murmurs, reaching out to touch Renze's chest. There's nothing off when his fingers trail smooth white skin under an open, billowy shirt.

Renze laughs. "I do not feel any differently, but this must be working?"

"You are astonishingly handsome," Ascelin laughs from behind us. "Far more so than usual. Actually, you look a bit like Elleph with the navy hair. Hot."

Renze shoots her the middle finger as she laughs. Noire and Diana arrive then, Noire bristling when he notices Renze. It's like he can sense Renze's predatory dominance, but he doesn't recognize him at all.

This is good, very good.

Renze spins slowly, rolling his shoulders as he paces across the dining hall toward Noire. I watch Noire tense and pull Diana behind him.

Renze stalks until his chest nearly brushes up against Noire's. "You do not recognize me, do you?" he questions as Noire tenses and balls his fists, ready to protect his mate.

"I do," Diana chirps helpfully. "Don't know how you managed this, but I would recognize your soul anywhere, Firenze."

"You have an unfair advantage, Chosen One," Renze laughs.

Noire looks from his mate to Renze, cocking his head to the side. "My gods, that's incredible," he murmurs, reaching out to touch Renze's nose.

Diana winks at him before rounding Noire and pressing her forehead to Renze's. "Whatever this tech is, I'm grateful for it. You look amazing."

Our group joins together, everybody taking one of Sante's disks and applying it. The pinch when it burrows into my skin makes me jump, but moments later, I stand surrounded by a beautiful group of people I don't recognize.

Arliss smiles at us. "Stunning. It would almost be a shame to turn any of you back. You belong at Oasis in these current forms."

"No need to be rude," I demand, stepping into Arliss' space as I lift my chin to him. "We were hot before."

"You are a curiosity, Achaia," Arliss whispers, unfazed by my teasing. "Your memories have not yet returned?"

"No," I confirm. "I remember being abducted, but I couldn't say by whom, or when, or from where."

Something about Arliss' focus today feels off and wrong to me. Maybe it's pure nerves from what we're about to embark on, but I can't be sure. Maybe it's an ability I had that I don't remember. But somehow, Arliss seems sick to me. The seizures are a symptom of a malady much greater than we know. I don't know how I know that, but I do.

Arliss snarls at the way I'm looking at him. "Whatever you think you know, you are wrong," he murmurs under his breath.

"Perhaps," I counter. "Perhaps not. If we can help, we will," I remind him.

Arliss gives me a heated look, then sidesteps me and gestures for us to follow. We pass through hallway after hallway before entering a giant, closed dome. Inside are hundreds of aircars. Older models and newer ones. And then a row of gigantic hovercabs big enough to seat the seven of us plus a few extra. Etu joins us, but I don't recognize the other three, and Arliss doesn't bother to introduce them.

Our host opens the nearest aircar and slides gracefully into the driver's seat. He depresses a button, and the side of the cab splits open into two doors, wide enough for us all to climb in.

"Time to go," he says. I look inside for my mates, steadying myself with their calming presence, even though I can't see them in their normal forms. Jet's skin is still tan, but the rest of him is unrecognizable—all the way to stark white, shaved hair.

We enter the aircar as Arliss turns from the driver's seat. "I will no longer be able to give you direction once we arrive at the sky city. Remember, we will go through security and take a train to my pod. There may be additional security there. That is normal. Don't make a scene. My group is always under my command while in Paraiso. Whatever you do, don't freak out about anything you see. Everything you witness in Rama's city, no matter how odd it may seem to you, is absolutely normal."

That's fucking cryptic, and I open my mouth to question him, but the hovercab leaps up and forward at the same time. Arliss puts it into a higher gear and takes a fast turn around the garage before tilting the vehicle up toward a hole in the ceiling.

My heart crushes in my chest as I scramble around for a seatbelt, despite being squished between my mates.

The ascent out of the garage and into the early-morning light is harrowing, but eventually, we climb above the clouds and level out. I grip the seat. I'm not meant to be up high like this, and an overwhelming sense of dread causes my stomach to tumble into knots. Still, I search inside for my backbone and will it to straighten. We are walking right into the lion's den; I need to be strong.

Arliss presses a long string of buttons on his dashboard before sliding gracefully out of his seat and joining us. "It is a long journey to Vinituvari. Relax. Fuck. Play games. Do whatever you like."

"Vinituvari?" Diana questions, her tone tense.

"Your home province, yes," Arliss croons. "She remains parked there for the party. You have not seen Vinituvari since she decimated it?"

Diana shakes her head, long blonde braids swinging from side to side in this new form. She sits back in her seat with a worried expression on her face as Noire threads her leg through his, pulling her into his chest to whisper in her ear.

She nods once, closing her eyes as they hold on to one another.

Goddess, this is going to be so fucking hard.

CHAPTER THIRTY-TWO
JET

The hovercab is so high above the clouds that we can't even see Lombornei below, but as we get closer to our destination, Diana tenses. I can't imagine how she feels, knowing we'll pass over her destroyed home province in order to get to Paraiso.

What do you need? I question into our family bond. I sense Noire's direwolf wants to shift and curl around her, protect and cherish her, and remind her we're all here for her.

I need to kill her, Diana barks back. I read her so strongly now that she and Noire are fully mated. Their powers have grown. He's reading everyone with ease, even more so than he did before. And Diana's wolf is crazy powerful. Plus, she's got the benefit of Cashore living inside her mind.

I can read Arliss now, she shares as Noire and I both look over at her. She continues on. *The friend he mentioned is his sister. In the past she helped him manage his illness, but then Rama took her.*

What else can you read from him, mate? Noire questions, reaching out to stroke a path down her chest as he purrs.

He's focused only on that, she whispers into our bond. *We need to keep an eye on him and his people; he'll betray us if he needs to.*

Noire wraps Diana in his arms, her back to his chest as he glances over her shoulder at me. *Achaia's memory?*

Nothing yet, I admit. *She's frustrated, but I don't think we can rush it. We've done what we can.*

He glances over at Achaia, currently resting against Renze's chest as she gazes out the window. The look on Noire's face tells me he's torn between feeling protective of her because she's mine but also wondering if she's less than us, somehow.

I didn't question your choices, I remind him directly into the bond he and I share. *Don't question mine.*

He places his hand over his chest and pats it twice, our signal that we're always on one side together, no matter what. It's something we started doing before the maze, even, and it's carried through.

I sense his thoughts turn to Ten, and mine follow. My direwolf is anxious under my skin, ready to find our youngest brother and release him from Rama's clutches. I can't imagine what she's put him through since we escaped, but it can't be anything good. I can only hope that when we get Ten back, he'll be in one piece physically, emotionally, and mentally. He grew up and came of age in the maze. He's so strong, but he's missed out on so much.

There's a break in the clouds, the hovercar dipping down below them for the first time.

"We're approaching," Arliss says. He looks directly at Diana. "Remember to keep it together, no matter what you see. Or you'll get us all killed." He gives her a sharp look before returning to the front of the hovercab.

She bristles but says nothing, turning instead to look out the window. She hisses in a breath as we all look down below.

I visited Vinituvari once with my father and once more with Noire when he took over Pack Ayala. We actually met Diana and her twin, Dore, at the time, although I don't remember much about Alpha Edson's children. I was more concerned with getting back home.

The sight below us is nothing like the rolling green, lush hills, and hardwood forests of her home province. The ground itself is black and charred, scorch marks covering everything as far as the eye can see. Through our pack bond, I sense Diana's distress rise and rise to choke her, and I stand in the hovercab, crossing it to pull her into a hug as Noire's rising ire fills our family bond, causing the hair to stand on my nape.

He will burn Rama to the ground for his mate to give her a moment of peace. And because she's Ayala Pack, I feel the same. Diana burrows into my chest, seeking comfort as Noire and I share a knowing look, his black eyes glittering in the low light. We will decimate Rama or die trying.

I sense my mates focus on me, realizing what's going on as Achaia notices the ground below. She hisses out a surprised breath. "This is Vinituvari? I pictured it so differently from all Thomas' teachings." She turns in her seat, looking across at us. "Diana, I'm so sorry."

Diana turns, her teeth gritted together tightly. "Be sorry, but be resolute,

Achaia. We will take Rama down, so she can never destroy anything like this again."

Achaia lifts her chin and nods once, an understanding passing between them as my mate's gaze darkens. "Never again," she confirms, her voice dipping into a dark, low tone.

The hovercab is silent for the next half hour. Vinituvari no longer exists. There's not a single sign of life anywhere; the entire province is scorched fields and cracked black ruins. The beautiful angular architecture Diana's father was so famous for designing is nothing more than stone and dust, as if Rama wanted to wipe all traces of Edson Winthrop off the map.

Except he does live on in Diana and in her brother, too—maybe.

The tension in the hovercab ramps up as we exit a fluffy white cloud, and Paraiso looms ahead of us. I can't hold back a snarl when I see the city from the air. I've only ever seen it from below, during the final fight when we escaped the Temple Maze.

Like this, it's horrifying and striking all at once.

The entire belly of the city looks like someone dug up a gigantic tree, bits of dirt and root trailing down beneath it. That's the weapons system we were lucky enough to survive. But above all of that, there are three distinct levels of what must be housing, and then lush gardens and high-rise buildings atop that. A giant spire sticks up out of the center of the city, surrounded by smaller ones on every side. The buildings are shaped to look like flames licking up into the sky. At the base, they reflect foliage that spills out into the streets and crawls up the buildings' sides.

We fly silently over multiple lush gardens and through tall high rises before coming to a cavernous hanger. Arliss pulls the hovercar into the hanger and expertly parks it. It's clear he's done this many times. Predatory focus hones my gaze—we're here, we're close. All we need to do is not lose our heads.

Arliss turns to us with a final warning look and presses the button for the hovercar's twin doors. When they slide open with a whoosh, a uniformed guard stands outside. He's human but so fucking big I'd guess he got served growth hormones from birth.

Arliss hooks his fingers into his belt lazily and grins. "Jentu, good to see you again. I brought the nose spices you asked for. They're in storage space B in the back."

"Don't know what you're talking about," the guard mutters but gestures for Arliss to exit the hovercab, leaning in as our host passes him by. "Many thanks, Builder."

"Take care of my vehicle," Arliss jokes back before beckoning us to follow.

We step out, Renze, Ascelin and I in the front and Noire bringing up the rear as always.

This whole experience is so surreal that I don't even know what to process first. We say nothing, trailing behind Arliss like ducklings behind their mama. I try to remember that his companions have been here before, and not to gape at everything with my mouth open like a fish. But it's hard not to be shocked at so much fucking tech in one place. Above us, the entire ceiling of the hanger is filled with screens, arrows flashing across them to direct traffic. It's almost like an upside-down runway, if I had to approximate it to something I've seen before.

We pass a screen-filled office with floor-to-ceiling windows where techs appear to manage the other operations related to the hanger. After that, we pass through a giant arched hallway filled with light. Screens embedded in the walls remind us of the huge celebration happening tonight, almost like advertisements for the party. I wonder if they ever advertised what happened in the Atrium.

I can just imagine it now—*Come join us for a thrilling night of revelry as Jet fucks fifteen virgins in a row! Visit the Atrium for tonight's show!*

My skin itches with the need to shift and run, to seek Rama out by scent alone and make her pay for seven years of bullshit.

I can't forget the way she looked through me that day on the train, that fateful day when she let her father trick us into believing he simply wanted to marry her off to Noire to cement his foothold on the continent.

But we were all foolish. Because she was the puppet master behind Alpha Rand, and he was nothing but a marionette at her direction. We all were.

We might still be.

"I'm so fucking excited about this party," chirps Etu to my right, clasping his fists together in excitement. He winks over at me as I hold back a growl. He probably *is* thrilled. He's never experienced Rama as I have. He has no idea what she's capable of. This is a means to fuck and get fucked for him. He's a one-dimensional person, and I hate him in that moment.

Arliss directs us through the advertisement-laden hallway, the screens too bright, too cheerful for my mood. The hallway opens, spilling into a massive train station, dozens of trains coming and going. But these are unlike the ancient railway cars Noire favored back home. These are high-speed bullet trains, full of fancy tech and even fancier people, walking around as if they have no idea what's happening to the rest of the world below Paraiso.

Suddenly, I have questions, so many questions. How many people live up here all the time? Who escaped Siargao when we got out of the maze? Which of her wealthy patrons did Rama take with her when she fled, and why?

I'm probably not getting answers to most of those, so I focus on keeping my eyes open and noticing everything I can about the station itself. Every detail could be significant in our quest to rescue Ten.

Behind me, I sense Noire does the same. Ascelin and Renze form a protective barrier around Diana as the Chosen One. Achaia walks in front of me and next to Renze, acting as cool as a godsdamned cucumber. If she's fazed by this city, she's not showing it.

"Train seven, my lucky number," Arliss sings as he bypasses the larger high-speed trains and heads to the last track. A single train car sits there, all matte-black metal without a single visible window. Arliss steps inside and gestures us in, pressing the button to close the train's doors as he turns to Etu with a grin.

Etu nods and goes to the front of the train, toggling a series of controls, so the car starts to move along the track.

Arliss gives me a wry smile. "Normally, I fuck all the way to the security checkpoint, but the angst rolling off you is putting a damper on my sky-high libido. You need to calm yourselves. You're here to party, remember? Put that face on and wear it well." He glances over at Diana when he says that last part.

She bristles and snarls but says nothing else.

I'll be fine, she snaps into our family bond. Noire and I reach out to comfort her at the same time, his hand on her lower back and mine on her upper.

Our end of the train car falls silent, whereas Arliss' group behind us chatters away about the party and other residents they're excited to see.

Ire and a need to maim and kill hit me like they used to hit me in the maze. Predatory focus has me turning to Arliss' group with a low growl. This isn't a rescue mission to them. We're nothing but a bunch of irritating, somber tag-alongs. They can't possibly understand the cruelty Rama is capable of, the psychological warfare she delights in delivering.

They'll be lucky as fuck if they never find out.

CHAPTER THIRTY-THREE
RENZE

Jet hovers protectively near Diana, Achaia standing just behind him against the train car's wall. We're the only ones upright as the car moves, too on edge to sit. The train speeds through a pitch-black tunnel before shooting out into the sunlight, shooting around the edge of the city. The entire wall of the train car is floor-to-ceiling windows, visible only from the interior. From here, it is easy to see how the spires at the center of Paraiso look like flames, reflecting the buildings and foliage around them.

This city is a work of art, and I would admire the sheer creativity and tech involved if I were not on such high alert. My focus is divided between my mates and the Chosen One—I will protect them at all costs.

The train rounds a sharp turn as we leave the outer edge of Paraiso and dive into the heart of the sky island. I'm shocked anew at just how large it is. Who lives here, and why? For how long? Hundreds of skyscrapers reach for the sun as its heat warms my skin.

"Still a lizard?" Achaia jokes, stroking my forearm softly. Looking over to see her wearing another face is an otherworldly experience. I would know her heart and spirit anywhere, though. She is mine.

I grin and flip her, pressing her front against the train's windows. "Any new memories coming to you, sweet one?" I whisper into her ear.

Achaia sighs. "No." I read her bitter disappointment as her head falls against my chest, her neck bared to my hungry gaze. "Random flashes of color crowd my mind every few minutes. Maybe my brain is simply trying to sort through it all. I'm imagining a little man in there looking at an enormous pile of papers and trying to figure out how to organize them."

"It will come," I murmur against her skin, reveling in the feeling of being able to touch her back without being shocked. Today it is even further healed, the wounds merely faint lines that criss-cross her back.

We watch the city pass outside the train car. By all accounts, Paraiso appears to be a thriving metropolis full of shops and stores. There are even humans here walking their dogs, strolling along busy streets.

It is so normal that I can scarcely believe it. And the tech. There is tech everywhere, screens covered in ads, and people holding tablets and phones. It is as if we have been transported back seven years into our history to a time when tech was pervasive in its daily use.

We enter another long tunnel, and Arliss turns to our group, dark eyes lighting on mine. "We are here. Security checkpoint first. Say nothing until I give you the all-clear in our rooms."

I nod, looking over at Noire. The pack alpha is gazing at Achaia with a neutral expression on his face. And once again, I realize that despite Achaia being part of his pack through her connection with Jet, she is a puzzle piece to him—he wishes to figure out how to use her to achieve his goals.

It is the same as it was in the maze. Noire does only what he must to ensure his immediate family is safe. In his heart of hearts, he is loyal only to his brothers and his mate. Gods above, he is an asshole.

When the train stops, he leans in to whisper in Diana's ear. She nods once, lifting her head and straightening her shoulders.

"We are with you, Chosen One," I remind her.

Diana turns to me with a soft smile. "As always, and evermore," she responds. It brings a smile to my face as Ascelin looks over at me, tears filling her eyes. It is a saying Cashore used with the two of us, a sign of the bond between a vampiri king and his First Warriors. He is here with us, even now. I pray his spirit guides Diana to help us make the right decisions in this dangerous place.

Ascelin shoots me a meaningful look and swipes the tears away, gritting her jaw as she rearranges her features into a more neutral expression.

When the train doors open, no one is there, but Arliss strides out with purpose. We follow as a chattering, happy group until we reach a small, enclosed room. I hate it immediately because there is only one way out should things go awry.

A massive blond figure steps up and grins at Arliss, and Achaia freezes next to me. Gods, it is the alpha from the market who trailed us and sent the spiders. I would recognize that sneer anywhere. The jagged scar across his throat confirms my suspicions. I don't risk a look at Jet, but the tension rolling from him tells me he recognizes this male, too.

He speaks, his voice full of gravel as if he's just awoken. "Good to see you, Arliss. Tonight's celebration will be something to remember."

Diana notices him the moment he speaks, stiffening like a board as she walks next to me.

"Wouldn't miss it for the world, Dore," Arliss purrs.

Diana stops so abruptly that Etu runs into her and nearly bowls her over.

"Careful!" Etu quips happily, grabbing Diana by the elbow to hold her upright.

Sandwiched between Ascelin and me, Diana's chest rises and falls rapidly, her eyes locked onto the male.

Her brother. I read the surety of it in her bond with us. The male who tried to take Achaia *is* Dore. We assumed it could be, but Diana's horrified aura confirms it.

Her chest heaves as her emotions spiral from horror to heartbreak to longing. Ascelin and I read her distress, but she lifts her chin and looks away, although tears fill her eyes.

Easy, I send her the sentiment through our bond. *Easy, my queen.*

Diana does not respond, but our group is tense as the blond alpha waves Arliss and the others through. Dore steps up to Diana as a security guard begins to pat her down. Her brother grins as he looks over her unrecognizable figure. "My, my, you're a pretty thing," he murmurs, purring as Diana lets out an irritated laugh.

I sense she's dying to bark back at him but doesn't want to risk him hearing her voice, even though the disguise should distort it.

The guard finishes patting her down, and Dore waves her through as I resist the urge to pull her into my arms and remind her I'm here for her. Instead, I get the same pat down treatment. As we make it through security, Dore calls out. "Arliss. Rama would like to see you before tonight's celebration. Make sure you are not late. Tonight is a big deal for her."

"Of course," Arliss hums.

I can't help but find his choice of words ominous as we follow Arliss quietly through a long dark hall, stopping at a small bank of elevators.

Between Ascelin and I, Diana trembles visibly, fists balled by her side as we wait.

Arliss gives her a pointed look and smashes the button to call the elevator. Our group is silent, a clear contrast between Arliss' happy companions and our tense court. We need to relax more believably than this if we are to succeed in our mission.

The elevator doors open, and Noire ushers Diana in, pinning her to the back wall as he buries his teeth in her neck. From any bystander's perspective, it looks like he can't wait to get his hands on her, which is probably typical of Arliss' group. But I see this for what it is; she is about to lose her mind, and he is doing the only thing he can to bring her momentary peace—giving her his bite.

A ding announces our arrival at the top floor. When the doors open, Arliss grabs Noire and Diana and shoves them into the room. He holds one finger to his lips and reaches into his tunic pocket, retrieving three small orbs. When he tosses them into the air, they whiz around the room and attach themselves to the walls. Glowing red dots on their surface flash to a vibrant green, and Arliss turns to us. "You can lose your shit now," he calmly instructs Diana.

The trembling in her limbs intensifies before she lets out a horrible, gut-wrenching sob. And then she buries her face in Noire's chest as he purrs his heart out for her, holding her tight.

"I'm so sorry, mate," he whispers as her tears wet his clothing.

Arliss looks at me. "I take it you all know Dore?"

"We do," I confirm, not sharing any further detail.

Arliss stiffens. "Perhaps you will be a better distraction than I thought."

I resist the urge to snap at him as I would have in the maze, where violence was the answer to everything. Diana needs me.

Ascelin and I stand protectively around her as she sobs, finally falling to the floor in Noire's arms. Arliss' group dissipates into the huge, open space as Ascelin turns. I sense she wishes to sweep the rooms, so I urge her to do so. I will remain with the Chosen One for as long as she needs me.

Jet and Achaia hover at my side, Achaia's fingers wrapped through Jet's much larger ones as they bear witness to Diana's breakdown.

After a time, Ascelin returns, and when she does, she reaches down for Diana, holding out a pale hand. "It is time, my queen. Time to reclaim peace and safety for this continent and our pack. Time to reclaim our brother and your throne. Rise, Diana."

Diana turns to Ascelin and grips her hands, pulling her to a stand as I marvel again at her strength.

"Cashore was right to pick you," I say proudly. "Ascelin and I are honored to serve you, Chosen One."

Diana's muscles tremble as her eyes flash white and then back to their usual blue, despite the masking tech. "That bitch will pay," is all she says as she raises her chin and looks at us both with a vengeful expression full of rage.

CHAPTER THIRTY-FOUR
JET

Our pack bond is a flurry of angry condemnations by Noire and grief-stricken distress from Diana. On top of that, I had hoped when we got here, we'd be able to hear Ten in the bond, but it hasn't happened. My immediate worry is that it means he isn't here on Paraiso at all. But I have to shove that aside and continue considering our plan, changing it as we gain new information.

Diana is a hair's breadth from falling to pieces. She hasn't seen Dore since Rama slit his throat in front of her, tossing him on a trash heap when they turned sixteen.

It's not like we didn't know seeing him was a possibility—we surmised he was the alpha from the market. But we didn't know that with certainty until right now, and we thought we left him behind at the vampiri court.

Achaia steps forward, her forehead pressed to Diana's. They stand still for a moment, drawing strength from one another.

I look over at my brother, but I've never seen his face so cold, so calculated. Noire is hot-blooded but smart. His mind is already spinning with possibilities, as is mine.

Glancing at Diana, I catch her eye. "I presume you want to get Dore out if we can."

Arliss steps in. "Dore is a sadistic asshole. He's lost to you. Whatever he was as a younger male, there's nothing of that person left. The things I've seen him do would stop your heart in your chest."

Diana grits her teeth but gives me a look, switching to our family bond. *We've got to try.*

First step is to locate Ten. Dore will probably remain close to Rama, I counter.

Ten first, then Dore, Noire commands into our bond. *I'm sorry, mate, but we know Ten's state of mind. He came here as a prisoner, and he has an entire life ahead of him. Dore comes second.*

Diana doesn't outright agree or disagree with him, but we can sense she's torn.

Anything new with your powers, Diana? I'm curious about what else has changed since she and Noire completed their bond during her heat.

Arliss is wondering how to use us. I don't know if I'm just not strong enough in my powers to read more, or if he's well-versed at warding off mind-reading. Even with Cashore's help, I can't access Arliss' thoughts. Shit, he might even be aware that I'm trying.

None of us look over at the enigma of a male, but I sense his focus on us anyhow.

Our host chooses that moment to go meet Rama, an act which in and of itself is a red flag to me. I watch him go, my gaze narrowed on his broad back as he steps back into the waiting elevator. He sneers at me as the doors close.

"Let's get ready for tonight," I encourage my packmates. Diana nods, grabbing her bag and heading for one of the small bedroom alcoves. Noire gives me a warning look and follows her as I turn to Renze and Achaia with a sigh.

Achaia places her palm on my chest; her touch is a comforting, soothing balm for my broken, aching soul. "We'll find Tenebris," she promises as I place my hand over hers. Renze steps behind her, laying his chin on top of her head as he looks at me. But in his gaze, I see the same thing—a promise.

I wouldn't want to do this without them.

~

The city is practically abuzz with excitement as night falls. Standing on a balcony overlooking the flaming spires, I marvel again at how incredible Paraiso truly is, even if I don't enjoy being here.

I haven't seen this much technology in seven years, so watching the shops, billboards, and cell phones is oddly disconcerting, like turning the hands of time back to before Rama threw my brothers and me into the godsdamned maze.

A door behind me slides open, and where I expect one of my mates, Arliss joins me instead. He paces soundlessly across the broad balcony, leaning against the railing as he gazes out at the city.

"Beautiful, isn't it?" he muses, looking fondly at his creation.

"Don't fuck us over tonight," I counter, turning to look at the mysterious male. "I know you've got your own reasons for being here. We won't get in the way of that. We'll even help you if we can, but don't throw us under a bus."

Arliss grins. "Remember that at least one of our goals is the same, alpha."

"A little more direct help would be nice," I murmur, not looking away from his brilliant eyes.

"I cannot attack Rama myself," he reminds me.

"Then give us a chance to do it successfully, and we'll get your *friend* back."

Arliss laughs, looking back toward the plush apartment. "Noire is here for one thing, Jet—to kill Rama. If he's able to free your brother, he'll do that as well. A distant third is Diana's brother. My needs fall somewhere after that. I'm under no illusions Noire will choose to help me if it comes to it."

"I would, though," I remind him. "That's why Noire and I are a good team. He's the asshole, and I'm the brains."

Arliss laughs again and shakes his head. "My only promise is to stay out of your way if I can."

"I have a favor to ask of you," I push on, opting to show Arliss a bit of vulnerability. Based on what I know of him, I think he'll bite. "If we fail, get Tenebris out if you can. He's brilliant, and he grew up in the maze. He is the best of us, and he deserves more."

Arliss gives me a curious look. "Brilliant, you say?"

"Brilliant," I assure him. "He's a scholar and a student. He would have known what Achaia's tattoo was. He'd love Oasis."

Arliss gives me a long, assessing look before glancing to our left. The giant spire there is Rama's reaching high into the sky above everyone else's.

"If I can, I will," he agrees. "Is he good looking?"

"Liuvang, Arliss," I spit. "Are you ever *not* thinking about fucking?"

He laughs and shrugs as my mind wanders back to our hostess for the evening. Goddess, I cannot wait to kill that bitch.

~

Half an hour later, we're dressed in formal wear, going back down the elevators. It's hard to reconcile the party vibe of Arliss' crew with the predatory need snaking its way through my brain. I sense Noire and Renze are feeling the same way—this is like being in a maze where the marks don't even know they're being hunted. My alpha nature takes over as I focus on what I see around me.

We return to the private train, zipping into the heart of the city. I'm in awe of the bright lights and the general bustle of revelers headed into the center of Paraiso. I'll say one thing for Rama, she knows how to put on a party. Which is good for us because it means we're more likely to go unnoticed right under her nose.

I've never been on this side of Rama's parties. Anger tightens my chest as I think about the thousands of times I was the *entertainment* at parties like tonight's. All the terrible shit she had me do, things that scarred me. I hold back a growl as my mates step close, Achaia's hand on the small of my back.

My concentration is torn in two different directions now that we're here. I'm intensely driven to protect Diana as my alpha's mate. I'm also overwhelmed with the instinct to keep Renze and Achaia safe. The undercurrent simmering beneath that is a vicious need to rip Rama's head from her shoulders and free us from her psychotic rule. All of that occupies my mind until the train car comes to a stop, and we exit into the glittering night.

I settle into a familiar cadence, leading our group as Noire brings up the rear, our mates in the middle. Renze and Ascelin are on either side of Achaia and Diana, not that the women are wilting wallflowers at *all*. But in a fight, I'd rather stick to the formation we know.

Arliss' group spreads out as we look ahead to a giant gothic building. It almost looks like a cathedral, horribly reminiscent of the eerie vibe of the maze. Flashes of fucking a man at death's door assault me, but I force them aside, wishing suddenly that I had uppers handy. They'd help me separate my past from what's happening right now.

No.

I don't need them. I need to focus, so I grit my teeth and remain vigilant.

Arliss leads our group up a concrete walkway to the building's front. Beautifully vibrant gardens spill onto the path at every turn as if Rama took my home province and transplanted it up here in the sky. Lights at the building's base cast their glow upward, highlighting the gothic edifice. It would be striking if every cell of my body wasn't so focused on the danger we're in.

Arliss' group runs and plays, thrilled to be at a party. It's a stark contrast to the rest of us, silent and on edge as we follow them.

We need to ease up, I bark at Noire through our bond. *We stand out like this, so different from Arliss' crew.*

Noire responds with a growl but pulls Diana into his arms and whispers in her ear as he slides a hand down her open-backed dress to cup her ass. She grips his arm, threading her fingers through his other hand as she leans into his attention.

Better, I encourage him, grabbing Achaia's hand as Renze stays the course to my left. Through my bond with Achaia and Renze, I sense their worried focus. Achaia, in particular, is lost in thought.

Huge double doors are wide open, and we sail through with the rest of the partygoers. Inside, two giant horse statues guard a short hallway. My whole group freezes at seeing them up close—they're exact replicas of the statues from the maze. They're a work of engineering that Diana's father created to keep her safe if she ever landed herself in the maze's halls, and now Rama has replicated them here.

Fuck, oh fuck. What are these programmed to do, I wonder?

Diana recovers the quickest, sailing past the horses as if she doesn't have a care in the world. The hallway opens into an enormous square room, open walkways lining each side up three stories, revelers looking down from above. The very back wall is an alcove, not unlike the one Renze first fucked Achaia in.

Memories hit me in rapid succession. Flying over a crowd while my blood rained down on the rich pricks below. Screwing more people than I could even count. Letting Rama's minions do whatever they wanted to my cock. Shaking my head, I crush those memories away. They won't serve me here, and I wish they'd fuck off.

"Arliss!" A woman's voice rings through the dark room, and we turn as one to face her. The crowd parts and a striking older omega slides through the crush of people, arms extended wide. "I always forget how well you clean up, old friend."

Rama.

It's Rama.

Standing not five feet from me. She looks exactly like the day I met her in Siargao, that long sheet of black hair slung over one shoulder. Dark eyes are focused on Arliss, who leans in and kisses Rama on both cheeks as she steps back, shadowed eyes assessing his group.

She winks. "Gorgeous new playmates, Arliss," she murmurs, giving us all a once-over. She's dressed in a long-sleeved, black silk dress, puddles of fabric falling around her feet. It cuts low in the front, her long pitch-black hair pulled over one shoulder, the swell of her breasts easily visible from the neckline.

Seeing her like that brings every horrible memory back to the surface, and I clench my fists tight to avoid launching myself at her right now. I won't do that yet; I can't, not without finding Tenebris first. Because if he's not here, she's got him hidden somewhere, and I need her alive to find out.

We're spared awkward pleasantries when Etu springs forward, bowing in front of Rama. "You look ravishing, mistress. A birdie told me you're making an announcement tonight. Is it true?"

His flattery pulls her attention away from us, but I don't miss the devious way she smiles as she strokes black nails down Etu's happy face.

"Indeed, my curious friend. Indeed I am."

CHAPTER THIRTY-FIVE
ACHAIA

I'm losing my godsdamned mind. The intensity of this party overwhelms me, and the woman who tortured Renze and Jet stands right in front of me, stroking Etu's face while she looks at him like a lion eyes its prey.

Her devious eyes flit to mine, but she bypasses me quickly before scanning the rest of our group with a haughty smile.

A memory hits me so hard that my knees buckle, and I'm forced to grab onto Diana's hand. Not wanting to give us away, I lean into her ear and nip at the lobe, trying to appear seductive like every other partygoer. I pray Diana understands what I'm doing, and thankfully she does, cocking her head to the side to give me better access.

I sense Rama's eyes on me before I hear the click of her heels departing, a vision slamming into me so hard I nearly scream.

Rama looks down at me with a cruel smile. "How does your magic work, my pretty? I'm going to pick every inch of you apart until I figure it out."

I strike at her, but my entire body is bound. I can't move an inch.

"It's useless to struggle," Rama laughs, nodding at someone I can't see because I can't move my head. "You've been here for years; haven't you learned not to try? The only thing ahead of you is pain." She laughs joyously, and then something stabs into my leg, opening my skin from my hip all the way down to my foot.

Merciful blackness overtakes me as my skin is flayed from my body.

With a jolt, I let go of Diana's hand, my breath coming in rapid, light pants as she leans closer to me. Jet and Renze hover at my side, peppering me with question after question.

"Silence," I hiss, needing a moment. What was that? A memory? Oh gods, it fucking was. Whoever and whatever I am, Rama is a key to my past. I look at Diana, who grabs my hand again and squeezes it. In her eyes, I see recognition and acceptance. Rama took something from both of us; she hurt both of us, and we have no time to unravel this right now.

"We are still here," Diana whispers into my ear, her lips soft against my too-cold skin.

"Let's go," I bark at Noire, who's watching the whole exchange with interest. He's still wondering if I'm a weapon, but if anything, that memory has me wondering if I'm just another victim—someone used up and spat out by the psychopathic madwoman who rules Lombornei with an iron fist.

Arliss turns to his retinue. "You know the drill, my lovelies. Fan out, enjoy yourselves. I will see you when I see you." Giggles and titters echo as his crew splits and disappears into the crowd. He turns to Noire with a meaningful look. "Let's go."

Silently, we follow Arliss through the crowd, which mills around expectantly. Drinks flow, and somewhere, the smell of fried pork and ginger wafts through the air. But all I can concentrate on is the warmth of Diana's hand as she holds mine.

We pass through the large room and into a corridor. Arliss leads us through hall after hall before stopping in front of a door and handing Noire a key card. "Take this down two levels. You'll find the cells there. There aren't many—remember this place is for parties. If you do not find him there, he is not on Paraiso."

Without another word, Arliss disappears into the darkness. Noire watches him go with a mistrustful, suspicious expression but scans the keycard as Jet, Renze, and Ascelin stand guard over our small group. An elevator opens behind us as Ascelin turns to Diana. "I will remain here with Renze in case this is a trap." Her white eyes move to Noire, who nods in agreement.

We step into the elevator, and I resist the urge to slump against Jet, instead steeling myself up against the railing. Mirrors line the elevator, and even though I wear a mask, I worry I look like a woman who's falling apart.

The elevator doors ping open, and we step into a pale blue, sterile hallway. Cells with bar fronts line one side of it, and that's all there is. Jet and Noire keep Diana and me between them, moving from one end of the hallway to the other. I sense Jet's distress before he speaks aloud. "Every fucking cell is empty. He's not here, and I can't godsdamned hear him. Fuck!" His roar of anguish cuts my soul before another memory slams into the forefront of my brain.

I slide down the wall to the floor as tears spill from my eyes.

A dozen warriors are lined up in front of me, their wrists and necks chained together. I stand in front of them as Rama's guards hold spears to the backs of their heads. Rama appears to my right, although I can't fully see her because my own neck is collared by something so large and solid that I cannot move.

She laughs once, and then I hear the sick thud of a knife sinking into flesh. There's a desperate gurgle and a high-pitched hiss, and my warriors scream as one. They flail against their bindings, but we are helpless against her.

"I gave you a chance." Rama smiles at me, shrugging her shoulders. "You could have avoided this, but you chose to fight." She steps to the next male, slicing her black claws across his throat as blue blood spurts from the wound. I let out an earsplitting shriek, but she just laughs again.

"Oh, we neutralized that particular magic when we bound you. Your scream will never again level a city."

In the hallway, Diana and Jet try to pull me upright as I struggle to understand.

"If she's going nuts, we'll have to leave her," Noire snaps. Jet bellows as Diana turns to her mate with a glare.

"She's remembering, Noire. Isn't it obvious?"

He growls as he shoves Jet away from him and stalks closer to me. "She's going to get us fucking killed."

Diana stands in front of me, so all I can see is the backs of her legs as Noire presses her, and thereby me, into the wall. Sound is muffled as he snarls something in her ear, but I manage to slide out from behind her, reaching a hand up for help.

It's Noire who pulls me upright, his teeth snapping in my face. Jet collars his brother around the neck, his claws at Noire's throat as I level them both with my most confident look. "I leveled a city with magic, Noire. I hurt Rama somehow. I don't know how or when I did it, but she had me imprisoned for it. In some way, I was a danger to her."

Noire's evil scowl morphs into a maniacal grin as he turns to his brother. "I told you she was a weapon."

"Get your fucking hands off her," snarls Jet, shoving Noire away from me.

"I'm alright, Jet," I reassure him as Noire shrugs, still eyeing me like I'm the next greatest chance to kill Rama. Maybe I am, maybe I'm not. But I straighten my spine and remind myself we came here for Tenebris, and whatever I do, I need to focus on that. I can fall to pieces later.

Diana hisses to get our attention, glancing at the otherwise empty hall. "Ten's not here. We need to reconvene upstairs and move on to the next phase of our plan."

We manage to make it back to the main floor, and Renze pulls me close to him immediately, stroking my hair from my face. *I'm here, atiri,* he whispers into our bond. This whole situation is too fraught with peril for me to return the sentiment. I'm focused purely on survival at this point, although my mate reads every emotion like a book.

Noire leads us back into the main room. This part of our plan was simple: find Ten, then kill Rama. If we didn't find Ten, we would capture Rama and find out where she put him.

Knowing we're about to try plan B has my senses heightened. The smell of bodies overwhelms everything else. But there's also champagne and pork belly and noise after too-loud noise. My mind is fracturing, and I desperately do not want to fall apart here. I refuse to be the weak link in our chain.

When I pictured my memories coming back, I didn't imagine it would be so painfully violent and awful.

The packed room falls silent as Rama walks onto the staged alcove at the front of the room.

She stalks from one end of the stage to the other, and it's easy to see she's an omega like Diana. She slinks in that same predatory way the other shifters do. Black eyes glitter with malice as she eyes the crowd.

After a drawn-out, tense moment, she speaks. "Tonight's party is special to me because I've been keeping a secret." The tension in my group is palpable as Rama looks to her left, blood-red lips parting into a seductive smile.

An enormous figure steps out from behind dark curtains, stalking across the stage with his eyes on Rama as Diana gasps next to me, uttering a single word. "Tenebris."

He's massive and elegant, even larger than Jet and Noire. Dark chocolate waves are slicked back, falling smoothly over his ears. Eyes the color of whiskey flash as he looks at Rama. He looks like Jet, but different still. I had imagined a younger brother, someone more childlike and innocent. But this? This is a grown-ass man. And he's looking at Rama like she's the water he needs to slake his thirst.

In front of me, Jet stiffens, hands balling into fists as his muscles begin to quiver in anger. "Not Ten, not Ten, not Ten," he murmurs over and over again. I reach out and place my hand on his back, but he gives no indication that he's noticed. Oh, fuck.

I glance back at the stage as horrible realization sinks in. Tenebris is dressed in a black tuxedo, a white shirt open to reveal his tan chest. He crosses the stage, not taking his striking eyes off Rama, and when he gets to her, he pulls her into his arms and wraps a fist in her hair, tugging her head back to nip a path up her neck. It's like he's completely oblivious to the room full of revelers all watching the show.

Oh, my fucking gods. In front of me, Jet and Noire are frozen in disbelief. Noire's chest rises and falls, and Jet can't tear his eyes from the stage, still mumbling under his breath.

On the stage, Tenebris tilts Rama's chin and kisses her deeply. Hoots and catcalls echo in the otherwise quiet room, and when they part, she laughs. The way she looks up at Ten is the look of a woman in love.

Our group is frozen as Rama smiles, threading her fingers through Ten's hand. He never takes his eyes off her, though, smiling as she addresses the crowd again. "This is my mate, Tenebris. Tonight, we celebr—"

I never hear another word because in front of me, Noire and Jet shift into their wolves and take off. They sprint toward the stage, which shimmers slightly.

"No!" screams Diana as the room descends into chaos and the screaming starts.

CHAPTER THIRTY-SIX
RENZE

Of all the things I could have expected to happen tonight, this revelation was not one of them. The plan was always to draw Rama away from the larger crowd, but seeing Tenebris kissing her ripped that plan into tiny pieces.

Diana shifts and sprints for Noire, and Ascelin slips after her as partygoers scream and flee the wolves, the room clearing as people scramble to escape. I grip Achaia's wrist because we decided if it came down to a moment like this, and any of our group needed to flee in order to give us a chance to come back and help the rest, that's what we'd do. And this is that moment.

The wolves reach the stage, but they hit a forcefield just like the one Rama hid behind when we faced off on the maze island.

Jet and Noire bounce off it before throwing themselves at it again, clawing and scratching as their brother pulls Rama protectively behind his muscular body. It is obvious he doesn't even recognize them, despite their shift forms. Diana and Ascelin try to drag them backward. It took dozens of horse statues to take the force field down the last time we met Rama. Three wolves and a vampiri First Warrior are not enough. We have already lost this godsdamned fight.

This is heading downhill so quickly that I know my only chance at saving them is to drag Achaia away and figure out a backup plan. Ascelin screams at me to run through our bond, knowing that's the only way we've got any chance. She claws at Diana, trying to pull her from Jet and Noire, who snarl as they back away from the force field, eyeing Rama through it.

There's an evil, unsurprised smile on the omega's face, Tenebris a protective wall by her side as he scowls furiously at his brothers.

Before I can even move, guards step out from the sides of the room and shoot at the wolves and Ascelin. Bullets pepper their skin as they turn into the room and begin to tear through the crowd. Rama laughs on stage as bullet after bullet sinks into the wolves and my partner. Achaia opens her mouth to scream, but I clamp a hand over it.

"We have to escape to have a chance at saving them," I hiss into her ear.

Achaia moans in terror as I drag her backward toward the nearest exit. A guard steps in front of us with a cruel grin as I hear a metallic clicking sound behind us. Gripping Achaia's hand tightly, I slip us across the room, but guards now stand at every exit. The crowd still runs in every direction, pressing up against the walls, but when I turn to look, all three wolves and Ascelin are down. The guards clamp metallic collars around their necks as the crowd falls silent, turning to see if the attack is over.

The shimmer in front of the stage droops, and Rama descends from the stage into the room with Tenebris as a protective shadow at her side. She laughs as she points to metal collars now clamped around Jet, Noire, and Diana's necks. Ascelin lies bloody on the floor beside Diana as guards shove Achaia and me toward the group.

Rama looks in my direction, black eyes focused on me as pain lances my side. Next to me, Achaia yells as the guards shock us with something. Pain radiates out from my brain as I reach for my mate.

We fall to the ground in agony as a zap under my ear indicates Arliss' tech is failing. Moments later, I look over to see Achaia's tan skin and auburn hair, sea-green eyes filled with tears behind her elegant mask. A guard claps a collar around my neck as I scratch and try to slip, but a gun is pressed to my forehead.

"What a joyous reunion," Rama purrs. "All my maze favorites are back in one place. By the way"—she points at the wolves—"the spikes inside those collars will continue to grow longer. If you don't shift into human form, you'll be impaled shortly. Your choice."

If Tenebris is shocked at her mistreatment of his pack, he says nothing while his focus is entirely on her. When she moves again, he follows her like a gigantic shadow.

Ascelin and the wolves are hit with the same electricity we were, and in moments, they're in regular form too. There's blood, so much blood, and even though we monsters heal fast, I don't know if they can this time. Guards drag their bodies closer together, clipping the collars to a long pole, so they're spread along it at regular intervals.

"Not him," Rama smiles, pointing at Jet, who snarls as he struggles to fight the collar.

Dozens of guards stand with guns and spears, ready to kill if they make a move.

Rama smiles wickedly as Achaia and I are shoved to the ground in front of our pack. Her glittering eyes fall to Noire as she addresses him. "I knew you wouldn't pass up an opportunity to come here, not since I took Tenebris. You may remember when you escaped the maze, and I shared how I see alpha mate bonds? Imagine my surprise when I realized Tenebris belongs to me. I had to take him, of course. Plus, the horses. That tech is a piece of genius."

Noire throws himself at Rama, but Tenebris headbutts him back, delivering a swift kick to his brother's gut as Rama laughs, dark eyes flitting to Diana. "Your father truly was a visionary ahead of his time. It was a shame to put him down the way I did, but he fought me at every possible turn. I couldn't stand for it."

Diana snarls and surges forward, clawing at Rama's face, but the movement drags Noire onto the ground next to her, falling awkwardly as the pole knocks them off balance.

Rama snaps her fingers, and a guard drags a chair in front of her. A second male grips Jet's neck and tosses him into the chair, Rama stepping to his side as Jet's eyes narrow at her. Guards surround the chair and yank his arms behind him, tying them to the chair's back as he scrambles and fights, snarling and snapping his teeth. He's no match for the numerous burly guards who make short work of binding him tightly, not with so many wounds peppering his body and the number of them.

My mind spins, trying to think of any possible way out of this scenario. I cannot fight my way out of this. *Think, vampiri,* I encourage myself. *Read what you can in the room. Use what you can.*

The sounds of a tussle reach my ears, and new guards drag Arliss in, collared and chained to a woman who could be the smaller, more feminine mirror image of him.

Rama laughs and snaps her fingers. "On your knees, Elizabet." The new woman scrambles, but guards force her down at Jet's feet. Jet's angry eyes flick to the woman and then back up to Rama.

"No," he utters, his voice full of shock and disbelief as a guard comes forward with a glass full of purple liquid.

The godsdamned uppers from the maze. She's going to put him back on them. Achaia and I scream for him at the same time, but pain blooms at the back of my head when a guard butts me with his gun.

Jet struggles, but the guards force his mouth open, pouring the contents of the glass down his throat as he bellows and fights tooth and nail, arching against the bindings but unable to escape them. Diana and Noire roar in anger, but there's nothing any of us can do as Jet's big chest heaves, pupils blowing immediately wide as he looks at Achaia and me.

Our bond is shredded with varied emotions, but Jet's run too fast to even process. He's already high as a kite, falling into his memories as Rama kicks Elizabet's foot. "Suck him off, Elizabet."

"What? No!" the woman shouts.

Rama smiles and slides her dress open, revealing a wicked dagger strapped to her thigh. She pulls it out and crosses to Arliss, stabbing him in the stomach as Arliss bellows and Elizabet screams.

"Oh, gods! No! Stop! I'll do anything, don't hurt him."

Rama doesn't bother to respond but gestures to Jet's lap, with blood still dripping from her knife.

"Ten, do something!" Diana shouts. But if he hears her, he ignores it, not even looking over at her plea.

Next to me, Achaia trembles as she watches Jet. His head lolls back, saliva dripping from his fangs as he snarls slowly.

The woman Rama called Elizabet looks up at her with a pleading expression. "Don't make me do this, please."

Rama grins. "Oh, this isn't for you, although I'll deal with you later. This is for Jet. He loves to put on a show, don't you?" Rama's dark eyes flick to Jet, who levels her with a glare of pure hatred. She laughs and stalks to Jet's side, and even though she leans into his ear, she says the words loud enough for us to hear. "I'm going to force her to blow you, and then I'm going to televise that to every screen on Lombornei. And the entire godsdamned continent will know that there is no escaping me. That it's useless to even try. Once that's done, I'll put you back in the fucking maze and watch as the remaining monsters tear you to shreds."

Jet doesn't look at her, he doesn't stiffen or respond, and I know the uppers are battering his system with endorphins. He had to be on them to perform all those years in the maze.

My heart beats rapidly in my chest as I watch the woman I presume is Arliss' sister open Jet's pants with trembling hands. She looks up at Rama once, but when Rama crosses to Arliss again, Elizabet moves with urgency, drawing Jet's cock out.

He's already hard, already performing like he did in the maze. He's lost to our past, to the terror he's tried so hard to overcome. "Don't touch him!" I snap as I lurch forward, desperate to get to him, but all it does is drag Achaia and me to the ground just behind Elizabet. Jet's eyes find mine, but there's no recognition there. He's gone.

Tears fall from the dark-skinned woman onto Jet's lap as she opens her mouth and sucks gently at his cock. A grunt leaves his lips as his eyes move to Achaia.

Jet, she moans into our bond. *Eyes on me, atiri. Focus on me.*

Rama wraps her fingers in Elizabet's black hair and shoves her face hard into Jet's crotch. "Suck harder, Elizabet. Let this be a reminder that your choices were never yours to make. If you wish to get to your brother and fix the damage I inflicted on his lungs, suck better."

Noire and Diana have recovered enough to try to scramble for Jet, but the spiky collars at their throat keep them from moving far. Blood already drips down both of their necks. Ascelin's eyes meet mine, and for the first time since she and I partnered as warriors, I read defeat in her emotion. Rama was many steps ahead of us. We have tried and failed. We were never going to succeed at this.

Long, terrible minutes pass as Elizabet works her mouth over Jet's cock. I ache to rip her from him, to pull him to my chest. Rama is taking his old wounds and flaying them open, forcing him back into his worst nightmares.

Achaia murmurs over and over to him through our bond, we both do, but he doesn't respond or even acknowledge us. He is lost to us, lost to Rama's torture.

"Come on, Jet," Rama croons in a sing-song tone. "It was always so easy to get you off. Everything turns you on, isn't that right? You're nothing more than an alpha whore." She presses the tip of her knife to his stomach, right where her guards stabbed him that horrible night.

Jet's pained grunting morphs into desperate panting as he squints his eyes tightly shut and explodes all over Elizabet's face, his hips rocking as his teeth gnash. Rama watches the entire thing with a sinister smile, and Tenebris an unmovable wall behind her.

Jet, I murmur into our bond. *I am here, atiri. I am here, my heart.*

But he doesn't respond, lost as he is to pain and uppers and pleasure.

When Jet's orgasm fades, Rama snaps her fingers again, and the guards snap Elizabet to the pole holding Arliss and me. Achaia stands tall in front of me, her eyes never leaving Jet, even as she tries to soothe him through the bond created by my bite.

Jet's eyes remain closed, the bond dim and silent. He is lost to us, lost to the memory of a madwoman's control. On the floor, Diana and Noire struggle, trying desperately to right themselves and unable to do so.

A dark figure approaches and when I look up, it's Diana's brother, Dore.

"Dore!" Diana screams. "Help us!"

His eye twitches at the corner, but even though Diana looks like herself again, he doesn't seem to recognize her—it's Achaia he's focused on.

"Hello again, princess," he growls before hauling a large bucket from behind his back. I smell water, and salt. He tosses the contents at Achaia, briny seawater splashing her right in the face, wetting her clothes so they cling to her generous curves.

Hello again, princess? Ice shoots through my veins, wondering what he means. He is speaking as if he knows her…

Achaia hisses in anger as I leap for her, dragging Elizabet and Arliss to the ground as I struggle toward my mate.

Dore looks at us with a smirk as Achaia starts coughing and sputtering, wiping the salty water from her eyes.

A rumbling fills the room, which is frozen as the quiet crowd parts, two soldiers pushing a giant glass box filled with water toward us.

Achaia falls to the ground, writhing as she grits her teeth in agony. Our bond is filled with her pain, and I double over as I live it through her emotions. Gods, the fucking pain. Daggers slice her, and she transfers all of that to Jet and me as I flail against the pole.

Diana screams my name over and over again. Jet remains frozen in his chair, his body jerking against the pain.

"If you would, my love," Rama purrs to Tenebris, patting him on the chest. The massive alpha crosses the room to Achaia as her dress splits down the front, her body arching as she screams. I flop onto my belly and dig my claws into the floor, trying to drag myself to her, but I can't haul both Elizabet and Arliss' heavy weights. Guards surround us, ready to shoot.

Tenebris reaches down and pulls Achaia into his arms, and the pain is so all-encompassing that I scream when she does. He stalks to the giant tank and steps up onto its side, tossing her in as I yell for him to stop. She snatches at his arms as he shakes her off, and then she claws at the glass as I try with every ounce of my power to drag myself to her.

Achaia's face is a contorted mask of rage and pain, and although Noire and Diana struggle behind me, we're helpless against the collars and a room full of guards with guns. I watch Achaia choke and gasp, inhaling water into her lungs. She's fucking drowning, and I can't do a single godsdamned thing about it.

I bellow and jerk at the collar, but a guard presses a gun to my head. "Be still," he snarls. I don't care. Jet is broken, and Achaia is dying before my very eyes. Hers widen, and she stills as the water fills her lungs fully, bubbles traveling a path from her mouth up to the top of the water.

Tears stream down my face. She can't be ripped from me like this. There has to be more—more time, more connection, more love.

In the tank, Achaia's dress slips off her shoulders and falls away, and her body sinks slowly toward the bottom of the box, her auburn hair waving as her last breaths leave her. A moment passes as she puts her hand sluggishly up to the glass. Pale green eyes flick to Jet, full of heartbreak before she meets my gaze again.

Love fills our bond for a brief, bright moment before her eyes close.

I roar as her body drops and touches the bottom of the tank, head lolling to the side. One last bubble exits her mouth and trails upward.

But then, a shimmer of blue dashes across her skin, there and gone so quickly that I am not even sure what I saw. It happens again and again as I blink my eyes, trying desperately to understand.

In a flash of blinding color, blue and green scales coat Achaia's skin, her body morphing and shimmering. I am so shocked by what I see that I cannot even focus on the danger around me, not on Jet's silence or Noire's seething rage. I cannot even focus on the gun still pressed to my temple as I surge forward toward my mate.

Achaia's eyes flash open, larger than before and now a brilliant, vibrant blue. Her nose flattens as her ears lengthen into long, sharp points. Fluttering, iridescent gills form a fan behind both ears. Spiky growths emerge out of her hair as it transforms from auburn to every possible shade of cerulean, long enough to curl around her waist. She screams as the spikes rise up out of her skin, but when they stop, they form a white crown filled with pearls on top of her head.

Lengthy legs cross and shimmer, and where she once had feet, long, elegant fins form.

She's a godsdamned mermaid. A real-life mermaid. Just like the mermaids at Arliss' but not bedraggled and desperate.

She's stunning. She's *alive*. An overwhelming need to go to her has me straining at the collar again, despite the gun to my head. Achaia's iridescent eyes flick to mine, and she puts a hand up on the glass. Where before she had shorter, blunt fingers, they're now long and spindly with sharp, blue claws.

"You were right," Rama murmurs to Dore with a triumphant look. "She removed the tattoo somehow. I owe you twenty."

"Told ya she would." Dore grins, sucking at his teeth.

Hearing that Rama would have thrown Achaia into the water, not knowing if she'd transition, has me ready to pull Paraiso apart brick by brick. I want to scream that she could have drowned right in front of me. But this is

Rama, and she cares about nothing other than inflicting pain and psychological distress.

Inside the tank, Achaia lets out a shriek I can scarcely believe comes from her. It's high-pitched but deeply resonant at the same time. I clap my hands over my sensitive ears as every glass in the room shatters, the remaining crowd shrieking in surprise. Dark claws now tip Achaia's fingers, and she digs them into the glass of the tank as she screams again.

The gills behind her ears flare, her crown shining as her skin takes on an iridescent hue. Our group looks shell-shocked, but Rama simply knocks on the glass with her knuckles, grinning at my mate. "Mermaid proof. You see, when you would not grant me access to the power of your city, I had to figure out a way to take you and keep you under my control. I learned a lot in those early days about the power of a mermaid queen's scream. You'll find your crown is missing a few pearls, my sweet. Suffice to say, this is one prison you will *never* find your way out of."

Achaia glares daggers at Rama before looking over at me.

I will get you out of there, I promise her into our bond, but just like with Jet, it's now silent and empty.

CHAPTER THIRTY-SEVEN
ACHAIA

The pain is so overwhelming that I don't know where I stop and where the hurt begins. I'm reduced to throbbing, slicing, unendurable agony, gasping for breath underwater. Except that I'm breathing as if I've been doing it my whole life. I can't remember my entire life yet, but it's flashing back in surging waves of remembrance.

Underlying the agony is a deep well of terror for my mates, for my pack. We walked right into Rama's trap, and when I think about it, how could this have ever gone any other way? She's been planning this since they escaped. We just hadn't sorted all the pieces out…

Flashes of light and color shoot through my mind as I struggle around a tidal wave of information. The box I'm in starts moving, but no matter how many times I shriek and claw at the glass, it doesn't shatter. My scream should be able to level this entire godsdamned city, but when I reach up to my crown, Rama's right. Half the pearls are gone; rough indents are my only reminder of where they should be.

"Party's over!" Dore shouts, waving a gun in the air as the guards part for the partygoers to leave. They flood out of the giant ballroom as guards yank my pack upright. Jet stares blankly ahead, and Renze can't rip his eyes from my face.

My powerful, strong mates are in danger. Rama is—yet again—trying to steal the happiness from us all. I can't allow it. I've got to get us the fuck out of here, because the man we came to save? He doesn't want it. In fact, he doesn't even recognize his own family. Now all I can focus on is getting us clear of this place.

One of the guards headbutts Renze, who snarls and spits venom at the man. The asshole falls screaming to the ground as I bang at the tank's walls, needing to get to Renze. Guards descend on my mate, shocking him with long, pointed sticks until he falls, dragging Arliss and Elizabet down with him. Elizabet screams when the guards yank the pole they're attached to upright, forcing them to their feet.

Just do what you have to, I urge my mates through the bond I can no longer feel. *Do what we must to survive. Look for any opening.*

My mates walk, their hands bound as the group moves at gunpoint out the back of the building.

Flashes of movement begin to intertwine with an array of colors as I sink to the floor of the box, back into the corner, my eyes squeezed tightly shut around sudden, searing pain.

The sea floor.

A kingdom.

Scales of every imaginable color.

I remember sitting on my throne, watching my people celebrate something momentous.

And then I remember being called to the surface to meet Rama. It comes back to me like a punch to the gut. How she wanted access to my city's magical core to power a floating island called Paraiso. How she was willing to give me riches beyond imagining if she could use our core to recharge her home. She didn't know that merfolk have no use for the riches of the land people. Her wealth meant nothing to me. But denying her the core cost me everything—the city, my armies, and my people.

She accepted my refusal but sent an army from another kingdom, arming them with superior technology. Rama decimated my warriors in a day and took my city for herself, abusing its power as she killed, maimed, and kidnapped. She massacred everyone who couldn't flee in time.

All of my memories flood back in minutes. After my capture, she tested and tortured me for four long years before selling me, broken, to traders. I remember how she asked a witch to put the prisoner spell on my back so I wouldn't remember where I came from or who I was. I remember her last words to me.

"I don't need to do any of this to you, Queen. I'm doing it simply because I want to, and one day, when we meet again? It will be glorious to watch you relive these horrors a second time."

I snarl as I watch Rama walk gracefully at the head of our group, through screen-filled halls and into an unlit tunnel. When the tunnel moves, it becomes apparent we're actually on a large ship of some kind, buried in its belly. My mates and my pack don't fight, but when I watch them, I know Renze, at least, is calculating the right moment to do so. We don't have the upper hand, but maybe something will change.

For hours, we fly. We fly for so long that the sun begins to come up again, blazing hot through the windows as it heats the saltwater tank I'm trapped in. And the whole time, I remember. I remember my entire life—my happy childhood, my ascension to queen, the natural death of my father, the king, and then that fateful day Rama came calling for me. My emotions take me on a ride from misery to distress to anger and back again.

Renewed movement drags me back to the present, and I look around for something, anything that could aid us in escaping.

Elizabet is allowed out of her collar long enough to put a compress on Arliss' chest, but his breath is short and stilted. He's suffering from a lung injury that probably requires surgery. Even allowing her to tend to him is a way for Rama to remind us she owns us now. There is nothing Elizabet can do to help Arliss. He will die a slow and very painful death without medical assistance. Even monsters can only heal to a point.

Guards surround our group in the belly of the ship. There is nothing we can do, not a single fucking thing, to help ourselves out of this situation.

When we finally come to a stop, I feel the ship settle onto the ground, and the back wall becomes a door, sliding open like a gangplank. My tank begins to move, propelled along a track as my pack is dragged upright by the long poles linking their collars together. We're shoved out of the dark ship and out into the sun, although I have to blink my eyes rapidly to understand what I'm seeing.

Oasis.

We're back at the Oasis. Except now, black smoke billows into the sky above it, and the front doors have a giant hole blown through their center. Someone was here before us, attacking Arliss' beautiful home.

Arliss stands with a pained hiss, his eyes intensely focused on Rama as she emerges from the depths of the ship with a yawn. "What have you done?" he snarls.

Rama turns to him with a grin as soldiers surround him. "Our partnership has outlived its course, Arliss. You were willing to betray me to get Elizabet back, so it's only fitting we part ways. I'm here for your tech. And I'm here because you aligned with my enemies and brought them to my home, hoping they'd hurt me. I'm here to hurt you."

Tenebris stands silently behind his mate, his eyes on her as his hand rests on her back. I can't reconcile this male with the stories Jet, Diana, and even Renze have shared. They told me he was the kindest of the Ayala brothers, the scholar, the one who carried the vampiri younglings out of the maze and comforted them when they were afraid. This is the alpha who purrs for children because he adores them, because he's good and kind.

I can't see how this male and that one could possibly be the same.

Jet looks over at me, and when our eyes meet, I want to scream as a flash of recognition passes through them. He's coming off the uppers and seeing me in my true form for the first time. *I need you*, atiri, I push into the dark bond. Jet blinks as if confused and looks away.

Think, Achaia, I urge myself, despite the memories that continue to rage in my mind. Scratching at the glass, I roar in anger, willing my scream to work on the glass. It shakes and creaks, but holds fast.

At the noise, Rama turns to me. "Oh, don't worry, sweet queen. There's a little something here for you, too; a reminder of how you will never rule again, simply because that is my wish."

Dread sinks like a rock deep into my belly as I scratch harder.

I'm too sick to my stomach to come up with a retort. Soldiers dressed in dark garb pile out of the hole in the front gates as Arliss starts to bellow, straining against black chains, his breath a pained wheeze.

The soldiers part, dragging all the people we met when we first came to Oasis behind them. The woman who gave us the first aid kit and the men we saw Arliss fucking on the dining room table. Every single one of them. From another section of the ship, guards drag Etu and the others who came with us to Paraiso, screaming down the gangplank and toward Oasis.

Etu sobs as he reaches for Arliss, trying desperately to work his way out of the grip of the guards. But he's just as helpless to escape as we are.

Below the bridge, mermaids roil the waters, claw-tipped hands grabbing at the soldiers' boots. They're kicked away, but when the first of Arliss' females is dumped, shrieking, into the water, it turns red as the mermaids hiss with excitement.

The vampiri and shifters are still chained by collars to long poles, and while they strain against their bonds, they can barely move without impaling themselves. Still, Jet and Renze both snarl and struggle as Arliss drags himself toward the front gates of Oasis, screaming for his people.

I claw desperately at the top of my tank, working my fingers into the metal as I scream, over and over. But my scream isn't enough to do anything but earn me curious looks from the mermaids as their eager maws open each time a new person is thrown into their waters.

Arliss never stops bellowing as the soldiers dump every person in his compound into the water, screaming, pleading for their lives. The waters run red with blood and offal as the mermaids shred everyone. Arms and legs are tossed from the waters up onto the bridge and immediately snatched by hands from the other side. The bridge itself is covered in mermaids, but I don't recognize them. These aren't my people, and even though I roar along with Arliss, the mermaids are in a feeding frenzy, and they will not stop until they're sated.

Rosu is in there. It's all I can think of as I watch the waters run red with blood, praying that my velzen somehow escaped before Rama's forces attacked.

An explosion rocks Oasis from the inside, black flames shooting up into the sky as Arliss falls to his knees, watching the destruction of his compound.

Minutes later, the soldiers part, and one man drags a final woman out by the hair. Sante kicks and scratches at the guard, screaming expletive after expletive as she fights. Behind her, another soldier carries Rosu, one hand fisted in his black scruff and another gripping the base of Rosu's tail. He's even bigger than when we left, but goddess, it's not enough.

Rosu snarls and snaps but can't find purchase as my cries rise until all I'm doing is screaming for him. The guards approach the edge, where mermaid faces already peer up, waiting for their newest meal.

"Don't touch him!" I yell at them, gill-framed faces looking my way. "Don't fucking touch him!" The mermaids grin, unblinking, as time slows. Rama's soldiers toss Sante and Rosu together into the water. My screaming shakes the glass of my tank as agony crushes my chest. The waters bloom bright red with blood as the walls of my tank vibrate under the weight of my scream. But they hold, even as I claw and scratch at the sides.

Jet and Renze throw themselves against their collars, but they're beaten back with shock sticks as Rama stands there with a wicked grin on her face. Tenebris is behind her, kissing his way down her neck as Rama sneers at the closest guard. "Gather the tech. Time to go home."

I'll kill her, I vow as I watch the red waters still. Bits of flesh still cling to the surface, but as I watch, fingers snatch the pieces from below.

I'll kill her the moment I get a chance. I'll take any possible opening, but she will pay for what she's done to my family. Sinking to the bottom of the tank, I watch, and I wait as grief consumes me, eating me from the inside out.

CHAPTER THIRTY-EIGHT
JET

In my mind, I'm back in the maze. I'm not mated; I'm just waiting to be told to go to the Atrium and perform. Just like I did earlier tonight. Except that they've given me no more uppers. I have to have them if I'm going to get through this. My brain aches, radiating pain throughout my body as anguish lances my heart.

But when they threw Rosu into the water, something snapped. *Rosu*. Oh, my gods. My mates, my family, they're in danger!

Renze is a frozen, furious statue across from me as Achaia beats her fists against the glass of a giant fish tank. She's a mermaid, a fucking mermaid. I can scarcely believe it. There's nothing familiar about the pale blue face, framed by rows of iridescent, spiky gills. She's elegant and otherworldly and a far cry from the bedraggled mermaids who just ripped Rosu, Sante, and everyone else to shreds.

My wolf howls under my skin with agony for the velzen.

For the millionth time, I snarl at Tenebris through our family bond. I can't feel him there, even though he's standing just behind Rama. I struggle against the uppers and the collar around my neck, but sharp points draw a hiss from my chest. Every time one of us moves or lurches, the spikes poke into my skin, my neck torn and shredded. I pray for uppers, knowing they'll bring me an escape from this reality, this horror that I'm living in once again. Then I pray to never see uppers again, because I need to get my mates to safety.

The guards push us at gunpoint toward the ship, but Arliss refuses to move, so they drag him by the collar. He grunts when the spikes burrow into the back of his neck, but still, he doesn't pick up his feet.

We're hauled into the ship's depths, and then we take off again.

In the maze, we never stopped looking for a way out, but I had accepted my fate. It wasn't until Diana came to release us that I allowed myself to *hope*.

My soul aches when I think about Rama imprisoning us again, mind spinning with possibilities. I know I should form a plan but the uppers make planning difficult. Despair soaks the edges of my mind as the hours pass. Noire and Diana are a watchful presence, collared to the same pole as me. We're all just...*waiting*.

Every now and again, one of us gets the urge to try something, anything. But movement sends sharp, stabbing pain through everyone else until we sit frozen and silent.

We fly until it's nearly evening again, and when we land, the back of the ship opens. The air is biting and cold, and it's pitch-black outside.

"Welcome to Nacht," Rama purrs, reappearing from the depths of the ship with Ten in tow. "Tonight's a big night; it's the night Tenebris and I will formally claim one another. Once I've basked in the glory of our bond, I'm going to pick you apart. I love it when my plans work out, and this one has been years in the making."

She stalks toward the row holding Noire, Diana, and me, kicking at Noire's foot as he glowers up at her. Guards hold electroshock guns pressed to Noire's chest as Rama leans in. "Imagine if you could have foreseen this all those years ago, Noire. Imagine if you had just taken my father's offer of marriage instead of shunning me."

"Never," Noire spits.

"It's a good thing," Rama continues on, stroking Tenebris' side as he passes us to stand just behind her. "Because when Tenebris came of age, and I realized he was meant for me, I would have had to cast you aside to have him. So really, you did me a favor."

Noire and Diana growl as we turn to Tenebris. "Help us, Ten," Noire barks. His alpha command rolls over Ten, who shudders under the weight of it but brings his eyes to Rama.

Ten, please, I murmur into our family bond. *Please help us.*

Ten turns to me with a vacant look, and it's then I realize the spindly legs of a metallic spider peek out from his shirt. I can't get a full view of it, but it's attached to his chest. Instead of the body being filled with his blood, though, it's pitch-black. Noire notices it the same moment I do but purses his lips. It's something, a piece of info we didn't have before. And maybe something we can use to get out of this.

I say nothing as guards shove us past Ten and Rama, down the gangplank, and onto an empty, black, cobblestone street. It takes my eyes a moment to adjust, and the uppers force me to take stock quickly. We're inside a cliff with giant stone arches holding up the roof above. Everything here is dark, just like the maze, although lights built into the arches themselves indicate the presence of others. It's a city, a veritable underground city built right inside the cliff face.

Closing my eyes, I listen intently. This place teems with life, although I can't see anyone. Ahead of us, a utilitarian, square building looms.

"Lock them up," Rama barks at the guards. "I have plans for the evening, but tomorrow is a big day." I wonder at the intelligence of locking us all together, but we must pose so little of a threat that she doesn't even give a fuck. I grit my teeth to hold in a sob. It's the godsdamned maze all over again. All of us together with no options. Except this time, there will be no Diana risking her life to come save ours.

Rama takes Ten's hand and pulls him in the opposite direction, and Noire loses his shit, throwing himself against the collar and dragging us toward Ten. Diana moans at the spikes that stab her neck. She's collared too far along the pole for me to reach her, but Noire freezes at the sound of her anguish, pausing even as he watches Ten stroll off into the darkness with one burly arm around Rama's shoulders.

"She's going to fucking claim him," Noire spits. "She's going to bond with him. Godsdamnit!" His shout rings off the stones as a guard slaps him in the back of the head with the butt of his gun.

"Shut the fuck up, and start walking," the guard growls, using a shock stick to get Noire moving. Our family bond is awash with seething fury from both Diana and Noire.

I struggle to find clarity around the high the uppers produce in my system. Searching for Diana, I think hard about what I'm trying to say. *Does Cashore have any insight?*

Diana's distress is practically tangible. She shakes her head, grunting as the spikes tear at her already broken skin. Ascelin and Renze both growl at her discomfort. It's not lost on me that the most dangerous monsters from Rama's maze are all here and all desperate to protect the one person willing to enter its depths to find us.

Behind us, Achaia cries mournfully from her tank, blue claws scratching at the thick glass that encases her. Her anguished cries are the only noise as we're pushed up the unlit street toward the looming, ominous black edifice.

We reach the front, and the guards shock us through the doors, pushing at the poles to keep us in line as we enter a huge, caged area. Cage. Another cage. Fuck no. Anger rages in my system, and I tense to flee, but Noire's harsh bark rings through the uppers.

"Hold, Jet!" Every muscle in my body is tensed to run, but I force myself to remember my pack.

Noire, my alpha.

Diana, my alpha's omega mate.

Firenze, the big vampiri who helped us escape.

Ascelin, his First Warrior partner.

Achaia, a voice whispers into my mind. *What of Achaia?*

I'm high enough to compartmentalize everyone in my mind, and I'm coming down fast enough to know I'm shutting my emotions off as much as I can. It's the only way to get through what's happening and what's going to happen. It's the only coping mechanism I have as I struggle between terror and resolve.

Renze breaks through the fog in my mind, a soothing presence in my consciousness. When I turn to my left, his white eyes are on mine. *What of our mate*, he presses again. *Do not lose us to your memories of the maze, Jet. We are here, we are now. Be watchful, atiri.*

The guards laugh as they use the poles to guide us into the huge cage. We fall into a heap when they shove hard, Noire bellowing with rage as Diana screams in pain.

"Sleep tight, assholes," one of the guards laughs, locking the door and following the other soldiers back out into the darkness.

I turn to face Noire and Diana, even though the spikes dig into my neck.

Noire's furious eyes find mine. "Stand on three. Let's take stock of the room." He starts a countdown, and Diana grips her collar tight as we lift to a stand. When she gets to her feet, I look around as much as I can without stabbing myself too horribly. Renze, Ascelin, Arliss, and Elizabet are locked onto poles like ours. We can barely move without intense coordination.

For an hour, we work together to make our way around the room. But just like the maze, there's nothing here to indicate a way out.

Just like the maze, there's no escape without a miracle.

CHAPTER THIRTY-NINE
RENZE

I wake with a jolt, pain lancing my neck as I look up at a white ceiling. Blinking my eyes quickly, I struggle to take in my surroundings. We fell asleep last night in a black cage, and now I am trussed up against a wall, my head lifted high, my feet barely touching the ground.

Ascelin is to my right, her white eyes on mine. "They drugged us in the night, Firenze. I heard a hiss, and then a cold mist rained down on us. That is the last I remember."

Taking quick stock of the room, I'm horrified to see that Achaia is no longer in her tank and Diana is not strapped to the pole between Jet and Noire. I struggle to look around but cannot see them anywhere.

"They must have been taken," Ascelin grunts as my movements cause the collar to stab her throat.

"Diana!" Noire bellows as he comes to, struggling against the bindings that hold him strapped to the wall. We are chained in a line on the cool surface, facing into a laboratory of some kind. Workstations fill the middle of the room. A large door swings open, and soldiers push two rolling beds in from another room.

Noire snarls as the guards pass us. Diana is strapped to one of the tables and Achaia, in human form, to the other. Jet is frozen next to me, mumbling under his breath when the wall slides open, and Dore steps in with a smile.

He passes us until he reaches Elizabet. He slips a key into the collar at her neck, stepping back as she falls out of it with a pained moan. She lands on dark tiles and clutches at her neck as Dore turns from her, heading back toward the doorway. "Up and at'em, doc. Rama wants the queens verified. You know what to do."

He stands with his back to the opening, watching as Elizabet rises on shaky legs, hobbling quickly to Arliss. She runs her hands under his shirt, which is covered in blood from his stab wound. He hisses as she turns to Dore. "He needs help!"

Dore grins, and it's the grin of someone so accustomed to seeing pain that he's unfazed by it. I recognize it because I saw it so many times in Jet and Noire in the maze. "Doc, I don't need to remind you what mistress will do to him if you don't do your fucking job. So again, hop to it."

Elizabet frowns but squeezes Arliss' hand. His head hangs limply; he's not awake yet. Or maybe he is barely hanging on. She turns from him with a glare in Dore's direction, pointing at Diana as she begins to come to. "You realize this is your twin sister, right?"

Dore snarls but keeps the maniacal grin as he shakes his head. "My twin died a long time ago, doc. Keep the chatter to a minimum."

I open my mouth to affirm Elizabet's point when the front wall of the lab slides back a foot and then to the side, revealing a bright hallway. Rama stands there with Tenebris just behind her. The moment they enter the lab, Elizabet crosses to her. "Mistress, I'm begging you. Arliss needs—"

Rama backhands the smaller female with a snarl, laughing when Elizabet falls to the ground with a yip. "Arliss is not long for this world if you do not do as I say, doctor. Confirm the test results of the queens. Now."

Elizabet struggles upright and nods, blood leaking from a cut above her eye. She shoves her long sleeves up to her shoulders and approaches a workstation as Ascelin's emotion demands my attention. My partner is focused and intent on what we've just heard.

The queens? It is the second time they have called Achaia that. But now Diana too?

That is a new tidbit of information I cannot hope to understand without more context.

Rama crosses the lab to stop in front of Noire, grabbing her dark hair and throwing it over one shoulder. It's bloody and swollen, but as she shows it off, Tenebris crosses the space between them to kiss it. She sighs blissfully, black eyes locked onto Noire's in victory as he rages against his collar, despite the way it digs into his neck.

"I'll fucking kill you!" he shouts.

Tenebris looks up from his place behind Rama. "If you touch my mate, I'll end you," he barks, pulling Rama behind his much larger frame. None of us are prepared for Tenebris to punch Noire in the chest, all the breath whooshing loudly from Noire's lungs as Noire snarls at him.

"It's me, brother," Noire barks. His alpha tone bowls Tenebris over, although he stands straighter and roars, fangs elongated as he snaps them in Noire's face.

There is a tense moment before Rama grabs Tenebris' hand, pulling him back toward her. "With me, alpha," she croons. Ten shakes his head and steps to her side, sliding an arm possessively around her waist, although he doesn't take his flashing eyes off of Noire. He does not even recognize his pack alpha, and my gaze falls again on the metallic spider legs peeking out of his shirt. They match exactly the spider we pulled from Achaia in the vampiri court.

Rama sighs as she looks at us, bound to the wall and unable to do anything to help ourselves. An evil smile splits her face before it falls. "We've got time for a little history lesson while Elizabet works."

Behind her, Elizabet hunches over one of the workstations, punching furiously at a keyboard despite the tears that roll softly down her brown cheeks.

Rama leans close to Tenebris, wrapping her arms around one of his as she rests her cheek on his bicep. "When I came of age, Deshali was at war with the monsters of the Tempang—a war no one was willing to aid us in," she adds, her tone dripping with disdain as she glares at Noire.

"My father, Alpha Rand, held the monsters off for a long time, but when it became clear we were losing, he made a deal with them—his daughter for a cessation of hostilities. He wanted peace so he could mine the gold from underneath Deshali, you see. And that was worth *everything* to him."

Rama shrugs as Elizabet grabs a tray full of empty vials and steps to Diana's side. The Chosen One struggles against her chains, eyeing the vials and a giant syringe in Elizabet's hand. Elizabet murmurs an apology under her breath and slides the needle into the crook of Diana's arm, drawing blood from her as she squirms.

"I lived in the Tempang for a year," Rama continues in a flat tone as she watches Elizabet. "The monsters did things to me that I cannot even explain aloud, but they made me a deal. A year in the forest, at their mercy, and the entire continent would be served to me on a platter. I owe them just one last thing. Well, two things."

She smiles wickedly at us before turning to watch Elizabet move on to Achaia. I press against the collar as her meaning sinks in.

The queens. She owes the monsters *two things*. Oh gods, she means Achaia and Diana. Achaia is still out cold, but Diana rages into the lab, struggling against the bindings holding her flat.

Elizabet moves to a workstation and plugs the full blood vials—one red, one blue—into a blood bank. I scent it from here, Acahaia's true blood, my fangs dripping venom as Ascelin snarls down the line from me. Elizabet punches at a keyboard before nibbling at the edge of her nail. Rama watches in silence, her dominance a weight over the room, before Elizabet looks up with a nod.

Rama laughs, turning to us with a victorious expression. "I think I'll save the surprise for tomorrow, but this just confirms the data my spiders collected—Diana and Achaia are the best candidates. And tomorrow, they will fulfill their destiny to the monsters of the Tempang. Gods, I cannot wait to see the looks on your faces when you realize precisely what that means."

Tenebris grips her hip tightly, pulling her back into his chest as he purrs in her ear. "I need you," he croons, loud enough so we can all hear, although he's focused completely on her. She turns in his arms, and Elizabet steps slightly away from them, tucking her hair behind her ear as she makes herself small, hunkering behind the next workstation over.

"Are you ravenous, my darling?" Rama purrs to Ten, wrapping her hands in his hair, yanking his head to the side as she bites her way up his neck. Her dark eyes are on Noire the whole time. She is torturing him by flaunting Tenebris in front of him. She has hated Noire since the day he denied the marriage proposal her father offered him. Even in the maze, she denied him everything she possibly could.

"To bed, mate," Tenebris commands, standing taller as he grips Rama's throat, forcing her head back with his thumb on her chin. She lets it fall as he kisses his way up it, then pulls her upright, leading her from the lab as Dore crosses to Elizabet, gesturing to the collar.

"Alright, doc. Back in you go."

"Gods, no," she moans. "Please don't, Dore."

"Have you ever known me to be generous?" he snaps as her eyes widen.

"N-no," she whispers, stepping up to the collar and clamping it back around her own neck. She cries when the points poke into already open wounds. I struggle against my own chains, but I can't move, no matter how hard I try to.

We need a miracle, presses Ascelin into my mind.

CHAPTER FORTY
ACHAIA

I come to, jolting upright, only to find I already am upright. In fact, I'm no longer in the saltwater tank but strapped to some kind of cross, back in human form although I'm wearing loose cotton clothing. I arch my back, struggling against bonds that hold me to the harsh metal, only to find Diana strapped to something similar off to my left. We're in a dark stone room, and nobody else is here.

"Diana!" I hiss. Her blonde hair hangs limply over her face as she shakes her head from side to side. Blue eyes flutter open before she startles like I did, screaming as she tears at the ropes binding her legs together and arms out to the side.

"What the fuck?" she barks out as I hiss her name. She turns to me frantically. "Where are we? Where's Noire?"

My heart shreds in my chest as I think about everyone else. "I don't know," I whisper. "The last thing I remember is sinking to the bottom of my tank and falling asleep."

Diana fills me in on the lab and Rama's ominous tidings as hurt and disbelief tear at my chest. We've got to get the fuck out of here. Whatever Rama wants us to do with monsters from the Tempang can't be good.

We look around the room, but it's pitch-black stone, not a window to be seen. "Gods, I hope we're not back in the fucking maze," Diana whines. "Anything could come through that door. A minotaur, a naga, the godsdamned humans."

"Don't get lost in that worry," I encourage. "Surely Rama didn't bring us to her home province just to travel right back to the maze."

"I put nothing past her," Diana huffs in a bitter tone. A door whooshes open to my right, and guards pour into the room. Without addressing us, they push the wooden crosses we're strapped to out the door and into the bright sunlight. Rama stands there with Tenebris, smiling cruelly when she sees us.

"Today is the day," she hisses. "I tracked you both for years, and the spiders helped me to confirm what I know to be certain. You are the queens I need to complete my promise. And now that you're both mated, you are ready to be delivered."

"Delivered to what?" I bark out, overwhelmed by the sheer amount of information she just shared.

"The Volya," Rama whispers, tittering again as if she's letting us in on a thrilling secret. She turns, walking backward as she points to her neck, encouraging me to look down. I can feel a thin collar around my throat, although I can't see it to examine it.

"What the fuck?" I hiss out, pulling at the bindings, which feel tighter and tighter as Rama laughs.

"Have you remembered what you did yet?" Rama questions, her dark eyes on me as Tenebris stalks in front of her.

Scoffing, I sift through my memories for any reference to what she's talking about. She takes my silence for encouragement to continue speaking as Diana and I glower at her.

"When you refused to give me the power from your city, I had you attacked. I hope you remember that, at least. A mermaid queen's power comes from her crown, although I didn't know that at first. It was a hard lesson to learn because when I tried to harness your power, you screamed."

We exit the bright hallway into the even brighter sunlight, and for the first time, I see Deshali in the light of day. The land is scorched and devoid of life. The ground itself smokes as if it's on fire from below. Everything, as far as the eye can see, is pitch-black and dead.

Rama sighs. "You did this to the land, Achaia. Of course, that's not your real name, although you never shared that with me. When we captured you the first time, before we learned the power of your crown, we learned the power of a mermaid queen's war cry. You leveled Deshali with one shriek. There is nothing left of my home province for miles and miles. Every single person was killed when you did that. I only managed to survive by snatching a pearl from your crown. Holding it saved my life."

The memory comes back in a flash.

Rama tries to tear the crown from my head as her soldiers drag me from the sea in a net. I let out a shrill, resonant battle cry, knowing I am dooming her entire province to immediate death. It was the only decision I could make; the only thing I could do in a last-ditch effort to save my people.

Somehow, though, she still won in the end. I gasp as the realization hits me. I did this to Deshali. The land is scorched and black because of me.

My mind flits immediately to Diana's home province, scorched and burnt just like this. But when I sift through my mind, I have no memory of leveling Vinituvari. Still, I shift uncomfortably against the wood, remembering how I decimated this place when Rama captured me.

Rama laughs. "You see? I adore being the evil villain, but I am not the only one here. After you leveled Deshali, I had only a small army left—beings who had been inside the mountain at the time. They helped me to build the city of Nacht back even greater while I amassed more troops. Eventually, I had enough leverage to lure Edson Winthrop into building the maze. That's when I met Diana and Dore. You remember, omega?"

Rama's dark eyes move to Diana, who snarls from the cross next to mine. She hasn't shared that story with me, but I'll have to ask it another time.

Rama says nothing else as we follow a trail down along the mountain until we reach the blackened valley below. I'm reeling from everything she shared, but I can't fall apart—not now. I look around at the destroyed earth, praying for something, anything I can use to get free of this mess.

Guards push Diana and me through a devastated town, one-level homes flattened. Gaping holes pepper every wall, every roof. Even the stone walls are burnt. After long, heartbreaking minutes during which I ache at the sheer level of destruction surrounding us, we come to a stop. I try to remind myself that monsters from the Tempang were at war with this province long before Rama captured me, but when I look around, I know *I did this.*

We halt in front of a huge three-story home, its front lined with delicately scrolled columns. Black char marks the front of it, the once-glossy doors splintered open. At the base of the steps, Ascelin and Renze are tied together, Noire and Jet chained next to them. Arliss and Elizabet are seated off to the right, still tied to a long pole and unable to reach one another. Elizabet scratches at her collar as Arliss' head rolls from side to side, his breathing rapid and shallow.

My heart gallops in my chest as Jet and Renze look up at me. Sweat clings to Jet's upper lip. He's coming down from the uppers again. I long to go to him, to help him through that for a second time, but Rama has taken every choice from us. The tank masked our mate bond, and I dig into it now, aching to connect with my mates. Renze strokes me softly through our connection but Jet is silent.

Rama laughs aloud just as the leathery beat of wings sends wind brushing across my face. I flutter my eyelids against the strength of it, struggling against the ropes binding me. To my intense horror, two figures emerge from the cloudy sky, landing with matching thuds on the front steps of the destroyed home.

I stare in horror at what can only be monsters straight out of the Tempang forest. They're tall, perhaps ten feet, with spindly, humanoid legs and arms and hollow chests. Sand-colored wings flare behind them before being folded up behind their bony shoulders, covered in long swaths of pale, rough fabric.

The bottom halves of their faces are human enough, although wide mouths full of sharp teeth stretch from one side of their face to the other. Where eyes should be, a flat expanse of bone extends from the center of their foreheads all the way to the side, curling onto horns that rise up above bald heads. Goddess help us.

They're…fucking horrifying. Despite having no eyes, they peer around at our group as if they do before finally landing on Rama.

The frontmost monster speaks, its voice a mixture of clicks and a rough, gravelly tone so low it's difficult to understand. "Young one, your timing is fortuitous," one of the creatures growls, looking at Rama. "You have brought the queens?"

"I have," she murmurs. "As promised, a queen of the land." She points to Diana, who snaps angry teeth in her direction. "And a queen of the sea." One clawed finger points to me before she hands two vials of what appears to be blood to the creature.

"You have done well, child," one of the monsters whispers. It hands the vials to the second, slightly larger monster who opens them and dumps the contents in its mouth. After just moments, it nods in assent, a long black tongue snaking out to lick its lips as it tosses the vials to the ground. Clawed fingers twitch as it levels its gaze on us.

Rama preens as the first monster turns its attention to Diana and me. "We are the Volya, protectors of the Tempang. Our forest is sick, and it requires a sacrifice, *your* sacrifice."

"Go fuck yourselves," snarls Diana as Noire throws himself against the chains.

"Why?" I press in an urgent tone, bringing the monsters' attention back to me. "What's wrong with the Tempang?"

"A betrayal," the larger one hisses.

"A murder," the second proclaims, opening its batlike wings wide as it flaps softly, the movement carrying it closer to Diana and me. It alights on a middle step, bringing it eye-level with both of us. Cocking its head to the side,

JET: A DARK SHIFTER ROMANCE

it sneers at us, saliva dripping from rows of conical sharp teeth. "The forest requires recompense. Royal blood for royal blood."

"Must fix…" the bigger Volya agrees, nodding its head in agreement.

Gods, I've got to think of some way to stall, to give someone a chance to pull a miracle out of their ass. Just then, Jet and Noire manage to spring upright in one fluid motion, rushing across the short distance and throwing themselves at the Volya.

Rama lifts a hand to stop her guards from intervening, simply smiling as Tenebris throws his body weight into the pole collaring his brothers. They fall to the ground bellowing as the collars stab them. When they struggle upright, Ten stands on the pole, effectively holding them trapped. "Please continue," Tenebris purrs to the Volya, Rama beaming as her mate speaks to the monsters.

We're fucked. We're so godsdamned fucked, not that it keeps me from shooting Diana a look and yanking at my bindings again. But it's no use, they're so tight, I can barely feel my fingers.

The Volya address Rama directly. "We will take the queens to the Gate of Whispers, and if the old gods accept their blood, you will be granted unspeakable power as we discussed."

Rama turns to Diana and I with an evil grin. "Unspeakable power…" A wild, joyful gleam in her eye sends my heart sinking in my chest.

CHAPTER FORTY-ONE
RENZE

Our situation grows more dire by the moment, and the rising angst rolling off of Ascelin is nearly enough to throw me over the edge. My mates and the Chosen One are in the gravest of danger, and my options are limited.

"Time to go, queens of the earth and sea," the shorter Volya whispers. Diana gasps, then screams, then looks over at me, her eyes vampiri white before a voice echoes out of her mouth, Cashore's voice, the voice of my dead king. "Arlissssss..." she hisses. "Arlissssss..."

Arliss and Elizabet look up just as Rama and the Volya turn in the direction Diana is looking. Dore, who has been guarding us, yanks the end of Arliss' pole and drags him toward Rama and her handful of guards. Tenebris steps off his brothers' pole and stalks across the clearing, standing in front of his mate, fists balled loosely by his sides as he readies himself to protect her.

Diana continues the refrain, her eyes a familiar vampiri white as Cashore's voice repeats the refrain over and over. "Arlissss...Arlissss...Arliss..."

"Shut her up!" snaps Rama, but when a guard reaches up with a shock stick, the Volya hiss and slash at him with six-inch claws, causing the guard to leap back.

Arliss lurches for Rama just then, feinting to one side as Elizabet is dragged along screaming. He just barely misses grabbing onto Rama, but Tenebris is on him in a second, pummeling Arliss' face and chest as Elizabet screams for him to stop. Tenebris lurches upright, grabbing Elizabet by the throat and lifting her high into the air as he snaps his teeth in her face. Elizabet pounds at Tenebris' chest as he shakes her like a rag doll.

"You presume to hurt what's mine?" His voice is unrecognizable as Elizabet beats her fists over and over again, her face turning a dark purple as he chokes her.

It's then I notice the smile on Diana's face and a dark, pitch-black stain spreading along Tenebris' chest, seeping through the thin white fabric of his shirt. Ascelin senses my change in focus and shifts forward. Dore grips the end of our pole. "You two are going nowhere," he snaps.

Elizabet's head falls forward, and Tenebris drops her to the ground as Arliss roars in pain, trying desperately to reach her and unable to because of how they're collared. Tenebris shakes his head in confusion, looking down at his chest and the spreading stain. He rips his shirt open as Rama comes around him, smiling. When she sees the metallic spider attached to him, dark liquid leaking out of its broken body, her smile falters.

Dore dashes from our side to Rama's, pulling her away from Tenebris, who shakes his head anew as if trying to clear his thoughts.

The Volya stand on the steps, watching dispassionately as the scene plays out before them. That is when I realize they will not lift a finger to help Rama, despite what's going on here. Perhaps without her knowing, she was just a pawn to them, simply a way to ensure they got the sacrifice they needed. Another time, I will dig into the questions I have about why they would even need Rama to do this on their behalf. But my focus is here now and the smallest of chances to save my people.

Tenebris grabs Rama's arm as Dore snarls, electrocuting him with a shock stick. Ten roars and lashes out, shoving Dore hard to the ground. The moment Dore is down, Noire and Jet spring as one, landing on top of Diana's brother as they fumble at his side for the keys to our collars.

On the tall crosses, Diana and Achaia struggle, but are unable to do anything but watch.

Rama shrieks in anger as Ten grips her throat, gesturing to the spider stuck in his chest. "What is this, mate...drugs? That's what this is, isn't it? Why?" His voice rises in anger as Rama scratches at his hand.

"Only to give you strength," she chokes out. "Only to make us perfect." Her dark eyes are blown wide, pupils focusing with predatory intensity as Tenebris drops his grip and wraps an arm around her waist, pulling her to his chest.

"You're trying to hurt Diana," Ten barks. "She saved my life! Why, Rama? Tell me."

"Means...to...an...end," Rama gasps as Tenebris shoves her away and puts both hands on his head, scratching at his temples as if he can't quite put it all together.

When he looks up, eyes narrowed at Rama, I know whatever was in that spider held some sway over him, and he's coming out of it fast. "Was that what our mating was, too?" His voice is angry as Rama backs up, wiping spittle away from her mouth with her hand.

"You did this to get back at Noire, didn't you?" Ten continues, grabbing the spider and ripping the now-empty body from his chest before tossing it at Rama. "It's always been about him. You wanted him, but you saw his bond with someone else. You hated what it said about you that you wanted him anyway, so you built a maze to torture him. And you took me to fuck with him even more. I'm right, aren't I?" He pauses for a moment, his dark eyes anguished as Rama looks around. "Talk to me!" Tenebris bellows. "Am I right? Was it about him this whole time?"

"It was never about him," Rama yowls. "It was always you for me, Tenebris." Rama backs toward the Volya, looking over her shoulder at them even though her eyes don't leave Ten. "Get me out of here," she commands the monsters.

The smaller of the two lets out a horrifying throaty laugh and shakes his head. "We needed you to deliver the queens, young one, and that is all. Our plan does not require your survival."

Rama snarls in anger as the scuffle on the ground continues, Jet and Noire both scratching at Dore's clothing in a desperate search for the keys.

"You're wrong," Rama hisses at Tenebris, backing around Achaia and Diana's crosses as she aims to put distance between herself and him.

"I'm not," he mutters disdainfully. "Because despite the way you took me, I claimed you with intention. So, I feel you in here." He pounds his chest once as Ascelin and I look toward the closest guards.

What I read from their emotions shocks me. They will not lift a finger to help Rama either. They are waiting for the tide of this fight to turn so they can safely escape this place.

Ascelin reads them at the same time and pivots our focus, slipping across the clearing as one to place ourselves between Achaia, Diana, and the Volya. The Volya roar, enormous wings beating the air as they leap over us, landing on top of both crosses and attempting to take off into the sky.

"Jet!" I scream my mate's name. If the Volya take Achaia from me, I will burn the Tempang Forest to the ground to get her back.

CHAPTER FORTY-TWO

JET

Renze screams my name just as Noire pins Dore's head between his thighs, squeezing the alpha's neck tight while I anxiously search his clothing for the key. I locate it and shove it into my collar, unlocking the godsdamned thing and tossing it aside. I unlock Noire's before sprinting to Renze and tossing the key at him. Noire leaves Dore passed out on the ground.

I jump up onto Achaia's cross to weigh it down with my body, slicing my claws at the Volya, who clutches her in its clawed feet.

Noire leaps onto Diana's cross, and together, we pull them back toward the earth as the Volya scream in anger, their voices rocky and monstrous.

Behind us, Tenebris has Rama in his arms, begging her to answer his questions. There's no fucking way we can let her get away, but we can't let these monsters take Achaia and Diana, either. My focus is torn. This has to end now.

Ascelin slips out of nowhere, stabbing a shock stick through one of the Volya's wings. It shrieks and hisses, slashing with its claws as she slips onto its back and shocks it again. The bigger of the two grabs for its comrade just as Ascelin disappears in a puff of smoke, reappearing on the other Volya's back. It manages to throw her to the ground as Noire and I shift into our wolves.

Our weight alone drags Achaia and Diana down as the Volya pair let out an earsplitting high-pitched call. Oh fuck, I hope there aren't more of these godsdamned things. The bigger one must be a guardian because the smaller one attempts to pick up both crosses and take off again, but the larger male swoops at us with the claws tipping every joint of his enormous wings. I barely miss getting stabbed in the head as Noire clings to the crosses behind it.

Renze, Ascelin, and I attack the guard Volya as Noire pulls Diana and Achaia down. His wolf is so big that the monster can't take off without help. Noire manages to slice his way through the ropes binding Diana, and she falls to the ground, shifting immediately and leaping up onto Achaia's cross, crawling up Noire's larger frame to bite at the Volya's clawed feet.

The monster bellows out an angry cry and shoots up into the sky, dragging Ascelin and Renze with him. He shakes them off, and they drop elegantly back to the earth, running to release Achaia.

Everything happens in slow motion, then. Diana's wolf sprints for Rama and Ten, even as Rama shrieks in rage, shoving Ten away from her. The bigger Volya swoops down, landing on Diana's back as she collapses into the dirt underneath his weight. Her wolf howls as jagged claws sink into her body, and then Noire is on the Volya, ripping and shredding. The remaining monster shoots up into the sky with an anguished scream.

Achaia is up fast, grabbing my hand as we run to Diana.

"Diana!" Noire bellows his mate's name as he shoves the broken, bloodied monster off her. She's shifted back to human form, deep wounds lining her sides and stomach. There's blood, so much blood, as she curls into Noire's arms with a sob.

Blue eyes move up to Noire's as Achaia grips my hand. "Kill her," Diana groans, her voice wavering. "Finish this, Noire."

Noire bellows with fury as he stands and turns, eyes wild as I follow his murderous gaze.

Rama and Tenebris are gone.

～

Ascelin slips to Noire, hissing to get his attention. "I will guard Achaia and the Chosen One. Go get your brother. End this, alpha."

Noire and I share a look as Arliss slumps on the ground by Diana, Elizabet examining his wounds. His breathing is still worryingly shallow.

I feel for Renze, and he's right there with me, urging me to move. Without a word, we take off toward Nacht. Up ahead, faint snarling echoes off the destroyed remainder of the buildings lining the street—Rama and Ten. We sprint through the ruined city until I hear a yip and the sound of a body hitting the ground.

Ten, we're coming! I press into our family bond. I can sense him there now that the spider's gone, but there's only seething rage and hurt, and he doesn't answer.

Up ahead in the street, Ten and Rama's wolves fight. He's so much larger than her that he's got her pinned as he snaps at her neck, dominating her. But she's older and more experienced, slicing her way along his belly as ribbons of blood well underneath the black fur.

She manages to throw him off her just as Renze bowls her over, Noire barreling into Ten's wolf. Rama lands on the cobblestones with a thud but leaps up quickly, her wolf lifting its lips into a sneer.

Ten's wolf sees Noire only as an attacker, despite his own focus on his lying bitch of a mate. He roars and backs up in front of Rama, shielding her from us. But now, she's under the attention of two alpha males in their prime and a very pissed off vampiri.

I'm in the maze all over again—hunting the mark with Noire, smelling that scent of fear as saliva drips from my teeth. That scent that all marks exude when they know their end is near saturates the air as I sniff at it, grinning at Rama.

Her direwolf freezes under my predatory focus, and I stalk closer as Noire shifts into human form and laughs. "It's over." He spreads his arms wide and takes a step closer as Ten growls, still guarding his mate.

Noire looks at our brother as Renze slips off to one side, preparing to attack. "She must die, Ten. You've got to know that. Whatever that spider was full of made you think she was yours. But it's a lie, just another game she played to fuck with us, to fuck with our family. It wasn't real."

Ten's wolf shakes his head, and Rama snarls at Renze as he hisses at her, white eyes flashing as he edges ever closer.

Rama shifts back into human form, clutching a wound in her side as she laughs and presses herself to Ten's side. "You're too late, Noire. I should have thrown you right back into the maze when I captured you. I won't make that mistake again."

I don't bother to shift or respond as the rapid staccato of hoofbeats reaches my ears. I cock my head to the side, screaming into my bond with Renze, and, inadvertently, Noire and Ten. *The fucking horses are coming!*

If we don't take Rama down now, we'll lose our chance. I don't know how many copies she could possibly have made of the horse she stole from us, but the resounding pattern of hoofbeats coming in our direction bodes poorly.

We spring into action all at once, Noire and I focusing on Ten as Renze slips behind Rama with a vicious smile.

Tenebris shakes Noire and me off as he tears a chunk of fur from my neck.

Noire commands him to stop through the bond, but he's still not answering, backing away from me with Rama hovering close behind him. Whatever was in that spider has begun to lose its hold on him, but he's still disoriented and protective. He thinks she's really his.

Renze slips around Ten in a flash, aiming for Rama with his claws out, but Ten swings around at the last moment, dodging between them as Rama shrieks in anger. She lashes out just as I join the fray, biting into Ten's scruff as I drag him away from Renze, giving my mate a shot at Rama just as Noire leaps for her. A dagger appears in her hand, and she lifts it high as something heavy barrels into Noire and me, crushing my lungs as it knocks me away from my brother. I hear a grunt from Noire, pain filling our family bond as we're all flung in separate directions.

I sense Renze attacking Rama, but Tenebris' protective instinct is on overdrive, and he manages to get his jaws around Renze's chest, snapping his teeth shut as Rama stabs Renze in the side with the wicked blade. Ten tosses Renze away from Rama with a throw of his enormous head.

Ten, no! I bellow into our bond, roaring as Renze lies broken and bleeding in the dirt.

I struggle for breath around the searing, crushing pain in my chest, watching as Renze yanks the knife from his stomach and grips it in his hand. He manages to get himself upright as I struggle to fill my lungs with air, a dark shadow looming over me. I look up directly into the face of a giant horse statue. It stands over me with its lips curled back, eyes glowing red as it sneers.

Oh fuck, she's won again. And she's going to take us and put us back in that hellish maze.

I can't.

I won't.

I'll die before I go back there.

Ten backs away from us, covering Rama with his big body. She laughs cruelly as she lays a hand on his side, sneering at us where we lie in the dirt. "You didn't think I'd ever be without backup, did you?"

A voice rings out across the cobblestones, clear as a bell.

"You didn't think that was *your* backup, did you?" Diana laughs cruelly from Ascelin's arms as the vampiri stalks up the street toward us, Diana cradled to her chest and Achaia following behind her, chin held high as her pale eyes land on me. She's desperate to run to me, and desperate to finish this.

Rama blinks rapidly, stepping away from Ten as she eyes the horse who hovers above me, snarling.

JET: A DARK SHIFTER ROMANCE

Diana's eyes move to Ten, her expression emotionless as she points at Rama. "Kill her, Tenebris. Remember the maze, brother. Remember what she did to us, what she did to you. For *years*."

Please, Ten, I push into our family bond. *Remember the maze. Rama isn't real. It was all a lie.*

Rama takes a step backward, only to find a line of metal horses blocking her from moving any farther. She looks swiftly from side to side, but she's caught, there's nowhere to go.

Painfully, I climb to my feet, holding my battered ribs as I keep one eye on the horse behind me.

Diana slips out of Ascelin's arms and limps to my side, gripping my arm as Noire hobbles protectively over to her, never taking his eyes from Rama.

Rama's eyes flit from each of us to the next. She looks at the closest statue. "Kill them," she commands.

The horse doesn't move, so she claws at Ten's arms. "Kill them, mate. They want to hurt us, to hurt me! They want to separate us just like I told you!"

Tenebris snarls as he pulls her into his big arms, one hand sliding around her waist as the other comes to her throat and squeezes possessively.

Noire stalks across the space separating us from Rama and Ten. "She has to die, brother. It could only ever end like this."

Ten snarls at our pack alpha. "Don't you fucking touch her, Noire!" His voice is a mixture of anguish and fury, but he recognizes Noire. He's coming back to us.

"There is no other choice," Noire presses on, taking another step toward Ten as Rama backs into one of the horses, her chest heaving.

"No!" Ten shouts.

"Stand *down*, Tenebris!" Noire roars with all the weight of a pack alpha's dominance. Every hair on my body stands at his command

Ten shudders and presses himself to his mate, shielding her from us as his chest heaves.

Ten, I whisper into his mind, watching whiskey-brown eyes flick over to me. The pain I see there crushes my soul, but this is our last stand, our last chance.

With my eyes locked to his, I share with him everything I endured in the Atrium. Every time Rama forced me to fuck someone or be fucked by someone. Every time her guards shoved uppers down my throat. Even the time she shoved a lance through me and forced me to rape a man while he bled out. I show Ten how the light faded from the man's eyes and how I slipped out of his body only to have Rama tell me to continue until I came. She delighted in being sadistically cruel. Ten never experienced that in the maze. I protected him from it as much as I could, but I'm letting him see it now.

My body aches and trembles as I relive it, and every emotion I feel fills our pack bond as Ten's jaw drops, his breath coming in great heaving gasps as realization fills him.

My brother's throat bobs as my memories continue to batter him, his grip on Rama tightening. He turns to her as we all stand, frozen and watching. "Why?" His question is simple, and heartbreaking.

Rama hisses and shoves her way out of his arms, but he grabs her immediately, yanking her back to his chest with a growl. His hands wrap in her long hair as he slants his mouth over hers, kissing her deeply. Tears stream down his face as she struggles to tear herself from him.

And then, in one swift move, he slices the claws of one hand across her neck, her blood spurting out of the fatal wound. With the other hand, he rips her head clean from her shoulders.

CHAPTER FORTY-THREE
ACHAIA

For one long, horrible moment, nobody says a fucking word. Tenebris turns to us with Rama's head in one hand as her body falls to the ground. The horses stand in a silent line behind them as Diana slumps against Noire, who cradles her from behind.

My mouth falls open at the sheer brutality of what we just witnessed. And another part of me revels in the death of the woman who sowed such hatred over an entire continent.

Tenebris turns to our group, falling to his knees, and that action spurs everyone into sudden movement. Jet and Noire fly forward, pulling their brother into their arms even as he starts yelling. It's an anguished gut-wrenching cry that shatters my soul for him.

Renze and Ascelin hover protectively near Diana and me, still on the lookout for the Volya to return. Diana looks over at me and smiles, even though she's cut to shit and bleeding from the wounds that line her core. "We did it, Achaia. We took her the fuck down, and she will never, ever hurt someone we love again."

"I'm in awe of you," I whisper.

"And I of you," she returns in a deep voice, her eyes gone fully white, telling me the vampiri king is speaking through her. "Your kingdom awaits you, queen."

A sense of knowing slaps me when he says that. My fallen, destroyed kingdom lies off the coast of Diana's home province. Will I be able to return there now? What will we do with Paraiso? Those are questions for another time.

"Thank fuck!" Elizabet's voice echoes off the cobblestones as she rounds the corner into the street, Arliss' arm slung around her shoulder. "Oh, gods. Is she gone?"

"She is," I confirm quietly, risking a glance at Tenebris, who's still in his brothers' arms.

"Good," Elizabet snarls. "We've got a medical kit in my lab inside the city. Help me get Arliss and Diana up there so I can heal them both."

Tenebris' screams have fallen off, and he stares into the distance as Jet helps him up. Noire crosses the clearing, his face distressed, and pulls Diana gently up into his arms. Without a backward glance, he stalks up the long cobblestone street toward Nacht.

Renze threads his fingers through mine as Ascelin crosses to Tenebris, reaching a hand out to him. I watch her give him a gentle smile, and when he looks up, recognition passes over his handsome, angular features. "Asc? You're here?"

"I am, Tenebris," she confirms, gripping his hand and pulling him upright. He's fucking huge, even bigger than Jet and Noire, and he towers over Ascelin.

A single tear trails down his cheek when she opens her arms wide. He folds himself into them, and all I hear are sobs.

∼

An hour later, we're in Elizabet's white, sterile-looking lab inside the mountain. Nacht is eerily silent as if every being here realizes their mistress is gone, and they've fled her tyranny. Elizabet flits from bed to bed, directing each of us to help patch up Diana, Renze, and Arliss.

Arliss' wounds are deep, but with a gigantic shot of pink liquid to the thigh, he begins to perk up quickly. Elizabet works on Diana next, cleaning her wounds and stitching the larger ones. Diana's skin is angry and irritated, but I'm amazed at how fast she begins to heal. Renze's gut wound is already healing too, but I'll never forget that moment when Rama stabbed him, and I thought he was dead. I lay behind him in the bed, holding him in my arms as I kiss my way along both muscular shoulders, reveling in the fact that we didn't die today.

"Tell me about the horses," I whisper when Elizabet turns back toward Arliss. Diana looks over from her bed as Jet slips behind me so we're all lying like spoons. I can't fucking believe Rama's gone.

Diana gives me a victorious smile. "Rama always played the game so many steps ahead. It's the main thing I learned from my time living under her rule. I knew there was a solid chance we'd be taken and end up in dire straits. We lacked so much information, I didn't see any other way it could work out."

Jet sighs and buries his face in my neck, grumbling. As his pack's strategist, I can't imagine how he felt trying to come up with a plan with absolutely no information to base it off of.

"You did what you could, brother," Diana laughs as she continues. "The only thing we knew with certainty is that she took one of my horses when she abducted Ten." I risk a glance across the lab to where Tenebris sits, staring blankly at the wall.

Diana's voice is firm as she shares. "Because my horses were programmed to protect me, I knew they'd follow as we made our way to Arliss and then wherever Rama took us, assuming we were caught. But they're not as fast as the ships. It took them longer. Then I just made sure to reprogram them to recognize others of their kind and destroy any with mismatched programming."

"Are you fucking kidding me?" I shout. "You might be the smartest, most devious person I know. Why didn't you tell us?"

Diana shrugs, but the smile on her face is wide and beautiful. "I had no way of knowing if she could look into anyone else's mind. I told no one but Noire." Her smile falls a little as she slumps back in the pillows. "The statues are programmed to protect Dore, too, so as soon as we can go back down and find him, we need to do that."

"I choked him out during the action," Noire growls. "Although, I'm sure he's up now."

Diana nods, and I know she's thinking of how Arliss told her that Dore is no longer the person she knew growing up. Diana looks up at Noire. "We have to find him and help him, mate. He's a victim, just like us."

"I disagree," Noire barks, "but if that's what you want, I'll help to a point."

Diana rolls her eyes, but Arliss speaks up as he shifts out of bed, shoving his tunic off his broad shoulders. Somehow, he looks bigger right now, almost larger than life, as his eyes take on a faint glow.

Elizabet grins. "Good to see you again, brother."

Arliss returns the look before glancing at us. "I required Elizabet's expertise to heal a virus Rama infected me with years ago. The injection you saw at Oasis simply kept it at bay, but this one just now killed it. That is one of the many reasons I wished to help Elizabet escape Rama. I have not been able to shift into my true form in years, and by the gods, I need it."

"Let me guess," I laugh. "You're a dragon?"

Arliss lets out a belly laugh that nearly shakes the room with its resonance. "Hardly, little queen," he chuckles. "I will let Elizabet explain as I clear this compound of any remaining inhabitants and retrieve Dore."

I smirk as his broad smile lands on me. "Hey, if you happen to see any spare pearls lying around, grab them for me, would ya?"

Arliss winks, and then his form shimmers and glitches and fades. Moments later I'm looking at a being made of pure smoke. One moment, it stands before us, and the next, he takes off out the swinging lab door with a wild scream.

The doors shut behind him as we turn in disbelief to find Elizabet smiling.

"What the fuck was that?" Jet shouts.

Elizabet's dark face breaks into a knowing smile. "Arliss is a carrow, the only one we've ever found anywhere. He's a being of pure energy, and in his true form, he can sense intention and hop between the consciousnesses of multiple beings. He'll be able to tell you what truly lies in Dore's heart these days."

Diana scoffs, and our group falls silent at the shocking news.

Jet turns from me and looks over at his youngest brother. "I have so many questions, I don't even know where to begin. Ten, have you ever heard of a carrow?"

Tenebris looks up, his stare blank. He doesn't acknowledge the question or answer it, and after a drawn-out, awkward moment, he looks away again.

There is a long road ahead of him to recovery if he even can. We all have that trial to face, because the ripple effect of what happened today will linger with us for years. Rama may be gone, but what lies ahead of us is a challenge of a different sort.

For now, I let my head fall back against Jet as Renze smashes us together. There is not a thing on this entire continent that could pull me out of this hug.

CHAPTER FORTY-FOUR
RENZE

The wounds in my side from Tenebris' teeth still ache, but there is joy in my heart. My mates are safe and whole, the Chosen One is healing quickly, and Tenebris is returned to us. I cannot say what will happen with Dore, but Arliss did return with him later that evening, trussed like a hog and being dragged behind the carrow by a rope.

A carrow. I have heard inklings of such a creature, age-old whispers, and rumors that popped up from time to time. I never would have thought one still existed, because carrow are not born, they're made. When a carrow's time comes to an end, he or she simply picks their successor and gifts their power.

Arliss, back in human form, tosses Dore, bound, into the center of Elizabet's lab so we may watch him like a hawk. The Builder looks over at Noire and Diana. "Once we get home, let's discuss what to do with Nacht and Paraiso. I'd like to come back and pick the tech apart with a team, once I can assemble it."

Noire shrugs. "Arliss, I don't give a fuck what you do with the tech you find here as long as you leave me alone when I go back home. And find Achaia's pearls if you can."

The pack alpha looks over at my mate, who dips her head in thanks as she beams. It warms my cold heart to see a breakthrough between them.

We agree as a pack that as soon as Diana is healed enough, we will return to Oasis and, from there, Siargao. My heart is broken for what we have lost on this journey, but I remain grateful for what I have.

As night falls, I curl up with my mates in a corner of the laboratory. Dore remains tied up on the floor, and we each take a turn guarding him and checking on Tenebris, who says nothing all night and does not sleep.

In the morning, Diana awakens, much improved. We locate Rama's flying ship, and between Diana and Arliss, we manage to get it off the ground and head for the Builder's home.

"I never thought past killing Rama," Diana admits from her place nestled in Noire's big arms. "But there still feels like a lot to do. Determine what to do with both Paraiso and Nacht, and restore power to all of Lombornei. It's overwhelming."

"I can help with all of that," Arliss purrs from his place at the ship's controls. "I will need some tech, and to return to Nacht, but I believe I can take down the restrictions Rama built from there. I have a few people in mind to join and help me."

Achaia shifts beside me. "I don't care what we do with Paraiso, but we need to unharness it from my kingdom. If that means the city has no other source of power, that's fine with me, but I will not let it leech from the merfolk any longer." She lifts her chin as Arliss turns in his seat.

"That would ground the city, maybe permanently. I can't be sure what changes Rama made to the tech we initially built." He clearly disagrees with her assessment.

Achaia smiles at him. "You're a genius, Arliss. You'll figure something out. It's time I returned my city to my people, wherever they may be. They were decimated and scattered when Rama captured me, but if I return, they will too."

Jet growls as he captures Achaia's chin. "You can't think to leave us on land to rule underwater, can you?"

"Not full-time," she laughs, planting a tender kiss on his lips. "But I need to check in from time to time. We'll figure something out."

Jet growls as our bond lightens from the inside out. I have claimed them both, but he has not officially claimed either of us.

I need it, I whisper into that tether, watching as Jet shudders and nips at Achaia's neck.

Still, a thread of sadness permeates it because Rosu is gone, ripped to shreds by Achaia's own kind.

Hours later, we step off Rama's ship and onto Arliss' sandy homeland once more. He sighs as he looks at the remains of Oasis, which still smolder. Crossing the bridge, he heads into the depths of his home with Elizabet. Noire, Diana, and Ascelin follow, keeping an eye on the still waters below the stone bridge. Achaia sighs and paces along the stones, her eyes on the water below.

A head pops up, matted green hair coated in mud. Wide blue eyes are her only visible features as the gills framing her ears flare out to the side. Achaia drops to a knee as Jet and I tense, ready to pull her from the edge. To my surprise, the mermaid swims slowly to us, sliding further up out of the water. She is beautiful like my Achaia but still deadly, her long limbs tipped in dangerous-looking green claws.

She cocks her head to the side as Achaia reaches down, filling her hand with water from the moat. She splashes it on her face and neck, and immediately her mermaid form appears, the crown pressing up out of her blue hair as iridescent scales crawl along her neck.

The mermaid clicks out a series of hisses that remind me of ancient vampiri before disappearing into the depths again.

Jet purrs and wraps an arm around Achaia's waist. "You can talk to them now?"

"They're trapped, stolen," Achaia murmurs. "They want to go home."

"Are they from your kingdom, *atirien*?" I question as she looks up at me, shaking her head.

"Another destroyed place, another people decimated by Rama."

At that moment, four more heads pop up out of the water, including a female with a crown identical to Achaia's. They stare at one another for a long moment as Jet and I watch in wonder. The queen circles closer, pressing her delicate, spindly fingers to a hole in her bone-white crown.

Achaia smiles and reaches up to her own. Iridescent pearls of every color line the front of her crown, some larger and some smaller. She pops a large pearl out and hands it to the other queen, who clutches it to her chest with tear-filled eyes. Moments later, another mermaid approaches the queen and takes the pearl, carefully placing it in the hole in the crown.

Immediately, the queen opens her mouth and sighs, and the entire gods-damned bridge shakes. Oasis itself seems rocked to the core as the queen shoots Achaia a pleased look, one white brow arched upward in glee.

Achaia claps her hands together joyfully, although her own expression is sad. The queen splashes off, and the others follow as I stroke my love's brilliantly blue hair. "What does it mean, *atirien*?"

Achaia sighs, her gills flattening against her hair. "Someone stole her pearl. The large pearls at the front of our crowns are the source of our power. Without a full crown of pearls, we cannot scream to protect in battle. Rama stole most of mine after I leveled Deshali," she finishes.

"And the smaller ones?" Jet presses, touching the pearls that line her crown and disappear into her gills.

"Ah," Achaia laughs, standing. "Those will help you breathe underwater so you can visit my kingdom with me." She pops a pearl out and presses it to Jet's ear. He hisses when the pearl takes on a life of its own, burrowing into his earlobe like an earring. Achaia slaps his chest. "Now, if you jumped into the moat, you'd be able to breathe underwater."

She places a pearl in my ear as Jet eyes the muddy, dirty water, which again ripples with movement.

A black snout emerges, and then pointy long ears, and the other queen shoves a dirty, disheveled body up onto the bridge.

Rosu flings himself into Achaia's arms, yipping as he spins and spins and spins, roaring with excitement as relief and joy flood our mate bond. Dirty brown water flies everywhere as he crushes himself to her and me and Jet's legs.

Jet drops down to the dark stones, grabbing Rosu around the body and burying his face in the velzen's wet, smelly fur. "Gods, we thought we lost you!" He purrs immediately, and Rosu returns the noise, and then we are a pile of wet velzen and bodies on the bridge. Rosu makes his way to each of us, licking and yipping his excitement as Achaia leans over and throws her arms around the other queen.

They exchange a series of hisses before the queen presses her forehead and nose flat to Achaia's. Then she takes back off into the murky depths.

I lie flat on the bridge, Achaia on one side and Jet on the other. Rosu zooms around us in ever-widening circles, yipping at the top of his lungs before throwing himself upon Achaia's chest, burrowing his face in her hair before letting out a contented sigh.

"How, *atirien?*" I question as she turns to me. Rosu smashes between us as his tail thumps lazily against my thigh.

Achaia laughs, stroking the tip of Rosu's ear where a pink pearl is now embedded. He nips at her fingers, his jaw open wide in a playful-looking grin. "She heard my cry," Achaia murmurs. "When Rama threw everyone in, she heard my cry for Rosu. She kept him for us, hoping we'd return. Gods, I wish I could have saved everyone."

Jet sighs, reaching out to tug Rosu's tail, then stroke Achaia's cheek. "You did beautifully, mate."

Achaia gives Jet a scorching look. "What's this talk of mates? I don't believe you've claimed me as such, Jet Ayala."

He rolls over me to get to her, pulling us both in close as he takes her mouth forcefully. When his attention turns to me, I sigh at the rough abrasion of his lips on mine. "I need to have you both." His voice is a lustful growl as his purr deepens. Rosu hops off me, looking toward the front doors as I stand, pulling my mates with me.

"Come," I command.

"Gods above, I need to," Jet agrees, hauling Achaia into his arms as Rosu trots ahead of us.

CHAPTER FORTY-FIVE
JET

Rosu wraps himself around my feet as I try to walk, curling in a figure eight over and over as if he can't get enough physical touch. The velzen comes up to my mid-thigh now, growing again even in the short time since we thought he died.

I take that moment to thank Liuvang for watching over him and my mates. I can barely keep my mouth off Achaia as Renze walks in front of us, leading us through the holes in the front doors and into Oasis.

My lips kiss a path along Achaia's neck as I pick her up, wrapping her legs around my waist. A purr reverberates from my chest as she leans in, long arms winding around me as her hands go to my hair. She grips it tightly as she drags my head to one side and bites her way up my skin.

Stopping at the nearest column, I shove her against it and devour her mouth, lust overriding every other emotion in my brain. We're alive. We're fucking alive, and Rama will never hurt us again.

"Need to claim you," I urge when we part. Renze hovers just beside the column, leaning up against it as he cages Achaia in from the side.

He growls as I place Achaia carefully in his arms, leaning in to bite his lower lip. "I want to check on Ten. Tease her, but don't let her come. Find a bed and I'll join you shortly."

With a low growl, I watch them go before feeling for Ten in our family bond. When I brush up against his consciousness, he barely acknowledges me.

It's not lost on me what he did for us at the end. Regardless of what was in the spider that Rama was drugging him with, and regardless of how horrible she was, he still claimed her. And then he ripped her head from her shoulders to protect an entire continent.

I've tried to speak with him several times since that happened, but he's been distant and aloof—like now.

Up ahead, Noire, Diana, and Ascelin are examining what used to be Oasis' dining hall. Arliss and Elizabet are nowhere to be seen, but Ten stands in one of the arched doorways, looking out into a smoking, palm-filled courtyard.

Rosù trails behind me, his nose practically pressed to my calf muscle as I join Tenebris, clapping my hand on his back. He stiffens and glances over, then down, his eyes going wide.

"A velzen," I share, reaching down to pick Rosu up. He wriggles in my arms as he leans over toward Ten, sniffing at Ten's chest before looking up with a hopeful expression. His long black ears twitch when Ten leans down, allowing the velzen to sniff his mouth.

"I've never seen one," my brother murmurs. Just getting a response from him is enough to send my heart leaping in my chest.

"We missed out on a lot, being locked in the maze and all," I remind him, willing him to remember Rama for what she was, not the bullshit she led him to believe.

He closes his eyes, his throat bobbing as his head falls back.

I press my shoulder to his as Rosu whines, rubbing his face against Ten's pecs. "I know better than anyone that trauma doesn't let go of us easily, Ten. I don't want to press you into something you're not ready for, but if you want to talk, I'm here."

He opens his eyes and glances over, reaching down to rub at the healing wounds on his chest. "Why did she lie?" he asks, almost more to himself than anything.

I sense it would do more damage than good to remind him that she was fucking psychotic, so instead, I hand Rosu to him, stroking my velzen's back as I rub my cheek along Ten's the way we used to. "We were terrified for you," I share. "I thought Noire was going to pull Lombornei apart to get you back, to give you a chance for a normal life."

Ten scoffs but brushes his cheek back along mine. "There is no normal in my future, Jet. Not like Noire with Diana. Not like you with your…mates?"

I sigh as his dark eyes find mine, full of misery.

Ten shakes his head as if dispelling horrible memories. "I'm going for a walk. I'll catch you later."

"Want some company?"

He pauses for a moment before shaking his head and handing Rosu back to me. "I don't."

Rosu and I watch in silence as he leaps over the edge of the balcony, landing gracefully on the scorched stone courtyard below. He heads into a dense thicket of trees as I watch him go, remembering something at the last moment.

"Don't go in the water, Ten. It's full of carnivorous mermaids!"

He doesn't answer, although he acknowledges me in the bond.

I have to hope there's a future where Ten is healed and happy, but healing is painful, and it's not a linear process.

I should know. I don't know if I'll ever fully recover from the horrors visited on me in the maze. But I'm sure as shit going to work toward that every day I can.

~

Rosu follows me through the charred remains of Arliss' home as I search for my mates. Like Ten, I suffered terrible trauma in the maze. But now? Now I'm choosing joy and happiness wherever I can grab it.

Pleasure slinks along my vampiri mate bond, Renze teasing me as he fucks with our woman. Achaia whines at me about how unfair he's being, and when I round a corner, my heart stops in my chest. Renze leans up against a wall, Achaia upside down in his arms. She sucks on his thick cock as he eats her roughly, her thighs clamped around his head.

Groaning, I shove my hand down my pants, pulling at my piercings as I watch them together. "Godsdamn, you two look good," I rasp. I watch Renze's forked tongue slide through Achaia's swollen folds, tickling at her ass as she grunts around a mouthful of him.

"You need a good chasing," I continue, crossing the small space to them. I haul Achaia out of Renze's arms and slap her on the ass as she yowls at me. She straightens up taller as I shove my body against hers, pressing her hard into Renze's chest.

He croons and bites his way along her neck as his black tongue snakes along her jawline.

Her cheeks flush pink as she gives me a haughty look. "Maybe I'd like to chase *you*, Jet."

Gripping her throat, I lean down and bite hard along her collarbone, sinking my fangs into her shoulder as her knees buckle. Renze keeps her upright as she sinks into his chest. "You're already caught between two monsters," I remind her. "We're gonna eat you alive, little queen."

"Gods, I love you calling me that," she moans.

"I want your real name," I press.

"I'll give it to you later if you're sweet," she teases. "But I love Achaia, and I want you to always call me that."

"What does it mean, *atirien*?" Renze presses, nipping at her earlobe as she bites her lip and gives me a devious look.

"It means 'watch out'," she laughs. "I was literally telling Thomas to watch out because the smugglers were dangerous. Not that he listened *at all*...," she grumbles, laughing as she reminisces.

I let out a noncommittal grunt as my eyes flick to my vampiri mate.

Renze's lips close over her shoulder, sucking at the blue blood that wells from the wounds as she hisses. My nostrils flare watching him. He's so intent on that heat, when my eyes flick to hers and she winks, he doesn't notice. He groans as he pierces her shoulder with his fangs, her true blood filling his mouth as I reach out, undoing the braid that holds his long hair piled high on his head. I wrap the braid around my fist and drag his mouth to mine.

Achaia's blood spills from his lips as I slide my tongue along one of his fangs, feeling it nick my skin, my blood joining hers. Renze shudders as he wraps one arm around her waist, teasing her nipples as we fight back and forth for the edge of power.

We pull apart, his eyes hooded as hers glitter with lust.

"Run," I snarl at them both. Achaia takes off first, sprinting into a burnt stand of trees as Renze reaches out to squeeze my cock.

"I know what you need, *min-atiri*. But after you have it, I'll need the same."

I bump him with my chest, growling. "You can fight me for it, mate."

He thumps the tip of my ear. "Remember whose bar belongs here. You are mine." With a slip of black smoke, he vanishes after Achaia.

Their footsteps echo softly to me, his barely audible, hers slightly more so. I count to thirty, and then I take off. His crisp scent and her depthless perfume guide me through the thicket, through hall after hall, until I reach a dark room, its doors blown off the hinges. One of them still smokes, but inside, my mates hide.

I hear a soft chuckle, and then a fist connects with the side of my neck. Renze drops down onto my body, pummeling me as I bellow and shove him bodily across the room. He lands on the bed with a grunt, arching his back to pull his shirt over his head.

I'm on him in the span of a breath, crushing him into an enormous, round mattress as I bite my way along his neck and shoulders, over his thick chest muscles, down his stomach to his cock. It juts proudly against the front of his pants as I unzip them, reveling in how it falls thick and heavy into my palm.

Bringing my fangs to the tip, I tug gently, Renze grunting as a shudder wracks his frame. Goosebumps cover his pale skin as he fists my hair, pressing my mouth further down his leaking cock. "Suck, Jet," he directs as I hum around the mouthful.

It's then I hear another titter, and I see Achaia leap over the edge of the balcony, sprinting across yet another sun-drenched courtyard.

"Bastard," I hiss at Renze, laughing as he slips out from under me to follow her.

A distraction.

Well done, asshole, I admit into our bond as Achaia flees ahead of us.

He catches up to her easily, and then they run before me, along the edge of the right side of Oasis, its sandy outer wall rising up the cliff in front of us. If Renze makes it to the cliff, he could easily escape up it with Achaia.

I can't have that.

Pumping my arms hard, I overtake them bit by bit, muscles burning as I watch her auburn hair flowing in the wind. The sweet musk of prey being run down fuels my intense focus, and I pump my arms harder as I sprint, knocking her down hard. We tumble once, twice before she lands flat on her back, chest heaving as she feigns indignation.

"Let me *go*," she cries, even as Renze leaps on my back and makes a show of choking me. I lean into his violence, shrugging him off as I hand him one of her wrists.

With a grin, he draws it up and over her head, leaning over her to sink his fangs into one of her veins. He sucks at it greedily as I bring her other hand to my mouth. I kiss each fingertip, then I nip and suck before moving my attention to her wrist. I bite that too, loving the way her body betrays her. Her eyes flash even as her hips thrust rhythmically against mine.

A victorious laugh tears itself from my throat as I yank her wrap dress open, baring her beautiful figure to me. "Mine," I grow. "Mine and his."

Achaia hisses as Renze crawls on top of her, shoving his pants down to his knees as he punches once with his hips, burying himself to the hilt inside her heat. His head falls back as she screams, and then his hands grip her ass as he pulls her hips up and begins to fuck her slowly, sweat breaking out across his back as his braid hangs long between his muscles.

I tuck it up over his shoulder before dragging my claws down his skin. Ribbons of blood follow my fingers, and Renze hisses when I lean in and lick my way up each cut. I smear his blood on my fingertips and reach between his ass cheeks, using it as lube to fuck him with my fingers. I'm not gentle. I never will be with him, but he clenches around me as he falls forward over Achaia, caging her in with one hand.

Shoving him further still, I spread his ass cheeks wide and spit on his back hole. He grunts as he slides agonizingly slowly into Achaia and back out. Gripping my cock in my hand, I tease him with it, rubbing the spongy head along his balls, following the line back to where I'm going to take him. Then I let my dick rub alongside his as his hips rock in and out of Achaia's heat.

Below him, she's up on her elbows, watching the show even as her lips part in pleasure.

"You're next," I growl. "Maybe I'll toss you in the water and fuck you in mermaid form. What do you think, my little queen?"

"I think we have a lifetime to fuck, and I can't wait to do it all," she growls back.

Renze gnashes his teeth in her face, his venom dripping down onto her heaving tits when I punch my hips hard and slip deep inside him.

"Fuck, *atiri*," I gasp. He's cool wrapped around me, his body temperature lower than mine. But he's so godsdamned tight, and his muscles contract hard, his ass stretched impossibly full as he slides into Achaia, then rocks back to meet me. And then he's impaling himself on my cock as he fucks her, pleasure building between us until he explodes all over us both, sending me into an orgasm that curls my lips back. Stars burst behind my eyelids as I fill him with my seed.

I don't even come down from that fucking pleasure for ages, and when I do, Renze sits back, his head on my shoulder as I kiss my way up it. "Remember what I said, *atiri*?" His voice is a menacing growl as Achaia cocks an auburn brow at me.

Laughing, I fist his cock, gathering the sticky cum and sliding my fingers inside Achaia's pussy. "I remember," I counter. "We said we'd fight for it, if you recall."

Achaia cries out as I shove Renze's release deep inside her, a sudden vision of her swollen with pups dominating my imagination.

"Alright, boys," she laughs. "I have to see it. Give me a show."

"Gladly, *min-atirien*," Renze purrs. But when he leaps to his feet, I'm already up on mine, running, knowing they'll chase. And I say my second thankful prayer to the gods in a long time because this chase is one I will gladly repeat for the rest of my days.

CHAPTER FORTY-SIX
TENEBRIS

I hear soft footsteps. Diana falls into a chair next to mine, looking through a hole in the balcony to a charred forest inside this walled compound. "Do you wanna talk about it?" she questions me gently, not looking over, not trying to poke at me through a new family bond I'm now aware of.

I guess she and Noire mated when Rama took me. Makes sense—they needed all the power they could get. I don't begrudge them that.

"Ten?" Her voice is strong but unsure. How much can she ask me? How much can she press about how I killed my mate to save my family?

The reality is that when I ripped Rama's head from her shoulders, I ripped my heart from my chest at the same time. Symbolically, of course. I'm horribly aware of its steady, depressed drumbeat. And I'm horrifically aware of the black, empty tether where I felt her until that battle.

How could you, I question into the tether. *How could you not trust me enough to share the whole truth? Why did you drug me? Why didn't you just tell me everything and allow me to love you despite your flaws?*

I'll never have the answers to those questions, though. I couldn't choose who my mate was; if I could, it would never have been someone who visited so much pain on my pack.

Still, a mate bond, once in place, is the strongest force in the universe for an alpha. I watched my father lose my mother, and that loss drove him to drink. And then it drove him to violence. And then Noire had to pack me, Jet, and Oskur up to live with Thomas until Noire was old enough to challenge our father and win.

It feels like another lifetime that I grew up and came of age in the maze. I can barely remember my pack from the time before. The maze is all I knew for seven years, and without it—without *her*—I'm lost.

"She wrote me letters," I admit, looking over at Diana finally. "The day I came of age, she started sending letters into the maze inside of books she thought I'd like."

"Oh, gods," Diana whispers. "That's grooming, Ten. You realize that, right?" Her voice is uncomfortable and horrified.

I shrug. I don't expect her to get it. I don't expect any of them to. Fuck, I didn't really get it myself until I woke up in her private chambers on Paraíso, and the mating bond slipped immediately into place.

Rama was a psychopath, but she was *my* psychopath. I knew what she was, but a bond can't be denied. Except, I *did* deny mine. I killed her.

Diana winces, and I look over sharply. Red spots bloom along her sides as her shirt immediately stains with the sheer amount of blood. We both shout for Noire, and he comes running, dropping to his knees as he yanks her shirt open. He takes stock of her reopened, leaking wounds and shouts for the doctor.

I don't know these people, I mean I've seen them, but I don't really *recall* them. Still, Noire seems to trust the dark-haired woman and the man who looks just like her. They move Diana into a half-destroyed laboratory and begin tending to her wounds again.

I hover at the edge of the group, Jet's velzen curling around my feet. He's small now, maybe fifty pounds, but within a month or two, he'll be larger than our wolves and twice as mean. Eyeing the gold bands around both his front paws, I frown. That means he's claimed.

Everybody wins; everybody has who they want. Jet's even got a pet now.

Turning from the group surrounding Diana, I hunch my shoulders as I duck through shrapnel hanging from the doorway.

"Fuck!" shouts the dark-skinned woman from behind me. "These wounds were healed. What the hells is going on here?" The dark-skinned man rubs his square jaw and looks at Noire.

"Not much is known about the Volya of the Tempang, but it's possible they poisoned her somehow."

Nothing I've ever read about the Volya is helpful in this situation, so I remain quiet. They're reclusive and they don't leave the Tempang.

Noire bellows with rage as Diana covers her face in her hands and screams. I know their anguish—every time they take a step forward, life shoves them further back, it seems. I'm familiar with that pain. It lives inside my body, taking up residence as I shove my emotions deep down.

"What are our options?" Noire questions the duo in his deepest alpha tone.

The woman looks at me, then back at my eldest brother. "There's only one place where anyone might know about the monsters of the Tempang—the library at Pengshur. We could go there to research..." Her voice trails off as Noire growls.

I turn back and watch dispassionately. I formed a kinship with Diana when we escaped the maze. But I feel very little now other than a deep and pressing need to leave this place and run until the ache in my chest leaves.

Watching the scene in front of me, the pain in my chest becomes a relentless, stabbing pressure that steals the breath from my lungs. Blood drips from Diana's wounds onto the floor, the ruddy scent of it stoking my predatory need. Once upon a time, I hunted her in the maze. It wasn't that long ago at all that she was nothing more than a sensual mark to me.

Now? Now, I feel very little as I watch her life source dripping in red rivulets onto the floor.

I turn from the room as Diana passes out from blood loss, the dark woman springing into action with a medical kit.

Leaving the melee behind, I pace through the sand-colored halls until I find an empty area. A stone bench faces the wide, dark river that runs through the center of the compound. Through a hole in the stone wall, I can see empty dunes stretching as far as the eye can see.

With a sigh, I look down at the scorched earth underneath my feet. I can't stay here. I don't *want* to stay here. I want solitude. I want to reclaim something of who I was. I want to remember the good parts of *her* that I experienced for a short time.

Reaching down, I scratch at the holes in my chest from Rama's spider tech. I haven't bothered to ask what was in the serum she infused me with, although Elizabet, the doctor, would probably know. Rama never answered that particular question in the end. She never answered *any* of my questions, even when all I wanted to know was why. The one thing I know for certain is that I would have been hers no matter what.

Rising to my feet, I head toward the hole in the wall, my feet echoing as I cross the small stone courtyard. I've never felt so fucking alone in my entire life.

Always alone. Now, I'll be alone forever. Nothing will ever complete that bond again. Growling, I leap across the dirty waters of the river and duck through the hole, nothing but a wide expanse of sand ahead of me as I begin to run.

TEN: A DARK SHIFTER ROMANCE
TEMPLE MAZE LEVEL THREE

MONSTER GUIDE

While I made up some of this world's monsters, a few are loosely based on existing entities. For the sake of those not familiar with monster lore, I'll quickly lay out the monsters you'll see and hear about in this book.

Vampiri - humanoid with exceptional senses, incredible speed and occasional psychic ability. They are pale-skinned with black claws, lips and fangs. Vampiri are venomous and drink blood.

Manangal - loosely based on the mythical filipino manananggal, a vampire-like winged creature that could separate it's lower half from it's upper to fly in search of prey.

Naga - Half human and half cobra, naga have humanoid upper bodies with a flared hood behind a distinctly snake-like face. Their lower half is that of a snake.

Gavataur - I made these up. Vaguely humanoid body with two arms and legs, but very tall and thin with saggy skin and a bull head, complete with horns. Ancient, wilder forms of the more modern minotaur. They are cannibalistic and non-communicative with hybrid monsters.

Velzen - Velzen are the vampiri court's version of a guard dog. Imagine a thinner version of a greyhound and fox mixed together, but all black with occasional white spots

Mermaid - We're not talking about Ariel, y'all. These mermaids have long, spindly limbs, rows of razor sharp teeth and hair/scales in all the beautiful colors of the sea. The mermaids in this book are carnivorous and hunt anything they can.

Carrow - A near-extinct monster spirit that can live inside any other monster breed. Identifiable only by a pale tattoo along the monster's jawline. Carrow have the ability to read intent and heart, and can vanish into a cloud of smoke to move through walls.

Volya - Volya are ancient creatures from deep within the Tempang Forest. Ten feet tall, their bodies are thin enough for their bones to be visible. A wide mouth features rows of conical teeth. Where eyes should be, a flat expanse of bone crosses their foreheads and then curls up and behind their heads. Horrifyingly, they've got leathery, claw-tipped wings as well.

PRONUNCIATION GUIDE

Ten - TEN-uh-briss
Onmiel - AHN-mee-EHL
Renze - renz (like friends)
Jet - JET
Achaia - uh-KYE-uh
Noire - Nwar
Diana - die-ANNA
Cashore - CASH-or
Ascelin - ASK-uh-lin
Vampiri - vahm-PEER-ee
Naga - NAH-guh
Gavataur - GAV-uh-tar
Manangal - mahn-ANG-ahl
Lombornei - LAHM-bor-NAI
Tempang - TEM-payng
Siargao - See-ar-GAH-O
Rezha - RAY-zhuh
Vinituvari - vin-IT-u-VAHRI
Deshali - deh-SHAH-lee
Dest - rhymes with west
Sipam - SAI-pam (like dam)
Nacht - KNOCKED
Arliss - ARR-liss

PRONUNCIATION GUIDE

Dore - Door
Velzen - VELL-zehn
Volya - VOLE-yuh
Evil - eh-VEE-zehl
Zakarias - zak-uh-RYE-uhs
Okair - oh-KAYR
Garfield - like the cat
Zura - ZUHR-uh
Kraven - KRAY-vehn
Anja - AHN-juh
Lahken - LAY-kehn
rahken - rah-kehn

Zura's Land

Tempang Forest

Carrow Village

Nacht

Moon Province
Library of Pengshur

the Adventurous Furyk 2023

CHAPTER ONE
TENEBRIS

I've died a thousand deaths since I ripped my mate's head from her shoulders.

Snarling, I shove overwhelming anger away only to have it rush back over me in waves so heavy and hard I fall to one knee in the scorching sand.

Rocking onto my heels, I lift my head to the sun, willing the intense heat to burn away the pain in my chest. It's so cutting and sharp that I can barely breathe around it.

Tenebris, get your ass back here. My older brother, Noire, barks into our family bond, calling me like a lost pup.

I suppose that's what I am.

Growling, I hop to my feet and sprint across the dunes instead. I'll run until I can't hear his voice. Until I can't feel my other brother, Jet's, pity. I'll run until Noire or one of his lackeys drags me back, clawing and kicking like every other day.

Noire's pack alpha command hits me straight in the gut as he demands my return again. Ignoring it, I rip my clothes off and shift into my direwolf, picking up the pace across the hot desert sands of this desolate province, so different from my own. I'm far faster in this larger form, sprinting over searing dunes as sand peppers my face. It stings, and yet I don't care.

My mind jerks me back to before I killed her, my omega mate. I drift to a memory of pinning her to the wall, both hands above her head while I knotted her. I remember the way our bond was so clear and full of pleasure. I remember burrowing my head between her breasts after the ecstasy faded, kissing her tenderly, her long, elegant fingers stroking my jawline before demanding another kiss.

An enormous flying shadow comes out of nowhere, barreling into me as all the air is knocked from my lungs. We tumble over a dune and down the other side. I lash out with my claws as the shadow swirls around me, a low chuckle emanating from within its inky depths.

I flop onto my back, shifting into human form, lips curled into a sneer.

The shadows reform as a hand reaches out for mine. "You look like shit, Tenebris," the bulky, older male croons.

I take a moment to look up and scowl at Arliss. He's nearly as big as I am but far, far older. Sapphire blue eyes flash as his black lips part in a wicked smile. Noire warned me about the devious carrow. He takes "every man for himself" to the extreme. Not that I really need the warning. Years of hunting prey in the Temple Maze tell me this male is a predator to be wary of.

He's vicious enough in human form, but in carrow form, he can read intent and travel around on a wisp of smoke. He is beyond dangerous.

Arliss tsks sensually, licking his lips when I get up. Standing, I'm half a head taller than him—and still naked.

"Don't look at me like I'm a piece of meat," I snap, slicing out with a claw-tipped hand.

He catches my wrist smoothly; he's been fighting for hundreds of years. Or so he says.

Arliss rolls his eyes. They're so striking against the pitch-black of his skin and hair. "You cannot continue running, Tenebris. You achieve nothing, and Diana worsens by the day."

Diana.

My one-time savior. My brother, Noire's, mate. My pack omega.

My mind helpfully supplies a memory of her entering the Temple Maze to free our pack and the vampiri clan.

That feels like a lifetime ago, before the day I realized our captor and the maze's creator was my fated mate.

Before I *killed* her...Rama.

Another memory assaults me. Opening my eyes after being kidnapped by her, only for her to smile at me. It was so real, so genuine, so godsdamned gorgeous. *"There you are,"* she'd said. And I knew what she meant. I was hers, bondmates in the ways of our people. True bondmates are rare, even among direwolf shifters.

And I *had* that, even if it was for a short time.

TEN: A DARK SHIFTER ROMANCE

A sob leaves my throat, and the first tear falls as I grit my teeth tightly together.

Arliss crosses his arms. He's a silent sentinel as the tears come hard and fast. He doesn't yell at me like Noire or try to hug it out like Jet. He simply waits for it to pass, and when it does, he jerks his head back in the direction of his remote, desert compound.

"Let us return, Tenebris. I have something for you."

"I don't care," I manage. I don't care about anything anymore, apart from running to escape the pain that clenches my heart so tight it feels like it'll burst at any moment.

"You will," he retorts, grabbing my hand as we disappear in a swirl of black smoke.

I scream into a tornado of wind and sand, falling to the ground when Arliss stops whatever the fuck he just did. Looking up, I see we're back at his home, the only building around as far as you can see in this wasteland of a province. There's nothing but sand and rocks for hundreds of miles until you reach the Tempang Forest on the northern end of Lombornei.

Staring at the long bridge that leads to the compound's entrance, I notice burn marks mar the double doors, and there's still a giant hole nobody's bothered to fix.

"She did that, you know," Arliss reminds me. "She liked chaos and control, Tenebris. Which is precisely why she drugged you to keep you with her, despite being your bondmate."

"If everyone could stop reminding me what a psychopath she was, I'd appreciate it." I can't stop thinking about how she infused me with a serum that did…something. She was mine, but she didn't trust me enough to allow me to be hers without drugging me, it seems.

Not that I can ask at this point, what with her being dead and all.

Without waiting for Arliss's response, I stalk down the steep dune and across the metal bridge.

Heads pop out of the water as the moat's mermaids watch us. Hair in every possible shade is matted from the murky, filthy depths. Long, pointed ears, wide eyes, and rows of sharp teeth are enough to keep me squarely in the center of the bridge.

"Beautiful, aren't they?" Arliss whispers as a chorus of snarls rings across the water. "Hush!" he snaps. "I will return you home soon enough, as promised."

The captive mermaids fall quiet at that, returning below the water's surface when I glance down at them.

A shuffling sound brings my focus back in front. In the hole blown into the front doors, a black-clad figure stands with her thin arms wrapped behind her back. She says nothing until we reach her, and then she gives Arliss a haughty, condescending look.

He reaches out to stroke Ascelin's cheek, but she swats his hand away like a bug. "Arliss, I have seen you fuck dozens of men and women on every surface of this compound. I am not your next conquest."

It's on the tip of my tongue to share how he looks at me the same way he looks at her, but I say nothing because I don't really give a fuck how Arliss feels or what either of them wants.

He laughs darkly but disappears in a puff of black smoke.

Ascelin, the beautiful vampiri warrioress, rolls her all-white eyes and slips her hand through my arm, clacking her long, onyx-colored nails together.

"I fucked him once," she whispers conspiratorially in my ear. "Just like I fucked you."

A shudder wracks my frame, but her sensual words don't spark desire as they would have before Rama. When we were escaping the maze, there was a time that I took what I needed from Ascelin's body. But all that was before I fully realized what awaited me outside the maze's walls.

Rama, my bondmate.

Ascelin's pale hand wraps firmly around my bicep as she guides me through opulent, sun-drenched halls and across tropical courtyards. There are obvious signs of a recent fight here too. The walls are singed, and scorch marks are all over the tiled courtyard. I don't really remember the actual fight, though.

She's silent, and I'm thankful that she doesn't remind me how terrible my mate was like everybody else feels the need to.

I absentmindedly rub my chest.

"Do your wounds hurt?" Ascelin questions. "Or is it deeper?" Her voice is gravelly but comforting, reminding me of how we formed a near friendship escaping the Temple Maze. She tried to save me during that final fight when Rama took me. Not that I wanted saving, exactly.

"*Everything* hurts," I whisper. Rama drugged me with a mechanical spider filled with some sort of serum. I'm still healing from ripping it off my chest once I realized what she was doing. If the serum vial hadn't broken during that final fight, I'd still be under its spell. I don't know how I feel about that.

She squeezes my bicep tighter, stopping us in place. A few hallways ahead, I hear the rest of my pack speaking in low tones.

Ascelin grips my chin, forcing me to look into her eyes. "You will overcome this, alpha. Eventually, you will find a new normal."

"There is no normal, Ascelin," I say, pulling away from her touch. "I tore my mate's head from her shoulders to protect everyone on this godsforsaken continent. There is no coming back from that, not for me."

Her white eyes fill with sorrow as she gives me a long, calculating look. Finally, she nods. I think she gets it more than the rest of my pack does. I had to do something unthinkable because the reality is my mate was an awful person—horrific, even. I knew that, and I made the choice to rid Lombornei of her, knowing I was killing myself at the same time.

My mind circles back to another memory of waking her with my tongue between her thighs. To the way she woke so slowly and then ravaged me in our bed.

Ascelin must sense she's lost my focus because she disappears into the hallway's shadows, leaving me to my thoughts.

A tug in my chest reminds me that my brother requires my presence. I always expect a sermon from him; it's what he did in the maze. But finding his own mate, Diana, changed him. Now he reads my emotions and intent better than ever, and there's a *slightly* softer edge to Noire that wasn't there before.

Although, as the youngest of the four Ayala brothers, I didn't experience his wrath as much as my older brothers since I was the pack baby. Noire was far harsher on the older two, pushing and shoving them to become the designations he needed for a strong pack. I was never meant to be part of his leadership crew. My three older brothers doted on me, even when I came of age.

That thought sends heat spreading through my core because when I came of age, Rama began to send me books and trinkets in the maze. It's when she started a seductive semi-courtship that lasted until I escaped. I didn't really understand it until I saw her for the first time in person. That's when I realized she was mine.

Growling, I shake my head to expel the demons of my memories, but, if anything, my body is even more focused on my dead mate, on the time we had together before I—

I shut that train of thought down, hard. When I enter the dining hall, conversation ceases, and everyone looks at me. Arliss is already there, seated at the head of the table. He steeples his fingers and gives me an appraising look.

"Your brother has plans to make, Tenebris."

I shrug my shoulders and sit at the far end, away from my pack. Jet turns and gives me a look, sending a tickle of affection through our family bond. The thing is, none of it sinks in. I don't give a fuck about making plans. Right now, my only plan is to keep putting one foot in front of the other to try to survive.

CHAPTER TWO

ONMIEL

"Onmiel, are you listening to me?" A low, teasing voice breaks through my thoughts as I look over at my mentor, Zakarias. His dark brows knit together over piercing eyes as he purses his lips. The very corners turn up, though, so he isn't mad. Of course, he's never mad at me. I'm his favorite Novice.

"I'm always listening," I chirp, pushing my reading glasses farther up my nose as I give him a haughty look.

"You said listening, but I believe you meant 'daydreaming,'" he corrects in a kind tone. The glare he gives me is equally haughty. He's full of shit.

"Yes, Daddy," I snark back, batting my long eyelashes. He's always joking about how he's older, despite the fact we aren't *that* far apart in age.

He snorts out a laugh, gesturing to the quiet book stacks surrounding us. "You are incorrigible," he mutters, mostly to himself.

"I'm also your favorite Novice," I whisper, looking around the library as he gives me a second warning glance.

"I have no favorites," Zakarias hedges.

"You do; it's me."

"I would never admit such a thing aloud."

"Don't need to. The eyes say it." I laugh. "Plus, you've let me deeper into the archives than any of the other apprentices. Just admit it." I sigh, leaning on my ornate wooden chair to rest both arms along the back. "You adore me."

Zakarias smirks but says nothing. And that's how I know I've got him.

Chuckling, I gesture at the giant, dusty tome on the wooden table in front of him. "How long are you going to stare at that ancient writing before realizing you can't read it?"

His happy smile falls, black brows dipping into a vee as a faint, anxious sentiment emanates from him. Ah, he is terribly angry about the perplexities of this particular book. "It reminds me of something, Onmiel," he says in a near-whisper. "It is on the tip of my tongue, and I cannot place it."

"Shall I take a look?" I offer quietly. Novices are not generally allowed in this section of the library without accompaniment by a First Librarian, but I'm miles ahead of the other Novices in my chosen topics of study—monster lore and languages.

Still, there seems to be some unspoken rule of the library—some books are simply off-limits to those of us who have not progressed through the training to officially become a First Librarian of the Ancient Library at Pengshur.

Gods above, that's a fucking mouthful.

But it's been my dream to become a First Librarian since I was much younger, maybe even the Master Librarian one day when I've learned enough to qualify.

Zakarias seems to consider it, then shakes his head. "Good as you are with languages, there is something off about this book, and I'd rather not. You have a way to go, young one."

I bristle a little at the comment, even though I know he means nothing by it. I'm not *that* young. I'd estimate Zakarias to be just twenty years older than me, and I've been through plenty of shit. I feel far older than my twenty-two or so years.

Not that he knows any of that.

Still, I can't push him into allowing me to take a peek. I know because I've tried in the past. He gets all bristly and weird, and there's just no point. I'd rather he remained in my corner for a time when I actually do bend the rules. Because that happens a lot, and he's always been willing to go to bat for me.

He must sense my frustration because his eyes soften, plump lips parting into a kind smile. His smile is his best feature—it lights up his face.

"You are learning quickly, my future librarian. It will not be long before you take up the official mantle. When you do, the entirety of the library will be at your disposal. I have complete confidence in you."

I nod absentmindedly, distracted by a ray of sun that comes through the plate glass window to my right. It highlights every mote of dust in the air, and I watch them twirl and dance as I put my chin in my palm. Next to the window, a light shines down on the column of books below it.

The entire continent of Lombornei has been without electricity for seven long years, but it was suddenly and inexplicably restored everywhere this week. Most of the librarians are scrambling to figure out how it happened. Plenty of theories are going around through the usual gossip channels.

I rather preferred it when our world felt a little more prehistoric and wild. People reading by firelight, not being connected to screens everywhere. It was heavenly for me. Technology is not my friend, so being unable to use it was awesome.

Zakarias stands and closes the dusty book gently, snapping his finger. I watch the book disappear into thin air and sigh. It's an odd ability that First Librarians develop once they're officially titled.

"Stuck it in your keeping room, eh?" I joke.

"I'll need to revisit it soon," he confirms.

I cross my arms. "Gods, I wish I could visit your room. I'd love to know what else you've got squirreled away in there. To be able to snap my fingers and magic me and my books away to a secret room? Hells, yes!"

Zakarias laughs. "Sometimes, I take Okair into my private room just to fuck him atop the books. It is *glorious*. That'll be you one day, Onmiel."

I give him a stern look. "Fucked atop your library stacks? No, thanks."

His dark skin flushes as red steals across the tops of his cheeks.

"Not *my* stacks, of course. I simply meant..."

I chuckle. "I know what you meant; I'm joking. I just want my own private keeping room, full of the things I want to read, where nobody can bother me. That and a nice coffee is all I need."

"It is a heavenly place to hide away from the world for a bit," he agrees.

We fall silent as we continue to pore through our books, cross-referencing data with the current paper we're researching. Occasionally, I look up at the long rows of tables lined between soaring stacks of books. The library is so tall that I can't even see the ceiling in this section. I imagine all the knowledge kept here and cannot wait to soak up every ounce of it. The Pengshur library is full of secrets and ancient magic, and I am obsessed with learning every last thing there is.

Onmiel, First Librarian of the Ancient Library at Pengshur. Here I come!

~

Hours later, I follow Zakarias along the wooden row table, looking at other First Librarians hunched over books of every size, color, and shade. I ache to know what they're reading, what they're researching, and what they're *doing* with all the knowledge they gain. Most librarians are knowledge-seekers, but First Librarians often serve the leaders of the realm as advisors. Still, anyone can come to the library and request to be assigned a librarian for a research topic. Some of the research programs go on for years and years.

Gods, I'd love to get assigned to one of the language-focused programs. Right now there's a whole First Librarian team cataloging a newly-uncovered ancient naga language. It's so fascinating.

My attention returns to the library around me. The only sounds are the faint page turns and the occasional rustle of clothing as we come to the exit. At the wide double doors that mark this section, a naga librarian slithers up to us, tapping Zakarias on the forearm but ignoring me entirely.

Ugh. One day, I'll have the distinctive triangular facial tattoo marking me as a First Librarian, then they won't ignore me like a bug. Stupid, ridiculous hierarchy.

This particular librarian has always been a conundrum for me. Naga don't love to mix with other monsters or half-breeds, and his huge, snakish body must be so unwieldy in the narrow rows of the library. I look up at the humanoid top half of his figure, only belying his naga heritage with the circular hood that flares at the back of his head. Slitted, catlike green eyes narrow on Zakarias as he crosses his muscular arms over his chest. He wears only a vest rather than the black tunic that would normally mark his rank.

"I need to speak with you, Zakarias," he begins. Just as I imagine a snake man would, he draws out the end of Zakarias's name into a long "s" sound, his forked tongue flicking out to lick his lips. His tongue is black, just like his hood and the snakelike portion of his body. He's always creeped me out a little bit, honestly.

Zakarias's voice is firm but calm. "Anything you wish to say to me can be said in front of my Novice."

Slitted eyes flick to me as the naga nods once, uncrossing his arms to hook his thumbs in the vest's pockets. He looks...uneasy? Behind him, the giant coils of his body draw tight together, as if he'd prefer to dive into them and hide from the world.

"I believe Rama is dead," he says abruptly, not taking a beat before he continues on quickly, "I cannot be sure, but..."

Zakarias and I hiss in matching breaths.

"Onmiel and I were discussing this yesterday," my mentor murmurs in a low tone. "We have all assumed that with the electricity back on, something happened to her."

The naga nods. "I was just speaking with Master Librarian Garfield, and he assumes it to be so. I'm considering leaving Pengshur as a result. What if this is another of her games?" The big librarian huffs, looking around as if

TEN: A DARK SHIFTER ROMANCE

Rama might have operatives hiding behind every musty stack of books. "I watched the nightly hunts she hosted in the Temple Maze. Now, the electricity is back when she cut it off for all those years. I cannot shake the feeling it might be time for me to return to my home province, far away from her and anything she might be plotting to do now."

What he says is very possible. She's psychotic enough to do that, I've heard. The reality is that for some reason that nobody is entirely sure of, Moon province, where Pengshur is located, is one of the few places Rama never attacked or even visited. I heard whispered voices once that she requested books from the Pengshur library, but who knows?

Zakarias looks up at the naga, straightening his chin. "If it's true that she is gone, then we are better off for it. It felt like only a matter of time before she turned her sights to Pengshur. Just imagine, for a moment, if she put her attention on the library..." Tears fill his eyes as he frets about the knowledge that could be lost if Rama brought her endless wars and bullshit here.

The naga doesn't look at ease as he lets out a soft hiss. "Perhaps she is gone, but something worse is coming."

His tone is ominous as Zakarias places a protective arm around my shoulders. "What could possibly be worse than Rama, Evizel?"

The naga shakes his head, his hood flaring wide as his forked tongue pokes out again. He looks down at me with a frown. "I do not know, Zakarias. But I cannot shake the feeling that this is the beginning of our issues."

I suppress a shudder as his emerald eyes narrow to slits. Without another word, he slinks back into the library's shadows and disappears behind a stack of books.

If there's something in Lombornei that's worse than Rama, I hope I never meet it.

CHAPTER THREE
TENEBRIS

Noire ignores my lackluster entry, focusing on the petite, dark-skinned woman seated at Arliss's right. His sister, Elizabet.

Her eyes go soft when she sees me look at her, but unlike everyone else, she's never treated me like I'm made of glass. I look away.

My big brother clears his throat, waving his hand for Elizabet to continue whatever she was saying when I came in.

She nods and leans forward over the glossy wooden table. "I can't heal Diana. I think we all realize that. I've tried everything I can think of, but she needs something I can't provide."

"Speak plainly," Noire barks.

Next to him, Diana stiffens but reaches out to place a hand on my brother's shoulder, her blond hair hanging limp against her thin shoulders.

A tic starts in Noire's jaw. I recognize the focused, predatory look on his face. It's like he thinks the cure is somewhere inside Elizabet, and he's ready to strip every bit of flesh from her bones to find it.

I should probably care.

Well, Arliss should care. He seems to be close to his sister.

It occurs to me that Elizabet wouldn't have lasted ten minutes in the maze. She'd have been ripped to shreds in minutes. I grit my teeth, thinking about it.

She lifts her chin and continues. "You need to go to Pengshur to the library there. They have healers and access to thousands of years' worth of research. Diana's injury is not commonplace. We need information that can only be found there."

"I'll accompany you, of course," Arliss decrees.

"A fucking library?" Noire's voice is barely above a snarl as he rises, planting both hands on the tabletop and looming over it. It's too wide for him to actually hover over Elizabet. Still, she shrinks back in her chair anyhow, casting a nervous glance at her sibling.

Arliss's expression goes cold and distant. "Sit *down*, Noire."

A ragged roar leaves Noire's throat, and it stabs like a dagger through the muscle of my chest. It reminds me of when Rama died, of how I screamed then. How it was full of anguish and emotion and horror.

That's the sound Noire makes now. His muscles tense and quiver. Elizabet stands and steps behind her brother's chair, never taking her eyes from my pack alpha.

"Noire, we need *help*, brother."

That's Jet—always the voice of reason, ever the strategist.

I'm barely involving myself, yet I'm exhausted thinking of how to control Noire and his temper. He's a flame that dances between pieces of dry kindling. Anything could spark Noire into a rage. He was always like this. He's the most calculating person I know.

My oldest brother jerks his head to Jet, and something imperceptible passes between them.

They don't bother to share it in our pack bond.

Not that I care.

Arliss unsteeples his fingers and rolls both eyes skyward as if he's thinking. Eventually, his focus returns to Noire. "I have a friend at Pengshur. He runs the place. Let us call and arrange to assign you a team to look for a cure. Garfield owes me a favor. I'm happy to collect on that now."

"And what'll I owe you after this is done?" Noire barks, defaulting to how he would have been in the maze, where nobody ever did anything for free.

Arliss grins. "Does it even matter, Noire? Diana's life is at risk. So, if I say you will owe me everything, will that stop you?"

There's a drawn-out, heavy pause. "No," Noire huffs. The glare he levels at our host would drop a lesser man to his knees.

"As I thought." Arliss grins, big white teeth making a show from behind ebony lips. "Let's go to my command center. We'll call Garfield."

"And then you've got another little errand to run, isn't that right?" Jet's mate Achaia's voice is fierce when she directs the question at him.

Our host rolls his eyes and huffs in irritation, shrugging his muscular shoulders.

"How could I forget, with you here to remind me so sweetly and repetitively." His voice is pure sugary sarcasm.

Jet's other mate, Renze, slips in a wisp of smoke across the room and reappears with a dagger pressed to Arliss's jugular.

"Speak to my mate thus another time, and you will lose your tongue, carrow. Perhaps without it, you will learn to be more pleasant."

Arliss's blue eyes narrow and focus on Achaia. He moves the dagger from his throat with one fingertip, shifts forward, and stands. When he jerks his head to the door, beaded braids tinkle around his broad shoulders.

I watch my pack and the vampiri follow him out of the room, but Jet lingers behind. He joins me and claps one hand on my shoulder.

"Come with us, Ten?"

I pause for a moment, trying to summon the energy to give enough of a fuck to stand up.

After a long beat, I do, trailing Jet and the rest of the pack through darkening halls. We head deep into Arliss's sandy compound until we reach a room full of monitors. Many of them are broken and trashed from Rama's attack. I was drugged then, so I scarcely remember it. Was I part of the group that blew holes in Arliss's home? Did I stand beside Rama when her soldiers threw every member of Arliss's family to the carnivorous mermaids in the moat?

I search my memory, closing my eyes as everyone finds a spot to stand or sit. But...I can't remember. It's hazy, like a lot of my memories these days. Even off whatever drugs she pumped me with, I can't seem to find clarity.

A beeping sound breaks through my thoughts, and a new voice echoes out of a speaker at the front of the room. A cracked screen blinks to life, and an older human-looking male with salt-and-pepper black hair appears. He squints at the screen momentarily and then smiles, but it looks forced. "Arliss, old friend. Haven't seen you in an age."

Arliss chuckles. "I'll write up the story of the last seven years of my life and gift it to the library. It would make for excellent fiction."

Noire bangs his fist on the desk in front of Arliss. "Get the fuck on with it."

When Noire appears on the screen, the male on the other end hisses in a breath. "Alpha Noire. So, it's true. You escaped the maze. We couldn't tell from what was televised."

Noire's focus turns to the male. "I'm coming to Pengshur, and I require your assistance."

Arliss shoves Noire back into his seat, and for a moment, I think there will be a scuffle. Again, Diana reaches for him, laying a hand on his chest.

Noir's focus turns to his mate. He pulls her carefully into his lap and buries his face in her neck, huffing softly. Our family bond is so tight it feels like splintered glass ready to shatter. I sense Jet's need to comfort our pack alpha. When I try to summon the same sentiment, I find I can't.

Arliss looks at the human again. "To make a very long story quite short, Alpha Noire's mate, Diana, was injured by a monster from the Tempang. She needs healing, and we cannot provide it here. Her injuries are extensive."

Garfield licks his lips and looks over at Noire, who's now glaring at him again. "Of course. The library has an excellent team of researchers, and we also work with local healers. But…" his voice trails off. I suspect what he's going to ask before the words leave his mouth, but it's still a knife to my gut that twists and turns when he says them. "You've escaped. So, is Rama dead? There are rumors."

For some reason, I force myself to stand there, wondering how Noire will explain what happened. Will he tell this man that I killed her?

"It's…complicated," Arliss hedges.

Noire breaks in. "If you cannot heal my mate, Rama will be the very fucking least of your concerns."

The male, Garfield, gulps and nods. "Of course, Alpha Noire. Please send any data you have about your mate's injury, and let me know when you'll be arriving. I'll pick my best team."

"See you soon," Arliss chirps in a cheerful tone.

Garfield grimaces, nods, and clicks off. The screen goes dark, and the room falls silent.

"You didn't want to tell him?" our host questions my pack alpha.

Noire snarls and rises with Diana in his arms. "I want him off-guard and worried. I don't want him to think the threat has lessened because Rama is gone. I will be Garfield's worst godsdamned nightmare if he doesn't find answers. And I want all of that at the forefront of his mind every second of every fucking day."

My older brother turns to me, his features twisted with frustration. "I need you to make this trip, Ten. You know about Pengshur. You've always been interested in that place. I'm counting on you to tell me if they try to fuck us over."

I glance at Diana, but her head lolls back in the chair. She can't stay awake for more than a few minutes at a time. So I nod and leave the room. I can't stay and listen to this any longer.

I'm just so fucking tired.

TEN: A DARK SHIFTER ROMANCE

Hours later, Ascelin joins me on the porch as the sun sets behind the dunes. For a split second, all I can think of is my home province of Siargao. This province is hot, but it lacks the humid resplendence of Siargao. A pang of homesickness overtakes me. Ascelin hops onto the stone railing, resting her hands gracefully on both lean thighs.

I look up to find her smirking at me, all-white eyes flashing with mirth. It still surprises me to see her smile. She was my enemy for seven long years in the maze. Being something close to friends now is...weird.

"Diana is not well enough to travel to Pengshur, but I will accompany you," she states as if it's the simplest thing in the world.

I shrug. "You mean you're coming to babysit me?"

"Not hardly," she purrs. "You are a grown male, Tenebris. But Arliss wants something from that library, and per usual, he's not forthcoming about it. I want to know what he wants, and so does Noire. So, I'm going with you."

"Gods, this reminds me of the maze," I grumble. "Everyone's got an agenda. Nobody trusts anybody. It's fucking exhausting. Why do we even give a fuck what Arliss wants?"

Ascelin's smile falls. The maze was kind to no one, which reminds me that my godsdamned mate created it in the first place. It was Rama who imprisoned us there and tortured us for seven years. I grew up in the fucking Temple Maze until Rama realized what I was to her. Even then, she didn't let me out. I had to escape on my own. What does that even say about her?

I shake my head as I struggle to reconcile what I know to be true about my mate from my brief experience as her lover.

"Tenebris?" Ascelin's voice is gentle as she reaches out to pat my arm. When I look back up, she gives me a soft smile, translucent black teeth glinting in the faint light. "You have not seen a library in years, my friend. Will you not be excited to visit the most revered library in Lombornei? All they do there is read, learn, and advise rulers and leaders. It seems like something you would enjoy."

I grit my teeth and nod. I don't need to tell her how the first time I took my mate was in a library in her quarters. A library she built for me with books taken from the famous Pengshur collection. A library I fucked her in dozens of times, spilling my seed as she fell apart on my knot, screaming my name, our mate bond ablaze with violent ecstasy.

The familiar ache reappears in my chest, and I rub at it, wondering absentmindedly if broken mate bonds can ever be healed. Or gods, maybe even turned off? But that train of thought leads me down a circuitous route of thinking. If I turn off my broken bond, will I forget her? Will I forget the perfect connection we had for such a brief time? Do I want that?

I don't know what I want, to be honest. I want to not be tired.

Ascelin must sense she's lost my attention for the second time today. She pushes off the railing and disappears inside. I don't need to focus to hear my pack talking about me just inside the doors.

"Ten."

Achaia's soft voice breaks through my thoughts as she joins me on the balcony. Goddess, it's one person after another, a steady stream of well-wishers hoping to convince me everything will be fine.

I look over at my brother Jet's beautiful mate. Luscious red hair falls in waves down her back, her green eyes sad when she smiles at me.

"Your mermaid form is so different from this one," I muse as I attempt to return the smile.

She winks conspiratorially. "To be honest, I miss the boobs in mermaid form. The boobs are really nice to have."

"That's not what I meant," I bluster, feeling a flush spread across my cheeks.

"Oh, I know." She shrugs, laughing as she leans against the railing. "I just think when someone experiences a loss, those around them tend to treat them like victims all day, and that shit gets old. Sometimes, you just need one person to act like the sky didn't fall on your head, and that one person is me."

A bit of relief threads through my system as I turn to her, leaning against the railing to match her stance. I can't ask her about what she lost because that'll lead to more stories about how crazy and vicious my dead mate was. Achaia tried—and failed—to kill Rama more than once after Rama decimated her clan. She's another person who lost literally everything because of my bondmate. Her victims are so numerous I can't turn without seeing one.

It's hard to wrap my mind around that most days.

"I could use your help with something," she says after a long beat. "I need someone big and strong."

I glance over my shoulder at my brother Jet, but he's currently wrapped in his other mate's arms. He passionately kisses Renze, the graceful vampiri warrior, sitting on the edge of the dining table.

Achaia follows my gaze and grins at them, then trills her fingers along my forearm. "Will you help me for a few minutes?"

I shrug again and gesture for her to lead the way. I follow her through lengthy, sunny halls until we come to a vast airship workshop I've seen once or twice. Arliss and Elizabet are there already. Elizabet holds a clipboard as she marks something off, checking a list. Arliss dwarfs her much smaller figure as he clips a giant glass box together at the corners with creaky metallic locks.

Elizabet's plump lips split into a smile when she sees us. It lacks the devilishness of Arliss's grin, but everything about him seems deviant, whereas Elizabet is a breath of fresh air. She's a scientist at heart, though, and Arliss is just...Arliss.

"Ah, you've found a helper. Thank you, sweet friend!" she says to Achaia. I wonder how the women have become so close so quickly, but I haven't been paying attention. Then again, Achaia seems easy to be around. She's thoughtful, kind, and strong. I'm glad Jet has her, even though it crushes my soul to see happy people continuing on as if my world wasn't decimated by a single moment.

Arliss gestures to the giant glass box in the middle of the room. "Tenebris, help me move this."

I stride across the junk and tool-filled space, picking my way over random pieces of shrapnel left over from Rama's attack.

"What's the box for?" I question as I shove against it, helping him move the entire thing to the far wall, which opens into a courtyard of sorts.

"Nothing just now," he grunts. "It will be full of mermaids soon. We will return them to their home sea on our way to Pengshur."

"That's right, and what else?" Achaia presses in a stern tone, following us with her arms crossed.

Arliss rolls his eyes exaggeratedly but winks at me before turning to her. "And I will apologize for accepting them as a gift, entrapping them with a spell, and keeping them in my shithole of a moat for seven years."

"And what *else*, Arliss?" Achaia presses further, green eyes flashing as she crosses her arms. "Don't make me threaten to shift and level this place. I could, you know..."

The hint of a smile tugs at my lips. Mermaid queens can let out a shriek that can obliterate armies with a single sound. It's a last-ditch protective effort, although I know Achaia leveled Rama's home province once before my mate took the pearls from her crown and stole that ability. Achaia's crown is full now, though.

I turn to her. "Mermaids swim great distances so fast. Can we not release them in the closest sea and allow them to return home more quickly?"

"We're not *that* fast," she mutters. "And they'd have to swim all the way down the coast and around Siargao just to come up the other side of Lombornei. It makes much more sense to deliver them with the airship. It's the least Arliss can do after keeping them in that—"

"Muddy, filthy, disgusting moat. I *know*," he cuts in, throwing his hands up.

"I have already apologized twice to you and thrice to the other mermaid queen."

"And I don't believe you meant a single word of it," Achaia snarls. "So, while I'm here, I will advocate for them until they are safe and away from your clutches. It's not natural for mermaids to be trapped in such a small body of water. The conditions they're living in are—"

"Deplorable. Yes, I *know*," Arliss hisses. Somewhere across the room, Elizabet chuckles. Achaia and Arliss fight like this every day, and I think the big male's sister finds it highly amusing.

"Mermaid cities typically cover several square miles," I think aloud. "And it's not uncommon for a mermaid to travel as far as fifty miles in a day. They'll be glad to be home, I'm sure."

Achaia shoots me a thankful look.

One of Arliss's dark brows raises. "How do you know about mermaids?"

Pressure crushes my chest inward, but I stand tall and cross my arms. "I wasn't born in the maze, Arliss. And there was a library in my room."

He opens his mouth to say something else but seems to think better of it.

"I'm going to bed," I murmur. The sun isn't even down yet, but I've lost any energy I had trying to muddle through this conversation.

"Come to dinner, Tenebris," Achaia encourages, stepping forward to stare at me with those shocking green eyes.

For a long moment, I look at her, truly look at her, this wondrous person mated to my brother and Renze. And I know I should *want* to get to know her. She's not a direwolf omega, but she's my brother's mate, which means I'm connected to her, too. If I listened hard enough, I'd hear her in our growing pack bond.

But I ignore that because I don't want to hear all the whispered worries and concerns in the bond these days. I don't want to join in on the fear everyone has for Diana's life.

I just want to go to sleep.

CHAPTER FOUR
TENEBRIS

Morning comes too fast. Sometime in the night, Jet packed a bag for me. It's sitting by the door to my room, and his scent is all over it. Early morning sunrays filter through my room's open balcony window. Noire tugs at me insistently through our family bond.

Asshole.

Groaning, I roll out of bed and change. I grab the bag without looking inside and head for the open-air dining area. Noire feeds Diana small pieces of meat, glaring at me when I show up. Jet and his mates look on in concern, whether for me or Diana, I couldn't say.

When I catch Ascelin's attention, she schools her heartbroken expression into something more neutral.

Ah, Diana then. The vampiri king connected with her in the maze. Of course they're worried for her. Even though he's gone.

Sort of.

I manage my way through a breakfast I don't care to eat.

Ascelin, Elizabet, Jet, and Achaia leave to load up the mermaids. Noire and Diana focus on me from across the table.

There's an impossibly heavy tension in our family bond.

"I'm counting on you, Tenebris," Noire begins.

Next to him, Diana's already pale face is more drawn than ever, her long, blonde hair hanging limp against her skull. She looks like a dead woman walking, and even in our family bond, she feels faint.

Noire almost looks like he's about to beg for something, but he continues on, his voice low.

"We three brothers are the future of Pack Ayala. It is our duty and gift to rebuild it. I want us *all* to have a chance to do that, Tenebris. You included, one day. When you're ready."

I shake my head. "I can't think about that, Noire, I—"

"I know," he interrupts. "I'm not asking you to. But you're still *here*, Tenebris. Your fate, your future still lies ahead of you. Not behind."

"Easy for you to say," I snap.

"No," he barks in a furious tone. "It's not easy for me to say that. Nothing about our journey has ever been easy, brother. Escaping the maze just brought us new godsdamned issues. We have to face them together."

Diana's blue eyes focus on me, and she gives me a reassuring smile. It's easy to see she's with Noire on this one.

"We appreciate you, brother," she says, her voice barely above a whisper. It sounds cracked and broken like it's hard for her to even speak. "We love you so fucking much, Ten. We're here for you, too, you know."

"I don't need anything," I bark.

"We need one another, now more than ever," she counters, her tone growing fierce despite her obviously waning strength. "We trust you, Ten, just as we always have. And you can trust us, alright?"

For a moment, I can't think of how to respond. Eventually, it becomes awkward, so I stand. I round the table and lean down to brush my cheek against Diana's with a soft purr. Despite everything that's happened, she's still my pack omega. I'm still drawn to protect her.

She leans into that touch, brushing her soft cheek against mine. Warmth steals through our family bond. There's satisfaction from Noire that we're connecting, and there's elated pleasure from Diana.

But being this close to her, I smell sickness. It seeps from her in inky, insidious tendrils that seem to creep around the room and congregate in the shadows.

She doesn't have long. I can sense it the way a direwolf senses any sick packmate.

When she pulls back, Noire takes her place and pulls me into his arms for a brusque hug.

"Love you," he says in his usual gruff tone. "Always have, always will, baby brother."

"You, too," I manage, wishing like hells I could snap my fingers and appear somewhere where we aren't exchanging heartfelt emotions. I can count on one hand the number of times Noire has told me he loves me.

I manage to extricate myself from his embrace and make my way to the front of the compound, where the long, metallic walkway leads over a dirty-looking moat. The water's surface roils, dozens of scaly bodies flipping and swirling. On the far side, resting on the dunes, is the enormous glass box from Arliss's workshop. Today, it's filled with clear water. Arliss and Elizabet stand in front of it.

Achaia and Jet stand next to them, and Achaia looks pissed. I head toward them, and by the time I get there, she's shouting at Arliss.

"You're such a godsdamned bastard, you know that?"

"You've said," snaps Arliss.

Next to them, Elizabet frowns at the water.

Jet taps me through the family bond. *Apparently, the mermaids arrived under some sort of enchantment that kept them from transforming to their two-legged form, and that's how he kept them trapped in the moat. Achaia wasn't fully aware of how it worked and she's going to rip his guts out through his nose if he doesn't fix it soon.*

I hadn't thought about why the mermaids didn't just shift and walk away from Arliss, or attack him in his sleep, but it makes sense if they're enchanted. I know Achaia can shift between mermaid and human forms, I just didn't give thought to why they *didn't*.

"I thought Elizabet sorted it already," Arliss grumbles.

Arliss's sister sighs, taps at her temple, and looks at Achaia. "I think I can actually fix this. Although Arliss failed to mention it earlier." She gives him a dirty look and jogs up the metal walkway past me.

Arliss groans as she goes, kicking at the sand with one booted foot.

When I join the group, Jet greets me with a toothy grin. "As soon as we figure out how to get the mermaids out, we'll be on our way."

I nod and head for one of two compact airships parked just beyond the moat, tossing my bag onto a metal bench inside. Jet and Achaia are going to accompany us as far as returning the mermaids and then they'll come back to try to stabilize Diana to come to Pengshur, if possible.

Ten long-ass minutes later, Elizabet returns with a vial of purple liquid. For the first time in days, I find myself interested in how this will go. I haven't spent much time with Arliss's sister—or anyone, for that matter—but I've learned she's something of a science whiz. It's why Rama kept her at the city of Nacht, forcing Elizabet to run experiments for her.

I grit my teeth as a memory of Rama backhanding the smaller woman assaults me.

Elizabet kneels down at the water's edge and dumps the purple vial out. Immediately, the viscous-looking liquid spreads across the surface, bubbling as water vapor rises off the surface. I leave the dark confines of the airship to rejoin the group for a closer look.

A crown rises up out of the water, covered in iridescent pearls of varying sizes. Wide, slanted eyes and a flat nose appear next, along with tapered, pointed ears. The mermaid queen swims to the edge and reaches out with spindly, claw-tipped fingers. When she reaches the sand, she hisses and sucks in a breath of air.

She jerks her head over her shoulders and lets out a string of hisses and clicks that remind me of Renze and Ascelin's language. I wonder if there's a common ancestor somewhere between vampiri and mermaids…

But then there's movement where the water laps at the sand, and that pulls my attention back to the current moment.

The queen drags herself up onto the sand. Obsidian scales shimmer and disappear, and her long, twin-tipped tail becomes two slender, shapely legs. She wiggles her toes with a gleeful smile and then stands, lifting her chin high. In this form, she reminds me of Achaia, but she's taller and thinner.

Behind her, nearly two dozen other mermaids begin to leave the moat, shaking off dirty, smelly water as they struggle to stand for the first time in who knows how long.

The predator in me realizes we're outnumbered, but that the mermaids are probably off-kilter, having not been on two legs in years. Even so, I widen my stance and ball my fists, ready for an attack if there is one. If the maze beat anything into me, it was to always be prepared.

The queen's fierce gaze flicks over to me and she turns, stalking across the hot sand. It must burn her feet; this province is hotter than the seven hells. But if it does, she pays it no mind. She comes to a stop in front of me, but Achaia steps between us and reaches out to place one hand on the other queen's shoulder.

I don't understand the words that leave Achaia's mouth next, but the queen's focus flicks to the behemoth glass box and she nods. Achaia gestures to a ladder on one side of the box. The queen strides on shaky legs to it and waits for the next woman to follow her.

I shift closer to Jet and Achaia, ready to protect his mate if something happens. These are her kind, but I don't trust anyone who isn't bound to me in some way. Achaia reaches out, loosens my fist, and threads her fingers through mine, pulling me close.

Touch.

A gentle, soft, woman's touch.

I never knew that with Rama. There was never any of that even in the middle of our mating. She was pure and violent delight, and not a shred of anything else. She hated anything soft, absolutely despised it and declared it as being weak.

I think I'll hate Achaia holding my hand, but I don't push her away. Jet says nothing in our bond, but there's a slow and tangible sentiment of pride. My formerly broken brother is proud of his woman.

I hate that. I'm not proud of mine.

I pull my hand from Achaia's.

The first mermaid climbs up the ladder and dives into the enormous tank. Nearly two dozen more follow. After long minutes, the queen stands at the base and a final head pops out of the water, a smaller one next to it. A child.

An ember stirs in the cold, dead fires of my heart. I don't give a fuck about anybody who isn't related to me, and even then, I'm having trouble giving a shit. But children have always been a soft spot. Maybe it's because I was a child myself when I saw every kid I knew massacred by Rama's goons. Maybe it's because I was a child myself when my godsdamned mate threw me in a maze of monsters to kill for her. Maybe it's because this world is a piece of shit, but children are the single shred of light and hope for me.

The woman and child leave the water, but when the child touches the sand, she squeals and leaps back with a pained cry.

The mermaid queen and I move as one, but I get there first, swooping the girl up into my arms. The mother and the queen scream at the same time, but I ignore them, focusing on the galloping heartbeat of the merchild I hold frozen to my chest. When I reach the tank, I heft her halfway up the ladder and stand to make sure she doesn't fall. She topples into the water, shifting back into mermaid form and pressing herself against the glass. One hand comes flat to it, and she gives me the tiniest of smiles.

The queen and the mother join us. She hisses at me, and I step back. She and the mother ascend the ladder and follow the child into the water. The tank is so full. It's not nearly big enough to comfortably hold two dozen mermaids, but it'll have to do, I suppose. Mermaids are always more comfortable in their natural form. Achaia will have requested the tank for them, rather than having them sit in human form. Truly, I think the only reason she stays in human form so much is for Jet's and Renze's sakes.

I watch the queen cross her now-spindly arms and glare daggers at Arliss.

He rolls his eyes and presses a button on a remote. Tracks on the bottom of the tank creak and groan as he moves it toward the larger of the two airships. He maneuvers the tank inside and secures it to the metal floor with giant chain hooks.

When I follow Jet and Achaia into the second ship, Renze appears out of nowhere. He stands, stroking Achaia's face as he kisses her.

Ugh.

Might wanna head to the other ship, brother, Jet says helpfully in our bond. *We'll be a minute.*

Wrinkling my nose, I leave my brother and his mates. When I turn to look at the compound one final time, Noire, Diana, and Ascelin stand in the hole in the gate. Ascelin looks to be saying her goodbyes. Diana lifts one hand to wave at me. Noire glowers, but that's his normal face.

Be safe, brother, he huffs into our bond.

Ascelin hoists her backpack over her shoulder and hugs Diana one last time. Then she turns and paces across the long bridge, striding into my airship and seating herself next to Arliss at the controls.

"Hello, pretty girl," he croons. Elizabet and Ascelin groan at the same time, but then Elizabet kisses her brother on the forehead and leaves the airship, waving goodbye to the mermaids and me.

Great. Third wheel with the couple who refuses to admit they're together. Fun times lie ahead for me.

I strap myself into a seat in the vaulted back with the mermaids. It doesn't take long for us to get under way. It takes even less time for Ascelin and Arliss to get into a shouting match.

I manage to drum up a notepad from under one of the seats, and I play tic tac toe with the mermaid child for an hour before she tires and swims into her mother's arms to rest. The queen watches me from the corner, eyes narrowed and dark blue lips pursed together.

There's no energy in me to engage with her or any of the rest of them, so I let my head fall back against the curved metal hull of the airship. Sleep overtakes me, despite having woken up not long ago.

Sometime later, I wake to the sloshing of water. Rising, I join Ascelin and Arliss at the front of the ship. Ahead of us lies a crystal-clear turquoise sea. Giant, blue waves splash up against pitch-black craggy rocks. The mermaids grow agitated, flipping and spinning, sending great sloshes of water onto the ground.

"Pipe down!" Arliss roars. "You'll be home soon enough," he tacks on under his breath.

Ascelin rolls her white eyes at him and punches one of the controls. A metallic croak echoes out from underneath the ship. Landing gear, maybe?

Five harrowing minutes later, Arliss lands the airship on a large rock with the back facing the water.

He stands and gestures to the mermaids. "Get out, fishes. You're home."

Ascelin stands and grips a fistful of his braids, yanking his focus to her.

"Can you not see the rocks look sharp as daggers, you asshat? Get them close to the water, at least."

His blue eyes narrow on her. "Did Achaia put you up to this?"

Ascelin doesn't bother to answer, but drops his braids as if they're venomous snakes. She grabs the tank remote from the dashboard and hands it to him. "They were promised front-door service, I believe." When she crosses her arms, Arliss leans in and snarls, backing Ascelin against her seat.

Shocking blue eyes drift down to her lips as he snarls. "It is high time to stop pushing me, vampiri. Fuck me or don't, I care not at this point. But press me further and you will see a side of me you do not care for."

"Been there, done that on all accounts," she barks, shoving him out of her face as she slips in a stream of smoke to the back of the airship.

Their banter makes me want to find headphones and go back to sleep.

Arliss uses the remote to maneuver the mermaid tank out of the airship. The scent of salt water fills my nostrils. It reminds me vaguely of Siargao, but it lacks the undercurrent of fried fish and that unique scent that's riverwater versus seawater. Gods, I think I miss home.

Jet and Achaia join us. They reek of cum and slick. Achaia's cheeks are flushed, and there's a sated, hazy look on Jet's face.

Gross.

I can't wait to get to the library if only to stop seeing mated couples every-fucking-where I turn.

By the time Arliss gets the tank to the very edge of the rocks, the mermaids are in a literal frenzy, spinning and whirling around the tank, crashing against the thick glass panels.

Arliss gives Achaia a haughty look. "Perhaps I should simply shoot out one side of the tank and splash them in?"

"Try it," Achaia snaps. "Maybe I'll just shove you in with them." She gives him a condescending look and heads to the tank, standing at the base of the ladder as the queen pulls herself out of the tank and descends it. They press their foreheads together and speak softly.

The queen stands guard as her people make their way to the edge of the rocks. They leap in with cries of joy, appearing with their heads above water to wait for her to join.

Two things happen almost simultaneously.

The queen lets out a shriek that splits my skull like a hammer. It shatters all four walls of the tank, and a giant shard breaks free and knocks Arliss backward.

Then, with seemingly inhuman strength, two of the mermaids snatch Arliss by the braids. He shouts and falls on his back, his head banging against the craggy rocks. There's a hissed intake of breath, and the mermaids drag him to the edge and over.

He lets out a raging bellow as he disappears from view, blood coating the rocks where they took him.

There's a moment of silence, and then Ascelin screams. I rush forward to look over the edge at the waters below. Blood blooms bright and red in the water, and her screams become wails of anguish.

I wonder if they're eating him.

Seems like it.

Or will they just rip him to shreds and leave him for the sharks?

Achaia joins us with a neutral look on her face. She looks neither surprised nor displeased at this turn of events.

Ascelin, on the other hand, is losing her mind and looks like she's about to throw herself into the expanding circle of red blood. She slips in a trail of black smoke to the edge of the rocks, wringing her hands.

I place my hand on her shoulder and push her back before she can do something stupid, something like I'm about to do.

Will they tear me apart if I toss myself in, too? What would that feel like?

I want to find out.

I kick off my shoes and leap over the edge into the roiling water.

~

Warm, tropical water covers me, muting sound as I enter the water. I open my eyes but can barely see anything. The mermaids roil madly around me, but I let out a roar that grabs their attention.

Arliss slashes out, but his movements are sluggish and heavy. He's drowning. There's a splash next to me, and Ascelin appears in the water with a dagger in each hand. A third splash reveals Jet and Achaia. Jet swims for Arliss, shoving mermaids away from the fallen male.

Blood fills the water.

So much blood.

Closing my eyes, I wait for a strike. A hit. Anything. Will they eat me too?

When nothing happens, I open my eyes, squinting them to try to see.

The mermaid queen glares at us, deprived of her revenge and her meal.

Achaia lets out a string of hisses and clicks. The other queen's gills flare angrily but she nods. She seems to decide it's not worth the fight because she lets out a horrible hiss and flits off into the darker turquoise water.

Death has no plans for me today, it seems.

I swim to Jet's side, grabbing a fistful of Arliss's shirt. Ascelin joins us, and together we manage to get him above water. It takes all three of us since he's heavy as fuck, but we're able to lug him to where we parked the airship.

We lay him flat on his back. Ascelin throws herself across his prone figure and starts mouth to mouth. He's bleeding from dozens of slash wounds to his torso.

Jet throws a furious look at me as I watch Ascelin trying to save the monstrous carrow.

"What the fuck were you thinking, Ten?" Jet snaps. "Diving in after him. You could have been killed. Is this the kind of help we can expect when you go to Pengshur? Because if this is what you've got to give right now, I'll go instead."

His fury is a slap in the face.

I wasn't thinking about Diana. I wasn't thinking about anyone. I just wondered what might happen. It was instinctive, more than anything, to follow Arliss in.

When I open my mouth to say something, nothing comes out. Jet glares at me, but I can't summon a response.

A coughing sound behind us draws our focus to Arliss, who chokes up seawater as Ascelin lays across him, seemingly trying to hold back a sob.

When he sits up, she slaps him across the face.

He grunts, whipping his head back toward her. He grips her cheeks, squeezing them together, and then he plants the most tender of kisses on her dark lips, falling to the ground with her in his arms. It's like they don't even know we're here. Ascelin sobs into the kiss, Arliss grunts in pain, and I watch on as he bleeds from dozens of deep-looking wounds.

Jet clears his throat, but I don't want to see this shit.

I turn and head back for the airship, dripping water and blood in a stream behind me.

CHAPTER FIVE
ONMIEL

I'm sitting on my apartment's small balcony, looking down the street at the southern entrance to the library when a sudden pounding at my door makes me leap up. Hot coffee spills down my legs as I hiss and grumble, pushing my glasses higher up the bridge of my nose as I stomp to the door.

When I swing it open, Zakarias stands there, out of breath. He steps into my cramped apartment, one palm placed dramatically over his heart.

"Onmiel, now that the electricity is back, *kindly* turn on your computer. I've been pinging you on the library's messaging app for half an hour."

My face flushes. He's told me this twice already. But to be honest, not only do I not like technology, I'm not that great with it either. I didn't grow up with it, and I'm not accustomed to how it works. I much prefer the days when someone who needs me would pick up a phone or knock on my door. Like… a week or so ago.

"Sorry," I murmur, grabbing napkins off the kitchen counter to wipe the coffee that's dripping down both legs.

Zakarias ignores that completely. "Get dressed quickly. We've got an assignment as a team!"

I jerk my head up at that. "An assignment? As a team?"

Zakarias's dark lips split into a grin, white teeth showing as the smile broadens impossibly wide. "A team! Meaning this is your final test before they grant you the mantle of First Librarian. ML Garfield wants to see us straight away."

"Oh my gods!" I shriek, throwing my hands up in the air and dancing around. "Are you serious?"

"As a heart attack," he mumbles, rubbing at his chest. "I ran all the way from the archives when Master Librarian Garfield called me in to tell me."

"Garfield called you himself?" I'm incredulous. ML Garfield rarely comes out of his keeping room, except for librarian meetings, I'm told. I've only ever met him a few times, and he looked through me like I was a wisp of wind.

"He did." Zakarias preens as he straightens the lapels of his collared shirt. "And he told me I could pick any of my Novices to assist."

"Knew I was your favorite." I wink.

Zakarias points toward my bedroom. "Get dressed quickly. He rang me half an hour ago, so..." His brown eyes dip pointedly to my robe.

That's all the hint I need to haul ass into my room and change.

I throw on my umber-colored Novice tunic, tying a sky-blue belt at my waist. Looking in my window, I fluff my shoulder-length peachy ombre waves, throw on a little matching lipstick, and thank the gods I took a shower this morning.

Tossing my notebooks and pens in my bag, I sling it over my shoulder and head for my small living room. Zakarias stands in the doorway, tapping his foot impatiently. The broad male looks so out of place in my pink and turquoise living room. I'd giggle if I wasn't so excited for his news.

I jog past him and out the door, hearing as he clicks the lock for me, and then we speed up the cobblestone streets toward the archives and the Master Librarian's Study, the long hall where ML Garfield's office is located.

Normally, I appreciate Moon Province's tropical beauty, but today, my mind is squarely on the gothic building that looms at the end of the high street.

"What do we know so far?" I question my mentor as he power walks past bustling shops, just as focused as I am on the library ahead.

"He was unusually cagey," Zakarias gripes. "Said he'd give me the details once we got there."

I grit my teeth but excitement fills me so fast I can barely stop from screaming with anticipation. I'm humming by the time we make it to the glossy black double doors that mark the archives, the non-public section of the library. A lone guard tips his white hat to us as we pass through the security station and head down a long, sunny hallway.

Zakarias makes a hard left down a hall I've never been down, the hall ML Garfield's office is on, and most of the First Librarians'. A gilded sign at the entryway marks it as the Master Librarian's Study. It's completely off-limits to Novices unless you've been requested and are accompanied by a First

TEN: A DARK SHIFTER ROMANCE

Librarian or the Master himself. The hall is lined with fancy, painted portraits of former Master Librarians. There are dozens of famed names I recognize from my Novice training.

I'm giddy with anticipation by the time we reach the end of the sun-drenched, windowed hall.

A giant maroon door looms before us, a white placard indicating we've reached the Office of the Honored Master Librarian Garfield.

If I can say one thing about the Library at Pengshur, they've got pomp and circumstance down. Everything about this place is designed to give it an air of dignity and academic excellence. I want into the inner circle so bad I'll do just about anything. Today marks a huge day in my slow-but-steady progress. I've been in the Novice program for eight years—it's definitely time to take the next step.

Zakarias reaches over and straightens my tunic, giving me a once over. I smile wryly. It's just as important to him that I be successful—not only because he adores me, but because it reflects well on him, too. I'm really fucking good at what I do, and he chose me for that reason.

My mentor takes a deep breath, then knocks twice.

"Come in," rings out a voice from inside, the tone gruff and impatient.

I wince as Zakarias swings the door open and sails through. Following behind him, I resist the urge to stare around at the office I've been dying to see inside for ages. Instead, I make direct eye contact with ML Garfield.

He sits behind a desk, except it's not a desk; it's more like a platform. It almost looks like where a judge sits in a courtroom. Stairs lead up to it from both sides, and the entire front is wood so I can't see what's behind it.

Garfield looks every bit the angry judge ready to mete out punishment.

Shit, I really need to learn to use the paging system.

Garfield's human, but his role at Pengshur is so important that he seems larger than life to me in his navy tunic, the scrolling Master Librarian tattoo visible on his pale cheek. Salt-and-pepper hair is slicked back effortlessly. If I wasn't freaking out about having made us late, I could definitely be ogling ML Garfield and his silver-fox good looks.

"I'll get straight to the point, as the clients are waiting," he begins in a harsh tone.

Next to me, Zakarias shifts from one foot to the other, but I lift my chin higher. This isn't the time to apologize or make excuses. I can offer a sincere apology after we get the assignment.

Garfield's sharp gaze moves to Zakarias. "Zakarias, I'm assigning you to a request from an old acquaintance of mine. His name is Arliss. He is looking for information on healing. Apparently, one of his companions was injured by a monster from the Tempang."

I open my mouth to ask a million questions. The Tempang? Nobody goes there, except Rama, who lived right on the edge until she built her city in the sky and flew that around instead. Shit, I wonder if this is connected to how our electricity came back on?

Garfield continues, "Arliss was unclear about their exact needs, but given your expertise in ancient methods of healing, I feel you're the best librarian to assist him. You chose this Novice as your second?" Eyes the color of the deep sea flash to me.

Zakarias nods. "Onmiel is exceptionally skilled in not only healing knowledge but languages and—"

"Good," Garfield interrupts. "I'll tell you now, he'll be accompanied by two of the monsters from the Temple Maze. You'll probably recognize them from the broadcasts, assuming you watched. One is a vampiri warrioress, and the other is Alpha Noire's youngest brother, Tenebris."

"Shit," blurts out Zakarias. "It's true, then. Rama must be gone? And the monsters are out of the maze?"

"I'll be blunt," Garfield mutters, ignoring the outburst. "Arliss is a wily asshole, and even though we have a long history together, he was not forthcoming on the details around the monsters escaping the maze. However, for the safety of the library and its librarians, I'd like to know more because I couldn't turn down this request. Arliss has been a Pengshur benefactor for a very long time. Assist as you can and find out what you can about the current situation with Rama and the maze's monsters. I want to know why and how the electricity is back on, and what future state I can expect for this province."

"You want us to spy on them?" I blurt.

Zakarias steps on my foot as Garfield sits back in his chair, steepling his hands together.

"I want you to *support* them, Novice Onmiel," he clarifies. "But find out what you can and report it to me. You wish to be a First Librarian yourself, do you not?"

When I nod to confirm, he opens his arms wide. "Your duty is not only to me, but the entirety of the librarian community. Arliss was vague on their needs. I know far less than I'd like, and while the library's duty is to assist, I cannot help but feel there is more to their story. That somehow, Rama herself is involved."

"Rama always left us alone, though," I counter because I feel like there's a hole in his tale and it's making the hair on my nape lift. "She never attacked us here, never took anyone from here. She focused on other provinces. Why worry now?"

ML Garfield stands, looming over the edge of his desk as he scowls at me. "Did she, Onmiel? If you feel that's the case, then I did my job of protecting the library very well."

Chilly fingers trace a path down my spine as I shudder and shrink back under the weight of his perusal. Is he saying what I think he's saying, that Rama was more involved here than I thought?

Zakarias steps in front of me. "We are up to this task, of course, ML Garfield. Are the clients in the Solarium now? We'll go immediately."

Garfield nods and gestures at the door. "There's a band for your novice just there. See she keeps it on while on assignment."

I dart to the door and grab the band, slipping it over my sleeve as I mutter a quick thank you. Then I follow Zakarias out without a backward glance. Even so, Garfield's eyes are on my back the entire way.

I can feel him.

○

"Onmiel, you must learn to hold your tongue," Zakarias chides the moment we're out the door.

I turn to him with a heated look.

"This assignment is huge," I agree, "and I'm grateful, but Garfield just dropped some very random information in our laps, Zakarias. You aren't the slightest bit worried? The monsters being out of the maze could mean a lot of things..." I think back to Evizel, the naga librarian, and how worried he was about what's happening.

Zakarias gestures impatiently up the hallway as we set off at a blistering pace.

"Yes, Onmiel. It means answers to the questions we've been asking ever since the power came back on."

"But—"

He cuts me off by raising a hand and giving me a warning look. "A First Librarian's duty is to the library, then to their partner librarians, and finally to themselves. In that order. Or have you forgotten our motto?"

"I haven't," I grumble as we pass through the entryway, where the motto is engraved over the door back out into the street. I give the engraved words a haughty look and fall quiet as we come to the steps of the eastern wing. We ascend them quickly and enter double doors, nearly jogging up the hallway until the Solarium comes into view.

The giant domed room sits between the archives and the First Librarian Hall. I love the Solarium, and it's the perfect place to meet the library's clients.

I sense monsters before I see the group. There's something about even half-breeds that sends butterflies tumbling around my belly. A sense of collected, barely-contained wildness hits me square in the chest as we round the corner. Three beings stand in the giant glass-domed room, looking up at the plate ceiling and the rain that's beginning to pour from the sky in buckets.

The first one to turn is a gigantic black male with long, braided hair. Bright blue eyes sparkle as thick, ebony lips part into a devious grin. His gaze travels from me to Zakarias and back, and the smile deepens.

I lift my chin and give him a polite smile. It is my sworn duty as mentee to a First Librarian to aid Zakarias in helping this group find what they came in search of. And I suppose to dig for answers for Garfield as well, although I'm not sure how I feel about taking on that mandate.

Next to the black male stands a striking vampiri woman with black braids that travel up over her scalp and down the side of her neck. They confirm her status as a vampiri king's First Warrior. I never watched when Rama broadcasted the nightly prey hunts in the maze, but I've heard the hushed whispers from other librarians. This female has killed dozens of beings in the last seven years, if she's who I think she is.

I resist the urge to shudder because she looks every inch a predator with her sharp, jet-black claws and focused, intense gaze. In person, her skin is nearly translucent. Her eyes are pure white, although I know a pupil and iris lie behind the protective covering. Thin, black lips purse into a frown when she notices my perusal.

The male smirks at her and reaches out to shake Zakarias's offered hand. "I'm Arliss, and this is my companion, Ascelin. That one…" He points to the third figure. "That is Tenebris, Alpha Noire's brother. Noire will be along in a day or two."

I turn to say hello but stop dead in my tracks at the third figure. He towers over the vampiri by a head or more, his huge body stacked with layers of muscle. I've never met a direwolf alpha in person, but nothing I've read about them prepared me for the way he dominates the room.

Broad, powerful shoulders taper to a trim waist. And gods, his ass is a work of art. Swallowing hard, I watch as he stares at the rain above us. It pelts the glass ceiling and slides down in giant rivulets. I know it's intoxicating; I've found myself doing the same thing from time to time. But I'm surprised he hasn't said anything or even noticed we've arrived.

"Tenebris?" The vampiri's voice is gentle as she addresses him, like he's a wounded bird.

Perhaps he's the one who was attacked, and they're hoping to find an answer here. Not all injuries produce visibly obvious wounds.

I straighten my shoulders, determined to be as helpful as possible.

The alpha male cocks his head to the side, and I catch a flash of amber eyes before he turns the rest of his body. Time seems to slow, or maybe it just does for me as I gaze at how fucking gorgeous he is from the front.

A thin tee does nothing to hide thick pectoral muscles or the dips and valleys of every visible ab. My throat goes as dry as the deserts of Dest, but I manage to drag my eyes quickly back up. Shit, he's looking at me. I expect to find wry amusement in his gaze, maybe wary interest, or even anger that I was staring at his beautiful midsection…but there's nothing there.

His pale eyes are blank of any emotion at all. Dark lashes flutter, framing how shockingly beautiful he is.

Where most men who meet me for the first time would at least give me a quick once-over, this male does nothing of the sort. Those stunning eyes move from me to the vampiri, who claps him on the shoulder.

"Tenebris, these are the librarians assigned to help us."

He nods once, but then those eyes go right back up to the rain as it pours onto the glass ceiling.

The vampiri sighs and grits her teeth.

I'm not sure what the issue is, but I am godsdamned determined to make my first assignment a fruitful one. These beings came here with a need, and so help me, I will fill it.

CHAPTER SIX

TENEBRIS

I don't know what sort of greeting I expected at the famous Pengshur library, but after Noire's threats, I half expected a red carpet. Or at the very least, the help of the Master Librarian himself. Garfield, I think his name is. Instead, we're presented with a First Librarian in a black tunic and his Novice, if I'm remembering their color system correctly. She looks barely my age, although she stands with the confidence of an older woman.

The rain pounding on the glass ceiling of the Solarium suits my mood. It mutes other sounds, soothing the pressure in my chest. I always loved the rain as a child, but then I didn't see it for seven years in the maze.

Somewhere along the way here, I've gone from inconsolable grief and exhaustion to anger, and that anger has set in good and hard. I'm furious at myself, furious at my mate, and furious at the world that fucked her so badly, she became the monster she had to be to survive.

So, I do something I started on the way here in an effort to distance my mind from her death.

I didn't see the rain for seven years because *she* imprisoned me. *She* imprisoned my family. *She* was an utter and complete asshole, and I had to kill her.

Still, thinking that feels disloyal, and it sends jagged strikes of pain through my gut so cutting I resist the urge to drop to both knees.

I grit my teeth and try to follow along, but it's hard to focus. The librarians introduce themselves. The male is Zaka—something. I don't catch the female's name at all. They gesture for us to follow them out of the room we're in. Ascelin paces behind me, watchful and wary as ever. She's worried I'm falling apart and unpredictable, especially after the scene earlier with Arliss.

She's right, of course.

When I was younger, I'd have given anything to make a trip to see Pengshur and visit the famous library. Now? Now, I don't fucking care. I'm somewhere between numb and enraged, but my emotions flip-flop one minute to the next. I think if I stop moving, everything will come crashing down, and I'll fall to the ground. I might never get back up if that happens.

The tall male librarian leads us down a long, windowed hall away from the big room they called the Solarium. Outside, foliage spills from hundreds of terra-cotta pots in a garden.

Diana would love it.

The thought enters my mind and dashes away again.

But then it comes back, curling around my consciousness.

Diana who faked her way into the maze under false pretenses, knowing my brother Noire was hers. Diana who screamed for me when Rama's monstrous machines dragged me up into the sky and away from my pack. Diana who's fighting against a terrible wound the Volya inflicted on her while I struggled to understand why my own mate would drug me.

Grinding my teeth, I let the anger flow through my system, and I visualize my pack omega. She's never done anything but try to help my family. She risked her life to save mine over and over again. She came onto Paraiso, Rama's sky island, to get me back.

I can do this for her. I can focus on finding a cure. If anyone in my pack is capable of understanding the knowledge here at Pengshur, it's me. Because the truth is I studied monsters for a long time in the maze, and my mate fed my addiction to knowledge by sending me books I'd enjoy.

I soaked up that knowledge, and now I need to use it to help.

Ascelin is a quiet presence behind me, but I wish she'd stop. I'm not going to take off running. I'm done trying to escape, for now at least. I'll help find a cure for Diana. But I don't know what I'll do after that. Maybe I'll take one of Arliss's many vehicles and go on a road trip, just disappear for a while.

Maybe I'll go back to Nacht, Rama's mountain city. It's where we spent our first nights together. It's where we cemented our—

I banish that thought the moment I have it, shaking my head. I can't go back to the dark, ominous city, right on the edge of the Tempang. I can't stand in the spot where I ripped her head from her shoulders. I don't think I'll ever be able to see Nacht again without thinking about killing her.

A door opens ahead, and when I lift my eyes, the female librarian is smiling at me as she holds it open, indicating I should go through.

She only comes up to my lower chest, but her face is uplifted as she smiles at me. Her eyes are kind. They're a shocking shade of pale gray, a weird combination with hair that starts at her scalp as a dark orange but fades to peach at the tips. It sort of matches her dark orange Novice tunic. I wonder if she did it purposefully. Maybe librarians have a whole style code I'm not aware of.

She tucks a strand of it behind one ear absentmindedly. When I step through the door, our eyes meet. Hers don't go to the ground, but she nips at the edge of her lip.

Sighing, I look from her into a tiny courtyard. It's full of plants, too. They burst from every surface, even covering the ground like a carpet. There's a large stone table in the middle of the room, and the male librarian sits at the head. The female rounds the table to hover at his side, grabbing a notebook from a bag slung over her shoulder.

Ascelin leans against the only spot in the wall with no plants, but Arliss and I sit. I guess they want another meeting.

The male opens his arms wide. "We'll quickly sync on your project here, and depending on any additional details you provide, Onmiel and I will begin our work. Master Librarian Garfield has already apprised us of what you're looking for at a high level." He gives us a concerned look. "But we need more information. I understand you want to know more about healing, but we need to know about the injury itself. How was it inflicted? How long has it been? What healing have you tried? Any details you can provide would be most helpful in directing our research."

Arliss sighs and steeples his fingers. "Volya. Just over a week. We've tried everything, and I have an extensive array of healing options at my fingertips. She heals because she's an omega, and then a day later, the wounds reopen. She is weak and does not have much time."

The librarian nods, but at his side, the female seems frozen at Arliss's words. When I narrow my eyes and observe her, her muscles relax, and she begins writing in her notebook.

"Not much is known about the Volya," the male librarian shares, glancing over at his assistant. "Onmiel, you're excellent with monster history. What do you think?"

She looks up, seemingly surprised he asked her opinion. But she turns to us with a serious expression, one scrawny forearm resting on the table as she lightly taps her pen. "The Volya are secretive. There's never been a half-blooded Volya to anyone's knowledge, for instance. They've always remained in the Tempang, so anything we have on them is from ancient travelers who braved the forest before the monster-human wars began."

Arliss huffs. "Are you saying there aren't answers to be found here? That would certainly be a first."

She shakes her head. "There are mentions of Volya scattered in hundreds of books throughout Pengshur, but it will take some time to find them." She looks directly at Arliss. "May I be blunt?"

"Please do," Ascelin purrs, pushing off the wall, "because my Chosen One's life hangs in the balance, and if we cannot find help for her here, we need to try something else."

The Novice purses her lips but nods. "It's possible there is help here, I can't be sure because I've never deeply looked into the resources we have on Volya. If the knowledge exists anywhere, it'll be here at Pengshur. But the reality is that your best bet is probably to find the Volya who hurt your friend, and to bargain with them for a cure."

"Not possible," Ascelin snaps. "We need another way."

There's a tense moment of silence, and it's so filled with worry for Diana that I feel my own mind receding back into the corners of my headspace. I'm trying to be angry, to push myself into that next stage of grief. But I keep drifting back to exhaustion.

"There's something else," Ascelin murmurs, tossing a paper on the stone tabletop. "A prophecy about the Chosen One. We always thought we knew the whole thing, but it turns out there were two halves. The second is in a language so ancient, there is not a vampiri alive who knows it. I'm hopeful it will tell us something that can save her."

The male, Zakarias, frowns. "How is a direwolf omega your leader?"

"You watched us in the maze, I presume?" Ascelin's voice is tense as I roll my shoulders and close my eyes to ward away the memories. When the male doesn't respond, she snarls.

"Then you'll have watched Diana risk her life to save her mate and his pack. And somewhere along the way, she found it in the goodness of her heart to save my court, to save younglings who have never seen the light of day. She carries my king's spirit, and so we will tear this place apart if it means finding an answer for her."

I open my eyes, sensing focus the way all predators do. When I look to my right, the peach-haired librarian is looking at me, but then she flicks those gray eyes over to Ascelin.

"I'm excellent with languages, so I'll start there." She looks at her mentor. "Zakarias, is that okay with you? I think I can be most helpful with that. You're better on the healing front."

He nods once but still looks uneasy.

If this obviously terrified male is the best Pengshur has to offer, I'm less than impressed.

"Does it bother you that we were in the maze, and now we're out?" My tone is laced with alpha edge. He shrinks back on his stool, shaking his head.

I focus on his gaze, or rather the lack of eye contact. He's looking everywhere but at me.

This male gives off a very prey-like aura, which makes my natural predatory instincts thump in my chest. Standing, I loom over him. He looks up, pupils flaring wide as his heart pounds in his chest. I'd almost swear he's about to start running, and I haven't chased prey since the maze. I'm surprisingly ready to run someone down, to rip someone to shreds. I want the destruction I mete out to match the way I feel inside.

I'm surprised when the female librarian steps in front of him, placing a hand on my chest. She pushes gently against me, the faint hint of a warning, until I look down at her. When I do, peachy lips tip into a smile.

"The library's systems are still coming back online now that the power is back. It will take Zakarias some time to find books on the Volya. Why don't I give you a quick tour and show you where you can work? Then we can tackle the prophecy issue."

For a moment, we stare at one another. I dare her with an imperious glare to push me again. But unlike the cowering male, this woman's smile simply grows broader. She's either incredibly brave or incredibly stupid.

Ascelin snorts. "You're just going to tackle the prophecy issue like *that*?" She snaps her black-clawed fingers together.

The librarian laughs. "Well, it's not likely to be that quick, but I'll do my best to impress."

Ascelin's black brows tilt upward.

Arliss rises to a stand. "A third request, then, once the first two are fulfilled."

That I pay attention to. I know Noire's curious why Arliss wanted in on this mission. It seems he's about to tell us.

The male librarian seems to have gathered his wits at that point, and he stands to match everyone else. "How can we help, Arliss?"

Arliss's normal leer is gone, replaced by a neutral look. "Information on carrow, if you have it."

Both librarians hiss in a breath, but it's the female who speaks first, her tone urgent.

"Why?"

Arliss shrugs. "My reasons are my own. But I'd like to learn more."

There's an awkward moment of silence before Ascelin snaps her fingers again "Let us go. Time is short, and Diana is fighting for her life."

Her life.

Those two words rush through my system like a dagger stabbing right into my heart. I think about how I watched the confusion and hurt and life die out of my mate's eyes. Lives are such finnicky things. They can be long. They can be short.

And I can't seem to find the energy to care about mine.

CHAPTER SEVEN

ONMIEL

This assignment is getting more interesting by the minute, although I sense Zakarias is deeply unsettled by our clients. We work with monsters and half-breed librarians all the time, but this group is different. Raw power ripples from them. I'd give my left arm that the black male is a carrow or suspects he is and wants to confirm it. I haven't seen him up close enough to tell if he carries the typical tattoo, but carrow are such an obscure and unusual monster to request information on.

I try not to envision these monsters killing people in the Temple Maze, but it's hard not to. They're dangerous, and their predatory awareness is obvious in the way they keep an eye on their surroundings. Plus, the way Tenebris loomed over Zakarias? I thought my mentor might shit his pants and run. It's unlike him to behave that way around a client.

Still, this is my first official assignment, and I'm really fucking excited.

I have so many questions for the group. How did they escape Rama's Temple Maze? Is Rama actually dead? How and who killed her? Is that why the power's back on? Then there's a long line of questions about the Volya. Volya don't leave the Tempang forest in the north of Lombornei, so how did they come into contact with the monsters? I'd wager all of the answers are tied together by some neat and pretty bow, but it doesn't seem they're going to be forthcoming.

Holding back my enthusiasm, I smile at our clients.

Zakarias grabs my hand and pulls me just outside. He looks terribly worried as he glances back through the door at them, then down at me.

"I'm concerned about this assignment, Onmiel." He peeks around the doorframe a second time, and I imagine all three monsters looking over at him.

"They can hear us," I remind him in a whisper. "And I'm not afraid. This is an excellent chance to help the pack that might have saved our continent from a psychopath. We should be grateful to them, right?"

He rapidly blinks several times, but his big chest heaves. I never took Zakarias for a weenie, so I'm a little surprised to find him so reticent right now.

When I nod my assent, he straightens his black tunic.

"I'll head to the archives and see about digging up books on the Volya, and we'll go from there. Are you sure you want to remain on this assignment, Onmiel?" His voice is wry and weary as if he's already tired from what lies ahead of us.

"Absolutely," I confirm, turning back into the room before he can remind me he thinks this is a terrible idea.

Opening my arms wide, I smile at the clients again. "FL Zakarias is off to start his research, so let's do a quick tour, grab a working room, and get you settled."

The vampiri woman grunts, and gestures toward the door. The males look at one another, and something unspoken passes between them.

Sighing, I fold my hands in front of my stomach. "This will go far better if you're open and honest with me about your needs. I sense you're holding back, but if there's critical information, it could help us find an answer quicker."

Arliss looks up at me with a shit-eating grin, the type of smile I'm sure has wooed many women into his bed. But that's not me, taken with a man who's so overtly sexual. I'm into nerdy, so he's barking up the wrong tree.

"You'll forgive us if we have trust issues, Novice Onmiel," he purrs. "If a time comes when you need to have additional information, we'll provide it, then."

I hold back a harrumph as I purse my lips and turn to the vampiri because of these three, she seems most focused on their injured packmate. When I lean in close, her all-white eyes narrow, black lips parting to reveal translucent black fangs. Gods, I bet she was terrifying in the maze. Vampiri hunt in packs, and I can just imagine her ripping someone to shreds with those teeth.

For the millionth time, I'm glad I never watched the televised nightly hunt. Hearing about it in hushed tones was enough.

She doesn't frighten me. "I trust you to know when I need further information, First Warrioress. You'll let me know, even when they're being dumb?"

She lets out a barking laugh, throwing her head back as the sharp noise slices through the air. When she's done laughing, she claps me jovially on the shoulder. "You can count on me, Novice."

"Onmiel is fine," I counter, giving her a stern look. I hate being called "Novice" because it reminds me that's what I *am*, even though I'm the best damn librarian here on several critical topics, ancient languages being my specialty.

I hear Zakarias's footsteps fade away as I gesture for them to join me. We leave the lush meeting room and follow Zakarias up the hall toward the archives. I pray I won't be embarrassed and get stopped by the guards if my mentor isn't with me, but it should be fine since I was assigned to this group. The band around my arm confirms it.

Still, as we approach the desk with a burly guardian seated behind it, I cross my fingers that he won't stop me and make me feel foolish.

I breathe a sigh of relief when he gestures us through, handing me a small manila envelope. Pushing glossy double doors open, I step into the archives, turn to my clients and open the envelope. Inside are three round metal pins, embossed with the library's motto. I dump them into my palm and show them to Arliss, Tenebris, and Ascelin.

"These pins go on your shirt. They'll mark you as guests and grant you access to the archives, which are off-limits to the general public. You won't be able to remove the majority of the books in the archives from their shelves as they're spelled to stay put, but you can walk around and view some of the research tools. I'll show you that in a minute. Let's go ahead and put these on."

I pass them out before pointing up the long hall ahead of us. "The archives are generally a quiet area. It's frowned upon to interrupt a librarian who's in the middle of their research. That being said, everyone here is helpful, so if FL Zakarias and I aren't around, you can ask another librarian to assist you."

"What is the point of being assigned to you if you may not be around?" Ascelin questions, eyes narrowed again. So suspicious, this one.

I give her a quick wink. "Even librarians have to pee sometimes, First Warrioress."

She snorts as if the idea of stopping anything to urinate is totally ridiculous.

I begin leading the group past a long row of books as I point fifteen stories above us. "Every floor up to the fifteenth is full of books and study rooms with the exception of the fifth floor, which is for librarians on assignment. It's living quarters as well as a garden. While Zakarias and I are assigned to you, I'll live at the library twenty-four hours a day."

"Zakarias won't?" Arliss questions, glancing up at the barely visible archives' ceiling.

Smiling, I shake my head. "As FL Zakarias's Novice, it's my role to clean up at the end of the day and to be on call for whatever you need. If something comes up, I'll notify him and he'll be here within fifteen minutes. We are dedicated to finding you answers." I look around at the group. "Let's finish up a quick tour, then I'd like to dive into everything straight away. You're welcome to explore the archives on your own if you want to."

Tenebris, who's been looking around at the books in awe, glances down at me, eyes the color of whiskey focusing with sudden intensity. "Thank you," he growls, and it's so low and sensual, all I can imagine is that big head between my thighs, thanking me for coming all over his pretty mouth.

Gods, I've got to get it together.

"You're welcome, Tenebris," I purr instead before turning and striding up the hallway. The row of books ends at a gigantic circular table, an ancient map of Lombornei that's been at Pengshur since it was built.

"The Magelang Map has lived at Pengshur for nearly ten centuries." I point to the wooden platform around it, a space between it and the map allowing for librarians to sit and study it. As we watch, a First Librarian seats himself, pinching in on the map's leathery surface to zoom in on a particular part of Lombornei.

I keep my voice low so I don't bother him. "This map shows the location of every person, city, and town on the continent, and is often used in research."

Arliss steps to the opposite side of the map and hunches over it, grinning as he plops a finger onto the map's surface. "Oasis."

Ascelin scoffs. "We could scarcely find you, yet if we had come here, we'd have found your precise location. That is frustrating."

Arliss shrugs. "I was trying to attract scholars with dirty minds, Ascelin, not beautiful vampiri First Warrioresses. I've always allowed my location to be shared with Pengshur."

I'm trying to keep up with their banter, but I'm obviously missing something. "Everyone's location is shared with Pengshur," I correct gently as Ascelin looks over at me.

"What about Rama's sky city, Paraiso?"

The blood freezes in my veins as Tenebris growls and looks at a stack of books, drifting away from us to examine their spines.

I had hoped not to cover the topic of Rama with them because there's so much that's unknown about what's going on, and because she had very little to do with Pengshur—I thought. ML Garfield's comments this morning have me thinking there's more to it, but I'm not sure yet.

"Even Paraiso," I acquiesce, leaning over by Arliss to scroll the map in my direction and spell it to zoom on the coast of Vinituvari. "It has been there for several weeks now, although that's not unusual."

"So, you kept tabs on her?" Arliss's deep voice is curious, blue eyes focused on mine even as Ascelin glances at Tenebris.

"I wouldn't call it tabs," I hedge. "Merely a curiosity, although I know there were some librarians here who watched her movements far more closely. But again, this province was unscathed by her, thank the gods."

Tenebris shoves his hands in his pockets and starts walking up a row of books as I resist the urge to call for him. Instead, I look at Arliss and Ascelin. "I had hoped to avoid this topic, given you and Tenebris were trapped in the maze. It's clear he doesn't want to speak about it, so I'm curious why you brought it up in front of him?"

Ascelin shifts back at my direct line of questioning, but tactful sincerity is a hallmark trait of a good librarian. The vampiri shares a look with Arliss, but he remains silent as she turns back to me. "We do not avoid the topic of Rama simply because we were imprisoned by her. Things are…complicated." She says nothing else, though. I can't help but wonder what part of their story they aren't sharing, and if it might have implications for our research.

I have a million questions, but Ascelin turns and strides up the row of books after Tenebris.

As she goes, Arliss grins and stares at her ass. When I catch him looking, he huffs. "What?"

Letting out a beleaguered groan, I leave him and trail my monster clients up a row of books, wondering why my first assignment couldn't have been something nice and easy. It scares me a little bit how something deep in my heart is thrilled about that.

CHAPTER EIGHT
TENEBRIS

I had forgotten how books smell. I had them in my room in the maze, but not this many. It's different.

As I walk slowly up the long row, perusing the beautifully bound leather titles, I can't resist leaning in to scent them. Gods, I love that smell. Without thinking, I reach for one entitled *On the History of the Mermaid Clans*, wondering if I might learn about my sister-in-law's people in it.

When I tug at it, it doesn't move. Right. Spelled. The female librarian mentioned that. It's disappointing though because I'd love to take that book and curl up with it for a day, to lose myself in its pages and not think about my real life. Part of me desperately hoped that coming to Pengshur meant I could hide from reality while Ascelin and Arliss sort out what Diana needs.

But then a wave of guilt slaps me in the face. I owe it to her to focus on finding a cure.

The female librarian stops next to me, looking up with a soft smile. She whispers under her breath, snapping and moving her fingers in a series of motions, and then she pulls the book I was looking at from the shelf and hands it to me. At the bottom of the spine, a golden number appears, embossing itself on the faded surface. She presses her forefinger to the number, and it glows gold for one brief moment.

Looking back up at me, she grins. "Had to catalog it on the list of books for this project. And to remember where to return it to once you're done." She gives me a wink before indicating we should follow again. Tucking the book under my arm, I rejoin the group. Ascelin and Arliss trail behind me.

The librarian smiles and points out to both sides with long, skinny arms. "The archives sunburst out from the Magelang Map. From there, there's a secondary ring that circles the archives' center. After that ring, the sunburst continues. Ten concentric rings make up the Pengshur archives. The public section of the library is even larger than that, housed in the building next to this one. From anywhere in the archives, you can follow the yellow arrows inlaid into the floor and get to the public side."

She turns and begins to walk backward. "It's unlikely a book we need will be on the public side, but it has happened from time to time, so we'll check publicly available books once we make our way through the archive collection." The librarian turns, and we follow her silently until we reach the outer edge.

I never imagined Pengshur would be so enormous. There must be millions of books here. I'd like to disappear and wander the ornate rows for a while, smelling them all.

The female stops in front of a tall door, its chunky golden handle reflecting bright sunlight coming in from somewhere.

She points at the handle. "These reading rooms line the outer wall of the archives, going up the first three stories. If a handle is gold, then the room is available. If it's black," she points at the next room over, "then someone is using that room. You can find a room you like, and I can assign it for the duration of your stay, or if you'd like me to pick for you, I'm happy to do so."

She swings the door open, and we get a look inside. The floor is a zigzag pattern of beautifully inlaid wood and a large wooden table takes up most of the room. The far side has a round window to the outside, and each side of the room is lined with empty shelves. A fireplace in the corner gives it a cozy, hidden library vibe—if I was feeling into such a thing.

"We do not care which room we get, Novice," Ascelin growls.

"Onmiel," she corrects. Ah, that's her name.

"I didn't think so," she chirps, "so I'll assign this one because it's got sufficient space to spread out." She steps into the room and places her hand flat on the wall, closing her eyes as she whispers yet another incantation. It's odd to me that she seems so unfazed by us, whereas her mentor was practically terrified. Maybe she just doesn't know much about monsters.

Her whisper is low, her voice throaty. It lacks the femininity of Rama's, but there's something far friendlier about Onmiel. Her ears are ever so slightly pointed, delicate and long. She must have monster blood somewhere in her lineage, although I don't sense that just looking at her. She appears human enough.

Arliss and Ascelin follow me into the room, and Ascelin perches herself on the table. "I am anxious to begin. Is there anything of the library we have not seen that we must?"

"Oh," Onmiel continues with a helpful smile. "There's plenty more to see, and if you were here for fun, I could spend two days showing you around. But I know you're ready to help your friend. What is her name, again, so I can address her properly?"

"Diana," Ascelin murmurs, and for half a second, I think I see tears in her eyes. But that can't be. I've never seen Ascelin cry. I don't think she even knows how. The tears are there and gone in a flash, but there's an obviously distressed expression on her angular features.

Loud footsteps break through my thoughts. The male librarian shows up with an armful of books. He places them gently on the table and nods at Onmiel.

"Tour's all done, we were about to begin discussing the translation," she tells him, her expression expectant.

He looks around, and I realize once again he's afraid. The unmistakable scent of fear rolls off him, reminding me of chasing marks with Noire in the maze. I suck in a deep breath, not really meaning to, and he shrinks back a little.

Ascelin joins my side and takes a book from the stack, examining it before she places it harshly back down. "You saw us kill in the maze, did you not?"

The male nods, and Onmiel joins him, a resolute partner by his side.

Ascelin senses the same thing I do: this male is deeply afraid of us. She sneers, letting her fangs descend as a drop of venom makes its way hastily to the floor. "You know what we are capable of, Zakarias. Perhaps it would be best not to dilly-dally."

He gulps audibly, but rounds the table, giving us a wide berth as he sets a book down in front of Arliss. "Our primary tome on carrow, Arliss. If you can tell me what you're looking for, I'll examine it for—"

"No need," Arliss interrupts, taking the book and heading for the door. "I'll be back later." Without another word, he leaves the room, jerking the door shut behind him.

Ascelin and I know he's a carrow, but I can't imagine what sort of research he needs to do. I ponder it for a moment, but then exhaustion sets in.

Onmiel turns to Ascelin. "Show me what you've got that needs translating, and I'll begin right away."

There's so much to do, and so much that hinges on us healing Diana. We've got to figure out what the second half of her prophecy means, and how to heal her at the same time. I'm sure the two are connected, and there's every chance the news won't be good.

I can't do more bad news right now, even though I'm struggling to find enough emotion to care about anything at all.

I sit in a chair in the corner and open my book, watching as Ascelin and Onmiel take seats at the end of the table closest to me. Ascelin pulls a piece of paper from her pocket and carefully hands it to Onmiel. "Long ago, the vampiri received a prophecy that our king would give his life to help a direwolf and that the direwolf would then allow the king to be born anew. That part of the prophecy happened during our escape from the maze. My king's spirit lives inside Diana Ayala."

Onmiel is silent, but it's easy to see the wheels of her mind turning. "I need the first half, written in its original language, if you can."

"Of course," Ascelin purrs. "Give me paper and a utensil and I will write it for you."

The librarian stands and opens a drawer in the bookshelves, bringing out pen and paper for Ascelin, who continues, "It turns out there was a second half, received by a vampiri seer, but it is in an ancient language even she did not know. She is hundreds of years old," Ascelin grumps. "It is unfathomable to me that this language is so old, she could not understand, but here we are."

Onmiel opens the paper and squints, then looks up at Ascelin.

The vampiri grimaces. "Because she did not know the language, she could only write it phonetically as she received it."

Onmiel sighs and sits back in her chair. "And there's no video or anything from when this person received the prophecy, I assume? Was it the same person who received the first half?"

"No, and yes," Ascelin growls, tapping razor-sharp claws on the desk.

Onmiel reads the words aloud, but they don't sound familiar to me either. She turns to Ascelin with a frown. "Do the words sound remotely vampiri to you at all?"

"No, so your guess is as good as mine, Novice."

"Onmiel," the librarian corrects once again.

Ascelin shoots me a grin, and I realize she's just fucking with the cheerful librarian.

I can't find it in myself to care as my thoughts turn to my dead mate and the loss of her touch.

"Tenebris." A sultry purr caresses my ears, my cock stirring slowly to life. *How the fuck can it be interested in something right now?* Everything hurts. Was I just fighting? A haze clouds my vision while a tight pull yanks at my chest.

TEN: A DARK SHIFTER ROMANCE

I reach down to feel for a wound but find something metallic attached to my pectoral muscles. I don't feel worry, though. I just feel...safe.

Someone says my name again, and her tone encourages me to move. I sit up and notice I'm in bed and the sheets below me are a black cool satin. They feel good against my skin. A blooming, warm sensation spreads in my chest, and my heartbeat picks up. It's almost like a sense of knowing that something important is happening to me. I can't seem to clear the haze in my mind, but I'm focused. Focused enough to swing my legs over the bed and find the woman that voice belongs to.

I register long, dark hair and elegant, angular features first. In the back of my mind, there's a niggling moment of uncertainty and surprise. A prickly sensation pokes at my chest, and that worry dissipates.

Desire unfurls in my gut, and my balls draw up tight against my body, my cock throbbing. My fangs descend as my focus narrows on the stunning woman in front of me. She's older than me by a bit, and it's so intoxicating I can barely stand it.

"Come here," I command, knowing, somehow, that she'll comply. The heady, hot sensation in my chest intensifies until I feel like I'll die if she doesn't come close. What does she smell like? I've got to know. Right fucking now.

Red lips part into a sensual smile, and she stalks gracefully across the space between us until she's almost close enough to touch. She stays just out of reach, though, almost teasing me. That won't do; it won't do at all.

Growling, I snap out with one hand, grabbing her wrist and yanking it to her lower back. I splay my fingers over the curve of her ass and pull her between my thighs.

She lets out a growl to match mine, this spitfire of a woman whose soul seems to call to me.

"Mine," I snarl as I bury my face in her throat and suck in great, heaving breaths of her.

"Yes, Tenebris," she purrs. "I am."

The squeak of a chair moving across the floor snaps me out of that memory. I can barely catch my breath. I don't even want to think about what came next. I can't go down the path of remembering how we bound each other.

Standing, I focus out the circular window. The city of Pengshur bustles below, people going about their daily lives, enjoying, loving, and experiencing as if my world didn't end a week ago, as if everything I loved isn't gone forever.

CHAPTER NINE
ONMIEL

I close my eyes and thrum my fingers along my forehead, something I do to encourage my brain to find answers. Ascelin turns to Zakarias, and he begins to explain how they can tackle the research together.

In the window, Tenebris stands silently, appearing lost in thought.

I stroke my pointer finger down my nose as I think. I've never translated something outside of its original language like this. Finally, I decide to read it aloud and send it to the other librarians here who specialize in obscure languages. Maybe one of them can point me in the right direction.

Whatever this language is, I've never heard anything like it. That's unusual, but there are so many variations and dialects of languages, it's not totally unheard of. Most librarians who focus on languages begin with just a few and then work on tackling the rest. At this point, I'm proficient in about twenty-five languages, but there are hundreds more to begin studying.

I stand and open another drawer, pulling out a small data tablet. Now that we have power back, this will be far easier. A week ago, I would have had to seek each librarian out in person to do this.

Reading the prophecy aloud, I send it to the identification codes of several librarian friends, including a few Novices like myself.

After that, I look at Ascelin. "I need to do some research in another wing of the library. Will you be alright here for an hour or so?"

"I'll go with you," Tenebris growls from the window, turning into the room as Ascelin's frown fades. He doesn't wait for an answer, just prowls out of the room without a backward glance.

Zakarias looks up at me, but he's careful not to bely any of his feelings as he looks back down at the stack of books on the desk.

Ascelin nods, too-white eyes narrowing. Having gained her consent, I leave the group to meet Tenebris. Light filters down from far above us, illuminating his face as he stands in front of a row of bookshelves, muscly arms crossed.

I've always been an empathetic person; I'm excellent at reading people. It's part of why Zakarias loves me so much. He's a brilliant librarian, but he lacks the people skills that come more naturally to me. Which is very obvious to me given how distressed he seems around our current clients.

"Are you alright?" I question the big alpha, who drops his arms, schooling his face to neutral.

"I'm fine, Novice," he growls.

"Onmiel."

"I'm fine, Onmiel."

"You don't seem fine," I press on. "Whatever's bothering you, I probably can't fix it, but if you want to talk about it, I'm here. Okay?"

"That another service provided by the library?" His voice is wounded and sarcastic as his blank expression becomes a glower.

"Not hardly." I laugh. "Most librarians are awkward at best and antisocial at worst. You've probably noticed that with FL Zakarias. I've always been a little different, I guess. I'm just saying, if you need a friend, I'm here for that."

When he doesn't immediately respond, I resist the urge to offer a hug. If anyone ever looked like they could use one, it's the monstrous male standing in front of me. I remind myself that he spent years in the maze. He was a child there, if I've done the math correctly after researching Pack Ayala. Tenebris would have had to be…ten, maybe eleven when Rama threw the Ayala brothers into the maze?

The little I know of the Ayala Pack is that they're a band of thugs, and they controlled the resource-rich province of Siargao, and thereby, the rest of Lombornei. Still, I can't imagine a child trapped in there with all the rest of the monsters.

"Come on," I encourage, waving a hand over my shoulder as I walk along the outer rim of the library. "You'll be an excellent assistant for an hour."

"Didn't say I came to assist you," he grouses.

I chuckle. "Oh, but you did. Some of the books in here are heavy as shit, and you've got super big arms. I can carry more back to the room if you'll help me." I turn to walk backward as the hint of a smile flashes across his handsome features. It's gone as quickly as I notice it, though.

He doesn't agree, but he doesn't take off into the stacks by himself either, so I'll consider it a win. Ten minutes later, we're nearly to the other side of the library and back down a row of books on ancient languages.

"Okay." I rub my hands together. "It stands to reason that if a vampiri received the prophecy, the language is some ancient form of vampiri, even though Ascelin didn't recognize it. It's as good a place to start as any."

Tenebris doesn't answer, but holds out his palms. I begin stacking books in them, trying not to stare at the way his biceps bulge as I weigh him down. I spell a dozen more off the shelves and hand them to him, and I don't miss the way his eyes light up as I fill his arms.

Gods, he's a nerd. I just know it. I'm about to tickle his nerd fancy, then.

I grin. "Most of the books in the library are made out of bovine leather, something like ninety percent." I waggle my brows. "But a lot of the older books are bound in skins from all sorts of monsters, including direwolves."

Ten scoffs, but looks down as I continue loading him with books. He's holding twenty or so at this point.

He looks lovingly at the stack, a curious expression on his face. I nibble at my lip before speaking because it's not really my place, except he looks almost entranced. "You know, you could apply to become a Novice here, if books are your thing. Which they seem to be based on the way you're staring."

He lets out a harrumph, but doesn't immediately answer. I give him a long moment, even shooting him a helpful wink of encouragement, but he looks away.

"Alright, then," I chirp. "Time for coffee and chocolate, and then we'll go back to the research room and dive in."

"Coffee and chocolate?" His tone is flat, and it's not lost on me that maybe he hasn't had a coffee or chocolate in a really long time. But if I'm anything, it's an optimist.

"A chocolate a day keeps the doctor away." I shrug.

"Not how the saying goes," he grumbles, but he hoists the book stack higher and follows me without further complaint.

Ten minutes later, we've visited the library's cafe and picked up coffee and snacks for the whole team. It might seem frivolous to do that when they're researching something so pressing and important, but they don't realize Zakarias and I truly will be here at all hours until their answer is found. We're either researching or assisting clients all the time.

A librarian's work is never done. Learn in order to guide.

That's our motto for a reason.

When we return to the room, I hold the door for Tenebris, who stalks through and sets the books carefully on the desk. I follow him with the drinks and food, placing it in the middle of the table as I look at Ascelin and point.

"That one's the Type-A latte, a vampiri barista made it when I asked what you might like."

She sneers but takes the drink and sniffs as I hand Zakarias his usual. He takes it without looking up as I place his favorite scone next to him on a plate. It's my job to keep him well-fueled and in possession of everything he needs to do his job well for our clients.

"Thank you, Miel," he mumbles as he flips a page, shoving his reading glasses higher up his nose.

Tenebris is already seated at the far end of the worktable, thumbing through a book absentmindedly. His dark brows furrow as he scowls but continues to flip the pages.

This assignment is going to be hard and prolonged if I can't break through to these folks and get them to open up a bit. I sense Zakarias and I have about half the information we need to really find an answer, but I'm determined to chisel away at their reticence with my sunny-ass disposition until I get what I need to figure it out.

They'll never see me coming.

CHAPTER TEN
TENEBRIS

Onmiel lays out a plan of attack, handing Ascelin and me both books on languages. She tells us what to look for. I admit it feels like hunting for a needle in a haystack.

Still, I lose myself for hours in the pile of books in front of me, only putting one down if the librarian requires it for something. She has an obsessed look on her face, and it makes me wonder if I looked like that to Noire all the times he let himself in my room to interrupt my reading.

Of course, he didn't know I was reading books sent to me by Rama, and he never questioned where I got them. Even I didn't realize what any of it meant at the time. How I'd wake up one day and know she was fated by the gods to be mine.

That thought produces a stabbing pain in my gut, so I stretch my arms over my head, letting my head fall back as I flex from side to side.

When I shift upright, Onmiel's eyes flick from my core up to my face. She bites her lip thoughtfully but looks over to Ascelin. "Ascelin, do you know how these words are pronounced when they were received? There's not a recording, but did you get this parchment directly from the person who received the prophecy?"

Arliss strolls back into the room with a cell phone in hand. "Nope, she was riding my thick cock at the time, but you may call Firenze to ask. He was there with the woman who spoke the prophecy."

Ascelin sputters and swipes at Arliss with her claws out. He sidesteps her with a smirk as he dials a number on his phone.

Onmiel doesn't miss a beat, taking the now-ringing phone, even as her pale eyes slide back to me. When the phone connects, she explains who she is and what she needs, but all I can think about is how she's speaking to my brother Jet's mate. Somehow, in the time my mate was taken from me, Jet managed to land two of his own.

I grit my teeth at how unfair it feels. I know nothing in life is fair, I was aware of that from a young age, but knowing what remains of my pack is all mated now has me wanting to rage and burn the library to the ground.

I was distraught when I killed Rama. But now, I'm angry.

I'm angry at her, at my pack, even at myself.

Why did she drug me?

Why did she put me in a position to be here, now, without her?

I'll never get answers to any of that, and when grief chokes me so hard I forget to breathe, I decide I'll leave and walk the library for a while. Just as quickly, I know I won't because Diana needs us, and anything I can do to save her, I should do. I will do.

Onmiel's voice breaks through my thoughts. "You'd like to speak with Tenebris?"

I give her a warning look, begging her to read it, and she gives me a thumbs up as she sits back in her chair.

"He's stepped out of the room for a moment, but I'll let him know to call you back later. Alright?" She hangs up, and Ascelin shoots me a knowing look.

"Take a walk, alpha," she encourages. "I will continue with the librarians and Arliss."

I can't think around the pressure in my brain, my focus narrowing as I shove my chair back and stand. Black dots crowd my vision as Onmiel stands and looks at me, her expression disconcerted for the first time since I met her this morning.

Her tone is low and comforting. "There's a garden on the exterior edge of floor five. If you go right, take the first elevator up. It's beautiful there. I think you'd like it."

I can't even summon a response, but I practically run from the room as memories flash and crowd my brain.

Rama on her hands before me, taking my knot so sweetly.

Rama calling my name for the first time before sliding a silky robe off her delicate shoulders.

Rama slipping her hands into my pants to stroke my cock while she whispered all the dirty things she wanted from me.

I sprint for the elevators, smashing the button to call it as I gasp like a fish out of water. I'm fucking falling apart, and right now, I can't summon enough strength to keep going. Not even to help.

The elevator slides open with a whoosh, and I step inside, grateful it's empty. I press the button for the fifth floor, and as soon as the doors open again, I run out, my head swiveling from side to side until I see a sign for the Pengshur Gardens. I don't stop to wonder how they've got a garden in the middle of the building. This whole place is imbued with ancient magic, built centuries and centuries ago.

I take off at a full-out sprint, ignoring the curious looks of other beings as I pass, focused only on getting to the sign up ahead. Passing it in a rush, I burst through double doors and into the middle of an actual forest. It reminds me so much of Siargao that I fall to both knees and gaze around. The foliage is a myriad of brilliant colors. Flowers cover almost every surface. Plants grow up from cracks in the bark of every single tree. It's a wonderland of verdant greenery.

I miss home, or what I can remember of it, anyhow.

Managing to stumble back to my feet, I rip my clothes off and shift into my direwolf. I lose myself to the forest for hours, running through valleys, leaping over logs and small rivers. I smell a larger body of water somewhere, but I don't stop to find it. I run until my legs are shaky and the tension has receded to the back of my mind.

I don't encounter anyone in the forest. Eventually, I find a sturdy, tall tree and decide to shift and climb to the top. I need to rest for a minute, and I'm curious how far up the forest itself goes. I haul myself up the thick branches, careful not to crush the beautiful vines that grow around the tree's wide, thick trunk. When I pull myself through the last layer of greenery and above the canopy, I let out a gasp of wonder.

Thousands of shelves line either side of the forest, soaring many stories up above to a glass ceiling that lets outside light in. I think I read once that Pengshur was famous for many reasons, one of them being the extraordinary gardens. It never occurred to me that any of those would be inside like this.

I sit at the top of the canopy for a long time, watching librarians bustle along the walkways in front of every story's-worth of shelves. Pengshur is a busy place, it seems. There's so much I don't know about it, and I find myself wondering what Onmiel might be able to tell me. Eventually, watching all the movement reminds me I'm not doing shit to accomplish my only mission. With a sour emotion overtaking my mind, I climb out of the tree and head back to find my clothing.

CHAPTER ELEVEN
ONMIEL

We research until the moon is high and Ascelin is cranky as shit. Eventually, I kick my clients out of the library with a kind reminder that they need rest, and most research requests take a few days.

Ascelin snapped at me, literally, but when Tenebris touched her shoulder and reminded her it was time to go, she relented. They seem…close. Honestly, I'm a little jealous. I'd love to be friends with the hulking alpha. He was quiet all afternoon after disappearing for a bit, lost in a stack of books and not engaging at all.

I never watched when Rama televised the hunts going on in the Temple Maze, but now, I'm wondering if I should have because I'm far less afraid of these clients than I should be.

After they've gone, Zakarias turns to me and sinks back into his chair, running his hands through his long braids.

"I should not have dragged you into this assignment, Onmiel," he mutters, more to himself than anything.

My blood chills, wondering if I've done something wrong, but Zakarias looks over and shakes his head.

"They've not mentioned Rama but now they're researching the Tempang's monsters. I've got a terrible feeling about all this," he whispers, his voice so filled with dread that I'm worried he's about to burst into tears.

"A librarian's work is never done. Learn in order to guide," I remind him gently, perching myself on the tabletop as I look at my oldest friend.

For a long moment, he stares at the intricately inlaid wood ceiling, but then he sits up and nods at me. "You're right, Onmiel, and it isn't a good lesson from me to you to second-guess assignments. I had just hoped your first official one would be something thrilling but not dangerous."

"Librarians get pulled into all sorts of situations, don't they?" I counter.

"That's true," Zakarias mutters.

"Why don't you head home, and I'll clean up," I offer.

He eyes the stacks of books left on the desk with a grimace but grabs his bag and heads for the door. I know he'd like to help me, but it's the unspoken rule between Novices and First Librarians—Novices do the grunt work. This means I'll be here a few hours still, reshelving and respelling the books, cleaning the room, and making sure we're prepared for tomorrow. I'll probably be here first, too, because I'm a dog with a bone when I have a mission.

Something niggles at me about this damn vampiri prophecy, but I can't put my finger on it.

The door swings softly shut behind Zakarias, and I pull out my datapad to see if anyone has responded to the group message I sent earlier. I'm still getting used to having the tech again, but I'll admit it's helpful to connect so easily. When I scan my messages, there's nothing new. I let out a huff of frustration, and then I look at the table full of books, reorganizing them by shelf in order from closest to farthest.

Grabbing the first stack, I head out of the reading room and slot the first book into place, whispering the standard incantation to keep it there until another librarian requires it. The magic of Pengshur is something Novices learn in our second year. There are layers and layers to it, and knowledge of Pengshur's spells must be earned. I can spell almost all the books in the archives at this point. There are only a few I can't call—banned books and books in private keeping rooms.

It takes me two hours to put everything away, but I love the library late at night like this. It's quieter than the daytime, although there are always people here; it's literally never empty. But it's peaceful, and after a crazy childhood, I need this peace like I need to breathe air. I've never felt so *me* as I did when I arrived at Pengshur for the first time and was accepted to the Novice program.

Eventually, I manage to reshelve the books we don't need and clean the room for tomorrow. I close the door and pace around the outer rim of the archives until I reach the elevator bank. From there, I take it to the fifth floor. When the elevator door opens, a broad hallway leads left and right, a desk centered in an alcove in front.

"Miel, girl! Spill the beans!" my human friend, Kassie, screeches from

TEN: A DARK SHIFTER ROMANCE

behind the desk when she sees me. Her head bobs as she leaps up off her stool and points one finger with rainbow-painted nails at me.

"About what?" I snort.

"About what?" she scoffs, rounding the desk to slap me lightly on the arm. "Those two huge hunks you're working with. I saw the black one take a book and disappear into the fifth-floor gardens. Tell me literally everything. There's been nonstop chatter today."

Nonstop chatter among the first-year Novices, she means. What they don't tell you when you enter the program is that you're not even allowed *into* the damn archives the first year. That year is spent tending the Novice dorms in the next building over and learning about the library's magic. Truthfully, it would be dangerous on the library floor without having a magical baseline. Visitors are allowed in only because they don't know the spells, and they're always accompanied, so they're safe. The archives are filled with magical artifacts and dangerous books.

"One of them was in the maze," I whisper as if Tenebris might show up here at any moment and hear me talking about him.

"Which one?" she gasps, bringing her hands to her cheeks excitedly.

"The hot one." I laugh. "The alpha."

She feigns a swoon and throws herself into my arms, looking up at me with big doe eyes when I catch her. "An honest-to-gods alpha? I die. What does he smell like? How tall is he?"

Giggling, I shove her upright. "Give me the key to my room, and I'll tell you."

Kassie grumbles but disappears behind her desk and grabs a key to room fourteen, my favorite. While I've never been on assignment before, I've often snuck up here and gotten room fourteen for a little shuteye. It's got a great view over the city, and I love to watch the nightlife.

When she levels me with a wry, displeased look, I chuckle.

"He smells clean, and he's probably two heads taller than me. But there's something different about predatory half-breeds," I admit. "There's a quiet focus to them that humans just don't have."

I think back to the way Tenebris stared at the rain just this morning, and heat flares between my thighs. Gods, I love a nerdy man, and beneath his somber exterior, I sense a dork waiting to shine. This library is just the place for that.

Kassie sighs, bringing my mind back to the present. "It's late as shit, Miel. Gah, I can't wait to pull all-nighters like this." She looks so wistful that I have to laugh.

"It's three a.m. you ding-dong. This is hardly an all-nighter."

"Yeah, but you'll be back at it by six, right?"

"Right," I grouse, remembering I should grab a few hours while I can. I give Kassie a quick salute, then head down the hallway to my room. When I open the door, there's a rush of wind and I'm yanked immediately to the side. Someone tosses me against the wooden wall. Pain bursts at the back of my skull as I bare my teeth at my attacker.

A low chuckle echoes from across the room as a standing lamp flicks on.

Ascelin.

She's now perched under the window, smirking as she crosses her thin, muscular arms.

I rub at the back of my head. "How'd you get in here and what the hells are you doing?"

"Warning you," she says, crossing the small room to get back in my space. "Stay away from Tenebris."

I choke out an irritated laugh, ire filling my chest as I try not to yell at her. "That'll be hard to do seeing as how we're working together to get you answers."

I try to force myself to remember this woman is a killer. I've heard stories of her eviscerating men—and women—with her bare hands. She's dangerous and unscrupulous. Somehow, though, I'm just really fucking irritated.

She collars my throat, shoving me against the wall a second time. "I mean stop considering him sexually. It is clear you find him attractive. But that sentiment is not returned."

Ah.

I open my mouth to respond, but a second figure pushes through the door.

Arliss. The bulky male turns to look at me with a grin, shoving his thumbs in his belt. "I see. Ascelin has already begun her interrogation."

"Not an interrogation," she snaps. "An interrogation would involve blood and torture. This is a kind warning."

"Kind, huh?" I scowl. "You could just ask me for a moment to speak, but in any case, you don't need to worry. My only priority is translating your prophecy so Zakarias can assist in the healing piece. Your friend's life is on the line, and I'm cognizant of that."

Ascelin lets out a low, threatening growl, venom dripping from translucent black fangs onto the ornate parquet floor. "See that you do, girl. Because—"

Arliss steps in front of me, blocking my view of Ascelin as he leans over me, throwing one arm above my head, his palm flat on the wall. Brilliant blue eyes scan my face, lingering on my mouth before they travel farther down.

It's a sexual perusal, nearly an offer. And I'm not at all interested. He's hot, but not my type in the slightest. Even so, my body reacts to the proximity of such a virile, sensual male so focused on me. I clench my thighs together, and Arliss grins. Ascelin peeks around his broad shoulder, her all-white eyes narrowing. This is the strangest interrogation I've ever heard of. They either want my deepest, darkest secrets or a threesome.

Maybe both.

Arliss lets out a low, rumbly growl, breathing deeply as he presses his body closer to mine. "Mmm, that's right, librarian. You could use a good fucking, couldn't you? How long has it been, my sweet?"

Snorting, I peer around at Ascelin. "Is he serious right now?"

"He is always serious about sex. He is a manwhore," Ascelin huffs. "As I was saying."

"Your message grows tiresome, Ascelin," Arliss growls. "Let us instead convince this pretty young thing to come to bed with us. Perhaps we can show her a good time, and then the moon eyes she has for Tenebris will be turned upon us instead."

Good *gods*. These two.

Ascelin rolls her eyes. "I'll remind you, Builder, that one ride on that cock was enough for me." She gives Arliss a reproachful look. Not that he notices because he's still staring at my mouth.

Builder? I wonder why she calls him that…

Milky eyes flick to mine. "And *you*. Stay away from Tenebris or you will not like the side of me you see."

I don't bother to agree with that. I'd like to be his friend if I can. Sometimes you meet someone, and your soul recognizes them immediately as someone you have to have more of. I felt that way the moment his golden eyes looked my way. It doesn't have to be sexual. In fact, it probably won't be. He seems caught up with other priorities. But being friends sounds great.

Ascelin slips in a puff of black smoke out my door, leaving me with Arliss as I resist the urge to grumble under my breath.

"It's so curious how completely unafraid of us you are…" he muses. "Is it foolishness or are you truly that brave?"

My lips curl up into a grin as I meet his lazy perusal. "Very little frightens me, carrow."

His eyes flash wide for a moment, and then they narrow. "You can't possibly presume to know I am one simply because I'm interested in them."

"You are, though. Aren't you? That's why you want the books?"

"What makes you think I am?"

I reach up and stroke one long finger down his square jaw, grinning.

"All carrow mark their successors with a practically invisible tattoo along the jawline. I couldn't see your tattoo in the Solarium, but it was visible in our working room. Were you aware you had it?"

A tic starts in his jaw, his muscle pressing against the pad of my finger. I drop my hand to my side. "You didn't know…" It's less a question and more a confirmation based on the frustrated look he wears.

He glances away, his expression clouded. He strikes me as a male who doesn't let others see a vulnerable side. It's on the tip of my tongue to comment on it, but even *I* know when to keep my mouth shut. Usually.

He shakes his head, long braids swaying before he turns a dazzling smile back on me. Thick, black fingers come to my hair and tug softly. His gaze becomes molten desire.

"What other secrets do you hide, Novice Onmiel?" He's practically purring, but I resist the urge to shut him down too harshly. If he wanted to talk more about the topic of his power right now, he wouldn't deflect.

I press both hands to his chest and attempt to push him from me, although he's too fucking big for me to move him very far. "Zakarias gave you our most well-known book on carrow, but there are a few lesser-known items I think might be more helpful. I'll make sure to bring them tomorrow. Plus, I'm always happy to answer questions, based on what I know. Monsters are kinda my thing."

"No matter." He shrugs his big, round shoulders and takes a step back. Both hands slide into the pockets of his tight jeans. "Back to the topic of Tenebris, be wary of the vampiri. I am the last person on Lombornei to ever dissuade two consenting adults from fucking, but there is a reason she is so protective of Tenebris. He's sacrificed more than you can ever imagine."

I haven't known Arliss long at all, but I sense he wears humor like a mask.

"I understand. I'd like to be his friend, if I can," I remind him. Then I shoot him a little smirk. "You can read what's in my heart, carrow, can't you? Take a peek."

Sapphire eyes narrow as he steps closer. There's an uncomfortable feeling inside my brain, like something's worming its way through. Smiling, I will myself to relax, and I concentrate on counting my fingers as his invasion of my mind continues. After far longer than it *should* take, the sensation abruptly ceases. I suspect he's unable to fully control his power for some reason. Either that or he wanted it to hurt.

"Find what you were looking for?" I can't resist another smirk as Arliss crosses his arms.

"You want to fuck him, but you're sincere in your desire to help us. You'd be happy to be his friend."

"Indeed," I confirm, giving him two finger guns to make my point.

TEN: A DARK SHIFTER ROMANCE

For a long moment, he stares at me, and then he leans in the doorway and crosses his huge arms, accentuating beautifully muscular biceps. Arliss snorts when my eyes drop to them. "Don't tell me you're not the slightest bit intrigued, librarian."

"Don't need to fuck you to find your muscles attractive," I counter as I lean opposite him. "I suppose I do find you somewhat fascinating. It's clear you're not exactly part of the Ayala pack, and I know you weren't in the maze. How did you all come to be connected, and why? Why don't you know what it is to be a carrow? Tell me all of your secrets, friend."

"I'm going to let you in on a secret, just not one of mine. It may help you navigate the next few days." He laughs. "Ascelin will not tell you this, and Tenebris likely won't speak of it."

My blood begins to freeze and boil simultaneously, starting behind my eyes and traveling down my spine as his gaze focuses, intent and predatory.

He leans in close enough for his lips to brush just over mine, his breath warm against my face. "Rama was Tenebris's mate. She is only dead because he ripped her head from her shoulders to protect his family. If he seems unmoored, it is because he sacrificed everything to protect the rest of us."

My hand flies to cover my mouth as tears fill my eyes. It can't be. She imprisoned him when he was eleven for gods' sakes!

And so it's true—Rama's gone. I can't even begin to think how to react to that news.

Arliss nods and rocks back onto his heels, crossing both arms. "I read his heart sometimes when he's unaware I am doing so. His is shrouded in darkness, Onmiel. You would do well to steer clear of him."

Arliss growls once, then turns and shuts my door, and I'm left alone with thoughts that spin my brain so hard, I slide down the ornate wall to the ground as they batter me.

CHAPTER TWELVE
TENEBRIS

I wake before the sun rises. The townhouse Noire rented belongs to the library but is located a fifteen-minute walk away. Ascelin and Arliss are nowhere to be seen, so I dress and leave. I consider a note, but they'll find me later. This early, the city of Pengshur is quiet, and I marvel at how different the architecture is from Siargao. My home province is all harsh, straight lines, and the over-water houses typical of a riverside city that's slowly sliding into the water.

This city, by contrast, is almost gothic in design. Every structure is ornate and scrolled, down to the glittering white street signs that tell me which direction the library is. It's ironic because the library building is impossible to miss. Where most of the structures here are six to eight stories, the library soars at fifteen or so. It's a beacon in the middle of town, and all roads seem to end at the library.

I roll my shoulders as the sun begins to peek up over the horizon, lighting up the giant white library building. It's stunning. If my life had been different, I would probably have petitioned Noire to let me come here and apply for the Novice program. Even as a pup, I was always obsessed with monster lore and reading every book I could get my hands on. It helped us in the maze, actually, because I knew every monster species' weakness.

That pulls a growl from deep in my chest, all my memories of hunting and killing rising to assault me. It prompts me to do something I started doing after my run last night—cataloging the things about my life that were fucked up because of my ma—because of Rama.

I'm aware it's a coping mechanism, but it's what I've got, so I start with my childhood. I think back to how she showed up at our pack home and slaughtered everyone she could, even the pups. I barely escaped with my life. Her goons caught me and tossed me in a bag in the maze. Noire found me when he woke up in the maze, too. Years later, she orchestrated an attack by another monster pack, and my brother Oskur was ripped to shreds.

Rama has been at the center of every horrible thing that ever happened in my life.

She never comforted me. She never reached out after doing something to hurt me. I screamed and sobbed and grieved when Oskur was killed, and she was never there for that either.

In fact, I barely saw her at all, except for the nightly message about our intended marks, our prey.

But when I turned eighteen, she began sending me books on every topic under the sun: math, monster lore, Lombornei's history. Noire wondered why I was always reading, but she stimulated my mind at a time when there was nothing else to do but the nightly hunt. We were her killers, her captives, her servants.

And then, eventually, I was hers in the only way that really matters to a direwolf male—bondmates.

When my memories threaten to get too sentimental, I remember that all of us Ayala brothers did time in the Atrium, me included, and it didn't stop when I came of age. The Atrium was all about the basest of instincts—sex. It was how Rama's wealthy patrons could touch and experience every sensation, safe from us monsters. It was a way for her to force us to perform in ways we never would have wanted to.

I wonder how my mate felt, watching me touch other women and be touched as well. Did it bother her? Turn her on?

It was fucked up, that's for sure. Growling, I turn my mind to Diana instead. She was the first omega I ever touched sexually, but that was before we all realized she was Noire's bondmate. Jet and I both had her, and gods she felt good. But we had to do it to pull Noire out of an impending rut.

I play our escape from the maze over again in my mind as I head for the library, up cobblestone streets still lit by oil lamps on giant white posts. That's Rama's fault, too, because she cut off the power seven years ago, and that affected literally every being on the continent. She thrived off of complete and total control. But in my short time as her mate, I never found out why.

The list of questions I have for her grows every day, but I try hard to shut off the way my mind wanders to that list.

Instead, I urge it to drift to the monsters in the Tempang, and I find myself wondering what their lives might be like? Vaguely, I remember the Volya who attacked Diana telling us the Tempang was sick. What did they mean, and how can a forest itself be sick? What would Diana and Achaia's lives have done to alleviate that?

The library looms in front of me. I've come directly to the archives entrance, and I'm able to make it through without assistance, thanks to the discs Onmiel gave us. The security guard keeps a wary eye on me. He must have seen me in the maze. I'm surprised we haven't gotten more strange glances, honestly, but I suspect some of the librarians never take their noses out of their books long enough to know what's going on outside of Pengshur.

In a way, the library feels hidden away from the rest of the world, and I like that. I feel like I could hide here for ages, and nobody would find me.

I pass through the entry hallway and the giant map we saw yesterday. When I stop to look at it, I shove down my own hesitation and pinch in off the coast of Vinituvari. Rama's flying city, Paraiso, should be there because none of my pack knew what to do with it. Well, I think it's more that Noire didn't give a fuck, and he never wanted to visit it again.

Arliss *must* be interested in the tech, as much of a collector and inventor as he is. But he hasn't seemed focused on Paraiso either. I haven't thought much about that until right now.

I pinch again at the map, but nothing happens. I guess I don't have the right magic, and that frustrates me. I want to know how the map works, to look at every inch of it. Even more than that, I want to know the library's secrets. Pengshur has been around for nearly two thousand years. The sheer amount of knowledge here is breathtaking.

Snarling, I step away from the map and find the long row of books that leads to our assigned reading room. Before I even swing the door open, I hear Onmiel muttering inside. When I open the door, she looks up with a brief flash of annoyance before smiling. That, at least, looks genuine.

"You're here early," she murmurs, glancing at an ancient-looking scrolled clock on the wall.

Damn, it's five a.m.

"Couldn't sleep," I grumble, sitting next to her. She's perched in the same place she was yesterday, tucked under the window. She sips a coffee and scowls down at the book in front of her.

Today, her hair is a brilliant blue, shocking and bright, although it fades to a pale cornflower at the tips of her wavy, shoulder-length hair. It's striking, but the orange was just as crazy-looking.

She's lost in thought, her glasses on the tip of her nose. She keeps scowling at the book and then scribbles on a spare notepad next to it. I grab the stack of books I was using yesterday and sigh. This work is daunting and tedious. I'd rather go back to the tome she gave me on mermaid clans.

Onmiel looks up at me before throwing her shocking hair up into a loose bun. Tendrils fall down around her heart-shaped face as she smiles again. "I need more coffee, so I'm going to run to the cafe. Can I get you anything, Tenebris?"

"It's just Ten," I correct. Rama and my father are the only ones who ever used my full given name, and it doesn't feel right for her to say it. Ten is so much more comfortable.

"Ten," she repeats, poking a pencil through the bun. "What'll it be?"

"I'll come with you," I murmur. "Maybe you can tell me a little more about the library on the way?"

She beams with excitement, pink stealing across her already rosy cheeks as I watch.

"I'd love to do that. What are you most curious about?" She stands and grabs a second pencil, shoving that through her bun as well. I wonder if she realizes there are now two there, sticking up out of her head like chopsticks.

I hold back the snort threatening to break loose and pace for the door, opening it as she steps quietly through. She waits for me just outside as I close the door, admiring the ornate black handle. Everything in this library is so beautiful and old, it needs to be treated gently.

"Tell me about the map. I tried to pinch in, and it irritated the fuck out of me that it didn't work."

Onmiel laughs, a tinkling sound that seems to echo around us as we follow the outer edge of the library and head for the coffee shop. Everything in here smells so good—I catalog old parchment and leather. I try to pick out anything non-bovine, but there's just so much.

"I'm gonna let you in on two secrets, Ten," she chirps, patting my forearm. "First, Novices aren't even allowed in the archives for a year because the magic is potentially dangerous if mistreated." She looks me up and down as if she's assessing me and then leans in like I'm about to hear a secret she can't say aloud.

Without thinking, I angle my head down to hear it because I want to know more about this place. Onmiel's lips nearly tickle my ear.

"I'll teach you how to touch the map if you promise not to do it when anyone's looking."

I shoot upright at that, incredulous. "You would? Even if it's dangerous?"

She shrugs and keeps walking, laughing when I jog to catch up. "I can tell a kindred spirit when I see one. You're curious about the library, which probably means you should apply to the program. If you want all the secrets, I

TEN: A DARK SHIFTER ROMANCE

mean." Her happy smile falls, but she plasters it right back on as we arrive at the coffee shop.

It's already bustling with librarians in tunics of all three level colors. I've read a few books about Pengshur. It's nice to have a baseline of info, although the reality of this place is so much more overwhelming than I could ever have imagined.

The Master Librarian who greeted us the first day is in the corner sipping an espresso, and he lifts it, inclining his head toward Onmiel as she responds in kind. She looks surprised to see him here, her eyelids fluttering before she smiles up at me.

I peruse the menu as we wait in line, but when he gets up to leave, there's a tangible sense of relief in the coffee shop. Onmiel watches him go and then turns to me secretively.

"ML Garfield is a super hardass; that's why everybody's thrilled he's gone. He's always been fair to me, but I'm a kickass librarian, so..." She shrugs again, and then it's our turn to order. I turn in the direction the Master Librarian left in, wondering how long he served here in order to get to his current station. He looks old as hells in person, even older than Thomas, my adoptive father.

We place our order and stand to the side to wait, and I lean against the wall as Onmiel taps one foot impatiently, long arms crossed. She's a stick, so different from Rama, who was all luscious curves. Rama was sex personified, the epitome of what a direwolf omega should be.

Onmiel is a pencil in human format.

She looks up at me and plants both hands on her hips. "What?"

"What, *what*?"

"You're staring at me like I'm some sort of maze prey or something."

Her casual mention of the maze has my hackles rising, but something about the teasing look on her face simultaneously puts me at ease. She's messing around with me, and I don't hate it.

She isn't treating me like a victim because she doesn't know everything I've been through. And she's not acting like my life was ruled by Rama and the maze because that's not her style.

I reach out to thunk the tip of her nose hard. "You wouldn't last twelve seconds in there."

"I might surprise you," she says bitterly before giving me a swift, playful punch to the side. I dodge it easily and grip her wrist, shoving it up behind her back as I bring my lips close to her ear.

"Nothing surprises me, Onmiel. I'd have been on you in less than a minute."

Shit.

I didn't mean to say that so seductively, but she straightens, giving me a serious look. Tugging at her wrist, she steps away, and I do my best to make light of my awkward comment.

"See? I haven't even chased, and you're on edge."

Her smirk is back as the barista delivers our drinks. "I'm just saying, I might look like a stiff wind could knock me over, but I'm scrappier than you think."

I grunt to keep from disagreeing but take a sip of the latte instead. The warm liquid burns on the way down my throat, but that burn feels good. It's a reminder I'm alive, and my family's alive.

Mostly.

Onmiel looks up at me with a smile. "So," she draws out the 'o' like she's about to tell me the gravest of secrets. "Arliss propositioned me last night. Is he always such a ho?"

I'm so caught off guard that I choke on the coffee and start coughing my head off.

Onmiel snorts and claps my back a couple times. "Poor thing. You're not used to my humor yet, but you'll come to love it. Everyone does."

There's a lump the size of an airship trying to go down my throat, but I give her a thumbs-up because it's all I can manage.

CHAPTER THIRTEEN

ONMIEL

When Ten pushes the reading room's door open, Ascelin scowls at me. The moment he turns his back to close the door, she pounds her fist into her open hand, her nose scrunched angrily.

I hear her message loud and clear; I just don't care. I've watched other librarians be bullied around by their clients just because of a whole "client is always right" attitude. I don't subscribe to that belief. It's like I told her—my primary focus is finding the information she needs. It's none of her business if Ten and I become friends.

I smile at her in the friendliest possible way. "Ascelin, we were here at the ass crack of dawn, and I didn't expect to see you for a bit. Would you like me to grab you another Type-A latte? You seemed to enjoy it..."

She doesn't bother to answer me, instead settling down on a chair. She reminds me of a cat hissing at unwanted affection.

Zakarias comes into the room, waving a quick hello. I set his drink down to the right of his book stack, smiling as he takes his glasses from his vest pocket and places them on the tip of his nose.

And then we get to work, Zakarias, Ten, and Ascelin hunching over the Volya books. I keep at my translation, having gotten a few tips overnight that might help. Hours after we begin, the door swings open, and Arliss shows up, a fresh round of coffees in his hands. He sets them down.

Standing with a smile, I move to the nearest bookshelf and pull a burgundy, leather-bound book off the shelf. I hand it to him with a meaningful look. "Lots of good info in here, Arliss. Let me know if you have questions."

He gives me a momentary look of surprise and clutches the book to his chest, then makes for the door again. I follow him out, the slippery weasel. I don't know why he can't research along with the rest of us, but I'd like to know.

"Where are you going?" I question, crossing my arms in what I hope is a motherly sort of fashion.

He presents me with that same shit-eating grin he flashed yesterday.

"Cut the shit, Arliss." I scowl. "Throw me a bone here. Why do you hide this?"

Blue eyes scan around us before he takes a step closer to me. "There are still those who would control a carrow if they thought they had found one. The only people who know of my existence are Ascelin's pack and now you. I would like to keep it that way because I might be the last of my kind."

"Meaning you can't pass on your gift?" I ask.

His expression falls, and he nods curtly.

"You never learned how? Or what…" I press.

He looks almost sad when our eyes finally meet again. "The carrow gift is a blessing and a curse, Onmiel. No one is meant to carry it forever. I would long ago have passed it on if I could. I need to know everything I can about it, as the one who gave it to me died during the transfer."

I sigh. "That's unfortunate. Most carrow function as mentors for a decade or two afterward."

"I'm aware," he replies in a flat tone. "How is it you know so much about this anyhow?"

I straighten my chin. "My life's work is a study of the monsters in the Tempang and the languages of Lombornei. This is literally what I spend all my time doing."

"What do you mean, monsters in the Tempang?" he presses on.

"You're actually *not* the only one, Arliss. An ancient tribe of carrow lives in the forest, but you'd have to journey there to meet and learn from them. They're highly reclusive."

An urgent look flashes over his face as he clutches the book to his chest. "I'm leaving immediately," he mutters, glancing around as if he's already thinking through the plans.

Angst hits me square in the gut. "You can't remove the book from the library, Arliss. Stay for a day or two and read that and its sequel. That'll tell you everything anyone on Lombornei knows about carrow. They're not friendly to outsiders; you can't just run up to the Tempang half-cocked."

"I don't do anything half-cocked, sweet one," he counters, right back to his old shit.

"Ugh," I groan. "I'm already exasperated by this macho-male horseshit. Can you not with me?"

Arliss throws his head back and laughs, and it carries throughout the section of the library we stand in. I hold back the urge to snip at him to hush. "You are a wonder, Onmiel. You'll be running this place in no time," he chortles.

"Seriously," I encourage him. "Stay a little while longer so you can read the books at least. I worry what might happen if you just traipse into the forest, even if you go in smoke form."

He looks shocked that I know about that. Arliss hesitates, but when he looks down at the beautifully bound book and then up at me, I know I've got him. He'll be staying with us for now, at least.

A wormy sensation of guilt wriggles around in my chest. I should tell Garfield about a lot of what my clients have shared—Rama's death and Arliss being an elusive carrow. But somehow, I find I'm not ready to do that. I want to help them first. If Rama's gone, then the worst of our fears are gone as well.

For now, it looks like I'll be keeping Pack Ayala's secrets.

~

Hours later, everyone's grumpy as shit. I've retrieved lunch for the males and another blood latte for Ascelin, who refuses to say she's hooked, but downs it in two seconds flat. I'll break through that prickly exterior if it's the last thing I do. I get it. She's protecting Ten because he's a treasure, and I see that now.

She's right to do it—Ten is amazing. He was helpful today, poring over the books and picking out bits and pieces of information that might help Diana. He works through the information far faster than Ascelin. He's got future Novice Librarian written all over him if I'm being honest.

I shelve that thought for another day, though, because this group has a big enough mission to accomplish first.

I'd love to help on the Volya front, but I can't speak to the intricacies of their medicine, and Zakarias can do the research better than I can. His background is in ancient healing techniques. Even though I excel in languages, this vampiri prophecy is punching me right in the asshole.

Nothing matches up.

Ascelin snarls and throws her coffee cup across the room. That makes me snarl in response because I'll have to clean the damn thing up. The warrioress leaps upright and paces aggressively in circles around the room. Arliss watches her dispassionately before turning his nose back to his book.

Ten and I can't stop watching her until finally, she breaks out a cell phone and dials a number. "Give me the Chosen One," she growls when someone picks up.

Moments later, her face softens. "Diana, how are you this day?"

I'm in awe at the change in her from one moment to the next.

"How are you feeling?" Ascelin probes, her voice gentle even as she frowns, pinching the bridge of her nose as she fakes a smile.

"Good, good. I am relieved it is a good day." The fake smile falls as she shakes her head. "No, Chosen One, nothing yet. We are putting together pieces here and there, but it is slow going." There's a momentary pause before she grits her teeth together. "Of course, if you feel up to the trip, please come."

Next to me, Ten tenses. When I look over, he's staring at the floor under his feet. Ascelin finishes her conversation and hangs up the phone, sighing as her head falls back and she focuses on the ceiling.

Ten breaks the silence first. "Noire's coming?"

"Achaia is taking them to an ancient mermaid city on the off-chance there is a healing salve of some sort. Once they do that, they will come here."

Ten nods again and then stands, excusing himself. I don't get a chance to ask if he's alright, but it seems like his brother coming is bad news.

Arliss looks up from his book to grin at me. "I can't wait to see you meet Alpha Noire, sweet one. He is *such* a fucking asshole."

CHAPTER FOURTEEN
TENEBRIS

I'm not anxious to see Noire, Jet, or their mates. The reality is that, even though we're desperately hunting for a cure, it's been nice to distance myself from my pack. Ascelin and Arliss aren't direwolf shifters. There's no mate or family bond tugging at me constantly. There's no Noire barking at me or Jet trying to hug me. There's no new sister-in-law to get to know. There's no kissing to look away from.

It's been fucking nice. I've had a few moments where I felt almost normal, aside from the moments where I catalog what a psycho my mate was in an attempt to distance myself from my ragged, painful emotions.

The sudden realization that I'm running away from everything douses me like icy water, and I turn back to the room. I can't run from my broken bond. I can't run from my family. And I shouldn't. What did Noire drill into us in the maze?

Family above everything.

He reminded us of that when we were escaping. In fact, we left the vampiri behind for a time, and half of them got slaughtered as a result. It was *always* Ayala Pack first. My older brother may be an asshole, but I know with certainty he would've burned this entire continent down to get me back if that's what it took.

Steel makes its way down my spine as I straighten and roll my shoulders, closing my eyes as I slump against a row of books. I index what I can scent around me. Leather, binding glue, thread, and paper of all sorts. Beings come and go, some scurrying and some leisurely walking. Echoes of voices make their way into my ears as I focus on the library itself.

This place has been a balm for my soul in the last two days, and I urge that healing sensation to spread to my aching heart. Rage seems to have made its way to the front of my mind in the last twenty-four hours, though, and it's a useful fuel. That and Onmiel's easy, immediate friendship.

When I get back to the room, it's tense, but she shoots me a glance, clearly asking if I'm alright. I nod softly, smiling a little before I seat myself next to her and look down at her work.

"Tell me about this," I encourage. "I need a break from the Volya stuff."

Her eyes sparkle and light up as she points down at the book and her paper. It's a list of symbols so intricate I can barely follow the scrolled lines and curves. When she opens her mouth and reads the first few lines aloud, I'm shocked at how stunning the language is. It's lyrical and beautiful, and I could listen to her speak it all day long.

"What is that?" I breathe.

Onmiel grins again and taps her pencil on the table before shoving it into her bun. Now there are three. Does she know? Is she that absent-minded?

I resist the urge to yank them all out as she starts looking around for another.

"This is Korsenji," she murmurs, stroking the page lovingly. "It's the language of the harpies, most of whom reside in the Tempang. You'll find the occasional harpy elsewhere, but they're highly territorial and very rare."

"Rama had one," I say without thinking. Diana told me that before we came here. A harpy told her how to find Arliss, and that information eventually led us to where we are today.

Onmiel gasps aloud. "Incredible. Hundreds of years ago, we had a harpy librarian, and she made this book for the library. Only a handful of people have ever studied it, though, because it's so incredibly complicated." She looks down at Ascelin's paper, the prophecy looming up at us from the fading sheet.

"I thought it sounded a bit like Korsenji, but now that I'm putting them side by side and matching the prophecy with the rarest of pronunciations from the book, I don't think so."

She sits back in her chair, huffing out a breath as she twists her bangs up and tucks them into the bun. She finds the pencils then and slaps me on the shoulder. "You didn't tell me I had three pencils stuck in my hair? Did I look like a doofus all day?"

I smile and look back down at the intricate language, the realization hitting me that finding the language this prophecy is written in is like finding a needle in a haystack.

TEN: A DARK SHIFTER ROMANCE

Ascelin and Zakarias stay til midnight, poring over every line in every book we have about the Volya. As it turns out, there's information squirreled all over the library. There are close to three hundred books for them to go through, and even stacking by relevance, it's a daunting task.

Eventually, Ascelin gives up and tosses another coffee cup at the wall before leaving. Arliss follows her out after shelving the book he's been reading all day. He and Onmiel share some sort of look before he gives her a mock salute.

Zakarias works with us for another half hour before giving up, and then Onmiel and I are alone in the reading room.

She turns to me after yawning for the third time. "You should get some sleep, alpha. If you can?" She's referencing how I mentioned this morning that I didn't sleep well last night, but I'm wired after a day of drinking coffee. I never had coffee until she gave me one, but I think it's safe to say I'm hooked.

"I'm going for a run," I muse aloud, thinking of the gardens up on the fifth floor. I felt like myself for a moment there, shifting into my direwolf and letting all that predatory focus eat up the emotions of my human body. Direwolves don't feel any *less* than their human forms, but they're able to focus on simply living, and that's a welcome distraction.

Onmiel gives me a thumbs-up and turns back to her work, so I leave and go upstairs.

Hours later, my head feels a little clearer, and I find myself wondering if she got to bed at a reasonable time. The plucky librarian seems to have no regard for her own wellness at all, something I can relate to because I haven't felt much of that lately, either.

I have a hard time falling asleep, with my mind picking and organizing all the information I learned today. There's got to be a cure for Diana somewhere or a faster way to get to it.

A sudden need to talk to her hits me, and I pad out to the kitchen of our rental to find Ascelin's phone. Diana picks up on the first ring. "Asc! Oh, Ten!" Her face is drawn and pinched, black circles resting under her eyes.

She's dying. It's obvious.

Noire appears behind her, squinting at the phone before he smiles at me. "Good to see you, brother," he growls.

"I wanted to check on you both," I murmur. "Diana, how are you feeling?"

Her half smile falls as she tucks her long hair over her shoulder. Noire's eyes move to her neck, his expression so pained that I almost hang up then and there. He presses his lips to her skin as her eyes close, and she sinks back like he's the only thing that can bring her comfort.

"We will fix this," I growl at them both. "You won't lose each other the way —" I stop before I can say the rest because I don't want to talk about it.

"Thank you, Ten," Diana whispers. "We did manage to get a coagulant from another mermaid kingdom with Achaia's help. So far, it's working to at least stall the bleeding, but I feel worse. Any luck with the research?"

I run one hand through my hair, running over everything we've learned about Volya so far. Eventually, I shake my head.

"There is something like three hundred books on Volya, and we're going over them line by line. Sometimes there are just mentions in a book, not more than a sentence or two. It's slow going, but if there's information to be found, we'll find it."

Noire growls as he pulls Diana into his lap and lays them both backward so I'm now looking at them from above. It's easy to see Diana's exhausted from this simple conversation. Her eyelids flutter shut, and she falls asleep as Noire looks at me.

"I need you to work faster, Ten," my pack alpha growls. "If I lose her, there will be no containing my rage. I'm starting to understand Father a little better, how insane he was after Mother died."

I think back to our asshole of a father. He was never kind to my three older brothers, but he doted on me a bit. Being the youngest had its perks, I suppose. But whatever goodness there was in him died with our mother. He never recovered.

That's how I know Noire will turn to the damn dark side if he loses Diana.

"How are you handling things?" Noire's surprisingly gentle question brings me back, his stare probing, even though he's hundreds of miles away.

How am I handling things? My mate was a fucking asshole, but I miss her. My only bright moments are the times with Onmiel when she treats me like I'm normal and life is normal, like every woman I love isn't dead or dying.

I don't know how to put all that into words, though, so I shrug. "The librarians are nice. They barely take breaks to sleep. At a minimum, they're extremely committed."

Noire nods, lost in thought, before he turns back to me. "We'll be there in another day or two. Elizabet is working on some concoction for Diana. As it is right now, I can't risk moving her too much. She's so fragile, Ten. The strongest person I know is reduced to almost nothing in such a short time. I feel like I'm losing my mind."

I can't think of anything to say to that, so I give him an apologetic look before leaning in the doorway to the kitchen. "I'm headed back over to the library now. Onmiel thought she cracked the code on the prophecy, but it was another dead end."

TEN: A DARK SHIFTER ROMANCE

Noire growls. "At this point, I could give a fuck what the prophecy says unless it's about healing her."

It seems to me it's likely all tied together, but I can't say for sure, so we say our goodbyes, and I hang up. When I set Ascelin's phone down on the countertop, I sense she's in the room. Turning, I find her leaning in the doorway, watching me in silence. Even at this hour, she's fully clothed in her warrior garb, complete with a knife strapped to her thigh.

"You ever *not* ready for war, Asc?"

She grimaces, gritting her teeth before she speaks. "How was she?"

"Not good."

"How much time do we have?" Ascelin's eyes are filled with tears, a reminder that so much has happened in the last several weeks. We faced off against the vampiri for years in the maze, although Noire protected me from that as much as he could when I was younger. But then the vampiri king, Cashore, gave his life to save Diana, infusing his soul into hers. Now, Diana has two vampiri partners who protect her like she's a goddess.

It's fascinating, and I find myself wishing I had time to learn more about their culture, and to talk to Cashore through Diana, to learn how things might be different in a pack of blended monsters.

But any of that'll have to come later.

"I'm going up to the library," I tell Ascelin.

"I will join you," she says, her voice so soft I can barely hear her. We leave the apartment and walk to Pengshur in silence.

When we arrive at the reading room, I growl. I can smell Zakarias inside, but there's none of Onmiel's bright, friendly scent. And no coffee.

Swinging the door open, I enter to find the male librarian head down, so focused that he doesn't even notice us enter. When I seat myself across from him, he looks up to greet us.

"I was able to speak with my partners at the Pengshur Healing Hospital. They are ready to act on anything we might uncover, so that is good news."

"Where's Onmiel?" I ask before he gets the chance to say anything.

He smiles kindly. "Miel would work herself to death if I let her. I asked her to grab a few hours of rest. She will be here again later."

Misery settles in my gut as I turn to Ascelin. "I need coffee. Want your latte thing?"

"Most certainly," she grumbles as she perches elegantly on the edge of her chair and opens her book to the last page.

I leave the reading room, irritated that Onmiel isn't here. I hope she comes back soon.

CHAPTER FIFTEEN
ONMIEL

Gods, I'm grateful Zakarias insisted I get a few hours' sleep because I feel like a new woman. The persistent caffeine headache I'd been nursing has finally dissipated, and my limbs don't feel like they weigh two tons apiece.

I've been so focused on translating this prophecy, and it's easy for a librarian to neglect their sleep schedule. It's worse for Novices since we carry extra responsibility during an assignment. Zakarias's schedule isn't much better than mine, but he's getting at least four hours more sleep every night.

I take an extra minute with my hair, curling the blue ends a little. Ugh, it's growing out again. My natural white color is nearly translucent at my scalp, which makes it look like it's floating. So fun because it appears I'm going bald when in fact, I can barely keep my crazy hair in check. It's always grown inexplicably fast like this. I hate it.

I look around my assigned room, gazing out the window onto the streets below. The city of Pengshur seems so happy with everybody bustling around. I swear, this really is the most peaceful place in all of Lombornei. Pengshur is its own insulated world, although ML Garfield's comment from two days ago still rings in my head.

If it appears that way to you, then I'm doing my job.

I should probably check in with him, but so far, there's really nothing to report about the monsters. I know Zakarias has been giving him daily updates, but I can't tell him Arliss told me that Ten killed Rama. It would be a horrible breach of trust, and if she's really dead, then the secret can certainly wait.

I'm still conflicted in my emotions about that. Direwolf bondmates are rare, and it's often said that losing one results in insanity in the other. How Ten puts one foot in front of the other is sort of amazing. Unless being mated to that psychopath wasn't all roses. But it's not like I can ask him…

Now that I know the horrible news about Ten and Rama, I'm more determined than ever to be a good friend, despite a rapidly growing and very inappropriate attraction to the muscular alpha. It can't possibly be a good time for him to start a relationship, and friendship is fine with me. It really is.

But is it? A little voice helpfully pipes up in my head. I grab the ends of my hair and twist them around my fingertips. Maybe there's a day in the future when Ten will have moved past his horrible loss and be ready to date. And if that day ever comes, maybe he'll remember the sexy, nerdy librarian who tried really hard not to stare at his super nice abs. And his super nice shoulders. And his super gorgeous ass.

I'm hopeless. At least, that's the conclusion I come to as I dress and grab my bag, heading downstairs for the reading room. To my surprise, Ten stalks out with a scowl. When he sees me, he grips my shoulder and directs me away from the room.

"Ten, what's going on? Are you okay?"

"Need coffee," he snarls, not letting go of my arm. He's clearly upset about something, but I don't want to push him, so I let him hold me like a wayward child all the way to the coffee shop. Eventually, I pry my elbow out of his grip and give him a stern look.

"You could ask pol—"

"That room is unbearable without you," he huffs. "Zakarias is trying to make small talk, and Ascelin snips at him every time he does. It's so tense. You're my barrier, so come help me fuel my new coffee addiction, and then come back and barrier for me."

I scoff, my mouth dropping open. I'm a *barrier*? I zip my lips shut as I ponder my response, but ultimately, I realize this is a good thing. I'd like to be Ten's friend, and if he counts on me, and if I can bring him peace? I'd love to do that.

Ten is a tense, seething presence at my side when we reach the ordering station. I order for the both of us, Zakarias, and Ascelin, too.

"What about Arliss?" I question as Ten scowls.

"Arliss can go fuck himself," Ten growls, crossing his arms.

The half-minotaur barista snorts, a gold ring in his nose moving with his

TEN: A DARK SHIFTER ROMANCE

wide, hairy muzzle. I used to find him hot until I met Ten. The barista rings us up to my library account, and then we turn to wait for the coffees.

Ten's silent, and I can practically feel the tension rising in him based on how his eyes move from side to side. He's assessing every being in here. Is he thinking of them like the marks in the maze?

When his breaths become shallower and his fists ball, I step close to him and place both hands on his immense pecs. Amber eyes flick immediately to my hands, then to mine, as I croon.

"Easy, alpha." I keep my tone low and friendly. "You can always come to find me upstairs if you need me." That's not technically true. He shouldn't be upstairs in the Novice quarters, but I've never been all that great about rules, something Zakarias has had to remind me about many times.

"Zakarias said you needed sleep."

"I did."

"I didn't want to bother you."

"You never will. Just come to room fourteen and sit with me. I snore like a hog, but I'm told it's adorable."

One corner of Ten's mouth curls up, pearly-white fangs descending as his pupils dilate. Is he thinking of me like prey? Gods, I wish he was imagining me in bed. But I'm one thousand percent certain that's not the case. He hasn't even told me yet that he killed his own mate. Maybe he never will.

Amber eyes focus on me as the black pupil recedes. He strokes absent-mindedly at the back of my hand with two fingers. After a few minutes of ridiculously intense eye contact, his breathing slows.

The barista bellows out my name, breaking the moment. Ten yanks his hand back but grabs the drinks. We head back to the reading room, but when we arrive, Ascelin and Zakarias are in the middle of a heated argument. Well, it's more like Ascelin snapping her creepy black teeth at my delicate mentor while he cowers in the corner.

Ten breaks them up immediately, shoving Ascelin so hard she flies across the room, although she lands with incredible grace. It's sort of fascinating if it weren't so terrifying.

"What's going on here?" I demand, looking from Ascelin to Zakarias and back again.

"We are running out of time," Ascelin roars. "The Chosen One is dying, and unless you help us find a cure, she will be dead in a week!"

I pad quietly across the room, grabbing Ascelin's hand and putting it against my chest. My heart pounds in my chest as Ten moves to stand behind me, a comforting presence, although I know he's focused on his friend.

"I will never stop until we find a cure for her," I reassure the distraught vampiri. "I can tell you love her so much, and this is really fucking scary for you."

Ascelin yanks her hand away. "Nothing frightens me."

"Losing people does," I whisper. "That frightens everyone."

No sooner have I said it than I realize what I just said, and I worry for Ten. But I carry on, even though I've just stuck my whole leg in my mouth. Opening my arms, I throw myself onto Ascelin, hugging her tight. "It's okay to be terrified, First Warrioress. But FL Zakarias and I are by your side, and I have a bit of good news."

There's a heavy pause, and then Ascelin buries her face in my shoulder and weeps like a child. I can't purr like an alpha, but I don't have to because Ten joins us, wrapping his big arms around us both. A rolling, deep rumble echoes out of his chest, vibrating against my shoulder and Ascelin's.

Gods, I've never heard an alpha purr. But I can one thousand percent admit it's sexy as hells. The noise vibrates through my entire body, my nipples pebbling as I resist the urge to clench my thighs together. Although, the sobbing vampiri woman in my arms puts a quick damper on my libido.

I hold Ascelin for a long time, and when she shows no signs of stopping, I step back and slap her lightly on the cheek. "Get to work, sister. Let me show you what I'm talking about."

Ascelin nods, wiping at both cheeks before she rounds the table to her seat again. She doesn't apologize to Zakarias, but he comes to stand next to me, looking over my shoulder as I flip my book around and turn it to her.

"See this language here?" I point to a line of angular markings in the book. "There are seven variations of this language. If your prophecy is not one of these seven, then it can only be one thing."

"What thing?" Ascelin bristles, even though we're narrowing down.

"Volya," I say in a strong voice, hoping I sound confident and professional. "If it's not one of these seven, it can only be Volya. Or I suppose it could be a language nobody's ever heard of, but that seems unlikely. Prophecies aren't typically delivered in unknown—"

"Onmiel," Zakarias murmurs. "That's enough, child."

I look over at Ascelin, and she's slumped in her chair, looking utterly despondent.

"Of course," her voice is an angry hiss. "Of course, it would be those fucking monsters. What are the odds of that being the case? And why did we not start with the Volya language?"

It's my turn to sigh and lean back. "Nobody knows the Volya language except the Volya. It has never been written down in any book in this library. I know because I asked to learn it when I started my studies, and I hunted high and low for it. It doesn't exist."

"We're going to have to go to the Tempang," Tenebris says, standing upright and crossing his arms.

"Godsdamnit," Ascelin mutters. "Tell me something I do not know."

~

Midnight comes and goes, and Zakarias has a breakthrough—an ancient text references a woman who was healed by a medicine man after a Volya attack. He sends a message through the library's system for any additional books that might reference the event.

Ascelin calls Diana and Ten's brother to let them know, and there's an almost tangible change in the feel of the room.

We break for the evening, but after Zakarias and Ascelin have gone, Ten remains.

He stacks books alongside me, and it doesn't surprise me in the slightest that he stacks them correctly.

Grinning, I look up at him. "After all this shit is done, and assuming Diana is okay, you're going to apply to the Novice program, right? You're doing this better than most second-year librarians."

Ten gives me a slight smile, then picks up the first stack as I give him a quizzical look.

"What?" he rumbles. "It doesn't feel right that you're busting your ass to help us. Plus, I don't sleep well anyway."

"Okay." I laugh, grabbing a second stack. "Then I'm going to teach you how to spell them back in place, and how to spell them out. But don't tell a soul I taught you because the magic is dangerous."

Ten's face splits into a huge, broad grin, and he puts his free hand on my lower back. I struggle not to sink into his warmth. Gods, I'm so sad he's had so much trauma and he's dealing with that. My heart is broken for him, but my pussy just wants to rub herself all over his face.

We make our way into the stacks, and I check each spine for the number, holding up my hand to Ten. "We make a fist like this." I wrap my fingers together, keeping my thumb on top of the other four. "And then we whisper the correct incantation to locate the book's spots. *Libris Actuis Localis*. You try it."

Ten makes a perfect fist and repeats the spell, and the number on the book's spine glows brightly. Without me even having to tell him, Ten follows the sensation that pulls us to where the book belongs. When we get there, he gives me a triumphant look. It's heady and beautiful and overwhelming because this is what he could be if given the proper environment to shine in.

I point to a shelf that doesn't look empty when he starts to appear confused, dark brows pulling into a deep vee above his striking eyes.

"Now it's *revertere ips manerit*."

"Can I say it?" Ten questions, looking around to make sure nobody's near us.

"Go ahead." I give him a conspiratorial wink.

When he repeats it, not quite correctly, nothing happens.

"Mah-nair-itt," I correct. "Not Man-urr-itt."

"Got it," he says, his fangs descending. Ooh, so he's feeling some kind of way about this little lesson if the fangs are a sign. I know enough about shifters to know it happens in a time of strong emotion. I love it. I'm going to convince him to join the program if I have my way, which I pretty much always do.

He repeats the incantation, and the books on the shelf slide apart. The one on top of his stack levitates and then shifts upright, slotting itself in its spot. Once it's in, the glowing number on the spine stops.

Ten turns to me with a little whoop of excitement.

You can take the dork out of the librarian, but you can't take the librarian out of the dork.

I grin and gesture for him to continue. It takes us an hour still, but we get all the books put away, and by the time we're done, Ten seems refreshed.

It's more than that, though. He seems good for the first time since I met him. He seems happy. It might not last because grief is a funny thing. It's not linear, and it's never really done. I know. Grief and I are close friends.

But if it's good right now, then it's still progress.

CHAPTER SIXTEEN
TENEBRIS

I should be exhausted, but I think I'm too wired and hyped on coffee to go lay down. Even Onmiel seems energized by having taught me something.

I look down at her. From my height, I can see the top of her head since she's so short. "Wanna go run with me in the garden?" I'm not sure what makes me ask it, but I think I'll be able to get a little rest if I do that.

Onmiel rubs the back of her neck but looks up with a wry smile. "As much as I'd love that, I think you mean in direwolf form, right?" She points down to her long, thin legs. "Athletic as I am, I'll never be able to keep up with you."

"You can ride me," I purr, not meaning for it to sound so incredibly sensual. But it does, and she stops in her tracks, crossing her arms as she narrows her eyes at me.

Onmiel's nostrils flare. She looks like she's trying not to laugh. "That sounds very sexual, Tenebris."

"I didn't mean it to," I say quickly, hoping I haven't made her feel incredibly awkward. "It would be fun, come on. It's not some big secretive direwolf thing. If I was still around my pack and there were pups, I'd give them a ride, too. Consider yourself a direwolf pup."

That seems to mollify her, even though it buries a dagger in my stomach.

My pack. Our pups. My friends.

All dead.

All dead because of Rama.

I hold back a growl because she'll never hurt anyone again. My heart paid the price, but Lombornei is safe.

"Okay." Onmiel's agreement brings me back to the present, and I smile. "You'll come with me?"

She scrunches her sloped nose and nods. "Yeah. I'm going to wrap my hand around all your neck fur, though. That doesn't sound comfy."

I do laugh at that because if she thinks that'll hurt an alpha like me, she doesn't know as much about us as she believes she does.

"Come on." I gesture for her to join me as I head back toward the elevator bank, debating if there's time for more coffee before the run. I'd better not, though. I should get some sleep before the rest of my pack arrives, assuming Diana is stable. Pack? Court? I'm not sure what we're calling ourselves these days, but I've heard both terms used.

Onmiel is a bundle of excitement all the way up to the fifth floor, and when we get there and enter the gardens, she grins at me. Then her cheeks turn pink as she tucks a strand of brilliant blue hair behind her ear. "You, uh, need to get undressed, right?"

Pulling my shirt over my head, I toss it on a nearby bench and grin. "Yep, unless I wanna walk out of here naked."

She grumbles something under her breath, but when I reach for my pants, she turns from me and walks away a few steps, looking studiously anywhere else.

"Alphas don't give a shit about nudity, Onmiel. It's sort of a side effect of shifting all the time. Someone in the pack is always naked."

"You might not, but I do," she chirps back. "I'll ogle you, and I don't want to be weird."

"Ogle me, huh?"

"Yeah." She laughs. "You're hot, Ten, but friends don't ogle their naked friends. I mean, not any more than is absolutely necessary."

I hear her heart pounding in her chest, galloping along at full speed as she works herself into a lather about my nudity. It's funny to me because I don't even think about it. Nudity doesn't equal sex for shifters, although I suppose if Onmiel were to actually stare at my dick, it might feel that way.

I shift into my direwolf and cross the small walkway, nudging her in the back with my nose. Like this, I experience her differently. When she turns, there's a surprised but joyous look on her face. She says nothing but reaches out to stroke both of my ears, which brings her chest nearly flush with my face. She smells…good.

Better than good. She smells sweet but a little tart.

When she scratches behind one ear with a little laugh, I butt her chest with my head and lie flat. She gets the message and gives me one final look. "You sure about this? I'm going to come away with handfuls of hair, so it's your funeral if you agree to it."

A low growl rumbles from my throat, and she takes my meaning, hopping lithely onto my back. She rocks her hips as she gets situated, squeezing me tight with both knees as her hands rest at the base of my neck. I take off at a slow canter, like a horse, to get her accustomed to the movement.

Onmiel leans forward over my shoulders and wraps her arms around my neck, and godsdamnit, she does wrap both fists in my fur. It pinches, but my direwolf is thrilled to have her on us. Alpha packs are affectionate with close-knit friendships. I've missed that, and he has too.

I run for a solid half hour before finding the crystal-clear lake I found that first day. Dropping to the ground, I shrug Onmiel off as she laughs excitedly.

"That was amazing, Ten! You're so fucking fast, I'm totally jeal—oh gods, what are you doing?" she shrieks when I shift out of direwolf form. My direwolf wants to play with her, to tease her, because he recognizes a kindred spirit.

Her cheeks flame red, and her eyes dart immediately to my cock, which hangs heavy against my thigh. I'm half-hard, knowing a female's examining me. I don't know if Onmiel's aware she is, but when I clear my throat with a haughty grin, she crosses over and slaps my chest.

"I told you I wasn't going to be able to not look. It's your fault for making me do it. I think you did that on purpose," she snaps, crossing her arms as I pick her up, and throw her over my shoulder.

"Don't gaslight me." I laugh. "I didn't force you to look."

It's nice to be playful, and it makes my direwolf happy—something he hasn't been since we ripped Rama to shreds. I jog straight into the lake and throw Onmiel bodily into the water, laughing as I dive under it to watch her.

She flails before finding purchase on the rocky bottom, and then she stands up with a glower as something blue runs in rivulets down her arms. "You are such an *ass*, Tenebris Ayala! Damnit, I just dyed that, too..."

Grimacing, I swipe two fingers up her arm, watching goosebumps cover it as I lift them to show her the dye. "I'm so sorry, I was just playing around, but I fucked up your hair."

As I watch, the dye runs in intense rivers down her hair. She gives me two middle fingers but dunks herself, shaking her head side to side as she runs her fingers through her long hair. When she comes back up, I gasp in surprise. Where her hair was a vivid royal blue before, it's now a shimmery, opalescent white. It shines like a pearl as she grimaces, pointing up at it.

"Do I look like an old lady?" She must hate the hair, based on the way she seems to expect me to hate it.

I take a step closer to her, picking up the ends and taking a look. Up close, it's actually every possible shade of the palest pastel, almost like a real pearl.

"I've never seen hair like this, Onmiel," I murmur. "What are you, if not fully human?"

"Nobody's ever seen hair like this," she grouses. "It's stupid to deal with. That's why you've known me for three days, and you've already seen it be two different colors. And I don't know what I am, sadly."

"It reminds me of my brother's mate, Achaia's, pearls. She's a mermaid queen, you know."

I splash Onmiel, who sticks out her tongue in a raspberry.

"So, what'll your hair color be next?" I turn on my back and float lazily around her. She's careful not to let her eyes drift to my crotch, where my half-mast cock still pokes out.

"I was thinking neon green," she smirks. "I'm already pretty noticeable in the library, but nobody'll be able to miss me with that."

When I think of how ever present she is in the library, I have to grin. I suspect even before we arrived, Onmiel was at the library as much as humanly possible.

There's a sudden movement, and I shift upright just as she throws herself on top of my head, dunking us both. Water shoots up my nose as I growl and remove her, although she's wrapped herself around me as she yanks at my hair with both hands.

Calling on my direwolf's strength, I lift her off me and toss her fifteen feet across the pond.

For half an hour, we play, but I notice my friend is starting to fade.

"Time to get you home," I mutter as I walk out of the lake. She doesn't even stare at my crotch before yawning and following me.

"Shit, we've got to be back in a few hours," she moans. "You want to just come sleep on my window seat? Or we could maybe get a room assigned for you."

For half a moment, I debate the merits of this plan. I'm not looking forward to the walk home, and I do have to be back here soon. But a bedroom with another woman? I don't know if I'm ready. But when my direwolf growls at me, I nod.

"Let's go. I'll stay with you."

"Good," she murmurs, her eyelids drooping. "You can shower because there's literally a fish scale on your forehead. Herk!"

Laughing, I peel the scale off my skin and flick it into the lake, shifting so she can get on top of me again.

The entire run back to the elevator bank, my direwolf preens at having Onmiel ride us. He likes her.

∼

Half an hour later, we've showered separately in the small room assigned to her. It's nothing more than a tiled bathroom, shower, and a small bed with a chair in the corner. A big, round window overlooks the city outside, with a bench seat underneath it. I sit there as she comes out of the bathroom, clothed, toweling her incredible hair.

When she smiles at me, it warms me from the inside out, and I pull my knees to my chest as I watch her.

"What?" she questions me with a suspicious smile, tossing the towel aside. "You look like you're about to ask me about the secrets of the universe or something."

Something deep inside me breaks, standing here with her. I want her to know me, to really know me.

"You don't treat me like a victim," I start, not sure I really want to go into this, but also desperate to talk about it. "Why is that?"

Onmiel grabs a fluffy gray sweater and pulls it onto her thin shoulders, flopping down across from me on the bench seat. She gazes out the window for a moment and then turns to me.

"I never watched what happened in the maze, but I heard about it, of course. The librarians and Novices used to talk a lot about all the maze's monsters. I don't pry because if you want to talk about it, you will. And I don't treat you like a victim because I've been a victim, and everybody pussy-footing around you does you no good."

"When were you a victim?" I growl, shifting forward as I lock my eyes on hers. A victim? Who hurt her? My direwolf prowls inside me, pushing an uncomfortable pressure into my chest. He hates this.

"It was a long time ago," she shrugs. "But everybody walked on eggshells around me after, and I hated it. Eventually, I left home because of it."

Gods, I've got so many questions about that.

"I'm sorry," I say instead, resisting the urge to pull her into my arms and run my cheek along hers. It's what I'd do for any omega in my pack, but I don't want her to think I'm being forward.

"Do you want to talk about the maze?" she asks softly.

For a long minute, I lean back against the smooth, burled wood and watch the city of Pengshur begin to come alive. Gods, we really do need to be back to the reading room soon.

"Another time," I growl finally, looking over to where she waits, her expression hopeful and then disappointed. "You need sleep, Onmiel."

"We need sleep," she corrects with a laugh. "You're welcome to sleep in the window or on my chair, or you can sleep in the bed with me. I sleep deeply, and like I said, I snore like crazy, I'm told."

A sudden possessive alarm trills in my brain. Who told her she snores? Who was here when she was asleep, watching her, protecting her?

I shove that thought away and nod, crossing the room and falling onto the bed, facing the window.

She lays down facing me and shoves a pillow between her knees, grabbing another one and clutching it tightly.

When I give her a look, she shrugs. "Can't help it. I'm a pillow whore. You should see the sheer amount in my actual apartment."

We fall silent as I smile, watching her eyelids droop. As she begins to nod off, I keep watching. I think she's asleep, but she reaches out and places a hand on my chest.

"One day, will you tell me why you looked so broken the day you arrived?"

I force myself not to look shocked. I felt broken. I am broken. Although every day seems to be a little bit better.

"One day, I will," I whisper.

CHAPTER SEVENTEEN
ONMIEL

My alarm goes off at some godsforsaken hour, and I flutter my eyelids open with a groan. A soft snore reaches my ears, and I flip over before remembering that Ten slept with me last night.

The early morning light illuminates his tan skin and dark brows. Chocolate waves are still slicked back from the shower, although one piece sticks straight up, giving him an almost comical look.

Gods above, he's so fucking handsome.

I wonder if I should leave him to sleep, but then I imagine the look on Ascelin's face when she asks me where he is, and I tell her he's passed out in my bed. Huffing out a laugh, I consider it, if only for the sheer pleasure I'd derive from fucking with her. I know she's killed people—a lot of people—but I just can't hold back when it comes to her. I like her, and I'm going to force my friendship on her despite her reluctance. She'll give in.

They all do.

Almost as if he can feel me willing it, Ten's eyes open, dark pupils widening as they filter the increase in light.

"It's morning," I whisper. "Unfortunately. Coffee?"

"Coffee," he growls, fangs peeking out from behind his lips. He rolls onto his back and reaches for my headboard, stretching out long as he points his toes and lets out a pleased growl.

Gods, help me, but I can't stop noticing the huge morning wood pressed against the front of his jeans. I think that thing would break me. It's so damn big. I read a shifter erotica once. They've all got a knot at the base that swells. That must feel like birthing a baby.

"Onmiel, what are you thinking about?" Ten laughs. "You're staring at my junk."

I don't know when we turned the corner from tentative friendship to sexual innuendo, but we've passed that corner, and we're hurtling toward the next one.

"I was just thinking a knot probably feels like you're giving birth if you're not an omega."

"Oh, I don't know about that." He laughs, rolling onto his side as he props his head in one hand. "My brother, Jet, is mated to a vampiri warrior and a mermaid queen. She takes both of them together. In the same hole."

I scoff. "Bullshit."

"Unfortunately, I've heard them. But in any case, you'll get to ask her yourself later," he replies, his tone suddenly wry. Amber eyes move back up to mine. He looks hesitant. "You'll love Jet and his mates. Achaia is fierce and kind. Renze and Ascelin together are hilarious. Diana is amazing, too. My whole pack is incredible. But my brother Noire is..." He seems to struggle to come up with a word for his eldest brother.

"A dick?" I offer helpfully. Ten sits up and stretches again, rubbing one big hand on the back of his neck.

Gods, I'd love to help with that.

"It's more than that." His voice is quiet, and I wonder if it's hard for him to talk poorly about his brother, being the pack alpha and all. "Noire is calculating and devious. He's always looking ten steps ahead. Just be wary of him. He'll use anyone to get what he wants, and he has everything to lose right now. He'd burn Pengshur to the ground if he thought that would get him an answer for Diana. He threatened Garfield with that before we even came. He'd do it, Miel."

A chill skates down my spine, imagining what that sort of male might be like.

"We better get him answers, then," I confirm.

Ten nods, but he looks lost in thought. We dress, leave the room, and head downstairs.

When Ten swings our assigned room's door open for me, I smirk when Ascelin's the only one present. She snarls as I enter with Ten right behind me. He's oblivious to her ire, but I hold back a smile as she turns apoplectic with rage. I can tell because her face gets a little grayer, all the dark blood rushing to it as she bites her lip to keep from screaming at me.

Instead, she turns to Ten with a lofty grin. "Tenebris. Your brothers will be here shortly. Are you ready?"

Oh, checkmate. The point goes to Ascelin because that news took all the wind out of my proverbial sails.

Ten stiffens, and I shoot her a shitty look. I open my mouth to say something, but Zakarias and Arliss come into the room together, mid-conversation.

"—sure we will be able to handle whatever—"

"I am certain you are not ready for Alpha Noire, First Librarian," Arliss snarls. "But you had better get ready with answers fast because he will not hesitate to use whatever means necessary to persuade you." Arliss uses air quotes to punctuate the word "persuade".

I think I see what's going on here. Ten warned me in the same way this morning. All that aside, I'm not here to let Zakarias or myself be bullied around by anyone. We are on the same mission as the Ayala Pack, and we are making progress, albeit slowly.

"We've got this handled," I interject, breaking Arliss's attention on my mentor.

At the same time, the door swings open, and a giant male steps through, pitch-black eyes flicking from face to face before landing on mine.

This could only be Noire. He looks slightly older than the male just behind him, even though he's a tad shorter. He's broader, though, all stacked muscle and an air of superiority. There's a sneer on his face, sharp fangs poking out from his upper jaw. He cocks his head to the side, and a flash of terror streaks down the back of my neck.

This male is a predator in every sense of the word. When Ten said Noire would burn the library to the ground without remorse, I found it hard to understand, but not after seeing him in person. Behind his steely, focused gaze is an air of insanity.

Noire is a male on the knife's edge of something, and I don't want to be in his path when he snaps.

"Brother," Ten murmurs, pulling me away from the door and behind him.

Noire doesn't move from the doorway, but the two males behind him push inside the small room, which now feels stifling. Next to me, Zakarias sounds like he's about to hyperventilate.

The second male looks like Noire but is a little taller, a little lankier. This must be Jet, the pack's strategist. Next to Jet hovers a slender vampiri male, blond hair braided away from his forehead and ear on one side in an intricate series of braids. They hang down his back on one side. He's a First Warrior like Ascelin if I read the braid pattern correctly.

So that must be Renze, one of Jet's two mates.

When nobody says anything, my mind wanders to such an unusual pairing. I've rarely heard of direwolves mating outside their species. But for Jet to take not only a vampiri but a mermaid queen. I wonder how it's changed their pack dynamics, if at all. Of course, I've wondered the same thing about Ascelin and her connection to Diana. It seems like the maze brought them all together in unforeseen ways, and I'm curious wha—

"Where are my fucking answers?" Noire keeps his voice light, but there's an intense undercurrent to the question.

Zakarias steps forward to stand next to me, wringing his hands. Gods, I hope he stops that. If there was ever a male not to be prey-like in front of, it's this one. "Alpha Noire, allow me to int—"

"I don't give a fuck who you are," Noire snaps, his voice rising in timbre. "I sent Ten here for one reason and one reason alone. Garfield assured me you were the best team, yet I've heard no good news. So, where the fuck are my answers?"

I watch the other brother's eyes flick around the room and refocus on his pack alpha. There's a long beat, and then Noire's eyelashes flutter against his tan cheeks.

Are they communicating through a family bond? They must be. If Jet is the strategist and the "nice one", according to Ten, I assume he could be talking his brother down. Or trying to.

"We're close," I lie. "We've made progress, but we're piecing information together from hundreds of different sources."

Black eyes narrow on me.

"Don't lie to me, girl." The promise of violence is heavy in his words. "Work yourselves to the bone if you have to, but find my fucking answers. You don't want to see me at my *persuading*, as Arliss said."

Oh fuck me.

"We won't need to go there," Jet breaks in, his tone calm but decisive. He glances over at Zakarias and me. "Because the librarians are going to fix this, right?"

"Of course," I tack on smoothly. "We are dedicated to finding Diana an answer." I purposefully mention the omega herself, even though she's not here. I want to remind this pack alpha that it's not him we're doing it for; it's his mate. That we know she's important, and our focus is on her.

"Good," Jet says, shrugging his shoulders. I watch the vampiri slip an elegant hand around Jet's waist and squeeze. The direwolf sinks almost imperceptibly into that touch.

It's fascinating.

Noire laughs bitterly, gesturing around the small room. "All of Pengshur at my disposal." Sarcasm drips from his tone, despite the hundreds of books in stacks around the room. He doesn't know or care about the organization system I've got going on here, how I'm cataloging every scrap of information we find.

My mouth goes dry as his focus moves to Ten. Noire cocks his head to the side, his frown deepening as he widens his stance.

"Of course, alpha," Ten purrs. And then, "That's not necessary, Noire."

What's not necessary? Watching this pack all together is like watching a well-oiled machine function at high capacity. I heard from colleagues who watched the nightly hunts that the direwolves were the veritable kings of the maze. Despite just four of them being there, they only lost one brother in seven years of hunting the maze's dark halls. Or so I heard. Ten hasn't mentioned a pack enforcer, and that's the primary role I don't see filled here.

Although having two vampiri certainly counts. I'm dying to ask about the dynamics, but now hardly seems the time.

"I said no, Noire," Ten snaps, reminding me there's a whole conversation happening that the rest of us aren't privy to. Zakarias simmers with tension next to me. I reach out and place my hand on top of his.

Ten continues in a respectful tone. "Go to our rental, alpha, please. I'll wrap things up and meet you there. I'd be happy to share what we've uncovered and what we're still hunting for."

Noire lets out a snarly, pissed-off rumble, but I hear the click of boots on the floor. The door opens, and footsteps tell me at least one person left.

There's a sigh, and when I look around, Ten, Jet, and Renze are still in the room. They exchange a look. Renze's dark lips split into a grin, translucent black fangs clearly visible. "Best to follow him, lest he rip a limb from Garfield to make a point."

Gods, if Noire is on his way to see Garfield, I think Garfield needs a warning. I step to the nearest comm and send him a message. Jet leaves with just a quick nod to me, disappearing out the door quietly.

"Firenze." Ascelin purrs, slipping across the room in a stream of black smoke. "How I missed you." I'm shocked to see her throw her arms around Renze and give him a big hug. They're all smiles, and it's then I realize not much is known about the personal habits of vampiri warriors. I could spout a dozen facts about the First Warrior relationship, but I don't think I realized there was a true friendship there as well.

Arliss strides to the door and reaches out, pulling Ascelin out of Renze's arms. The tall vampiri grins, but Ascelin slaps Arliss on the cheek. Despite that, he doesn't let her go. Instead, he grips her chin and turns her to face me.

"Look how beautiful she is, my sweet. Let us tempt the librarian. She could use a good fuck after meeting Noire. You've had an eye on her since we arrived."

Gods, he is insufferable.

"Fuck off, Arliss," Ten barks, pulling me back behind his larger frame. "She's told you no a dozen times at this point."

I peek around to see what happens, and Renze winks at me. "It seems I have missed quite a bit since being parted from my First Warrior partner. Asc, let us retire to our temporary rooms. I have many questions for you, friend."

"Ugh," Ascelin groans, slapping Arliss again. "Enough with your tiresome games, carrow."

"You love me," Arliss sniggers, squeezing her butt before shoving her away from him and into Renze's arms.

Then, to illustrate a point about who he is, I suppose, he disappears into a wisp of black smoke and out the door.

"Fuck me," Ten sighs. "This is going to be a long day."

He's right about that.

CHAPTER EIGHTEEN
TENEBRIS

The rental's kitchen is crowded with this many people in it. Jet and Achaia cook fish while Renze and Ascelin hover around Diana. They seem relieved to be together again as a First Warrior duo. Diana's sitting at the head of the table, watching us in obvious misery.

I don't know where to turn first, but I wish Onmiel was here. I'm awkward around my family; I want things to go back to how they were before the evidence of Diana's illness was so present in front of me.

Crossing the modern-looking kitchen, I sit next to her. Noire hovers behind his mate, holding a cup of water and reminding her to drink.

Renze gives Diana a look. "It is time to change your bandages, Chosen One."

Diana's eyes flash white. The vampiri king, Cashore, speaks from inside her in a deep, commanding tone. "It is nearly time for me to return to my Zel, First Warrior. Do not delay me."

Noire bellows, but I can see he's resisting the urge to grab Diana by the throat and shake her to get at Cashore.

"Is this new?" I gasp, looking over at both vampiri.

Renze nods. "Cashore seems to believe it is time for him to move on, but we do not know how to extricate him from Diana without killing her. I have never heard of something like this. His spirit may very well be giving her strength."

Diana gasps, eyes rolling back to the normal, vivid blue. "Gods, he's strong," she complains. She shifts forward, and Noire sets the water on the table, pulling her shirt off her shoulders as I avert my gaze from her high, round breasts.

As my eyes travel down her ribcage, misery sinks into my stomach. Both sides of her core are lined with gaping slash wounds. The skin around them is black and mottled, poisoned.

Renze leans forward and applies a pink salve directly onto one of the wounds as Diana hisses and immediately begins to cry. Noire grits his teeth tightly as he strokes her cheek with the back of one hand. She cries all the way through the treatment, gasping when Renze has finished. Noire gently closes the wrap around her, and she falls back against the chair.

"Is this the treatment Zakarias found, or what you got from the mermaids?"

Achaia joins us, her brilliant green eyes flashing as she looks from me to Diana. "The mermaid treatment was a simple coagulant we often used. The sea is full of sharkfolk, even more than mermaids. Can't have lots of blood in the water." She gives me a wry grin as she grips the back of Renze's chair. "It can't do anything for the poison, though."

"What news from the library?" Noire barks, black eyes practically drilling holes into my own.

I sit up straight under my oldest brother's heavy, angry gaze. "Nothing new to report. The librarians have combed through about half the books referencing Volya, and they're ninety-five percent certain the prophecy is also Volya, but no translation exists."

Noire curses under his breath as he looks over at Jet. "So, we make a plan to capture one of the bastards so they can fix this."

"Perhaps that is exactly what the prophecy would have us do," Ascelin murmurs. "There is no way to translate it. Our only option is to ask the Volya themselves. There is almost no way for this plan to work."

"We've done it before," Diana reminds her. "But I can't ask you to risk your lives, especially with Cashore trying to dip out."

Ascelin leans over, rubbing Diana's hand with her own. "You will always be the Chosen One, Diana, even once Cashore has left you to be with Zel. That will never change. You will always be our queen."

A heavy silence falls over the group as Diana looks over at me. "Can we change the research focus to Volya defenses? We need to know what we're up against if we're going up there."

"Of course," I agree. "I'll ask Onmiel tonight."

"Onmiel?" Noire's voice is light, but there's something animal about how he says her name.

I fully expect Ascelin to have a sarcastic remark, but she's entirely focused on Diana, still rubbing the back of my pack omega's frail hand.

For a moment, the kitchen is silent. Somehow, despite the fact I killed Rama and freed our continent, it feels like that was just the beginning of something bigger. I can't stop thinking about how the Volya said the Tempang was sick, and I have to wonder if Diana's somehow tied into all of that. Maybe that's what the prophecy is about.

The moment breaks when I stand. I've got to talk to Onmiel. I've got to tell her everything I haven't shared because if there's any chance that information could save Diana, we have to take it. I wouldn't have thought my killing Rama had any bearing on our research, but I just don't know anymore.

When I turn to leave, Noire bristles through our family bond, his direwolf snapping angrily at me.

I spin in place, giving him a reassuring look even as I refuse to bow to him. I've lived a lifetime in the last two weeks. He may be my pack alpha, but the days are long gone when Noire can lord his power over me.

"I'm going back to the library to speak with Onmiel," I say quietly. "I'd like to share all of this with her in case it sparks an idea. I'll be back in a little bit."

Again, I expect Ascelin to make a derogatory comment, but she looks up at me, her white eyes filled with tears. My pack is falling apart as Diana's health fails. I always knew the pack alpha and omega were its heart—that was why my father losing his mind was such a devastating blow for us. But to have sacrificed my mate and still lose everyone else? I can't.

When nobody says anything, I leave my family behind and jog back toward the library. Onmiel isn't in the reading room or the cafe, so I make my way upstairs to her room. When I call her name, she doesn't answer, but I hear a soft, low whine.

Her voice sounds pained. Oh, fuck, gods. What if she's hurt?

Without thinking, I shove my shoulder against the door, knocking it half off its hinges as I barrel into the room.

The first thing I notice is that she's naked, an enormous tattoo covering her entire back. The second is that she's wearing giant cat-eared headphones, eyes squinted tightly closed. Now that I'm in the room, I can hear faint music.

Oh gods, she didn't hear me come in. She rocks back, impaling herself on a gigantic ribbed dildo stuck to her headboard.

My cock stiffens as she rocks forward off the dildo. I see it's coated with her juices. This entire room is soaked in the candy-coated, tart scent of her pheromones. I should leave. I need to. I—

My brain goes to my dead mate, and I feel like an asshole. But I've spent a lot of time in the last few weeks attempting to retrain my brain to remember what Rama was to everyone else.

There isn't a kinder person in the world than Onmiel.

I spin this around, trying to make sense of a deep, building attraction between us. I want to lower myself onto the bed and take charge, to press her back onto that dildo and take control until she breaks apart.

But it would ruin our friendship because I'm fucked up about killing my bondmate.

Suddenly, Onmiel's eyes spring open, and she screams, reaching for a sheet to cover herself as I throw my back against the wall and look away.

"I'm sorry!" I shout. "I thought you were hurt."

"I'm not hurt. I'm masturbating!" she yells back, wrapping the sheet as she grabs the dildo and shoves it under a pillow.

"Fuck, I'm sorry," I groan, willing my cock to lie flat. Instead, it throbs harder at the idea of me joining her in that bed, maybe tossing her against the headboard to fuck her.

Rama liked that, being manhandled by me.

Gods, I'm so fucked up. I feel like I'm cheating on my dead mate while also being attracted to my closest friend. And I'm still standing here like a creep.

I look up at Onmiel, her white hair glowing like a light in the small room. "I'm sorry, Onmiel. I needed to talk to you, and I thought you were hurt."

She huffs and stands, letting the sheet drop to the floor as she places both hands on her hips with a scowl. "You said nudity wasn't a thing for shifters, so I'm going to embrace that and act normal. Hand me my clothes, would you?"

I blink as I try not to stare at her beautiful godsdamned figure. She's thin and athletic whereas Rama was all curves and soft skin.

Both of Onmiel's dark red nipples are pierced through with bars. There's not a single hair on her entire body, her swollen pussy visible as I struggle to swallow. Slick honey drips down her thighs.

I hold my breath.

"Ten," she murmurs, breaking the moment as I drop my eyes. I'm standing on her godsdamned clothing.

I drop down, grab the tee and jeans, and hand them to her. When our fingertips touch, I bite the inside of my cheek to resist grabbing her and pulling her to me.

I've got to get the fuck out of here before I do something I'll regret. Locking my eyes on her face, I give her what I hope is an apologetic look, but she turns and shimmies into the jeans. I can't help myself, crossing the room to run both hands carefully down the tattoo on her back.

"What are you?" I murmur as the tattoo shocks me.

TEN: A DARK SHIFTER ROMANCE

"You know what this is?" She turns her head over her shoulder, and the look on her face is so sorrowful that I want to pull her into my arms and comfort her until it's replaced by the usual joy. Instead, I do what I swear I'd do with any omega in my pack; I lean down and rub her cheek with mine, purring softly.

"Prisoner tattoo," I mutter. "Achaia had one, and they had to cut it off to release her mermaid form."

"Gods, that's fucking awful. There's a serum to remove them, but it's an ancient magic. Only a few species of beings know it exists."

"Is that how you know?"

Onmiel sighs, making the tips of her breasts brush against me. But when she looks up, her face is distraught. She's forgotten about the nudity because whatever she's sighing about must be something terrible.

"I don't know, but sit down, Ten," she encourages, pointing at the window seat. "There's a lot about myself I haven't shared, but I'd like to now."

Fuck.

CHAPTER NINETEEN

ONMIEL

I'm simultaneously sweating and freezing to death. Sweating from the masturbating and the embarrassment of Ten seeing that. I was legit about to scream his name because it's totally fine to jack off to my hot friend whose pecs I want to lick.

But I'm freezing because I'm about to share something with him I've only ever told one other person at the library.

Ten grabs the T-shirt I've forgotten about and pulls it over my head.

"If your tits keep touching me, I won't be able to concentrate. I'm sorry."

I blanche and pull my arms through the sleeves, crossing them as I look up. "Ten, I—"

He throws his palms up in the air. "I shouldn't have barreled in here. It was an invasion of your privacy, and I'm sorry I did it."

I nod, but I'm not really sorry. I wish he would have joined in. Was he standing there for long? What did he think?

Crossing the room, I flop down in the window seat and pick at a hangnail as he sits down opposite me.

"Gods, I'm really nervous," I whimper. Ten laser focuses on me, his head cocked to the side, and then he reaches out, grabbing my waist and pulling my entire body between his legs. I'm facing him, seated between his knees, our bodies so close together.

He leans down and rubs my cheek with his, a soft, rumbly purr rolling out of his chest. With one hand, he strokes my sweaty hair back behind my ear. "Alpha packs are physically affectionate. Does this bother you?"

"No," I murmur. The reality is that as a single librarian, I have very little physical contact. Even a hug feels damned good.

"Tell me everything, Onmiel," he whispers, his fingertips drawing a path from my ear down my chin.

I suck in a breath and look out the window. "I don't know what I am, and that's the truth." Patting my shoulder, I glance over at the handsome alpha. "I've had the prisoner tattoo for as long as I can remember. Typically, it keeps the person from remembering anything about their life. Unless you tattoo yourself, which I did."

Ten pulls me a little closer, his forehead pressed to mine as his purr intensifies.

"I killed someone." The words are so godsdamned hard to say that I can barely get them out, and I don't miss the way he stiffens like a board. What he'll think of me now is anyone's guess.

Now that I've said it, everything comes out of me in a flood of words.

"I don't remember most of my life, but I remember killing my sister. It was an accident, but I had some kind of power I couldn't control. It ripped my family apart when she died."

Ten gasps and moves his hands to my thighs, which he squeezes once.

"I'm sure I'm not human. Not fully, at least. When Zura died, I couldn't stay home," I sob, the tears streaming. "So, I placed the tattoo on myself, leaving just enough memory that I would know what I'd done and wouldn't try to remove it and risk hurting someone again. I left," I add as the tears become a torrent. "Because I couldn't stand the looks on my family's faces, knowing I killed her."

A gut-wrenching sob leaves me then, both hands coming to my face as Ten sits stiffly across from me. I can't even focus on his rapid breathing.

"If you want to get the fuck out of here, I get it," I shout. "I'm a murderer, Ten. I'll still help you find a—"

Ten's warning growl stops me—its tone low and menacing. Memories of Zura's death flood my brain as the tears continue to fall, wetting my shirt as I debate my next move. I shouldn't have told him. I should—

"I killed my bondmate, Rama." That's all he says, and he says it simply like he's telling me what sort of latte he had this morning.

My eyelashes flutter as I struggle to focus on him around the tears.

"She was a psychopath; I know that," he admits with a shrug. "But she was mine. Still, she did things that I couldn't live with. She hurt everyone I loved, and she would have destroyed this continent. I killed her because she couldn't be allowed to hurt anyone else." He looks up at me as the first tear falls down his bronzed cheek. "I had to choose her or my family, and I picked my pack."

I don't even know how to respond because Arliss told me that, and I don't want to throw him under the bus, except I can't to lie to Ten.

"Arliss told me the day I met you," I whisper.

Ten growls and pulls me into his arms, our bodies pressed tightly together as he wraps his arms around me. "He's such an asshole, so I'm not surprised."

"We're both fucked up, aren't we?" I whisper into his neck as he strokes my back, careful not to touch the tattoo itself.

"I don't want to be," he admits quietly, his lips tickling the shell of my ear. "I want to be normal if that's even possible. You've built a life here," he reminds me. "Despite your tragedies. You have a good thing in Pengshur."

Usually, I agree, but I can't stop sobbing as I remember my sister's death and how it all happened so quickly, yet in slow motion at the same time. I can't even remember what she looked like anymore, or my family, for that matter. I just know I hid myself away so I couldn't hurt anyone else. Never again.

For a long time, Ten holds me. And he cries, too. We fucking cry until we're cried out, and he still holds on like I'm his lifeline, purring the entire time.

Eventually, I look up at him. "You came here for something less dramatic tonight. What was it?"

Ten's eyes are puffy from the tears, but he rubs my cheek again.

"I have more information from my pack. I was hoping sharing it might spark an idea. Diana's dying, Onmiel. She's fading fast."

Extricating myself from Ten's big arms, I stand up and grab my pack, giving him my best librarian look. I've got to focus on something, anything other than my dead sister and Ten's dead mate.

He swings his legs off the window bench, leaning over them with an elbow on each knee. Whiskey-brown eyes focus on me as a little spark returns to them. "You think we need a coffee?"

I nod.

I'm going to ask for a shot of tequila in mine.

CHAPTER TWENTY
TENEBRIS

As we walk to the cafe, I fill Onmiel in on anything we haven't explicitly told her already. I relive the Volya attack while avoiding talking about the moment I killed Rama. I rehash everything the Volya said, although some is a little fuzzy to me because I was so focused on the mechanical spider my mate was drugging me with and finding out why she would do that.

Onmiel is quiet as I share what they've tried with Diana healing-wise and how Cashore is trying to leave her.

When we order and I've blurted everything out, she turns to me with an incredulous look.

"You did all of this while dealing with your own grief?"

I give her an uncomfortable look, agreeing. We shared so much earlier, but I don't want to rehash it now. It all feels too tender, and I'm not ready to talk about that part again.

Onmiel seems to realize that, though, because she reaches out and holds my hand, standing quietly while we wait for our drinks. When she lays her head against my shoulder, I wish I were shorter so I could put mine on top of hers. In the short time I've known the plucky librarian, she's wormed her way right into my soul. I think she might be the best friend I've ever had.

Our coffee arrives, and we head back to the reading room.

"Noire wants to go up to the Tempang, capture a Volya, and force them to heal Diana."

Onmiel gives me a thoughtful look as I open the door to the reading room.

Noire, Jet, and Ascelin stand inside, Noire with his arms crossed as he glares daggers at us. Pitch-black eyes move from my face to the coffee in my hand before he sneers at me.

"So, this is how you're trying to save Diana? Getting coffee with the librarian…"

It's obvious Noire's about to fly into a godsdamned rage, but I'm too old for this shit, and I'm a head taller than my older brother at this point. Straightening my spine, I let out a warning growl as Jet takes a step closer to us, ready to pull us apart if we fight.

Ascelin appears from somewhere and quietly moves Onmiel out of the way as Noire bumps me with his chest. Despite his slightly shorter height, his pack alpha dominance bowls me over. Our family bond is tight with seething anger, even though Jet's trying to remind us we're all working toward the same end goal.

"I'm going to say this once, Noire," I tell him in a calm, collected tone. "Onmiel and I are here almost twenty-four hours a day, poring over books and research to find an answer—any answer. Sometimes, all we find is a singular line with information, and that leads us to the next book. I haven't slept more than two hours since I got here, so don't press me."

Noire lets out a bellow of rage that knocks several books off their shelves. Onmiel winces as they fall to the ground, spines cracking. I resist the urge to slap him for his irreverence.

Snarling, I grip Noire's throat and pull him even closer, snapping my teeth at his face. "Simmer the fuck down, brother. You're being an asshole, and I won't stand for it. I'm doing everything I can to help you save your mate while grieving the murder of my own. Don't say a godsdamned *word* to me about how hard we're working."

Onmiel hisses in a breath and rushes to my side, too quickly for Ascelin to grab her. She shoves her way hard between Noire and me and looks up into my eyes. "Ten!"

I don't look away from Noire, who's glaring daggers at me. Onmiel rubs at my chest. "We don't have to talk about this, Ten," she murmurs. "Let's just get started, okay?"

My eyes flick down to hers as I nod, glaring back down at my big brother. Onmiel turns, still standing in front of us. I dare Noire with a scathing look to do anything to hurt her. I swear to the gods, I will pull him to shreds if he touches a hair on her head.

"What are you?" he snaps instead, noticing the way her hair is so white that it's incandescent in the low light of the reading room.

Onmiel lets out a low chuckle, her tone wry. "I don't know. I sealed my identity in a prisoner tattoo a long time ago. But it doesn't matter now because we need to help your mate, and Ten has just filled me in on your possible change of plan."

Ascelin snarls. "Did you place Achaia's tattoo, then? We were told there's nobody left on this continent aside from the Tempang's monsters who know how to do this…"

"I've only ever placed one," Onmiel murmurs, rubbing at her shoulder. "The one on my own back. Can we get back to work, or is this critical to finding help for Diana? I don't know what I am or why I could do it, and I have no way to find out. I'd rather not even focus on it now."

Noire says nothing, leveling her with a stare that's dropped grown men to their knees. But Onmiel doesn't wither underneath it. Instead, she gestures for us to follow, even as Noire mutters under his breath about us wasting time.

"Not a waste, I promise," she chirps, walking backward as we head toward the center of the library. When we arrive back at the expansive Magelang Map, I know exactly what she's thinking.

She points to the map and then looks at my brothers expectantly. "The Magelang Map has lived here for centuries, and it'll show the location of every person on Lombornei if you know how to use it." When Noire shrugs, she rolls her eyes and carries on. "So, if you want to find a Volya, we can use this map to locate them. Volya don't leave the Tempang, so they'll be in that area of Lombornei."

Noire's face lights up when he realizes what she's saying. He leans over the map as she pinches in, and the paper face of the map appears to zoom in closely on the edge of the map closest to the province of Deshali.

All I can think about is how I'm dying to know what magic powers the map. Who made it? How does it work? And how can I learn it…

Gods, I hope she doesn't zoom into the city of Nacht because if I have to see my mate's dead body on a map, I'll lose my shit.

Thankfully, Onmiel scrolls the map along the edge of the forest near Nacht. "From what we know of Volya, they live deep inside the Tempang, but if you know anything about the ones who hurt Diana, we might be able to use that information. There are several Volya clans we know of," she clarifies.

Jet straightens, sucking at his teeth. "They called themselves the protectors of the forest and said the Tempang was sick. Does any particular group deal with that?"

Onmiel shrugs. "Most monsters of the Tempang are secretive, and many have never left the forest or interbred with humans. If we don't know of the species, it won't be listed on the Magelang. But we've also been reading a lot about the Volya in the last few days. From what we've gathered, it's not so much a certain clan but a particular class of Volya who care for the forest. Unfortunately, caring for the forest could mean a lot of things."

Jet grumbles as I lean over the map. "What if we had a name?" I murmur. I sift through vague memories from my time with Rama as she planned those final days. Somehow, I was lucid, but not. I was there for her, for our mating. I was there as I watched her bring years of plans to fruition, but my emotion was totally focused on her and her alone.

I wonder for the hundredth time what was in that godsdamned spider she poisoned me with.

"Lahkan," I say, the name coming to me as Onmiel hunches over the map. She murmurs an incantation as she pinches in, and the map zooms across the Tempang to a point where the land curls around the sea like a finger.

"Godsdamnit, they're at the far end of the fucking continent," Noire rages, his voice echoing out over the books. Onmiel and I turn to shush him at the same time as he gives us withering looks.

On the map, a small label indicating "Lahkan" hovers over a village. The map won't zoom any closer than we've got it, but the beast who hurt Diana is *right there*.

"We can't run off half-cocked, Noire," Jet warns in a low, gentle tone. My pack alpha is about to lose his shit, seeing the name of the male who hurt Diana right in front of us.

Noire's glittering dark eyes focus on Onmiel. "You've got twelve hours to tell me anything we need to know about the Volya. We're leaving for the Tempang after that."

Arliss appears out of nowhere, clapping Jet on the back. We whirl to face him. I haven't seen him much, and he's just strolled in like he never left.

"If you're going to the Tempang, I'm going with you," he announces. "Was going to go alone, but if I can be helpful to Diana at all…"

"Bullshit," I snap. "You haven't opened a book to help us the entire time we've been here. Why are you coming? Because it's not to help my pack omega."

Arliss scowls at me but eventually shrugs, even as Noire balls his fists. I can tell he wants to pound Arliss into dust, but the reality is Arliss is really fucking strong, and I don't know who'd win that fight. Jet told me they fought once, and it only ended because Arliss had some sort of health episode. Even that is related to Rama because she poisoned him, too.

"I have my reasons for going, but just like on Paraiso, when our goals are aligned, I'm on your side."

Onmiel gives Arliss a shriveling look. "If you want information about what we discussed, the Volya will not help you. When you get to the Tempang, you'll have to part ways."

Arliss narrows his eyes as he points to the map. "Be a dear and show me where I might find what I'm looking for, librarian."

CHAPTER TWENTY-ONE
ONMIEL

I've never felt so strung out in my life. I'm exhausted from sharing with Ten, I'm overwhelmed by the sudden appearance of his brothers, and the force of Arliss's current command is practically tangible.

"Stop with the magic," I bark at him, his power scratching at the edges of my mind. I haven't told anybody about him being a carrow. For all I know, this whole group is already aware, but if he's going to fuck around with me in front of everyone, I'll happily toss him right under a bus. Dickhead.

The uncomfortable sensation dissipates, and I shush him aside with one hand. The pack parts, and I lean over the forest on the other side of the Tempang, the northeastern corner. Whispering an incantation under my breath, I pinch in on the map. Just like before, it zooms to a lake. I didn't look for a particular person; all I know is that carrow live in that area.

Pointing to the spot, I glare at Arliss. "That's where you'll find answers, as long as you've paid attention to the resources you've been given in the last two days. You cannot simply show up and hope for the best."

Everyone is silent as Arliss inclines his head at me, not saying another word. Eventually, he looks over at Tenebris. "You freed me when I could not free myself." His voice is low, almost kind, as he talks. "If you want my help, I will lend it for a time. Once it's done, I'll move on."

Ten cocks his head to the side. "We need every extra hand, Arliss. Thank you."

Something momentous is happening here, this reforging of alliances between the mysterious carrow and the direwolf pack. Behind everyone,

Ascelin stands in silence, her cell phone tightly gripped in her hand. It rings, and she jumps but picks it up with urgency.

"Chosen One, are you well?"

White eyes move to Noire, who grabs the phone and starts purring.

"What do you need, omega?" His voice is sultry and comforting, all sensual, dark promise. He listens for a moment before growling softly. "I'm coming, Diana." He tosses the phone back to Ascelin. "She's not feeling well. Let's go home and change the bandages again."

Pitch-black eyes turn to Ten. "I'm counting on you, Tenebris."

He strides off into the darkness without looking back, Ascelin a dark shadow silently trailing him. The other alpha turns to us with a soft look, his dark eyes locked onto Ten.

"How are you, Ten?" His voice is deep and concerned, but Ten takes a step closer to me.

"Fine," Ten barks. He doesn't sound fine, and the skeptical look on his brother's face indicates he realizes that, too. He smiles softly at Ten, though, and doesn't ask again. Instead, he turns to leave.

When everyone's gone, I catch Ten's eye.

"Your family's intense."

He snorts out a frustrated laugh. "Intense isn't the half of it, Onmiel." When he falls silent, I look back at the Magelang Map, wishing it could give us some sort of clue as to how to help Diana.

"We've got to be missing something that can help her, Ten. I just feel it." I mutter the words to myself more than him. At the end of the day, Zakarias and I are working hard to find answers, but I'm starting to worry it's not going to be enough. I know Zakarias checked in with ML Garfield after Noire showed up earlier. It almost feels like the whole library is tense and quiet as it waits to see what the violent alpha might do.

Ten crosses his big arms and leans up against the map as I try not to stare at the corded muscle of his enormous forearms. I've noticed in these last few days that shirts don't fit him. He's just fucking huge.

"Hear me out," I start. "This will probably sound unconventional if you haven't been around the library for a while."

Ten chuckles and bites the inside of his lip. "Well, I can't wait to hear this, Onmiel. Spit it out."

"Okay," I start. "You know it's common for librarians on assignment to work insane hours. Sometimes, you get really stymied doing that. There's a secret-ish room in the basement where we go to dance and do other stuff. It doesn't have a real name, per se, but it's pretty much the breakthrough room."

"Is this like a dungeon, or…" Ten looks like he can't decide whether to laugh, cry, or run away.

Does he think it might be like the maze? Oh, hells no.

"Not like the maze," I rush, hoping it doesn't seem like I'm asking him to do something that might remind him of where he came from. "I'm not explaining it well. Why don't we just go, and you can see. It's a way of opening your mind to other possibilities."

"And we haven't been there before now because…" His voice trails off.

"I think we thought we had more time, to be honest." It's a shitty answer, but it's the truth. We knew Diana was badly hurt, but I don't think Zakarias or I even realized she's hanging on by a thread. And maybe she wasn't when they came here, but it seems obvious she is now.

Ten stands tall and gives me a look. "Let's go, librarian. If we need to do this thing to have some kind of a breakthrough, let's do it."

Nerves jangle around in my stomach as I shift from one foot to the next. "Okay, but I want to warn you, the breakthrough room is a little wild."

"Wild?" Ten looks down at me with a mischievous glance.

"Yeah, it's, umm. Well, people pretty much let loose in there."

"So…drugs and fucking?"

A nervous cackle makes its way out of my throat as Ten places a hand on my lower back. "I'll be fine, Onmiel. Sex and drugs don't bother me. Remember the whole nudity conversation?"

I do, and to be honest, we've already seen one another naked. Not that I'll be getting naked in the breakthrough room, but still.

"We'll go and hope Noire doesn't come back to hear we've left our post to go do this. But I swear, it's led to some of the biggest research breakthroughs to ever come out of Pengshur. It's worth a try."

"Diana's worth it," he confirms, following me as I hang a left around the Magelang Map toward the opposite side of the library.

"We've never even come over here," Ten muses as he reaches out to stroke a row of books.

I'd love to stop and tell him all about these, but Diana's situation is dire, and I can't help but feel we're missing some brutally obvious connection.

We make it all the way to the outer rim of the library before stopping in front of a flat expanse of wall. I feel around the edge of a nearby painting, depressing a small red button as the wall swings on a hinge, opening like a secret lair from a superhero book.

Ten grinds his teeth as I step in, and when I turn, his eyes are locked on the dark hallway. Immediately, I wonder if this is like the maze, and it's too horrible to ask him to do this.

"There's another way," I offer, stepping back out.

Ten growls and takes my hand. "Come on." He pulls me back into the hallway and follows it toward the steady beat of music. The hallway is lit by the very lowest of lights, but Ten guides me like he's done this a million times. It makes me wonder if he was like this in the maze—focused, protective, and unafraid.

And how does he feel about the fact that the person who imprisoned him was later revealed to be his bondmate? I can't fucking imagine, but I squeeze his fingers tighter to let him know I'm here for him.

At the end of the hall, we come to a glossy black door, much like the rest of the doors here at Pengshur. Rounding Ten, I swing it open, and we move forward onto a platform that overlooks a giant subterranean club. A dancefloor takes up most of the middle, a deejay spinning electronic music from a stage in front of us.

I point to the outer rim, where small alcoves are built in. Ten follows my gaze.

"Those are research alcoves. Sometimes, librarians will bring their team down here with their work."

"Or other things," he murmurs, his eyes moving with focus to the alcove next to the one I just pointed at. The U-shaped leather alcove is currently hosting an orgy, and I half expect to find Arliss in the middle of it.

Ten lets go of my hand and crosses his arms. "Now what, Future First Librarian Onmiel?"

I laugh at him calling me the title I'm desperate for, but it's also hot because I can imagine him saying it in a seductive way in a bedroom conversation. But then I remember everything we shared earlier, and sobering reality crashes down on me.

"Time to dance," I chirp, pulling Ten down the stairs behind me. When we get to the bottom, one of the other Novices runs up and throws herself into my arms, pulling away, only to gape at Ten in surprise.

"Is this the hot alpha from the maze?" she whisper-hisses as Ten and I both stiffen. Without pulling her eyes from him, she digs around in her pocket and presses a small bag into my palm. "Find me later if you want to have some fun."

I roll my eyes as she gives Ten a suggestive wink, then slips off into the darkness.

"Friend of yours?" Ten's voice is dry, although I can see he's holding back a smile.

"Fellow Novice," I shrug, showing him the small bag she handed me. "But this could be fun. They're nose spices. They help you relax, allowing your mind to do the work of getting around your roadblocks."

Ten looks skeptical as I barrel on. "It's super common down here, although you'll almost never see them upstairs. It's a breakthrough-room-only sort of thing." Gods, maybe he thinks I'm a druggie now.

His striking eyes move around the room, narrowing as he takes it in. He looks uncomfortable as fuck. I'd give my left arm to know what he's thinking.

"I wish we had a family bond," I grumble as I cross my arms. "I'd love to be able to talk to you without having to shout in this loud-ass room."

Ten's gaze flashes back to me as he nods at the packet dangling from my fingertips.

"Let's do it."

"Are you sure? There's absolutely zero pressure to," I remind him.

"What can I expect?"

"You'll feel happy and high for a few hours, and then you'll be back to normal."

"Alphas burn hot, Onmiel. It might not affect me at all."

Alphas burn hot. Godsdamn, everything he says turns me on, even though he's not trying to.

For a long moment, I don't respond, but Ten's smirk widens. I swear I think he's messing with me on purpose, but it's probably just wishful thinking.

I break the moment as I lift the bag up, pulling the tiny drawstring open.

"Bend down here," I shout, pinching powder between my fingertips.

Ten leans down, his forehead almost touching mine.

"I'm going to blow this in your face, okay?"

"Do it," he growls, his long fangs poking at the edge of his lower lip.

I blow softly, the purple powder coating his nose and mouth. His tongue slides out to lick at where it covers his lips, and then he takes the pouch from me. Ten repeats my action, and I breathe in deeply, pulling the drug into my system as I wait for the moment it hits.

"It takes a minute to hit me," I laugh, "but most people feel it within about fifteen seconds."

"I've got nothin'." Ten laughs, and then that smile falls, and his chest rises and falls more rapidly. I watch his pupils widen until they take over nearly the whole pale amber of his iris. Ten's fangs descend from behind his upper lip, poking into the lower one hard enough to draw blood.

He reaches out, gripping my throat in his hand as he pulls me flush with his chest. There's a wild, focused look in his beautiful eyes as he squeezes me so hard that I struggle to breathe.

"Is this a fucking aphrodisiac, Onmiel?" Ten's voice is ragged and on edge, throaty and dangerous.

Oh shit, oh fuck. I hope I haven't just dragged him into the basement and given him an aphrodisiac. He'll think I'm doing it on purpose.

I hate the direction this is going.

"I've never heard of it being that," I gasp out. "We have other shifter librarians, Ten! Oh gods, I'm so sorry!"

His grip loosens as his lashes flutter. Ten shakes his head and grumbles something under his breath, but I can't hear it over the din of the music. He looks behind me at the packed bar and even more crowded dance floor, and then the drugs hit me.

"Come, Onmiel," Ten growls, pulling me toward the music.

And come I do.

CHAPTER TWENTY-TWO
TENEBRIS

I'm high as fuck, focused on one thing alone—the music. Deep, throbbing beats pull me by the dick to the dancefloor as I drag Onmiel behind me. I'm horny and uninhibited, and everything feels so good as long as I don't focus on the room itself.

This place is a dark stone grotto. It's the maze all over again, and that fractures my mind so hard the only thing I can do is focus on a second thing—my librarian. She's high now, too, her pupils a galaxy of black with starbursts of gray at the edges. She positions herself in front of me and starts dancing.

The music is fast but sensual, pulling and swaying as we rock to the beat, not touching but not looking away from one another. She grabs my hand and spins herself, cackling the whole time. I struggle against the urge to pull her lithe body to mine to feel her.

Mate.

The word flits through my mind, there and gone like the stab of a knife.

Rama.

I remember Rama screaming my name the first time I took her, how she fell to pieces on my knot.

No.

Not now.

And never again.

Growling, I step away from Onmiel and rock my hips to the music. I've never danced. I've never even heard music like this, and it's so fucking beautiful. Sensual. The notes smash down my spine like the strike of a hammer, jolting my body with their intensity. The drugs make it feel like the music is coming from within my body, taking over every nerve ending as sensations too numerous to process war for my attention.

My head falls back as I rock and sway. It's like fucking but not, and everyone around us is doing it, too. This is a sea of writhing bodies.

I look back up. In front of me, Onmiel dances with the female librarian from before. They hold on to one another, swaying seductively with their lips hovering together. If my dick wasn't already as hard as the stone walls around us, I'd stop to watch them move. Onmiel grabs the other woman's throat and pulls her in for a kiss, her pink tongue slipping between the other librarian's lips as she sucks it.

A groan falls from my throat as I reach down to adjust my cock. I'm going to fucking knot myself, high on these drugs, and watching the intensity of the room play out. I don't know if the nose spices are an actual aphrodisiac or if my inhibitions are just gone, but there's nothing but an intense sense of pleasure as I move to the music.

Hands circle my waist, and I smile, but then I realize Onmiel is making out with the other librarian, so it's not her hands on me. I'd bristle, but I'm too high to care. All I know is one hand slides up my shirt, and the other reaches down for my dick, and I let it happen. It feels so good as I leak precum like a godsdamned waterfall.

A second hand joins the first, traveling down into my pants as the drugs push me higher until all I can do is focus on the hands now stroking my cock with even, measured pulls.

Onmiel's scent flares in the tight space, and when I look up, the other librarian is gone, and Onmiel is focused on me. Her beautiful gray eyes are locked onto the hands in my jeans as I pant, my mouth open. The pleasure builds, my balls tightening as I throb into the hands of a faceless being.

Gods, this is so fucking hot. Onmiel stares at me like she's ready to worship me, and I want it.

I rip my pants open, my cock falling out heavily as there's a whispered "yes" from the being pressed to my back.

Onmiel gasps. Is she enjoying this show? I focus on her because I can't focus on this pitch-black room that reminds me of the maze and my dead mate. I focus on the pleasure because my mate was a complete asshole, and she doesn't deserve my time or energy.

She never deserved it.

I find myself wondering, again, if a mate bond can be broken by magical means. I think I want that.

Because the woman in front of me is watching me get jacked off, and all I can think about is how I wish the hands were hers.

I want her. Gods, I do.

When I look down and realize the hands now stroking me with expert tugs are a man's hands, I grimace and pull away. It's not my preference, and while I don't care who fucks anyone else, men don't interest me.

There's a soft whine behind me, but the hands disappear, and then I'm standing in front of Onmiel. She drags her eyes back up my body, her breath a rapid staccato as her nostrils flare. Strobe lights send a rainbow of colors across her face, white dots ringing what remains of her iris. I could fall into the black pools of her pupils and swim for hours.

You want me, I think. *And I* want *you, too.*

It's a realization that spins my head as a waitress shows up with a tray full of shots. I grab two without thinking, stalking forward to hand one to Onmiel.

She licks the salt at the rim and then throws the glass back, tossing it to the floor as her muscles begin to tremble.

Oh, sweet girl, I could eat you alive.

Instead, I press my chest to hers, purring as I lick the edge of the glass, gathering the salt on my tongue. Then I wrap my fist in her beautiful long hair and yank her head back. The back of her skull hits my palm, and her throat bobs. Every predatory instinct I have screams at me to rip at it with my teeth.

My direwolf wants her blood, my cock bobbing between us as I lean down slowly. I drag my tongue up her neck once, depositing the salt. And then I lick and suck my way back up it, pulling her skin into my mouth as I groan around the sheer taste of her.

Sunshine. Tart candy apples. Pure pleasure.

Take her, a voice whispers at the edges of my mind as I startle, but I'm too high to sort out who. It feels like a problem for later.

Onmiel goes limp in my arms until I clamp my teeth around her throat and bite hard. My direwolf preens in my chest, eager for more, even as surprise burrows somewhere at the back of my mind.

I shove that away. I can't dwell on the past. I can only focus on the now. And my now is looking really fucking good.

Onmiel's hips rock against my thigh with steady, even punches, her hands gripping my arms as I bite and suck my way back down her neck. I'm a hair's breadth from coming all over her clothing, so I release her hair and move that hand to her upper back. The other goes to her ass as I help her grind on me.

I rock slowly to meet her. It's a sensual dance, her clothing rubbing all over my cock. We don't look down. We don't need to. This euphoria is so all-consuming that I can barely breathe around the intensity of it.

Onmiel gasps as her cheeks turn pink, her plump lips falling open as she begins to shudder and moan.

My gods, she could come like this, I realize.

Do it, a voice murmurs again in the back of my mind, even as a memory wars with that intention.

Snarling against that push and pull, I shove my hand down the side of Onmiel's pants and push the front far enough down to slide my cock between her thighs. The moment it slips through her slick, soaked heat, we both groan. Her hands come to my T-shirt and twist as she holds on to me. This isn't the ideal height, though. I'm too tall, so I grab her ass in both hands and wrap her around my body, my cock rubbing her clit with every roll of my hips.

Onmiel presses her forehead to mine, her lips almost touching mine. And she never looks away. Not as her body coats me in slick juices. Not when her breath begins to rise, her muscles tightening in my arms. Her scent floods my nose, so heady and beautiful that I salivate.

She doesn't even look away when that pleasure crests, and she floods my dick with her sweet honey, throwing me into an orgasm so hard, I lean back to roar. My bellow is lost in the crowd, melding with the beats as she leans forward and screams into my chest, clenching her thighs around me as her orgasm prolongs.

Moments later, we come down, and I can't decide if I should throw her to the ground and fuck her or leave and take a freezing shower. Everything smells of her release. She's nowhere near sated, and my direwolf knows, prowling in my chest as if he can't stand not taking more.

He's never been this active, this present in my entire life. I've never read about this in a book. Our wolves are a sentiment, not a separate being.

Take her, I hear again.

Oh, my fucking gods, is it him? My direwolf?

Good. Very good.

Shifters' animals don't speak to them; they don't have a voice.

Pleasure rumbles through my system, a sudden, intense desire to start this all over, but Onmiel pushes out of my arms, zipping up her pants even as I whine, watching all that honey disappear from my view.

She slaps my chest, looking up at me with a thrilled expression. "Ten! I've got an idea."

CHAPTER TWENTY-THREE
ONMIEL

I'd be a godsdamned liar if I didn't admit to still being halfway high, but that gorgeous fucking orgasm opened a door somewhere in my mind. I didn't intend for it to escalate to that, so I'm going to move right along like we didn't just dry hump until we came all over each other.

But I've got an idea. An honest-to-gods idea. I practically sprint from the breakthrough room, up the stairs and down the long hall, and back out into the library. Ten rushes out behind me, and then we're flying together through the aisles, passing the Magelang Map and hooking a hard left. We come to the exit.

Ten gives me a quizzical look. "We're leaving the library? Why?"

"Not the library, just the archives," I whisper-hiss in excitement. "I'll tell you on the way. Come on."

He doesn't ask anything else but opens the wooden doors as I sail through, pointing down another burled wooden hallway to a second set of doors.

"That's the public section of the library. Anyone can visit there, and there's no magic keeping the books in place."

Ten looks ahead. I barrel on. The public section looks a lot like the archives, but it's larger. It's also dead this late, although we pass the occasional librarian as we head for a giant circular staircase in the middle. Stopping at the bottom, we look up.

"At the top of the public section is an archive of gifts. Anything anyone has ever gifted the library lives here."

"And you don't have access to this in the archives?" Ten's voice is confused as we start trekking up the stairs, moving quickly from one inlaid wooden step to the next.

"It's not connected because everything is cataloged when it's gifted. Master Librarian Garfield is our ML now, so he's responsible for cataloging each gift and deciding if it needs to be in the archives or not. Sometimes, the decision is that it's not dangerous, not secretive, or not librarian-only information, and so the item or book remains in the public section."

Ten catches on quickly. "So, you're saying the library could have been gifted something that ML Garfield just didn't think was important enough to put in the archives."

"Could be." I look up at the sexy-as-sin alpha, hoping he's as embroiled in this as I am and definitely not thinking about the way we almost just fucked.

Ten's beautiful eyes are focused on me, narrowed with intensity. His nostrils flare. He's still a little high, I can tell. Shit, I am too, but it's fading fast as my excitement builds.

"It's totally possible there's nothing to find here," I caution.

Ten puts one hand at the base of my spine, urging me faster up the stairs, even as my muscles begin to tire.

"We have to try," he murmurs.

We make it to the eighth floor and rush to a circular bookshelf in the middle. There's a small reading room on the inside of the ring that people can sit in and peruse the books.

"How do we find anything about the Volya here?" Ten's tone is morose as he strokes the spine of one of the books.

"This is where the library's magic comes in handy." I chuckle. "While there's no magic keeping books on shelves in the public section, I can use my magic to hunt for what I'm looking for. Like this..." I place my hand on a spine and murmur an incantation, and the book wiggles a little bit but doesn't move.

I point at the spine. "If this one had contained a reference to the Volya, it would have popped out of the shelf."

Ten grins. "Teach me. I'll help."

I quickly show him the incantation, and we start at opposite ends of the bookcase. For half an hour, we go through the books one by one, and then we move to the next row and the next. It's arduous, painstaking work until Tenebris comes around the corner with a triumphant grin, a black leather-bound book in his hand.

"This one popped out." He shrugs, his grin growing larger as he hands the book carefully to me. My hands shake with excitement as I press a button on the bookshelf, and a panel swings open, revealing the small reading room inside this column of bookshelves.

"This place is amazing," Ten mutters. "I could spend years uncovering all the library's secrets."

"I hope you will." I laugh, entering the reading room and taking a seat at the tiny table inside. Ten props himself on the edge of the table, crossing his legs at the ankle as he watches me. His pupils are still blown wide from the drugs, his breathing quick and shallow.

"One day, when all this bullshit is over, I hope I get the chance to come back, Onmiel." There's such a serious look on his face. I can't help but wonder if he means for more than the library. It feels like he's saying he's coming back for me, too, and while that gives me hope, anguish settles in my chest, curled like a cobra waiting to strike at my heart. I don't deserve him, this perfect, amazing man who feels like he fits me so easily.

It's a cruel, fucking twist of fate that I'd find the him at the most imperfect time.

"I don't want you to leave at all," I whisper, not even meaning to say it out loud.

Ten looks down at the floor, and I ponder apologizing for making this awkward, but instead, I turn to the book and begin flipping through its pages.

When he says nothing, I want to slap myself for opening my dumb mouth. I push the thought aside, focusing on the book in front of us.

"It's an account of the gifts given to the library in the last ten years," I murmur as I carefully look through the various lines. I point out the columns to Ten as he leans over. "This is ML Garfield's handwriting, so you can see here and here where he noted what the gift was and who gave it, if that's known."

"People give anonymous gifts?" Ten's voice is low and curious as he leans over me to examine the page more closely.

"It's less common," I share. "Most beings are happy for the library to list them as donors. Occasionally, we'll receive something that just shows up on the doorstep."

"Seems sketchy," Ten grumbles.

I can't think of anything to say to that. Ten spent seven years locked in a dangerous maze, fighting for his life. I'm sure everything unknown could present a danger there. It must be hard to stop thinking that way.

Frustration sends a pinch of pain between my eyes as I growl. Ten slides down into the chair next to mine. "Let me, Miel."

My eyes dart up to his. "You've never called me *Miel*." I can't resist the grin that splits my face.

Without missing a beat, he keeps flipping the pages, concentrating on the book, although the very edges of his lips curl into a smile. "That was before you came all over my cock while high on nose spices."

Oh, fuck. Fuck. Fuck. I thought we were going to just pass right on by that. I mean, I'll never forget it, but I don't want him to feel pressured. I nibble at my lip, but I can't think of a damn thing to say once again. My cheeks must be redder than cherries right now.

"Found it!" Ten chirps, setting the book carefully down. He points to an entry from eight years ago.

"Unnamed Volya gifted the library with a vial of blood. Remanded to ML Garfield for safekeeping." I look up at Ten. "We don't know if Volya blood would be an antidote for Diana, but a good physik might be able to craft something from it. I know that much from helping Zakarias with medical research."

Ten stands with a little whoop. "Let's find Garfield now. We've got to get this vial immediately."

I huff out a breath, thinking. "The library has a physik on-call, and Garfield is sometimes in his office very late. Let's try that first, and if he's not there, we'll buzz him on the messaging system."

Ten gives me a hopeful look. "I'm going to call Noire and let him know we might have an option before we haul Diana up to the Tempang."

I smile as I look back down at the book, running my fingers across the beautiful ink. Ten grabs his phone and dials his brother, talking in excited tones as I flip through the rest of the book, making sure nothing else has been mentioned about Volya. Finding nothing, I watch Ten instead.

Realizing I should update Zakarias, I stand and go to the screen buried in the back of the circular bookshelves, calling up the messaging app. I'm still awkward with the tech, but I can figure out the basics.

Grumbling under my breath, I punch in Zakarias's code and force through an urgent message detailing what we've found. I wait, listening to Ten answer a barrage of questions from his brother. He hangs up as I stand in front of the comm screen. Zakarias sends a message back moments later.

Buzzed ML Garfield to meet at his office. Coming now.

Ten looks at the message and beams at me. "We have hope for the very first time, Onmiel. Thank you." His beautiful eyes drift down to my lips. Gods, I wish he'd kiss me. I can imagine just how good it would be when he looks at me with that predatory gaze.

"Ten," I whisper.

He doesn't acknowledge he's heard but plants one palm above my head on the wall as he leans in.

"What are you doing?" I manage as he tugs my head back with a hand in my hair.

"Alpha packs are affectionate," he murmurs, bringing his nose to my neck and inhaling with a soft, pleased groan. "I'm excited and relieved, and I want to connect with you."

I can't ask the question I want to know the answer to, which is that this seems like more than an affectionate hug. There's an underlying sexual current to this that's so strong that I could easily drown in it.

My heart pounds in my chest. It's so damn loud I know he can hear it. "Are you like this with your sisters-in-law, then?"

Ten chuckles, low and throaty, as he purses his lips. "We rub cheeks and hug, but if I scented Diana's neck like this, Noire would remove my head."

Why are you doing it to me, then? That's what I want to ask.

Except the answer is obvious to me now. He's attracted to me the same as I'm attracted to him. The bigger and more important question is, is he ready for something? I'm going to wager *not* after murdering his bondmate in the last month.

"I wanna chase you, Onmiel," he breathes out. Tawny eyes flash with need before dropping to my mouth. His lips part, his fangs descending. His nostrils flare, and he sucks in a deep, slow breath. Time slows to a halt, and sound muffles. There's nothing in this moment but the male in front of me, looking at me like I'm the sun at the center of his universe. I want that with every fiber of my being.

But fierce realities batter me, reminding my heart that he's still grieving, and he's still a little high, and to initiate something with him now isn't right. I press myself harder to the shelf, trying to get away from the overwhelming *everythingness* of Ten when he's focused like this.

He must sense my hesitation because his eyes shutter. He presses off the wall with an unhappy frown and turns toward the opening. "Ready to go?"

Fuck no! That's what I want to shout because I'm desperate for more of that connection with him. But now that neither of us is riding that all-encompassing, drug-aided high, I'm more cautious of anything that might be taking advantage of him.

Instead of voicing any of that aloud, I sigh. "Come on, alpha. Let's find the Master Librarian and see if we can save Diana with this blood."

CHAPTER TWENTY-FOUR
TENEBRIS

Warring emotions spar in my mind as we leave the public section of the library, passing back through the long hall toward the archives. I know where I'm going now, so my focus is on Onmiel, who's silent by my side, her strides long and purposeful.

I want to stop and toss her up against the wall, to have a conversation about everything that happened in the breakthrough room, just now, and everything that's been building up between us.

Friendship. Support. Partnership.

Something *more*.

In my chest, my direwolf presses against the breastbone, anxious to break free and touch her. He's never been so active in our connection. Shifting was always a thing I could do, but in direwolf form, I was always *me*. Direwolf shifts always reflect our emotions, but they don't have their own separate thoughts.

But mine seems to, all of a sudden. He has his own preferences, and his choice is not to beat around the bush but to start something with her right now.

And then there's the achy place in my chest that misses my dead mate. That can't stop thinking about how I killed her. I can't forget how she pleaded for mercy in our bond, but having that connection meant I could also feel that seedy undercurrent of lies beneath her plea. It was like ash filling my mouth and choking me. If I had given Rama mercy, she'd have stabbed all of us in the back a moment later. I know that. And I've worked hard to remind myself of that, hoping it would somehow shred the stupid bond I share with her. It still hurts.

My direwolf quiets as the memory of Rama takes over my thoughts. Did the serum she kept me drugged with hurt him? How does he feel about that? Why is he making his desires known just now?

But now isn't the time to explore what's going on with him. I'll eventually return to Pengshur and research if other alphas have experienced this. I'll ask my brothers and my adoptive father, Thomas, too, but it's new. It's…weird.

When we arrive at the entry to the archives, Zakarias is there with an excited look on his face.

"Well done, Onmiel! My goodness, I am so thrilled to have a real lead." He looks up at me. "Fingers crossed, alpha."

I give him an understanding look, and then I follow them both through the center of the library, passing the Magelang Map and out to the other side of the archives. We'll exit the archives and then—

There's a sudden hiss and the sound of scales slithering across wood. I freeze, grabbing Onmiel's arm.

Zakarias turns to us with a confused look.

I glance around urgently. "Is there a naga here?"

I killed two naga in the maze, and I'm coated with their death mist, a pheromone that'll announce to any others that I'm not to be trusted. Smelling like that pheromone is a fucking death sentence. If there's one here, it'll try to kill me.

Time slows as the doors to the archives open, and sure as shit, a gods-damned naga slides through, speaking with another librarian. He's huge with a large, round, black body. His humanoid upper half is crested with the round hood common among his kind.

We all pause. The naga's head whips in our direction. His slitted eyes meet mine, snakelike, flat nostrils flaring as his tongue slips out, flicking the air as he tastes it.

"Onmiel, run!" I shout as I shove her and Zakarias away from me and sprint in the opposite direction, hoping to distract the naga as I shift into my direwolf.

An ungodly roar shakes the bookshelves around me.

I hear Onmiel and Zakarias's panicked screams as the shelves start to fall, the naga giving chase.

"King killer!" he shrieks. It's deafening as I try to lead him away from my friend.

He's nowhere near as big as the naga in the maze, but it took our entire pack to kill that one, and we barely survived it.

I race around the outer rim of the library, hoping to pull him into the hallway leading back to the public area; it's emptier than the archives. There are faint, far-away screams as those in the archives flee the fury of the raging naga. He chases me without giving thought to the library itself. I hear the splintering of wood and the tearing of books from their shelves.

An entire bookshelf flies past my head, tumbling over itself as the naga catches up, his whispered hiss right behind me as I push my direwolf harder.

Away from her, my wolf rages in my chest. *Then fight.*

I barrel through double doors and into the hallway before a swipe of black claws knocks me into the wall. I'm up before my feet even hit the ground, pushing off the wall to leap at my attacker, slashing my claws across his chest and face before sprinting away.

He roars and raises up high on his long body, his chest shaking with anger as he rattles the tip of his tail. The hood behind his head flares open wider, revealing a red and black scrolled patterned tattooed along the inside. This specific pattern marks him as a naga scholar, but any naga is dangerous.

His eyes blink slowly, his forked tongue tasting the air as he slithers quietly up the hall toward me.

"You killed him. You!" He points a black-clawed finger at me. "King killer. You are a king killer."

I scream for my brothers in our bond, praying they can feel me from this far but also hoping Onmiel called them. If I can keep him talking long enough, Noire will get here, and I won't have to do this on my own.

I hear footsteps pounding behind the naga.

I can't answer him in this form, and there's no fucking way I'm shifting to talk this out.

Fight, my direwolf growls.

Crouching, I flick my tail from side to side. The naga coils, preparing to strike. He balls his fists as his upper body sinks lower, preparing for maximum impact.

Behind him, the double doors swing wide open, and Zakarias runs through. Onmiel is right behind him, her pale face flushed, gray eyes wide with terror.

"He won't recognize you!" she screams at Zakarias, even as her mentor barrels toward the naga, waving his arms to get its attention.

The naga whips around, and I take that moment to strike, leaping onto his hood and slashing. I rip and tear my claws down the back of it, trying to get around to his neck. His hood is a series of massive muscles, flaring as he bucks and writhes, his body ripping and curling.

I hang on for dear life as he flails around the hallway.

There's a grunt. Onmiel screams. A glass window shatters as the naga's body goes halfway through it. I'm tossed to the wall, sliding down as he lets out a rattling war cry. Onmiel is pressed against the wall to my left, twenty feet from me. Slitted, furious eyes move from me to her. He's no longer the male she might have known. The pheromone that coats me has turned him into a wild beast with no logic left, save to kill in revenge.

There's an immediate shove in my chest, and my direwolf takes over, all consciousness narrowing to Onmiel, who looks horrified as she edges toward the door with a knife in her hand.

Good girl, I think, *for grabbing that from somewhere.*

The naga strikes like a flash, but I catch him right before his teeth sink into her, clamping my fangs around his throat as I sink deep into the muscle. His arms come around me, and he whips from side to side, smashing us up against the ceiling, down to the floor, against both walls and then the plate-glass windows. I hang on, refusing to let go as I crush his throat, praying Onmiel's out of the way of his writhing coils.

Screams echo around me as pain blooms in my core. He's digging his claws in, trying to rip me from him before he dies. Then there's a flash of shock, and blood fills my mouth. Ascelin hisses from behind the naga's head. My eyes dart up to my friend and the knife she's just driven into the naga's skull.

We fall to the ground in a heap as the naga's rolling movements slow. But my direwolf never lets go of his throat, not until the last drop of rich blood spills over my muzzle. Not until the rapid beating of his heart slows, and I'm coated in sticky, smelly naga blood.

The screaming intensifies. My direwolf recognizes the voice as Onmiel's. We quickly assess the enemy, ensuring it's dead before he'll let go of its throat. I faintly hear my brother, Ascelin, and others all shouting, but Onmiel is my only focus. I shift, naked and covered in blood, and look for her. She's running to me across the floor, slipping in pools of slick blood.

I fly to her, ignoring the pain in my sides, grunting when she throws herself up into my arms, squeezing my neck so tight I can barely breathe. In my chest, my direwolf purrs, bigger and louder than he ever has before.

"Are you okay?" I grit out in a hoarse, anxious voice. I try to pull away to get a look at her, but she's gasping for air in my neck, sobbing as she wraps her legs around my waist like a vice.

"Thought I lost you," she cries. "Gods, Ten, I was so fucking scared for you." Her crying escalates as I stroke her hair, sensing my pack joining us. Noire scratches at the edges of our family bond, checking in with me. I don't answer.

TEN: A DARK SHIFTER ROMANCE

Onmiel safe, snaps my direwolf, grabbing my attention.

"Tenebris!" Noire commands aloud. "Look at me!"

I glance over, my eyes flashing with anger as my older brother scowls. The hallway is a fucking wreck. Every window is broken, blood dripping from every visible surface. I'm cut to hell. People stand all over, staring at the smashed wood panels and artwork that's fallen to the floor.

Onmiel safe, my direwolf snarls, leaping inside my chest as I gasp at a sudden streak of pain from deep in my belly.

"Take care of this, Noire," I command my older brother, turning with Onmiel in my arms.

"Where the fuck are you going?" he shouts after me as I pass quickly through the archives, Onmiel still clutched tightly around my neck. I head for the elevator bank, ignoring the increasing pain in my side as I mash the button for floor five. I drip blood all over the elevator and hallway, but all I can focus on is getting her somewhere private, cleaning her, examining her.

Need make sure she safe, my direwolf presses, less urgently now that I'm obeying his desire.

Onmiel's door still isn't locked after how I entered the room earlier, so I sail through and into her bathroom, ripping her clothes from her lean body as I turn on the water. When I try to set her down, she shakes her head and clutches tighter to me.

"I need to examine our wounds," I whisper, and with a sniffle, she drops out of my arms. She turns immediately, rooting around under her cabinet, presumably for a first aid kit. I reach for her waist, pulling her to me as I drag us both into the shower.

Pain wells up hard and fast as I whine and slide down the wall with her in my arms. The endorphins that fueled me through the fight are leaving now, and in their wake is bone-snapping pain.

I run my hand over every inch of my librarian, and she's covered in scratches, but she's unhurt otherwise.

We protected, growls my direwolf, slinking back deeper as he leaves me, content that we kept her safe.

"Ten, you need a doctor," she cries softly. "You need stitches."

"No," I say, pulling her to straddle me while I bury my face in her neck. Her scent calms me, wrapping me up in a comforting, warm blanket as my muscles slowly relax. "Sit with me," I growl.

"Okay," she whispers, resting her head on the side of mine as the water streams down us. "Let me wash this blood off you, at least?"

I grunt out my disagreement as I hold her tighter, relishing the connection. Pain wells up so hot I resist the urge to scream. I'll heal fast; I'm an alpha.

But the naga got me good with his claws. Already, my body is knitting together the worst of the injuries from the naga's claws, but it fucking hurts.

I have very little time before Noire barrels his way up here and drags me back down to answer his questions. But right now? Right here? My focus is on the librarian who has so quickly become the light at the end of my tunnel.

For ten long minutes, water washes us both clean, and then Onmiel insists on scrubbing every bit of blood from my body. I lie in the shower, slumped, as I watch her hands move over my skin, touching and probing at the wounds. I could lie here and watch her touch me for hours, I realize.

I know what you look like when you come, I think. And what's more, I want to know what you look like when I'm knotted inside you and pleasure hits. The rush of her being in danger has me feeling possessive and protective. She's safe, and now I want to fuck.

I do. I want her. I've half-ass fought it since we met. The timing is bad. I'm still broken up about my mate, and I'm on a mission to save my pack omega. The timing is *shit*, actually. But when has this world ever given me good timing on anything? The answer is never. My life is what I choose to make of it.

But the reality remains. Despite all of that, I want Onmiel, and it's that simple to me.

When she's done, I take the soap and bring my hands to her neck, lathering as I grip her throat, using my fingers to wash away the last remnants of blood. I move to her shoulders, swirling my fingers over her beautiful skin. When I bring them to her breasts, cupping each one as I pinch and pluck at her nipples, her head falls back, hips moving in my lap.

Growling, I drag my fangs up that slender column of her neck, following the sting with my lips and tongue. Onmiel sighs happily until a banging at the door indicates my brother has, indeed, arrived.

Noire doesn't bother to wait after the knock but enters Onmiel's space and hovers in the doorway with his arms crossed. I snarl when she tries to cover herself, but I don't move us.

Noire smirks at what he sees before his dark eyes fall on my wounds. His voice is surprisingly neutral as he looks at me. "It's a shitshow downstairs, brother. Take a moment, but we have a pile of trouble to deal with."

I growl, and he understands, leaving us as the water in the shower begins to run cold.

Onmiel looks up at me, her expression sad but resolved. She leans in and rubs her cheek along mine before planting a soft, tender kiss on my jawline. When she stands and exits the shower, I can't pull my eyes from the tattoo on her back or the gentle swell of her ass. She disappears into her room to get dressed as I realize I have no fucking clothes up here, and mine are downstairs covered in blood.

Another figure appears at the door, and I hear low voices. Onmiel appears in the bathroom doorway again with clothes for me.

"We keep some on hand for librarians who run out. You're probably too muscular to fit in these, but it's better than nothing." She hands me the items and turns into the room.

My direwolf preens at her words, and despite the urgency to get downstairs, I just can't stop godsdamned touching her.

She pulls a shirt on, her movements stiff and jerky when I press myself to her back, wrapping an arm around her waist. She's hurting and scared, and I want those emotions to dissipate. I want her usual joy and happiness because it's infectious. I want her laughter. I want all the pencils in her hair, to watch her bite the tip of one as she pushes her reading glasses up the bridge of her nose. I want all that like I want to keep breathing.

Purring, I bring one hand up between her small breasts and kiss the side of her neck over and over.

"I would never let anyone hurt you," I growl into her ear. "I will always protect you."

She turns in my arms, and while I can sense she wants to say something, she holds back.

Outside the door and down the hall, Noire clears his throat. Onmiel senses my change of focus and slips out of my arms. She pulls her pants on and threads her fingers through mine.

"Let's go, Ten."

Nodding, I let her pull me from the room, even though all I want to do is hide away and bury myself in her light, in her happiness.

Her, my direwolf rumbles. *Onmiel mine.*

CHAPTER TWENTY-FIVE
ONMIEL

I've never been so terrified in my life. I've known Evizel for years. While we've never been friendly, I wouldn't have pegged him for a killer. The only way that would happen is if he scented someone who had killed another naga.

Oh, gods. I know there were naga in the maze, so I come to the only conclusion I can. Ten's killed one. If I had watched the fucking hunts, I'd have known that, and I could have warned him. I could have stopped all of this. It's not a commonly known fact about naga but I knew it. Guilt chokes me so hard I gasp for breath.

Another one of Ten's secrets uncovered, I suppose. He's like an onion I keep peeling back the layers of. And every time I get to a new level, I find deep wells of hurt. I can't imagine knowing your mate was fine with allowing you to deal with so much godsdamned agony.

I can't let go of his hand as we leave my assigned room and meet his brother again. Noire gives me the first less-than-hateful look I've seen since I met him. "The Master Librarian wants to speak with you immediately."

I struggle to swallow around the lump in my throat. Half the library was ravaged when Evizel went crazy. I can imagine exactly what ML Garfield wants to talk about. I could sob for the thousands of books we'll have to patch together after his rampage.

We're silent as we enter the elevator bank and return to the first floor. Librarians run every which way as they examine the damage and pick up stacks of books and fallen shelves. I can't think about that right now. Because now that I'm not so utterly focused on Ten getting killed, I'm remembering how Zakarias ran to stop Evizel.

My heart begins to pound as we round the outer edge of the library to the hallway toward the public sector. The double doors fly open, and an elderly librarian presses through, retching onto the floor as my heartbeat picks up fast.

"Zakarias!" I shout as I run through the doors.

Behind me, Noire growls at his brother. "She'll need you. Go."

I'll need him? What for? Oh fuck. I can't help the sensation of falling as I run through drying puddles of sticky blood toward ML Garfield, who's huddled with a dozen other librarians in front of one of the many shattered windows. Every one of the long plate-glass windows is blown out, giving us a view into the darkness outside.

Garfield's dark eyes turn to me when he sees me coming, and he puts up both hands to stop me. "Wait, my child. Let's talk."

I rush past him to where the others are peering out the window, talking in hushed tones. Below us is the Sunken Courtyard, a deep pit that many librarians use for meditation. It lies mostly underground, and it's four stories below the first floor of the library.

I fly to the window and lean out. Below, at the bottom of the pit, Zakarias lies face up, lifeless eyes staring at the sky as raindrops begin to pour out of the middle-of-the-night clouds.

No.

It can't be.

A wail leaves my mouth even as I claw at the edge of the window, cutting my hands on the glass.

"Somebody help him! Help him!" I shriek, even though I know he's gone. I feel like I'm reeling and falling as I scream. Big arms pull me in close, a rolling purr vibrating against me as I scream over and over and over.

Zakarias is dead.

~

Time loses all sense of meaning for me as people come and go. It takes a godsdamned crane to move Evizel's body. Every surface is coated in blood and a sticky scent I know is his death mist. Anyone in the room when he released it is now covered, including me. We'll probably never be able to have another naga librarian because the entire library will be a trigger for them.

Gods, Zakarias is *dead*.

I let out a cry of anguish as Ten pulls me closer. There are voices all around us, his whole pack, I think. Noire's there, of course, but Ascelin, Jet, and even Arliss show up.

A huge figure drops to a knee next to us, and when I manage to drag my eyes from Ten's shirt I see Jet.

His dark eyes are kind as he gives me a soft smile, handing me a bottle of water. "Drink something, sweetheart. Ten's gonna get you out of here. You don't need to be here right now, okay? We will handle this."

I nod and stand. My brain is frozen in time, remembering that moment Evizel's body spun over and over in the room and sent everything flying. And that brings me back to the memory of my sister, Zura, dying. It's the only memory that haunts me on a daily basis, and what happened tonight has that imprint front and center.

Tears stream down my cheeks as I look over to see Noire's mate, Diana. I haven't met her in person yet, this woman who's at the center of bringing Ten to Pengshur. It's obvious who she is, though, with the way Noire hovers so closely by her side.

She's speaking with Ascelin, pointing at something. I think she's helping to direct the workers who now flood the hallway.

My mission demands my attention, and I push out of Ten's big arms long enough to find ML Garfield. Tapping him on the shoulder, I wipe the tears away from my cheeks.

He turns with a somber, consoling look, pushing his glasses farther up his nose.

"We were meeting you tonight about a reference in a book. Did Zak—did FL Zakarias tell you the details about the blood?"

Garfield gives me a quizzical look but then sighs. "You are an excellent librarian, Onmiel. You do not have to do this tonight, but I understand your need to fulfill your duty." He reaches into his pocket and pulls out a small vial of what appears to be blood. "I knew the day would come that you'd ask for this. I hope it helps."

I can't even comprehend his cryptic message as I take the vial and approach Diana, handing it to her and Ascelin. The omega looks half-dead with dark circles under her eyes. Ascelin watches her with something akin to terror on her face.

"I don't know if this will help you, but there's a solid chance. It's Volya blood. If there's an antidote to be found at all, it'll be here. A good physik can use this to help you. Zakarias had the connections to help you with this, but—"

Relief splashes across Diana's face as she clutches the vial to her chest, her face pale and drawn.

"Thank you, Onmiel. I'm so sorry we haven't met," she whispers. Her voice is frail and hoarse. She's wasting away; that much is obvious.

"Call a healer immediately," I direct Ascelin. "They'll be able to tell you in twelve hours if it'll help. If not, you can leave for the Tempang tomorrow."

The elegant vampiri nods, but I can't stay here any longer. I don't have to because Ten sweeps me up into his arms for the millionth time today, and we leave everything behind. I hear Noire call him, but he doesn't bother to respond, although I know he could in the family bond they share. Instead, he goes right back up to my room, pulling me into his arms and tucking my head under his chin.

"I'm so sorry, Onmiel," he whispers into my hair, stroking my back and side as he threads his legs through mine. "I'm so fucking sorry. If I hadn't—"

"Stop," I command him, sitting up as he props himself up against my headboard. "You fought for your life in the maze. What Evizel did put you in danger, and I was fucking terrified for you. What he did isn't your fault. You protected everyone, Ten. You—" I can't go on to say anything else because I'm so overwhelmed with the memory of Evizel snapping at me and Ten leaping in front.

"You could have died," I whisper. *And Zakarias is dead.*

My face crumples, and I hate it. I'm not a weak person. But this day has taken me on an emotional rollercoaster from hells, and I don't have any expectations of handling that well. Ten purrs and pulls me flush with his chest, wrapping his legs around mine as our foreheads touch. The tip of his nose brushes mine, our lips so close.

Oh my gods, is he going to kiss me right now? After everything that happened?

My lips part because all I want is to feel good.

Ten growls, brushing his lips across mine as his golden eyes bore into my soul. What is he thinking, feeling, wanting? I'm dying to ask but terrified to.

A knock at my broken door pulls a growl up out of his chest, but he stands and deposits me gently in the pillows, stalking to the door before he moves it out of the way.

"May I see her?" It's ML Garfield. Oh, fuck me. I don't want to fall apart in front of the Master Librarian, not any more than I have. I leap out of bed, but Garfield comes into my room, shaking his head. "Do not rise on my account, NL Onmiel. There is something I wanted to give you, a letter that came with the blood gift from the Volya."

"Why not give it to me earlier?" I question as I take the faded cream envelope from him. There are no markings on the front.

"It was neither the time nor the place," he says in a kind tone, turning to look at Tenebris and then back at me. "When the blood was gifted to us, I made sure the letter and blood didn't need to remain together, and so I gave the blood earlier since you made a remarkable discovery for your clients. The letter is purely personal."

"You're being obtuse," Tenebris growls, taking the letter from me to examine it.

Garfield sighs. "I knew there would come a day I would give this letter to Onmiel, and that day has finally come."

"You're making no sense," Tenebris reiterates, pointing to the door. "We'll deal with this tomorrow. Tonight, she needs rest."

Garfield nods. "There is no rush, Onmiel. But when you have questions, find me."

All the strength leaves me then, and I sink back onto the bed as Ten sets the letter down on my bedside table.

"You want to read it tonight?"

"I haven't known it existed for years and years, and my mentor is dead. Nothing in that letter can change what happened today. I'll read it another time."

Ten gives me a look and slides back onto the bed, pulling me into his arms. He starts purring, and I'm lost to the darkness, falling into a deep and dreamless sleep.

CHAPTER TWENTY-SIX
TENEBRIS

I hold Onmiel for hours until the sun is high in the sky and finally dipping again. She sleeps the entire time, snoring softly with her fists wrapped in my shirt. I use that time to think because what we're doing, this isn't friendship. This is so much more, and I'm struggling with how I've gone from being destroyed over killing my bondmate to wanting another woman in a relatively short time.

My direwolf sits up and growls when I think of Rama. He begins to pace in my chest anxiously.

Hurt. She hurt. His voice is deep, his words broken. I've never heard of anything like this.

Who's hurt? I question, wondering if I can speak with him and if we can have an honest-to-gods conversation. I've never heard of a shifter being able to do this. Our wolves are more of a sensation than anything.

Hurt me, he snarls into my mind. *Bondmate hurt me. Cruel mate. Bad mate.*

A sense of wrongness washes over me in waves that choke the breath from my lungs. There's so much anguish that threatens to break loose. I have so many questions. How did she hurt him? What exactly did she do? And why? Did she know my direwolf was different? Would I have eventually become another experiment to her? Did the fucking bond matter at all? Does it even matter now? If I start something with Onmiel, will the bond tear it apart?

I'm unsettled that I don't have an answer for any of that.

Onmiel shifts in my arms, stirring, and when I go to move away, my direwolf startles and pushes up against my ribs. *Take. Hurt go away.*

Wait, is he *still* hurting? I ponder the question, but he doesn't answer. Onmiel's beautiful eyes pop open, going wide when she looks at me and scoots back. "What's wrong? You look worried…"

"Nothing," I murmur, standing to go to the window and look out. "You've been asleep all day, Onmiel. Are you hungry? Can I get you anything?" My direwolf preens in my chest as I rub at it, wondering what the hells is going on with him.

When she rises and stretches, joining me, I sit in the window seat.

"Have you ever heard of an alpha's direwolf having a separate consciousness from his?"

Onmiel startles, glancing to where I'm still rubbing absentmindedly at my pecs. "Is that happening to you?"

I confirm with a slight nod.

She sighs, gritting her teeth. "Maybe a mate bond thing?"

Hearing her say the word mate sends me growling and my direwolf preening for attention. Onmiel blanches. "I'm sorry to bring her up, Ten."

"You don't have to dance around that topic with me, Onmiel," I reassure her. "He didn't start speaking to me until *this week*. I find that significant."

She folds her arms over her knees and pulls them to her chest, away from me. My direwolf snaps in my chest, hating how she folds in on herself. Gods, he's going to get insufferable shortly.

"Maybe that takes a while to develop after you mate someone," she whispers. "I've never heard it mentioned about shifters, though. They just…shift, I thought. Can Noire do this?"

I shake my head. "Noire's never mentioned it. Jet hasn't either, although I suppose they probably wouldn't have bothered to cover standard mating procedures with me given how things happened."

There's a sudden pang of sadness, a sense of loss when I think of all the growing up I missed out on in the maze. I came of age there, my eighteenth birthday punctuated only with me being chosen by Rama to kill the mark that night—an elderly woman thrown in for some stupid fucking reason, I'm sure. I'll never forget her terror or my promise to make it quick and painless.

She thanked me before I broke her neck.

If I'd been living a normal pack life, on my eighteenth birthday, my brothers would have gotten me rip-roaring drunk and pierced my cock for my future mate. I find myself wondering how they would have done it. Most alpha piercings are highly elaborate.

I did end up getting hammered drunk the night of my birthday after I killed that night's mark. Jet rubbed my back while I puked my guts up in the toilet and sobbed for hours. Rama was the source of all that pain. She must have known I was hers, then. I'd come of age, a fully adult direwolf male in his prime. But she never came for me. She never did a godsdamned thing to help.

Even when I came out of the stupor after being captured in that final fight to escape the maze, she never apologized. Not a single time. She just carried on with our connection as if all our history was something she didn't need to bother to address. I was so bond-drunk and drugged up that I couldn't even fight it. I fell headlong into mating her without another thought.

I don't think I could regret anything more than I regret that.

My cell rings, and Onmiel falls quiet. We're dancing around a conversation about my dead mate and just how much Rama does or doesn't have control over my present.

"Noire," I growl out my brother's name.

"We're at the hospital with Diana." His tone is gruff. "The physiks and healers are working on a serum based on the blood, and it's looking good, but we'll be here all day. Please thank Onmiel for us until I can come in person."

"Done." I smile softly at her. She can hear him because he talks so damn loud into the phone.

"How is she?" His voice quietens.

"It's hard," is all I say, but Noire gets it. Of course, he does. He led our pack through seven years of hell in the maze. Seven years of bullshit brought on by my godsdamned mate. A switch flips in my brain. She might have been mine in a fated mate bond, but I didn't *choose* her, and if I could undo that fucking claiming, I would. Rama might have belonged to me spiritually and emotionally in ways that matter, but I do not choose her *now*, and I won't let her control a single thing about my future.

It's freeing to think that, and my direwolf curls up contentedly in my chest, seemingly pleased we're on the same page about her.

Noire and I hang up. I look out the window to see the library's flags at half-mast, indicating a death of their own. Onmiel watches the flags wave softly in the breeze, her face tense.

I hate to see that look on her beautiful, delicate features. There should be only joy and excitement.

A ping makes her jump, but she unfolds herself to cross the room and read the screen on the library's tech. She blanches, her hand coming to her throat before she crosses the room to me.

"There's a releasing ceremony for Zakarias tonight. ML Garfield wanted me to know."

I can't resist bringing one hand to her hip as the other tilts her chin up, pulling her between my thighs. "Do you want to go?"

"Of course," she whispers, but her voice wavers even though she lifts her chin. She moves her hands as if she'll put them on me but seems to think better of it. I hate it.

"Don't hold back around me, Onmiel," I demand. "Just be how you always have been."

She nods but doesn't touch me, and my direwolf yowls in my chest. His position is crystal clear, at least. Taking her hand, I guide it to my chest. "Can you feel him, Onmiel?"

He purrs and presses against my chest, threatening to force a shift so he can touch her, but I suspect she can't tell any of that.

There's a cracking sensation deep in my chest, surprising me with its intensity. I fall off the window seat and onto my knees. Pain and shock slam into my brain as my shift takes over in a flash of light. It happens so fast that I'm standing there in direwolf form before realizing I've fucking shifted.

Holy fucking hells.

He took over. My godsdamned wolf took over.

Onmiel takes a tentative step back as I huff and pant, struggling to understand how he was able to control me. It's unheard of. It's not possible. Except, he just did it.

I work hard to get up to speed fast, trying to sense his intention. I don't want her to be in danger; she's been through enough. But I don't read malice from him, and I'm in too much shock that he forced the fucking shift to do much about it. He wants to be close to her. I see her through his eyes, but I'm disconnected, somehow. He's in total control, pushing her with his nose back to the window seat.

She sits with a soft smile, stroking one of his ears as we shove our nose in her lap and inhale. Gods. Oh, fuck. This is probably the last thing she wants, for a giant direwolf to scent her this way. Does she know how sensual this is for us, for him? Her scent explodes against my senses, filling the forefront of my mind with promise.

My direwolf sniffs his way slowly up her body, reading her hurt, her despair. He rubs his enormous cheek along hers with a mournful whine then lays his head in her lap, his ears flat. He purrs the whole time, and I don't bother to try to stop him or attempt to take control. I'm reeling that he could do this, and I'm in complete wonder that it didn't frighten her in the least.

Ours. He growls in our bond. The bond that's always silent because shifter wolves aren't a separate fucking consciousness.

Except mine suddenly is in the last few days.

We sit for a long time, my direwolf purring his heart out for Onmiel. She strokes our fur, ears, and nose, and her scent morphs into something more peaceful. Eventually, I make my presence known, telling him I'd like to be in my human form again, and he allows me to shift back as she looks up with a wry grin.

"Guess he really wanted an ear scratch, huh? This is new, right? He pushed that?"

I suppose she picked up more of that than I thought.

"Yeah. It's new. I've never heard of that. He just…took over."

She looks up with big eyes filled with tears. "I think he thought I needed him, maybe? We'll find answers for you, too, Ten, if that's what you want. Fingers crossed the serum works for Diana, but today, I need to focus on Zakarias's releasing ceremony."

I pull her into my arms, unable to keep my damn hands off her. Everything about her pain calls to me. I've always been like this, though. I can't stand to see a gentle person or child in pain. Noire's always said I'm too nice, too empathetic, but secretly, I know he believes it's a strength. He admires it, not that he'd admit it aloud.

"I'll come with you," I grit out as I run my hands over Onmiel's lithe, tense figure. Little by little, she relaxes, arms crossed and chin laid on top of them as she looks up at me from my chest. "If you want me to," I add, worried she might not want me there. Zakarias wouldn't be dead if I hadn't been in the library.

"I always want you to," she murmurs, pale eyes locked onto mine. We say nothing, but I shift her higher as I touch and stroke her, my direwolf preening at the attention, at the way she's relaxing in my arms. But it's more than that because an undercurrent of desire threads through her usual scent, and I'm hard for her.

"Onmiel," I growl, hauling her farther up until her breasts are crushed to my upper chest, and I'm looking up into her face.

"What is it, Ten?" Her voice is soft, almost desperate, as she hovers above me. Does she even know her hips are rocking against my upper stomach?

I know what you look like when you come, I muse again. *I've seen you fuck yourself on a godsdamn replica of an alpha cock. You want me.*

I slide one hand up her back, over her shirt, so I don't agitate her tattoo. The other comes to the back of her head, and I pull her close, close enough for my lips to brush hers.

Onmiel goes tight and loose all at the same time as she tries to push back, her expression worried. "Ten, are you su—"

I silence her concern with my lips, nipping at her plump lower one as I tug it gently. A soft whine greets me as I grip her jaw and force her mouth open wide. And then, I let myself go. All the thoughts and worries I could have in this moment disappear as I slick my tongue over hers, tasting her silky heat.

"Open for me," I purr when she's still too hesitant. She's wrapped up in her brain around what's happening, and I want her to let go.

Gray eyes flash with need, and then she relaxes into the kiss. Heat streaks along my limbs and pools in my groin. I can't do tender, so I unleash, biting and nipping, feral in my need for her.

Onmiel claws at my chest as I plunder her mouth, growling because I want to be inside her in every way possible. I want her joy, her release. I want to drown in her honey. And she smells so fucking good right now, so sweet and bright. So godsdamn needy.

And it's all for me.

Sitting up, I shift myself so she's straddling me. Onmiel's lips are swollen and red from the attention, and I attack them again. I want her marked and smelling like me, and every time I suck at her tongue, my direwolf focuses more intensely.

She drips arousal through her jeans into my lap, coating me as our bodies clash together. I need more of this delicious friction, more of her sweet pussy kissing my dick. I need her to come at least once before we leave for this horrible fucking ceremony.

Growling, I shove her jeans down. I toss them aside and then she's rocking her soaked folds up and down my hard length. I can't tear my eyes from the sight as I grip her throat and kiss her again. I'm going to come so fucking hard like this, finally kissing her.

This connection, this is everything.

When I slide a hand around her ass and coat my fingers with her sticky arousal, she jolts in my arms. But the moment I slip two fingers into her ass and stroke, she explodes all over me. My name falls over and over from her lips, and hearing it sends me headfirst into mind-obliterating pleasure.

I clamp my fangs around her neck, biting hard as I come, coating her with release as my balls tighten and throb. The thick knot at the base of my cock begins to expand even though I'm not inside her.

"Fuck, Ten," she gasps. "What do I—"

I cut her off with a growl, directing her hand to my knot, the swollen area at the base of my cock. She can barely get her fingers around it as it swells, but the sensation of her gripping it, her fingers tight and warm, is enough to get me off again as I snarl and snap and throw my head back with a yell.

Onmiel strokes my knot, aided by my much larger hand until my cock stops spurting cum all over the damn place. She shuffles back off my lap and looks down. It's fucking messy, but I don't stop her when she begins cleaning me with her tongue. She licks her way around my knot as I groan, feeling it harden again. When her lips kiss a trail up my throbbing dick, I chuckle and pull her back into my lap.

"You keep doing that, and we won't make it out of here, sweet girl. Alphas have sky-high libidos. I'll go all night if we're not careful."

Onmiel laughs, and it's finally joyous, but uncertainty returns far faster than I'd like it to.

"What is it?" I encourage. I want no miscommunication between us, no being unsure of feelings. All I had with Rama were falsehoods. I won't accept it now, and I don't always read social cues well after spending my formative years in the maze. I need transparency.

She nips at her lip. "I just…is this all too soon for you, Ten? We have chemistry, absolutely. We have friendship. Is this the best time for…" Her voice trails off as she gestures to the mess in our laps.

"What we have isn't just friendship," I remind her. "We built it on friendship. We built it on trust. We built it on godsdamned coffee, Onmiel."

She bursts out laughing at that, giving me a wry grin before she slips off my lap and discards what remains of her clothing. My direwolf preens at the sheer amount of cum she's coated with. It drips from her lean stomach muscles and down her swollen pussy lips onto her thighs.

She grins at me. "Well, I guess if it's built on coffee, who can argue that?"

"I'm serious," I say, pulling her to me as I rise. "We can take this slowly if that makes you more comfortable, but make no mistake, Onmiel, I want to take *everything*."

The look she turns on me is pure heat before her eyes flash away. "We're not done talking about this, Tenebris."

Gods, hearing her say my full given name makes me hard, and my cock leaps, bobbing against my thigh as she holds back a grin. When we met, I told her to call me Ten, but hearing the whole thing now has me aching with need.

"You using my full name gives me sexy professor ideas," I admit. "I'm a simple male, Onmiel. I want simple things. I want to be cuddled. I want to feed each other and run in the moonlight. I want to be fucking adored by the person I *choose* to spend my life with." I purposefully don't use the word mate because there's too much recent connection with that word, and I refuse to choose the woman who wasn't any of the things I want for myself.

Onmiel's smile grows wider, and she crosses the room, grabbing a spare set of clothes in my size out of the closet. "I ordered these for you when it seemed like you wouldn't be going to your apartment anymore."

"Why would I?" I laugh. "When I can stay here and have cuddles for days? And talk books. Don't forget the books."

"Never forget the books," she agrees with a laugh, pulling on dark jeans and an umber tunic. When she reaches for the sky-blue Novice belt, I take it and tie it around her midsection.

Her happy expression falls, but I've smothered her enough today, so I pull on my clothes in silence, watching her. She goes to the mirror and dabs a little color on her cheeks, pulling her still-white hair up into a messy bun on top of her head. When she pulls tendrils down over both ears, I can't resist kissing my way along the side of her neck and down her shoulder.

"I can't stop touching you," I admit. "You draw me in like a godsdamned magnet, Onmiel."

"You must have a thing for dorks," she laughs. "Like recognizes like?"

I grin because most people wouldn't assume my scholarly tendencies based on my appearance, but I genuinely am the ultimate nerd. Give me books and coffee all day long, throw in some kids to be goofy with, and life is perfect.

I like quiet, too, although I suspect there's not much of that in my future.

CHAPTER TWENTY-SEVEN
ONMIEL

I'm literally overwhelmed with emotion, but Ten joking with me like every other day brings some levity to it all.

And that kiss.

Gods.

I'll never recover from it because it was even more incredible than in my numerous fantasies about him. Ten is a masterful kisser. He's commanding and in charge and totally aware of every reaction, every feeling. Kissing Ten was an emotional epiphany followed by orgasming like a damn waterfall.

I honestly needed that, and he knew it. I'm a little more relaxed now, despite what we're about to do. My brain is reeling with all the information we've uncovered in the last twenty-four hours, but I'll dumpster dive through it later. I can't deal with it right now. I'm just grateful that I'm not dealing with it alone.

My face is puffy from all the stupid crying, so a quick swipe of mascara makes me look human again. I've cried enough to last me a lifetime in the last twenty-four hours. I'd like to be done with that. My sister, Zura, is top of my mind as I finish getting ready to lay my mentor to rest.

Ten's standing in the doorway, enormous arms crossed as he watches me, and despite how pleased he looks, there's a worrying, niggling part of my consciousness concerned about our connection. It's so good, so right, so godsdamn *deep*. But I don't want to be the rebound or someone he latches on to because I'm *alive*. I want something real, and I think that could be what's between us, but it'll take revisiting the conversation another day.

Today isn't the right time.

He must sense my hesitation because he crosses the room and rubs his cheek along mine. "I'm here for you, Miel. Just you." His words are a balm to my cracked, bleeding soul as I lean into his touch and sigh. I want to let go and really sink into this more-than-friendship thing, but I'm scared.

"We're going to address this hesitation later," Ten growls in my ear, nipping softly at the skin just below it. "And I'll keep reiterating to you what I said earlier. I want to know where this goes, sweet girl."

Godsdamn, I'm loving my new moniker. I want to get a T-shirt made with that on the front and wear it every damn day. Librarian praise kink chic. That's my new thing.

We make it back out of my assigned room, and reality hits again. The library is noisy, and people scurry back and forth. Many have been crying if their puffy faces are any indication. I groan as Ten's hand comes to my lower back.

"We'll deal with this later," he reminds me. "Let's honor Zakarias now."

"His mate, Okair, will be there," I whisper softly. "We'll have to pay our respects to him."

Ten nods but takes my hand. "Do you want me to stay out of sight? Do you think it would hurt Okair to meet me?" He means because of his role in Zakarias's death. But the reality is there's nothing easy about death, and hiding Ten won't change that.

I shake my head in disagreement, and we don't speak as we leave the library. Outside, hundreds are gathered in the street, holding candles as they walk toward the square where all releasing ceremonies are held. Ten doesn't let go of my hand, and eventually, most of his pack joins us, walking behind as we pace through the somber, stone, quiet streets of Pengshur to the very last square at the edge of town.

I've always loved this square. It's in the older section of town, and the shops here are quaint and cozy. Zakarias and I spent hundreds of hours picking through fabrics, shopping for antiques, and having coffee with Okair. That's why they settled here, even though it was as far as he could possibly be from the library.

Okair stands on a raised platform, his thin shoulders hunched as he openly sobs. Dark hair flops in waves over his chocolate eyes, red-rimmed from crying. In his hand is a small box. I know when he lights it, it'll morph into a beautiful lantern. Once his is released, we'll all release ours. Someone comes around and hands us releasing boxes.

Master Librarian Garfield stands next to Okair in his formal navy tunic, one arm around the younger male's shoulders as he cries. His anguish rings out around the cobblestone streets, seeming to echo off the buildings until it sounds like the whole city mourns Zakarias's loss. I realize every-fucking-body in the entire square is crying, including me, and when I look up, Ten is too. He's not distraught like me, but tears roll down his handsome face as he watches Okair.

Is he remembering everything he lost in the maze? I know one of his brothers died there; I remember hearing that much from the other librarians who watched the nightly hunts. Maybe he's even thinking of his mate right now. Oh gods.

I'm hit with a sudden hatred for the woman the stars picked to belong to him. She let him languish in the maze. She let him kill and be hurt, this sweet alpha who cries for a male he barely knew. If Rama were here right now, I'd rip her godsdamned head from her shoulders for ever causing Ten a single moment of pain.

Fuck her. May she rot in all seven hells for the rest of eternity.

Garfield gives a moving speech that I instantly forget, and then Okair sets off his lantern. I watch it catch the wind and billow up, hovering just above him before it makes its way slowly up into the night sky. As one, the crowd lights their own lanterns, sending them up to join Okair's. I know my librarian friends are here, but I can't summon the energy to find anyone.

For a long time, the square is silent. We stand until the last of the lanterns have blown away on the breeze, and then the crowd dissipates. ML Garfield catches my eye and gives me a solemn wave, leaving Okair's side as people begin to form a line to express their condolences.

"Onmiel, how are you holding up?" Garfield has a reputation for being shrewd and almost cruel, but he's been so kind that I'm starting to think of him a little differently.

"Everything hurts," I reply honestly as Ten pulls closer to me. "But we'll honor him every day."

Garfield nods as Ten's brothers join us. Noire gives me a quick once-over, then glances at the Master Librarian. "Onmiel's work resulted in a serum that's helping my mate as we speak. She's the best she's been since she was attacked. We have your librarians to thank for that."

Garfield gives me a pleased smile and claps his hands together, a tear traveling down his weathered, pale cheek. His voice is the hint of a whisper when it comes out. "Zakarias would have been so proud, Onmiel. You were his favorite, you know."

I choke back a sob, leaning against Ten as he begins to purr for me, crushing me to his side as the crowd slowly disappears. Garfield turns from us. "Forgive me. I've spoken with Okair, but I'm going to retire early. I've got some arrangements to make regarding our other loss."

Evizel. Gods. I'd forgotten about the naga librarian who was just as beloved as Zakarias. Evizel had been here for ages and ages. Garfield takes his leave, and Ten turns to speak with his brothers. Eventually, they leave too, and then it's just Ten and me.

"You want to speak with Zakarias's mate?" Ten's voice is cautious and low but understanding.

"I do," I murmur. "I have to tell Okair how fucking sorry I am. They were like my family, the first people to befriend me when I came here."

Ten falls silent, guiding me to the now-short line of beings waiting to speak with Okair. I watch him as he greets each one, and it's not lost on me how this process isn't for the family of the person who died. A wake is for the people who feel the need to say something or give their final goodbye. I've been on the receiving end of these things; I know how fucking awful it is.

My mind wanders to Zura and everything that happened after she died. I'm sure there was a wake then, too, but I can't remember. The prisoner tattoo keeps a huge majority of my memories locked away. I kept just enough of them to remind me how I never want to access that power again. It's for the best.

My heart is broken anew for Okair and Zakarias by the time it's our turn. There's almost no one left. When Okair sees me, he breaks down, pulling me into his arms as he squeezes me so tight I struggle to breathe.

I squeeze him back, crying over and over about how sorry I am. I don't even know how long we do that, but I sense Ten standing off to one side as he watches us.

When Okair and I part, his eyes darken when he notices Ten.

"You're the alpha Evizel was chasing, aren't you?" Okair's voice is flat as he grits out the words.

Ten nods and steps closer to us. "I'm so sorry for your loss, Okair."

Okair sucks in a deep breath as if he's steeling himself to rail into Ten for being the cause of Zakarias's death. But then all the fight goes out of him as he looks from Ten to me. "It hurts so bad, Onmiel. I don't know how I'll go on without him."

Ten croons, his purr strengthening as he joins us, placing one big hand on Okair's thin shoulder. He says nothing, but I know he's trying to comfort the other male, even though he doesn't know him. He's doing it for my benefit, I suspect.

Okair looks up at Ten as tears stream down his face.

"People don't leave you forever, Okair. Part of them will always remain." Ten clears his throat awkwardly.

My blood freezes in my veins. I feel like I'm going to be sick, bile rising in my throat at Ten's words about losing people and how we're never done with them.

There's silence as Okair watches us, but finally, he snuffles and reaches into his pocket, handing me a small envelope. It matches the one Garfield gave me earlier, a fact I struggle to comprehend. What is with this shit?

"Zakarias held this for you at your request. I thought you might want it back now that he, that he…" He loses the ability to say anything else as I take the envelope and tuck it into my back pocket. It's thick like there's an object inside.

"Thank you," I mutter as another mourner pushes into us, anxious for their time with Okair. I give him one last hug before Ten and I turn to leave.

It was foolish to think I could have him. Rama had her hooks in him for years. That doesn't dissipate in a week of friendly nerd banter.

People don't leave you forever, part of them will always remain.

Those are the words that came straight out of his mouth.

I'm such a godsdamn fool.

CHAPTER TWENTY-EIGHT
TENEBRIS

Onmiel is stiff and silent as we leave the nearly empty square. This part of Pengshur is beautiful and old, and I'd love to explore it with her sometime, but right now, she's…hurt? Is that what I sense?

It must have been my words about losing people. I meant what I said to Okair, but losing people doesn't keep us from seizing happiness. I had hoped that would be meaningful to her in a positive way, but if anything, she looks more visibly distressed by the moment.

"Onmiel," I murmur, putting my hand on her forearm to stop her. When she turns with a hurt look, I tilt her chin up and press myself close to her. "How did you take what I said? I want no miscommunication between us, so tell me."

She crosses her arms, but I don't let go of her chin. She's going to tell me if I have to stand here all night and wait for the truth.

"Miel," I whisper. "Talk to me. Don't hold back. Not from me."

"The way you talked about how you felt when she died…" Onmiel's voice falls off as her eyes meet mine. "I've felt that before when I lost my sister. I felt it to a degree, losing Zakarias. But I've never lost a fated bondmate, Ten. It's only been a few weeks for you."

"You never had a fated mate who tried to destroy the world, either," I counter. "I was a fucking mess after I killed her, that's true, but—"

Onmiel interrupts me. "You said we're never done with those we lose. I can't come second to your dead bondmate, Tenebris." She pulls her chin from my fingertips with a sigh. "I'm not saying you need to pick her or me, Ten. Gods, I'm not that person, I swear. We have a real connection and incredible chemistry. That's true. I'm just saying maybe you need time to truly grieve Rama, even if she was a total asshole."

I bark out an angry laugh at her summary. "She *was* an asshole," I clarify. "She hurt everyone and everything I ever loved. She hurt me over and over, even after she knew I was hers. She never fucking apologized, and the moment she had me in her clutches, she drugged me until I stood there and almost allowed her to murder my brothers and their mates. Does that sound like what a bondmate should do? Because if it does, I don't fucking want it. I don't *choose* her."

Onmiel blanches. "I don't want to fight with you, Ten. I just don't want to pressure you or get my heart broken because I'm gonna level with you right now—I'm falling for you. For better or worse, I'm halfway in love, and I don't think I'd recover if we got serious and you weren't done grieving her."

Her words are a splash of cold water, followed by the slow burn of delicious heat in my core. My direwolf preens about what she said. In love? She's falling in love?

Am I? We talked about taking this slowly, but could I be in love with Onmiel?

When I don't immediately answer, she rubs my forearm. "It's a lot, and I shouldn't have laid that on you. I need a night to myself to think. Why don't you stay with your pack tonight? Check on Diana. Find me in the morning, and we'll talk, alright?"

I can only nod as I mull over her words. When she walks off into the fading light, I watch her go, but I'm still rooted to the spot. She's falling in love?

Her admission sends warmth curling through my chest, wrapping around all those places that have hurt since I killed Rama. It's like she's banishing all that darkness little by little, simply by virtue of being who she is.

I walk through Pengshur's quiet streets. The whole city seems to be mourning its loss.

Half an hour later, I arrive at our rental. Diana's back from the healing hospital, and finally, she looks improved. She rises gingerly out of her chair to rub her cheek with mine when I come in the door. Ascelin shows up next, throwing her arms around me as she hugs me in silence. Ah, my other friend—I've neglected her lately.

Jet comes around the corner with Renze's arm slung around his waist. "Brother, we've missed you. Is Onmiel alright? She's not with you?"

Something in my chest bursts with joy that they ask about her, that they seem to hope she came with me.

"She wanted a night alone," I admit. "There's a lot going on."

"Ah, you had a fight with the hot librarian, then," Ascelin comments. "Come in the kitchen and tell us everything." Behind her, I see Arliss at the stove. I'm surprised he's still around, but I suppose he's staying true to his word to remain until our task is done.

I suspect Noire will bark at me to spit it all out, and I'm not anxious to rehash the last forty-eight hours, but all he does is pull Diana into his arms and give me a shrewd look. He kisses his way up Diana's neck as she leans into him, our family bond awash with bright joy. For the first time in a while, I can feel Diana's pack omega strength underlying and supporting the rest of us.

Arliss enters the room and sits across from Noire at the opposite end of the table. I get the sense they've been arguing over which end is the head.

"How is our favorite librarian?" Arliss croons, biting into a piece of white bread as everyone sits at the table. It looks like they were just finishing up a late dinner. Achaia pops up out of nowhere and sets a plate down in front of me as I thank her.

I've been so blinded by grief that I've failed to really absorb how strong my pack is now—a mix of shifters, vampiri, and even a carrow, not that he considers himself part of us. I feel like I've had my head in a deep hole for ages, and I'm just realizing how much has changed.

There's still an achy scar in my chest when I think about Rama, but it's faded, sandblasted away by Onmiel's joyous friendship.

"Brother?" Jet presses me again, laughter apparent in his dark eyes. "Wanna tell us what's going on?"

That encouragement is all it takes to open the floodgates.

Our whole story spills out. How I connected with her, how she discovered the blood, and what happened with the naga and Zakarias. The conversation we just had. Once I open my mouth, it feels so godsdamned good to share with my pack that I can't stop. I haven't had a pack since I was seven, not one that consisted of anything more than my three brothers.

By the time I'm done blurting it all out, Arliss and Ascelin are giving one another joking looks.

"Time to pay up, vampiri," Arliss purrs, kicking Ascelin under the table.

I give them an irritated look; I hate to be a foregone conclusion.

Diana leans over to grab my hand, pulling it into her lap as she strokes my forearm. That's when I realize just what being part of a happy, full pack is like. I don't remember this from my youth, but this touch, this connection?

That's what shifter packs do. I fucking missed it. I missed out on it for all of my formative years.

Godsdamn that woman I refuse to call my mate any longer.

"Ten?" Diana's voice is tentative as she scratches the back of my hand. "This is sort of the moment where Onmiel needs a grand gesture. She needs you to chase her, to show her that you want her and that Rama is in your past—and will remain there."

I look around the table to see my whole pack nodding.

Even Noire gestures to the food in front of me. "Finish eating, brother, and then get your woman and bring her here. I'd like to thank her for saving Diana's life. And I'd like to get to know her."

Smiling, I look down at the food as my pack starts talking around me. It feels good to be with them like this. Arliss and Ascelin needle one another back and forth. Jet is watching his mates make out with one hand down the front of his jeans. Diana and Noire laugh with everyone as we poke fun at Jet.

I'll finish eating and go find Onmiel. Making that decision feels good. And for the first time in a long time, I'm not waiting for the other shoe to drop.

CHAPTER TWENTY-NINE
ONMIEL

I return to my assigned room and sit at the window, watching Pengshur at night. There's a bustling market just outside the side entrance into the archives, but even that seems slightly less busy this evening. The death of a librarian is a big deal to the whole city, and most vendors respect that by keeping the night market low-key.

I'm exhausted from the day but too wired to sleep. When I look around, all I see is Ten every-fucking-where. I see him sitting in the window seat, curled around me in the bed, naked on my shower floor with his soapy hands on my tits.

Godsdamnit. Figures I'd meet the right man at the worst possible time. The red flag of his dead mate was so damn big, waving right in my face, but I happily chose to ignore it because the connection was just *there*. It was so *right*.

I'm the biggest dummy in all Lombornei.

Growling at my own stupidity, I look at the letter Garfield gave me. I'll open it, but not here. I've got to get out of the room. I want my apartment and my blankets and my great view. I need comfort.

It's not lost on me that what I really want is Ten, but I refuse to call him. He's probably enjoying time with his family, who he's barely seen since they arrived, focused as we've been.

Grabbing the letter, I stuff it in my pack and leave the library, heading for my apartment.

When I arrive, I throw open all the windows, letting the sights and sounds of Pengshur at night filter in through my open windows. I make a coffee in my tiny, pink kitchen, grumbling about how much less excellent it is than the ones at the library. And then I wonder if anyone is around to make Ten a coffee because he loves late-night coffee.

I physically slap myself and then take the letter out onto the balcony and fall into one of the plush, oversized chairs that overlook a busy square. Vendors selling to-go booze shout out at the passersby, and it's all I can do not to scream down to them that someone died today. Shut the fuck up and go home! Apparently, this part of town has no qualms about disrespecting the heaviness of the day.

Life goes on; I know that. It always goes on because life is for the living, not those who are already gone.

Grimacing, I tear the envelope open and pull out a single aging sheet of paper. It's folded in half, the heavy handwriting visible from the exterior. When I open it, I choke on my coffee, hacking and slapping my chest until I can set the cup down.

It's my godsdamned handwriting.

I blink rapidly, and then I read the letter in fucking disbelief.

H*ey, you! Hey, me? That's wild.*

I'm sure you're wondering why you wrote yourself a letter and ML Garfield gave it to you, right?

Grab a coffee and settle in. This is a crazy story, but I promise it's 1000% the truth.

You're a Volya, Onmiel. That's what the prisoner tattoo is keeping in. You hide yourself because of Zura's death, which you hopefully remember. If you're reading this letter, it's because you had a need to know more about your past. You asking for the vial was the only condition under which Garfield was allowed to give it to you.

I'm sure this all seems very vague, but you spelled your tattoo in two ways. Drink the vial, and you'll remember everything. Just don't drink the second one unless you're ready for the tattoo to come off...

P*.S. There's a vampiri traveling orb hidden under a loose floorboard in the bathroom. Just in case you need it...*

. . .

TEN: A DARK SHIFTER ROMANCE

Signed, yours truly (literally)

Scoffing, I sit back in the chair and sip my coffee in disbelief. This is my fucking handwriting. But me? A Volya?

I close my eyes and sort through my memories. But my fucking memories are vague on purpose. Vague remembrances of loving parents and siblings. The only memory that's aged well is the accident that killed my younger sister. That was my fault, and it's something I will never ever forget or get over. That's why I spelled myself the way I did. I wanted to be clear on how I killed her, even if it was an accident. I couldn't risk losing control by digging up my past, and I wanted that guilt to stay with me.

Zura died because of me. Nobody else ever needs to.

Slowly, pieces move and shift into place, and I realize I gave away one fucking vial of blood to Diana. What if, by finding out more about myself, I could know precisely how to cure her?

Oh, fuck! I shoot upright. If I could at least remember, I could translate the godsdamned prophecy.

Ugh, there were two vials. The letter references two vials. Suddenly, I remember the envelope Okair gave me at the releasing ceremony. I snatch it out of my back pocket and open it with shaky hands. Is it possible I really planned this far ahead on the off-chance I'd need to know my history? What kind of fucking kismet is that?

Inside, a tiny vial of bright red blood shines, sinister in the low, late-night moonlight.

I reread the letter a dozen times, but it's pretty straightforward—drink this to regain my memory. Memories I locked away for a good fucking reason, I'm sure. But having those back means I can finish my mission and ensure that Diana's healing works. It means I can help figure out what the prophecy says.

I can help Ten achieve his goal because all of this will close a chapter for him. And maybe, selfishly, I hope another future chapter will open where he and I get to write our own book.

The steps are simple.
Drink the vial.
Translate the prophecy.
Save Diana.

Closing my eyes, I pinch the stopper off the vial, steeling myself before I throw it back and swallow.

To my surprise, the blood doesn't taste like anything at all, but it burns like hells on the way down. I fall to both knees as I choke on it, my throat on fire. Then my back feels like flames crawl across it as the blood works its magic to release one layer of the scrolled black prisoner tattoo. Inch by inch, the magic streaks like predatory nails down my back, removing the dark spell I used to conceal myself in human form.

I fall to the ground, gasping for breath as the pain lances down my back. It's so insanely hot and hard that all I can do is scream and writhe on the porch, gripping the railing as the magic releases. The agony goes on for minutes that feel like hours, yanking and pulling as it unlocks whatever I locked away.

When the stabbing sensation recedes, a soothing, cooling feeling replaces it, coating my back in what I can only imagine is the healing nature of my own blood on a wound inflicted by me.

Sobbing, I roll over and pull myself back up into my seat, wiping tears and snot away as I steel myself for the memories.

They come back in a flood, choking and drowning me as I relive my entire life in a flash. I was right to hide myself away for the last eight years.

I'm a monster. I'm a godsdamned monster.

CHAPTER THIRTY
TENEBRIS

I've barely finished dinner when Jet cocks his head to the side.

"Someone's coming, running. I think it's Onmiel."

I'm up and to the front door, swinging it wide as Onmiel barrels through, her face pinched in terror. She stalks past me, shoving me aside as she runs up the hall toward the dining hall, calling for Diana.

Diana appears in the entryway, looking concerned, then weirded out when Onmiel drops to both knees and shoves Diana's shirt up. She inhales deeply over the healing wounds and then falls onto her butt, shaking her head.

"Fuck. Godsdamnit!" She leaps to her feet and looks at Noire. "The blood won't cure her, not permanently, because it's not from the Volya who injured her. The only reason it helped her at all is because it's mine. Lahken's my father, and he's a healer, so I carry some of his ability."

"Wait, what?" Diana and Noire roar at the same time as my entire pack crowds around her. I go to her side and reach for her, but she shies away from me, turning and lifting her shirt to show my brother her tattoo.

"Oh, fuck. Not that shit again," mutters Jet as Achaia sinks back into his arms with a wary look.

"I'm a Volya," Onmiel snaps. "I spelled myself to stop from remembering horrible shit I did when I was younger and couldn't control my magic. I spelled myself so I couldn't hurt anyone. But I left myself a letter in case I needed to remember. I left it as a safeguard in case my family ever needed me for something. An emergency parachute of sorts."

"And how does this have anything to do with Diana?" Noire snaps.

Onmiel reaches into her pocket, grabbing a piece of paper which she hands to Noire.

"The vampiri prophecy, remember? The second half? We learned it was written in Volya, but I couldn't translate it. I removed the first layer of my tattoo so I could figure out what it said." Her eyes go wide with unshed tears as she looks up at me and then back at Diana.

"When the dead come to life, the king will sacrifice the queen. A common enemy must die. Only then will there be peace."

"You must be joking," Ascelin hisses. "Do we assume the king's sacrifice means Diana?"

"The Volya who injured her marked her," Onmiel whispers, her voice hoarse. "He could have deposited a killing poison with his claws, but he did this so she'd have to find him to get well. He did this, knowing you'd venture back to the Tempang. This was his last-ditch effort to call Diana to him, so he must assume she's the queen or the common enemy."

"And we are certain he could mean no other sacrifice, no other enemy?" Ascelin sounds doubtful but horrified as she looks around the room.

"The Volya are peacekeepers," Onmiel whispers. "While dangerous and reclusive, we are responsible for the peace and safety of the forest. Lahken has never fought anyone, not in my entire life. If Diana was marked like this, he thinks he needs her for something. It's hard to say if it's this specific prophecy, but it was given to you, so…"

"He said the forest was sick, though," I counter. "Could there be some enemy there?"

Onmiel shakes her head. "Many beings in the Tempang have enemies, but the Volya generally keep the peace. They simply don't *have* enemies."

"What if *you're* the enemy?" Noire purrs, his voice low and calculating, bringing me right back to our time in the maze. "You said you did terrible things, things bad enough to hide yourself here under that godsdamned tattoo."

"I'm a monster; it's true," she whispers, crossing her arms as she slumps into the wall for support. "I won't deny what I did, but when I left, my family begged me not to go. I thought it for the best, but that hardly seems like something you'd do with an enemy."

Diana turns from us, her hand over her mouth as if she can't even fathom the words to say while she flees the room.

Onmiel looks to Noire urgently. "Gather your things. We'll leave in the morning, and I'll go with you. You can't approach my father with Diana like this. He'll think nothing of tossing her right in the Gate of Whispers, and then you'll be fucked."

"The what?" Ascelin snaps, both hands on her hips as she glares at the librarian.

"The Gate of Whispers is the mother of all life in the Tempang. It's…" She waves her hands around like she isn't sure how to explain it. "The gate is our deity, created by the old gods who ruled the Tempang when the rest of the continent was nothing but dust."

Noire ignores that and leans in close, even when I push myself between him and Onmiel. He pokes his head around me, not caring at all that my big body blocks him from her.

"Hear me on this, Volya. If Diana receives so much as a scratch during this adventure, I'll burn down the entire Tempang and your family with it. There is nothing I won't do to see her fully healed."

"As you should," Onmiel agrees. "I'd do the same if I were you. But all I can do now is give you a fighting chance, right?"

Noire looks at Onmiel as if he can't tell if she's telling the truth or not, but after a tense moment, he turns from us and follows Diana into the depths of the house.

"You sacrificed your personal well-being to give us the truth," Ascelin voices. "I am in awe of you, librarian. Thank you."

She nods. Ascelin turns to Renze with a meaningful look. "Let us prepare, First Warrior. We have much to do."

My pack parts ways as Onmiel turns to me with a resigned look. "We could have gotten to the truth so much faster, Ten. Godsdamnit!" She stomps her foot and shakes her head, huffing.

"Are you alright?" I keep my voice low and soothing as I resist the urge to pull her into my arms and kiss the tension from between her brows. My direwolf paces in my chest, scratching and yowling at me to smother Onmiel in affection, to fuck that anguish away. I still haven't mentioned his development to my brothers. Somehow, it feels like it's between Onmiel and me.

When I can't hold back any longer, I reach for her waistband and pull her flush with my chest. "Are you *alright*?" I reiterate.

"I'm not," she mutters, looking up as she finally places both hands flat on my chest. "I'm not alright at all, but I will be."

"I'll be there every step of the way," I reassure her. "And my direwolf. He's losing his mind right now about the stress rolling off you."

Onmiel's plump lips part into a dejected smile. "No exploding out of there. It'll be okay," she whispers, rubbing between my pecs as he preens deep inside me. She looks up at me with a hopeful expression. "Run with me in the moonlight before we embark on this awful fucking quest?"

I nod as I open the front door and pull my shirt over my head. "You think your father won't stop to listen to you?"

"I'll make him," she confirms, following me into the darkness. I get naked and shift into my direwolf, who immediately presses his head between her pert breasts, purring his godsdamned heart out as I lay down, belly to the cobblestones.

Onmiel crawls on top of me, fisting her tiny hands in my fur as I take off. We run up the street and out into the countryside. I run for a solid hour before I slow, stopping at a small overlook before I shift into human form again. Pulling Onmiel into my arms, I seat us so we can look down at Pengshur, the library a glittering white landmark in the middle of town.

"I'm there every step of the godsdamned way, Onmiel," I say again to drive the point home as I pepper kisses down her neck.

"I meant it when I said I was a monster," she mutters from her spot between my thighs. "The things I've done, Ten…"

"More than your sister?" I press, rubbing at one of her knees as she sighs, pulling them up tight to her chest.

"Isn't that enough? Killing your loved one? You did it to save people, Ten. I did it because I was hotheaded and foolhardy, and I thought I could control a power I barely even understood. She died because I was a fucking idiot."

"And you've made yourself pay the price ever since," I remind her. "You can't change that, Onmiel. You can only move on."

We fall silent as the moon reaches its peak. Eventually, she starts yawning. "I've got to go home and pack. I'll be back bright and early."

"Want some company?" I lick and suck my way along her exposed shoulder as she shudders in my arms.

"I just…I need a minute, Ten. I'm fucking reeling, and I just need a few hours to grab some sleep and hopefully wake up with a clearer mind. My brain feels like it ran a hundred miles today."

"I understand," I whisper, even though my direwolf howls at the idea of being parted from her for even a few hours.

Eventually, she starts to nod off in my arms, so I shift and run back, dropping her at the archives. She gives me a sleepy wave goodbye, and then I jog back to the apartment. I pack and shower and lie down for a few hours, knowing she'll be back soon.

∼

TEN: A DARK SHIFTER ROMANCE

Rough hands shake me awake what feels like mere minutes later.

"Ten, get up. We've got problems." Noire's voice is gruff and irritated. I leap out of bed, shaking the sleep out of my limbs as Ascelin appears in the doorway with a baleful look in my direction.

She reaches out, handing me a slip of paper. When I open it, I recognize Onmiel's handwriting.

Ayala Pack -

I've gone ahead to the Tempang. I'll admit to not sharing the whole truth yesterday. You journeying into the Tempang is practically a death sentence. Even with me to escort you, the reality is that my father won't wait to hear about Diana or the vampiri prophecy. He'll toss her into the Gate of Whispers without a backward glance simply because the gate has been calling her.

If I go alone, I can talk to him. I'll get a vial of blood for her, and I'll share the prophecy with him. We'll find another way. But I can't risk you.

Any of you.

Meet me at the edges of the Tempang if you must. But whatever you do, don't fucking come in, I beg you.

Ten, I'm sorry it had to be this way. This is the only chance I have to protect all of you and heal Diana for good.

I'm a half day ahead of you, so chances are by the time you read this, I'll already be well on my way to getting a cure for her.

See you soon,
Onmiel

The roar that leaves my chest shakes pictures off the wall as they fall to the ground, shattering. My muscles tense, and I grit my teeth. My direwolf rages in my chest, and finally, I can't hold him anymore. I scream as I fling myself back against the wall.

My direwolf explodes out of my chest, taking over as Noire grunts in surprise. I shove past him and sprint downstairs and out the door. He rages, demanding answers in our family bond. I ignore every command, running to Pengshur.

I barrel through security and into the archives, running every fucking level to be sure. There's nothing left of Onmiel but her lingering scent in our reading room and her assigned room on the fifth floor.

She fucking left. I can't believe it.

Except, I can. She's put her personal safety and well-being behind everything else to find a cure.

I sprint back to the house, shifting as I barge through the door. Inside, Jet hands me a pack, giving me a wry look.

"Now that's out of your system, we going to get your girl?"

"Right now," I snap. "We go for her right fucking *now*."

"Good," Noire growls as he comes around the corner. "Because Arliss is here with his ship, and it's time to go. And I want to know what the fuck happened with your direwolf. You weren't trying to shift, and it happened anyway. Care to fill me the fuck in?"

"Later," I growl. We've got a long ride ahead of us, even in Arliss's airship.

"Not later," Noire commands. His tone slaps me right in the face, tightening our bond until I struggle to breathe around it. He's gotten so strong since mating Diana, and that's obvious to me now. His pack alpha demand is almost impossible to ignore.

Turning, I roll my shoulders and growl. "We'll have plenty of hours on the ship to talk about it, brother. Not fucking now." Fury rolls in waves off me, my direwolf pressing up against my breastbone. He's furious and terrified. He wants Onmiel, and I'm losing control fast.

Noire's black eyes narrow, drifting down my body. He steps forward, and I'm vaguely aware of Jet and Renze coming closer. I don't know whose side they're on, but I let out a warning growl anyhow. Noire steps until we're nose to nose, then he leans in and scents me. It's an invasion of my space, and the resonant growl that erupts from my throat is a warning from my wolf to his.

Get the fuck away from me.

He shifts backward. "On the way, then, Tenebris. But rest assured, I want answers. Do you pose a threat to my mate like this?"

I snort at that. The last thing I want to do is hurt her. But my wolf is ready to rip into Noire for getting in my fucking space.

"Let's go," I bark.

Noire nods, dismissing me. I stalk back into the street where Arliss now sits in one of his giant mechanical airships. Double doors swing open as I strut inside and look ahead.

I'm coming for you, sweet girl, I think to myself. *And when I get you back, you're never leaving these arms. I didn't tell you I was obsessed with you, and I only hope I get the chance.*

CHAPTER THIRTY-ONE
ONMIEL

I look up at the Tempang in front of me. I haven't been home in years, but the forest has changed. Where the trees used to be a beautiful dark green, all lush, ancient ferns, and creaky vines, they're different now: they're visibly sick, black, and decaying. When I left, the forest was reeling from Zura's death, but it was still a healthy place. This is something different entirely, and I have a sneaking suspicion, *somehow*, I'm the reason why.

Sighing, I pull my pack higher over my shoulder and begin walking. It's a long way to the Volya village in the far northwest of the Tempang, but it won't be long before Father learns I'm back and retrieves me. It's the one thing I can count on.

The moment I cross from Deshali land into the forest, an eerie sense of foreboding snakes down my spine. The forest is dying. Not just sick, as I was told, but on its deathbed. I choke back a sob, wondering if my magic is responsible for all this. I don't have access to it, not in this form. I can only access it in Volya form, but I won't risk that unless it's a last resort.

If it turns out that I caused this when I killed Zura, Father will never let me leave. I'll have to stay here to fix what I broke. My only hope is that I can barter my life for a cure to Diana's illness. I can't let Ten's pack come into the forest; I've got to get to my father first.

Almost as if on cue, leaves rustle in a clearing up ahead. A gigantic, weathered figure appears. He's nearly ten feet tall, all long, spindly pale limbs, still cloaked in oatmeal-colored robes. His wide mouth, full of sharp teeth, is pursed disapprovingly. His rahken, the wide, flat bones that cover where a human's eyes would be, are angled together. Horns rise up behind them. His are the biggest in our clan...

I remember being proud of him as a child.

"Daughter," my father murmurs in ancient Volya. "You have returned."

"I didn't know," I say, inclining my head as I join him in the clearing, a single tear tracking a path down my cheek. "Is this me? My magic?"

"It is far more complicated, Onmiel," Father hisses, his voice soothing as he folds his hands in front of his waist. Even the wooden crown on his head seems to be fading, the wood dark and chipping at the edges as if it's already dry and dead. His wings look paper-thin, folded to his back and held slightly off the ground.

"Why not come for me?" I question. "You knew where I was going. If I did this, why not come for me?"

Lahkan lets out a laugh, but there's no mirth to it at all. "I will show you, daughter, why we could not leave. You will not believe your eyes when you see the horror that has haunted the Tempang since your departure. Come, let us go home. There is much work to do."

"Wait," I hedge. "I need something. I'll stay and help fix this no matter what, but you hurt a friend of mine, an omega. There was a prophecy about her, and I need your blood to heal her."

Father pauses and gives me a curious look. "Her life is hers to guard, Onmiel. If she comes and asks for the cure, I will provide it if you wish. But know this, Diana Ayala and the other queen were called by the gate herself. I will sacrifice them if I must."

My father glares at me, and there's ripe condescension on his angular, pale face before he gestures for me to follow. "Come, Onmiel. The forest will let us know if your friends arrive. In the meantime, there is something you need to see."

Gods, I hope it takes Ten a day or two to get here. That'll mean I've got that long to sort this out before I have to tell him I can never leave the Tempang again. Because worst comes to worst, Father would toss even me into the gate if it meant fixing the forest. Forest first. That's the Volya mission. Anything for the forest.

Even if it means sacrificing the future queen of the Volya clan.

CHAPTER THIRTY-TWO
TENEBRIS

I stand at the front of Arliss's boxy airship, tapping my foot as I stare out the glass-paned side window at our rented townhouse. He's taking his godsdamned time prepping and I'm ready to get on the road. He and Ascelin are in the middle of a standoff.

"My lap would make an excellent perch," he purrs, rubbing the top of his thigh suggestively. Asc gives him the middle finger and sits in the co-pilot chair, propping her feet up on the front. Arliss frowns at the mud on the bottom of her boots, but when her black brows lift, he says nothing.

"Cut the shit and get going," I snap. "She's ahead of us by hours. She could be in danger."

Arliss turns in the bucket seat and crosses his legs, bringing both hands to one knee as he gives me a condescending look. "In danger from her own family, Tenebris?"

I don't have an answer for that because I don't know if Onmiel is in danger. I just know she's risking herself for my pack, for people she barely knows. She's the most selfless, kind person I've ever met, and I'm dying without her here.

My hands tremble with the physical need to touch her, so I press them to the glass and look out, my forehead touching the cool surface as Arliss spins toward the front and puts the airship in gear.

Behind me, my pack lounges on the hovercar's benches. Diana lays down on one, her head in Noire's lap as he strokes hair away from her sweaty forehead. Jet, Renze, and Achaia occupy another, huddled closely together as they watch Diana with worried expressions despite their light chatter. Their black velzen, Rosu, lays at their feet and watches me, his long tail swishing lazily from side to side. I haven't seen him until right now, but somehow, I find his presence comforting.

My wolf recognizes a kindred spirit in the young predator, not that he looks young anymore. Several weeks ago, he was equivalent to a medium-sized dog. Now, he's about the size of a small pony. He's growing fast as hells, an indicator of the general sentiment of danger around our pack. His growth rate is in direct proportion to how often he feels his people need protecting.

If Onmiel were here, she and I would talk about that, and she'd have some quippy remark about velzen from a book I've not had the chance to read yet.

Why didn't you just take me with you, I think. It's not lost on me that I had a mate who wasn't fully honest with me. I don't want it to be like that between Onmiel and me.

I chose her, but now she's gone, too. What's worse is that she didn't feel she could tell me the whole truth. And I'm so fucking sure it's because she thinks it'll protect me in some way. She knew if she told me her plan, I'd insist on going with her.

Because the reality is that it happened fast, but I'm fucking obsessed with the beautiful librarian. I'm obsessed with everything about her. Her wild, white hair, gorgeous gray eyes and dorky expressions, her love of coffee and terrible rhythm when she dances.

My direwolf whines in my chest, and the noise echoes out of my mouth as I press my forehead harder to the glass, willing the airship to develop warp speed and spit us out at the mouth of the Tempang. I've got to get to her.

"Ten." Noire's voice is pure pack alpha command. He wants to know about my wolf now that we're on the way. I knew he wouldn't drop it, but I find myself not wanting to share. Noire's command has never bothered me, but right now, it rankles. Deep inside, my wolf paces and snarls. He dislikes Noire's command, and that unsettles me. I've never had trouble listening to my brother before.

When I turn, my eldest brother gestures to my chest, his dark eyes narrowed.

"What happened upstairs?"

He's referencing how when they told me Onmiel had gone ahead without us, my wolf forced a shift and took over, running the city looking for her. I let it happen, crazed with fear and need.

"My wolf has developed his own voice," I admit, crossing my arms as I lean up against the glass.

The airship is silent as everyone absorbs my words.

TEN: A DARK SHIFTER ROMANCE

Jet's eyes narrow as he internalizes what I said. "As in he has thoughts that are separate from yours?"

"He speaks to me," I confirm. "It started when I came to Pengshur."

Now, both my brothers are staring at me like I've got a dick sprouting out of my forehead.

Noire looks over at Jet. "You ever heard of something like this?"

Jet shakes his head and leans back, nudging Renze with his shoulder. "You?"

Renze cocks his head and looks at me like I'm a scientific specimen. "I have not, but that does not mean it isn't more common in alpha history, perhaps. We could venture to the vampiri court and ask our whisperer, but it would take time away from our mission. Something to consider once we have healed the Chosen One."

"Can you speak back to him?" Diana's voice is weak, but she shuffles upright and slumps against Noire's shoulder.

His eyes fill with worry as he wraps an arm carefully around her. She seems worse today, even though she improved yesterday and the day before. Dark red circles underscore both blue eyes, her cheeks sunken and her breathing shallow. She's on death's door, and if she reaches that threshold before we get to our destination, Noire will pull this fucking airship to pieces and kill everyone.

"Did he speak to you about Rama?" Arliss's question catches me off-guard, but I confirm it. The dagger that usually stabs me when I think about my dead mate is less noticeable now. She might have been fated to be mine, but I didn't choose her, and she was terrible in every possible way. I don't choose her now, and even if she were standing in front of me, I don't think I'd want her.

When I don't expand on my answer, Arliss shrugs and turns fully around to face me. "Since Diana's brother, Dore, was under the influence of the same drug as you, I asked Elizabet to run tests on it. Dore is still locked up at my compound, and I need to understand if his mind will ever be salvageable."

Diana is quiet at the mention of her twin. I'm equally perturbed. Dore was Rama's right-hand lieutenant, but she drugged him the same way she drugged me.

"And?" I wave my hand to encourage him.

Arliss's blue eyes flash with focus. "It was a hallucinogenic. It would have kept you and Dore in a perpetual state of struggling to focus. What's worse is it would have left you both susceptible to her suggestions."

I can't say I'm surprised at that. When the mechanical spider injecting the drug into my chest broke, the brain fog was a bitch to get clear of. Dore was probably on drugs for years. He may never recover.

What I am surprised at is how it doesn't feel like the betrayal it was. I grieved, then I got mad, and now I'm numb to the horrible shit Rama did to me. That was a past me, and I don't want to focus on that now.

After a quiet moment, I expand on my confirmation. "My wolf says she hurt him."

I shrug as I turn to look back out the window. Nobody speaks, but the airship is tense. Noire and Diana are bondmates. He knows the depth of that devotion, the intense need to protect and care. Diana would kill anybody who posed a real threat to Noire, that's the conviction of a bondmate. That my wolf feels our bondmate hurt him is unfathomable.

Need her, my wolf growls in my chest. *Need Miel.*

I know, buddy, I try to console him. The airship behind me is silent as a grave. Nobody knows what to say about him or what it means.

My entire pack, smart as they all are, is stunned into silence.

CHAPTER THIRTY-THREE
ONMIEL

I follow Father through the glade and out of the dappled sunlight. I took an ancient vampiri traveling orb here, something I apparently squirreled away in my apartment when I first arrived at Pengshur. Gods, I really did plan for every eventuality, assuming I'd have to come back here one day and relive my fucking godsawful memories.

The forest's sickness seeps into my very bones like a disease. The Tempang used to radiate peace and vibrant, verdant health to me. Now, every tree, every branch, every vine looks defeated and angry.

My father, Lahkan, comes to a stop in front of a broad tree, placing his weathered, pale hand on it as he murmurs an incantation under his breath. The tree's bark parts and opens into a doorway, glowing a sickly green from the inside out. Traveling trees should glow brightly.

Father's horns slump in defeat when he sees the way I stare at the tree.

I choke down a sob as I follow my father inside the small opening. Once we enter the tree, the space seems to expand, another glowing doorway opening on the tree's now-cavernous interior. I follow him through a series of passageways. Traveling trees are all one giant, interconnected organism that only Volya have access to. They allow us to move quickly all over the Tempang. As moderators and peacekeepers, it's imperative to our success to reach any of the forest's constituents fast.

Our footsteps are barely audible against the smooth bark floor of the tree's hallway. Ahead of me, Father's strides are sure and quick, but there's a slight limp to his gait that wasn't there when I left the forest.

"Father, are you injured?" My voice echoes in the hollow chamber as he looks over his shoulder, his flat profile visible as he shakes his head. It's so familiar. I've seen him look over his shoulder thousands of times. Being here with him hurts deep in my chest. Zura always took after him in looks. Looking at him now is like staring into her face.

Shame and grief sweep me up in a torrent.

"Simply getting older, daughter," is all he says. If he can sense my inner turmoil, he doesn't address it.

When it's clear he's not planning to expand on the topic of his limp, I reach for his hand and tug it, stopping us in the hallway so I can look up at him. Volya have no eyes, just the flat, wide rahken bones that cover where eyes would be. Our rahken allow us to better connect with the sentiment of the forest, connected as we are.

"Father, what's going on here? Please, talk to me."

Lahkan sighs and squeezes my fingers, which might be the most affection I've ever experienced from him—Zura was always his favorite, they were so similar in personality and appearance.

He shakes his head, his enormous horns nearly reaching the sides of the traveling tree's hall. "It will be easier to show you, child, because once we begin discussing this, you will have many questions. I would rather just show you everything."

It's a cryptic answer, but he turns, indicating the conversation is over. I follow him in complete silence for another five minutes, and then he takes a sharp right. This path leads to the far northwestern reaches of the Tempang, an area filled with dangerous, ancient creatures. Kurasao ice dragons, giant spiders, and some of the more ferocious centaur tribes. Even the Volya rarely venture there.

Goosebumps rise along the surface of my skin as Father stops in front of a door to the exterior and turns, a wrinkled finger pressed to his lips. "Quiet, child."

I nod, my stomach tumbling into knots as the traveling tree opens, depositing us into a part of the forest I haven't been in since my sister and I were much younger. This part of the Tempang should come with its own warning. It borders the area where my people live, but the creatures who make their home here thrive *only* here.

I follow Lahkan out of the tree, rubbing anxiously at my elbow as the door seals closed behind us. In human form like I am now, I'm nothing more than a snack to the sorts of monsters who inhabit this sordid corner of the Tempang. Not to mention Father doesn't look to be in great shape to defend me. Volya can be dangerous, and we all know how to fight, but Father is definitely well past his best fighting years.

The jungle in front of us is burnt and blackened, even the earth beneath our feet is scorched. Vines hang from the trees, but where they used to be a dark, healthy green, they now glow as if lava runs through them, red fire peeking out from cracked skin. But that can't be possible.

Wrong. It's so fucking wrong. I suck in a breath, but it barely fills my lungs as I take in the devastation around me.

I whip around, the sensation of fingers on the back of my neck so real, so tangible, I'm certain someone will be standing there. But there's no one. Father grips my wrist and pulls me to his side, snaking around the traveling tree and pulling me up a black dirt path to the top of a small hill.

Below us, a valley opens up. My mouth falls open. There used to be a river here and a vibrant forest that spilled over the banks into the water. Now, every tree is torn down and the earth is scorched every possible shade of brown. The earth itself is cracked open, streams of what looks like lava running underneath the dirt.

I clap my hand over my mouth. Father points down into the valley. At one end, there's an encampment, and all sorts of monsters mill around. I watch as a group of centaurs stomps at the water's edge. They turn from it, and everything is wrong. They don't look…normal. Flesh hangs from their bones, their movements jerky. Beyond them, the valley is filled with a dozen different monster species—species that normally never come close to one another if they can help it.

No matter the species, they move in that same, herky jerky way. Skin hangs from visibly protruding bones. Fire seems to run underneath their muscles, dripping down their limbs to pool wherever they step.

I open my mouth to ask my father what in the seven hells I'm looking at, but he puts his hand over my mouth, indicating I should be quiet. I follow his gaze to the opposite end of the valley where forges blow flames sky-high. There's a clanking sound, and even though it's far, I can barely make out centaurs pounding metal with giant hammers.

Weapons. The motley group below us is making weapons. But why? These monsters never congregate together, much less form any sort of army. The Tempang doesn't work that way. Every monster species has a territory of sorts, and most don't overlap in the slightest.

My father looks down at me, his face set into a mask of sorrow. He scoots back on his stomach before standing, gesturing for me to follow. I glance once more at the dark valley, filled to the brim with unrecognizable monsters. I don't know what this is, and I've never seen anything like it.

I jog quietly after my father, a sense of relief flooding me when the traveling tree opens and then seals shut behind us.

"What's wrong with the forest?" I demand of my father. "What were those...things?"

My father turns to me with a hardened set to the bones that split his face in half.

"The undead, Onmiel. The undead are ravaging the Tempang, and we cannot stop them."

⁓

I stare at my father in obvious confusion, struggling to comprehend what he just revealed.

"Undead? What do you mean? How can that be?" My blood chills as it pounds through my veins, so loud I can hear it in my ears. My breath comes in stilted gasps, my lungs struggling to move oxygen through my veins.

Lahkan indicates we should get going, and I follow him as he moves quickly through the tree's hallways.

"My warriors are ready to speak with you when we return home. We have much to catch up on, Onmiel. I wanted you to see this first because it is nearly unbelievable."

My mind is still reeling from what we saw in that glade, bodies dripping fiery blood, skin and flesh hanging from their bones. Red, visionless eyes.

I miss Ten.

The thought is there fast and flashes away as I hold in a groan. There's nothing I want more than his big arms to comfort me. I want his inquisitive mind to dig into this with me. I want him by my side. But also, I want him as far as humanly possible away from those things.

Father's being cagey, and as much as I'd love for Ten to be here to back me up, I'm terrified for the Ayala Pack to come to the forest.

I'm not a fool; I know they're on their way. There's no way Ten would let me go willingly, but I have to try to fix this. Diana is running out of time. But so is my forest, and somehow, it's my fault. I know it. That knowledge is curled around my heart like a snake waiting to strike. Father hasn't said as much, but I know he will. I can feel it.

All those thoughts dissipate when the traveling tree opens again, depositing us into a familiar, shady glen. I look up at the trees above, noting how unchanged they seem. This part of the forest still looks healthy and sentient, like we passed through an invisible barrier, and the Tempang here is still happy. The trees are a brilliant green, their leaves shimmering in the early afternoon light. Moss covers their trunks up as far as my eyes can see. It's exactly like it was the day I left.

I struggle to swallow around the lump in my throat.

There's noise ahead as Father exits the tree, his pale robes swaying softly behind him. He tucks his wings tightly to his back and his hands into his sleeves as he heads for our village.

I gulp as I watch him go. Somehow, my magic is the cause of this. I feel it in the way the trees here seem to tighten and shrink back at my presence when I step out of the tree.

They know something.

They recognize the same evil in me that I unleashed when Zura was killed. It was an accident, but my power is nearly limitless and totally uncontrollable. The Tempang may look like a simple forest—however, it's anything but. It's alive in its own way, and it's the Volya's mandate to protect *it* and the Gate of Whispers.

Closing my eyes, I concentrate on the gate herself. Before I hid my true form away behind my tattoo, I could always sense the gate and her connection to the Tempang. Now, when I focus on finding her in my mind's eye, I see nothing. I feel nothing. Running both hands through my long hair, I huff out a breath of frustration.

"I'll fix this," I mutter under my breath, placing my palm on the closest tree trunk. It shudders slightly under my touch. I jerk my hand away, looking up to see the tree's leaves quivering in the wind.

The forest is afraid of me.

I violated its trust when I tried to control and channel my unusual ability to communicate directly with the gate. That violation left mayhem and death in my wake. I deserted the Tempang to protect my clan, but it seems all I really did was leave behind a mess. I didn't face what I did, and that mistake has haunted everyone I love since.

Sick nerves bundle in my stomach, threatening to make me vomit. I hear my name called in a sharp tone and then a softer one. "Miel? Miel!"

It's my mother's voice, and that, at least, makes me feel good for the first time. My mother is one of my favorite beings in the entire world. She and I have always been so similar, whereas Zura was more like Lahken.

When I turn from the tree, I see my mother's slim, elegant figure dashing up the path, sunlight filtering through to shine on her. She hasn't aged a day, her broad mouth curved into a joyous smile as she runs to me.

I sprint from my spot, arms open, and jump up into hers the moment I'm close enough. Our bodies clash together, and because I'm so much smaller in this form, she wraps her arms all the way around me, crushing me to her chest. I inhale my mother's scent, all woodsy sunshine, like the forest itself is infused in her very skin.

"I have missed you so much, daughter," she whispers, swaying from side to side as if rocking a small child.

Laughing, I wipe the tears away and lean back to look at her. There's such evident joy on her face in the way she's smiling and how her horns are curled up high behind her forehead. I've always loved her horns. Where Father's are shaped broad and wide like a bull, Mother's slide back along her hairline like some kind of gorgeous, curly arrowhead. All Volya horns are different, but hers are so beautiful to me. Zura and I used to drive wooden aircab toys along her horns as children, playing loop-the-loop on the bone.

Zura's were just like hers, maybe the *only* way they were alike.

I suck in a slow, steadying breath. She sets me down and grabs my hand in hers.

"What happened here, Mother? It's my fault; I know it. The trees don't want my touch."

Her happy smile falls, and she nods. "It is not your fault, Onmiel, but we do believe your magic caused what's happening. Come. Father is with Kraven. We will celebrate your return over dinner, but for now, there is much to catch up on."

Kraven.

There's a name I haven't heard in ages. My former betrothed until I killed my sister and called off our engagement.

Mother pulls me by the hand toward the village, stroking my long, white hair with the other.

"You look good, Onmiel. Better than good. You are striking in this form, and your soul is peaceful. Tell me everything about your last eight years."

"Time for that later," I murmur as our village comes into view. Volya already gather around, gasping in shock when they see me. Most faces are angry, although they school them neutral as we approach. This is not a joyous homecoming, no matter how pleased my mother is to have me back.

I killed a clanmate, broke an engagement, and fled the forest, leaving behind whatever this current devastation is. I had no idea, but I suspect they don't want to hear about that.

We enter the village in silence. Mother keeps her hand firmly in mine in a silent show of support. It gives me a moment to look around at the village I grew up in.

It hasn't changed a bit. Multiple levels of beautiful wooden cottages are built into the broad efek trees. Dangling ropes and ladders connect each home to the next. The village appears to be the same size as it was when I left.

TEN: A DARK SHIFTER ROMANCE

I would have expected a few more houses by now, but maybe there are less children.

"Onmiel."

A masculine, gravelly voice breaks through my thoughts, calling my attention to what's in front of us. Mother halts, her claw-tipped fingers still threaded through mine.

My former betrothed stands in front of us.

Kraven.

Gods, he's still attractive despite the years that distance us. He's now taller than Father by half a head, long horns spreading wide before curling backward in what I'd call lazy circles that end in vicious iron-tipped points. He's packed on the pounds since I left, far more muscular than the gangly young male who courted me all those years ago. I used to daydream about stroking his horns while we fucked, but that seems like a lifetime ago.

That was back when Kraven smiled, if only for *me*, during stolen, secretive moments deep in the forest.

He's not smiling now.

Father tucks his hands deeper into the billowy sleeves of his robes, scowling over my shoulder. I hear footsteps, the crowd dissipating as he turns that scowl back to me, letting it fall away. He looks so tired, the rahken bones that cover the top half of his face sagging as if he doesn't have the energy to even keep that expression.

"Daughter, now that you have returned and seen the creatures, we need to tell you what you have missed."

"What you *caused*," Kraven corrects, crossing his enormous arms.

Okay, then. There's a significant amount of blame in his tone. I need to catch up fast.

Lahken glances at his second-in-command with an exasperated look.

"We are losing this war, Lahken," Kraven says softly. "She needs to understand the severity."

"Spit it out, then," I snap, disliking how the blame has fallen on me without me having a clear understanding of what's happening. "I'm back to help, so tell me everything."

"Come," Kraven snarls, turning from us and hunching slightly, his muscles flexing before he leaps up onto the first floor of the main Clan House.

Mother sighs but pulls me into her arms, leaping to follow him since I can't do it in this form. Father joins, landing gracefully on the front porch of the Clan House, where he holds his most important meetings.

"Thanks," I huff when Mother puts me down. There are a lot of ladders in my future since I can't leap between tree houses the way my clanmates do.

I walk into the enormous structure, a place I haven't been in almost ten years, not since Zura's death, not since the Volya leadership council voted not to kill me for my crimes.

It was an accident, they agreed.

Not that it made anyone feel any better.

Which is why I took myself out of the equation by leaving.

The Clan House is built into the middle of a massive, broad *efek* tree, its branches winding through the soaring, open room. A long, wide table in the middle is covered with maps and weapons, small vials of blood and other serums scattered here and there. They must have been working to heal someone before I arrived.

Kraven lays a map flat on the table's edge, pointing to the part of the forest Father and I visited earlier. "The demon queen rules there now, creating the monsters Lahken took you to see. They're infecting the forest piece by piece, and while the Gate of Whispers is doing everything she can to prevent them, they are a virus. We don't have long before the queen takes the gate, and then we're well and truly fucked."

I blink around the incredible amount of information he just shared, opting to start at the beginning.

"Demon queen? Taking the gate? What in the fuck?"

Kraven turns to me, the set of his rahken angry and resentful. "That is what we call her, Onmiel, yes. When Zura was killed, and you spoke to the gate, we didn't realize, but your power brought her back. You reanimated her, and nobody realized until it was too late, and you had gone."

I fall backward into a chair, looking from Kraven's handsome face to my father's and finally my mother's.

"Is it true?" I whisper. Every muscle in my body quivers, my lower lip following suit. Tears fill my eyes and threaten to spill over. Zura's alive? I brought her back?

My mother will tell me the truth without blaming me.

"Zura's alive?"

"No," Mother murmurs, shaking her head as her horns sag. "She is simply *returned*, child. She is reanimated, she is sentient, and she is preparing for war."

CHAPTER THIRTY-FOUR
TENEBRIS

"We're here." Arliss's voice cuts through the tension in the hovercar as I pace its length for the thousandth time. Ascelin vacates her seat next to him and pats it for me. I lower myself into it so I have the best view of the forest ahead of us.

Rosu pads up from the back and lays his head on my knee with a soft whine. I look down, surprised again at how fast he's growing. His fuzzy, long head covers half my thigh at this point.

I stroke my fingers between his doe-like black eyes as he begins purring. Inside my chest, my wolf responds in kind. He's always recognized the velzen as a friend, but it seems now more than ever, he appreciates the comfort.

We fly low over the scorched earth of Deshali, Rama's home province. Achaia leveled it with a war cry when Rama imprisoned her, and the ground doesn't appear to be recovering at all. I know there should be a pang in my chest, knowing we're closer to where we left her dead body. But instead of the grief that used to hit me, I feel only sorrow for the way things were between us.

I no longer want what she forced upon me.

Ahead of the airship, the Tempang Forest looms.

A dark, gloomy sense fills me as I look at it. Onmiel asked us not to follow her in. I'll give her anything in this world she wants, but that's one request I can't grant. It terrifies me to think of her going in to get help for us without a care for her own safety.

Then again, it doesn't surprise me at all. Onmiel is too selfless for words.

Gritting my teeth, I look at the edge of the forest, a depression settling in my soul that she felt the need to take this on by herself.

In my chest, my wolf stirs and whines, pressing against my ribcage to the point of discomfort. He's as worried for Onmiel as I am, whining and licking his lips in my mind's eye.

Behind me, Diana and Noire begin to argue. Noire's voice is barely above a snarl.

"I'm not risking taking you in there, omega. I'll go with Ten, Arliss, and Ascelin, and we'll return with a cure."

"Like hells you will," she barks. "If you're going, I'm going, and that's all there is to it."

Rosu hovers at my feet, letting out a soft mewl as he plops his shaggy butt on my shoe and focuses on the disagreement. Achaia and Renze join me to watch the show.

"Diana," Noire growls, standing to his full height as I turn to watch their showdown. Even near death, Diana's strength rolls off her in tangible waves. Despite being in obvious pain, she rises and butts against Noire with her chest, a deep growl rumbling from her throat. Her direwolf is bigger and meaner than Noire's, which is really saying something. Jet told me that when they fight, it's no-holds-barred. Their bonding triggered a strengthening in them both.

Diana isn't afraid of Noire; she never has been. Not even when Rama dumped her in the maze to be killed by us. We did hunt her, but nothing turned out the way we expected it to.

"We're partners, Noire," she reminds him, the harsh look on her face morphing into something more delicate, more pleading. "If we can't fix this, if we can't find a cure, or if Onmiel isn't successful, I want to spend every possible minute with you. You can understand that, can't you?"

I've never heard my brother whine, and I've never seen him crack under pressure, but he looks ready to fall to pieces as he collars her neck and pulls her into his arms, burying his face in her throat.

"Diana," he moans, his voice broken as I gulp back my own anguish. Watching them reminds me of those final moments with Rama, how I felt our bond fray and snap and shatter. I thought I'd die, then. Even now, it hurts to see another pair of bondmates and to know their bond is good and strong.

The only reason I'm even put back together is the woman who came into the Tempang to face monsters on behalf of my family.

I can't let Onmiel take this on by herself.

Arliss says nothing this whole time, but per usual, he's in our corner so long as it serves him. I'm aware of that, so I don't count on him. I know he's

TEN: A DARK SHIFTER ROMANCE

after information on carrow, and Onmiel told us a tribe lives here in the Tempang. It wouldn't surprise me if he deserts us at the earliest opportunity.

He sets the airship down gently several hundred yards in front of the forest, looking over at me with a wry expression.

"Don't want to take my ship in there and risk losing it. It might be our only means of escape." He says as if this is sage advice, but I suspect Arliss doesn't know that much about the Tempang. I, on the other hand, have been studying it since I was a child. My monster fascination began by learning everything I could about the forest, and it's never stopped.

"Arliss," I begin. "If the forest wants to take us, there will be no escaping. You cannot even begin to fathom what lives in there."

"Don't need to," he grumbles back. "I'm helping you, and then I have my own mission, remember?"

"Hopefully, those two things remain aligned," I growl. He might be traveling with us, but Arliss isn't technically part of our pack, no matter how close he and Ascelin seem to be at times.

As if to illustrate that point, she reaches out and aggressively slaps the back of his head.

He snarls and whips around, but all it does is anger her. She snaps her teeth at his jugular, and he leaps back just in time to dodge a slice of her claws.

They might as well be middle schoolers smacking each other around but secretly in love. I don't have time for this shit right now.

Slinging my backpack over my shoulders, I pound on the hovercar's doors. If the little I know about the Volya is true, they'll find us the moment we cross into the Tempang.

Rosu slinks out of the hovercar and stands quietly by my side, his dark eyes focused on the forest ahead. Jet, Renze, and Achaia join us. Achaia glances around at the blackened earth, her expression sorrowful. Renze leans close to her ear and whispers something. I watch her vivid green eyes close as she presses her cheek to his lips, seeming to seek comfort. Rosu twirls around them, winding through their legs or trying to. He's getting too big for that, and he nearly knocks Achaia to the ground when he tries.

It doesn't stop her from giggling or making cooing noises at the mammoth velzen.

I'd swear he's even grown since we entered the airship, but I don't know what's really possible for a vampiri velzen. He's part guard dog and part cat, but he'll be a warrior if he needs to be.

Noire exits the hovercar holding Diana's hand, although she looks ready to drop. Black circles under her eyes give her a ghostly appearance. She has hours, maybe a day or two max. My wolf can sense it.

Noire's eyes follow mine, and despite Diana growling at him, he picks her up in his arms and cradles her to his chest.

I can't watch how beautiful they are together any longer, so I turn and head for the forest, Rosu by my side. My wolf is anxious to get in there, to shift and run and rip the entire Tempang to the ground to find Onmiel. I don't think I'll breathe easy until I find her in one piece. And then I'm going to toss her over both thighs and spank her ass until it's raw for leaving me like she did.

My pack follows in our usual formation, and I have to say it gives me strength to have us all together. The Tempang is full of monsters, but the worst ones are right here, and they're on my side.

I stop in front of the thick treeline. It's almost like the forest can only grow to a specific point, and although it tries to spill over onto Deshali land, it just can't. Every root, every limb, every branch stops in a line as if held back by an invisible forcefield.

Jet growls next to me, "You want to do our usual formation in there, Ten?"

He means how I'm always in front, he and the vampiri cover the middle, and Noire brings up the rear.

Through our family bond, I poke at him. *Think Noire can focus on the rear right now?*

Jet's solemn eyes come to mine before he calls out over his shoulder. "Noire, stay in the middle with Diana so the vampiri can help protect her. I'll take your usual spot."

Noire says nothing but pushes through our small pack, surrounded by the vampiri. It's a testament to how sick she is that he didn't bother to fight Jet's suggestion. Jet gives me a worried look, his chocolate eyes flashing with concern.

"I will join you," Arliss croons, following Jet to the back. I'm sure he'll be looking for the first godsdamned opportunity to leave us, but I can't find it in myself to care.

I turn to my pack with a warning look. "Whatever happens, listen if I give you a command, alright?" Noire gets a serious, pointed look from me. "Even you, brother. In the Tempang, consider me your alpha. I know things about this place you can't fathom, and that could save us. It's fucking dangerous. Worse than the maze, even."

Noire's eyes are narrowed as he considers my words. Finally, he inclines his head to the side. "Noted, baby brother."

He hasn't called me that in ages, not since I broke double digits. But something about it warms my heart. For all that Noire is a fucking asshole, he was there every step of the way for me. He made a big deal out of every birthday by getting me rip-roaring drunk, even in the maze. He pushed through unbelievable odds to get me out of that hellhole. And then he crossed a continent and staged a coup to release me from her clutches.

Love you. I murmur it into our family bond so all my brothers and their mates can hear. I haven't had a chance to get to know Achaia well, but I'm including her because she's family now. And I hope there's a near future where I get to know the mermaid queen who saved Jet from his own demons.

There's a moment of silence, and Noire shifts Diana in his arms. She's practically catatonic, her lips open as she breathes through her mouth.

"Let's go," he growls. "We don't have much time."

I reach out to stroke a stray blonde lock from Diana's cheek. If she were upright, I'd rub my cheek along hers, but Noire's right. We've got to get moving.

I take the lead, stepping from Deshali land into the forest as my pack follows me. There's no visible barrier, but the moment we cross into the Tempang, the scent of ancient forest slaps me. There are trees growing out of trees, mushrooms as tall as I am, and vines slithering on their own across a barely-there path.

"Careful not to touch the vines; step over them," I caution. "They'll grab you if they feel you."

The vines can sense the vibration of our footsteps, but as long as nobody touches their surface, we'll be alright.

I'm focused, keeping an eye on everything around us. Still, my thoughts go to Onmiel. I'm fucking pissed she left and terrified she'll get hurt. We were building something, something important. I want to know where that 'something' will take us.

I lead for half an hour before I sense something is following us. I can't hear it or see it, but my wolf knows it's there. I let the pack pass until Arliss and I are eye-to-eye.

I cast a look around, but I can't see anything obviously amiss. My direwolf paces anxiously, though. Arliss seems to have come to the same conclusion I have, based on the look he gives me.

"Can you shift into carrow form and do a quick circle."

He hands me his pack and shifts into a slip of black smoke, dashing off into the trees. We continue to move forward quietly, but the sense that we're being followed doesn't leave me. If anything, it builds until there's pressure in my chest, and I'm resisting the urge to shift and attack. Around us, the forest has gone silent.

A sudden crashing sound puts us all on high alert. Noire barks for us to be steady in our family bond.

"It's Arliss," Jet hisses just as the bulky carrow bursts from between two trees in human form.

"Run!" he bellows, taking off up the slim path as I hiss at everyone to move. But what bursts through the trees just after Arliss makes my heart skip a beat. My wolf snaps against my breastbone the second we see it.

It's a centaur, but there's something horribly wrong with him. Muscular flesh hangs from his bones as rivulets of fire drip from fissures in his black coat. The rivulets drop from his belly as he takes a step toward me, and then the fire spreads to the trees, soaking into the nearest vines even as they struggle to move away from it.

A flash of realization goes through my mind. The Volya said the Tempang was sick. Is this what they meant? I've never heard of anything like what I'm seeing.

The centaur's crimson, cracked lips split into a sneer as he grips a long, jagged spear tightly in his hand. The tip of the spear drips with the same smudgy black essence as his body.

No touch, screams my wolf inside before urging me to flee from this being.

The centaur and I face off as I pull a dagger from my belt, lifting it high in hopes I can give my pack a head start. We can't outrun him without shifting, but despite the state of him, I suspect we won't make it far.

I relay all this to my brothers just as the centaur lunges, striking out with his front hooves as I dart to the side.

Up ahead, Ascelin and Arliss yell for Onmiel, hoping she's close enough to hear us. The centaur's head never turns to focus on them, though. Fuck, there must be more.

He slashes out with the spear just as he kicks rapidly with his front feet. Hooves dig into the tree above my head, chipping giant chunks away as I slice at his stomach, watching the muscles split under my blade.

The centaur rears backward with an ungodsly roar, nipping at his own side as black sludge drips from my knife.

As I watch, the goo begins to travel up the blade itself toward my hand.

Oh, fuck.

The centaur laughs, even as his slippery-looking intestines begin to spill from the gash in his stomach. I turn and fling the knife, burying it between his dark, glittering eyes.

Initially, he doesn't even react. After a tense moment, he yanks the knife out and glares at me, gaze full of bloodlust.

When I turn and run again, his laughter rings out behind me.

TEN: A DARK SHIFTER ROMANCE

Go, my wolf screams in my chest.

∼

Hoofbeats pound behind me but I don't dare turn and look. I smell water ahead, my entire pack sprinting toward it. Maybe we can lose the monster there.

I burst through the dense undergrowth into a clearing to see Noire diving through a small waterfall. He disappears behind it along with the rest of my pack.

Good, they're hidden.

My wolf bursts out of me, forcing a shift, at the same time the centaur clears a fallen tree and slams to a halt, gripping his long spear.

No touch, my direwolf snarls. *Wrong. Male wrong.*

I crouch low, waiting for my brothers and the vampiri to emerge from behind the water. I did a shit job of paying attention to what weapons, if any, we brought. But I can sense my pack distributing them behind the curtain of water. Thank fuck for Jet and his ability to plan for almost any scenario.

There's a flurry of activity in our pack bond, and then Jet and Noire refocus on the monster.

The centaur takes a few steps toward me and bellows, lifting his spear high. He throws it with shocking force. I'm able to sidestep it but he darts forward at the same time, swiping at me with a knife that's appeared in his other hand. I dive to the side and roll around him. He grabs the spear from where it thunked into the ground and turns. The force of his turn pulls guts and a plump, swollen organ through the hole in his side. The dark mass falls to the ground and then slithers off into the trees like it's sentient.

The fuck?

I've never heard of anything like this in all of my reading. I'd heard the Tempang was dangerous, but this? This is something unnatural. I don't know how to fight this.

Before I can say anything in our family bond, a percussive blast echoes across the pool of water in front of the falls. The centaur's head explodes into a black mist.

I fall back and away from him, rolling to ensure none of the offal reaches me.

Ascelin, Jet, and Noire run to my side. Asc holds a big-ass gun. She must have gotten it from Arliss because it's not from our pack.

She grimaces and holds a hand out for me. "Are you alright, Ten?"

I take her hand and nod, shifting and pulling to a stand.

Noire rounds me and steps to where the centaur's headless body now lies, crumpled in a heap on the ground.

"Don't get too close," I hiss. "It's infected or something…"

As we watch, the centaur's body begins to sink in on itself, almost like it's disintegrating in front of us. The black slime that covers it pools into long, thin strings and then begins to slip over the ground, disappearing into the forest.

Ascelin hisses and clicks out a string of words in vampiri before whistling for Renze. He jogs out from behind the waterfall and joins us to watch the last of the centaur disappear.

Moments later, the trees at the very edge of the clearing begin to fade from brilliant green to gray and finally black. They're dying right in front of us.

Jet and Noire watch the scene unfold in silence for a minute, and then Noire turns back to the waterfall.

"Let's get ahead of whatever the fuck this is and try to find the librarian. We need higher ground to make camp if we don't find her before dark."

He strides off toward the waterfall and re-emerges with Diana in his arms. He's followed by a concerned-looking Achaia and a frowning Arliss, who must've stayed hidden to protect Diana.

We fill them both in on what just happened, but what can we even say? Something monumental is happening here, and even though I've never been to the Tempang, I know this isn't normal. Even in the maze, I never saw a monster take a hit like that male did and keep moving.

An hour later, we haven't seen another centaur. We haven't seen any sort of animal, but we've managed to find another clearing with steppe-like, defensible outcroppings that should be a good spot to park for the night.

I'm frustrated that there's been no sign of Onmiel, but I don't know much about Volya. I don't even know where to start to find her.

Need little woman, my wolf growls. *Need Onmiel.*

I know, I say mournfully, rubbing at my chest. *We'll find her; I promise.*

He growls and curls up in my chest, falling asleep almost immediately. It's an odd sensation to feel his rumbly snores when I'm awake. It's almost like his consciousness is separating further and further from my own. I still don't know what to make of that.

When the hair on my nape lifts, I whip around to see Arliss unrolling a backpack across the steppe from me. Blue eyes are narrowed to the spot where my hand is still on my chest. Not much is known about carrow either, so I don't know what he's doing, but he's doing something. Examining me, maybe.

A scratchy sensation pokes at the edges of my mind, and I suspect it's Arliss fucking with me, somehow. I'm not in the godsdamned mood, so I let out a warning growl and unroll my own pack as far from him as possible.

Achaia and I gather wood, then start making a campfire. Jet drops to his haunches next to his mate, his dark eyes focused on me. "What do you make of the centaur, brother? You're the best read of any of us. Can we expect more of th—"

He's cut off by a gut-wrenching squeal. It's shrill and pained and then cuts off with a gurgly squelching noise. Our pack is up and in formation in two seconds, Diana and Achaia protectively placed between me, my brothers, and the vampiri.

There's a moment of silence, and then the bushes just below our flat outcropping explode in a flurry of motion. A dozen wild boar flee something just behind them, another centaur. No, two.

Fuck.

They haven't seen us yet, but it's just moments before they do.

A muscular chestnut female throws her spear, and it lodges in the gut of one of the boar, who goes to the ground in a cloud of dust and blood, squealing. The centaur grins triumphantly before looking up to see us. We're a solid twenty feet above the ground, but that puts her just six or eight feet below us.

She and the second centaur, another male, step closer to where we are and grin. At their feet, the pig screams as black sludge drips from the spear and sinks into its wound. It shudders, its cries growing more pained by the moment.

I don't take my eyes off the centaur.

Noire barks commands in our family bond. We're ready to fight our way out of here if we have to.

Then the trees part again, and more horse-like men and women join the two staring at us. The boar rises from the ground, its body now covered in tar, dripping rivulets of fire onto the forest floor. It turns beady red, flame-filled eyes on us, and snarls.

Rosu returns the angry noise, dropping to a crouch.

Oh, fuck.

CHAPTER THIRTY-FIVE
ONMIEL

The sun is just starting to fade. Gods, I miss Ten so fucking much. A shadowy figure appears in the doorway to the Clan House just as Kraven opens his mouth to deliver more bad news, I bet.

"The shifters have arrived. They are being attacked by Zura's centaurs."

"No!" I shout, leaping from my seat to run to the edge of the treehouse.

Kraven appears next to me with an angry huff, throwing one arm in front of me. "Stop, Onmiel. You can't possibly help with this. I will retrieve them, whoever is left alive."

Without another word, he leaps from the porch and sprints off into the forest, a host of warriors behind him.

In a panic, I turn to my parents. "I've got to go help them; I can't let the forest kill them. I came here for this pack!"

"We know, Onmiel," Father reminds me. "Kraven will find the queens. Be patient, child."

"Not your strong suit, I know," Mother says in a gently chiding tone. "Those who are meant to join us will."

I hate that fucking saying. It's a nice way of saying sometimes, people die, and so when you never get to see them again, you weren't meant to.

Growling, I yank at my hair as I jog out of the Clan House. I trot along the front porch and move quickly down the long ladder. It's thirty feet from the plank platform to the forest floor, but I make my way to the traveling tree where they'll have to emerge.

I'm fucking pissed I couldn't keep up with Kraven, and without being in my Volya form, I can't open the tree, either.

The pack would have had to enter the forest at the Deshali border, even though I begged them to wait for me. I fucking knew Ten wouldn't, and now they're in danger. I had hoped I was far enough ahead of them to take care of things before they arrived. It seems I was very fucking wrong.

I pace back and forth for a full quarter hour, terror clawing at my insides. There's a wooden creak, and the traveling tree splits wide. Two figures tumble out, fists flying so quickly I can barely see who's who. I leap out of the way as two bodies fall into the glade. I recognize Ten's mop of waves immediately, but Kraven's hands are around his neck as he throttles him.

I open my mouth to shout at them to stop, but the rest of Ayala Pack and my father's warriors spill out right after them, the traveling tree zipping closed behind them. Noire pops upright with Diana in his arms. Ascelin leaps forward but slams to a halt when Noire's arm flies up, catching her in the chest.

"What are you—" she shouts but follows Noire's nod.

Kraven's on the ground now, one of Ten's hands around his throat as the other yanks on Kraven's horns, smashing his head to the ground.

"Where is she?" Ten bellows.

Gods, he's going to rip Kraven's head from his shoulders.

"Ten!" I shout. "Ten, stop!"

Ten's head snaps to the side, eyes narrowing as his nostrils flare. The whiskey color of his irises is fully black. I've never seen him like this, out of his mind like a wild predator. He looks at me like he wants to eat me alive, and for the first time since I met him, I'm afraid.

Still, he's *Ten*. My Ten. And he's here.

He leaps gracefully off Kraven and looks at me. My father and the other Volya run to join us. Kraven leaps up in a flash to continue the fight, but Ten pays him no mind. Despite my fear, I run the short distance between us.

"Sweet girl," he growls, opening his arms wide as I leap up into them, his warm, comforting scent wrapping around me like the very real hug. He crushes me to his chest, both arms around my waist, as he purrs loudly, burying his face in my neck. He gulps in breath after breath like he forgot my scent and just needs it again.

"I'm sorry," I whisper. Was it just this morning I left Pengshur to come here and get ahead of him?

"You're in trouble," he huffs into the skin just below my ear. "So much fucking trouble, Onmiel."

I hold back a chuckle because Ten hauls me higher up into his arms and turns from everyone, stalking toward my mother and father, who stand shocked as they watch me wrapped around the big shifter. There are social norms when greeting Volya, but none of those seem to matter right now. I'm just so fucking relieved he's here and he seems to be in one piece.

I open my mouth to say something, but Ten continues past my parents as if they're not there, through the throng of onlookers and across the middle of the village. He heads straight for the Clan House in the center and leaps up onto the first level, stalking to the center, where he sets me carefully down on the broad table.

Ten's eyes don't leave mine, his dark pupils still wide as he steps back, never breaking the heated look. He backs up until he hits the wall, letting his head fall back against it as he licks his lips. "Why'd you leave?"

"Ten, I—"

"I mean, why'd you leave *me*, Onmiel? You can't possibly have thought I'd let you come do this alone."

"I hoped I'd have a cure and be out by the time you came for me," I admit. "The note explained the gate's prophecies. It's dangerous here for Diana and probably Achaia, too!"

Ten waves my explanation away, pushing off the wall to stalk back across the space between us. He shoves my thighs wide and plants himself between them, gripping my throat with his thumb pressed to my lower lip.

"We'll sort that out together," he commands, his voice going hard and low. "Never leave me like that again. Do you understand?"

I nod, submerged in Ten's dominance. I could no sooner deny him than my next breath, and when he leans even closer, using his thumb to press my head back, I let it fall.

His other hand is there, waiting, and his long fingers dig into my hair, wrapping it around his fist as he holds me caught in his arms. I squirm as his hips press to mine, the long outline of his erect cock rubbing against my clit.

Gods, I missed him *so* much. It's stupidly crazy to miss a person so much when you've known them for such a short time. And it's even more stupid to miss someone who just lost their mate in the last few weeks.

A squeak and a sigh fly out of my throat when Ten's lips come to my neck and bite hard enough to draw blood. His soft, warm tongue follows, sending a trill of nerves jangling up my spine.

"I need to hear your agreement, Onmiel. Say 'yes, alpha.'"

"Oh gods," I moan. This is so hot. I'm having one of the worst days of my life, but I'm so relieved and overwhelmed and amazed he's here, and this demanding tone is too much. "Yes, alpha," I state simply, grinding my hips against his. He leans further over me, pressing me against his forearm, and holding me up with his immense strength. I'm caught, and there's nowhere I'd rather be than right here.

Beautiful eyes come to mine again as he presses his lips gently to mine. "Never, Onmiel," he reiterates. "Rama never considered me a partner. She lied, schemed, and planned. She hurt me, *and* she hurt my direwolf." His voice breaks as he continues. "You aren't her, and I thank the gods every day for that. But if you leave me behind like that again, I'll wear your ass out so hard you won't sit for a week. Are we clear?"

Oh, fuck. Oh gods. He feels like I left him behind, the same way it sounds like Rama did. I didn't even consider that when I left. I left to *protect* him. Tears fill my eyes.

I open my mouth to reassure him that I would never, ever do that to him, but he closes his lips over mine, his tongue probing deep, and I lose all ability to think. Nothing exists outside of the exquisite dance of Ten's lips on mine, his kiss full of desperate need as he clutches me closer. One hand is still wrapped in my hair, and the other slides down my back and into my pants.

His fingers press all the way down to my ass, and he settles them there as his kiss grows more frantic until he's eating me alive, our bodies wildfire against each other. It's like we can't get close enough; it's like we need to become one in order to be whole. I've never been so fucking gone for a man like I am for him. It's exhilarating. It's *terrifying*.

Ten rips his mouth from mine and shoves me back, removing his hand from my pants but grabbing my waistband and yanking it down. The move sends my father's maps and papers flying, but Ten growls and jerks me to the middle of the table, crawling on top of me like a predator, his eyes on my breasts and stomach.

He drags them back up, pupils back to full black. With a snarl, his fangs descend, and he yanks my jeans all the way off, tossing them aside.

My gaze darts to the left. My parents or Kraven could show up at any moment. I never introduced anybody. His godsdamned brothers are right outside, but—

"Eyes on me," Ten commands, holding my gaze with his. He dips low, shoulder blades contracting as he buries his face between my thighs and sucks hard at my pussy lips. He pulls gently before sliding his tongue between them and sucking again. I've never had a male eat me out this roughly, and I'm dying from the overwhelm of Ten's stubble as he rubs his chin along my inner thigh and buries his tongue inside me.

My head threatens to fall back, but he growls, gripping my ass hard as he spreads me wide and turns his attention...lower.

All I can do is cry out as fireworks bundle and build in my core, my hips desperately thrusting to meet him. But I'm caught in his hands, forced to submit as a cry echoes out of my throat, his name falling from my lips as I struggle to breathe.

Soft lips suck at my pussy again before his tongue circles my clit, and when I gasp, Ten goes wild. He bites and sucks and tongues my clit until I explode in an inferno of ecstasy, screaming my fucking head off as I wet the table—and my father's maps—with a spurt of release.

Ten groans and grips my ass so hard I can feel bruises forming, but when his tongue spears deep inside me, and he shakes his head side to side like a godsdamned animal, I come again.

And then I come a third time when his mouth closes gently on my clit and rubs in soft, tender circles.

After wrenching three heartstopping orgasms from me, Ten sits up and slides a hand to possessively cup my sex.

"Never again, my sweet librarian," he growls. "Never leave me like that again." He utters that last command in nothing more than a whisper as I throw myself upright into his arms, wrapping my entire body around his again. I want him so much, to give him the same pleasure he gives me. I need to touch every inch of him, but I can hear shouting outside.

Ten pulls back from me, smiling as he strokes my hair over my shoulder. "I should never have given you space after we ran last night. I won't make that mistake again, Miel. Am I clear?"

Tears fill my eyes as the emotions from today hit me all at once. Devastation at leaving him behind, relief that he's safe. Determination to save Diana. Horror at what I left behind when I fled the Tempang all those years ago.

"Ten, there's so much to catch up on. There's more than Diana's prophecy. It's so much worse here than I thought," I whisper.

"I'm here for you," he reminds me. "Now, let's go back out there as a united force and get Diana healed. That's my second priority. You are my first."

If I didn't think my heart could physically burst in my chest, I know now it can. And if I didn't think I could fall in love so quickly, I've now been proven wrong because I'm in deep with Tenebris Ayala.

And that scares me more than anything I've ever done in my entire life.

CHAPTER THIRTY-SIX
TENEBRIS

My wolf paces in my chest, needing more of Onmiel. He's possessive and demanding now that we're here and she's within reach. It's just like the last few days in the damned library—I can't keep my hands off her. I'm obsessed, and as I follow her down the ladder to the glade in the center of the Volya's village, I find myself trying to remember if I was obsessed with Rama like this. And if I was, was it chemically induced, or was it because of the bond? I don't even care anymore.

I'll never have answers to that, and it doesn't even matter at this point. It's just that, while Onmiel wants me with every fiber of who she is, she's still worried about my dead mate. I can sense that the same way I sense she's struggling with whatever happened between this morning and right now.

There's a tense, anxious set to her trim shoulders as we approach the group to find Noire bellowing at two Volya.

It doesn't take a genius to guess what he's roaring about, but his dark eyes snap to me as he clutches Diana tightly to his chest.

"If you're done fucking the librarian, tell these motherfuckers to heal my godsdamned mate before I burn the entire Tempang to the ground."

Diana's no longer awake. She's slumped to his chest, her arms and legs limp as if her life has already drained away. I don't think I've ever seen Noire so unhinged.

Now that I'm not focused on reconnecting with Miel, I fall into my usual place in front of my pack. I don't give a fuck that this is her family. They've done nothing but put mine in danger, and I won't stand for it.

The two Volya turn to face us. One's a male, and one's a female. And based on the devastated look on the female's face, I'm guessing she's Onmiel's mother. Still, Miel addresses the male first. A wooden crown rises up between his curled horns, symbolizing him as the Volya king, then. Her father. I vaguely remember him from the last fight with Rama, but at that point, Rama was my only focus. This male is nothing but a blur in my memory banks.

"Father, please," Miel murmurs, dropping her head in deference. "I'll stay and fix this, but help Diana. I'm begging you." Her tone is respectful and cautious. I fucking hate it.

The Volya king frowns, the flat rahken bones that cover his eyes dipping in the center to form a vee. He may not have eyeballs, but there's no mistaking the disappointed, angry set of his expression. Sharp teeth gnash together as he considers Onmiel's plea. He glances over at the big fucker who came to get us and promptly insulted our entire pack.

Asshat.

"We've come a long way," I purr. "You *will* do this for us." I refuse to believe there's a future where we let Diana die.

The Volya male who fought me on the way here bristles and snarls, but there's a chorus of answering, furious hoots and growls from my pack.

"I'm not asking," Noire shouts again. "I'm telling you to fix this unless you want to have a feral fucking alpha rip this entire village to shreds."

The Volya king cocks his head to the side. I do recognize him now. He was there when everything went down with Rama. He didn't bother to try to save her, despite working with her, which makes me angry. All he wanted was to snatch Diana and Achaia and drag them back here. I pull Onmiel closer to me, ready to protect her if I need to.

Next to me, she shivers. She's giving off a nervous, anxious energy. I place my hand on her back, not taking my eyes from her father. After a long, tense minute, the king turns and gestures for us to follow, heading to the gigantic treehouse we just came from. The queen pauses for a moment, her focus on Onmiel. Her rahken are slumped in what looks like worry, but it's hard to be sure. Onmiel says nothing, and the older female turns to follow the king.

Stay focused, Jet reminds us in our family bond. *Stay alert.* I'm in front like always, sweeping my head from side to side as I watch for any signs of an attack.

A dozen Volya warriors surround our pack, but it doesn't matter. We've fought against worse odds, and I'm ready to if we need to do it again now. Curious faces, young and old, peek out from houses built high into wide trees surrounding a big, open glade. I notice a huge firepit in the middle. Something cooks on it, but the food has been deserted now that we're here.

The Volya king and queen leap up to the first floor of the biggest treehouse. Onmiel heads for the nearest ladder, and I follow behind her. Noire climbs up behind me, one-handed with the other around Diana's frail figure. When we arrive at the top, Renze and Ascelin flank them. Jet takes Noire's usual position behind all of us, Achaia in front of him. It's not lost on me that at the end of the day, Achaia alone could level this place if she wanted to. I wonder if the Volya are even aware that of all of us here, she's the most powerful...

I set Onmiel down on the wide, wooden plank floor. She blanches when one of the Volya warriors grabs the soaked maps and tosses them on the floor, giving her a disapproving look.

Inside, my wolf preens with pride.

We did this, he purrs to me. *Make her wet. Make Miel ready.*

We'll do it again later, I reassure him, sensing him retreat deeper inside again now that he's not so worried about finding her.

Lahken climbs onto a throne at the head of the table, perched a level higher than everyone else. Onmiel takes a seat next to me. I drop down next to her, dragging her closer so that I can hold onto both muscular, tense thighs. She's trembling and afraid. I'd rather put my mouth on her again to take some of that anxiety away, but she's hovering on a knife's edge, it seems.

"Set Diana Ayala in the center of the table, please," Lahken instructs Noire.

My brother growls, but climbs carefully to the center and seats himself, Diana's upper body resting within the cocoon of his muscular arms.

"It would be better if you were not close to her," the king drolls.

"I dare you to pry me from her," Noire snaps. "Your people did this to her. Fix it."

"Noire," Jet murmurs in a gentle tone. "We did it, alpha. We're here." *Calm the fuck down,* he shouts in our family bond.

My eyes rove continually around the room, watching how the warriors focus on guarding Lahken. Good. They won't be ready for us, if we need to fight our way through them.

Noire bristles, his grip never loosening on Diana, who groans softly from within his arms, clutching his shirt on one feeble hand.

Lahken swirls one hand in the air in front of himself, focusing on Diana. "I did not give Diana this injury; it was my second-in-command. You killed him."

I sense Noire holds back from whatever he wants to say, but Lahken continues.

"He had one mission if our meeting went awry—poison Diana Ayala or the Queen of the Sea to force you back here. We had no choice. We knew the gate was sending out prophecies about queens, but we could not travel the broader continent to retrieve them."

The snarl that rips out of Jet's throat sets my teeth on edge. He's standing on the other side of the table, Achaia wrapped in his arms. Renze is by their side, looking simultaneously bored and furious.

"I don't need a godsdamned history lesson. Fix it," Noire finally shouts. Our family bond is tight to the point of snapping. I want to stand to be ready for the fight that feels imminent, but I don't want to let go of Onmiel. She's practically vibrating with terror at this point. My wolf perks back up in my chest, focused on what's going on around us and ready to take over.

Onmiel stands and steps onto the wooden table, picking over maps and stacks of paper before dropping to both knees next to Noire. I'm on the edge of my seat, ready to rip her away from my violent brother, but when their gazes meet, his is desperate and hopeless.

She reaches up and cups his jaw carefully, rubbing his stubble with the pad of her thumb.

"We did it, Noire. We can fix this. Do you trust me?"

Noire's throat bobs. To my incredible horror, his dark eyes fill with tears that start to spill over onto his tan cheeks. Onmiel wipes them away carefully. Jet's gaze flicks over to me, but I can barely pull my eyes from Onmiel. She wraps one arm around Noire's waist and grabs Diana's hand with the other, clutching it to her chest.

"Go ahead, Father," she encourages.

You could hear a pin drop in the tense room, Lahken saying nothing as he stares curiously at his daughter.

After what feels like a lifetime, he reaches out with one hand, swirling it through the air in an intricate design. It's almost like he's drawing an invisible picture or a rune. I can't see anything happening, but the temperature in the room heats until a bead of sweat rolls down my face.

His movements grow quicker, a low chant leaving his pale, leathery lips. I don't understand the words, but Onmiel nods along with him.

A black mist begins to rise out of Diana's body. It's barely visible at first, but then it collects and pools into a dark sludge that hovers above her like a cloud. The mist writhes and spins like a snake swallowing itself. Lahken's voice grows louder until he's shouting the same words over and over.

There's a loud pop, and the sludge explodes into a fine mist and rains down onto the tabletop.

Diana shoots upright with a gasping scream, swiping at her clothes like she's crawling with insects.

Onmiel scoots out of Noire's way just as Diana turns in his arms, her face pale and drawn, but her eyes once again full of life, full of concern.

"Noire, are you—"

My pack alpha's lips crash into hers as he falls flat on his back, both arms clasped tightly around her. He kisses her like it's the last time he'll ever touch her, and watching them sends stabs of pain through me. I did the very same thing, not long ago, and it was the last time I ever kissed Rama. I hate that I'm even thinking about it. I hate the way she drifts into my brain sometimes when I don't want her there.

I shudder. Onmiel slips off the table and back into her chair, looking at me with a guarded expression.

The room feels tense, everyone silent as Noire and Diana stop kissing.

Lahken rises from his throne and opens long, spindly arms wide. "Welcome to our village, Ayala Pack. We will find temporary homes for each of you, but in return, you will help us heal the forest."

Renze is the first to speak up. I'm sure the second half of the Volya prophecy remains top of mind for him. "Speak plainly. Are you a danger to Achaia or Diana?"

Onmiel's father turns toward him, the bones that form the upper half of his face splitting into what looks like a scowl. It's shocking how expressive his face is despite having no eyes. The look he gives doesn't reassure me. I pull Onmiel closer as his scowl deepens.

"There was an accident, long ago," he begins, addressing the entire table.

Onmiel is stiff as a board next to me, her muscles trembling. I know instinctively what Lahken's going to share. It must be the story of her sister dying because she looks agonized about hearing it.

"My daughter Zura was killed, and in her grief, Onmiel attempted to use her ability to communicate with the gate to bring her sister back."

"Is that even possible?" Ascelin breaks in. "I have never heard of that sort of power."

Lahken shakes his head. "It is incredibly rare, even for a Volya. Only twice in history has a Volya received the gift of communication with the Gate of Whispers, who is mother to us all." He turns again, his expression a little softer this time. "Very little is known about that power, so none among us could even guide her. Typically, the gate communicates with us through prophecy…" His voice trails off and he pauses, looking at his folded hands.

"Onmiel's request to revive Zura did not work, so when she asked to be allowed to leave the Tempang and find her way among the half-breeds and humans, we were distraught, but we understood." Lahken suddenly looks years older, his horns drooping as he examines his hands again. When he looks up, he releases a sigh that sounds like the weight of the world is on his shoulders.

"We did not realize that Zura *did* return, just not as we knew her. She is undead and is building an army to take over the Tempang."

"What in the actual fuck?" Diana barks out.

"Why?" I question

Lahken nods at the outburst and turns to me. "The gate is the giver of life. I believe Onmiel has more than just the power to communicate with the gate. It's my belief that she channeled the gate's life-giving power into Zura. But we are not meant to return to this plane. Where Onmiel sought to give life, she brought only death."

There's a sob next to me. Onmiel throws her head back and covers her face with her hands.

My wolf snarls in my chest, demanding I pull her into my lap to comfort her. I hold her close, and she goes limp in my arms, tucking her face up under my chin. My wolf purrs loud enough to shake the chair underneath me.

Lahken isn't done. "Zura's former protective power became a formidable weapon when the gate brought her back. She cloaked the Tempang in a barrier. We cannot venture farther than the town just below Nacht. We are stuck here while she attempts to poison the very well from which all life on this continent is derived."

Jet growls from his seat next to Onmiel. "When you say stuck here…does that apply to us now that we're here?"

Of course, he'd focus on that first. I'm so horrified by this whole story and the tension rolling off Onmiel, I can't decide where to focus.

"It does," Lahken confirms. "The barrier has grown stronger. We used to be able to visit Nacht and now we cannot even do that, so none of you will be leaving either, I'm afraid. Not until Zura is defeated."

"So, what's the fucking plan?" Jet presses on, standing as he crosses his arms. "Why haven't you been able to defeat her yet?"

Lahkan sighs again and tucks his bony hands into his long, wide sleeves. Next to Onmiel, her mother is stiff as a board. Her wings are tucked up tight behind her back, her lips clenched tightly together. She stares across the room blankly like she's seeing a ghost.

The asshole of a male who fought me in the tree glowers at Onmiel before speaking, his voice angry and accusing. "We have been able to capture her once or twice, but she is almost constantly surrounded by her guards. If they bite or impale you, or if their black slime enters your body, you become one of them." His rahken stiffen and press against his head. "We have seen it happen over and over."

TEN: A DARK SHIFTER ROMANCE

Jet snarls. "Tell us again why she gives a fuck about the gate?"

The male answers Jet's snarl with a matching one of his own. "We assume she is drawn to its power, since Onmiel channeled the gate's power to revive her. The truth is that we do not know. We know only that she has been unable to breach the surface of the gate to poison it. If she is eventually able to poison the Gate of Whispers, all of Lombornei will fall..."

The giant, vaulted treehouse is silent as we take in what he just said. After a tense beat, Jet glances over at me with a wry frown. "Why are we always saving the continent, us Ayalas who never even cared to leave Siargao?"

Noire stands from the center of the table, Diana still in his arms. Although, he's holding her close now rather than holding her up. He walks across the tabletop and hops carefully down, depositing her in a chair. Jet, Renze, and Achaia are at his back. He glares over at the volya king.

"I haven't forgotten your part in Diana's injury. You tried to steal her from me once." Noire's eyes glitter with malice as his fangs descend, poking at his mouth. When he speaks, a shiver steals across my shoulder blades at the power in his voice. "Try to take my mate or my brother's mate again, and I'll kill you myself. Are we clear?"

The asshole next to the king snarls, a wide mouth full of cone-shaped sharp teeth snapping in Noire's direction. I bristle instinctively, gripping Onmiel tighter. She's no longer sobbing, but I'm at my wits end with this entire conversation. I'm ready to fight for my pack, banish this threat, and comfort my woman.

It's Diana who speaks first and breaks the tension. "We'll help you if we can, but let's agree now that this is a partnership. It's like my mate said: we won't be your victims. You don't know us, but rest assured, we're more than capable of laying waste to this place if we have to."

"It would do you no good," Lahken murmurs, shaking his head at her. "But I understand your need for a semblance of control. You have my vow, for now, that no harm will come to you or the sea queen."

"You tried to take us once," Achaia barks from behind Renze. "I want to know precisely what you planned to do and why you assumed it would fix anything at all."

The Volya king shakes his head but slumps against the wooden throne and puts his spindly fingers on the side of his face. "The gate demands blood, Queen of the Sea. She has sent prophecy after prophecy out into the world pulling the strings of fate across our continent. When she sends prophecies, the Volya receive a copy. We know the gate foretold Diana Winthrop's connection to Noire. We knew it spoke of sacrificing queens, and that is why we engaged with Rama to bring queens here. The gate demanded we sacrifice queens of land, sea and air, and we were prepared to offer either or both of you."

Achaia's expression goes from shock to fury in the span of a second. Renze's muscular arm slides around her waist, his focus on the Volya warriors as he snarls. All I hear is Rama's name ringing in my brain.

These are the beings who made her what she was, who hurt her and shaped and molded her into a fucking monster. And then they used her for their own godsdamned purposes.

I've heard enough.

I stand, glaring at the Volya king. When I speak, my voice echoes through the otherwise silent room.

"We stay only in support of Onmiel. Lift a finger against my pack, and you will regret the day the gate brought us here. Am I crystal clear?" My direwolf snaps his teeth behind my breastbone, ready to make his point as known as mine.

Volya warriors crowd around the king, but he merely sighs and nods his head in agreement. "Understood, Tenebris Ayala. For now, we are partners in this. Let us take a step back and start with formal introductions. Today has been unexpected and…trying."

Onmiel's body's shutting down, quivering as she looks at her lap. It's easy to see she's overwhelmed by all of this.

"Introductions later," I growl. "We need to regroup."

Lahken nods. "My wife, Anja, will assign you housing. Dinner is being prepared. Tomorrow, the work begins. Onmiel *must* fix this, or we are all doomed."

"Got that," I snap, disliking how he puts the responsibility squarely on her head. My wolf and I have a deep and pressing need to protect her from the entire world, and that includes her father and the asshole standing next to him who's looking at Onmiel as if she's his.

◦

Twenty awkward minutes later, we've each been given a small treehouse of our own, all in a row leading off the main circle of homes in the village. Noire and Diana disappear into theirs without a backward glance. I sense Jet has questions, but I can't entertain them right now. Ascelin goes with Arliss, although the irritated look on her face tells me Arliss is likely to get an earful. I'm a little surprised he's still here, now that Diana is healed.

My pack bond is flooded with emotions ranging from fury to anger to intense focus. It's the maze all over again. No matter what the Volya said, I don't fucking trust them.

Take a few minutes and regroup, Jet purrs into our bond. *We need a plan.*

I follow Onmiel into our assigned house. She hasn't said a fucking word since her father dropped the bombshell of her story. Wordlessly, she grabs a sweater from her backpack and wraps herself up. She studiously avoids my gaze, tucking her hands into the sleeves, her shoulders hunched as she examines the small space. The house is built around the interior of a broad tree, and all the furniture is carved from the interior of the tree itself.

I can't focus on how cozy it is at the moment, though, because she takes a step or two and just stops, her head falling forward. I hear the tears before I see one fall and splat on the polished wooden floor.

My wolf springs out of me then, taking over as we pad across the small space and butt into her. She turns with a fake smile as we shove her down onto the floor and lay our much larger weight on her lower half. My wolf plasters his head to her stomach, purring his heart out as she cries and strokes his nose.

Her arms go up around our head, and then she's clutching onto us like a baby monkey, sobbing. Like this, he's in charge, and he snuffles at her neck and chin, licking the tears away as they pool in the dip at the base of her throat.

She cries for a solid ten minutes, her face red and puffy as frustration and fear bleed from her. Eventually, the tears slow and subside, and she's wiped out, exhausted. She shimmies out from underneath us as we rise to stand in front of her, pressing our face to her chest.

"I'm gonna draw a bath," she says finally. "Gods, I'd kill for a coffee."

That makes my wolf huff, and when she gives us a quizzical look, we pace to my pack and pull out a bag of coffee grounds and a stack of filters. I shove at him, pushing him with my consciousness until he lets me shift back into human form.

"Ascelin packed them for you while I was raging around the library."

Onmiel's eyes flutter with worry but she smiles. "She's grouchy as fuck, but I think she loves me." Pale eyes dart up to mine. "Wait, raging around the library? What about the books?"

I do laugh aloud at that. Despite what I just said, she's worried about the godsdamned books.

"I didn't touch the books," I confirm. "I just ran and looked for you. When it comes to Asc, the more she loves you, the grouchier she is," I confirm.

"Like with Arliss," Onmiel whispers conspiratorially, seeming like herself for the first time since I got here.

"Just like with Arliss," I agree. When we fall silent, she begins to worry at the edges of her lower lip. "Tell me about the bath," I press. "How do we do that? Somehow, I imagine you snapping your fingers and it appearing out of thin air because I don't see any pipes around here."

Onmiel barks out a laugh before gesturing at her lithe form. "I don't have that sort of magic. Conjuring a bath out of thin air isn't one of my strengths. Unlike bringing people back from the fucking dead." Her voice goes low and mournful, but I tilt her chin up.

"You only brought her halfway back," I joke. "Don't give yourself too much credit."

Onmiel laughs, despite herself, and lets her cheek rest in my palm. "My family is so pissed."

"And I don't give a fuck about that," I remind her. "Anyone who isn't Ayala Pack is our enemy, even if they're related to you. Don't forget that, sweet girl."

"They're my family, Ten," she corrects, emphasizing the word.

"They might be, but they tried to rip mine apart," I growl. "The maze taught me one important lesson, Onmiel. Trust no one but my people."

She frowns and tucks a long strand of hair over her shoulder. I sense she disagrees, but I didn't come here for her family, and I don't care about the Tempang. I want out of here, and if we have to help them to accomplish that, that's the only reason I'll do it.

She frowns up at me. "I missed you so much, even though I saw you early this morning."

I reach out and stroke my fingers down her throat and along her collarbone. "We should always have been doing this together."

"Now, you're all stuck here," she presses on. "Even Diana, and we know what the prophecy said now. There's a very real chance this goes south for her. Or Achaia. I suppose the prophecy could be about her, even though Jet isn't a king."

"Whatever it is, we'll get through it together," I remind her. "We both need a bath, sweet girl, so tell me how to draw it, and then I'm going to feed you and fuck you, and we'll fix this tomorrow."

"Feed, fuck, fix?" she jokes with a wry look. "You make it sound easy, Ten."

CHAPTER THIRTY-SEVEN
ONMIEL

There's a hornet's nest of thoughts buzzing around in my brain, but I show Ten around the small treehouse. All the guest houses are the same: one main room with a seating area and small kitchen and then a bedroom with a swinging platform bed covered in plush woven sheets and downy pillows.

He follows me into the bathroom, where there's a secondary room with a toilet. The primary space holds a tub carved right out of the wood. This whole place has pipes; they just run up through the tree and aren't visible. I twist the water knob on as Ten laughs about how normal it is. He expected magic, but the guest houses are equipped for non-magical guests. Volya being the keepers of peace in the Tempang means we often entertain dignitaries or royalty from the Tempang's various kingdoms and clans.

It's so strange to be home. The village itself looks exactly how I left it. But my clanmates stare at me as if I'm the source of all their ills, and I am, in a way, even if I didn't mean what happened.

"Do you want to talk about it?" Ten's voice is low and reassuring as he wraps a big, warm arm around my middle. His lips come to my neck as one hand pulls my sheet of white hair over my shoulder, tucking it on the other side.

"I didn't think I'd bring her back," I admit. "I was distraught, and I asked the Gate of Whispers for help to fix what I'd done when Zura died. But nothing happened, of course. I can't use the gate's power. I mean, I didn't think I could. I just know I cried my eyes out and went home, and Zura was still there, shrouded for burial. I left after that to go to Pengshur, and that's the last I heard of it. But they were stuck here, this whole time, fighting her."

"You couldn't have known," Ten reminds me.

"I know that." I turn in his arms. "But everyone here suffered because I lost control of my magic in the first place. Why I thought I could fix anything is beyond me, but I was young and foolish."

"And grieving," Ten presses.

"Sometimes, we do funny things when we're grieving," I comment. Ten doesn't miss the insinuation, leaning up against the doorway and crossing his arms as he gives me a look.

"I'm not grieving Rama."

"How could you not be?" I press on. "It's been what, two or three weeks?"

Ten's lips purse into a thin line, but he reaches around behind me to cut the hot water off. Steady hands pull my shirt over my head and shove my pants down. Then he undresses himself and helps me into the tub, joining me so water splashes up over the sides and onto the wooden floor.

He makes a point to seat himself across the wooden tub from me, muscly arms resting along the side. Gods, he's so fucking beautiful like this. I wanted him the moment I saw him, staring up through the glass roof at the rain.

Eyes the color of the perfect cup of warm, caramel-infused coffee drift to mine. "I want to have this conversation now, Onmiel, because I want you to be clear on my stance. We've mentioned this before, but we're going to dive into the nitty-gritty tonight."

"Okay," I breathe out, my pulse skyrocketing at the way Ten licks his lips. He's rocking a kick-ass stubble that accentuates his square jaw and dark hair. He's never looked hotter to me than he does right now, whiskey-brown eyes flashing with focus as he shifts in the tub, reaching for a bar of soap. He crosses the tub and straddles me where I sit on a ledge that's built into the inside of the basin.

Large hands come to my neck as he rubs the soap gently on it, kneading my stiff, tired muscles with his big fingers.

"The worst thing I've ever done was kill my bondmate. I thought I'd die from the pain of it. I wished I did, in those first days after she was gone. Especially when I watched Noire and Diana. They're bondmates, too," he points out. I could have guessed that, though. Their love is practically an obsession.

"Was it like that for you, the way Noire and Diana are?" This is one of the many questions I want to ask but am terrified to know the answer to.

"In a way," he confirms. "But I was also drugged the entire time I was with her. I guess she didn't trust that I'd love her without that chemical addiction, or maybe she just wanted me compliant. I have no idea what it would have been like if we'd just been two people bonded by the fates with nothing else between us."

"Will you not wonder for the rest of your life?" I can barely get the question out as Ten's strong hands move to my shoulders.

He shakes his head with an easy, slow smile. "I won't. And it took meeting you to realize it." His beautiful eyes come to mine as he washes my chin and the skin just under my ears. "She never trusted me, never supported me, never backed me up. She hurt me and my wolf over and over again with her lies and deceit.

"She came into my home and killed my friends and family, and then she groomed me like a godsdamned predator until I came of age. And somehow, this world thought it made sense for her to be my bondmate. But the reality is that she would never have been my *choice*. I'm glad I killed her because I would have lived my entire life under her thumb, not as her equal in any way."

His gaze locks onto mine with such intensity I can barely breathe. I want to believe every one of these words because they speak to the truth I feel in my soul.

He continues. "Mark my words, sweet girl. I have a choice now, and I choose you. Every fucking time I get the chance to, I'll choose you."

I want to believe what Ten is saying with such ferocity that I can barely fathom it. I want him to be my sunrises and sunsets and every moment in between, but there's still a niggling doubt.

"Spit it out," he laughs. "You're still worried. Be blunt, my coffee-loving librarian."

I fist both hands and cover my mouth, almost afraid to say the words aloud. "Do you worry you've gone from being obsessed about her to obsessed about me? Don't you think you'd be better off being alone for a while and learning who you are without a partner and without the maze?"

Gods, I feel like an asshole for asking that question, but it's at the root of what I need to know. I don't want Ten to get hurt; I can't let that happen. Ten is a fucking national treasure, and he should be protected as such.

Ten's eyes narrow, falling to my lips. "I'll never not be obsessed with you. And the reason I'm obsessed with you is because you're perfect for me. If I could have built the woman I wanted for myself out of all my hopes and dreams, it'd be you, Onmiel. Dorky, hot, loves books, enjoys adventure, fascinated by learning, kind, and addicted to my knot."

I laugh aloud at that one, despite his serious tone. "I can't be addicted to your knot; I've never ridden it."

Ten's responding laugh is so deeply sensual that heat floods my system.

"You will, Miel," he growls.

I clamp my thighs together.

He grips my throat and squeezes, pulling me flush to his chest. "My perfect woman, we're going to rectify that situation tonight, and once you've had this knot, you'll stop worrying. I'm going to bury my teeth in your throat and take from you, Onmiel. What do you think?"

I make a choice then, one I desperately hope won't bite me in the ass. I choose to believe Ten when he says he wants me, that he's obsessed with me, and it'll only ever be me. I choose him because I need someone who's 100% in my court, and there's nobody else on this continent who will be there like he will. I choose to put my trust in Ten, simply because he asked me to.

"Give it to me," I growl, throwing my arms around his neck as he begins to purr.

"Oh, my good, sweet girl," he croons. "Are you ready to get dicked down by a big-ass alpha?"

"Gods, yes. We'll see how it compares to my dildo," I snark.

Ten roars with laughter and stands, pulling us both out of the tub and stalking into my bedroom. He tosses me in the middle and climbs on top of me, his cock swinging against his leg as he lowers himself to rub it through my already-slick folds.

"It's bigger than your dildo, Onmiel," he growls. "A whole lot fucking bigger."

CHAPTER THIRTY-EIGHT
TENEBRIS

Onmiel's eyes are hooded with lust, and while I don't feel her in a mate bond, I read her body language like a favorite book. She's relaxed, comfortable. I am her safe haven, and as long as I live, I'll work to deserve her.

She's worried I'm obsessed with her, and she's right to be. I *am* besotted. Deep inside, my wolf preens at having her in my arms.

Little mate good. Make her happy.

I'm done wondering how he's got his own thoughts about the matter. I'd rather lean into his presence and use it to my advantage to get us out of here and somewhere safe.

Yes, our little librarian is perfect, I confirm. He purrs louder at my agreement.

She arches her back, my little hussy, pressing small breasts closer to my face as I nuzzle them with a low, needy growl. I drag my stubble along the underneath of one soft mound before pulling the hard nipple between my teeth. Onmiel hisses, and it makes my balls draw up tense and tight.

I'm finally going to fuck her. I'd be a damned liar if I didn't admit to having thought about this many times since we met. Not that first day or two, but as time passed and we became friends, my brain and my wolf went there so fast.

Thin hips notch and grind against mine, my cock sliding along her wet heat as she teases me. We were friends first, even though we were friends who wanted to fuck. We've never discussed her likes or dislikes in the bedroom, but based on what I saw when I barged into her room in the library, my girl likes a tease.

Reaching my hand around her waist, I flip her onto her belly, loving how she presses her ass back to meet me.

"You're my favorite book, Miel." I stroke my fingers down the length of her spine, watching goosebumps trail in their wake. "I want to turn every one of your pages, sweet girl. I need every one of your chapters to include my story."

She groans when I hover over her and begin kissing and nipping my way up her back. By the time I get to her shoulders, she's keening underneath me.

"Gods, Ten," she cries out. "I never knew book-sex talk could be so fucking hot." She lets out a little whine.

Chuckling, I collar the back of her neck, pushing her down harder into the soft sheets. Her tattoo shocks me, but the pain travels through my system and spreads between my legs, morphing into a heatwave of searing pleasure.

"How do you want me?" I growl into her ear, my voice rough and needy. I'm going to give it to her hard, but I want to hear her ask me for it.

Onmiel pulls her hair over her shoulder, pressing up on her elbows so she can rub her cheek against my jaw. "I want you unleashed," she whispers, her voice tentative but teasing. "I want you wild, alpha."

Laughing, I rear back and grip her hips, thrusting against her slowly, my cock spearing between her thighs as she moans. She coats me in sweet honey, her breaths quick, her eyes squeezed shut as she grips the sheets.

I want to tease her for hours until she detonates on my cock, but I'm losing control, watching her below me.

Growling, I grip her neck and flip us again, pulling her into my lap with a snarl. I grab both thighs and lift her before yanking her down onto my waiting cock, filling her in one deep punch of my hips.

Onmiel's head falls back, lips open in a silent scream as her pussy clenches over and over around my girth. I'm big, even for an alpha.

"Too much," she gasps out. "You're too much, Ten. Gods, I'm dying…"

"I'm exactly right." I laugh, guiding her up off my dick and back down slowly. Her channel relaxes the second time I impale her, her legs quivering as I revel in finally touching her like this. My mind flashes back to doing this with Rama, how she and I were a catastrophic whirlwind in the bedroom.

Will Onmiel like that? Would she like the things I like? Because I like it really fucking rough.

I think Onmiel would enjoy anything I dish out, so I snarl and pull her off my cock, tossing her against the wall as I slip back between her thighs with a hard thrust. She cries out, her pussy spasming around me as her chest heaves.

TEN: A DARK SHIFTER ROMANCE

"You ready for more, my sweet?" I purr, picking up a slow, teasing pace. In, out, in, out. Onmiel wails every time I thrust back in, her hands clawing at my chest as she tightens around me again. "You're gonna come from this tease, aren't you?" I question, growling in her ear as goosebumps spread along her pale skin.

Sure as shit, her head hits the wall as she grits her teeth and screams, and the way her pleasure rings out in our room sends me over the edge. I snap my teeth around her throat and bite, fucking her through one blistering orgasm and into another, her blood filling my mouth as she thrashes in my arms.

I don't come, focused as I am on her ecstasy, but as her release fades, we fall back to the bed with her on top of me. Onmiel's eyes are glittering jewels of intensity in the low light of the cabin. Her upper lip curls into a sneer as she growls at me.

"More, alpha," she demands. "I need a whole lot more of that."

"Done," I snap, yowling when she grips my cock and seats herself on me with a cry of pleasure.

An hour later, I've taken her four times, and the heat between us is just slowing to a simmer. I carry her into the bath and fuck her there, cleaning her as I go, and when she finally begins to drift off in my arms, I watch her sleep.

I don't trust the fucking Volya, and I'm on edge for my brothers and their mates. Safety is an illusion.

Even so, for the first time in a long time, I feel something close to peace with Onmiel snoring in my arms. Deep inside me, my wolf purrs his agreement, and together, we hold her for hours.

∽

Brother. Jet's gentle nudge in our bond has my eyes blinking open. I fell asleep with my girl, and it felt good. *You awake? I want to do a little reconnaissance.*

Be there in five, I grumble.

Onmiel is still fast asleep, her pink lips parted as she snores. She's had an absolute shit day, and part of me doesn't want her to see me taking stock of the village she grew up in. These might be her people, but there's clearly no love lost between them after what happened with Zura. The only one who didn't appear to place all the blame on her shoulders is her mother.

I hop quietly out of the treehouse, not bothering to dress. Noire, Jet, and Diana are there waiting. Diana looks amazing, and I pull her into my arms for a quick hug and cheek brush.

"You look good, omega," I huff into her ear. "Healed."

When we part, she squeezes my arm. "I *feel* good, thanks to Onmiel. I'll thank her later." Blue eyes take in our surroundings. She's as watchful as I am. Noire never takes his eyes off what's in front of us. The strength of their connection is almost tangible in our family bond, like they're the bedrock the rest of us are formed on. I hadn't realized that was missing with her being sick. There's something supremely comforting about having it back. She's a peaceful river of honey easing harsh feelings and worries.

Jet jerks his head toward the dense forest at the end of our "street". *Usual formation, I want to circle the whole village and get a sense of what this place is like. I don't trust these fuckers not to try something with the girls again, and I'd rather not have to rip Onmiel's family to shreds.*

I nod and call my wolf. We shift easily and jog toward the outer edge of the village, slinking off into the dark forest. He's happy to be free and as anxious as I am to get a sense of the Volya. Like any potential threat, we need to know everything we can about them. My brothers shift behind me, although Diana remains in human form, padding along beside Jet. Noire is back to his normal position, bringing up the rear.

We walk for almost an hour in ever larger, concentric circles. As far as I can tell, there are no defenses and no traps unless there's something magical I can't see. I wouldn't put it past the Volya after watching Lahken heal Diana with a swirl of his hand. Unfortunately, there's no way for us to know much about their magic.

They seem clean, Jet growls into our family bond. *I don't sense anything amiss.*

Let's go through the village itself, Noire says. *I want to lay eyes on the people. I thought I saw children, and that says a lot about their intent.*

I'd shudder at how callous he is about children, but he's right. Slinking beneath the treehouses, I direct us to the center of the village, where the large fire pit is. Embers burn brightly underneath three large pots that bubble with something that smells delicious. Half a dozen Volya in long, pale robes are cutting vegetables, stirring what's in the pot, and talking in low tones.

One of them steps carefully to the side to make way for me when I appear next to her, but a quick incline of her head seems respectful enough. A child runs from between two houses and joins her. She keeps the child on one side, but they don't leave. Instead, she gives the child a long, wooden spoon and sets her the task of stirring what they're cooking.

"It's soup," a low voice barks.

I turn to see Kraven, that fucker, leap out of the big treehouse in the middle and land gracefully on his feet. He stands and crosses the clearing to the firepit, glaring down at me from his much taller height.

"Well," he snipes, "are you sufficiently regrouped to do something about Zura? Or does it take direwolves longer to get their shit together?"

My wolf snarls just as a softer voice echoes across the clearing.

"Kraven, you're needed by the king." It's Onmiel's mother, who leaps out of the Clan House, too, and crosses to us. She tucks each hand in her opposite sleeve and gives Kraven an imperious look, her chin held high.

I follow it up with an equally snide look of my own, my brothers and Diana coming to my side.

Kraven snarls at me, thin lips splitting to show off rows of conical, sharp teeth. He's a dangerous predator attempting a show of force, and I'd love nothing better than to rip him a new one. But I'm not an idiot, and eviscerating a warrior who's temporarily aligned with us isn't a good idea, no matter how much I dislike him.

When I don't back down, he turns and inclines his horns low at Onmiel's mother.

"My queen," he murmurs, sidestepping her and leaving.

She doesn't watch him go but turns to us with a smile. It reminds me of Onmiel's smile, for all that her mouth shape is totally different. She walks around the edge of our group, seeming to examine us until Diana finally steps in front of all three of our wolves.

"What are you doing?"

The queen grins even bigger and then reaches out to Jet, laying her hand between my brother's eyes. He jerks back, his lips pulled into a snarl, but she pays him no mind.

"Your wolves are strong, which is a good and lucky thing." She turns to me. "Yours feels different, though." With a shrug, she lifts her hand from Jet's face and moves to me. "May I?"

I push forward enough for her palm to connect with my nose. Her skin is warm and soft, and she rubs gently at the bridge of my snout.

"As I thought," she says in a kind tone. "We have not been very good hosts, so I will attempt to rectify that now. There were many Volya clans; now, very few remain, and those hide far from here. Our clan is the most connected to the gate. We are her guardians and her wards. As such, most of the Volya here have some element of power. Mine is that I read auras." She looks at me, her rahken bones held high. "Your aura is different from everyone else's, and I think that is because of your wolf."

Onmiel's mother leans in closer, her lips nearly brushing my ear. "You are different, are you not?"

My wolf preens but doesn't sense anything amiss about her. I don't bother to shift to answer.

My brothers and Diana pepper our family bond with questions, but I can't focus enough to answer them either.

"How so?" Diana questions.

The queen straightens up and smiles. "Half-breeds descend from the direwolves of the Tempang, who could not shift and live their lives in wolf form. There are many packs, and we have interacted with them many times through the years. Tenebris's reminds me of theirs, although why that should be, I cannot say."

"I was there when he was born," Noire shifts to snap. "I watched him come into this world from our mother's body. What are you saying?"

The queen holds up both hands in apology. "I do not mean he is not your brother. I mean, simply, that he is something other, as well."

I've heard enough. I don't know or even care why my wolf is different right now. I'd like to dive into it, but I want to do that with Onmiel when we're away from all this bullshit, and she's safe and happy. Everything is on hold until then.

I pull away from her mother and head back for the treehouse. I've been gone from her for too long.

Even so, I sense the queen's focus on me as I leave, and it's unsettling.

CHAPTER THIRTY-NINE
ONMIEL

I wake in the morning, wrapped tightly in Ten's arms. I couldn't have fathomed this a few days ago, but here we are, acting like we're… together. Which we are, I suppose, because he chose me, and I decided to take him for a man of his word.

I'd be lying if I didn't admit to worrying that he killed his bondmate—a bond fated by the stars, according to shifter lore—just weeks ago. But I won't do to Ten what she did. I won't deny him the chance to make his own choices or be an active partner in a relationship. So, despite my misgivings, I'm leaning into what we are.

I'm just praying I don't get my heart trampled on and ripped to shreds as a result. I resolve to enjoy him while I have him because there's every chance that fixing what Zura is doing to the Tempang is an effort that'll kill me…or all of us.

"You're scowling," Ten murmurs, reaching out to stroke his long fingers down the bridge of my nose. "What're you grumpy about?" Chocolate eyes spark with mischief, despite the serious question. His eyes are so godsdamned beautiful.

"I was thinking about Zura," I admit. "How I created her, and what I might need to do to…put her back or whatever."

Ten sighs, but more than anything, it sounds upset for me. The stroking doesn't stop, but he shifts closer and shoves one muscular calf through my legs.

"Want to tell me something about her from before?"

"She liked daisies," I offer. "And she was a daddy's girl. She and Lahken were very close."

Ten frowns. "Wanna go deeper than that, sweet girl? Or is surface level what you've got energy for right now?"

I take a moment. I've just woken up, and the stressors of last night are piling up around me again.

Ten pulls me close to his chest and tucks my head under his chin, his stubble tickling my scalp. A purr rumbles from deep in his chest, vibrating against my skin. It's so comforting, even though I'm not an omega of his people. I feel safe here, wrapped in his arms. Like no matter what bullshit is happening outside the window, Ten will never let anything happen to me.

A sudden, irritated growl joins the purr, and he sits up in bed. "Someone's coming. That big motherfucker who tried to fight me."

"Kraven," I groan, sitting up to pull my clothes on. "He's father's right hand now, I guess."

"We killed the other one," Ten murmurs. "When Diana was injured."

I frown. I knew Etren my whole childhood, and to hear he's gone is a blow. But I can't start counting sins based on what's happened between my clan, the shifters, and the vampiri. I'll be here all day if I start adding up where everyone went wrong, starting with myself.

A sharp rap at the door announces Kraven's presence, and then he lets himself into the front room, despite a warning snarl from Ten. Anxious to put myself between them and ward off any more fighting, I leave the bedroom and incline my head to Kraven in the way of our people—forehead down, sliding my fingertips out and along the horns I don't have in this form.

Kraven returns the gesture, his rahken curving in irritation when he notices Ten emerge from the bedroom behind me. I wonder how he feels about all of this. I broke off our engagement to leave the Tempang, but it's been eight years since I saw him.

Kraven's focus moves back to me. "Your father requires your presence in the Clan House as soon as you can. We'll take breakfast there, but we need a plan. Immediately."

Ten presses himself to my back and kisses my shoulder tenderly. "I'll come with you, Miel."

Kraven says nothing, but I can tell he's intensely irritated that Ten's offered to join. With a last withering shake of his horns, he turns from the room and leaves, leaping off the open porch.

"Don't like him," Ten growls into my neck, peppering me with possessive kisses and light nips. "If we were still in the maze, I'd kill him for looking at you the way he does. Maybe I'd have cornered him in the church and ripped him to shreds on the altar. What do you think, my sweet?"

The picture he paints both chills me and makes me wet. That Ten would protect me like that makes me want to toss him on the ground, but I think he's right that he doesn't know how to be outside the maze with normal people, especially surrounded by danger. The library was its own insulated world, but being in the Tempang is different; it's dangerous.

"So, you can tell there's a history there."

"Of course." Ten chuckles. "I bet he doesn't know shit about book spines, though. Or the magic of the Magelang Map. Or how you like your coffee."

"Or where my clit is," I whisper conspiratorially, giving Ten a teasing wink to relieve the moment's tension.

He snickers as he slides a strong hand between my thighs, his thumb rubbing a gentle circle over my still-sensitive mound.

"I know where *everything* is," he says. "And I intend to explore it further tonight. I've only just begun to catalog every inch of you, Onmiel, and I am far from done."

"Deal," I breathe out as I press both hands to his chest. "I'm glad you're coming today. I might be home, but I feel ganged up on here because of what happened." It's hard for me to admit that how I hoped if I ever returned home, it would be under happy conditions. The reality is, I left a mess behind me, and it's my job to clean it up. I understand why my clan isn't happy to see me. But it was also an accident, and had I known, I'd have returned far sooner.

"I've got you," Ten reminds me, gripping my chin as he slants his mouth over mine. His tongue probes softly inside my mouth, teasing me because he knows *exactly* what to do with that tongue. I moan as the kiss deepens, the big alpha pulling me into his arms as one hand goes to my throat and the other wraps through my hair.

"Fucking love this hair," he growls, pulling on it to expose my neck to his hungry gaze. Everything about Ten is predatory, but the way he eyes my neck —which still bears evidence of his bite—makes me hot. "I loved it the moment I saw it in the lake." He presses a kiss to the scabs from where he bit me, and I resist the urge to tear up a little bit.

"You think we'll ever get to visit the library again?" I left without a word to anyone, not even ML Garfield. As far as they all know, I shirked my damn duties and disappeared. But this was more important. Ten's *family* was more important.

A vision of Zakarias and I studying comes to mind, and I almost drop to my knees at the wave of grief accompanying it.

Gods, Zakarias. I'm so sorry it ended the way it did.

"It's hard to imagine what'll come next after all of this." Ten waves one hand around, gesturing out the front door. "But I want to go back there when we're done if you do. I want to explore the library and learn, and apply to the Novice program. Maybe even Novice for you once you become a First Librarian. What do you think about that?"

My cheeks heat when I imagine all the teaching I could do to Ten in my private keeping room if I ever get the chance to make one.

"You've got a deal, sir," I huff out. His lips on my neck turn needy as Kraven clears his throat from outside my treehouse.

Ten huffs but kisses my swollen, tender lips. "We'll continue daydreaming later. For now, let's figure out how we can fix this and get the hells out of the Tempang."

I nod, letting him pull me to the front door. We leap down to join Kraven, who glowers at us both, his rahken set stiffly against his head.

Minutes later, we're back in the Clan House, and the rest of Ayala Pack is filtering in to sit. My father sits at the head of the table, glancing around as Jet and his mates take a seat next to Ten and me. A huge black velzen sits by Achaia's side.

Father turns his focus to me and the pack. "Our time is running low. We need to capture Zura and return her to the grave. When she is gone, the undead army she created will follow her. To kill a snake, you must cut off its head."

My brain swirls with anguish and distress at hearing my sister talked about like this, but I try to remind myself the monster out there killing the Tempang isn't her, not anymore. The Zura I grew up with adored the forest. She would hate what she's doing now.

My brain flits back to a memory of us walking through a traveling tree, laughing about boys. I can remember playing with her in sun-dappled glades and how the forest's animals were always drawn to her protective power. She was so fucking kind, so good. She was the best of us, really.

And I destroyed all of that.

"Do we have other allies?" I question, my voice impossibly small. I try to remember I'm the daughter of the Volya king and that I was fated to be the queen one day when Father passes. Lifting my head, I speak a little louder. "Will others come to help us?"

Kraven shakes his head, arms crossed as he stands behind Father's left shoulder protectively. "Many of the old clans you knew are now decimated. Even the carrow have tried and failed to help us. At this point, most of the remaining monsters have migrated to the northeastern side of the forest, hoping to steer clear of Zura's armies, although we know she sends scouts."

Arliss sits up at the mention of carrow but doesn't voice any questions aloud. His pale eyes drift to me, but when he shakes his head once, I know he doesn't want me to say anything. His carrow tattoo is visible if one gets close enough, but I doubt anybody here would be looking for such a thing.

"We came in at the southern tip of the eastern edge of the forest," Ten says. "Centaurs attacked us. Were those scouts? Or is her army that far? And how are you safe here, so close to where she's building that army?"

Kraven gnashes his teeth. It's obvious he hates answering a question for Ten, but he does it anyway when Father gives him a curt nod.

"The Gate of Whispers protects us and the network of traveling trees. We have a symbiotic relationship of sorts, so the gate will do what it must to keep this Volya clan safe. But even She can only do so much against Zura. She has already attempted to poison the gate more than once."

Poisoning the gate. Oh my fucking gods. I put a hand to my mouth as I absorb Kraven's words.

Ten's big hand wraps around my thigh and squeezes. I let his warmth sink into me, bringing me strength as I lay my hand over the top of his and turn to my clan.

Jet speaks up next. "What are Zura's patterns or schedules? What's our best way to catch her? What haven't you tried yet, in terms of killing her?"

I hiss out a breath. I can't believe we're talking about my baby sister like this. It's her death all over again—that rushing swirl of terror and the sinking pit of realization. Between this and losing Zakarias, I'm fucking drowning.

Father nods. "Zura often remains guarded in her valley. Her scouts go into the forest, and then the armies move to take over lands and turn more monsters. Once her army has captured their conquests, she joins to turn the leaders."

"Turn the monsters?" Noire's voice booms across the quiet room. "I'm gonna need more specifics. Exactly what is she turning them into?"

My father sighs and cocks his head to the side to look at Noire. "Onmiel's specific magic is an ability to communicate with the Gate of Whispers, as I mentioned. She always understood the gate, even as a young child. But somehow, when she asked the gate to bring Zura back, it worked. But we are not meant to return to this plane when we leave it, and so she came back as something dark. If Zura or any of those she has turned are able to infect you, you are no longer the person you were. You become like them."

"Like a virus," Jet announces. "She's spreading her condition like a virus. But you have to wonder if the other beings are actually dead like her or just hosts for that black sludge we saw on the centaurs."

My father and Kraven give one another looks, and it's clear to me they've not had this train of thought. At the end of the day, I'm not sure it even matters.

I look up at my father, seated at the head of the table. "How can you be sure that killing Zura will stop the spread?"

Father slumps back on his throne, bringing a hand to his forehead as he rubs at the top of his rahken. He looks so tired; I feel bad for even asking the question. "The gate told us, child."

"Through prophecy?" I stand, surprised. I can count on both hands the number of prophecies the gate has given us during my lifetime.

Ten stands with me, one hand on my back below my tattoo.

"Let me see the message."

I sense the Ayala Pack is confused, so I look around at Ten's brothers and their mates. Even Arliss looks fascinated by this entire meeting. He's quiet, for once.

Ascelin speaks up, addressing me. "Why does this appear to concern you, librarian?" Her white eyes are narrowed.

I huff in frustration. "The gate doesn't prophesy with any regularity. She is simply the well from which all life began in the Tempang and from there, the rest of Lombornei. Our clan's duty is to keep peace here in the forest, all of which considers the gate to be our mother."

Renze steps forward. I've barely spoken to the tall, austere vampiri, but he's an undeniable predator, especially focused like he is right now. "What's this about the gate sending a prophecy, then?" He addresses my father directly.

Father sighs, his rahken slumped. "As Onmiel shared, the gate is the original mother of all life on Lombornei. The gate trusts us to maintain peace here. Her prophecies are few and far between, and it has been that way forever. But once Onmiel left, the gate began sending us prophecy after prophecy."

"How many?" My voice barely rises above a whisper.

Kraven turns and focuses on me. "Since you left us, the gate has issued over five hundred prophecies."

I suck in a jagged breath. Five-fucking-hundred prophecies?

"I need to see them," I demand.

"Show us." Noire's barked command stops me in my tracks. I dart a look across the table at him. There's a cruel tilt to his lips, even though his hands are slung casually into the loops of his jeans. The Clan House is silent for a long moment, but then my mother rises and gestures for us to follow. I go immediately, not wanting to waste a single moment.

Mother leaves the main room and walks up a tight hallway behind

TEN: A DARK SHIFTER ROMANCE

Father's throne. The hallway empties into a wide, circular room, filled floor to ceiling with scrolls and notebooks. She paces to one wall, and I see the hundreds of notebooks she and I made together over the course of my lifetime. Every one appears to be here, except now, they look full to bursting.

She grabs a notebook from the shelf and hands it to me. She hands a second to Ten right behind me and then more to his brothers.

The book she handed me is bound in dark blue leather with caramel stitching. I remember the day we made it—Zura helped, something she wasn't normally happy to do. She found bookmaking tedious and preferred to make herself scarce when we did it. But on this particular day, she was mourning the loss of a forest nymph, and she helped without us even asking.

Tears fill my eyes at the memory of her long, elegant fingers carefully stitching the pages together.

I open the book to find it stuffed to the brim with hundreds of tiny sheets of paper.

"These are gate prophecies," I whisper, holding one up for Ten to see. Chocolate eyes are filled with concern as he looks at the small page.

From somewhere behind him, Noire snorts.

"You expect me to believe that an ancient gate sends you a sheet of fucking paper with the future of our continent written on it. All of this—" He gestures to the wall of books behind me. "All of this is what's written in our future?"

I shake my head. The gate is hard to understand for anyone who didn't grow up in the Tempang.

Before I can explain that prophecy isn't an exact science, even for the gate, he lifts a page and scowls, tossing it to the ground when he can't read what's on it.

I kneel and pick it up, reading it aloud. "A queen of the land, a queen of the sea, a queen of the air, I demand all three."

His dark brows furrow into a deep vee. "I've heard that before. Here we fucking are, I suppose. Doing the gate's bidding by bringing queens right to you. I've seen enough. We're leaving."

I stomp my foot, frustrated. "You can't, Noire. You don't understand."

Ten wraps one muscular arm around me and turns to face the rest of his pack. Behind them, my parents and Kraven stand casually by the door. Gods, this is exhausting.

My father speaks before I can even begin to explain how I'm viewing this.

"Before the tragedy, the gate only delivered a prophecy every few years. It was rare. We always took what she told us as Gospel because prophecies were so scarce. But now? Many of these prophecies contradict one another. The only way I can explain this is to say that the gate seems desperate to find someone, anyone who can fix this. She is doing everything she can to protect us and the forest, and thus life outside the forest as well."

I rub my chest and think about the gate, wishing I could feel her the way I used to. In this form, I can't feel her at all.

Father grabs a book and flips through the pages. He seems to be looking for a particular prophecy, and after a few moments, he finds it and hands it to Diana.

"I believe this one may be about you, omega." His focus shifts to her chest. "And the spirit you carry which does not belong to you."

Diana takes the page and reads it, her pale face going even paler. She hands it to Noire and gives my father a curt nod.

"Shall we release him, then?" Father continues.

"Can you?" Diana's voice is firm. Noire's arm comes around her waist as he cuts my father a skeptical look.

Father nods. "It is a type of healing, so yes, my power will allow me to release the vampiri king's spirit from you."

"What if we still need him?" Noire asks casually.

"I don't, alpha," Diana's voice is steady. She turns to him and strokes pale fingers down his dark cheek. "Cashore has wanted to go for some time. I think he stuck around just long enough to get me well, but he's anxious to reunite with Zel."

I have no fucking idea what's going on here, but I watch in disbelief as my father takes Diana's other hand.

"He fulfilled his duty to you, child. He received a vampiri prophecy decades ago from the gate. We have a copy of it here somewhere, I'd wager. But now, he is done. Other spirits are not meant to live with ours for very long."

"I understand," Diana says with a soft smile, placing one hand over her heart. She closes her eyes. Noire pulls her closer. I'd guess they're sharing something in their bond, and I wish to fuck I could listen in. The whole gods-damned pack is probably talking right now, and I'm not getting a word of it.

For painful, long minutes, nobody says a word. Then Diana opens her eyes and gives my father a quick nod. "I'm ready."

Father places his hand on her chest and dips his head. Diana's mouth opens, and a voice leaves it—a male's voice—it's sinfully seductive and beautifully deep. It's the voice of a confident male, a leader. Ascelin slumps back against Arliss, and Renze goes white as a sheet.

"My warriors, I will see you in the halls of our fathers. For now, I must find my Zel. Go, thrive, protect. I trust you to guard the Chosen One now and always. I am so proud." The voice trails off, and when I look at Ascelin, blood tears streak down her white skin, black lips quivering as she stares at Diana, whose eyes are rolled into the back of her head.

"Goodbye, old friends," the voice comes again.

Father murmurs low under his breath, and then Diana's eyes snap open. She grits her jaw and places a hand over my father's. When she speaks, her voice cracks on a sob. "He's gone. Th—thank you, Lahken. He's wanted that for a while."

Father removes his hand and squeezes hers once. "It is my duty, omega, and my honor. I know the concept of the gate and her prophecies seems odd to you, but until now, she has never been wrong."

"She'd better be wrong about the sacrificing the queen piece because that's not an option," Noire barks. "Not now, not ever."

My father says nothing but looks around the room with a sigh. "I hope you are right, Alpha Noire, and that, somehow, it will not come to that. But I cannot know the gate's mind, not truly."

Noire's glittering black eyes move to me, and he grins. "*You* can't. But she can."

CHAPTER FORTY
TENEBRIS

Jet is already barking ideas into our family bond. Ascelin cries softly behind him. Arliss swoops her up into his arms and disappears back up the hallway on a wisp of black smoke. If any of the Volya are surprised to see him morph into a carrow, they don't show it.

Onmiel looks up at me, and I see the same determined look I saw on her face in the breakthrough room.

"What do you need, sweet girl?" I pull her close to me by the belt loops and tuck a strand of pearlescent hair over her shoulder, gripping the back of her neck.

"I'll try to communicate with the gate. Just come with me?" Her voice is sure and confident. It's the first time she's sounded like herself since we arrived here.

"We will all accompany you," her father says, but she shakes her head.

"Just the pack, please. It'll be easier for me that way."

Her mother frowns sadly, but her father nods. Lahken leaves the room, but Onmiel's mother crosses it and places a hand on her daughter's lower back, careful not to touch the prisoner tattoo.

"Call for me if you need me, daughter. Alright?"

Onmiel nods and rubs the back of her mother's hand softly. "I will, Mama. I'll be fine; I'll be with the pack."

"I know, child."

With that, the queen sidesteps my brothers and leaves as well.

Onmiel peers around me. "Are you all coming? Or what's the plan?"

"Fuck yes, we're all going," Achaia laughs. "The pack that slays together stays together, right?"

"Ugh," Diana groans. "That's your worst joke yet, bitch."

Achaia snorts out a laugh. "Oh, come on. We've been through the seven hells together. If we can't laugh about it, our only option is to cry, and I'm really, really tired of doing that."

Renze strokes her hair, his expression thoughtful. "Speaking of crying, I would like to check on Ascelin before we leave."

"Don't bother," I bark. "Arliss has it covered."

"Literally," Achaia whispers.

"Fucking hells." Diana laughs. "I'll grill her about it later. I need the deets. For now, Onmiel, we'll follow you?"

"Yeah, of course," my sweet librarian murmurs. "Let's go. It's about an hour from here."

Kraven growls. "I will join you to activate the tree."

Onmiel thanks him, but I have to resist the urge to slap him for his tone.

We follow her out of the village to the main traveling tree. Kraven presses his hand to it, muttering the incantation that opens it wide for us to step in.

For half an hour, we pace through the glowing green pathway inside the tree. Eventually, it spits us out into part of the forest that still looks healthy. Despite that, Onmiel looks anxious.

We remain in pack formation with Kraven on the outside, just in case something happens.

Onmiel is quiet as she leads us through the sun-drenched forest to a clearing. It's nearly as wide open as the street between our row homes back in Siargao. In the middle of the clearing is a giant stone disk with a turquoise, rippling surface. It looks like some sort of otherworldly portal. A matching round pool in front of it is filled with water.

"This is the gate?" I look to Onmiel.

Gray eyes are wide and worried, but she nods and points to the structure.

"The standing circle is the gate herself. The pool in front is where I used to play as a child." Her pale brows knit together in frustration. "Normally, I can sense how she feels when I'm here, and I suppose I do to a degree. But it's muted."

"We'll give you a minute," I encourage her, stepping closer to my brothers. I don't want to pressure her with my presence, and she already looks frustrated.

We stand quietly in the clearing as Onmiel walks a circle around the gate. She dips her long fingers into the pool of water and frowns.

"What is she doing?" Diana questions Kraven as we stand in the shadows of the forest, watching Onmiel.

Kraven sighs. "Onmiel always said she could talk to the gate, but I never believed it until Zura was killed. Who knows what she is doing now…"

"I'm starting to see why it didn't work out between you," I bark. I brush past him, slamming my shoulder into his as my wolf lets out a deep snarl.

He flares his leathery wings wide and snaps sharp teeth at me, but I ignore it.

Stalking across the forest floor, I join Onmiel, where she now sits on the edge of the round pool in front of the gate. I stop just behind her, looking over her shoulder. The pool's water is crystal clear. I can even see stones at the bottom of it. It's…peaceful.

"I can't hear her loud enough," Onmiel murmurs, stroking the water with one hand. "Usually, I can hear her talking to me. I can feel distress, but I can't get anything deeper than that." She sighs in frustration and gestures to her body. "It's this godsdamned form, Ten. I can't communicate with her like this."

She glances over her shoulder at my pack. "We need to consult with my father because I don't know how to do this. I think I need his help."

I don't know what to say, so I rub her thigh in gentle circles. She stands on the edge of the pool and brushes her cheek against mine. It's such a direwolf thing to do, so I'm surprised, but I lean into that touch.

I purse my lips for a kiss, and Onmiel grants my unspoken request. Her lips are warm against mine, her tart, candy-apple flavor bursting against my tongue.

"Let's get back," I murmur. "We'll talk to your father and go from there."

She nods, but she's lost in thought.

CHAPTER FORTY-ONE

ONMIEL

"Daughter." Father's voice breaks through my thoughts as I stand with the pack inside the Clan House. We just got back and shared with Father how I can't communicate with the gate, although I sense her tumultuous emotions.

When I turn, there's a mournful set to his rahken like he's about to deliver yet more bad news. I don't think I can take it.

"What is it, Father?"

"We need to remove your tattoo, child, at least a portion of it. You are too fragile in this form. Perhaps, you could communicate with the gate in Volya form."

My blood freezes, and Diana's hand comes to the middle of my back. He's right. I suspected as much but he's confirming it.

Father presses on without waiting for a response. "Your sister is powerful, Onmiel. If you face her in human form, I am not certain we can protect you, and you are our only chance to win this war. The gate has said as much." He gestures around us at the prophecies laid out on the floor and every other available surface.

Achaia looks sharply up at my father. "I didn't realize you could partially remove a prisoner tattoo. I thought it was all or nothing." Ten told me that she had one that hid her mermaid form, and they had to cut it off her back in order to free her.

Gods, I can't imagine.

Father nods. "Because Onmiel placed her own prisoner tattoo, she can undo it in layers. She must have removed a layer in Pengshur in order to remember us."

"Right," Achaia presses. "But she doesn't *want* to fully remove it. How many layers are we talking about?"

"There are two more between me and my full form," I mutter, looking up at my father. "You know I can't go back to that form. I was uncontrollable, Father. There are no guarantees I could handle my power now."

"I know, child," he agrees. "But I fear there will come a day very quickly when we will have to return you to that in order to win this war."

I shake my head as I stare up at the man who raised me. "It's got to be a last resort."

"We are there, Onmiel," he whispers back, his voice kind. He understands how dangerous it is to allow me in my natural form. There's a reason I locked myself up under layers and layers of magic.

Diana pats my father on the arm. "Lahken, give us a minute? We need a moment for girl talk."

My father inclines his head and disappears without a word. His words ring through my mind as I watch his pale robes sweep the floor behind him.

Diana sits at the broad table and bends forward over it, giving me a curious look.

"What are you really afraid of unleashing, Onmiel? It's more than just the ability to talk to the gate, isn't it?"

I shudder. She's incredibly perceptive, especially now that she's well. I've watched Diana and Noire since they arrived. They're perfectly aligned in every way.

Would Ten have been like that with Rama under different circumstances? The very thought of that makes my heart clench tight in my chest.

I miss him. I wish he wasn't with his brothers right now. Wrapping my arms around my torso, I slump against the table and look at the girls.

"The Gate of Whispers isn't good or evil; she just is. She contains light and dark and every shade of gray in between. I've always understood that about her. When I was a child, I felt I could communicate with her, and eventually, I began to foresee her prophecies before she sent them."

Achaia smiles. "That's badass, Onmiel."

I shake my head. "Nobody thought so at the time except for Zura. She always believed in me, that my power to communicate with the gate was a gift. We loved to play by the gate. We both felt peaceful and comfortable in her presence."

I gulp. What I'm about to share is more than I've ever told anyone. I wish Ten was here to hear it, but now that the girls have encouraged me to share, I don't want to stop. I feel a pressing need to get the words out until I can't even speak anymore.

"Zura and I were playing by the gate one day, and a tiny forest cat was chased into our clearing by something larger. The predator probably saw us and gave up the chase, but the little cat was gravely injured. It basically flopped in the dust and died right in front of us."

"Oh gods," Diana says in a tight tone.

I barrel on because the words are flowing now.

"Zura was hysterical; she was so sensitive to death and particularly anything to do with animals. We were sobbing, and somehow, I just knew that where we had seen death, the gate could bring life. I grabbed the cat and put it into the gate, and I asked her to heal him."

The girls sit rapt, listening to my memory.

"I didn't think it worked at first, but then the cat leaped out of the gate. He wasn't like before, though. His eyes were red and wild. I didn't know what to do. He went for Zura first because she was closest. He ripped her throat out and then took off into the forest. She died in my arms, coughing on her own blood."

"Fucking hells," Achaia whispers. "You know that wasn't your fault, right?"

"It was, though," I murmur. "I couldn't control my power, and she died because of that. I carried Zura back as fast as I could, and I told my parents everything, but none of it made a difference. Father tried to heal her, but she was gone."

Tears stream down my face at reliving the worst day of my life. "For three days, I sat by her side. On the fourth day, a council of Volya elders agreed I should be allowed to leave the Tempang. Normally, the punishment for what I did would be binding within a prisoner tattoo to lose access to one's powers. I opted to bind myself, and they allowed it. That was eight years ago. I left the Tempang and traveled to Pengshur, and I've been there ever since."

The girls are silent, and I can't help but feel that silence is damning. I turn to go, but Diana lays a hand on my forearm and grips it hard. She rises to a stand, which puts her nearly a head over me. She looks down, blue eyes hard and bright.

"Listen to me and listen good, Onmiel. What happened to Zura was an accident, and you did everything you could to make it right, but you were alone. You are not alone now, do you understand? You're here, and you're one of us, and not a single member of our pack will rest until we right this wrong alongside you." She pauses.

I didn't realize I needed to hear those words so badly until she said them.

"Thank you," I manage.

Diana pulls me in for a quick hug. Achaia rubs my back at the same time. I try hard not to burst into fresh tears, but eventually, I extricate myself.

"I need to talk to Ten. I just…"

"We get it. Go find your alpha," Achaia says. "We're here when you need us."

I nod and leave the friendly women behind, descending the ladder.

I miss the library so fucking much. I felt more alive at Pengshur than I ever have anywhere else—even here at home with my family.

Surprisingly, I hear my mother's voice as I scale the ladder and appear in the doorway.

The view there warms my heart until I think I might burst. My mother sits gracefully at the small table in the main room, Ten seated across from her with his legs folded at the ankle. He's looking down at an ancient, weathered book as she points something out. They both turn when I enter, Ten rising from his seat to cross to me.

He pulls me into his arms, wrapping my legs around his waist as he takes my mouth tenderly, his soft tongue probing the tip of mine. It's the kiss of a lover who knows your body like the back of his hand. It's unhurried and perfect, and I hope there's never a day I can't have this.

"Missed you," he murmurs when we part, despite my mother sitting right behind us. If I've learned anything about Ten in the day since we came here, it's that he doesn't give a fuck what anybody else is doing or who's near us. If he wants to touch me, to kiss me, he takes every opportunity. I've never been more grateful for him than I am right now.

My big alpha sets me down with a devious smile. "Your mother was showing me some of her books from your family library." I have to laugh at that.

"She is a prodigious journaler." I chuckle, following Ten as he sits back down and pulls me into his lap.

"I can't read this," he reminds me, long fingers stroking across the ancient Volya words on the worn, weathered pages.

"I was just translating for Tenebris." Mother smiles. "I hope there will come a day in the future when we can teach him ancient Volya so he can read about your adventures for himself."

There's an achy crack in my heart watching my mother and my alpha connect in a way that's so meaningful to me. I reach out to stroke the book, too, my fingers brushing against Ten's.

"When I was a child, Mother was always writing, always chronicling what happened in the forest. She wrote about peoples' actual lives, and she wrote made-up stories, and this is why I love books." I turn to face Ten, pressing one hand to his chest. "She taught me to bind books, and when I got old enough, I made all her blank ones so she could write. Including this book," I finish in a soft voice, reaching out to touch the familiar pages.

Mother beams as she looks at us. "I am so glad you are home, Onmiel. I know the circumstances are terrible, but there is nothing more heartwarming for a mother than to have her child in her arms once again."

I beam back at her. "After we get through this, I'll make you new books if you'd like?"

Mother claps her hands together, her rahken parting into a mischievous expression. "Perhaps Tenebris can assist you? He should begin to learn some of our ways, should he not?"

"I'd like that," Ten breathes, one big arm tightening around my waist. He tenses behind me and then sighs. "Noire is poking at me. It's time to go, sweet girl."

"I've got to let down some of my tattoo first," I grumble, looking up at my mother. She nods, unsurprised.

"Your father is just worried for your safety, my darling girl," she says confidently, her earlier smile falling. "Zura is incredibly strong, and it would crush us to lose you." She cocks her head to the side. "Do it now, Onmiel. I will remain here with you."

When I falter, Ten strokes his fingers down my side, bringing his lips to my shoulder. "I'm here too, Miel. I'm not going anywhere."

"What if I go crazy?" The question is out of my mouth before I even mean to say it.

Ten grips my chin and turns me in his lap, his amber eyes serious as he gives me a chiding look. "I don't want to hear any more of this self-doubt. You're the strongest person I know. You can do this. For yourself, for me, for your family, and for your forest. I believe in you with all of my heart."

A single tear tracks down my cheek, but he leans in and licks it away with a laugh.

"Will you still have eyeballs?" he chuckles, thumping the tip of my nose as I guffaw, sitting up a little straighter.

"Probably not," I titter, nerves jangling in my belly as I slide off Ten's lap and hold my arm out to my mother. When I look back over at Ten, there's nothing but confidence in the way he looks at me. "Better get your last look at this face," I joke. "It might be different here in a moment."

"I'll still love it, though," he whispers before reaching out to lock his fingers with mine.

Love. Gods, Tenebris Ayala wants me. Could I be any luckier? I don't think so, and that knowledge alone steels my resolve. I will do this, and I will fix what I broke because I need a long life to love him. I need years and years to explore him, to fulfill him, to enjoy him.

I nod at my mother, who draws one long claw across the vein inside my wrist. Hot, sticky blood wells immediately up to the surface, and my magic screams in my veins to be released.

"Careful, child. We will help you stop taking blood when it is time," Mother reassures me.

"You can do this, sweet girl," Ten croons, a purr picking up that fills the room as I squeeze his hand.

My hands shake, but I bring my wrist to my mouth and suck at the wound, blood filling my mouth. The moment the blood hits my tongue, awareness of my magic fills the forefront of my brain. There's a sudden deep awareness of the Tempang, too. Everything sounds louder to me, and it sounds wrong. The bird cries, the animal grunts. It's all…poisoned.

Zura's doing this. She's poisoning the forest, and even though she is my own creation, she must be stopped.

Magic thrums in my veins as I suck harder at my wrist until I feel my mother pull it gently from my teeth.

An uncomfortable, dark sensation worms its way through my mind. The gate. She calls me just like she used to. But where she always brought me comfort, there's now inky darkness. Everything is wrong, and she is so, so afraid.

"That is enough, child," Mother says. I yank my hand from her and put it back to my mouth. More power. I need more power. I need to stop Zura, and my power isn't enough. I need to channel the gate like I did before but in reverse. Where I brought Zura back to life, I need to return her.

I *will* return her.

When Mother draws my hand away again, I snarl, an angry yowl leaving my mouth as my body shifts, pain lancing through me as the prisoner tattoo begins to melt away. I fall to the floor against the pain, but Ten drops down next to me.

"We're here, Onmiel. We're right here, and you are so fucking beautiful. I'm here."

Magic screams through my veins, filling me. I haven't accessed or been aware of my magic in years, and now that I have it back, that heady need for more is a constant ache in my chest. The tattoo feels like glass shards ripping at my back as it fades partially away until all I can do is cry at the pain.

Ten's big arms come around me, his purr filling the room as it picks up in intensity. I want more blood, I ache for it, to release all that magic. To find

Zura and take care of this now. My magic and the gate created her, and I'm drawn to her because of it.

"Focus on me, Onmiel." Ten's voice is all alpha command, brooking no argument. His purr draws me out of my desire for blood as he repeats his demand. The world reduces to nothing but Ten—his scent, his purr, the strong, corded muscles of his arms. Everything fades but him, and I feel a little bit like myself again. After long minutes, the pain in my back ceases, and I look up.

Ten's handsome face lights up, full lips curving into a smile. "Godsdamned beautiful, Onmiel. Well done."

I preen under his words, despite my mother standing right behind me. I sense her moving, her hand coming to my shoulder.

"Daughter, I am so very proud of you. I'll give you and Tenebris a few moments. Everyone is gathering outside. Join us when you can."

I nod, turning to her with a soft smile. Her robes billow behind her as she steps gracefully out of the treehouse, leaping off the front platform and disappearing from view.

Ten strokes my hair, wrapping it in his fist as I realize that I'm suddenly the same height he is. I look down, cataloging all the other changes. I'm still humanly pale, although my arms and legs are longer, thinner like the Volya. Long claws tip both hands, and when I reach up, my face is still human, but long horns curve alongside my scalp.

"You've still got eyeballs." Ten laughs. "But they're a brilliant amethyst purple now like you're lit from within by a star. Gorgeous." His voice is reverent as he strokes my hair. "This is the same, still long and white."

"I miss the neon orange," I grumble.

"You can put it back if you adore it." He laughs. "But for what it's worth, the white is fucking hot."

"Good thing I'm hot in all forms," I snark. Ten laughs and reaches his hands up to stroke along my softly curved horns. Heat floods my system as my pussy contracts, a gasp leaving my lips as I curl my hands around Ten's shirt.

"Gods. Oh, fuck, Ten." My voice is deeper in this form, throaty and sensual. All Volya are sensual, sexual beings, but I forgot just how true that was. Even though I was a horny hussy on the best of days.

"Mmm. So they're sensitive." Ten's fingers still stroke and tease my horns as my head falls back, my neck bared to him.

"Bite me," I command, needing more than this horribly inconvenient tease. Now that I'm partially back in my real form, need has me at the point of pain. I need to be filled and used by him. I ache for it. My soul recognizes his, and I won't be happy until I have him. Tasting my power for the first time in years has me drunk and inhibition free.

I have to have more of him.

Ten's mouth closes over my throat, fangs punching through the skin far harder than he ever did in my prior form. It's difficult to breathe like this, but he bites harder, then releases it and makes his way down my throat, licking at the hollow at the base of my neck.

"I'm not gonna make it out of here if we keep this up, Miel," he growls. "You're going to be unhinged in this form, I can tell."

I let out a growl I don't recognize as one hand comes to Ten's throat and squeezes, my mouth hovering over his.

"Need you, alpha."

Ten purrs and drags my body closer to his, not backing down.

"You want to dominate me, Onmiel? Have you forgotten I'm a fucking alpha? That I grew up in a brutal, terrible place? That I could rip you to shreds with my bare hands?"

A possessive snarl leaves my throat as Ten laughs, cocking his head to the side.

"Much as I'm anxious to continue this fight for dominance, people need us," he sighs, taking my hand as he steps back. The long outline of his thick cock is evident against the front of his pants.

I want to drop to my knees and worship it. I want to learn what I can do to him in this form.

Ten yanks at my hand. "Come on, dirty girl. There'll be time for that later. Let's go hunt your sister."

CHAPTER FORTY-TWO
ONMIEL

I follow Ten out of the treehouse, leaping down next to him as his pack turns. Diana and Achaia both gape at me.

"You look fucking badass," Achaia says, walking across the space to join us. Like this, she has to look up at me. Achaia walks a circle around us and pretends to fan herself. "How do you feel, Onmiel?"

I have to smile at the perky queen. No matter how dark this adventure gets, she maintains a surprising level of humor. I know she could annihilate the forest if she had to. She's our last resort. Between that and the growing velzen at her side, she's plenty badass herself.

Nearly the entire clan has gathered, so it's probably a good thing I didn't just start fucking Ten upstairs. Gods, I want to. I need to. I'm more predatory in this form, monstrous and dominant.

I recognize a familiar soul in Ten's wolf. It's almost like I can feel him roaring inside Ten's chest, wanting to get out and command me, fight me, and claim me. He wants to chase and take me. I can tell that from the way my alpha stares at me and licks his lips slowly, suggestively.

Noire glares at my father. "So, how do you imagine this going?"

Kraven comes to the forefront of the group and gives us all a haughty, cold look.

"The Dead Queen spends time at a lake near her lands, and occasionally near the Gate of Whispers. None of our plans ever work as expected, so instead, let us focus on a goal. Onmiel's presence is likely to surprise her. Let us use that to our advantage. We will distract her guard to give you an opening. Kill her if you can."

It sounds so simple when he says it like that.

It's anything but.

I haven't seen my baby sister yet, but it's anybody's guess what'll happen when I do. Despite what's going on in the forest, it's hard to imagine being able to kill her, no matter what she's doing to it. Everyone seems to believe I'll have to, but—

Ten's hand comes to my lower back and slips up my shirt, skirting the edges of my tattoo. He strokes me softly and then brushes his cheek against mine.

"I'm here. Here for every moment, Miel." His purr rumbles between us. It's the louder version that happens when his wolf is actively focused on me, too. Something about knowing I have them both at my side helps me focus.

I'm a bundle of nerves as I follow my clanmates and the pack through the traveling tree. We decide to try checking at the gate first, and already, she calls to me. There's a desperate tugging sensation deep inside my chest, so heavy I rub between my breasts to ease the pressure.

In this current form, closer to my full, natural form, I sense the traveling tree's distress. The very ground beneath my feet seems to quiver with anxiety. The forest is sick, hanging on by a thread, and that sickness seeps into my bones.

It's a real mindfuck, honestly. I did this. I thought I was just communicating with the gate, but somehow, I channeled her power and caused this. It's up to me to fix it. We're a small group, but if Father is right, a large army can't move on Zura without being seen.

It makes sense, but given what I've seen so far, I'm still terrified. Whatever magic Zura is using to poison the forest is something ancient and dark. She didn't have that sort of magic when she was alive, so somehow, when I brought her back, I gave it to her. Or the gate did. Or maybe her own protective power just got twisted when she came back. I don't know.

My sins are piling up on top of my head so hard and fast, it's difficult to breathe around the weight of them.

Ten is a silent, steadying presence by my side as we walk quietly through the distressed, dying forest. The trees here are sickly and gray, their leaves either blackened, wilting, or gone. Zura has eaten this land up, and everything about me aches to turn the forest green and healthy again if it's even possible.

I grip my spear as we follow Kraven through a dappled, dark glade. He stops behind a group of boulders and turns, his focus intent.

"The gate is just ahead. Zura's guards usually remain out of sight. We need to capture her quietly." He turns to me. "Onmiel, you'll need to distract her. We'll grab her while she's focused on you."

I nod. The pack is silent. I imagine they're all talking in the bond. I wish I could hear them, but I know they've got my back.

The trees here are scorched and darkened, already destroyed by Zura's magic. I sigh and look around, reaching out to touch a tree before thinking better of it. Everything in this part of the forest drips with the black, sticky tar my sister is using to poison the Tempang. The sludge seems almost sentient, lifting off the trunk to reach for my hand.

Ten tickles my side.

"No touching, Miel. I'm going to shift until we see her, then I'll change at the last moment if you distract her."

Nodding, I grab his pack as he shifts and stalks slowly into the depths of the forest. There are no sounds. No bugs, no small animals. The forest's usual noise is simply gone. Pools of black tar lie all around us. I don't remember seeing this when the pack and I came to the gate before.

Ten's brothers and Diana shift and disappear into the trees with Rosu. Achaia remains by my side with Renze, Ascelin, and Arliss. Nobody says a word as I lead them through the trees toward the gate.

Eventually, it comes into view. My heart thumps wildly in my chest. The gate's pull is even stronger here, like she's screaming for help. It's all I can do not to run to Her and do something, anything.

Achaia and the vampiri remain out of sight behind me. I round the gate's pool and Zura is there, kneeling at the edge as she swirls one black finger in the water. I suck in a breath at seeing her for the first time.

This is my sister, but not. Her skin is mottled and dark, her rahken missing giant chunks with blast marks marring their smooth surface. Her hair is stringy and limp, her clothing torn and wet.

Her throat is still ripped open from the wound that killed her, and dark slime leaks out of the shredded flesh, sliding down her body and wetting her clothes. She is utterly focused on the pool of water in front of the gate, her black lips parted into a sneer.

I feel like I'm having heart failure. My muscles quiver with the need to run to my sister. I want to pull her into my arms and apologize for turning her into this, this *thing*. The Zura I knew would never want this, would never accept it.

As I watch, black goo drips from her fingertips onto the rocks that surround the gate's pool. The sticky deposits snake along the stones and then slither into the forest of their own accord.

The gate is practically screaming into my mind at how wrong this is, sending a chill of goosebumps flashing across my skin.

Zura, I'm so sorry.

Around us, there's nothing but a terrible and heavy silence.

I take a few more steps around the pool.

"Zura," I murmur.

My sister pauses but shudders. She remains kneeling but swivels her head to face me. A river of lava runs down the crack between her rahken. She snarls and pulls her hands from the gate's pool.

The gate breathes an audible sigh of relief in my mind, but there's still so much tension, so much wrongness in my sense of her.

Zura rises, slow and creaky, her dead bones and muscles unable to move smoothly. Tar drips from her as she takes a step toward me, her lips splitting into a cruel grin.

"It's me, Miel," I whisper. "I'm home, sister. Talk to me, please."

I don't know how sentient Zura even is in this form. Is she driven by a baseless need to conquer? Is she capable of forethought? Is she purely reactive? It's hard to say.

I'm fucking terrified as she descends the pool's steps and takes a few steps toward me. My brain screams at me to flee this danger. I steel my spine, knowing the pack is here if everything goes south.

"I'm so sorry, Zura," I say softly. "I'm sorry for making you like this."

Zura cocks her head to the side, and a look of fury crosses her face. It's there and gone in a moment, and that's when I realize that despite her not speaking, she's scheming. It's obvious in the way her focus shifts around me, like she's sensing the forest and the encroaching danger of the wolves and vampiri.

My sister straightens tall and purses her lips, whistling a string of discordant notes that echo harshly into the quiet forest.

She throws her head back and laughs, and that's when everything descends into chaos.

Spiders the size of aircabs ripple from the bark of the trees behind Zura. They were hiding in plain fucking sight, and I didn't even see them, but as they descend in droves down the trees, black sludge follows in their wake.

Zura sprints for me, raising a dagger high as she shrieks out a stream of curses in ancient Volya.

I'm frozen in fear as I watch her, spiders filling the clearing behind her. Something bursts through the trees behind me, and I hear the pad of footprints.

I pull myself up onto one of the direwolves without pausing to figure out who's who. Rosu lets out a shrill yelp and darts off into the forest with Achaia on his back. Volya warriors tumble through the trees with spiders right behind them.

And we flee. Zura's laughter rings out, echoing off the gate herself.

The spiders give chase, leaping from the trees above and following our path, crashing through the underbrush.

In front of us, one of the Volya warriors runs for the nearest traveling tree. If we can't get to it, we stand no chance.

A spider swings out of nowhere and impales him with the stinger on its back end, disappearing into the underbrush with a great, heaving crash. His scream of pain cuts off on a squelch.

Kraven roars and sprints ahead. Next to me, Arliss evaporates into dark mist just as a black spear flies through him, thunking into a tree ahead.

I scream into the wolf's fur at how helpless I feel. Kraven shouts out a spell, and a tree in front of us splits wide, its glowing green interior a beacon for safety.

Kraven pauses as the vampiri and wolves rush into the tree, not stopping. I'm in last with Arliss and another Volya bringing up the rear. We slide into the tree, but just as it begins to close, a black hand—my sister's hand—grabs the Volya by one of his horns and yanks him backward. The tree closes tight on his leg, trapping him. There's a terrible scream, and then the leg drops to the ground, severed.

Kraven lets out a bellow of anger and tosses his horns against the interior of the tree in frustration.

My heart pounds, my chest rising and falling so fast. I can't seem to pull the breath into my lungs as I fall to the ground and stare at the leg.

Jet shifts and paces to the tree's door, eyeing the leg. "Is it infected? Do we need to get it out of here?"

Kraven turns to him with a scowl but looks at the leg.

I clap a hand over my mouth as they kick at it. No black sludge leaks out of it. Nothing emerges to attack us.

This is all so wrong, I'm physically sick to my stomach.

It's also clear to me what I need to do. I'm the only one who can stop Zura. The gate reassures me through our connection, whispering a chorus of anxious yeses into my mind.

I hop upright and into the depths of the traveling tree. Ten is an angry, seething presence at my back, but he says nothing. Everyone follows as we return to the village and head directly for the Clan House.

My father sits on his throne, speaking in low tones with my mother.

"She's poisoning the gate," I say. "The gate is barely holding on. She told me."

Father shifts back in his wooden throne, one hand over his rahken as his horns slump.

Ten moves to stand next to me, slinging one big arm around my hips. Behind us, I can almost feel the packs' anger. But underlying all of that is the gate's terror.

Father's voice rings clear as a bell across the Clan House space. "You know what you must do, Onmiel. Your true form's power is the only thing left in the Tempang strong enough to stop her. I have to believe you are capable of that. If you brought her here, you can send her back."

I nod. I want to believe that, too. "If you'll help me control it, I'll do it."

"Of course, child," Father says. "Let my warriors recoup for a few hours. We begin again shortly."

I nod and turn to find the whole Ayala Pack staring at me. I don't have words for them right now, though, so I brush past them without saying anything. What could there even be to say at this point?

CHAPTER FORTY-THREE
TENEBRIS

For once, my pack bond is quiet. I think we're all still in too much shock that Zura orchestrated a trap. I'm still buzzing with anger at the memory of Zura streaking toward Onmiel to attack. I'd swung her up onto my back, but I could have lost her today.

We cross the clearing in the middle of the village and head down the side street that houses all the guest homes. I swoop her into my arms, leap up onto the front porch, and carry her through to the bedroom.

She smiles back at me, although it's forced and weary. And that's the moment I know I'm in love with her. Despite Rama and the hold our bond had on me. Despite the fact that I've known Onmiel for such a short time.

She's good and kind and powerful and sexy. She's sarcastic and goofy. She loves books and coffee, and she's been enamored with me since the moment we met. There's a reason for that, a reason she was drawn to me so completely, even when I couldn't see it.

And I almost lost that today.

I fucking refuse to lose her. Not now, not ever. In my chest, my wolf pants with the exertion of fighting and running and the need to cement her to us.

I open my mouth to tell her that, but she takes my hand and points above us with the other.

"Climb with me?"

I smile and follow as she crawls up the tree trunk on the far side of the living room, out a skylight in the ceiling, and up through the branches. Grinning, I hop up and dig my claws into the bark, following her up. There's a beautiful view of the village, but even that disappears into the darkness once we're at the very top of the tree our house is built into. The leaves rustle quietly around us, still healthy in this part of the Tempang.

When we reach the top, I find a small platform built into the topmost branches. It sways softly as the tree does.

"Are these for sleeping?" I join Onmiel as she settles down onto the flat surface.

She gives me a saucy look. "And other things."

Heat floods my chest as my wolf growls.

Careful, friend, I caution him. *You won't fit up here.* He slinks back into the recesses of my mind, comfortable and relieved to be in her presence.

She lies back and folds her arms behind her head. "Every Volya home has a platform like this. We believe the gate made it because Volya souls come from the stars. They enter our bodies at birth, and when we die, we become part of the forest." Onmiel turns on her side, her head in one palm, as she smiles at me.

"Zura and I used to come to sleep up here together when we were children. We used to imagine which stars would be our own children someday." Onmiel's voice goes soft. I sense her thoughts turning dark again. Today was an epic clusterfuck.

I pull her into my chest and stare deep into her beautiful, gray eyes.

"When I was a pup, I watched my father lose my mother. They were bound like Noire and Diana, and while all direwolves hope to find their soul bond in that way…I was afraid of it happening to me."

She strokes her fingers down the bridge of my nose. I nip gently at them, sucking on her fingertips. But I can't start fucking her; I've got to tell her how I feel. I want her to go into what's next with the full knowledge of what's in my heart.

"When I came of age and Rama started sending me books and letters, I didn't get it. I didn't understand the soul bond until after she'd kidnapped me when I woke up in her bed. I saw her, and something just…clicked."

Onmiel's silent. I don't want to hurt her by talking about Rama, but I want her to know how I feel.

"When I started to realize she was drugging me, I felt betrayed, broken. And then Jet showed me what she forced him to do in the maze. All the terrible shit she put him through just because she could." I pause, overcome by all the things he never told me about. I knew the Atrium room was a fucked-up sex-slave palace, but I didn't know the lengths Rama went to just to screw with him simply because she could.

I press on. "Killing her was the worst thing I've ever done." My voice breaks with emotion, but I grip Onmiel's throat gently between my fingers. "And I thought I'd never come out of that grief. But then I met you."

Purring, I reach down and thread Onmiel's legs through mine as she looks at me wide-eyed. Her heartbeat trills fast in her chest. I want to sync it to mine until we're bonded in every possible way we can be.

"You have surprised me at every turn, Onmiel. You snuck into my soul with every look, every joke, every time you needled Arliss, every fucking cup of coffee. I couldn't deny an immediate, incredible connection."

Her throat bobs under my hands, tears filling her eyes as I pull her closer, pressing our foreheads together. I want to breathe the same fucking air she's breathing.

"I'm in love with you," I whisper. "I fell so fucking fast, Onmiel. And despite what's in our past, there is nobody on this continent I'd rather build a future with than you. I want it all. Your happiness, your joy, your safety."

"Ten, I—"

I silence her with my lips on hers, and where I expected to make this a sweet kiss, the stress and insanity of our day turn my lips hungry. I can't get enough of her, and so I attack her with my mouth, nipping at her tongue and sucking her lips between mine.

"I wanna fill you with my cum and make babies, Onmiel, when we're free of all this," I snarl as my wolf sits up and takes notice.

Pups. Yes.

He's just as sure as I am.

Placing Onmiel's hand on my chest, inside my shirt, I tip her face up to look at me.

"You're mine, in here. My wolf knows it. I know it, and I will spend every day for the rest of my life worshipping you, pleasuring you, and loving you. Wherever you go, Onmiel, I'll be there."

Tears stream down her face as a joyous smile parts her beautiful lips.

"I don't know what'll happen when I undo the rest of the tattoo," she admits. "It could be a fucking shit show. But for the next few hours, make me forget?"

I growl as I flip us, using my knees to spread her legs apart.

"It would be my honor," I growl, dipping down to lick my way up her neck.

I don't know if I'll ever call Onmiel my mate because I don't want her to associate that word with Rama and everything that came before. To me, she's more. Because Onmiel is my choice, and choice is all that really matters.

"You're my fallen star, Onmiel," I growl into her neck, nipping at her sensitive skin as she lets out a soft, needy moan. "You came down out of that sky for me. We didn't know it, but I was on this earth, enduring every day. And every one of those fucking days brought me to you. I'm the luckiest alpha in the world."

Onmiel thrusts her hips hard against mine, greedy for more.

"I need to claim you, sweet girl," I growl.

"Later," she gasps, struggling when I pull her hands above her head and capture them in one of mine. "After we fix this…"

"Now," I snarl, biting at her neck as I unzip my jeans with my other hand. "Need you tied to me, Miel."

"Gods, Ten," she groans. "Fuck me, please!"

I give her a stern look. "Leave your hands there, little star."

She nods, twisting her fingers together as I reach down and slide her pants off, tossing them to the side. I hover over her waist, breathing her in as she cries out with need. Purring louder, I slide my tongue down into her sweet pussy, circling her clit once as her groan falls off into a pant. Onmiel's knees fall open wide as I feast on her, one small hand sliding through my hair as she grips it in a fist.

"Gods, Ten," she gasps out. "You feel so fucking good!"

I purr as I suck at her clit, pulling it gently between my lips, and then I press both knees down to the ground, holding her with my weight as I attack that sweet pussy. She belongs to my wolf and me in ways Rama never could have.

"You are everything to me," I growl, pausing for a moment to drag my stubbly jaw along her inner thigh. Onmiel's muscles quiver as she tries to rock her pussy up to meet my mouth and can't.

"I'm gonna give you this tongue," I murmur. "I want you soaked for me when I slide this big alpha cock into you. You ready, my love?"

Onmiel lets out something between a plea and a wail as I kiss her clit and then thrust my tongue deep inside her, curling it up to rub against her g-spot. She detonates the moment I do, screaming her pleasure into the quiet night as I purr my heart out. I watch every one of her muscles tense and tighten through the throes of her orgasm, and even though we don't have an alpha mating bond, I imagine she feels my devotion, so I send her my love just like I would if we had that connection.

I suck at her pussy until she's coming again, and when she finally shudders and relaxes, I smile and snake an arm around her waist. Onmiel nuzzles into my neck before biting me hard, really fucking hard, drawing a growl from my wolf and me. He typically recedes when I'm touching her sexually—it's something for my human form—but that bite, godsdamn.

TEN: A DARK SHIFTER ROMANCE

When I look down at Onmiel, her pupils have overtaken the shocking iris of her beautiful eyes, and there's a feral, unhinged look on her face.

"I need to fuck you," she snarls, darting forward to bite at my lip.

I whine at the pleasure and pain that shoot through my system as she reaches down and roughly strokes my erect cock.

Gripping her throat, I use the arm around her waist to flip her and push her head down into the smooth wood surface of the platform.

My wolf joins me, watching her as she waggles her ass at us, taunting, teasing.

"How about getting fucked by a wolf, Miel…would you like that?" I don't know what the fuck I'm doing, but I know my wolf wants to mount her as badly as I do.

And I'm going to let him.

CHAPTER FORTY-FOUR
ONMIEL

My entire body is a livewire, despite coming twice all over Ten's beautiful fucking mouth. I fantasized about him the moment I saw him that day in the Solarium. But the reality of him is better than every daydream.

And he loves me.

He loves *me*.

The part of me that worried he was moving on too fast, getting too obsessed, is gone. I trust him to know his mind and his heart. I believe every word that comes out of his mouth. I don't know how I fell so fucking fast; I just know it started that day I saw him standing in the library, watching the rain patter on the glass windows above us.

Gods, I hope we get to go back one day. The Tempang might be my home, but the library feels like it's meant for Ten and me.

His voice brings me back into the moment, overwhelmed as I am by everything he shared.

"What do you think, my sweet girl?" he growls. "My wolf wants to take you like the animal he is."

Oh gods. It shouldn't be so hot, but I nod.

The moment I confirm what I want, Ten's big body comes down over the top of me, his hips pressing into mine, his enormous cock sliding between my thighs. Except when his hands come to either side of me, wolf claws grip the smooth wood. Soft fur brushes against my back, sending a trill of alarm and need through my core. He's half-shifted, and I'm about to be taken by a direwolf.

Whining, I press back into him as he brings his lips to nuzzle my neck. But when his tongue snakes out, tasting my shoulder, my neck, my upper back, it's not Ten's tongue. It's bigger, rougher.

Ten's attention turns hungry and fierce, his teeth and tongue dragging over my shoulders and back as he tastes every inch of me. I rock back as much as I can but half-shifted like he is, I can't fucking move. I can't get him where I want him, but as his thick cock bobs between my thighs, dripping precum onto the wood below us, I snarl.

"Fuck me, Tenebris," I command.

There's a low, confident laugh behind me. His voice is different like this, full of gravel, seductive, wild, and utterly breathtaking. Not for the first time, I wish we shared a bond like Diana and Noire, something to allow me to see inside his mind, to feel his soul.

"Steady, Onmiel," Ten commands. And then he grips the base of one of my horns, squeezing it tight as he yanks me back onto his waiting dick.

I scream at the intrusion—his cock has ridges in this half-shifted form, and they drag along every sensitive nerve ending in my pussy. But then his big claws stroke my horn, and I'm lost. Pleasure sweeps over me in waves as Ten pounds into me from behind, bringing one hand to grip the back of my neck. I'm caught and fucked, and I can't even think around how good he feels.

A low growl lifts the hair on the nape of my neck as Ten leans forward, his hips pistoning as he pushes me flat down onto the platform. He grunts his pleasure as my muscles clench around him, my hips slamming into the wood below me. Ten is everywhere, his lips and sharp teeth at my shoulder as that hand continues stroking my horn. Gods, I never knew it would feel so good to have him touch them.

An orgasm rushes through me like a tidal wave, and I squirt all over his huge cock as Ten lets out a bellow that's half howl and half roar. I tighten around him as the pleasure drowns me, but he's not done. If anything, that release unleashes him, and he fucks me hard and fast with zero regard for how much bigger he is. He's wild and untamed, and then in a moment, he flips me, and I'm treated to a view of Ten.

I gasp when I see him. He could be an ancient werebeast like this. His eyes are narrowed, golden slits, and his snout is fully wolf, leading back to long, tapered ears. But his body is somewhere between—covered in thick, chocolate fur but still Ten's muscular form. But then behind us, a long tail lashes angrily from side to side.

Ten's lips are curled back, revealing enormous fangs that drip saliva down onto my stomach. Everything between us is a mess, and as his slitted eyes focus on me, heat builds between us again.

Clawed hands come to my knees, and he presses my thighs up to touch my chest.

"Mine." The growl that rumbles out of Ten's mouth is barely human at this point. And somehow, I know his wolf is pushing further and further through.

"Yours," I confirm, pushing up onto my elbows as his ridged cock slides along my slick, used pussy. I whine as he nudges at my entrance with a broad, flared head, and then he's sinking to the root inside me once more, his head thrown back as he pants.

He picks up a brutal, punishing pace as he leans over me, his tongue snaking out to lick every inch of my upper body. His big wolf tongue curls around my nipple and tugs, and I'm lost, wrapping my hands around his broad neck as I scream out my release. The world goes starry and black behind my eyes as pleasure robs me of the ability to even speak.

I don't even realize I blacked out until much later when Ten is curled around me in full human form, stroking my thigh lazily.

"Must have been good," he rumbles in my ear, nipping my lobe as he slides his hand between my thighs. "You're still so wet, my fallen star."

I scoot closer to his chest, loving how his chest hair tickles my back. Everything about him is so masculine, so alpha. He's perfect in every way.

"We've got to get started soon," he reminds me. "I insisted they let you get a few more hours rest, but we can't wait any longer, according to your father." Ten's tone turns sour so I flip over to face him.

"I've got this, and even if I don't have it, you'll help me, right?"

He strokes my hair out of my face and smiles. "I'm there for every moment, Miel. Anything you need, okay?"

∽

I follow Ten down out of the tree, hating that every step brings me closer to reality and its consequences. All I want to do is hide up in the tree for the rest of my life with him, basking in his love and happiness. But I can't because all this goodness around us is dying.

When we reach the ground, my clan stands there in solidarity. Ten's brothers and their mates are there, too. Even Ascelin and Arliss have remained, although I know Arliss is anxious to visit the carrow and learn. His time might even be running out, but he's staying here instead, and that means the world to me. I give him a thankful look, watching his dark lips tilt up into a smirk.

I don't miss the way Ascelin looks up at him, and even though she plasters a neutral expression on her face, there's a longing in her eyes I can't help but notice. There's more to that story, I'm sure of it. I just fucking hope I fix things so they get to enjoy one another if that's what they want.

Looking at my clan, I notice Kraven is watching the two of them closely, his rahken knitted firmly together at the top. Father steps into my view, laying one clawed hand on my shoulder. He pats it lightly. "Your mother and I will take the women and children to the carrow in the northeast part of the forest. We will make our last stand there if you—" his voice trails off as my mother joins him, wrapping her arm around my waist.

"We believe in you, child," she whispers in my ear. Father gives me a curt nod. My clan parts around me as Ten shadows me into the clearing in the center of our village.

Butterflies rocket around like vultures in my stomach, eating away at the lining when I think about what I'm going to do.

Ten comes around me, holding my hands.

"I'm here, Miel. The whole time, my love." His whiskey-brown eyes burn a hole into mine as he helps me lift a wrist to my mouth. I bite deeply, sucking at my own blood, and just like before, power fills my veins, thrumming as my head falls back.

The gate speaks into my mind clearer than she ever has.

Come to me, daughter. Take what's mine. Return what's lost. Come, come, come.

I don't remember falling to the ground; I just know that I'm there as knowledge and magic fill my veins, and the world around me starts to change. My parents' faces blur, then everyone begins to scream, and the last thing I see is Ten's worried expression as I let out a guttural, animalistic roar of pain.

CHAPTER FORTY-FIVE
TENEBRIS

Everything happens so quickly. Onmiel's eyes roll into the back of her head, and then her body changes. Rahken form over her eyes as she curls in on herself, screaming and writhing on the ground.

"She is enraged," hisses Arliss as he appears beside me. "I can almost taste her power. She wants blood."

The wrongness of it scratches like nails in my mind, but Arliss has the gift of reading intent. He is reading hers now and does not like it.

"Bind her quickly!" Lahken screams, directing Kraven and the other warriors. They form a circle around us as my pack moves in to surround us.

I snarl and stand over her. She's defenseless like this, in the middle of changing. But Arliss is right; she's not in control. I sense it. Still, I won't allow them to hurt her.

Kraven and the others back up, although he still holds a spear aimed at her. I snap my teeth at him, shifting into my wolf and hovering over Onmiel.

She rolls underneath me, screaming as her body changes. There's a cracking sound, and when it stops, she rises from the ground in full Volya form. She's not any bigger than she was before, but where before she had those incredible striking eyes, now, I'm looking at rahken like her father's and a cruel, thin-lipped mouth filled with razor-sharp teeth. Saliva drips from them as she glances around me at the warriors holding spears pointed in her direction.

A low, menacing growl leaves her lips. I reach for her, horrified at the way she shudders from my touch. She snaps at my hand, so I pause, even though Noire screams at me to get out of the way.

"My love," I try to soothe her. "It's me. I'm here. We're doing this together, remember?"

Onmiel cocks her head to the side but then throws her head back and lets out an evil cackle. It reminds me so much of the way Zura laughed at the gate that I shudder and step back.

A shrill noise rings through the forest. We all pause, and Onmiel goes quiet, her head jerking in the direction of it. She cocks it to one side and then the other, and then a throaty, murmured "yes" echoes out of her mouth.

Someone rushes toward us, shouting, "Zura comes!"

The village devolves into a frenzy of rushing Volya. The king and queen guide the women and children to the closest traveling tree. I can barely focus on that as I beg Onmiel to see me, to hear me.

Noire grabs my arm, but when she sees him, Onmiel lets out a percussive roar that knocks us all flat on our asses. The scurrying around us increases as her arms swing wide and a crack appears in the ground around her, the earth falling away as she separates herself from us.

I stand at the edge, watching the crack widen as the earth carries her away from me.

"Onmiel, please," I beg, reaching out for her. "It's me, my love. Let's do this together."

A distant roar comes again, and then the crashing of hooves.

Noire grabs my shoulder. "There is no time, brother! Zura is attacking!"

I shout for Onmiel, but in the moment I turned to look at Noire, she disappeared. The spot she stood in is empty, and only a rustling in the bushes on the far side of the village gives any indication of where she might have gone.

"No!" I bellow, screaming as my brothers drag me from the clearing.

A herd of undead centaur barrel into the open space, and I thank the gods that all the women and children have already escaped.

Black, sticky spears fly. The Volya warrior next to me falls to the ground, impaled, sludge overtaking his body as he jerks. I don't stick around to watch him become like the rest of them.

All we can do is flee as dozens of centaurs fill the village and chase us all the way to the tree. The traveling tree's door closes, but a black spear lodges in the opening, and tar drips off it, slinking toward us like a snake.

"Run!" shouts Kraven, taking off into the tree's depths. We sprint for a solid ten minutes until we don't see the slime anymore. Kraven stops and turns, but it's Renze who speaks up first. He strokes Rosu between the eyes,

TEN: A DARK SHIFTER ROMANCE

but Rosu remains watchful, focused on the darkness of the passageway behind us.

"What now, Tenebris? We hunt your woman and make her see reason?"

I look around at my pack. My brothers stand ready to fight. Their mates look on with resolute expressions. Even Arliss is still here and focused.

"I need you to join me," I say. "We need to find Onmiel and support her. She'll do the right thing. I know she will."

A pair of all-white eyes flash at me from across the traveling tree's hallway. I meet my friend's gaze and give her a look I hope she can read, but when Ascelin smiles, revealing two rows of translucent black teeth, I return the look.

She's with me, I know it.

"We are ready to hunt by your side, Tenebris," she purrs.

Good, I say into our family bond.

"She'll be at the gate," I whisper. I don't know how I know, but I do.

My pack trails quietly behind me, but we're on high alert. That sensation brings me right back to the maze. I'm in front as always, Jet, Renze, and the girls in the middle, Noire bringing up the protective rear. I was never safe in the maze, of course, but with my family at my back, I was never worried either.

I'm worried now, though. Worried for the sexy, perfect woman who captured my heart when I didn't even know that's what I needed. Now, she's lost to her power and its darkness, and it's my job to pull her out of that.

She did the same for me.

CHAPTER FORTY-SIX
TENEBRIS

"We are here," Kraven says coolly, brushing past me when the traveling tree opens to deposit us into a dark, desecrated glade.

I half shift, calling my wolf to the surface; my senses are better like this, anyhow. Noire comes to my side, barely contained surprise evident on his face. Direwolves don't halfway shift; it's just not something we do.

"What's the plan, brother?"

"Find Onmiel. Help her kill Zura. Try not to get killed in the process." The voice that leaves my mouth isn't mine, and I didn't even think those thoughts. It's all him, focused as he is on our mate and getting to her as quickly as possible. We don't wait for anyone as we stalk into the underbrush.

Behind me, I hear Jet's voice in a grumbly, low tone.

"That isn't a fucking plan; it's a death wish. We need an actual plan, Noire."

The thing is, Onmiel doesn't have time for us to plan. I search for her in a bond, but I can't feel her the way I always felt Rama. Still, I continue on because I will never stop looking for her as long as I live.

There's a faint light ahead in the jungle. The occasional tree is still verdant and green, although streams of sticky black tar drip from branches in front of me. They hit the ground and slither off into the forest. Lahken was right. This is our last stand because Zura's magic is right here at the godsdamned gate, the home of life on our entire continent.

I scent the air as we come into the gate's clearing. The shallow pool in front of it is still pale blue and clear, the water undisturbed by Zura. There's no sign of the Zura or Onmiel.

"She is not here," Kraven snarls, grabbing one of his horns and yanking at it in irritation.

Turning to my brothers, I give them a look.

"Standard formation," Noire barks. "Ten, you're up front. Everyone else, fan out in the middle. I'll bring up the rear with Arliss and Kraven."

Kraven turns with a scowl and nods.

"If you find her first, drive her to me," I command, my voice otherworldly as the gate shimmers in front of us.

What I'll do when we find her is anybody's guess. I don't know how to make Onmiel see that she can do this, that she can harness her power and save us all, but I have to try.

My pack splits off into the forest as I scent the air again. There's the crisp tang of Volya magic, so much stronger in this form. I sense my brothers and Diana shift into their wolves, then disappearing off into the forest. Rosu slinks next to me with Achaia on his back.

The thrill of the hunt fills my chest, my muscles trembling with the need to move and seek, to find my quarry and corner her.

I'm coming, Miel, I send out into the universe. I only hope she can hear me.

∼

For two hours, we patrol an ever-widening area around the gate. Frustration is at an all-time high when I catch a whiff of something, my wolf locking onto a scent.

Little mate close. Something wrong. My wolf's voice is an urgent warning in my mind. I'm on high alert for any sign of Zura and her armies, but the forest waits with bated breath. I half expect Zura to pop out from behind the next tree and stab me.

Instead, Onmiel is just ahead. We're deep in the forest, but I smell water. My family bond is awash with concentration as Renze slips in front of us.

When he returns, stopping in front of me, I pause.

"She is up ahead on the banks of a small lake. The Dead Queen is coming; I heard her."

Nodding, I break into a run and pump my arms to get to her, to have time with her before Zura shows up, and we need to be a united force.

I slide to a stop when the edge of a cliff looms ahead of me. Forty feet below, a crystal-clear pool of water shines with the midday sun. Onmiel stands waist-deep, focused on the water below her. Her hand darts into the water, and she pulls out a huge fish, ripping its head off as blood sprays her rahken and horns.

A growl of appreciation for her in predator form rises from my throat.

Mate strong. Mate good, my wolf reassures me.

Arliss appears in a stream of smoke next to me. "She is not herself, alpha. She is agitated and frustrated. Be cautious."

As if she can hear us talking, she looks up to the cliff's edge where we stand. She doesn't seem to recognize me, though, although she doesn't look away as I follow a trail down the side of the cliff, meeting her on the beach.

Stay back, I tell my family through our bond. *Give me a minute.*

"Onmiel," I purr, crossing the pebbled shore and wading into the water.

She backs up with a low growl, ripping into the fish's belly as wet innards spill down her chin.

"My fallen star."

She cocks her head to the side, feral in this form. Anxious energy radiates from her. Arliss was right. She's not in control of her emotions like this, tasting her power for the first time in eight years. I just need to get through to her to bring her back to me.

I take another step. I'm five feet from her. "I ache to touch you," I admit. "You are so fucking beautiful like this."

She drops the fish, wiping blood from her mouth and takes a step closer to me, eyeing me as if she might attack.

"You can do this, sweet girl," I whisper, remaining still.

She comes up to me, almost close enough to touch. I need to show her something to remind her she's mine, that I trust her, and that I always will.

I close the distance between us but don't touch her. Her body tenses and tightens, ready to fight or flee.

I let my head fall back, a sign of trust. A long moment passes, then two, during which Noire bellows at me not to show her my godsdamned neck, not to get killed being a stupid fucker, but a warm tongue dips into the hollow at the base of my throat.

I sense my pack flying down the hill to tear me from her, but I can't be bothered to focus on them.

A ragged groan bursts from my lips as her tongue snakes straight up my throat, sharp teeth closing on my chin and biting hard enough to draw blood.

I resist the urge to yank her to me and have her right here in the water.

"Your power, my love," I whisper. "We need your power. Your sister is coming."

That intoxicating tongue traces a path to my ear, sending goosebumps along my entire body.

I reach for her, wrapping an arm around her waist.

"Ten?" Onmiel's voice is worried and afraid.

I crush her to me, gripping the back of her neck with one hand. "We need you, my star." I bring my head up, locking eyes on her face.

She sputters, looking around us. "I, I don't remember coming here, Ten. I'm not in control like this. I—"

"You can be, my love," I encourage her. "Focus with me. I'm right here. You can do this, Onmiel. I know you can."

An angry shriek echoes from above.

Onmiel snarls when a black-tipped spear flies through the air, narrowly missing my head. It clatters off the stones behind us and falls to the ground. Her focus moves to the cliffs above us.

I follow her gaze to where Zura stands, blazing red eyes narrowed on us, the threads of her black dress waving in a non-existent breeze. It's like she's floating through the air, and up close, she's even more horrifying than what I previously saw. Zura says nothing, her mouth opening in a silent scream as she lifts one hand, pointing toward us.

Noire snaps from the beach. "We can't fight off a godsdamned army, Tenebris. Is she ready?"

I press a hand to Onmiel's lower back, but she leaps from me with a hiss before turning to her sister again. She's a predator, utterly focused and drawn to her sister like a magnet.

She's lost to me, even as another spear flies through the air. I catch it and spin, throwing it at the first centaur, who barrels down the rocky path toward us.

It hits him square in the chest, exiting his back with a horrifying squelch. He laughs and pulls the spear from a gaping hole, tossing it lightly in his hands, ready to throw again.

We really can't kill a fucking undead army. We need a miracle.

"Protect Onmiel," I bark at my pack. "Get her to Zura, no matter what." I turn to my mate, even though she's not focused on me in the slightest. "I'm with you," I murmur low enough for her to hear. "We're all with you, Miel."

She lets out an ungodly roar and takes off, sprinting up the path toward the approaching army. We take off after her, and I pray to every god and goddess I grew up with to watch over her alongside me.

The moment it's clear Onmiel's not slowing down, Zura's entire army moves as one, like a flock of birds. They round her, but she pays them no attention as she runs for her sister.

Jet barks a command at Achaia.

She opens her mouth and shrieks, sending a percussive wave that flattens

TEN: A DARK SHIFTER ROMANCE

the army in front of us. They fall to the ground, rolling and stumbling as they struggle to rise. Rosu sprints next to me with Achaia on his back, her face screwed up in concentration. We're right behind Onmiel. As the undead begin to rise, my pack and the Volya warriors slash, removing heads where we can. The bodies rise and run, but headless, they can't focus. And more importantly, they can't bite and turn us.

Achaia lets out a second deafening scream, and I crouch while the army falls to the ground again.

Zura leaps to her feet, a spear in her hand, as Onmiel gets close.

Behind me, my pack keeps slashing and attacking, but we're outnumbered by hundreds of monstrous, undead soldiers.

My heart pounds in my chest, the only sound in my ears is my own blood rushing through my body.

A centaur dives for Onmiel just as she nears Zura.

I bellow, but with a wave of Onmiel's hand, he disintegrates into dust.

Oh my fucking gods. Is she channeling the gate's power in reverse?

"*Yes!*" Kraven shouts. "You can do this, Onmiel!"

If she hears his sudden support, she says nothing, focused as she is.

I watch the sisters clash together, Onmiel's larger frame knocking her sister to the ground.

Zura lets out a scream of anger.

Everything is chaos as Achaia levels the army to the ground a third time, only to watch them rise again. More undead stumble out of the forest to join the horde. We can't keep going like this.

Zura slices black-clawed fingers across Onmiel's face, and I watch the dark sludge ooze into the wound. Oh fuck, oh gods. If she infects her, that's it.

I sprint for Onmiel, screaming for her to remember why we're here.

With a wave of her hand, Onmiel disintegrates the row of monsters closest to her. They disappear into a fine mist that coats the ground as she scrambles to fight Zura.

Onmiel screeches and throws herself on top of her sister. When she waves her hand over the smaller woman, nothing happens. Zura doesn't disintegrate like the others.

Zura kicks Onmiel off her, leaping up with a black, dripping dagger in her hand.

Time slows as Zura brings the dagger up and drives it through Onmiel's chest.

Onmiel's rahken lift in surprise, then her horns slump, and she drops to both knees with the hilt of the dagger sticking out from between her breasts.

I roar, my wolf taking over. I grab Onmiel by the neck and drag her from Zura.

Kraven throws an iron net over the Dead Queen, yanking it tight until she falls to the ground in a heap. Around us, soldiers still rage, but Achaia knocks them down, and my pack picks them off.

I half shift and haul Onmiel into my arms. Blood spills from her lips. Her focus drifts past me to the fight. She waves her hand in an intricate symbol, and the entire army explodes into mist.

CHAPTER FORTY-SEVEN
TENEBRIS

Behind me, Kraven lets out a roar of triumph. I can't focus on that, though. Fear tears through me as I look at Onmiel, slumped against my chest.

One of her hands wraps into the fabric of my shirt. "The gate requires sacrifice," she murmurs, her eyes fluttering closed. "A queen of the land, a queen of the sea, and a queen of the sky."

It's the prophecy all over again, and it chills my blood to hear her repeat it now. Is the gate telling her this?

"No, fallen star," I whisper into her ear. "Not today. But we *are* going to return Zura to it."

"Won't work," she mutters.

"It has to," I purr. I stand with her in my arms and look over my shoulder at Kraven. "Bring Zura. Follow me."

It's an alpha command from my wolf, who takes over. My pack follows in silence. Our family bond is full of anguish and heartache for Onmiel. Rosu pads quietly next to me, Achaia slumped in a heap on his back.

I pace through the thick underbrush, ignoring the black sticky tar that follows us like a virus. Despite killing Zura's soldiers, our fight isn't over.

I need to get to the gate and end this. I don't know what'll happen after that, but I can't watch Onmiel die or turn. So, I'm going to beg the gate just like she did. Spare her because she saved everyone.

I send my intention out before we even arrive at the gate, hoping it is sentient, that it can hear me because I belong to Onmiel, that it can see what we're trying to do.

The only sound is Zura yowling and scratching, but Kraven silences her with a backhanded slap, dragging her behind him in the net.

We enter a traveling tree, and Kraven directs us through it. Exiting, we walk until the gate looms ahead of us. Onmiel's body is limp in my arms, the wound in her chest filled with the black sludge from Zura's dagger.

By the time we see it, I know what I have to do.

I stop next to Kraven. "Give me Zura."

He hands me the rope. My pack watches as I approach the gate portal.

How are we doing this, brother? Noire questions into our pack bond. *Let us help you.*

I don't immediately answer. Zura thrashes and screams as I pace to the gate and ascend the steps. When I step into the pool, Kraven rushes to the base of the platform.

"You cannot step into the portal, alpha. It will kill you!"

Noire sprints across the clearing and commands me to stop with the deepest alpha tone I've ever heard from him. Normally, that would cripple me. But now? My wolf shrugs it off and focuses on Miel, limp and dying in my arms. I pull the dagger out of her chest and toss it away.

I'm knee-deep in the pool when I turn to my family, watching their expressions of confusion turn to abject terror.

"I love you all so fucking much, and I'm sorry it has to be this way," I start. "Long live Pack Ayala." I stride across the pool and up the two steps to the Gate of Whispers's big, round portal. I surge through, dragging Zura with me.

The only sound I hear is Noire raging behind me.

And then, nothing.

∽

A sense of calm fills me, the worry about my family left behind. They will live and thrive, even if it's without me. Onmiel saved our entire continent. My pack and the Volya will flourish. I know all of that just like I know my own name. Somehow, after coming into the gate, I sense it in the way Onmiel must have.

It's a peaceful sensation, like a warm hug wrapped around my soul. I'm still half-shifted, my direwolf refusing to be parted from Miel.

There is no sound, there is nothing but the draw of the gate, and as I look at it, I hope it can hear me.

I could never leave her, I admit. *I will be by her side forever in this life and the next and the next. We return Zura to you, but in her last moments, I want Onmiel to have peace. And you are her peace. I know that now.*

The surface of the portal we came through shimmers as if the gate Herself is laughing.

Cool water flows over me, even though I'm not getting wet. There's a splashing sound, and Zura falls through the gate behind me.

Without a word, she rises and lifts her hands to look at them. Sticky, black tar melts off her, tendrils of color returning to her skin. Worm-eaten flesh heals and reattaches to her bones. Her thin lips part in awe as all the death flows away from her, and what's left is beautiful life.

After a few long minutes, she stands, cocking her head to the side. When she smiles, it's broad and happy, the picture of health. She puts a finger to the side of her mouth in thought. "You are not what I pictured my sister with, but it is right. Can you feel it?" She gestures around us, laughing. It's a lyrical, happy noise, and it sends an ache through my chest when I think about Onmiel losing her so long ago.

"But we are together now, are we not? Together forever." Zura laughs as if she heard my thoughts, turning from me as my eyes follow her.

I gasp. Where there was nothing around us, we now stand in a pastel forest. It's a mirror of the Tempang, but not. Everything is the color of cotton candy, and as I look in awe, Zura strides off, motioning for me to follow.

"They used to say the gate killed those who entered it. That the old gods who live here are full of wrath." Zura speaks over her shoulder. "But I think Onmiel always knew the truth. The gate simply delivers those who enter it into what's next. What is next for you, Tenebris Ayala?"

I clutch Onmiel tighter to me as I follow her sister. I'm too overwhelmed to even respond to her question.

Zura turns when we arrive at a pale pink waterfall, her focus on Onmiel in my arms.

Where the dagger stuck out of her chest before, the wound is gone. I feel peace when I look at her. I should be heartbroken and terrified. Where has that emotion gone? Did the gate take it? I hug Onmiel tighter.

Zura looks at me. "She was always the best of us, you know. The kindest, the smartest. I wanted to be her when I grew up."

I give her a brief smile, but worry is beginning to push through the peace I feel. Dropping to my knees, I set Onmiel gently on the ground.

Zura joins us, laying one manicured hand on her sister's head. She strokes bloodied hair away from Onmiel's face and sighs. "It is time for me to return to the stars, Tenebris. Tell Onmiel that I forgive her, that I love her, and that we will pick daisies again one day. Tell her I approve."

She reaches out and ruffles the fur on top of my head, pinching one of my ears playfully.

"Goodbye for now," she says. "I will see you in the next life, brother."

I watch as Zura's skin begins to shimmer and flake. Where her hand was, she seems to be disintegrating into thin air. She seems happy about it, humming as she sits with us. It doesn't take long. A minute or two, and Zura is gone. The pastel forest around us is peaceful and quiet, and a sense of knowing hits me again.

When the first bit of Onmiel's skin and mine begins to shimmer like Zura's, I bury my face in her neck to remind her how in love I am. How it's always been her from the moment my wolf decided it. How he slapped me around to help me realize it, and how all I want to do is make her happy for the rest of my days.

I watch us drift away, the colors of our souls dancing and mingling together on a faint breeze. It grows stronger, whipping my hair as we become one and disappear into the sky.

And then there is nothing but peace.

CHAPTER FORTY-EIGHT
DIANA

Noire rushes past me, sprinting for the steps to the gate. Anguish fills our mate bond so completely that I can't breathe around it. He runs smack into Jet's broad chest, bouncing back with a furious roar. I grab his arms from behind, trying desperately to stop him from throwing himself headfirst after Ten into the Gate of Whispers.

"You cannot go!" Kraven shouts, joining me to haul Noire away from the gate's pool.

My mate yanks his arms from me and shoves Jet, but Renze and Ascelin join us until we're all piling on top of Noire, who rages, snaps, and snarls as he struggles to follow Ten.

Oh my fucking gods, Ten. After all of this, after *everything*, he's gone.

I know in my heart Noire will never recover from this.

"Mate," I cry out. "Noire! You can't go! Stay. I need you!" I throw that last bit in as a final resort, feeling like a total ass, but Noire can't follow Ten into the gate, or I'll lose him forever.

A resonant explosion knocks us flat on the ground. I blink my eyes wide, trying to understand what happened, but the forest is silent.

I struggle to sit up, but Achaia pulls me up next to her, squeezing my hand. Even Noire has pauses. In front of us, streaks of green seep out of the Gate of Whispers and up over the edges of its pool. Smoke in every possible color erupts from the gate in streams that dash into the trees.

We're all so shocked that we say nothing.

"The trees," Arliss hisses. "Look at the trees."

My entire pack looks around in wonder as decay and darkness disappear and healthy color returns to the forest.

The clearing around us is silent until a wail rises up. Noire. Goosebumps crackle down my skin to hear the way he howls. His voice cracks, his wolf screaming in agony at Tenebris's loss.

Rosu joins him, raising his nose to the sky, his ears flat as he howls. It's a long, mournful sound that rings out over the stones, covering the forest with all-consuming heartbreak.

Tears stream down my cheeks as Noire slumps to the ground, falling forward onto his knees as great big sobs wrack his giant frame.

The vampiri move aside, and Jet sits back on his heels, gasping for breath with a hand on his chest. I move to Noire's front, plastering myself to him. He doesn't say a word, doesn't even look away from the gate, but tears slide in a torrent down his cheeks.

"Mate." I scratch at his chest, willing him to look at me, to remind himself that I'm here for him, no matter what he needs, no matter what insurmountable thing hits us next.

Ten is gone. Onmiel is gone.

"The king will sacrifice the queen to the gate," Achaia whispers. "Do you think it meant Ten and Onmiel? She was the Volya's future queen, so he'd have been—" Her voice trails off like she can't even finish the sentence.

He'd have been king.

I try to process the idea of it, but Noire's sanity is unraveling in front of me. Big muscles tremble as he pulls to a stand, still not looking at me.

"Not Ten," he growls, his voice breaking, fists balling by his sides. "Never Ten." I've never heard Noire this broken, this angry. Our family bond is frayed to the point of snapping. Agony floods it until I can't stand it. He's the fire to my water, and together we bolster our pack. But white hot agony streaks through our bond, choking me until I can barely breathe.

Noire is shattered by this, and I don't know if it'll ever be possible to put him or our pack back together without Ten. We've overcome every gods-damned obstacle, every impossible feat thrown at us—first the maze, then my injury, then a zombie queen intent on taking over the whole continent. But this?

This I can't even comprehend.

"The barrier entrapping us is gone," Kraven whispers. "Can you feel it?" He looks around in wonder, but I can't fucking focus on that right now. I don't give a shit.

I don't even know what to do next, but I scramble to think of something.

My pack stands silent and shocked, but I'm the godsdamned pack omega. It's my job to support every one of my people.

Even my alpha.

I stroke my fingers down Noire's face, but he still quivers with rage, his black eyes narrowed at the gate.

"Noire." Jet's voice is urgent, and when we turn, his eyes are on the gate, too.

Kraven joins us, one hand gripping a sword as we gaze at the gate's surface, which now ripples.

"What's happening?" I demand of the big warrior.

"I don't know," he grits out. "I have not seen this nor heard of it. Step back, everyone."

Despite his warning, Noire surges toward the gate and manages to fling himself into the pool. I scream for him, but it doesn't make a difference. He sloshes toward the portal as I scramble after him, desperate to pull him to safety.

The pale blue surface of the gate shimmers again, and then a set of broad, leathery horns appear. They push forward and up out of the portal as if whatever's coming out has to duck to make it through. Wavy chocolate hair appears next, and then a figure that would be Ten if he were twelve feet tall and half Volya.

Horns twice the size of Lahken's curl up and away from Ten's forehead. His eyes glow pale blue like he's lit from within by the gate's power. He's clothed in a simple tunic and pants, his form as muscular as ever. Pointed black claws tip his hands and feet. This not-Ten stares silently at us, his enormous chest rising and falling with slow, measured breaths.

"Tenebris?" Noire's voice cracks as he stumbles forward until he's standing just below the monstrous male.

Kraven paces up the pool's steps and stops next to me, the look on his face incredulous as he stares. "The Prime," he murmurs, his voice barely above a whisper. "The king of all that is. The gate has never given us a Prime in all of Volya history. There are only foretellings from many generations ago. I never thought to see it happen."

I'm still clinging to Noire as Ten watches us.

"What does that mean?" I hiss. "Is this Ten or no?"

"Yes and no," Kraven continues. "He is your brother, but also the alpha of alphas, the king of vampiri, the regent of naga regent. He is the king of *everything*. He is the gate incarnate. The ultimate protector. The light and the dark combined into one."

Kraven falls to his knees in the shallow pool, his head dipping respectfully.

Ten moves toward us with otherworldly grace. He steps into the pool, towering above us in this form. I sense my pack joining us, but I can't look away from Noire, and he doesn't look away from Ten.

Not-Ten looks down at me, a soft smile splitting his face. "Hello, Diana."

I step forward until I'm next to Noire, threading my fingers through his. "Hello, Ten. Assuming you're still Tenebris of Pack Ayala."

Not-Ten smiles, and it's the comforting smile of a parent to a young child.

"They are all my packs, my clans, my kingdoms." He shrugs as if it's the most obvious thing in the world, but when his glowing eyes light on Noire, I press myself closer to my mate. Rustling behind us tells me everyone else has dropped to the ground, too.

Ten looks behind us and grins at my mate. "You know, everyone else is kneeling for me, Noire." Ten's tone is all lyrical joy as he gives his oldest brother a teasing look. Is this really Ten, this giant beast of a man with horns wider than an aircab?

Next to me, Noire shifts from one foot to the other and reaches out, placing his hand on Ten's chest. "Is it really you, brother?"

Ten laughs. "Yes and no, alpha."

Noire frowns. "How much of the Tenebris I know is left?" His voice is just as commanding as it ever has been, a deep resonance that seeps into my bones and makes me want to show him my throat.

Tenebris laughs again, but it's not harsh and angry; it's more melodic than anything. "Everything you knew remains, brother. There is simply more of me now."

Moving slowly, my mate drops to one knee, never pulling his eyes from Ten. I drop with him, watching in shock as the strongest male I know bends the knee for his youngest brother.

"Only ever for you," Noire whispers, his voice so low it's barely audible. "Only ever for you, brother."

Ten smiles and places a hand on Noire's shoulder. "The gate blesses you and yours, Alpha Noire. I will be there to see all of those happy moments, brother."

A surge of emotion crashes through our mate bond as Noire stands and pulls me to his chest.

Ten turns from us and faces the gate as a second figure emerges.

Onmiel.

Goddess, I'm so fucking relieved to see her. I sprint forward before anyone can stop me, throwing myself up into her arms the moment she's through.

Noire goes tense in our bond, but I couldn't stop myself if I wanted to.

Onmiel wraps both arms around me and sighs, whispering in my ear. "Being dead was weird for a minute, but I've got some cool new powers. I can feel them."

I let out a hysterical cackle as she lets me down, crossing the pool, and descending the steps with Ten following her. The clearing breaks out into chaos as the Volya surround her and pepper her with a million questions. When she raises a hand, Kraven and the Volya warriors drop to the forest floor again, bowing low.

"That's enough." Onmiel laughs. "Please rise, and don't do that every time you see me. I'm still me, sort of."

Ten wraps his arm around her, snaps his fingers, and then they're both in normal-sized form, although they've still got incredible horns.

Jet slides an arm around Onmiel and hugs her. "We're so fucking glad you're safe."

"Me, too," she whispers, radiant, glowing blue eyes moving to Ten, who gives her the happiest look I've ever seen on a male's face.

"So, the prophecy was never even about Diana or Achaia, then?" Noire questions.

"No," Ten confirms. "It was always Miel, because she is the queen of everything—land, sea, air, and all that lies between."

A bubbling laugh rises out of my throat. That godsdamned prophecy has been a noose around my neck for what's felt like ages. But it's done now, gone.

I watch Ten and Onmiel reintegrate with the group and smile. For the first time in a long time, I feel safe. I'm not dreading what's next. I'm not worried about some madwoman stealing my happiness and ripping me to shreds. For the first time in a long time, I can think about the future.

And that future is intoxicating.

CHAPTER FORTY-NINE
ONMIEL

There is so much love around us, but I notice something new, something amazing. I feel Ten in my chest, and when I think about him, he turns to look at me. The gate unleashed us and gave us a gift I could never have imagined having—a bond that allows me to feel and experience him as a true mate should. Every bit of his emotion, his needs and wants? I can sense all of it.

My mate and his wolf have a few things on their minds.

Ten looks at his brothers with a quizzical, almost amused expression. "I need to return to the maze to release the monsters."

At his proclamation, the shifters and vampiri explode in a flurry of indignation. I think Ascelin is the loudest, her brows all the way up to her hairline as Arliss laughs from his spot next to her. It's not lost on me that he has yet to leave us to find his own way with the other carrow, but now that Ten and I are what we are, we can help him.

There's a sense of knowing in my chest, driven home by my sacrifice to the gate. I am her, and she is me. The entire continent is connected to my very bones. I feel a need to protect and cherish everyone and everything. Every monster, every being, *everything*. It's all my family now. Ten and I have a duty to protect Lombornei. The gate is no longer alone; she has us—the first Primes.

Noire is still raging about Ten's maze comment. "You've got to be fucking kidding me," he bellows. "We can't go back there! It's dangerous, and whoever's left has been weeks without food, Ten. You'll be ripped to shreds. Don't ask me to watch that."

Ten laughs, and I join him, taking his hand.

"They will not hurt us, Noire," I reassure him. "You don't even need to come; we'll be fine on our—"

"Like hells," he snaps back, crossing his enormous arms. "If you're going, I'm going."

And like that, it's settled. Nobody seems willing to disagree with him.

A tug pulls my focus in the direction of Arliss. I give the bulky carrow a grin.

"I need to find my parents, and they are hiding with the carrow, Arliss. Fancy a trip to meet your kind?"

There's a tangible look of relief on his face, but he gives me a brusque nod.

Half an hour later, our group emerges from the traveling tree into a clearing. I watch color seep back into the trees here, and I hear a titter. A child hiding in the bushes. A quick flash of smoke surprises Noire, and he growls as a child appears in human form right before us. She's young, maybe six or seven, and seeing her fills my heart to the brim.

"Call your kind," I whisper to her conspiratorially.

Arliss joins me, practically quivering with the desire to finally get answers about who he is.

The child darts off into the trees, and we follow. Moments later, several pops of smoke deposit three carrow in front of us. They see Ten and me, their eyes blowing wide, and they drop to the ground in deep bows.

"Is this gonna happen everywhere?" Noire deadpans. Diana shushes him, and I try hard not to laugh at how quickly he returns to his naturally abrasive demeanor.

I do turn around and give him a saucy wink. "Yeah, alpha. Better get used to it. You look pretty good on your knees."

Achaia giggles. Noire scowls.

It feels…normal.

There's a crashing sound in the forest ahead, and then my mother breaks through a group of Volya warriors and falls into my arms, sobbing. Father is right behind her, and the moment he sees me, he drops to a knee in deference. His wings tremble with the force of sobs that wrack his spindly frame.

"Father," I murmur.

He rises, and when I open one arm wide, he tucks in for a hug.

I don't know what the future will hold, but I know that this is just the beginning.

Eventually, we leave the carrow to return our people home. Arliss remains with them, but Ascelin comes with us. I'd have sworn she wanted to stay, but even with the vampiri king's spirit gone from Diana, neither vampiri seems willing to stray from her side. To some degree, she will always be their Chosen One, and Cashore's absence doesn't seem to have changed that.

As for me, I don't see a future where Ten and I spend all our time in the Tempang, even though it's the Volya way and the gate is here. That's a conversation for another time, though. For a day, we remain with my family. We rest and eat, and then it's time to free the monsters in Rama's maze.

My very soul tells me to call them home, to set them free and right Rama's wrongs against them.

Noire bitches the entire ride from the Tempang to the verdant, stunning island the maze is built under. He doesn't fall silent until we enter its dark halls.

It's such an odd thing to be inside the dark, damp maze where Ten was a prisoner for seven years of his life. I no longer harbor hate toward Rama for what she did to him, even though I can't understand it. I'm just thankful he's mine to love for the rest of our long lives. The gate has never produced a prime, although it was foretold eons ago. I suspect we will be around for a good long while. It's a good thing, too, because the Tempang needs our help to fully heal.

"I cannot believe we are doing this," Ascelin hisses as we enter a cold pine forest, snow covering the ground. There's a snuffling in the woods, the sound of hooves, and then a gavataur bursts through, its head lowered and a wild look in its red eyes. I read its pain the moment I see it, and my heart breaks for its confusion and hurt.

"Hush, my child," Ten whispers, walking toward the monster. He reaches out and strokes between its eyes. The creature falls back, cocking its head to one side. The pack is tense behind us, but when the gavataur raises its head and lows, I smile.

"He's calling his people to follow," I tell the pack. They look positively terrified, but Noire refused to allow us to come without him. I don't think he wants to let Ten out of his sight, despite the fact that Ten and I are now the most powerful beings on Lombornei. We have every power the gate has ever given. It's near limitless.

I know we'll be good stewards of those gifts.

We spend hours in the maze, collecting what's left of the monsters imprisoned there. The humans are gone, something Noire preens about. Ascelin and Renze are highly unsettled by a trail of manangal that follow us. The moment we lead them out of the maze, most of the monsters take off, with the exception of a basketful of baby naga Ten found hiding in the depths of a heated pool of water. Turns out that when the pack killed the naga queen during their escape, she was pregnant.

It takes us hours to get to the far northwest corner of Lombornei, Rezha province, to reunite the babies with the naga court there. The king and queen bristle when they smell the death pheromone, but being prime has its advantages—namely Ten having time to explain what happened and deliver the babies to their homeland.

Once that's done, we return the pack to Siargao and what remains of Ten's extended family. He's crushed immediately between an aging omega and her alpha who both sob when we show up on their doorstep.

When they finally let him go, Ten pulls me forward. "Thomas, Maya, meet Onmiel, my mate." Ten grins. "Thomas and Maya raised us after Father died."

My eyes fill with tears when I think of all Ten lost before we met, but Maya pulls me in for a crushing hug, thanking me over and over for returning Tenebris to her.

Eventually, a herd of vampiri children rushes through the house and crowd Ten, dragging him into the street to play with a ball. If they notice he's got horns, they don't comment on it.

Diana joins me as I watch him go, linking her arm through mine. Achaia takes my other hand, holding it to hers as she smiles at me.

"Noire has always said Ten was the best of us: the kindest, the smartest, and the one he wanted to carry on the Ayala name. I never realized it until now, but Ten is the heart of our pack, Miel. You are now, too." Diana's voice wavers a little bit as Achaia lays her head on my shoulder with a little nod.

"Our sister. Our perfect, dorky sister. You're not going to stop being nerdy now, are you? Your love of coffee and books hasn't disappeared, has it?"

I laugh as I shake my head and groan. "Gods, coffee and books sound so good right now."

Ten looks up at me from the middle of the street, his beautiful lips curling into a smile, and I know exactly what he's thinking.

We spend a full day with the pack before taking Arliss's airship back to Pengshur. When we arrive at ML Garfield's office, he doesn't bat an eye, letting us in without a word.

For two hours, we share our story, and Ten requests to be officially allowed into the Novice program. Garfield immediately promotes me to First Librarian, with Ten as my Novice, but when we ask to have Ten fast-tracked out of that ridiculous first year, Garfield declines.

"We can't bypass the process for anyone. We never have in the thousand years since the library was founded."

I laugh because now that I'm the prime, I know everything about the Volya who created the library ages ago and left it in the capable hands of half-breeds they trusted to guard the secrets held here. I'll have to find a new area of focus because I'm now an expert in monster lore and languages. Another gift from the gate, it seems.

When we leave ML Garfield's office, I give Ten a devilish look. "Coffee, my love?"

Ten threads his fingers through mine and plants a scorching kiss on the side of my neck, huffing just below my ear.

"Our first coffee together as mates. I want it, Miel."

It feels like he's talking about far more than coffee, and we both know it.

I don't think I've ever been so happy in my entire life.

CHAPTER FIFTY
TENEBRIS
SIX MONTHS LATER

I've thoroughly enjoyed six months of bliss, traveling back and forth between the Tempang, Siargao, and Pengshur. I don't feel much different than I did before I took Onmiel and Zura into the gate. Even so, things aren't the same. I have an awareness of *everything* now. When I meet someone new, I read their soul like a book, and I know if they're good…or not. I can communicate with and understand any species of monster. Most of all? A deep-seated need to protect and serve everyone underlies each decision I make.

It's an odd feeling, but the need to heal my world is threaded through me as deeply as my own blood. That and Onmiel. She's part of me in a way Rama never was and never could have been. Because at every turn, Onmiel was my choice, all the way to the very end. So much so that I gave my life for hers, and that love allowed the gate to bring us back and make us her partners, her stewards.

I focus on how fucking much I love my fallen star as she sinks onto my hard cock, throwing her head back at the bliss that rockets through our bond.

Our bond.

I didn't realize I gasped it aloud, but everything between us is more heightened since the gate. Every sensation, every touch, every emotion.

"I feel you," she cries, clenching around me as I try not to spill too fast.

Snarling, I grip her thighs and guide her on and off me until we're both a feral clash of fangs and claws. She grasps my horns tight in her fists and strokes them until I unload my seed into her womb, praying it takes root fast. I want a million babies with this woman, and I want them immediately.

Onmiel slumps in my arms as I carry her to the tub, and then I wash her hair, kissing her all over. We eat dinner with her parents in the village in the Tempang, and then I take her to the closest traveling tree.

She sighs as she looks around us. "The forest is healing; can you feel it?"

I growl as I pull her to me. I will never get enough of her. I've been obsessed for ages, and it never goes away. "I feel it, little star," I murmur. "You are an excellent guardian, but I have a surprise for you."

"Is it coffee?" she whispers surreptitiously.

I have to laugh at that. No matter how much coffee we bring when we come to the Tempang to visit, it's never enough. The water here doesn't make the coffee taste like it does at the library, which is where we really consider home.

"Follow me." I laugh, nipping at her ear as I pull her into the tree.

"Anywhere, anytime." She laughs back, tickling my side as we head into the tree's depths.

I take a left turn.

Onmiel pinches me playfully. "Where are we going, Tenebris?" She infuses authority into her voice, but it only serves to draw a purr from my chest. My wolf and I love it when she uses our full name. He's different since the events at the gate, too, but it feels right to me. He was always different from other wolves because I'm different. I was meant for something more. And now? Everything is perfect.

I don't answer but pull her faster, and when the tree opens, and we see my family's smiling faces at home in Siargao, Onmiel squeals with delight. She leaps out of the traveling tree and throws herself into Achaia's arms and then Diana's. Then my whole family shouts as they take turns hugging her. We haven't been home in two months, and Noire says he never wants to leave Siargao again.

Jackass.

But now, there's a look on my brother's face I haven't seen before. Something protective in a new way. When I glance at Diana, I know what it is.

Congratulations, brother, I murmur into our family bond. *Don't be like Father.*

Jet and Renze laugh in the bond. I imagine he's been insufferably proud.

Noire scoffs but preens, giving me a snide look as I watch Diana share the happy news with my mate.

We think Zura's a good name, Diana whispers into the bond. Onmiel's joy at the news is palpable in our family bond.

Noire sidles up to me. "We never pierced you, you know." His alpha purr is pure evil. Jet comes to my side and grips my shoulder. Then they're both manhandling me, and although I could fight them with my newfound strength, I don't. They've been planning this for a while, and I don't want to take the wind out of their sails.

Renze helps Jet and Noire drag me into the kitchen. Onmiel follows with a slightly concerned look on her face. Rosu pads after her, whining at what they're doing. My wolf senses him, reaching out to let him know we're alright. He's remained enormous, a perfect protector for my family when I'm not around.

When my brothers toss me onto the kitchen table, and Thomas rounds the table to hold down my shoulders, Onmiel raises a brow and crosses her arms.

"Family tradition," I snort as Noire unveils his piercing kit.

"Damn, this shit hurts," Diana laughs as she grabs Achaia's hand and heads back up front. "We don't wanna watch!" she hollers as she goes. Ascelin rolls her eyes just as hard and follows the other girls out the door, and then it's just my mate, my brothers, and Thomas.

Thomas deftly yanks my pants down far enough to expose my dick. With a practiced, clinical touch, he holds it by the head.

Noire grins at me as he threads a curved piercing onto a long needle.

The first piercing slips through the skin underneath my cock as I bellow, pain shattering up my core. I thrash, and Noire growls.

"Be still, brother. You know you'll heal fast. Don't be an asshole."

Fifteen horrible minutes later, a row of bars line the underneath of my throbbing cock, and I'm trying not to fall apart at the seams.

Jet slaps an ice pack to my chest and hands Onmiel another. "Brutal, I know. But trust me, brother, when you and Onmiel do the thing for the first time, you'll think you're losing your mind from how good it feels."

"I'll take your word for it," I croak out, reaching for my girl, who slings one arm around me and leads me to the front of the house.

"Nice of you to let them do that," she whispers into my neck.

"Thought you might like it," I say. "I wanna spend a night here and then go home."

To the library, I mean. I'm halfway through my first Novice year, kicking everyone else's ass because I mentee with the best First Librarian ever. Smiling at her, I pull her in for a kiss as my pack cheers from the front steps of Noire's brownstone.

Later that night, after an amazing dinner, Onmiel helps me to bed and checks on my dick. It's hard for her like it always is but bruised and swollen. It'll be better by tomorrow, but for tonight, sex is off the table.

It doesn't stop me from pulling her on top of my face and making sure she gets off a few times, though. Nothing will ever stop me from that. I'm obsessed with my fallen star. And that's never changing.

~

The following morning, we say goodbye to the pack and take the new traveling tree right to Pengshur—my second surprise. I've been growing the two new trees for six whole months to make our travel easier. We emerge just outside the library in a grove ML Garfield's been helping me keep secret from Onmiel. When we walk out of the tree and into the busy street, she claps her hands together and throws herself into my arms.

"Ten! I can't believe you did this. You're such a sneak!"

I bury my face in her neck and breathe her in the way I always do when I need to feel grounded. Love spreads along our bond, overwhelming me the way it always does.

"I don't think there's ever been a man who loved a woman like I love you," I whisper, wrapping her legs around my waist as the busy street behind us continues on, oblivious to our happy moment.

She chuckles, kissing the tip of my nose. "I love you, Tenebris Ayala."

"Good," I huff. "Because we haven't fucked in your keeping room yet, and I want that today."

Onmiel throws her head back, glorious white hair swinging as I wrap my fist in it and carry her into the library. Her gaze turns heated as she looks at me, one pale brow curling upward. "I always knew you were a nerdy freak."

I grin. "You're right, my sweet. You've *always* been right, Onmiel, about everything. And most especially about you and me."

"Mhm." She laughs, pressing her soft lips to mine. "Take me there, Tenebris."

"Yes, ma'am." I smirk, heading through the dark halls, through the smell of musty books and the sound of a coffee machine.

Heading home.

+++++

I bet you're sitting there wondering how a fellow book lover came up with something as cool as the keeping room but didn't even let you see it! Well, you're in luck. As soon as I finish the spicy keeping room epilogue, it'll be available to newsletter subscribers!

TEN: A DARK SHIFTER ROMANCE

Sign up for my newsletter to get every freebie bonus epilogue straight to your inbox!

BOOKS BY ANNA FURY

DYSTOPIAN OMEGAVERSE
Alpha Compound
The Alpha Awakens, Wake Up Alpha, Wide Awake, Sleepwalk, Awake At Last

Northern Rejects
Rock Hard Reject, Heartless Heathen, Pretty Little Sinner

HOT AND COZY MONSTERS
Haven Ever After
Getting It On With Gargoyles, Tangling With Trolls, Partying With Pixies

Scan the QR code to access all my books, socials, current deals and more!

@annafuryauthor
liinks.co/annafuryauthor

ABOUT THE AUTHOR

Anna Fury is a North Carolina native, fluent in snark and sarcasm, tiki decor, and an aficionado of phallic plants. Visit her on Instagram for a glimpse into the sexiest wiener wallpaper you've ever seen. #ifyouknowyouknow

She writes any time she has a free minute—walking the dog, in the shower, ON THE TOILET. The voices in her head wait for no one. When she's not furiously hen-pecking at her computer, she loves to hike and bike and get out in nature.

She currently lives in Raleigh, North Carolina, with her Mr. Right, a tiny tornado, and a lovely old dog. Anna LOVES to connect with readers, so visit her on social or email her at author@annafury.com.

Printed in Great Britain
by Amazon